Brave men of Albion, arise!

The treacherous Aurorans threaten our lives and our livelihoods, but we shall not cower!
Take a stand in defense of your home Spire and stop the blaggards in their tracks with
THE READY ARMS SENTINEL long-range aetheric rifle.

This finely crafted weapon lets you stand tall and aim true, maintaining pinpoint precision
at an incomparable 150 feet, whether in the skies above or on the surface below.
The dual-trigger firing mechanism, requiring both mental and physical commands,
ensures maximal intention in every shot.

Let the Aurorans quiver before our might, and tell Old Tusky the instrument
of his destruction was manufactured here in Albion by Hinton Arms!

Choose courage! Choose honor! Choose Hinton Arms!

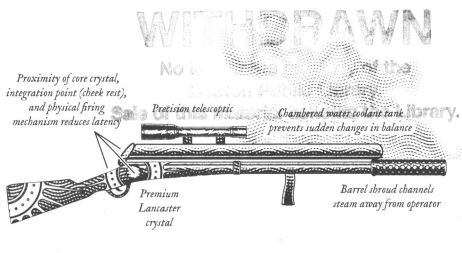

Proximity of core crystal,
integration point (cheek rest),
and physical firing
mechanism reduces latency

Precision telescoptic

Chambered water coolant tank
prevents sudden changes in balance

Premium
Lancaster
crystal

Barrel shroud channels
steam away from operator

THE ESTEEMED
HINTON ARMS
MANUFACTORIES
FOR THE DISCERNING DEFENDER OF ALBION

The
Olympian Affair

THE
OLYMPIAN
AFFAIR

THE CINDER SPIRES

JIM BUTCHER

ACE
NEW YORK

ACE
Published by Berkley
An imprint of Penguin Random House LLC
penguinrandomhouse.com

Endpaper and interior illustrations by Priscilla Spencer

Library of Congress Cataloging-in-Publication Data

Names: Butcher, Jim, 1971- author.
Title: The Olympian affair / Jim Butcher.
Description: New York : Ace, [2023] | Series: The Cinder Spires
Identifiers: LCCN 2023022193 (print) | LCCN 2023022194 (ebook) |
ISBN 9780451466822 (hardcover) | ISBN 9780698138032 (ebook)
Subjects: LCGFT: Novels. | Fantasy fiction.
Classification: LCC PS3602.U85 O49 2023 (print) | LCC PS3602.U85 (ebook) |
DDC 813/.6--dc23/eng/20230526
LC record available at https://lccn.loc.gov/2023022193
LC ebook record available at https://lccn.loc.gov/2023022194

Printed in the United States of America
1st Printing

For Bru and Fenris,
who kept me from going entirely mad during the pandemic,
fuzzy friends and snugglers of the highest quality.

And for the furry angels everywhere,
who do so much to make human life
richer and warmer and better.
Go do something sweet for your animal friends.
They've earned it.

Aetherium Fleet

Rough Survey
of the Near Reaches

COMMISSIONED 336 A.R. BY HIS MAJESTY

ADDISON ORSON MAGNUS
JEREMIAH ALBION

✦ *Pike*

✦ *Spire Dependence*

Spire Dalos ✦

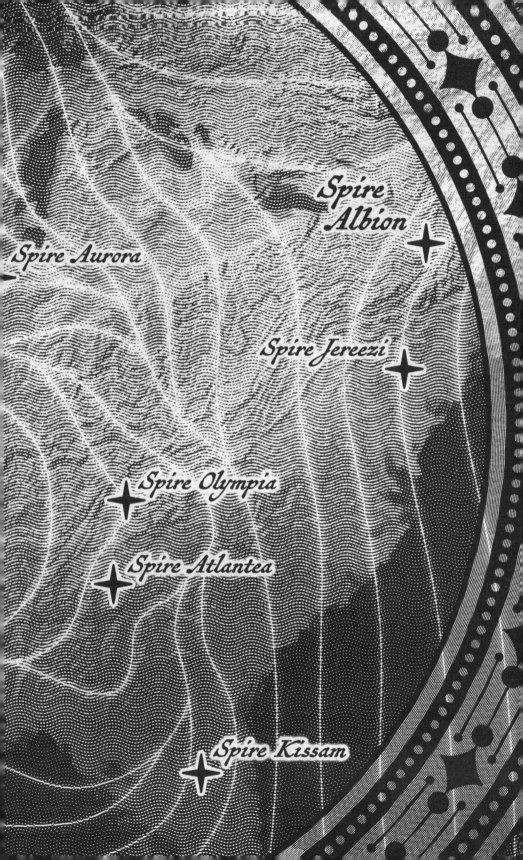

Spire
Albion

Spire Aurora

Spire Jereezi

Spire Olympia

Spire Atlantea

Spire Kissam

THE
OLYMPIAN AFFAIR

■ ■ ■ Prologue ■ ■ ■

Flamecrest, Spire Aurora

Colonel Renaldo Espira, resplendent in his gold-and-scarlet dress uniform, stalked through the streets of Flamecrest, uppermost habble of Spire Aurora. Though the city-sized space could have housed far more people than it did, it was more of a royal palace in itself, beneath the lean, hungry rule of His Majesty Juan Francesco Tuscarora del Aurora, Spirearch of Aurora and master of her scarlet-starred Armada.

Flamecrest had changed in his time in the Armada's service, Espira reflected, and not for the better. The Ashen Halls of the Armada, headquarters of the service, remained as they had always been, stark and spartan and gloomy—but the rest of Flamecrest blazed with the light of hundreds of thousands of brilliant lumin crystals. They flashed and rippled through various colors and patterns, as always, though the artists the palace chose to arrange the specific palette of light had grown steadily more unrestrained in their tastes, and the current light arrangement created an uncomfortable suggestion of the buildings of Flamecrest blazing in a smoky inferno.

Espira's nostrils flared. The smoke was all coming from the new vatteries. Acres of space had been cleared and devoted exclusively to the new masonry buildings, which produced red light and black smoke in equal measure, and where the new ember-colored crystals were produced in numbers far greater than should have been possible. The new vatteries stank. Greasy, chemical-smelling smoke lingered in a semiopaque pall on the floor for a block in every direction around them, and the air smelled of acrid things that would sear the flesh and burn the eyes if exposed to them.

The Ash Guards walking in a box formation around him marched Espira past the vatteries—but instead of turning down the street toward the palace, they took him on a different route, passing the palace and the Ministry of Intelligence and clear on past to the Etheric University.

Espira shuddered as they passed through the copper-clad steel gates of the university.

His stomach twisted and turned as memories of two years past flashed through his mind. Cold and smoke and fire and blood—and sometimes outright horror—all centered around the calm face of the most terrifying etherealist Espira had ever met.

"Someone looks like he's eaten from a tainted batch of meat," murmured a woman's voice.

There was a motion in one of the severe, gloomy alleys between buildings—the brightest lights resulted in the darkest shadows, Espira supposed—and a lean woman as tall as most men appeared from them. She wasn't a great beauty, but there was a rakish, magnetic quality to her that more than compensated. She wore an aeronaut's leathers over a man's tunic. Her face and neck showed an aeronaut's light-beaten skin, and crossed belts on her hips carried half a dozen compact pistols along with a broad-bladed fighting knife.

"Captain Ransom," Colonel Espira said stiffly.

She fluttered her eyelashes at him in a parody of coquettish behavior. "Oh, please, heroic Colonel, call me Calliope. Aren't you pleased to see me?"

"Not particularly."

She opened her mouth as if shocked, and then grinned widely. "How rude."

"I thought I'd best take the opportunity to do so now," he said, "as I might not have much opportunity in the future."

Captain Ransom's smile became brittle. "Ah, that explains your expression, then. Intelligence often results in a sour stomach when one can see what is coming." She fell into pace beside Espira, taking long, confident strides.

"You've been summoned too," Espira said, frowning.

"In my experience," Captain Ransom said, "the reward for a job well done is generally to be given a more difficult job. The fastest ship in the sky is at Spire Aurora's disposal. For the proper price, of course."

Espira frowned at the woman. She dressed and comported herself like a barbarian from Pike, but she clearly had wit and an education as well. She had chosen to discard the mores of modern society. If doing so had disturbed her confidence, it didn't show. He had to look up at Ransom slightly to frown in disapproval, of which he disapproved.

"Second fastest," he said diffidently, "according to my observations."

Something stiff slid up her spine, but her smile didn't change. "We shall see." She gave him a look that said she had guessed the general direction of his thoughts, and her smile became sunny and sharp again. "Go ahead," she said. "Ask."

"Ask what?" Espira said as politely as possible.

"Whatever it is that's rattling around in there," she responded affably enough. "Colonel, you may be a capable commander, but I advise you strongly against playing cards."

Espira straightened and sighed. "Have you seen the madwoman since Albion?"

Ransom chewed on one side of her lower lip for a moment before answering. "Colonel," she said finally, "the answer to that question could be worth your life. Do you want it?"

Espira cocked an eyebrow at the woman.

If she hadn't seen the etherealist, there'd have been no reason to be evasive—so she'd given an answer to him without actually giving it to him.

"I get in less trouble when I keep my teeth together," he said. "You would too."

Ransom tilted her head back and laughed, and, damn the woman, it made Espira want her to do it again. "How likely does that seem to you, Colonel?"

"About as likely as me being given a quiet post at the academy after being summoned to Flamecrest in the middle of the night, Captain." He paused. "Or you being hired for honest work."

She laughed again. "I have no *objection* to honest work, provided it doesn't get in the way of business." She narrowed her eyes. "Have you met Tuscarora?"

"His Majesty?" Espira asked. He quieted a flutter in his belly and touched his fingers lightly to the Star of Gallantry, Aurora's second-highest military honor, pinned in golden glory on his left breast as the highlight of his commendations. "Only during the award ceremony. I've never spoken to him."

"We didn't speak the first time I met him either," Ransom said, though her tone filled the sentence with wry, lazy libido. "Stay in my shadow, and I'll give you what cover I can."

The Ash Guards paused at the gates to the university. Passwords were exchanged and the gates slowly rolled up. Espira fought off a yawn. Then they were through the gates and walking through the silent campus, past the row of dormitory buildings, through the amphitheater, and into the teaching and research halls. The guards took them to an inconspicuous building whose doors were heavily fortified. The password exchange took longer there, but eventually the doors were unbolted and opened, and the group proceeded into the spirestone building.

They were taken to the basement. Espira had rarely been on the campus and never in this building, but from what he could see of the laboratories and workshops they passed, he guessed that they were in the School of Medicine.

The guards took them up a couple of staircases, down a nondescript hallway, past two more checkpoints of squads of the black-robed Ash Guards, and into the observation seating of a surgical theater.

Inside were only three people.

The center of the surgical floor was occupied by an enormous glass tank full of what looked like water. A man stood beside the tank, before some kind of control panel, his hand on a brass dial. Cables ran from the control panel to long copper rods that thrust down into the tank and the fluid it contained. He was head and shoulders taller than average, like most warriorborn, and by the same token his build was both athletic and muscular. Hair stood sparsely upon his head and face, his forearms and the backs of his hands, all about the same short length, so that he resembled some kind of bipedal spider. His feline eyes, able to see in the darkness with perfect clarity, were set at slightly different angles, and it was difficult to tell on what they were focused. His bare arms were steady on the controls and covered in a tapestry of pockmarks, each one raised from the skin beneath it and shaped roughly like the tip of Espira's little finger. His name was Sark.

A woman floated in the tank, submerged completely. An air hose had been run out to her, and her lips were sealed around its mouthpiece. Dark hair as long as her body floated like a storm cloud around her, lifted by some kind of current running through the liquid. She was as innocent of clothing as a newborn—and some . . . thing . . . was in the tank with her.

It looked like an amorphous blob of urine-colored gelatin moving slowly. It might have passed for some kind of oceanic debris, except that it was moving against the current in places, and it had wrapped its translucent body completely around the woman in the tank, folding her gently into its very form.

The woman twisted one hand so it was palm up and lifted it, and in response Sark slowly turned the dial higher.

Suddenly she thrashed, her body arching in a weird paroxysm that struck Espira as both arousing and utterly unsettling. Her body strained against some unseen force, gathering in tension and seemingly helpless motion—and then suddenly convulsed, her mouth opening in a scream that spat the mouthpiece of the breathing tube clear of her lips and sent a thick, dense column of bubbles rushing toward the surface.

Madame Sycorax Cavendish, master etherealist and agent of Spire Aurora, writhed in either pain or ecstasy. Espira could not tell which.

"God in Heaven," Captain Ransom breathed from beside Espira. "The lunatic did it. She actually did it."

Sark lifted his hand from the dial and turned toward the tank.

"No," said the third man in the room calmly. He was seated in a cushioned chair that had evidently been brought into the surgical bay so that he could watch the procedure from extremely close range. "She will not die for minutes at the least. I want her to have control for as long as possible."

Sark paused and stared hard at the man for a moment.

Then he subsided and returned dutifully to his station.

In the tank, Madame Cavendish thrashed, screaming in silence, bubbles eventually slowing and thinning.

Juan Francesco Tuscarora del Aurora watched her intently. He had been an assault Marine in his youth, one of the big, muscular types the Admiralty favored to spearhead infantry attacks—work usually reserved for warriorborn—and at the time it had been a scandal that the heir to Flamecrest would associate with such creatures. Twenty years had passed, and he was at the end of his youth, with silver peppering his dark beard if not his long, wavy hair—and there was a mountainous quality of patience and power to the man that his reputation for aggression and swift action utterly belied. He spared a short glance up at the entrance to the observation seating, and Espira and Ransom both bowed at the waist. Tuscarora inclined his head in reply and gave a curt beckon with one hand, gesturing toward the row of seats down nearest his chair.

Espira dutifully approached his King, and Ransom came with him.

"Sit," said Tuscarora. "Mister Sark, tea for our visitors, if you please."

The warriorborn stared at the woman thrashing in the tank, her eyes bulging now, focused on someplace that was not within mortal sight. Then, without expression, he turned to a tea service set prepared nearby. He poured two cups, placed them on saucers with small dishes of honey, and brought them dutifully to Espira and Ransom.

Espira found himself staring in quiet horror as Madame Cavendish drowned, and he took a sip of tea. "Thank you, sire. Excellent."

Cavendish's thrashing began to slow and become increasingly spasmodic.

She was dying.

Beside him, Ransom stared hard at the glass tank. She adjusted her teacup on its saucer, and when she lowered her hand, it came to rest with her fingertips on the grip of one of her pistols.

"Don't," Espira breathed. "Fire a weapon in here and the Ash Guards will kill you without asking questions."

"They'd try," Ransom replied. She glanced back at the guards still present. There were only four—but there were plenty more where those four came from, and Espira watched her consider her odds of making it out of the secured halls of the university in one piece. She apparently came to the same conclusion he had—and she took her hand away from the gun.

"That should be sufficient for now, Mister Sark," Tuscarora said. He took up his own teacup and sipped as Sark suddenly became a blur of motion, returning to the control panel and turning the dial down to zero with anxious deliberation.

When the dial reached its base point, the stuff around Cavendish in the tank suddenly went liquid and limp. It began to fall slowly toward the floor of the tank, taking Cavendish with it.

Sark put a hand on the lip of the eight-foot tank and simply leapt up and into it as if it were a bathtub. He plunged into the water and seized Cavendish, kicking and pushing at the urine-colored gelatin until she was free of it. Then he hauled the etherealist out, tossing her over a shoulder and carrying her back out of the tank and to the surgical bay's floor.

Sark dumped the woman unceremoniously on her back. Her lips were a shade of purple that Espira had seen only in corpses. The warriorborn henchman rolled her onto her side, made a fist, and struck several careful, precise blows to the woman's back.

On the third such blow, she clenched her entire body as water flew from her mouth. She coughed and gagged, choking, and it took Espira several uneasy seconds to recognize the sound coming from the woman's lips.

She was laughing. Choked, half-drowned, wheezing, hysterical laughter.

Tuscarora sat perfectly still in his chair as Sark tended to her. It took Cavendish a few minutes to compose herself—and then she managed to rise. She prowled over to where a robe had been folded and was waiting for her, her motions sensual, as if she were fixated on the simple pleasure of moving her body. Cavendish slid into the robe, her dark eyes distant and dreamy, her dark hair falling like a banner to the ground, and then she took a slow, deep breath.

She turned to pace toward Tuscarora. Three feet in front of his chair, she sank to her knees and bowed her head. Her hair spilled over the floor around her.

"Madame Cavendish," Tuscarora murmured. "Report."

"Thank you for allowing me time to complete my task," Cavendish said. "We have been met with success, my lord. Complete success."

Tuscarora had electric green eyes, the legacy of an intermarriage with the royal house of Atlantea four generations back. They studied Cavendish carefully. "You're certain?"

"The colony at Dependence is destroyed," she said. "Nothing of the skyport remains."

"We shall see," Tuscarora said calmly. "The *Conquistodor* will already have dispatched troops to verify your claim."

Cavendish looked up at him slowly. "You sent a ship?"

"Obviously," Tuscarora said. "Before making a move so bold, we must be absolutely certain of our capabilities. Don't worry, madame. You will have ample opportunity to rehearse before opening night."

"My lord?" she asked, her tone carefully polite.

"The other Piker colonies, of course," Tuscarora told her. "Destroy them in addition to one of Albion's outposts. I desire a thorough proving of the weapon's efficacy."

"But, sire . . ."

The King of Aurora tilted his head and said, "I believe you told me, not a moment ago, that the test was a complete success."

"Yes, sire," Cavendish said.

"Anyone can hit a target once by simple luck," he said. "Someone with skill can do it repeatedly."

"I . . ." Cavendish took a deep, wheezing breath. "I understand, my lord. Your will shall be done."

"Good," he said. He turned to Ransom. "Calliope, dear, see to transferring this equipment to your ship. Mister Sark and Madame Cavendish are to supervise."

Captain Ransom tensed, rose, and bowed. "Of course, sire."

"Oh, and, Calliope?"

"My lord?"

"Remove the explosive charges in your hold."

Captain Ransom stiffened. "Sire?"

"If you have a conflict with Madame Cavendish, you'll just have to talk it out like an adult," he said firmly. "No such further measures are to be taken. Am I understood?"

Her jaw tensed a couple of times. But she bowed in acquiescence. "Perfectly, Your Majesty."

"Good," Tuscarora said. He rose from his seat and paced with slow, calm dignity toward the surgical theater's exit. "Colonel, with me."

Espira had to clamber over the guardrail and down to the surgical theater floor, and hurry to catch up to the King. Tuscarora didn't adjust his pace. Others adjusted theirs to suit him.

They exited the surgical theater into a service hallway dimly lit by occasional lumin crystals. Espira matched his strides to Tuscarora's.

"You don't like the new research, do you, Colonel?" the King mused.

"It isn't my place to judge, my lord," Espira replied.

Tuscarora grinned, a shockingly human expression. "You don't." He shook his head. "Neither do I. But there's no time. What's coming will drown us all if Aurora doesn't master the skies, and swiftly." He clenched his hands and released them again. "Colonel, I have another job for you. It isn't pretty, and you won't like it. But I have to send someone, and it might as well be one of our best. During the raid on Albion, your command performed beyond all expectations. I hope that you can do it again."

"I will serve the Spire, my King."

"Good man," Tuscarora said. He paused and looked at Espira for a moment. "Are you married, Espira?"

"No, my lord."

"We need to get you a wife," mused Tuscarora. "Hardly appropriate for a man of your status to be a bachelor."

Espira's heart thudded. "Sire?"

"I have a third cousin," Tuscarora said. "She'll not turn heads, but she's intelligent, a ferocious student, and wealthy. She'd make you a fine wife."

The air spun. Espira shuddered. He had grown up in Habble Izamel, one of the most crowded, impoverished, and violent levels of all of Aurora. If he married into the royal family, even one of the cadet branches, it would mean wealth and influence beyond anything he had ever dreamed of. More than that, it would mean security. Espira had enjoyed the honors bestowed upon him and the fetes given in his honor, but he had known all the while that the very same people singing his praises would howl for his blood even more loudly if he failed the Spire somehow.

Everything he'd ever earned could be taken away from him if he lapsed in his duty, and he'd find himself right back in Izamel, struggling to eat.

Tuscarora watched Espira as he thought it through.

"If I succeed," Espira said.

"If you succeed," Tuscarora said, nodding, "you and I will be as family."

"And if I fail?" Espira said.

"Don't," Tuscarora said, amused, drawing the word out into multiple syllables. His smile faded. "I would be disappointed."

Espira took several more steps. He supposed he could turn down the mission—but doing so would effectively put a noose on his career. He'd never be more than a colonel. And then he would, most likely, be destroyed by some political scheme or scandal cooked up by a status-hungry major or commander.

In the Armada's officer corps, one's status was never static. One was always driven, up or down—and Espira refused to be driven back down to Izamel.

"What does Flamecrest require of me, sire?"

Juan Francesco Tuscarora del Aurora grinned, his jewel-tone green eyes sparkling.

▨ ▨ ▨ Chapter 1 ▨ ▨ ▨

AMS *Predator*, Colony Spire Dependence

Captain Francis Madison Grimm, commander, AMS *Predator*, strode down the length of the deck, doing what an airship's captain all too often found a necessary duty— waiting calmly. The ship's crew had gone to general quarters in predawn, nearly eight hours before, with breaks for no more than two men at a time, and those only for biological necessity.

Mists hovered thickly over the ship, for it was barely more than a thousand feet above the lithosphere—that elevation where the growing things of the hellish surface world reached out branches, tendrils, and various other structures that could threaten a ship's physical integrity. Grimm could scarcely see from one end of *Predator* to the other, much less what might be happening to the armed away team of the Spirearch's Guard currently deployed to the colony Spire below.

Grimm climbed the steep ladder to the bridge and strode over to where the ship's pilot, Mister Kettle, leaned easily back against the pilot's brace, his wrists draped over the ship's steering grips, fingers hanging loosely. He was relaxed despite the hours of waiting. Kettle was a brawny, bearded veteran aeronaut. The skin around his eyes was permanently a bit lighter than the rest of his face where his goggles had shielded him from the glare of the light of the open sky far above. His forearms looked like ham hocks, and he wore his fleece-lined cold-weather aeronaut's coat unbuttoned and open in the warmth at this altitude. Sweat had run tracks down his face and neck.

"Skip," Kettle drawled easily as Grimm approached. "We should have seen or heard something from the team by now."

In response, Grimm calmly, deliberately removed his pocket watch from where it resided in his waistcoat, and he consulted its face before polishing it, closing it, and returning it to its pocket. "They're barely outside the mission window, Mister Kettle," Grimm said. "I think we shall not wail and gnash our teeth quite yet."

"Aye, Skip," Kettle replied. "But beggin' the captain's pardon, I'd be happier if Sir Benedict had sent up a rocket by now."

"I'm sure if Sir Benedict had need of us, he would have done so," Grimm replied. "Meanwhile, I'll not leave us sitting fat and happy on an unguarded docking platform. Any Auroran who ran a patrol past it would blow us to splinters."

"If they could see us in this soup," Kettle growled. A boarding ax, his weapon of choice in most ship actions, hung from a loop on his belt, and on his left hand he wore a gauntlet—a cage of copper wire wrapped around a heavy leather bracer and connected by straps and wires to the heavy leather strap that held the weapons crystal against his palm. "If the enemy comes close enough to see us in this, we'll be biting one another's noses off before anyone can aim a cannon."

There was a sudden hiss, followed by a swift trilling sound that seemed to embrace a rapid series of sharp clicks in its volume. Something flashed by in the mist off the ship's prow, a lean, sleek mass almost five yards long supported by an impossibly fine-looking webwork of glittering wings. Its body trailed a pair of long, fine talons beneath it.

Kettle's breath exploded out of him in a huff of surprise, and his gauntlet came up so he could track the creature's path as it glided by through the mist—and was gone.

Other trills echoed those of the first creature, somewhere out of sight, hauntingly sourceless in the endless grey.

"That's the fourth time that one's come by," Kettle said, his voice pitched low. "And I've seen half a dozen more, one of them even bigger. Skip, if we're down this low when it gets dark, we'll lose a dozen men to mistsharks."

"We'll be back in the aerosphere in time to see the sun set," Grimm assured him. "XO to the bridge, if you please, Mister Kettle."

"Aye, sir," Kettle replied firmly. He leaned over to one side to swing a copper-clad speaking tube to within range of his mouth so that he could bawl, "First officer to the bridge!"

In less than half a minute, there were firm boot steps on the main deck and then the sounds of the XO coming up the staircase to the bridge, at the prow of the ship, where the pilot could see the most sky around the vessel. *Predator* was a light, armed transport outfitted a little more heavily than the average Aetherium Fleet destroyer. Swift and agile, she was equipped with both an etheric web and wind sails for running outside the main etheric currents—and her guns could speak with an authority that could have challenged the batteries of a minor colony Spire like Dependence. Even now her own guns were trained down in the general direction of the colony, and they had been for hours, their crews waiting suspended in a state between fear for their lives and utter boredom.

Grimm noted several members of the gun crews nervously tracking the XO's progress with their eyes instead of doing their duty, and he scowled them back down to their posts as the heir of the House of Lancaster came clomping up the stairs, her boots striking the deck beneath her far more sharply than was strictly necessary.

Gwendolyn Margaret Elizabeth Lancaster was a petite woman

who had acquitted herself ably in a trade where few females tried their hands—yet were always about in small numbers. Granted, most of them were warriorborn and outcasts from society in the first place, but Gwen had thrown herself into the work with a will, starting two years ago, after *Predator's* role in the capture of the *Itasca*, the storied Auroran battlecruiser now rechristened the *Belligerent* in a clear signal to her former masters of Fleet's intentions toward Spire Aurora.

Miss Lancaster wore an aeronaut's leathers that matched Grimm's own. The pattern was based upon the Fleet officer's uniform but rendered in black leather with silver skull-motif fittings rather than the dark blue and gold of the Fleet. The garments made her look like something out of a melodrama—and she had, in fact, been portrayed as a melodramatic heroine of Spire Albion in a number of productions about the opening conflict of the current struggle.

One that hovered precariously upon the brink of open war.

Miss Lancaster attained the bridge, came to attention, and snapped off a proper Fleet salute to Grimm. As per usual, there were smears of engine grease upon one of her cheeks—even after her elevation into the illustrious ranks of the aeronaut officers' corps of Albion, she was frequently to be found arguing with the chief of engineering, Journeyman, over *Predator's* systems. "Captain. We've had reports of mistsharks circling the ship from all quarters now, and the ship's glass makes it less than an hour to sundown."

"I'm aware," Grimm said calmly. "I'm going to consult with the etherealist, XO. Take the conn."

Lancaster braced to attention. "Aye, Captain, I have the conn."

Kettle glanced back at them both with naked skepticism.

"Problem, Mister Kettle?" Gwen asked.

"No, ma'am," Kettle drawled. "It's just that every time you're on the conn, things seem to get interesting, Miss Lancaster, ma'am."

"I beg your pardon, Mister Kettle," Gwen said sweetly. "But what exactly are you saying?"

"Just saying we didn't *have* to go in on those pirates at three to one, ma'am," Kettle said. "We might have tried another way."

"I said, 'Take me down their throats so I can blow their guts out,' and that's precisely what we did," Gwen replied firmly.

"Usually, it's ships what got all that armor that do such things, ma'am," Kettle retorted. "Since if the pirates had been a bit faster to get back to their guns, or the shroud had failed, we'd have been blown to tiny glowing pieces at that range."

"But they weren't faster, and it didn't fail," Gwen said. "And we all made out like bandits on the salvage of the two that didn't explode, and here you are complaining."

Kettle looked back and grinned. He'd added more gold teeth in the past few years, one of them set with a tiny lumin crystal that glowed like a star, and the gold hoop in one ear had gained a red gemstone the size of a baby's eye. "There, now you sound like a proper officer, ma'am."

"Eyes out, tongues in," Grimm said, giving Kettle a glance. "If the away team has encountered the enemy and been unable to signal us, then the enemy could know of our presence and could be in the process of hunting for us. Let's not make it easy for them."

Lancaster frowned. "Do you think that's what's happened, Captain?"

"It is one possibility," Grimm said, and lowered his voice pointedly. "One easily enough ensured against, eh?" He put a finger to his lips and climbed down from the bridge.

The temperature had dropped noticeably, and through the mists the quality of light had become warmer as the sun headed for the horizon. Night would not be far away, and the ship would need another thousand yards of sky beneath her to climb up out of the regions where the aerial predators of the surface world cruised. That distance would carry them out of range of the signal rockets of the away team. Grimm would be willing to leave the team overnight if he could be assured of their safety, but the communication would have to happen before night fell. Otherwise, he'd have to assume that nothing had gone terribly wrong.

And that was an assumption that Grimm would rather not make.

He knocked at the door of the passenger cabin, waited a beat, and then opened it enough to say, "Miss Folly, a moment of your time?"

"Oh, yes, do tell the captain he is welcome, of course," came a young woman's rather breathless voice. "Please tell him to come in."

Grimm opened the door to find the table in the little cabin set for tea for two. One of the seats was empty, though the teacup before it had been filled and prepared. In the seat opposite was the ship's etherealist, dutifully wearing her safety straps, which were attached to the chair, which was itself secured to the ship's deck.

She wore an odd mishmash of clothing: a quilted buckskin Piker jacket with merry-colored holiday trim over several layers of tunics of Atlantean silks in various unlikely colors, and a hooped, petti-coated skirt without an overdress. Her hair had been divided into two halves starting at the part in the center of her head. One side had been dyed with a flat black ink of some kind, and the other bleached almost white. Both sides had been drawn back into a braid that formed complicated whirls of light, dark, and shadow. Between the asymmetry of her colored hair and her different-colored eyes—one pale blue, the other apple green—it was enough to make her direct gaze disconcerting to those who did not know her.

"Miss Folly," Grimm said, "I have come to a quandary, and I wonder if you might help me resolve it."

After listening to Grimm's words, Folly straightened in her chair, then turned to address a jar of small, expended lumin crystals sitting on the table next to the teapot. "Of course. Tell the captain I am at his service." Folly smiled at the empty seat across the table. "I do beg you to forgive this interruption— Oh, so very kind."

Grimm drew up cautiously, looking from Folly to the empty seat and back. Etherealists were well-known for their uniquely unstable personalities, but Grimm had seen enough to know that Miss Folly's madness had a great deal of method to it, and he was not prepared to discount her strangeness as simple oddity. "Am I interrupting? I do beg your pardon . . . um . . ."

Folly smiled and shook her head. "Please let the captain know that I'm taking tea with *Predator* this afternoon. She seemed so tense and to need someone to talk to."

Grimm saw no evidence of anyone in the chair, but that didn't mean that the etherealist was out of her mind—or at least, no more so than at any other given time. Before now, Folly had certainly coaxed performances out of the ship that seemed to indicate that the vessel was more than merely the sum of her parts—that business with the ship's shroud withstanding the broadsides of three enemy vessels, for example. And no airship captain, no matter how educated or refined, could entirely escape the superstition of shipboard life. All in all, he found it wiser never to disrespect Miss Folly's oddness. "As always," he said, "please convey to her my ongoing gratitude and admiration."

"The captain knows perfectly well that *Predator* is entirely sensible of his feelings and supports his command," Folly replied, her tone fondly reproving. "But she's worried that the men haven't had a proper meal and that there are several mistsharks coming far too close to the ventral lookouts as shadows lengthen."

Which was information Miss Folly should have had no way of knowing, Grimm mused. The quiet words passed up the line to officers would not have reached this cabin, and the door had been shut all day. And yet somehow the young woman knew what was happening around the ship. Her awareness should have seemed damned unnatural, but after two years' worth of her regular presence aboard, he tended to regard such matters much as he did the effectiveness of the ship's grapevines—word would get around regardless of what anyone wished. It just so happened that in Miss Folly's particular case, the only other apparent participant in her grapevine was the ship herself.

"Part of my problem," he assured her. "I need to know if the ship can show us anything of the shore party. We can't remain at this altitude for much longer, and we should have heard from them by now."

Folly put down her teacup with a sharp clink. "Oh, goodness. That is worrisome." She turned to the chair across from her and leaned forward, speaking in a confidential murmur. Then she paused and tilted her head as if listening to a similarly pitched reply. Then she addressed the jar of crystals again. "Please tell the captain that *Predator* will be able to display significant sources of etheric power to him—the weapons crystals of the shore party's gauntlets, for example. She will show them to you as sources of red light upon the inside of the ship's shroud as she has before."

"Excellent, Miss Folly," Grimm said. "Thank you."

Running with *Predator*'s shroud up would put wear on her core etheric systems, but the additional knowledge to be gained by the vision those same systems could offer (with Miss Folly's assistance) was priceless.

"Make sure the captain knows," Miss Folly said before Grimm could withdraw, "that the smaller a power source is, the more difficult it will be for her to sense. He must bring the ship in closer to the colony if she is to show him what he wishes to see."

"How close?" Grimm asked politely.

Miss Folly murmured to the empty chair and listened gravely. "I believe the distance she means is several hundred yards? And . . ."

She listened again. "*Predator* says that she thinks she may have heard another vessel earlier in the hour, though she cannot be certain."

Grimm lifted both of his eyebrows and then felt them tighten as tension sank into his shoulders. "My thanks to *Predator*, then, Miss Folly, and to yourself," he said as politely as possible as he rushed from the guest cabin and back out onto *Predator's* deck.

Grimm hurried back up to the bridge, where Kettle and Lancaster stood ready for action, safety lines lashed taut.

Lancaster took in the look on his face immediately, and her brow furrowed with concern. "Captain?"

"Miss Folly is of the opinion that another ship is in the area," he said in a hushed tone. "We're going in to look for the shore party. Guns and lookouts to keep their eyes sharp, XO. Spread the word quietly and signal the engine room to bring up the shroud."

Both of Grimm's fellow aeronauts tensed visibly. An airship's protective shroud was costly to operate. Ship captains never signaled for their use unless they were expecting trouble.

"Aye, sir," Miss Lancaster murmured, loosing her safety straps and vanishing from the bridge after a quick salute.

He heard her descend to the gun deck and begin hurrying along it, speaking in a low, urgent voice to the starboard gunnery officer and first crew before hurrying to the forward gun emplacement. She would proceed from there to the port-side gunnery officer and first crew, and rely upon the officers to spread word down the ship's flanks.

"All right, Kettle," Grimm said, stepping into position beside the pilot and snapping his own safety lines onto the hooks positioned to receive them. "As soon as we're rigged, take us in closer to the Spire. Let's see if we can get a look at anything."

Once again, the lean, unnerving form of a gliding mistshark went through the occluded air not ten yards away. Kettle tracked it with his keen-eyed gaze and then growled, "We stay here much longer, we'll get to look at plenty, Skip. They're getting closer. Sunset's got them riled up."

The XO's boots thudded quietly on the ladder up to the bridge, and before she could get all the way up, Grimm murmured, "Rig the web for maneuver on the quiet."

"Rig web for maneuver on the quiet, aye," she breathed, and rushed off the deck to relay his orders to the riggers and topmen. Within half a minute, the ship extended her masts, unfurling them from her flanks and belly. Within another half minute, her reels had unlimbered short lengths of heavily reinforced ethersilk webbing through the guide rings set along the lengths of the masts, and Grimm felt the ship quiver with life beneath the soles of his boots.

Kettle took the steering grip in his hand and signaled the engine room by moving the throttle forward. Grimm could feel it as the engine room sent electricity to the web, sending it to float weightlessly from the tips of the masts to catch upon the etheric current flowing through the area. The short lengths of web were more heavily charged than a length of sailing web, and they were able to provide propulsion in much heavier, more intense bursts that were a great deal harder on the ship's core power crystal but much more suitable to controlling the ship in precision maneuvers.

Grimm didn't bother to give Kettle more direction than he already had. The ship's pilot had more years on the decks of airships than Grimm did, and the man would have taken only so much direction in any case. Kettle knew what he was about and would react appropriately to any problems. Grimm let the man do his job, readjusted his safety straps, stepped over the safety rail, and leaned forward, off the prow of the ship, trusting that the straps attached to his aeronaut's harness would keep him from falling off the ship and into the mists. Then he scanned the swirling grey mist for any signal from *Predator* herself.

Predator glided gracefully toward the tower and down as engineering cut power to the main lift and trim crystals and sent more current to the etheric web, drawing the airship slowly ahead. The ship's shroud disturbed the mist slightly as it went through, appearing in brief flickers as a spherical field of barely visible green light stretching around *Predator*'s spars and timbers.

Grimm swept his gaze around the sky in a steady pattern, though the mists made visibility much beyond the shroud a dicey proposition. There was a gentle wind from the south-southeast, and it pushed the ship forward a little. The sound of it changed subtly, and Grimm felt himself tense. They had to be near the Spire, the only thing large enough to alter the air currents.

And then a point of scarlet light appeared in the air at the limit of the shroud.

Grimm clenched his jaw. Even as he watched, a dozen additional points of light appeared farther behind the first.

Then the shriek of gauntlet fire split the twilight, and a second later, the howling shriek of long-gun fire echoed through the air.

The first point of light began to move, bobbing back and forth in a serpentine weave. The pursuing points of light spread out into a ragged firing line. Grimm clutched the line so hard his knuckles ached. Someone was on the way out of the Spire and being pursued by others. The shore party had been only four people—Benedict and three other warriorborn, convicts from Spire Albion's woodcutting camps. If anyone on the team was still alive, it would make sense to assume the shore party had run into opposition in numbers and was under fire.

Grimm called up his memory of Spire Dependence's skyport. It was identical to those in every other Spire—a cylindrical tower two miles high and two across. As a fledgling colony of Spire Albion, Dependence had only three berths for visiting ships, two warehouses, a light-grade anti-ship battery for fending off raiders and pirates, and a portmaster authority's building. Having assumed the original point of light that had emerged from the ramp leading down into the first habble of the Spire was the shore party, they were sprinting straight toward the edge of the Spire.

The light kept bobbing, weaving. The sound of long guns screaming their fury intensified.

And there was a sharp, clear hissing sound as a red signal rocket screamed out of the sky perhaps half a mile ahead and above them, its crimson glare bright enough to be seen even through the mist. The flare hung in the air and began to fall slowly—it was from a military illumination rocket.

Grimm's belly went cold. The signal rockets he'd issued the shore party would have burned bright green.

Another airship was operating near the Spire. And there was no way to tell who she might be or how heavy.

Predator was an anomaly as a vessel: she weighed a little more than an Aetherium destroyer, and if one squinted one's eyes hard enough, she might be mistaken for a (very) light cruiser. She was an armed merchantman, sixteen guns, seven etheric cannon mounted along each flank with heavier chase guns mounted fore and aft. More important, given the overpowered nature of her core lift crystal, she was one of the nimblest ships in the air—an excellent advantage since she utterly lacked physical armor. Miss Folly's odd ability to interface with the ship gave them still more of an advantage over other vessels of her class—but Grimm had no illusions about *Predator*'s ability to trade blows with a heavier vessel.

The entire reason one built larger, heavier ships was to make fights unfair for smaller, lighter ones, after all.

Grimm gave himself perhaps a second to formulate a plan and another to consider its weaknesses and logistics. Then he hauled himself back up onto the deck calmly, tightened his safety straps, and took up the speaking tube.

"Engineering, bridge," Grimm said firmly. "Emergency dive." He hung the speaking tube up and folded his hands behind his back as he tracked the points of light.

The one he presumed to be friendly dove off the side of the Spire and began to fall.

"There's our wayward lieutenant," Grimm said. "Mister Kettle, dive."

Kettle whipped his head around to give Grimm a half-second wide-eyed stare. He gave a frantic look at the dive bell used to warn the crew before such maneuvers took place. Grimm stared back at him evenly. The men had been at general quarters since dawn. They were all supposed to be secured—but long hours had a way of wearing away at discipline. Without a warning, if a man was on his way to the jakes or if he stood up from his gunnery chair to stretch, he might suddenly part company with the ship.

Miss Lancaster, for example. She was moving about the ship on her duties. But then, that was why Grimm had always been a stickler for discipline in combat situations. She was meticulous about her personal shipboard protocol. Or she had better be. If she wasn't, she was about to place herself at the mercy of gravity.

But in the silent mist, ringing the bell would alert any enemy within a mile to *Predator*'s presence, which could conceivably kill them all.

So, without a warning, the ship suddenly dropped from the sky.

Kettle wrestled the steering column, his broad, scarred knuckles steady on the U-shaped grips, hauling her about and orienting her rounded nose down. There were startled screams from the men, and Grimm thundered, "Silence!"

Soon, the wind was the only sound to be heard and the ship began to buck and vibrate.

"Sorry, darling," Grimm murmured to the air. "We can't have fun today." He took up the speaking tube again as he tracked the plummeting dot in front of him, off the port beam. "Mister Journeyman," he shouted calmly. "Watch the altimeter if you please. Best speed to thirty feet off the ground at the base of the Spire, maximum power to the shroud. We've got another vessel at hand."

"Aye, Skip!" shouted the engineer in reply. "Hard landing at the base of the Spire!"

Grimm felt it when the ship's plunging descent began to slow, felt the deck buck in disappointment. *Predator* loved combat dives. She sang with every line and spar when she was allowed to gather enough speed—but that extra noise was exactly what he wanted to avoid. The other vessel might simply be a trader coming into a quiet port, but with someone shooting at the shore party, Grimm didn't want to take chances.

The ship flashed past the Spire Dependence skyport and . . .

Grimm saw it for only a pair of seconds, through the mist, as the ship dove past the roof of the Spire.

The skyport was gone.

Not burned.

Not blasted.

Not destroyed.

It was gone.

Bare, dark spirestone was all that remained. No batteries, no berths, no ships, no buildings. No ruins. No bodies.

Just gone.

God in Heaven.

What could have done *that*?

A dozen half-obscured figures wearing ethersilk fighting vests and civilian clothing and carrying long guns could just barely be seen on the roof, thanks to *Predator*'s helpfully provided dots of red light, but Grimm was too far away to tell more than that.

Grimm jerked his attention away from the sight and onto the point of light, which was still falling.

"If that's the lieutenant, he's dead," Kettle called over the still-fierce wind.

"They went down on parachutes," Grimm replied calmly. "I presume the lieutenant repacked them at once and is employing them to escape."

"Weren't there four of 'em that went down?"

"The etherealist can only make *Predator* show us their power crystals," Grimm replied. "There might be more people than crystals."

"More people going splat," Kettle said darkly.

Suddenly, the point of red light slowed in its descent.

"Hah, there, you see?" Grimm said. He gripped Kettle's shoulder hard. "Bring us down near him. Haul up at about thirty feet. We'll throw down a line. Then we'll head for open sky and back home."

"If the elevation logs are right," Kettle said darkly. "If they're forty feet off, Journeyman will stop us ten feet underground."

Grimm pursed his lips as the vast clifflike side of the Spire rushed by. "Have you ever taken an Aetherium survey? Faith, Mister Kettle. Albion's bean counters never sleep."

"Doctor to bridge," came a dull voice from the speaking tube.

Grimm took up the tube. "Bridge."

"The XO has sprained her wrist, Captain," Doctor Bagen reported laconically. "She had two safety straps secured but one of them broke in the dive."

"Damned cheap Dalosian leather!" piped Miss Lancaster's outraged voice from the background.

Grimm grunted. One functional hand would mean that moving

around the ship safely would be a slow process for her as she laboriously attached and detached safety clips to the various bars and attachment points throughout the ship, but this was exactly the kind of experience she needed if she was to be a proper combat officer—even if the Aetherium itself would never accept her. There were a number of highly competent armed merchant marine captains who happened to be female, but the old ways still held out in the proper military. Regardless, Grimm needed the XO's eyes and brain, not her hands. "Wrap it up and send her to me. Bridge out."

Grimm kept his gaze on the skies above, though he could see little enough in the mist. It was an ingrained habit. He *knew* an unknown ship was up there—and he had seen enough things go wrong in service to Albion to place any bets on the notion that said ship was a friendly one.

"Land," Kettle muttered a long moment later as the ship's descent slowed and eventually came to a halt—about half as far off the ground as they should have been.

Kettle glanced over the side and eyed Grimm darkly.

"I didn't tell him to land *on* the ground," he told the pilot mildly. "Faith, Kettle. But not blind faith."

One of the gun crews broke out of their position to rig a line and toss it over the side; they moved carefully so that no sound of metal on metal rang out. The ground was broken and covered mostly with sparse low grass. The land at the base of a Spire was kept clear for a hundred yards in every direction, since residents occasionally tossed things out. Beyond that, in a thick ring all around, would be the ruined outbuildings of a deserted Spire's logistical staging area. Beyond them, Grimm knew, would be what remained of a wall placed there with the intent of shutting out the things that dwelt on the surface.

The walls were not terribly effective at doing so. There was a reason most of the folk who lived there were either warriorborn or convicts.

Spire Dependence hadn't been big enough to have the outbuildings occupied by more than a token force of foresters, and the shells of various structures that hadn't been used in centuries stood silently in the mist.

Grimm watched the line. Evidently whomever they had tossed it to had to be hauled up. Several of the crew heaved and rapidly produced a bloodied Lieutenant Sorellin-Lancaster.

Sir Benedict was dressed in civilian clothing as well, or at least he had been. His clothing was covered in long cuts—had been slashed to ribbons, really—and at least part of him had been opened up along the way, Grimm believed, judging from the amount of blood soaking the rags. Sir Benedict was a tall man with a thick brush of tawny brown hair and muttonchops and the vertically slitted green-gold eyes of a cat, the telltale marker of the warriorborn. He looked grim and exhausted.

He was also covered in . . . Grimm blinked.

The man was covered in kittens.

There must have been a dozen of the little beasts. They were clinging to him, all over his shoulders and back and hips, with three or four of them in his arms, and they looked around alertly as Benedict climbed slowly onto the ship and began setting them down one by one.

There were rushing footsteps, and Miss Lancaster, trailing an unwinding spool of cloth bandage from her wrist, flew from the doctor's cabin and across the deck to Benedict—only to come to a hesitant halt as she reached him.

"Benny," she breathed. "God in Heaven, what happened?"

Sir Benedict carefully set the last kitten down on the ground. The dozen of them just sat down right there around him, none of them more than an arm's length from his feet. The tall young man reached behind him, wincing as if the movement pained him, and produced a diplomatic courier's pouch from his belt, where it had been wrapped in the ragged remains of his jacket. He held it out to Gwen, who took it in her good hand, blinking.

"Into the safe in the captain's cabin if you please," he said, his voice haggard. He offered her a weary smile. "Mission accomplished. How was your day?"

"We must get you to the doctor at once," Miss Lancaster insisted. She took a step toward him, reaching for his arm.

Twelve small kittens, none of them more than five pounds, flattened their ears and hissed.

Miss Lancaster stopped and said, "My goodness."

"It's all right," Benedict sighed. He leaned down and started making cat noises.

Ears perking forward, the kittens all turned and looked at him as he did. Then they looked at the XO. Then they flicked their ears as a group and started pointedly ignoring her.

"I really *must* learn to speak Cat," Miss Lancaster muttered.

"Sir Benedict," Grimm said from the bridge, "anyone else to pick up?"

Benedict stared blankly at Grimm. The aeronaut didn't know what had happened to the younger man, but Sir Benedict's eyes were exhausted, bleak. "No."

Grimm nodded. "Get him to the infirmary, XO. And get back there yourself. Bandages are expensive."

Miss Lancaster looked down at her wrist, from which the bandage trailed for yards behind her, and her face flushed. "Aye, sir."

Grimm nodded and began to turn to give Kettle the order to ascend and leave—when the door to the passenger cabin slammed open, and Miss Folly rushed out.

"Where is the captain?" the etherealist breathed. "He must know at once!"

"Miss Folly!" Grimm called.

The young etherealist focused on him, her eyes wide. "Please tell the captain that we found more power sources," she said in a thin voice, then simply pointed up.

Grimm followed her indication.

In red light, on the inside of the ship's shroud, there was . . . an image. An illusion of light. It was as if someone had somehow painted out of red flame a ship with three blazing stars at her core. He could see her silhouette, a few sparse details—like a sketch of a ship dashed off by a rough but accurate hand.

Grimm's stomach dropped. That wasn't an enemy destroyer or cruiser. It wasn't even one of the larger warships of the line, the heavily armed battlecruisers and battleships. Grimm recognized her lines. There were only nine of them in the entire Auroran Armada, after all.

That was the *Conquistodor*.

An Auroran dreadnought.

A ship with twenty times the crew and forty times the firepower of his own vessel. A ship hung with copper-clad steel armor, with a shroud that a tiny foe like *Predator* couldn't hammer through if it had all day. The multiple decks of heavy guns of a dreadnought would utterly obliterate *Predator* in a quarter of a salvo, if not less. She was a veritable mountain of armor and firepower that could launch at least a couple of frigates a third the size of *Predator* along with a mass of Auroran Marines.

Conquistodor could swat Grimm's ship like a fly.

And that ship was, if *Predator*'s representation was accurate, already well within range and drawing steadily nearer.

■ ■ ■ Chapter 2 ■ ■ ■

AMS *Predator*, Colony Spire Dependence

This was not a moment for rash action, Grimm thought.

This was a moment to think.

He had a minute or so—enough time to make a single move.

Grimm invested seconds in simply staring at the enemy vessel and observing it more closely.

The dreadnought must not have seen *Predator* yet. If it had, *Conquistodor* would have blown them to flinders already. As Grimm stared at the image of the oncoming airship, he noted another detail: the enemy vessel was coming almost directly at them, head-on. If *Conquistodor* had spotted an enemy ship, she'd have rotated to present her broadside rather than aiming only her limited chase armament (which was larger than *Predator*'s broadside) from the dreadnought's bow.

Further, the enemy ship wasn't coming precisely at them. It was off by several degrees—which meant that *Conquistodor* wasn't hunting them specifically. It was blind, bad luck, then, that the dreadnought had cruised close enough to be a danger.

Grimm had four options: run, fight, hide, or wait.

Fighting was out. Simply running wasn't an option either—by

the time they reeled in the maneuver web and reeled out a sailing web, the enemy would have destroyed *Predator* and been halfway through supper. Given the enemy's course, waiting and remaining still wasn't an option either.

Grimm felt Kettle's eyes on him. The grizzled sailor watched him, jaw tensed, eyes patient, gaze flicking between his captain and his potential death.

Grimm nodded once, reached for the speaking tube, and said firmly, "Bridge to engine room. I want the quietest direct ascent you can give me, Journeyman. If we make noise, we're all dead."

"Aye, Skip," came Journeyman's unconcerned voice—he hadn't seen the enemy vessel from the engine room.

"Take her up easy, Mister Kettle," Grimm said, resecuring his safety straps. "Our Auroran friends have delicate, passionate psyches. Best if we don't disturb their evening meal, eh?"

"Aye, Skip," Kettle said in a subdued tone. He took hold of the steering grips with one hand and with the other moved the lever to throw more power into the ship's ascension.

Grimm felt the soles of his boots press hard against the deck beneath him, and *Predator* began to rise. Grimm kept track as his ship simply rose from the ground, supported by the lift crystal at its balance point at the ship's core. The suspension rig would be under great strain at the moment. Spars and decking and bulkheads creaked and groaned under the strain, but for all of that, the little ship left the earth behind her swiftly, rising with a grace few others could match. The enemy ship was coming nearer, and they were rising to meet it.

Grimm felt like some poor insect trying to avoid a hungry chicken; a singing silver tension for his crew made his shoulders tighten like barrel hoops.

Predator matched *Conquistodor*'s altitude, barely outside visual range, and the massive dreadnought's bulk absolutely dwarfed Grimm's tiny ship. Then they began to rise above her, and Grimm let out a slow breath, beginning to believe that they might escape.

And then a cat let out a yowl of outrage from somewhere in the direction of the infirmary.

There was a moment of stunned silence when Grimm hoped that the piercing sound would go unnoticed.

And then, from less than a hundred feet below him, a lookout shouted in Auroran.

Seconds later, alarm bells began ringing on *Conquistodor.* Seconds after that, the steam engines of the dreadnought bellowed to life, roaring as it brought its combat maneuver thrusters online.

Grimm seized the speaking tube, caught Kettle's eyes, and called calmly, "Bridge to engine room. Maximum ascension now if you please, Mister Journeyman."

Kettle nodded once, clamping his jaw and bracing his legs, and then slammed the lift throttle all the way forward.

Predator surged with power, and Grimm staggered, dropping to a knee while Kettle grunted with effort against his brace and kept his feet. The mist swirled around them and a sudden breeze from *above* arose as they ascended, Grimm's ears swimming with painful pressure.

Grimm thought furiously.

What happened next would depend greatly on the enemy commander. It stood to reason that the enemy had spent their day much as Grimm had—hiding in the mist, watching, listening. They too would be tired, tense, and wired up for combat. They too would be wondering about the composition of an enemy vessel, wondering if they were there to swat a fly or fight for their lives.

Had the enemy lookout gotten a clear look at *Predator?* If she had, then she would simply roll, present a broadside to the sky, and more than likely annihilate them, even firing blind, from this range. He had to get higher above *Conquistodor*. Dreadnoughts were great, wallowing beasts when it came to maneuver. If he could keep above where his enemy's cannon could elevate, even with a dreadnought's limited maneuver capability, he had an excellent chance to escape.

"Serpentine, Mister Kettle," Grimm noted. "Try to keep us directly above her."

"Stay in her blind spot, aye," Kettle replied, and threw power to the port-side maneuver web. The ship dragged itself abruptly to the left just as Grimm began to stand again, and he grabbed onto both safety lines to save his balance as *Predator* continued to rise. A moment later, Kettle hauled the ship the other way.

From below, the sound of *Conquistodor*'s turbines redoubled, and Grimm put himself in that captain's place. He would know that the enemy was present, but little more. He'd expect to be facing a Fleet ship, Grimm felt sure, but *Conquistodor* could battle any Albion, and her captain knew it. Dreadnought captains were chosen for their cool in the heat of battle, where they were expected to stand in the middle of the deadliest combat known to man without flinching. And the King of Aurora chose his captains for their hunger and aggression.

If Grimm had been in charge of that ship, he'd have sent maximum power to the lift and trim crystals and pointed every thruster he had straight down. Dreadnoughts weren't terribly mobile—but they were powered by three core crystals ten times the size of *Predator*'s, and what they lacked in footwork they more than made up for in raw power and endurance. *Conquistodor* could probably match the ascension rate of any ship in the Fleet.

It was, Grimm reflected, once again an excellent thing that *Predator* was not a Fleet vessel—she was the personal armed craft of

His Majesty Addison Orson Magnus Jeremiah Albion, Lord Albion, Spirearch of Albion, and he had bought her with a brand-new lift crystal meant to keep a far larger battlecruiser mobile in aerial combat.

Predator's only mobility-related problem in battle was not tearing herself apart with her own maneuvers, so powerful was her lift crystal, and at the moment, she rose swiftly, the mists turning from threatening storm cloud grey to bronze to glowing orange.

"Topmen to the masts!" Grimm bellowed. "Run out the sailing web!"

Officers relayed orders to the men. The heavy maneuver web was retracted, and moments later the far finer, longer, wider sailing web ran out, ethersilk webbing springing weightlessly from the ship as the vessel ran electrical current along its length. The web began to spread as they rose, and Kettle bawled instructions to the crew, who struggled against their own apparent weight as the ship continued to rise.

"Maximum power to the web if you please, Mister Kettle," Grimm said. "Set course for home. Let's show them our heels."

As Kettle grinned, he showed Grimm the glowing crystal set in his tooth. The ship's pilot "angled the sails" of the ship's web by adjusting the amount of electricity flowing to the dorsal, ventral, port, or starboard web, and *Predator* leapt forward as the web caught the etheric currents flowing through the skies and drew them forward.

Predator broke free of the mists and into clear skies as the sun was setting in an enormous roiling cauldron of flame. She turned her prow away from the sun, etheric web sending wavery shadows across the deck as *Predator* banked slightly and danced across the seething surface of the mists.

Moments later, the vast shape of *Conquistodor* came boiling out of the mists as well, cloud streaming off her flanks as her blowing engines roared, thrusters sending the clouds into a frenzy. She was facing the wrong way, and Grimm could imagine her captain's frustration at seeing such a tiny, agile foe leap away from his grasp after it had practically sailed right down his gullet.

The vast dreadnought wallowed through a slow hundred-eighty-degree turn, but by the time she finished and started running out her web, *Predator* was a mile away and sailing forward at nearly double the best speed that *Conquistodor* could manage.

"Think she'll launch her chaser ships?" Kettle asked Grimm.

It was a viable question. In her captain's place, Grimm might.

"I hope not," Grimm said.

"Think they can hurt us?"

Grimm shrugged. "Word is the new cannon that the Aurorans are using are about fifteen percent more effective at tearing down shrouds than ours. If they can get their frigates close enough to burn down our web and keep launching rockets to signal the dreadnought, they could run us down."

Kettle grunted. "We'd have to kill them."

"We'd have to kill them," Grimm agreed. "I hope he doesn't launch."

The Auroran captain might have been aggressive, but he was also cool, Grimm noted. *Conquistodor* completed her turn and came to a halt, and then her flags dipped a yard and returned to position—an airship captain's tip of the hat. The man was not in the right ship to pursue a vessel like *Predator*, and he was smart enough to know it.

Grimm felt a victorious surge of energy wash through him and sternly suppressed it from showing in his face or manner.

"Bob the stern flag!" Grimm called out, and *Predator*'s flags dipped in response. The tiny ship couldn't have challenged her foe in battle, but neither could mighty *Conquistodor* claim laurels in a footrace.

"Let's not get arrogant, Mister Kettle," Grimm said. "Once you've got your heading, take us into the mist. I'm not feeling too proud to run and hide."

"Neither am I, Skip," Kettle drawled in response. He paused, then said, "Ain't many men who would stop and think with that many tons of airship bearing down on her."

Grimm paused and eyed the pilot.

Grinning, Kettle pulled down his goggles against the waning sun and tugged his forelock. Then, broad hands steady on the grips, he took the ship back down into the mists, and the ship left any real possibility of death by enemy action far behind. "You saw their skyport, Skip?"

Grimm set his jaw. "I saw."

"What in the name of God in Heaven could do that?" Kettle said.

"You fly the ship and keep your mouth closed, so no one sees that damned lumin crystal," Grimm said, meeting the man's eyes.

Kettle noted the serious look and nodded. The man would keep his teeth together about what he'd seen. "I read you, Skip."

"Good man," Grimm said. "Make sure the crew knows too. We are but simple aeronauts. We'll have to see what wiser heads make of it all."

Kettle bobbed his chin firmly. "Aye, Skip."

Grimm unfastened his straps and prepared to leave the bridge. "Best speed for Albion while I sort out the damage. No games. Just keep us in the mist and running in a straight line. I'll get Marley to spell you in two hours."

"Best speed in a straight line home, and anything the Aurorans have can eat *Preddy*'s dust, aye," Kettle said firmly.

But Grimm noted that the man's eyes tracked back over his shoulder toward Spire Dependence, haunted.

*　　*　　*

Grimm strode directly to the infirmary, where Bagen was dutifully attempting to wrap the XO's wrist. The doctor had already lit the room brightly with lumin crystals against the coming night, and the fiery mists outside the cabin's portholes made a smoldering, beautiful background.

"Outrageous!" Miss Lancaster was saying. "Look at him!" She gestured with her wounded arm, then let out a yelp that drew a level, exasperated stare from Doctor Bagen, a man in his late fifties with bags under his eyes that gave him a mournful appearance.

Grimm looked across the cabin to where Sir Benedict reclined on a surgical table, alert but clearly exhausted, covered in smears of scarlet and bloodied, tattered clothing. The dozen kittens were all up on the table with him, calmly seated upon his body or next to him, watching the room with bright eyes.

"Captain," Miss Lancaster protested, "tell the doctor to tend to Benny!"

"Superficial wounds on Sorellin, sir," Bagen mumbled. "And those little things won't let me close without going for my eyes in any case. If she keeps waving that around before it's wrapped, it's not going to heal."

Grimm considered, nodded, and said without rancor, "XO, once you have ceased waving your arm about and allowed the doctor to tend to you, please review the Fleet manual on battlefield triage so that you will know not to overrule your medical officer when he is performing his duties to standards."

"But, Captain," she began.

Grimm eyed her, jaw set.

The XO looked startled for a moment. Grimm was not surprised.

He had met Lord Lancaster several times. The man was not a disciplinarian. That was perfectly appropriate for a civilian—but unacceptable in a Fleet officer.

"Doctor, I hesitate to be so bold, but . . ."

"Of course, Captain," Bagen said quietly. The doctor nodded to the XO and departed from the cabin.

Grimm turned to the kittens on the table around Benedict and said, "Excuse me."

A double dozen eyes focused on him intently.

"I must address my junior officer," he told them in a slow, clear voice. Cats did not speak any languages besides their own—but they seemed to understand others well enough when need be. "What is said has nothing to do with any of you."

From the corner of his eye, he saw the XO swallow and then scowl. Good. It might be profitable for Miss Lancaster to be a little uncomfortable for a moment.

Grimm turned to face her and said, "Miss Lancaster." He paused. "Gwen. You have been an able student during this cruise. I daresay we have even become friends."

Her face colored slightly, but she nodded in response without looking away.

"Fate has already cheated you out of the chance to be on the bridge during enemy action today," he said. "Don't compound the loss by earning the ill will of one of your fellow officers. Bagen has served on airships longer than you've been breathing. In here, he outranks everyone but me. Clear?"

"Clear, sir," said the XO. Her eyes were flat with pain from her wounded arm, but her voice was steady. "I wanted to give you a reason to send him out."

Grimm beetled his brows at the XO and exhaled. "And that's the way you chose to do it?"

Her cheeks reddened a bit more brightly. "But look at him!"

Grimm did eye Benedict for a moment. Bagen had cleared away the clothing from his upper body, and the man was covered in unusual six-inch-long cuts in tiny rows of five.

Dozens of them.

"The cats," Grimm breathed. "They were holding on to him when he jumped from the top of the Spire. And when he opened his chute . . ." The tiny cuts would be deep, Grimm feared. If he assumed five claws per paw, twelve cats meant that the man had borne something well over two hundred tiny cuts. The blood loss might not be overwhelming, but the pain and inflammation would be serious—not to mention the likelihood of some kind of infection. Treating the warriorborn's wounds would involve copious amounts of alcohol, and Grimm winced in sympathy. But Bagen's analysis had been correct. Benedict was in no immediate danger.

"Report," Grimm said quietly.

Miss Lancaster grunted and produced a diplomatic courier's case from her belt. "For the Spirearch," she said.

Grimm took the case, considered it, and then calmly broke its seal and opened it.

"Sir!" the XO protested.

"This isn't Fleet," Grimm said. "I am the captain of the Spirearch's personal armed vessel, after all, and he doesn't choose such men for their lack of initiative." He opened the dispatches and began to study them.

"Is that what you're going to tell the Admiralty when they have you up on charges?" the XO asked drily. "That's a sealed diplomatic case."

"I am the captain of the Spirearch's personal armed vessel AMS *Predator,*" Grimm said.

"Meaning what, precisely?"

"My title is nebulous. Its powers must therefore be nebulous too," Grimm said, reading. Then he added more seriously, "I've never lost crew because I knew too much about what I was getting them into, XO. We're going directly to the Spirearch in any case. He'll decide whether or not to hang me."

"You think he finds you valuable enough to overlook your flagrantly violating the law."

"Yes, obviously," Grimm said.

Miss Lancaster nodded, frowning. "Then I might as well do it too," she said, and took up dispatches of her own. She held her wounded arm quite still now, Grimm noted.

"Atlantea has fielded a new dreadnought," Grimm reported. "They are shaking down with the entire First Fleet in the Mistmont Range."

"That's near Olympian territorial markers," the XO noted, her voice tense. "Very near."

"Atlantea is reminding the Olympians that they would rather they didn't join the war on our side," Grimm agreed.

"You don't think they've thrown in with Aurora, do you?" Miss Lancaster asked worriedly.

Grimm shrugged. "They're our second-largest trading rival. They would prosper if Albion fell, much like Aurora."

"Olympia would suffer under that arrangement," the XO noted.

"But will they fight to avoid it?" Grimm noted. "That is the great question of the hour."

"Three more colony Spires have gone silent," Miss Lancaster noted, her brows furrowing. "Beyond Dependence. Which makes four, I suppose."

Grimm frowned, then extended his hand, and the XO passed him the dispatch. He scanned it quickly. "Piker colonies," he reported. "Lightly armed like Dependence. And they're reporting . . ." He frowned.

"One hundred percent casualties," Miss Lancaster said in a sickened voice. "That can't be right, can it?"

"If it is," Grimm said quietly, "it means that whoever is behind the attacks killed Piker children."

"I don't understand," the XO said.

"Pikers are . . . intense about their young," Grimm replied. "They raise them on airships. Don't let them cause trouble. And God in Heaven find a Way for anyone who tries to hurt one."

There was a groan from the table. Then Sir Benedict made a soft, catlike sound, and the kittens perched on him moved aside. He sat up slowly, wincing, but even though he moved gently, a dozen of the scabbed-over wounds opened and oozed fresh scarlet. He lifted a hand to run it over his hair and said, "Is there any more water?"

Grimm rose and seized a ewer, then dumped a quart of water into a tankard. The warriorborn accepted it gratefully and drank.

"When you're ready, tell me," Grimm said.

"Don't take too terribly long if you please," the XO added. "My arm's beginning to vex me."

Sir Benedict flashed a faint grin at Miss Lancaster. "Dear coz," he said, "in this moment, why in Heaven wouldn't I be thinking about you?" He tipped the tankard again and drank the last of the liquid before looking up at Grimm with still-haunted eyes.

"As you can," Grimm said. He sat down on the doctor's bunk, his elbows on his knees, his hands clasped loosely, and waited.

Sir Benedict didn't really want to talk about his day, Grimm decided. But the young warriorborn was disciplined. He closed his eyes for a moment and then said calmly, "The team dropped at sunrise. The colony had been destroyed."

"I saw the skyport," Grimm said.

Sir Benedict nodded. "The inside . . . There was no one left. No witnesses. Just a few hundred of these large, stinking slugs about ten feet long and an Auroran rifle company scouting the place." His eyes flickered darkly. "I lost all three of them."

Grimm shook his head. "What do you mean, no one left?"

"Gone," Benedict said. "The whole habble still in place. Everyone gone."

"God in Heaven," Miss Lancaster breathed. "What happened there?"

"The only ones who saw it," Benedict began slowly. His eyes dropped down to the kittens.

"Good Lord," Grimm breathed. "And what do they say?"

"That they're willing to negotiate," Sir Benedict said drily. "But only with the Spirearch himself."

Grimm took a step toward the table and considered the little tribe of kittens. "We are transporting visiting dignitaries," he noted.

"So it would seem, sir," Benedict said.

"And they have critical knowledge of what would appear to be a new weapon of some kind."

"They do."

"I don't suppose they've shared it with you."

One of the kittens, a little grey-and-brown tabby with whiskey-colored eyes, gave Grimm what he thought seemed to be a very patient look. The kitten made a mewling sound at Benedict.

"He says he was born in the morning," Sir Benedict reported hesitantly. Then he added apologetically, "But not *this* morning, Captain."

"I see," Grimm said gravely. "In that case, I will assign you to the guest cabin with your, ah, delegation once the doctor has seen to"— he glanced at Miss Lancaster and spoke firmly—"everyone."

"Yes, Captain," the XO said, her face drawn. She passed the dispatches she held back to Grimm, and he packed them up in the case. "Sir . . . if Olympia accedes to Atlantea's wishes, the smaller

Spires in the Dalosian Federation will all have no choice but to stand down. And now Atlantea has seven dreadnoughts. And Spire Aurora has nine. We have only eight to match them both."

"Thorny," Grimm agreed. "But chin up, XO. Albion has overcome worse odds."

She gave him a forced smile. "Yes, sir."

Grimm opened the cabin door and waved Bagen back in. Then he nodded and gave the two wounded young people a reassuring smile and strode out to put the dispatches in the safe in his cabin.

"Thorny" hardly began to describe matters. "Desperate" might have been a good deal closer to an accurate description of the situation Albion found itself in. But then, Grimm reminded himself, he had only an incomplete view of the field. The Spirearch, doubtless, would have gathered every scrap of information he could. He would doubtless be acting upon it.

And Francis Madison Grimm, and AMS *Predator*, would doubtless be involved.

This time, Grimm had every intention of finding out exactly what kind of mess he would be expected to take his crew into.

He slapped the dispatch case against his leg and strode purposefully across the deck to his cabin.

■ ■ ■ Chapter 3 ■ ■ ■

Skyport, Spire Albion

Sergeant Bridget Tagwynn of the Spirearch's Guard strode up the transport ramp to the Albion skyport, her boots striking firmly on the spirestone floor. She wore one of the new dresses that Gwen's seamstress had made for her; it was a rather close-fitting affair in a soft sky blue fabric with a complementing pale silver-grey bolero jacket that occasionally made her feel like a cloudy day.

One shoulder of the jacket had been carefully reinforced, and the jacket's structure itself had been built around a load-carrying harness. Bridget's friend Rowl rode along on her shoulder, his front claws sunk comfortably into the padded shoulder piece, his back legs clawing into the padding down her back. He was a ginger tomcat of magnificent size and pelt, two stone if he was an ounce, and his bright green-gold eyes watched everything moving around them as Bridget emerged into the open air of the skyport and reached the security checkpoint.

The guard was a Fleet Marine, a fresh recruit from the look of him. He was as tall as Bridget, an even six feet, and she thought he looked rather charming in his deep blue uniform.

"Oh," said the young man as she approached. "You're Lady Tagwynn."

Bridget threw back her long wheat-colored braid and laughed. "Hardly that. The House is just Father and me now. We don't even have any retainers."

The Marine tossed her a salute and grinned. "Admiral Tagwynn was a great hero of Albion, ma'am. His House seems noble enough to me." He stepped back and waved her through.

Bridget made herself keep smiling. It was somewhat tiresome that her great-grandfather's legend remained so powerful in the Aetherium Fleet. Neither she nor her father had been to the Fleet Academy, after all. They ran a vattery and grew the finest meats in Habble Morning, but some would insist on reminding her that she had what seemed a largely coincidental connection to Albion's history.

After they had passed the young man, Rowl flicked his tail in irritation and said, "I take note that the Marine on duty did *not* seem to recognize *me*."

"Now, now, Rowl," Bridget said soothingly. "I'm sure he meant you no insult whatsoever."

"Hmph," Rowl said. "I think you should challenge him to a duel and beat him senseless."

"Rowl!"

"He has insulted my honor," Rowl said firmly. "And I am a prince of my people. It would be beneath me to discipline a common soldier. You do it."

"I shall do no such thing," Bridget replied firmly. "Duels are not to be fought over such trivial matters."

"Duels are meant precisely for trivial matters!" Rowl replied. "You have refereed several of them now, and they are never fought for anything but ridiculous human reasons."

"Are you calling my own duel ridiculous?" Bridget asked.

"Kings and Spirearchs rudely decided to have a war first, so you never actually fought it," Rowl said. He considered her question. "But yes, it would have been."

Bridget threaded her way around a gang of longshoremen unloading cargo from a wallowing Atlantean merchantman with scarcely a popgun armament. "We are not at war yet, Rowl. There are steps to be taken first in the hopes that the conflict might be averted. Shall I explain it to you again?"

Rowl yawned, unconcerned with Bridget's viewpoint. "Your ships hunt their ships. Their ships hunt your ships. It is a war."

"Those are ships capturing merchant targets," Bridget said. "We go after their traders. They come after ours. It is not open war yet."

"Typical," Rowl said. "Humans must dance and talk and write and shriek to work themselves up to a proper war. I'm certain if you'd simply clawed their eyes out at the very beginning of the conflict, it would be over by now."

"If we'd simply rushed them, it *would* be over by now," Bridget said, "but not in our favor. Spire Aurora is quite strong."

"Your ships have been not-warring for two years."

Bridget arched an eyebrow. "Meaning?"

"A cat would have ended it by now," Rowl said.

"We aren't as capable as you?" Bridget asked.

"Precisely."

"We dither?"

"Endlessly."

"To be fair, it *is* rather a tangled problem with multiple theaters and axes of complication."

Rowl yawned. "To humans."

"And how would you solve the Aurora problem?" Bridget asked, amused.

"Tear out his eyes," Rowl said promptly. "This Auroran King. Let us see how aggressive he is when he must walk with a cane."

"Ah," Bridget said. "But Tuscarora has many rivals. If we weaken him, one of them, like him, will depose him and continue the war."

"Tear out *his* eyes," Rowl said promptly.

"And when he is replaced?"

"Then do it again," Rowl said with great patience. "Eventually, they will learn. Or they will all be blind. Either way, they are no longer a threat."

Bridget considered this wisdom and sighed. "I'm afraid the Aurorans might object to all this eye tearing."

Rowl sniffed and gave her a haughty look. "I can't be expected to think of everything, can I? Humans will simply have to become less incompetent or more manageable."

"I do not see myself visiting a beating upon that poor Marine for you," Bridget assured him. "But I am working on it."

"I shall not hold my breath," Rowl replied. He abruptly leaned his head against Bridget's cheek and pressed firmly against her, purring.

Bridget fought off a smile but carefully leaned back against the cat.

"You are more manageable than most," Rowl admitted fondly.

"Why, thank you," Bridget replied. "That was hardly insulting at all."

"You have not precisely earned it," Rowl said. "But I am *quite* fond of you. And that makes up for a very great deal."

They continued through Albion's frenetically busy skyport. In the two years since agents of Spire Aurora had attacked Spire Albion, trade had been severely hampered, thanks to the destruction of the secondary skyport at Habble Landing. While trade between Spires was largely unimpeded, trading between the habbles inside of Spire Albion had been greatly slowed. The inability to transfer cargo rapidly and efficiently between the various habbles of the Spire had brought logistical chains to a grinding halt for months and robbed

Albion of much of the internal efficiency that had given it such an advantage in trade over its most aggressive neighbor.

Rebuilding efforts continued, of course. Landing's skyport could take a couple of ships already, and work continued every day to expand its capacity, but it was crippled by desperate demands to use what little space it had and by the general impact of the struggling economy.

There were still empty slips here and there. The ongoing war on shipping meant that airships often did not reach their original destinations. But other slips were currently filled with captured merchantmen flying Auroran flags, and they were being sold; gutted for parts, especially precious etheric crystals; or refitted for use in the Aetherium or merchant fleets.

Bridget continued walking calmly and confidently, not altering her pace as she came closer to *Predator's* docking slip. She rounded the corner where *Belligerent* had been magnificently prepared for war. Command of its battle group had been given to her captain, Commodore Bayard, who had captured her in a daring battle of wolves against a great bear and who had stubbornly resisted promotion to the full Admiralty.

She did not permit her expression to change as she passed *Belligerent*, though her heart began to pound a great deal faster and she could hardly keep herself from hurrying ahead. When she finally passed *Belligerent's* stern, her steps faltered, and her heart nearly stopped.

Predator had returned. The slim, graceful ship rested in her docking slip in the bright light of morning sun illuminating the mist, dewdrops sparkling on her spars and rigging. Evidently she had arrived in the night, since there was only a skeleton crew aboard. Grimm made it a habit to dismiss the majority of his crew for leave the moment *Predator* was docked and unloaded.

Benedict had returned.

Bridget nervously patted her braid, twitching it back and forth a little, hoping to settle it. She adjusted her skirts and jacket as well. Then, while brushing a bit of straw off of one of her boots, she realized that she was behaving like a silly schoolgirl waiting to meet her beau. She came to the foot of the ramp up to the ship and waved at the sailor on watch—in this case, young Mister Stern, who had been promoted to lieutenant after that hideous mess over the Forest Seas that Gwen had led them into.

In the breath before Gwen had given the order to open fire, a ship had appeared in *Predator's* blind spot. Stern had been the officer who at the last instant gave the starboard guns the order to retarget the enemy. Without his quick thinking, his considerable daring, and a little luck, everyone aboard *Predator* would likely have perished. The slim, wiry, under-height young man had earned himself a scar next to his eye, a white streak through his hair, and abiding respect from the crew in the same hour.

"Hello, *Predator*," Bridget called.

Stern gave her a big grin and waved back. He was dressed down in his aeronaut's leather breeches and a loose white shirt in the relative comfort of the Spire's skyport. "Hello there, Miss Tagwynn!"

"Permission to come aboard?" Bridget called.

Stern beckoned. "Granted!" As Bridget clomped up the ramp, he nodded at the cat on her shoulder and said, "Mister Rowl."

"Hah," Rowl said in Bridget's ear, pleased. "That is still not accurate, as I am a prince, but that human is more appropriate than the last one. He may live."

"He says good morning," Bridget translated, smiling at Stern.

The lieutenant winked, but then his face grew more serious. "He's here," he told Bridget. "Infirmary. He was torn up a bit, but he'll be fine."

"Oh," Bridget said, her stomach suddenly twisting. Grimm's stoic influence on his crew meant that the men frequently understated difficulties when speaking about them. "How do you define the word 'fine' if you please, Mister Stern?"

The door to the infirmary opened, and Benedict emerged onto the ship's deck. The lean young warriorborn moved carefully, dressed much as Stern was with the addition of clean white bandages basically everywhere that he wasn't covered by his clothing.

"He means," Benedict said, wincing, "that I will live, with a great many scars to remind me of my questionable judgment."

He met Bridget's eyes and the young woman felt a small sun rise in her chest. She smiled and walked over to him. She took Rowl from her shoulder and set him on the deck carefully. Then, just as carefully, she put her arms around Benedict in what she would have considered a shocking display of public affection only two years ago.

She felt his arms go around her in return, and she closed her eyes. He pressed against her, smelling of liniment and fresh soap, and she held him, feeling the silent, muscular power of him—and a sense of quiet desperation in the way he held her.

She broke away enough to look up and meet his eyes, asking silently.

His green-gold feline eyes were haunted. "I lost the team," he said.

"Auroran Marines?"

Benedict nodded. "They had a warriorborn. He beat me. Outthought me. Outfought me. Killed my team."

She touched one of his bandages. "What happened?"

"I had to jump off the Spire and take a chute down," Benedict said.

Bridget felt herself shudder in terror. "What?"

He shook his head. "I can't talk about it here. But I need your help."

"Why?"

As if in answer, kittens began appearing from the infirmary. One by one, a dozen of them simply gathered around Benedict's feet and looked up at him.

"These fellows," he said. "They saw what happened. I spoke just enough Cat to offer to take them out of Dependence. They were hanging on to me when I jumped."

Bridget drew in a slow breath. She imagined all of those kittens' claws digging into Benedict's flesh when he opened the chute, and her belly quailed. "God in Heaven, Ben."

He gave her a faint smile. "Stings. Little bit of a fever, is all. I'll be fine."

Bridget took a step back from him and knelt down to eye the kittens. "Goodness. All these young . . ." Then she paused, frowning, and glanced at Rowl.

"Faugh," Rowl said in disgust. He turned his back on the other cats and sat indignantly.

One of the little cats took several steps from Benedict and settled down; it was a black-and-white female who could have curled up comfortably in the palm of Bridget's hand. The cat gave Bridget a steady, even aggressive look and curled her tail around her paws primly.

"You are the half-soul's mate," said the little cat.

Bridget blinked. "Excuse me?"

"No," said the cat peremptorily. "I am Saza." She spat the name as if furious.

A second little cat came to sit just behind Saza and to her left. He was a little grey-and-brown tabby, of slightly odd proportions, and everything about his demeanor seemed absolutely calm.

"This," said Saza, "is my second-in-command, Fenli."

"It is a pleasure for me to meet you both," Bridget said.

"Yes," Saza replied. "My people will require many things if you wish us to tell you what we saw."

Bridget traded a glance with the tall warriorborn, who only smiled.

"I am sure some kind of bargain can be reached," Bridget said. "You'll need to speak to—"

"Longthinker," Saza said firmly. "He has a name among cats. As do you, Littlemouse."

"Cats," Rowl said. "Barely."

Saza arched her back and spat, and the other eleven little cats, not kittens, followed suit.

"Halflings," Rowl spat back. "Don't make me eat every one of you."

"Rowl!" Bridget said, appalled, as she rose. "We will do no such thing to our guests."

"*I* did not invite them," Rowl replied haughtily, and stalked away with his back rigid as the tiny cats slowly eased back down.

"Well, then," Benedict sighed.

He leaned into Bridget again and rested his forehead against hers. She leaned back and closed her eyes for a moment. He was covered in injuries, and she was positive he was downplaying his discomfort, but he was back and he was alive and she could breathe in the scent of his skin.

Thank God in Heaven.

"What now?" she asked him.

"The kittens have us over a barrel," he said. "We take them to the Spirearch."

Chapter 4

AMS *Predator*, Skyport, Spire Albion

Grimm had finished his tea and just put on his coat when the door to his cabin opened and the XO knocked belatedly and came in.

"Skip," Gwen said, "we're ready."

Grimm nodded once, settled his long black leather aeronaut's coat around his sword, donned his captain's peaked cap, and went to the safe. He opened it, took out the courier's pouch, tucked it beneath an arm, and strode out of the cabin. He'd slept less than two hours during the entire night previous, but that was more than he got many nights when on mission.

Gwen fell in on his right, a step behind him, and Folly was immediately behind her. Sir Benedict and Bridget Tagwynn, together with Rowl and Sir Benedict's entourage, were waiting outside the infirmary.

"With me," Grimm said briskly, and the pair fell in behind them. The cats followed, staying in an orbit around the tall young warriorborn and Miss Tagwynn.

Grimm took them through the skyport, dodging through carters and stevedores and aeronauts alike. The crowd of cats drew a few stares but little more. Tension amongst everyone in the skyport was high. Crews manned every single battery Grimm passed, with spotters vigilantly scanning the misty skies for the approach of any enemy vessel.

Even as Grimm watched, signal rockets coursed down from the mist and were answered. As a merchantman descended, every gun defending Albion tracked its path. Grimm could well imagine the desire of the ship's crew to obey all instructions scrupulously rather than being blasted into glowing splinters by the batteries.

Grimm led the party out of the skyport, down into Habble Morning, and toward the First Lord's Palace, which was housed in the same building complex as the old university. Grimm presented his orders at the gates, and the group was led into the complex, down several long halls, and into a spacious chamber filled with growing plants. Overhead, a lumin crystal of tremendous size was mounted on a moving track; it was meant to simulate the light of the sun. The room was warm and the air thick with the smell of green growing things.

Seated at a table in the center of the garden, evidently enjoying his breakfast, was the Spirearch, Addison Orson Magnus Jeremiah Albion. He was a man of medium height and blocky, inconspicuous build, with greying hair and a short beard. A slim man all in black with greying hair stood behind and to one side of the Spirearch, dark eyes calm and observant.

The Spirearch glanced up from his book at the approaching group, then down, then rather sharply up again, focusing upon the small constellation of cats following Sir Benedict. He stared at them intently, then slowly straightened, dog-eared a corner of a page, and closed the book, then set it aside.

Grimm marched up to the table and saluted. "Sire." The crew bowed and Miss Folly made a lovely curtsy to the Spirearch.

"Captain Grimm, welcome," the Spirearch said. "Sit down, Captain, and your people too. Vincent makes an excellent breakfast."

"Ladies and gentlemen, you heard His Grace," Grimm said, suppressing ninety percent of a smile.

"Good morning, sire," Gwen said brightly, taking the spot to Lord Albion's right.

Grimm sat down beside her, noting that the XO had positioned herself to intervene between her captain and the Spirearch. Grimm rather fancied that Miss Lancaster would run out her guns toward her Spirearch before she would her captain, but then he might be underestimating her. It was entirely possible she had decided she might need to manage them both.

"My word, Lieutenant," the Spirearch murmured as Benedict sat down. "You had an interesting trip, it would seem."

Benedict glanced at the Spirearch, gave him a brief nod, and said quietly, "I found the bag. I had to take it from a group of Aurorans with Marine training."

"And they'd brought a bloody dreadnought to support them," Miss Lancaster added seriously.

Grimm put the courier's case on the table and slid it over to Miss Lancaster, who passed it on to the Spirearch.

"Mmmmm," the Spirearch murmured, his eyes resting on the case. "I'll need to hear it all. This calls for additional tea, I think. Vincent?"

"Ladies and gentlemen?" Vincent inquired, and then fetched tea for everyone as they indicated their desires.

"First things first," Albion said. "What did the butcher charge us?"

"All three members of my team," Benedict said.

Albion exhaled. "The enemy?"

Benedict shrugged. "They had a platoon. We were four. I don't know how badly we hurt them back."

The Spirearch nodded. "Your crew, Captain?"

"We slid out just ahead of them," Grimm replied. "No casualties for either party."

Albion nodded, opened the dispatch case, and took out the letter inside. He lifted his eyebrows upon viewing the state of the case's seal and leaned forward slightly to glance past Miss Lancaster to Captain Grimm.

Grimm met Albion's gaze without flinch or challenge.

Albion arched an eyebrow, snorted quietly, and opened the letter to begin reading.

Grimm traded a look with Miss Lancaster and winked at her.

She worked furiously to suppress a smile.

"Continue, Sir Benedict," the Spirearch murmured as he read.

"We dropped down to Dependence three mornings past," the warriorborn reported. "The colony had been destroyed."

Albion looked up sharply. "How so?"

Benedict shook his head. "All the people were gone. Just gone. The skyport too."

Albion stared intently at him, then at Grimm.

"Gone," Grimm reported. "Scraped clean. Buildings, docking slips, batteries, everything. Nothing left but spirestone and some scraps. I've never seen anything like it."

The Spirearch's handsome, genial face suddenly became as hard as stone.

"Are you sure of what you saw, Captain, Lieutenant?" he asked them, leaning forward slightly. "Are you absolutely sure?"

Grimm nodded once.

"Yes," Benedict said.

"Did you see what had done it?"

They both shook their heads.

"But they did," Grimm said, pointing at a black-and-white kitten who had leapt up to the tabletop beside Benedict.

"Ahhhh," the Spirearch said, drawing out the sound. "That explains it."

The kitten paced calmly across the table to the Spirearch, sat down primly with her black tail curling around her white paws, and made a number of cat sounds.

"Yes, obviously," Albion said. "Just as I assume you understand me."

The little cat looked pleased and made more sounds.

Benedict made a choking sound.

Grimm frowned, looking back and forth between Benedict and the little black-and-white cat.

"This is Saza," Benedict said. "She is the chief of her tribe. She, ah, speaks her mind rather directly, sire."

"Your offer is very generous, but I feel I can maintain leadership of Spire Albion well enough on my own," the Spirearch informed Saza seriously.

The kitten looked skeptical, but she replied.

"That is entirely reasonable," the Spirearch said. "Prime territories are already claimed by a number of local tribes. Establishing a place for your tribe will require time. That said, I am certain it can be Arranged."

The little cat sat up straight suddenly, her eyes widening, and asked a sharp question.

"I am well aware of the nature of that word in this context," the Spirearch said. "I maintain a number of Arrangements with your people, and if you are willing to assist me, I am willing to forge a new Arrangement."

Those words seemed to galvanize the kittens. They began to leap up onto the tabletop as well; there the little furry creatures studied the Spirearch with bright eyes as they settled down before Benedict.

Saza said something else.

"That will be up to Sir Benedict," the Spirearch said carefully. "I understand that he is bound to your tribe now, but his living arrangements will by necessity be up to him."

Saza flicked her tail and looked disgusted. Then a little grey-and-brown tabby walked up and sat down next to her, purring. She flicked her ears toward the male kitten and subsided, leaning slightly against him.

"I will do everything in my power to find a new home for your tribe here in Spire Albion," the Spirearch said, "if, in exchange, you share your knowledge of what happened to your former home."

The kitten made a chirping noise.

The Spirearch raised his eyebrows. "After you have your new home, you'll tell me."

The kitten looked smug.

"Understandable," Albion sighed. "Ours is a dangerous world." He glanced at Benedict and opened his mouth.

"I've already spoken to Miss Tagwynn," the warriorborn assured the Spirearch. "She's already taking word to Chief Maul."

"Excellent, thank you," the Spirearch said. "Vincent, I believe there is fresh fish in the cooler, is there not?"

The lean man in black nodded. "Of course, sire."

"If you would please lead Chief Saza and her people to the kitchen and get them a good meal," the Spirearch said, "I would be grateful for the assistance."

"Of course, sire," Vincent said. He turned to Saza, bowed, and said, "Chief Saza, I am Vincent, the Spirearch's valet. If you and your people would accompany me, I will see to it that food is made available."

Saza chirped to the other small cats, and they promptly gathered around Vincent. He departed from the room haltingly. Cats being cats, there were at least two or three in the immediate path of Vincent's feet at any given time. He managed to leave after a long-suffering glance at the Spirearch.

As Vincent withdrew, Albion scanned over the papers Sir Benedict had acquired. The man read with what seemed to be nigh-supernatural efficiency. The Spirearch's eyes flicked left and right only half a dozen times per page, despite there being many more lines of text. It took him a couple of moments to read the entire packet. After that, his eyes went out of focus for a full minute as he buttered a scone with slow, methodical movements.

His eyes came back into focus as he ate the scone, a bite at a time, though he looked like he was thinking furiously the entire while. By the time he had finished the scone and patted the crumbs from his lips with a napkin, the Spirearch had a small smile on his face.

"I take it you see the shape of things to come, Captain," he said then.

"Prognostication is for etherealists, sire," Grimm replied. "But it looks to me like Atlantea is preparing to change their posture from a neutral stance to one that favors Spire Aurora."

The Spirearch reached for his tea and nodded calmly. "If we find ourselves pitted against the fleets of both Spire Aurora and Atlantea, we shall have a difficult time of it."

Miss Lancaster coughed and then said, "Rather an understatement."

Albion smiled without mirth. "Captain, you know of the summit council in Olympia in a week's time?"

Grimm inclined his head. "Diplomats from Aurora, Spire Atlantea, here, and Pike are meeting in Olympia to determine trade patterns for the next five years."

"And the results will help determine the shape of the war to come," Albion said.

There was a sudden long silence around the table.

"You're sure?" Grimm asked.

"Tuscarora is giving us very little choice," Albion replied. "And if he's acquired a weapon that can wipe out a Spire's defenses and upper habbles, it's just become imperative that we rob him of every ally possible, while securing all those for ourselves that we can beg, borrow, or steal."

Grimm nodded. "What are my orders, sire?"

"I'm sending Lord Lancaster to speak for Albion," the Spirearch said.

Gwen drew in a breath and squared her shoulders. "Ah."

Lord Lancaster, the head of House Lancaster and its irreplaceable crystal vatteries, was the prime minister of Albion. He had a well-established reputation as a diplomat and ambassador who had a knack for drawing functional solutions from impossible situations.

"His mission will be to secure alliances against Aurora," the Spirearch said. "The Senate has decided to send him to Olympia aboard *Belligerent*, and Commodore Bayard is to be seconded to him as his diplomatic deputy."

Grimm lifted both eyebrows. "Bayard? Alex is an excellent battle commander and an exceptional duelist. He's hardly a diplomat."

"Shall we not cast stones, Captain?" the Spirearch said in a dry tone.

Grimm shrugged comfortably. "I'm not. Doesn't change that you're sending him to do a job he isn't suited for."

"Even if I tell you that Tuscarora is sending Rafe Valesco as the deputy to his own diplomatic team?"

Sir Benedict let out a low whistle.

Gwen looked back and forth around the table and asked, "Who is Rafe Valesco?"

"Aurora's most proficient duelist," Benedict said. "Warriorborn, noble blood. Has killed something like two hundred men and women in duels."

"Closer to three," Albion noted.

"God in Heaven," Gwen murmured. "Then . . ."

"Yes," Benedict said.

Grimm frowned and tilted his head at the nobles.

Benedict explained. "Tuscarora is sending him as a demonstration."

Grimm folded his hands on the table and scowled. "That's why you're sending Bayard."

The Spirearch spread his hands. "Alex is our most successful duelist, and Tuscarora's tactics are not subtle. He wishes to show the other Spires his strength. He wishes to show them Albion's weakness. He wants Olympia and the others to be too afraid of Spire Aurora to take our side in the coming fight, and to ensure that, he means to make an example of the man who defeated and captured *Itasca* with a trio of cruisers."

"And one privateer," Gwen muttered sullenly.

Albion showed his teeth for a second. "The world is largely unaware of *Predator's* contribution to that particular situation. I think it's best if things remain that way."

"I don't mind going unnoticed," Grimm said. "It helps avoid trouble."

"Tuscarora wants to show the world that they dare not come to our side and that we are too weak to resist him," the Spirearch said.

"Are we?" Grimm asked bluntly.

Albion regarded Grimm for a long moment before he answered.

"I can't answer your question, Captain, until we know the outcome of the summit council. If Tuscarora makes a good show of strength, he may well convince them that he is right. If he sways Atlantea, Dalos, or Olympia to his side, the odds against us become a great deal steeper."

"What about Pike?" Benedict asked.

"They've never had a proper fleet," Grimm replied, shaking his head. "They have very limited crystal vatteries, so they can't put a regulated fleet together, and their ships are always going to be smaller and slower than those of Spires with more resources."

"But there are a lot of them," Gwen noted.

"Real ships of the line will swat them from the sky," Grimm said. "The Pikers are brave to the point of lunacy, they can be in a lot of places at once, and they can cause havoc on anyone's merchant shipping. But they're privateers. They're overmatched against proper warships."

"Pikers rarely concern themselves with the affairs of other Spires," Albion noted. "No particular virtue in it. They simply don't have the resources to waste on such matters. The university's analysis estimates that they'll join whichever side will get them the most profit."

Grimm grunted. "Sire, with respect, have you ever sailed on a Piker ship?"

Albion tilted his head. "I have not."

Grimm rubbed at one of his eyes with a finger. "Sire, Pikers live rough and hard. And without a real Spire of their own to protect them. It makes them fiercely loyal to one another. Maybe more than someone from Albion could easily understand."

Albion narrowed his eyes. "You disagree with the university."

Grimm nodded toward the dispatch case. "The colonies that were attacked were the Pikers'. They'll be furious. As long as whoever wrecked them wasn't us, we'll have a natural ally."

"It wasn't us," Albion said calmly. "At least, to the best of my knowledge, which in this particular instance is comprehensive." His eyes became remote. "Happily, since Aurora's raid, there's been considerable unity of purpose within Albion."

Grimm stared at the man, thinking.

A horrible thought occurred to him. Two years before, the general stance of Spire Albion toward Spire Aurora had been one of appeasement. After Aurora's raid on Albion itself, that attitude had become a great deal angrier and more martial. Albion had demonstrated the keenness of his perception on several occasions. Had he seen the attack coming? Had he *allowed* it while taking steps to mitigate its possible deadly outcomes?

Hundreds had died in the raids and in the fires that followed them. It could have been tens of thousands, but the quasi-criminal Guilds had been forewarned and taken action to organize evacuations and fight fires—and then acquired quite a bit of property in the aftermath. "Fire sale" meant something entirely different when a criminal organization was handling firefighting efforts.

Hundreds of lives had been lost, but Albion was now on a footing to defend itself against Spire Aurora's incursions, leaving little opposition to the war effort. Aurora's preemptive attack had seen to that.

But suppose it could have been stopped?

Shouldn't it have been?

Grimm pushed away the faces of crewmen lost during that action. He wasn't some blushing virgin. He'd known what he was about when he'd joined Albion's service. The man might appear as some genial old academic. He was not one. The cats called him Longthinker. Albion's eyes were made of one-way glass. They never gave away any hint of his emotions, and they were always watching.

Albion was a crafty and dangerous snake. He had a wealthy and powerful Spire to prove it. Grimm would simply have to hope that the Spirearch was *their* snake.

Grimm found Albion's eyes on him. The Spirearch watched him steadily as he thought, and Grimm felt certain that the man had guessed much that was on his mind. Albion merely met the aeronaut's eyes calmly, directly. Grimm supposed that the man had never, to his knowledge, pretended to be anything else.

He appreciated that kind of integrity.

Grimm nodded. "I take it you have a mission for us, then."

"Indeed," the Spirearch said. "I would prefer not to test Bayard's skills against this opponent at this time. You're going to deny the enemy a battle if possible. *Predator* is to accompany *Belligerent* to the summit council. There, you will place yourselves at the disposal of Lord Lancaster and Commodore Bayard. You will see to it that they are protected. Assume that Tuscarora's people will do or say absolutely anything to make sure that Valesco and Bayard meet and that Bayard is killed. You are to take all necessary action to disrupt any such attempt. Prevent the duel from happening if possible and carry out any orders or assignment that Lancaster and Bayard deem necessary to the success of their mission. They'll have all the usual resources at their disposal. Consider *Predator* and her crew as extraordinary assets to be expended to ensure the success of the diplomatic mission."

"Expended," Grimm said.

"I don't mind if you and your people come home in one piece, Captain," Albion said in a calm, even tone, his expression gently pained. "But the plain truth is that the outcome of this summit is more important than your lives. I need people who understand what that means."

"And you believe that's me," Grimm said.

The Spirearch smiled sadly. "That is my conjecture."

"I will never be that man," Grimm said.

"You can't be anyone else," the Spirearch countered gently. "As I recall, I once told you the reward for work well done, Captain."

"More work," Grimm noted.

"More work," Albion replied, nodding. "And more difficulty. Expect to have Master Ferus's and Miss Folly's skills at your disposal. Coordinate with Commodore Bayard. You depart in two days."

■ ■ ■ Chapter 5 ■ ■ ■

Hinton Manor, Habble Morning, Spire Albion

Abigail Meredith Heloise Hinton, Duchess Hinton and mistress of the Hinton fortune, judged Bayard's face with a languid smile, met his eyes very directly, and murmured, "Are you ready, love?"

Alex's voice came out in his low, pleased growl. "For you, Your Grace? In every season, at every bell."

Abigail lifted her dueling sword in a calm salute, and Bayard mirrored her. Hinton Manor's upstairs dining hall had been cleared for use as a salle years before. As it happened, the salle adjoined Abigail's bedchamber.

Which, she thought with satisfaction, had really worked out quite well.

Alex attacked, as he always did, and she let him, testing his mood through the speed and nature of his attack. Their evening workouts were the practice of decades at this point. He hardly needed to inform her about his day when they could cross blades instead.

She caught a tentative thrust, defeated his riposte with uncharacteristic ease, took a dainty step back, and arched an eyebrow. "I beg your pardon, sir. Are you quite sure you remembered to attach the rest of you to your sword arm this evening? Shall I come back when you aren't so far afield?"

Bayard eyed her for a moment, then sighed and lifted his sword in signal of a touch. "I beg your pardon, Your Grace. I allowed myself to be distracted."

"By something other than me?" Abigail challenged him merrily. "When I'm right here in front of you? That's a rather bold thing to say to a woman with a sword in her hand."

She stepped forward without warning, her blade darted out, and she forced Bayard to step back to buy enough time to catch the sudden thrust. She escaped his binding counter and drove him back half a dozen paces with flicking thrusts, finishing with a cut to his left arm that sent a slender ribbon of lace floating into the air and to the floor between them before he could escape. He defeated her position and circled, and they both came to guard reversed from their original positions.

"Fair point, Your Grace," Bayard said. "I would hate you to think me inattentive."

His sword arm blurred, and Abigail had all that she could do to rely upon pure instinct to defend herself against him. In that, at least, she operated without doubt. She had fought and danced with Bayard for too many years for him to hold many surprises for her now. Steel chimed cleanly upon steel as she caught a small family of slashes half an inch from her skin, much to the disfigurement of her maroon bolero jacket. By the time they had parted from the exchange, her blouse showed through the coat in ribbons of white.

She lowered her sword with disgust, turned it sideways, and tossed it at Bayard's chest. The dark blond man caught the weapon with a grin as Abigail gave him a very prim look. Then she calmly removed the ruined jacket, never looking away from his eyes. She sighed, considering him. Then additionally unbuttoned the blouse's sleeves and rolled them up away from her forearms.

"Shameless," he murmured, watching her with open admiration.

"Beast," she replied, smiling.

Alex gave her a lazy smile in return. He gallantly dropped to a knee and offered her the hilt of her sword, his own held behind his back, parallel with his spine.

Abigail put her hand on the weapon—and immediately lunged forward with it, toward him, in as treacherous a maneuver as she could conceive.

Bayard lashed into motion, his open hand batting the blade aside as his own sword sprang in a circle, its point whirling around to orient itself on Abigail's right eye. She melted before the blade as it came at her, her momentum carrying her forward and to one side. She meant to step clear of the exchange, but somehow Bayard's foot was there, tripping her.

She fell, spinning to bring her sword clear—and wound up on her back with the tip of Bayard's sword resting upon her cheek.

The tip of her sword, in return, made a solid dimple on the front of his aeronaut's leather trousers.

Bayard glanced down at her sword, then past it at her legs. Her skirts had fallen open rather immodestly.

"Well, then," he murmured, "shall we call this one a draw?"

She curled her mouth into a smile and moved her legs so that a bit more of them would show. He inhaled rather sharply and the tip of his sword moved suddenly away from her.

Abigail drew her own blade's tip slowly away from Bayard—and then drove it forward again.

His reflexes were incredible, but she had spent years honing her own against him, and he wasn't fast enough to escape without her blade kissing the skin along his belly. He hissed as flecks of pink showed on his white shirt.

Bayard stared at Abigail with wide eyes for a moment, confusion showing on his features. Then his eyes narrowed in comprehension.

"One cannot help but note that Your Grace trains with special fervor today," he noted.

Abigail lifted her sword to examine the minute drops of red on its tip. "I should hope so, I daresay."

"I take it you heard about the man Tuscarora is sending for me," he said drily.

Abigail smiled sweetly. "Yet I did not hear it from you."

"Yet. So you try to gut me, Your Grace?" he said more gently with something like real pain in his voice. "That hardly seems fair."

"La, I barely pinked you," Abigail said, flicking the sword's tip to one side to clear it. "If you could not defend yourself against me, Sir Bayard, you have no business whatsoever representing Albion against Aurora's finest. If I was capable of wounding you and preventing you from attending the summit, it would be my duty to Albion to do so."

His eyes softened somewhat, and he stepped closer. He lifted his hand to cup her cheek, and she felt the fever heat of him through the gentle roughness of his hand. "To Albion, eh? Are you sure you weren't trying to protect me?"

She closed her eyes for a moment and leaned her cheek against his hand. Then she met his gaze again and said, "Do you need protection, Commodore? Against a meek little kitten like me?"

Bayard growled in mock displeasure and leaned a little closer. She lifted her face to meet his kiss—and then at the last instant disengaged and spun away, laying the flat of her blade across the backs of his legs.

Bayard yelped and came away to a guard position, and she mirrored him.

"Pay attention," she said. "You didn't think it would be that easy, did you?"

"My lady," Bayard replied, "you are many, many things."

He pressed forward suddenly, and Abigail found herself on the defensive and then suddenly wedged between Bayard and the salle's wall. She was intensely aware of the scent of him, sweat and leather and the oil on his sword, and of the feeling of his hard, lean body pressed against hers.

She twisted her body, trying to free her blade from where he had it pinned, and he countered by moving his own, one of his thighs suddenly pressed between hers, so that her breath caught in her throat and she felt color flood her face and throat.

"You are many things," he repeated in a low growl. "'Easy' is not among them."

And this time when he kissed her, she didn't try to get away.

"You're not falling asleep on me, are you?" Abigail murmured.

"I wouldn't think of it, my dove," Bayard declared gallantly and without opening his eyes. "Not for all the crystals of"—he yawned—"Lancaster."

The lean, quick bantam of a man stretched out lazily, and Abigail took a moment to simply admire him and the network of scars, from battles and duels, that laced his body.

"Oh, no, you don't, Alex." She laughed. She rolled atop him, straddled his hips, and dug a knuckle into his bad shoulder, smiling.

The man let out a yelp of reaction, winced, and then relaxed and leaned into the pressure with a faintly pained expression on his face.

"I do heroic labor like that, yet you won't let me rest? You've become hard-hearted and merciless in your possession of me."

Abigail arched an eyebrow at him. "Passably heroic, I suppose. But you'll sleep till dawn if you stay, and tonight you mustn't. I'll join you on *Belligerent* in the morning."

"Mmmph," Bayard said.

He sat up and stretched again—deliberately showing off, she thought. Abigail felt her heart warm for the arrogant, dear fool. When he opened his eyes again, she kissed him firmly and lingeringly on the mouth.

Alex enjoyed it for a long moment before she drew back and he opened his eyes, blond hair falling in mussy curls over them. "Now, what was that for?"

"I appreciate you, Bayard," she said, sliding her arms comfortably around his neck. They were well matched in size, though she was generally the smallest person in any given room. "If you were a little taller, I might even marry you."

He smiled at her, though there was a touch of sadness in his expression. "You'd be bored with me in a week."

She put her hands on either side of his face. She couldn't marry him. No matter how much either of them wanted it. His eyes let her know that he understood, accepted, and still did not like her reasons why.

"For all that you know, I'm bored with you now," she said archly instead.

He grinned, touched his heart, and mimicked a fencer's salute with an extended finger before dropping his weight back onto his arms behind him and regarding her with pensive eyes. "You're worried," he said.

She met his gaze and tried to still the little quiver of apprehension that threatened her when she considered the possible outcome of the next few days in Spire Olympia. She stared at him and said simply, "Valesco."

"I have been ordered by the Admiralty to avoid a duel," Alex replied primly.

Abigail tilted her head and gave him a very cross look.

"And Albion asked me politely not to," he added in a placating tone.

She sighed.

"I often avoid them," he protested. "I duel only when there's cause."

"Oh," she said.

"*Some* cause," Alex insisted. "For goodness' sake, Abby, it's not as though I do it for fun anymore."

"And the fact that Valesco is the only one around who has won more duels than you has no effect on your thinking whatsoever and never has?"

He rolled his eyes and then offered her a rakish smile. "Mmmm. A palpable hit, madame. What promise do you ask of me?"

She leaned forward and kissed him firmly between the eyes. Then she sat back and met them and said quietly, "Be wise."

He winced. "Oh. Ask for something less harsh, I beg you."

She placed one fist on her naked hip.

His expression sobered. "Believe it or not, I do know how to work in a group," he said. "Albion's right. It's better if we deny them the opportunity for high drama. I can test that arrogant braggart another day."

"You're sure?" she asked intently.

"Yes," he said.

She studied his expression, her own worried, and then suddenly clasped him close. She felt his arms go around her, strong and warm, and she shivered and leaned against him. "That man isn't coming to defend his honor or test his skill. He's coming to murder you. He could take you from me, Alex. I would prefer it if he was denied the opportunity."

"This isn't the right time," Alex said after a moment. "We can agree on that much, love."

She leaned her head against his and held him a little tighter. "Thank you. It was a point I felt it important to be clear upon."

"We are," he said.

"If I begin to think you are mouthing platitudes," she warned him, "I may stab you."

He seemed undisturbed by the threat. "I would never."

"I'm quite serious."

"So am I."

He toppled to one side on her spacious bed in her luxuriously appointed chamber, taking her with him. Abigail felt her heart skip a little beat in excitement as they tangled together. Even after all this time.

"I'm not a foolish young officer any longer," Alex murmured to her.

"Naturally not," she said. "You're a foolish senior officer."

"Senior?" he demanded, his tone feigning outrage.

"Apparently," she said tartly. He kissed her, and for a moment the world melted into a blur before she drew back and said, "They made you a commodore. There are no dashing commodores. It's a logistical impossibility. And you get sleepy if you don't take a nap."

He did something that made her draw in her breath sharply.

"What about when I do that?" he asked, his voice lazy.

"It's a good thing ours is a mmm-mindless affair," she said a little hastily a moment later. "Yours only ever has the one thing on it."

His hands moved, and her breath caught in her throat as her heart began to beat harder.

"I'm sorry, my love," he purred. "Could you repeat that?"

She attempted to and couldn't. She did manage to say, "Damn you, sir," before she spun to him and kissed him again, hard.

And after that, neither of them spoke for a good while.

Abigail walked Bayard out and kissed him good night at the door, as she always did. The servants and staff ignored them, as they always did. She closed the door behind him herself and leaned silently against it for a moment, as she always did.

And she felt outraged and disappointed that he was not staying in her bed.

As she always did.

Honestly, Abigail thought, if she didn't love the fool so very much, this would all be a great deal easier.

The simple dark gown went on easily, along with the dark cloak and hood, and she slipped out a side door, through her house's garden, and out into the night. It was a quick, cool walk through the darkness of the Spire, lit only by a spangling of lumin crystals, especially in the tradesmen's quarter. She paced up to the back door of a plain smithy, which was like a dozen others in the capital. Then she unlocked it with her key and let herself in.

"Finally," murmured a tired male voice.

"I told you my talk with Bayard would likely run late," Abigail said archly.

As she took off her cloak, someone breathed on a lumin crystal and set it down in the center of a table in the workroom.

Two men sat at the table.

The first was a tall, spare man with a steep widow's peak in his dark hair and silver-white streaks like frost at his temples, which gave his head a rather oblong look. He was dressed in an excellent suit of charcoal grey, and the signet ring of House Lancaster rested upon his right forefinger. He was perhaps fifty and seemed entirely unamused.

"I don't see why you haven't gotten married," he said testily. "Honestly, Abigail, at your age."

"Mostly to tweak the noses of prudes like you, Simon," she answered sweetly.

"Please, it's late enough," said the second man at the table. A slender fellow with greying hair, he was dressed all in black. His name was Vincent, and most people thought he was the Spirearch's valet. "Shall we not lose more sleep bickering?"

Lord Lancaster raised the fingers of both hands in acquiescence. "Yes, yes, we all have things to do before our ships depart."

Vincent nodded gratefully to the other man. "Lady Hinton?"

"Alex intends to avoid the duel," Abigail reported. "Of course, where duels are concerned, Bayard's stated intentions and lived choices are occasionally incongruous."

Vincent winced. "That seems a rather severe qualifying statement."

"He's sincere," Abigail reported, "and not easily manipulated. But he is a warrior in a sense I'm not sure either one of you can readily appreciate. It is not in his nature to avoid a challenge. But neither is he trained or inclined to this sort of subtlety, and I fear that the enemy may find a way to provoke him if he is not guarded."

Lancaster arched a brow. "By more than me, you mean."

"My lord," Abigail said delicately, "with respect, your experiences have simply given you no personal frame of reference for the kind of danger he faces on behalf of the Crown."

"Mine have," Vincent said simply.

Lancaster frowned and began to object.

Vincent interjected. "This is my area of expertise. They're going to play as dirty as it comes, Simon." The slim man studied Abigail calmly. "Lady Hinton will be able to be at Bayard's side more readily than you during the summit, regardless of the time of day. It will leave you free to focus on your own tasks."

Lancaster spread his hands. "Very well. My purview is the negotiating, not the skullduggery. I yield to the pair of you."

"Wise," Abigail said, smiling. She turned from Lancaster to Albion's spymaster. "We must consider the very real possibility that the duel will occur, despite everyone's best efforts. There are some lines beyond which Bayard will not be pushed."

"Then steer him around them," Vincent said bluntly.

Abigail narrowed her eyes and put a brittle lightness in her voice. "Are those my directives, my lord? To betray Bayard's honor on behalf of the Crown?"

The spymaster ignored her tone entirely. "Your directives are to accompany Bayard. Keep him clear of a duel," Vincent said seriously. "Take proactive steps to disrupt any plans the enemy intends."

Ah. An instruction with latitude. Abigail felt better about matters immediately. "That last can be done readily enough at least. Anything else?"

"Yes. Assume things will fall apart. Be ready to adjust when they do."

"Life would be desperately dull if they didn't, dear Vincent," Abigail said. "And you and Addy wouldn't need me half as much as you do."

Chapter 6

Skyport, Spire Albion

I'm not going to rely on rain barrels or waste time scooping up clouds," Grimm said firmly to the carter. "I need those tanks filled."

The brawny man glared up at Grimm sourly from his water cart, shielding his eyes against a rare day of clear sun in the Albion skyport. "Look, Captain. A broken pump is a broken pump. Bring me barrels and I'll fill them."

Barrels that Grimm did not own and might be forced to purchase at the last moment, doubtless at exorbitant prices, possibly from the carter's cousin. Grimm glanced aside at *Belligerent*, whose crew was already clearing its docking slip of carts and crates and preparing to make sail. Bayard's far larger ship had needed considerably more in the way of supplies, and it had little more access space to load it than *Predator* had. Grimm and his crew had cooperated in making sure traffic had kept moving to *Belligerent* at the partial expense of *Predator*'s preparation speed.

No matter, Grimm decided. He could leave at dusk and catch *Belligerent* by dawn if it came to that. He would rather be forced to such a measure than let such a scam be perpetrated upon the Spirearch's pocketbook. He supposed he would have to deal with the man.

The poor bastard had it coming.

"XO?" he called.

Miss Lancaster appeared out of the dash and bother of a hundred twenty men making familiar preparations swiftly. In her black uniform, she was as immaculate and professional as any other Fleet officer. She saluted. "Sir?"

Grimm nodded toward the recalcitrant water carter and said mildly, "Inspire competence?"

Gwen turned her eyes to the carter and narrowed them. Then she speared him with a brilliant smile and started stalking toward the gangplank, her boots thumping firmly on the deck.

Grimm winced in empathy, on the off chance the fellow was merely being sincere rather than opportunistic. When Miss Lancaster began moving in a direction, it was the labor of a dozen habbles to stop her, occasionally more. But there would, by God in Heaven, be water in the tanks before *Predator* sailed. Grimm was certain of that.

Lieutenant Stern hustled up to Grimm, dodging two men lugging a heavy side of vattery-grown beef, and saluted. "Captain, Mister Journeyman's compliments, and he reports the new chase armament is installed and under power. He says it will be ready to test as soon as we've cleared Albion's twelve-mile limit."

"Excellent news, Mister Stern," Grimm said, grinning, and he clapped the young man on the shoulder. He considered the young man affectionately. "That will be your work, I think, Lieutenant. Make sure the new guns perform as advertised. Draw from stores to build a pair of target buoys if you please."

"Sir!" Stern said, grinning, and saluted. "I'll get it done for you, sir."

"Of that I have no doubt," Grimm said. Then he scowled. "Look sharp, mister. We have a ship to sail."

Stern threw him a quick salute and dashed off down the deck, moving with a bit more swiftness and energy than when he had approached. Grimm saw to the loading of the new cooling box, a coffin-sized affair that was kept cold on the inside by some ingenious mechanism attached to the ship's power systems. It was packed with meats that would remain frozen for weeks at a time, as effectively as if they'd been dropped off on a glacier.

"Skip!" called a voice. "Anyone seen the skipper?"

Grimm poked his head up above decks and spotted Journeyman peering around. "Here I am," he called.

"Visitor for you," Journeyman said. "Lady. Says she's in a hurry and you're to make time for her, as you know perfectly well you ought to."

Grimm felt his eyebrows rise. Miss Lancaster was handling the water situation, so . . . "Ah. Lady Hinton, I assume?"

"The same," said Journeyman respectfully. "I showed her to your cabin, Skip."

"Well done. Thank you, Journeyman."

Grimm strode to his cabin and entered to find the exquisite Abigail Hinton waiting calmly inside, her hands folded over her fan. Today she was wearing a bustled dress of royal blue with a matching bolero tailored to her well-muscled figure, and though she was three years Grimm's senior, but for the lines at the corners of her eyes and mouth she could have been a maid. Her hair, a mix of auburn and red-gold, had been bound into a thick braid, and her hat was decorated with a pair of dragon plumes that would have cost a crewman six months' pay, their oil-slick colors rippling hypnotically when she so much as breathed.

"Ah," she said with a warm smile, turning to Grimm and extending her hands. "My dear captain. However have you been, Madison? I've heard so much about *Predator*'s exploits."

Grimm took her hands, then bowed over one and brushed his lips against her gloved knuckles. "Your Grace. Do you truly find it necessary to be so . . . linguistically extravagant with my crewmen?"

"La," Lady Hinton said, waving a hand. "We're all in a rush, and if one wishes rapid access to the voice of God on an airship, then one needs to give the crew the impression that God has been naughty and must now answer to someone of importance."

Grimm suppressed a smile. "Alex would feel a need to attend extra services just to hear you speak so."

Abigail sighed. "Blasphemy has always felt natural on my lips. The poor dear."

"May I offer you tea?"

"Most kind. My God, I'm simply dying."

Grimm bowed and made them tea with the clever Dalosian kettle that connected to the ship's power systems and heated water rapidly with a coil of glowing metal. "I probably don't have any of the blends you're most used to," he apologized to Lady Hinton.

"Nonsense," she said. "I've been with Alex long enough to appreciate an aeronaut's world. You know that, Madison."

"Honey?"

Abigail's face lightened and she fairly glowed with pleasure. Honey was difficult to find and often expensive, even for one of her exalted status. He made the tea to taste and they both sipped.

"Now, then," Grimm murmured.

"So direct," Hinton replied, amused.

"As you say, Your Grace, we are all very busy," Grimm said in a mild tone. "Taking an airship to a foreign Spire is no matter for partially paid attention."

"And I am interfering in your preparations?" Abigail asked.

"Only in the most charming and doubtlessly benevolent way," Grimm replied.

She gave him a wry look, then a very direct one. She put her cup down on its saucer and frowned for a moment before speaking.

"I don't like you very much, Captain Grimm."

"I am well aware, Your Grace," Grimm replied.

She nodded. "I assume you feel the same way toward me?"

Grimm took a sip of his tea before answering. "Honestly, Your Grace, I hardly know you. I have no particular feelings either way, but Bayard's good graces are enough for me. And I've never seen you be unkind to him."

"Even after my consortium changed shipping regulations on vat-sand and copper crystal? That must have cut into your profits rather badly."

"I saw no reason to take that personally. Every independent captain was affected the same way. And besides"—Grimm gave her a faint smile—"we made up the difference capturing pirates."

Lady Hinton tilted back her head and laughed, though there was something bitter down in the bottom of it. "A fighter. Like Alex."

Grimm dipped his head in acknowledgment. "As you say, Your Grace."

Hinton stared around the captain's cabin for a moment before she sighed. When she spoke, her voice had the cadence of someone speaking words that had been said in private many times before. "This shouldn't have been your ship."

"Perhaps not," Grimm said.

"I bought it for Alex," she said.

"I know."

"I bought it so that he could begin a trading empire."

Grimm nodded. "*Predator* makes House Bayard a nice return on their investment every year."

She exhaled. "One ship was to be the beginning. He was supposed to . . ." She shook her head.

Grimm refused to let himself wince in sympathy. Abigail Hinton, social mayfly that she was, had backbone, sharp eyes, and an excellent brain. She would not receive pity well.

"He was supposed to found a trading empire," Grimm said quietly.

"Expand and grow wealthy. Until the House of Bayard was powerful enough not to be subsumed by House Hinton when you married. Instead, after I got drummed out, he gave it to me." He shrugged. "You feel some resentment toward me because here I am running around in the ship you meant to change Bayard's life, not mine. Which I should think would be quite frustrating for you on a purely emotional level." He paused and glanced at her. "Is that about the size of it, Your Grace?"

Abigail stared at Grimm for a long moment before she said, "You don't look terribly intelligent, I must say, Captain."

"And rarely feel that way," Grimm assured her. "But it's not a hard picture to see if you know the people involved. It would take forty House Bayards to match the Hinton fortune. And you're both the principal heirs of your Houses. If he wed you, House Bayard would be folded into Hinton."

"Making him the Bayard who presided over the end of his House and Name," Abigail said quietly.

"So?" Grimm asked, watching her.

Lady Hinton made a face at him. "Captain, I know we have never precisely enjoyed each other, but please do me the service of assuming that I am not an utter fool. I very much doubt he would survive such a thing, certainly not as himself, and I am rather fond of him. What do you think?"

Grimm thought she was exactly correct. The last son of a small House of great honor, Alexander Bayard had always borne a heavy responsibility on his shoulders. He was the youngest remaining member of his family, and Grimm knew that the profits from *Predator* went directly into supporting a number of his elder cousins and his parents' younger siblings. Pride in his House and its Name had always driven Bayard to strive for excellence in every way that Grimm had been able to observe. It had been a tremendous advantage to him in his career.

Perhaps it had been less of an advantage elsewhere.

Grimm considered the Duchess. "Do you think it would have destroyed him as thoroughly as if he had turned himself into a coin-counting merchant instead?"

Hinton gave him a look of sullen anger that melted slowly into a kind of sad acknowledgment of Bayard's character. She nodded grudgingly. "Perhaps so."

"Lady Hinton," Grimm said carefully, "I had always assumed that these matters were unspoken ones and would remain so. But may I assume your purpose here is not to enumerate and elaborate upon the ways in which you are not fond of me?"

She gave him a faint smile. "I am glad you do not find me quite that malicious."

"Yet," Grimm said amiably.

She let out a quick, silvery laugh.

Grimm bowed his head slightly, smiling. "Why are you here, lady?"

"I hope that you know," she said, "that I love Bayard with all of my heart."

"Obviously," Grimm said.

Some of the stiffness eased out of the woman's shoulders. "Shall we make things simple and take that for granted? Just as I will take for granted that he is your friend and brother, and you would rather strike off your own hand than turn it against him?"

Grimm stared at Abigail for a long moment before he said, "You don't seem to be that perceptive, I must say, Your Grace."

Abigail extended a forefinger and lifted it up, mimicking a fencer's salute. "Oh, touché, Captain."

"We both love Alex," Grimm agreed.

"And we both want his good," Abigail pressed.

Grimm tilted his head. "Of course."

She nodded. "I'm worried about him, Madison. I came here . . ." She fretted at her dress with her hands, then picked up her tea again to conceal the lack of stillness. "I came here to ask you to protect him."

Grimm felt an eyebrow rise. "Bayard is my friend. Of course I'll do that."

Abigail shook her head fitfully. "I don't mean generally. Of course you'll do that." She put the tea down, rose, and paced the cabin. Finally she stopped and stared resolutely out a porthole. "I want you to protect Bayard from Bayard."

Grimm set his tea down and put his hands carefully on his knees. "What do you mean, Your Grace?"

She folded her hands. "I simply cannot abide the idea of Bayard sacrificing himself for Albion," she said. "I am perfectly sensible of the fact that at times Albion will require sacrifice. I simply prefer it to be someone other than Bayard upon the altar."

Grimm blinked mildly. "You would have me as his scapegoat, then?"

"You seem an entirely honorable man, Captain," Abigail replied. "Perhaps even a good man. But if I had to push one of you off the side of an airship . . ."

"How awkward," Grimm noted. "I should think I would jump to save us all the embarrassment."

Abigail smiled faintly. "Alex would never allow it. He'd die for you, Madison. The fool would jump first." She stared at him steadily. "What really happened to the two of you back on that ship?"

Grimm stared back and tried not to think of those hideous days when he had been a lieutenant in the Aetherium Fleet. "It's all in the public record," he said calmly.

"La," Lady Hinton said irritably.

Grimm held up his hands. "You did indeed ask a courtesy of me. Very well." He paused to consider his words carefully. "I gave my word not to speak further about what happened on the *Perilous*. The Admiralty wanted the matter burned and scattered. It should be. That's all I'm going to say."

Lady Hinton sighed, her dark eyes frustrated, but she nodded toward Grimm. "I conjecture it must be rather difficult, bearing the weight of such secrets." She turned to Grimm and said simply, "Bayard is a born hero, which is the larval form of a dead hero. Don't let him be one. If I cannot have him as a husband, I will at least not have him molt."

"I should prefer it if no one died, heroically or otherwise," Grimm assured her, "and I will labor in that direction as diligently as I know how." He rose and offered her his hand.

She took it uncertainly.

"I love him too, Abigail," Grimm said. "Try not to worry about Alex too much. He's been handling himself in difficult situations for a very long time."

"And so have you," Lady Hinton said.

"And so have I," Grimm agreed. "I'll allow no harm to come to him if I can stop it, Your Grace. You may be assured of that."

"That is not what I ask," she said. "What I want is someone nearby him who I know will choose Alex over Albion. I came to you because you know what it is to be scorned by them. By us." She met his eyes and her face pleaded with him in an expression that did not match her calm, steady voice in the least. "You're his friend. Be his friend first. And Albion's man second. That is what I ask."

Grimm inhaled and exhaled slowly. "I am not sure you appreciate, Your Grace, exactly how weighty a request that might be."

"You might be surprised, Captain," she said. "Honor is not so airy a thing that only high-flying aeronauts can see it. Which is more important to you, Captain? Your friend? Or your Spire?"

"I don't see that they are necessarily two separate things," Grimm replied.

Lady Hinton stared at him intently for a long beat before she straightened her clothing and said firmly, "I suppose we shall see which of us is correct." She nodded. "Captain, you would not have this ship but for me and for Bayard. That is a fact we can, I think, agree upon?"

"We can."

"Then for me, and for Bayard, Captain Grimm, please. Do as I ask. I would see him have a brother beside him, not merely a fellow officer."

Grimm frowned. "Your Grace, I don't see that they are necessarily two separate things either."

Lady Hinton exhaled through her nose. "Stubborn," she said, her voice firm. "Exactly like him."

But her eyes were approving.

"Captain," she said, nodding.

Grimm rose and bowed. "Lady Hinton, I will promise you this. While I live, Bayard will never stand alone."

She drew herself up, her eyes widening slightly.

"By God in Heaven," she said, "you mean that."

"Yes," Grimm said.

The wrinkles at the corners of her eyes deepened. "The pair of you. How." She exhaled a little laugh and strode out of the cabin, leaving a waft of expensive, excellent perfume in her wake.

Grimm stared after Lady Hinton for a long moment, wondering what she knew that he didn't. She felt Bayard needed a friend, did she? Someone who would choose Alex over Albion?

He couldn't help but wonder why a woman like Abigail Hinton wasn't planning to do it herself.

■ ■ ■ Chapter 7 ■ ■ ■

Silent Paws Territory, Habble Morning,
Spire Albion

Bridget Tagwynn and Rowl walked slowly down the air tunnels leading toward the portion of the access tunnel network claimed as a home by Rowl's clan, the Silent Paws, the premier cat clan of Spire Albion. (Though, Bridget thought, every single individual cat she'd ever met considered himself the premier cat of the premier tribe of whatever Spire he or she happened to be standing in, so she supposed that the Silent Paws' claim was, by its very nature, somewhat dubious. Not that she would ever mention such a thing to the Silent Paws' clan chief, Maul, or his son, Rowl.)

She wore lumin crystals as earrings, a birthday gift from Gwen, and they lit her way with a wavering light that often became partly veiled by locks of hair escaping from her braid.

Behind them trailed Saza and Fenli. The little tuxedo cat swaggered arrogantly behind Rowl and Bridget, and her second, Fenli, followed behind her, the little grey tabby's body language contained and confident.

"I don't see why everyone does everything Longthinker wants," Rowl complained bitterly. "He isn't particularly large or magnificent, even for a human. He couldn't defeat anyone in single combat." Rowl paused and then added in casual insult, "He is not dangerous."

"I think," Bridget said carefully, "that if the Spirearch of Albion were so readily removed from his position, he would not be in it."

"In a competent system," Rowl acknowledged, "that would be true. But humans have built Albion."

Bridget lifted her eyebrows. "Rowl," she said, "why do your people call the Spirearch 'Longthinker'?"

"I have not considered it," Rowl said loftily.

Bridget eyed her furry friend. "Rowl," she said seriously, "you are the Prince of the Silent Paws."

Rowl did not, quite, stop to preen. "I am."

"And Albion has been your clan's ally and conspirator, has he not?"

"He has," Rowl admitted testily.

"I know that your view of humans and mine are very different," Bridget said. "And they should be."

"Humans are not aware enough to truly understand a cat's perspective," Rowl assured her. "Most of us do not consider your poor sight, hearing, and smell to be your own fault."

Bridget no longer really had to repress frustration at Rowl's choice of words. Cats were very direct little souls, with scant sense of what humans would have called "tact." If one wanted to associate with them, one rather had to accept feline judgment. It was not generally so bad, once one learned to compensate for the cat perspective. Most cat complaints about humans were understandable, once one comprehended how imperfectly cats understood human culture and society.

"I think it would be wise for the Prince of the Silent Paws to consider his tribe's allies at greater length."

Rowl's tail lashed in annoyance. "That is Maul's duty," he said.

"It is certainly the duty of the chief," Bridget acknowledged. "One day, Maul will no longer be chief."

Rowl looked anywhere but at Bridget. "In many years."

"Perhaps," Bridget said. "But there is war on the wind. And many terrible things happen in war, Rowl. Maul might be kill—"

"He will *not* be killed," Rowl snarled vehemently. "My sire cannot die."

Bridget walked for several steps in silence, not bothering to challenge this statement, and let the silence answer Rowl. Then she continued as if he hadn't interrupted her. "He might become lost. He might be called away. If those things happen, the Silent Paws will need their prince to act as chief."

There was a soft sound, and Bridget found Fenli scampering along next to her, staring up at her with wide, intent eyes.

Rowl eyed the smaller cat sourly and swerved a step toward Fenli as they walked. Then he raised a paw and menaced the smaller cat with a possible strike.

Fenli simply made eye contact with Rowl, entirely without malice, and neither moved to defend himself against the strike nor stepped out of the way.

Fenli's boldness seemed to disconcert Rowl, who lashed his tail in agitation and moved to put Bridget's legs between himself and the little tabby.

Bridget blinked mildly at this interaction.

"I do not care for halflings," Rowl said. "There is no honor in beating them, because they are tiny."

"Rowl," Bridget protested, "they are our guests."

"They are *Longthinker's* guests," Rowl said sullenly.

Saza promptly trotted on stiff legs to catch up with Fenli, her back arched, her fur standing up. "Do you think we are afraid to fight you? You might as well be a clumsy, overgrown human!"

"Oh!" Rowl spat, his fangs showing, his long ginger fur fluffing out threateningly. "You take that back!"

"Human!" Saza singsonged at Rowl. "Human, human, falling over his own paws!"

Rowl pounced toward Saza, who as if weightless bounded away, touched lightly on Bridget's knee, and flew like a bird up to her shoulder.

Bridget flinched. The tiny black-and-white cat couldn't have weighed much more than five or six pounds. She had seen Rowl quite readily dispatch multiple opponents about the size of Saza and Fenli, and they'd had deadly venomous bites.

"That is *my* human!" Rowl howled. "Come down from there at once!"

"Big, clumsy human!" Saza caroled.

Rowl started slamming his shoulder against Bridget's knees. "Trespasser! Intruder!"

Saza's claws dug into Bridget's shoulders for purchase.

"Rowl!" Bridget exclaimed.

"Human, human, human!" Saza sang.

"This is too great an insult to be borne!" Rowl thundered.

Bridget, a human who outmassed the pair of cats four or five times over and had a knife and a gauntlet and combat experience to boot, found this entire conversation to be in terribly poor taste.

"Human!"

"I will not be mocked!" Rowl stated, gathered himself, and hurled himself at Bridget's chest.

Saza spat at him, flew off Bridget's shoulder, and darted off to one side and into a tiny air tunnel. Rowl kicked Bridget in the belly to push off her, and darted off after Saza.

Bridget didn't quite fall down but wound up holding her belly and staring helplessly after the pair of cats. "Oh, dear."

Fenli paced calmly around her, then sat down in front of her, bowed his head in an almost human fashion, and said, "Now that the unreasonable people are off doing unreasonable things, the reasonable people can talk in peace."

Bridget felt her eyebrows rising. Then she straightened and sat down cross-legged in front of the little cat, arranging her skirts around her folded legs the way a cat would her tail. "Forgive me if I must ask a few questions to understand."

"One cannot drink water when one's stomach is full," Fenli replied amiably.

Bridget blinked.

"Ask," the little cat clarified.

"I thought Saza was your clan chief," Bridget said.

"She is, always," Fenli said in a pacific tone. "She is a great hero to our tribe. We love her unreservedly." Fenli's tail twitched, just at the very tip. "She is, however, sometimes difficult. How do you find Prince Rowl?"

"I love him," Bridget replied, "and he is sometimes difficult."

"I find that chiefs often are unreasonable," Fenli said. "Don't you?"

Bridget found herself smiling helplessly. "I suppose most of us think that from time to time."

"Then perhaps those of us who are less difficult should handle these matters ourselves and spare them the trouble," Fenli suggested diffidently.

Saza shot out of a vent and across the tunnel, yowling. Rowl came barreling along behind her, spitting in fury. Both vanished into another side vent.

"Being a chief seems exhausting," Fenli observed. "I am sure that what they are doing is necessary. But as I am not a chief, I do not understand it. Perhaps you and I can find a solution together. I find that if I produce a viable solution to a problem and bring it to Saza, she can often simply approve, and then it can be implemented without disturbing her business as chief."

Bridget found herself smiling. "I see. My plan is to take you to see Chief Maul of the Silent Paws. They are a large and prosperous clan who dwell here in Habble Morning. Chief Maul is an older and very serious chief who does not—"

Rowl and Saza went by in a howling storm again, although Rowl was panting rather heavily.

"—readily engage in such expenditures of emotional energy."

"Ah," said Fenli. "Older, then. A warrior chief?"

"Very much so," Bridget replied.

"Then his concerns will be territorial, focused upon resources," Fenli said. "Will he be willing to grant us a territory, or must we fight for our place?"

Bridget was a bit taken aback, not by the question but by the absolute serene confidence with which Fenli asked it. "I don't think you want to fight the Silent Paws. They are large and healthy, and there are hundreds of them."

Rowl burst out of a side vent and slid to a halt on the tunnel floor, breathing hard and looking around wildly.

Saza darted out of the tunnel behind him, leapt on him, raked his haunches with her rear paws, and zipped away lightly.

Rowl howled and went after her.

Fenli regarded Bridget with a pleased look. "Most humans do not take the time to speak to us. They do not wish to know anything about our world. This is very novel." He looked after the vanished chiefs. "Our world is not kind. We choose not to lie down and die in the face of danger, Littlemouse the Drinker."

Bridget tilted her head. For a cat to give a Name to a human was a significant gesture—one that did not often happen outside of an Arrangement. At least, not among the Silent Paws. Either Fenli and his clan were different, or the little tabby thought a long-standing relationship was in the offing.

"Our home was destroyed," Fenli continued calmly, "but we live. We must have a new home if we are to survive. Therefore, we will fight, even hundreds, if we must. What choice have we?" He considered the tunnel. "Besides, Saza likes to fight."

"So does Rowl," Bridget sighed in a tone of agreement. "Perhaps it would be better if you and I spoke to Maul alone."

"Thank you, Drinker. To me, this appears to be a plan reasonable people would make," Fenli concurred.

Bridget had never before visited the Silent Paws' home territory without Rowl at her side. By the time she and Fenli appeared in the large tunnel juncture where Chief Maul held court, she and Fenli had gathered a small crowd of curious warriors and hunters and kittens.

Chief Maul, upon hearing of the dais arrangement Chief Naun of Habble Landing established in his audience room, had consulted with Longthinker upon an appropriate action. In the end, he and Longthinker had agreed that a more reserved and stately position seemed appropriate, so instead of a row of cast-off furniture that ascended in height, a scholar's desk had been neatly positioned against one wall of the spirestone tunnel. The middle drawer to each side of the desk stood open, and within each sat a large and magnificently furred Silent Paws warrior as a bodyguard.

Atop the desk sat Chief Maul, a ginger tom like Rowl, but heavier with muscle and marked here and there with scars of battle. He regarded the approaching human and the little cat with her gravely.

"Greetings, Littlemouse," Chief Maul purred in rumbling greeting. "How is Wordkeeper's health?"

"My father is well, sir," Bridget replied. She said "sir" in Albion; there was no equivalent polite honorific in Cat. "He remains content with the Arrangement and desires slow enemies and healthy prey for your people."

Maul flicked his ears in pleasure. "Excellent. The meat he contributes to our sick and our caregivers brings life. We will continue to protect his vats from scavengers." He fluffed out his fur proudly. "Also, I have a new kitten. He must see it and tell me how fine it is."

To be offered a visit with a cat's kitten was to be all but a member of his clan. Bridget felt a surge of pleasure for her father. He would be deeply honored by such an invitation, and she found herself smiling broadly at Maul. "I will take word to him, Chief Maul. I'm sure he will be delighted to see your new kitten."

Maul regarded Fenli steadily. "This is well. Now, I must ask you who this stranger you bring before me is. And where is my son Rowl?"

Bridget briefly outlined the plight of the cats from Spire Dependence. "And so, sir," she said, "Longthinker asks you to consider whether a territory can be found for this clan, in exchange for them sharing the information about the enemy's weapon."

"A matter of human war," Maul said. His voice was heavy. "Longthinker has been teaching me about human war. Your people must keep track of so many things. When cats go to war, we have to consider only tactics and our battle spurs." He gave a faint shake of his head. "Longthinker asks this?"

"Yes, Chief Maul."

Maul regarded one of the cats seated in the drawers. "Fetch me a Rememberer."

The bodyguard cat flicked his ears and flowed out of the drawer and down a tunnel. He returned a moment later with an elderly female cat, her dark fur marked everywhere with silver. She padded slowly up to the desk, leapt carefully up on it, and sat down by Maul.

"Maul," she said without his title.

"Meen," he replied fondly, and went to her. The two rubbed cheeks, and Maul said to Bridget, "This is my mother, Meen."

"Oh. How do you do, Meen?" Bridget said politely with a little curtsy.

The elderly cat observed this and then eyed Maul.

"She is behaving with respect," Maul clarified.

"Ah," said Meen. She regarded Bridget and said, "I am well, human child."

"Meen, the northeast tunnels. Who remains of the Shadow Stripes?"

"Shadow Stripes?" Bridget asked, picking up on the subtle intonation that indicated the name of a cat's clan. "I've never heard of them."

"There was a clan war when I was young," Meen said. "The Shadow Stripes lost." She flicked her tail thoughtfully. "They were confined to a quarter of the habble by the terms of victory. The hunting there was not sufficient to support a clan, so most of them drifted away until few remained."

Maul rose to pace languidly. "Mmmm. Yet they are a clan, and by right of surviving the war, their territory remains theirs. The question must be asked. How many remain?"

"To my knowledge," said Meen, "only their chief. He is even older than me."

"That is ideal," Maul said. "It would require the word of a chief to allow these newcomers to dwell there. Send for him."

"He will not come," Meen said. "He does not even live in the northeast tunnels anymore. If she would speak to Chief Farr, she must go to him."

Bridget glanced at Meen. "If that is what is necessary, that is what I will do."

Maul lashed his tail, regarding Fenli steadily. "Not until I know where my son is, Littlemouse."

It was at that moment that the crowd of cats that had gathered around Maul holding court began to stir and part.

Prince Rowl entered. He was covered in scratches, and his soft fur was lumpy where blood from them had clotted in it. There were visible fresh scratches on both ears. He walked in stiffly, though with tremendous dignity.

Beside him and perhaps a whisker's width behind him walked Saza. The little tuxedo cat was limping rather badly on one leg, with a gimlet look in her eye and a nice set of raked wounds across her chest.

"My sire," Rowl said, coming to sit down calmly in front of the desk.

"My heir," Maul rumbled. He tilted his head and regarded Rowl and the diminutive Saza. "Are you well?"

"I have been testing the newcomers," Rowl said in a sullen tone.

"And?" Maul asked.

Saza lifted her little chin proudly.

"They fight well," Rowl said, then added hastily, "For their size."

Maul's ears focused forward as he compared the two of them. "*She* fought *you*?"

"I am a cat," said Saza proudly.

Maul considered this response and then looked at Bridget. "If they made a good showing against Rowl, they aren't weak. That's something." He sat down and yawned dismissively. "You may consult Chief Farr. If he agrees to allow them within the northeast tunnels, they may stay."

Bridget could just imagine the reaction of Gwen or Captain Grimm—and quite probably Vincent—to this answer. They would demand to know why the cats weren't cooperating, behaving like allies, and leaping to the aid of Albion. They wouldn't understand, of course, that this was *exactly* what complete and unswerving support looked like—to a cat.

"Thank you, Chief Maul," Bridget replied with as much respect as she could summon. "Where might I find Chief Farr?"

Maul looked at Meen. The elderly cat wrapped her tail primly around her paws and said, "Why, in the woodcutting camps, of course. You must look for him outside the Spire. On the surface."

Chapter 8

IAS *Mistshark*, Somewhere over the Sea of Trees

Colonel Espira finished the last page of Lord Albion's treatise on group airship logistical operations, closed the book, and frowned meditatively.

"Well?" asked Ciriaco. The warriorborn Marine sergeant had declined promotion to the ranks of the officers after being decorated for his actions in the raid on Spire Albion—as a proper Auroran warriorborn was expected to do. As a result of playing by Aurora's silent rules, he had been richly rewarded and feted as—an appropriately humble—Hero.

To be declared a Hero was to be strapped with a very comfortable muzzle. Part of Ciriaco's new status as a Hero of Aurora was the imprimatur of the noble classes. Ciriaco now had the grace to socialize with the highest caste of Auroran society, and as a result it was no longer shameful for Espira to share a cabin with the fellow he had worked with for a decade.

"He's methodical," Espira told his old friend. "Thorough. But not hidebound. I think the man is a genius at scheduling." Espira leaned back. "Frankly, I find it terrifying."

Ciriaco was better than six and a half feet of lean, hard muscle, so when he sat up abruptly and stared at Espira, his movement was rather leonine. Espira would have found it intimidating if he didn't trust the man.

"Terrifying?" Ciriaco rumbled. "Why?"

Espira spread his hands. "When you step back from it, war is about deliveries. We deliver ships and men with the appropriate equipment to the same place at the same time, with their guns all pointed in the same direction."

Ciriaco scowled, dark brows heavy under silver hair now worn in a long, decadent, not strictly regulation style. It was an acknowledged privilege of the warriorborn whose competence had caused them to grow too powerful to be contained by anything less than overwhelming social pressure. It was, in effect, a badge of his rank as a Hero and one of the most powerful warriorborn in the Marines. Espira thought he was, in many ways, still a fairly simple, direct soul who preferred a stand-up fight to any kind of negotiations.

"Suppose I can see that," Ciriaco said, squinting.

"So, whoever can deliver the most men and matériel to one place at one time wins," Espira said. "It strikes me that a man who is skilled at scheduling would be rather well able to do that."

Ciriaco snorted, drew his knife, and inspected the wax seal over its razor-sharp edge—exposing it to open air would cause it to oxidize in hours. "Running airship deliveries is one thing. Running a war is another."

Espira grimaced and countered. "Moving ships around is moving ships around, old friend. Albion doesn't have to be a fighter himself. He's got people like that Captain Grimm for that. He understands logistics better than any of my instructors at the academy, which means he also understands what he could do to *our* deliveries."

Ciriaco considered this statement for a moment, then shrugged and answered in a practical tone. "You fight someone who is slippery, the way you beat them is to close, pin them down, finish them quick.

Don't give them a chance to get clever. Albion's got eight, nine dreadnoughts, tops. We've got that, and Atlantea has a bunch more besides. Knock them down and kick their guts out."

"Between the two of us, I suspect His Majesty agrees," Espira said. "But the Albions are every bit the aeronauts we are. We can't simply throw the dice and attack them. Otherwise, even if we win, we might be so weakened that Atlantea or Dalos or even Olympia starts getting ideas."

"Politics." Ciriaco spat and shook his head. "The more dancing around we do, the more it favors Albion."

Espira grimaced. "Politics does not always allow for the most direct solutions. At times, compromises with ideal doctrine are necessary. And His Majesty is known as something of a dancer himself."

With a snort, Ciriaco replaced his knife in its sheath. "War ain't the sort of place where you compromise, Ren. That's just another word for your men dying when they don't got to."

Espira grimaced. "You're not wrong," he said. "But the reality we must face is that—"

The relative silence of the midmorning was split by the sound of the ship's bell sending up a steady clangor. Aeronaut boots began to thud all over the *Mistshark*'s hull.

Espira and Ciriaco exchanged a glance. Then they leapt to their feet, put on their aeronaut's leathers, and strapped themselves into their safety harnesses. Both had spent enough years aboard airships to be very nearly as proficient with operating them as the aeronauts themselves.

"I'll find out what's going on," Espira said. "General quarters and ready arms for the platoon. Time them. This is an excellent opportunity for a drill regardless."

Ciriaco took out his expensive silver stopwatch and checked that it was wound. "Very good, sir."

Espira nodded, reached up to clap the man on the shoulder as he went by, then hurried out onto the deck of the *Mistshark* and found an airship readying for battle. Crewmen rushed up and down the length of the ship. Gun crews piled into their emplacements, and gunnery officers bawled at laggards to get into place. Topmen headed into the masts, port and starboard, dorsal and ventral, where they would act as needed to make sure the lengths of etheric web that powered the ship were deployed and retracted smoothly; all the while, they'd be hanging miles above the hellish surface, protected from lethal falls only by their wits, sinews, and safety lines.

Espira clipped a safety line to a guide rail and worked his way down the deck to the ship's bridge at the prow. He had to step around a rushing gunnery officer and duck aside as a boarding party went rushing together into the armory to arm themselves, just as Ciriaco would now be belowdecks arming the Auroran Marines.

Espira reached the steep staircase leading up to the bridge at the same time as a woman in a lavender dress, and his belly went cold.

Madame Sycorax Cavendish had her long, glorious hair bound up tightly beneath a silver leather hat rather too small for her head. Her severe, lovely features had grown leaner and sharper in the two years since the raid on Spire Albion, giving her the hungry look of a half-starved cat, and when she stopped to regard Espira, her dark eyes were calm and cold.

Cavendish was an etherealist, a deadly one. All etherealists had difficulties relating to normal life. Those difficulties made most of them rather odd. The etherealists behaved in ways that seemed mad to most people who saw them, and they engaged in any number of ritualistic behaviors to compensate for their intellectual and emotional challenges. It also made it necessary to walk quietly around their foibles if one was to work with them, and Espira was familiar with at least one of Cavendish's points of irrationality: the woman observed the rules of courtesy as if they were a blood sport—one she was more than willing to participate in should one's manners slip.

Espira made a gallant bow to Cavendish and doffed his cap. "Madame Cavendish, after you."

"So kind, Colonel," Cavendish murmured, and stepped past him to the staircase. She went up the stairs smoothly with a flicker of boots and ankles and a very small smile that told him she'd noticed him looking. He waited a prudent moment after she'd ascended to the bridge, and then followed lightly.

The bridge was occupied by five people: Calliope Ransom; the ship's pilot, a Dalosian fellow with few teeth; Ransom's broad-shouldered, warriorborn first mate; and a couple of scrawny youths in cast-off leathers and resized safety harnesses. The last two were evidently runners needed to carry the captain's orders to the rest of the ship.

Espira strode up to Ransom. Standing with her legs braced apart, the *Mistshark*'s captain held a spyglass to her eye, staring out at the open sky. Espira put his hands on the rail and squinted, but the distance was too great for him to see much: a number of what appeared to be airships were very near to one another, and their relative motion and attitudes suggested they were in combat, not forming a convoy.

"God in bloody Heaven," muttered Ransom through her teeth, staring through the spyglass, "what am I looking at?"

She lowered the spyglass but continued to gaze at the distant shapes, her expression sickened.

Espira stared at her for a long moment, the cold feeling in his stomach growing queasier. "Captain?" he said finally.

Ransom started with a little jerk of her body and shot an oblique glance at him. Then she offered him the spyglass and waved her hand vaguely out at the battling ships, her expression still somewhat dazed.

Espira took the spyglass and swept it around the sky until horror filled his vision.

An airship was under attack.

She was a potbellied merchantman flying a Dalosian flag, her hold made for storage, not speed. She was armed with four light cannon per deck, for while no merchantman wanted to do battle with a proper man-of-war, every captain of such a vessel needed enough armament to defend against simple pirates. Light armament was the most tactically and economically effective compromise, but that weaponry hadn't been anything like enough to hold off half a dozen corsairs acting in concert.

Corsairs were dedicated pirate airships meant to hold only troops and weapons, much like military vessels—only a good deal smaller than even frigates and much smaller than modest merchant ships like *Mistshark*. The pirates on a typical corsair would attack a merchantman, burn down her web, board her with superior numbers and ferocity, dispatch or capture her crew, and leave enough men behind to sail the captured vessel and its cargo back to their home base. Life on a corsair was crowded, violent, and miserable, and the things the crews of such ships did to relieve the terrible pressures placed upon them by their lifestyle were the things of nightmare.

Espira felt sickened as he watched the crews of three corsairs hurl themselves onto the doomed merchantman, and its crew began to fight for their lives. Then he realized *why* he felt sickened.

The crews attacking the merchantman were not human.

The *corsairs* attacking the merchantman were not human.

The ships had not been built from timbers and beams and planks and boards. They had been built . . . Espira stared. He did not *know* how they could have been built, for the hulls were smooth and natural and lined as if they had simply been grown into the desired shape out of some bizarre grey tree. That shape itself was unnatural, vaguely mimicking the look of an airship, but with the dimensions either exaggerated or understated, so that the whole of the ship looked both familiar and unsettlingly odd.

Especially since there were no masts. No web. No visible means of propulsion of any kind.

Even as Espira watched, a fourth corsair warped in and cast out hooked lines. A sullen orange light rippled through the lines in the hull of the bizarre ship; sparks of static electricity snapped and popped along its length as if the ship's hull itself was catching and harnessing the same etheric current that drove *Mistshark*. The corsair grappled onto the merchantman and hauled it in, and . . . boarders began leaping across to it.

They were larger than humans, at seven feet, and a hunchbacked seven feet at that. They had heavy, forward-leaning builds balanced by thick slabs of clublike muscle for tails extending behind them, and heavy chests and weirdly wide shoulders leading to unnaturally long arms ending in three-fingered hands. Their skin was . . . a greyish leathery crust coated with growths of etheric crystals of some kind glittering in the sunlight, and they bore both gauntlets and sidearms. Their faces were long muzzles lined with rows of snaggled, crocodilian teeth, and their eyes were invisible behind bands of crystals that seemed to grow from the sockets.

Espira had never seen anything like them. Never heard of anything like them.

"God in Heaven," he echoed Ransom unwittingly. "What am I looking at?"

Espira continued to peer through the spyglass, glad that his view was distant and grainy. Because what the enemy did to the crew of the Dalosian merchantman was not something he wanted to see. He lowered the spyglass, his belly twisting.

There was warmth beside him, and he turned to see Madame

Cavendish staring out at the boarding action, her eyes remote, her expression distant.

Ransom's hand gripped the rail. The first mate stepped up beside her, stared hard out at the action with feline eyes, and rumbled, "Captain?"

Ransom wasn't a handsome woman, Espira thought, but it was easy to see the keenness of the mind operating behind her highly expressive face, and *that* made her look intensely interesting.

"They're human," she decided crisply. "They're in trouble. We're going in." She considered, then added judiciously, "And we'll make them let us choose a reward."

Espira huffed out half of a laugh.

Ransom arched a brow at him.

"You're going in to save a merchant from pirates," Espira said, "so that you can pirate them yourself."

Ransom's teeth showed. "I am a much more reasonable shark than the current bunch."

"It's six to one," Espira noted. "And we have no idea about the six."

"Ships that size can't have much of a shroud, and I have an excellent idea about the one," Ransom said, her smile widening defiantly. "Sound maneuvers. I mean to blow the two loose ones out of the sky and pick off the boarders as they try to disengage. We'll put sharpshooters on the dorsal mast and let them kill any boarders on the deck." She made a hungry sound deep in her throat. "And I want one of those corsairs. How do they do that?" She shot a glance at Espira. "Can I count on your men?"

"That's a Dalosian ship," Espira said. "Auroran Marines have no cause to be fighting for them."

"That's a human ship," Ransom countered. "Politics is cute. But get reality straight. People need help."

"And you need a prize."

"And I need a prize," Ransom said, grinning. "I find it so reassuring when the right thing is also the profitable thing."

They were toying with each other, of course.

After the last ten days, the last several colonies, neither one of them could stomach the thought of standing by and doing nothing. Espira was a soldier. Ransom was a professional mercenary. Neither found any pleasure or honor in the slaughter to which they'd been indirect parties.

"Reassuring, eh? Then you'll find it comforting when I assure you I'll take ten percent for my men and any intelligence for the Armada," Espira said easily. "And a corsair for myself."

Ransom threw back her head and let out a belly laugh. "Done." She turned aside and began giving orders to the pilot.

Espira took another look through the spyglass. The merchant-man's crew had retreated belowdecks. The enemy was sending climbers down to try to cut through the ship's wooden hull. *Mistshark* was too far away for Espira and the others to hear the howls of gauntlet and long-gun fire, though the superheated projectiles could be seen in flashes of various colors of light. The enemy boarders soaked up fire as if they were clad in the heaviest ethersilk armor, though Espira noted that boarding axes and cutlasses had done their work well enough. Several still forms attested to the fact that the strangers were not immortals.

He lowered the spyglass and turned to go belowdecks and order Ciriaco to break out the gunpowder firearms, an order sure to make him immensely unpopular amongst his men. Well, if they'd done their maintenance on their weaponry sufficiently, they'd be safe enough, wouldn't they? Well-maintained rifles hardly ever exploded— and if gauntlet fire wouldn't impress their foes, perhaps three-quarter-inch ball would do the trick.

He turned to go and simply froze, staring at Cavendish.

The etherealist's eyes had . . . had changed.

They had been a warm brown when Espira had met the woman. Now they were a kind of eerie bronze, and . . . and . . . structures had formed in them. As if the colored irises had been replaced with a spread of quasi-crystalline bronze frost. The woman's mouth was locked in a rictus, and her spine had gone quaveringly tense, rigid.

"Too soon," she said under her breath. "It's too soon."

The ship's bell sounded maneuvers, a frantic trill that gave the crew ten seconds of warning to secure themselves before the ship began to do things like abruptly dropping in a free fall. Espira hastily secured all three of his lines to different attachment points nearby.

"Captain," Cavendish snarled into the silence that fell instantly after the maneuver bell, "stand down!"

Ransom whirled on the etherealist, her eyes narrowed, her safety lines taut and neat around her. "Excuse me?"

"This is an excellent opportunity for a tactical test," Cavendish hissed. She turned slowly, her unsettling eyes glinting in the light. "Resist your gluttonous urges, Captain. I claim those ships for Tuscarora."

Ransom stared coldly at Cavendish, but the etherealist ignored her with a demure smile and turned to descend calmly from the bridge.

"God in Heaven," the pilot muttered, "she's not even wearing a harness."

Cavendish gave the pilot a venomous look—and flicked a finger.

The man suddenly froze, his body quivering, and it took Espira a second to realize what was happening. Somehow current had overloaded the insulation in the steering column and surged up through the handgrips and into the poor pilot.

The man twitched helplessly, the muscles in his jaw bulging as they clamped shut harder and harder.

Ransom moved instantly, drawing her knife, slashing the pilot's safety lines, and violently kicking the man away from the steering column. He hauled the steering grips with him before his hands, scarlet and burned, were torn away from them, and the ship yawed sharply to the side.

Espira lunged for the steering column, shoving his forearm against it to prevent the current from locking his grip on it, but the surge of electricity had apparently ended. He heaved the column more or less back into the neutral position, and the *Mistshark* stabilized.

Ransom moved as smoothly and automatically as any animal, taking the steering column from Espira with a nod of thanks. Then she stared hard after Cavendish while the first mate scooped up the groaning pilot and bore him quickly from the bridge toward the ship's infirmary.

The etherealist gave the aeronaut a tiny smile. "That man is of no station to speak about me in such a familiar and blasphemous fashion. I implore you—don't make me kill any of your crew with their own ship, Captain. Do stand down. And stay well back from what is about to happen."

Calliope Ransom glared at the etherealist. She still wore her pistols on her hips. One of her hands twitched, and Cavendish smiled mockingly.

Ransom stilled her hand and let out a slow breath. Then she said, "There's no point in fighting. If that's the mission, just tell me. There's no reason for drama."

"Isn't there?" Cavendish shivered and swallowed, sliding one hand to her stomach. Then she nodded, smiled faintly, and turned to descend dreamily from the bridge and walk toward the hatchway through which she could go belowdecks.

When Cavendish was almost to the hatchway, Ransom murmured, "I rather wonder what would happen if I ordered power to the lift crystal cut right about now." She moved a shoulder suggestively. "Slice to port. Let her fall."

"I don't know. But she'll have thought of that," Espira replied firmly. "She's mad. Not stupid."

"No, she's not. Yet we are professionals, Colonel," Ransom replied, "not flunkies to be smacked about. I'll not tolerate that woman again, Espira. If my man dies, the gauntlet's already been thrown."

He frowned. "Tuscarora would not be pleased to hear that."

"Tuscarora knows where my boot would go if he said as much," Ransom shot back.

Espira suppressed a surge of real panic. People like Captain Ransom were useful to Spire Aurora precisely because they were independent minded, drew their own conclusions, and took action on their own initiative. If the woman who had casually seduced Tuscarora and walked away took it into her mind to arrange a three-minute air bath for Madame Cavendish, she would do it—and as much as Espira might sleep better at night with Madame Cavendish dead, she was an irreplaceable part of a weapons system necessary to Spire Aurora.

"Captain, I understand your frustration," he said, and met her eyes frankly. "But you know how volatile etherealists like her can be. For the sake of this mission, be patient a little longer. I'm sure His Majesty will reward your restraint appropriately."

Espira had not said out loud, *Put off your revenge until it is a little more convenient to Aurora, and I'll make it worth your while.* But Ransom tilted her head sharply, studied his face, and read his expression easily enough. Calculating, she glanced after the vanished Cavendish with narrowed eyes and then back at Espira.

"You're a fool," she said a beat later without malice. "Believing in him."

"His Majesty is well known to reward loyal service with loyal leadership," Espira replied.

"He's a fool too," she said drily.

There was a deep, deep sound. A moan that vibrated through the air and shook the spars of the ship. It died away in a long, despairing wheeze.

Everyone on the *Mistshark* went utterly still.

Espira felt his stomach twist and writhe as it had at the last several colonies. Something disturbed the air, a hideous stench that wafted against his face, and the mist beneath the ship stirred and surged upward in whirls as something vast moved through it.

A moment later, the moan came again—this time from ahead of them, heading toward the battle and away from the ship. Espira felt a little burst of hysterical relief that came hand in hand with a bellyful of molten lead ingots of shame as he regarded the doomed Dalosian merchantman and its attackers alike.

"To Hell with this," Ransom said roughly. "I don't need to watch it again."

"No," Espira agreed quietly. "Neither do I."

But neither of them moved.

It was over in moments. Nothing remained. Not the enemy ships. Not the Dalosian merchantman. Nothing any of them did made the least bit of difference.

And a minute after that, there was a woman's delighted laughter from belowdecks.

Espira wanted to vomit.

He found himself staring at Ransom. The woman's expression matched his own.

"You were ready to go in with me, weren't you?" she murmured.

Espira ground his teeth. "After this cruise. Yes."

Ransom nodded and squinted out at the now empty skyline for a long moment.

"Some cruises can do that," she said in a rough voice. Then she blinked and said more brightly, "Ginger tea, Colonel?"

"Please, Captain," the Marine said.

Something flickered in the woman's dark eyes: amusement and interest. "My cabin. Half an hour. Wash."

Chapter 9

AMS *Predator*, near Spire Olympia

The journey from Spire Albion to Spire Olympia took a little less than five days, and Grimm had the crew spend the time holystoning *Predator*'s decks, masts, and hull. The soft sandstone scraped off the surface layers of the wood, revealing the unstained beauty beneath, and the ship shone brightly in the sun on the journey. The scent of freshly exposed wood filled the air as they prepared it to be resealed, and the crew spent the trip in high spirits, their overlapping work songs and merry shouts filling the skies around the ship.

Predator had sailed in mighty company. AFS *Belligerent*, whose mass dwarfed *Predator* to insignificance and whose armored flanks could endure broadside after broadside from the smaller vessel, cruised along with very nearly as much speed and ease as *Predator* herself. Bayard's ship had five times the crew of Grimm's and three decks of cannon twice as powerful as *Predator*'s on each flank. Her half dozen chase guns were the same heavy cannon as the broadside armament of a dreadnought.

And yet, Grimm thought, for all that ship's speed and endurance and power, the reason she flew the scarlet, blue, and white stripes of Albion and not the sky blue bars and scarlet stars of Aurora was because the little ship he commanded had slipped a knife into the battlecruiser's mighty guts. It had required no small degree of trust between himself and Bayard, the sacrifice of too many good crewmen, and the loss of two light cruisers to get the job done, but the former *Itasca* now served the Aetherium Fleet.

While the loss of a single battlecruiser was not insignificant, neither would it be a decisive factor in the coming war, but the capture of a storied vessel with a long history was a blow to the morale of the Armada and a similar boost to the morale of Albion, whose Fleet had handled the heavy warship with a handful of light vessels. Sending the captured vessel out to be displayed at the summit council was a political statement of its own, demonstrating Albion's prowess to the world and all but daring Aurora and her aggressive monarch to try something else.

"Hell of a big ship," Kettle noted to Grimm from his post at the steering grips. "But I wouldn't want to holystone it. Or seal it up again after."

Grimm grinned at his pilot and looked over to where *Belligerent* cruised five hundred yards off the starboard beam, forty yards below *Predator*. Her etheric web, many times as vast as *Predator's*, gleamed and shone in the sun. Crews labored at beautifying their ship much as Grimm's men had; they would make an impression upon arrival at Olympia.

"Time to Olympia?" Grimm asked politely.

Kettle consulted his pocket watch. "Call it ten hours." The pilot nodded out toward the horizon off the ship's port side. "See?"

Grimm turned and squinted to see not one, not two, but half a dozen other ships in various positions in the sky, all on virtually the same heading *Predator* currently followed. More attendees to the summit council, then. Grimm got out his spyglass and checked banners. The ships hailed from a quarter of the continent: the Dalosian

115

Federation with its white star on a red-and-blue field; the Pike Alliance and its white skull on a black field; and the Olympian Council, a green field with a golden laurel wreath centered on it.

"Lot of people coming to dinner," Grimm noted, then bellowed easily, "XO!"

Word went down the ship, and a moment later, Miss Lancaster arrived, her face smudged with grime and grease from the engine room. How she managed to dirty her face but not her uniform was an ongoing mystery Grimm felt sure he lacked the intellectual or emotional capacity to solve.

"Skip," she said breathlessly. "Mister Journeyman's compliments, and he says he's finally got the engines tuned right, sir."

"Only took him two years," Kettle drawled easily from the steering grips.

Grimm grunted. "Did he finish those buoys for Mister Stern?"

Gwen hesitated for half a second before answering. "They're ready, Skip."

Grimm turned on her and raised an eyebrow. "That wasn't my question, XO."

Miss Lancaster grimaced. "Sir, the chief engineer claimed he was too busy following your orders to aid the lieutenant, sir. I redelegated it to myself on my own initiative to make sure it got done."

Grimm stared at the XO for several seconds. He used the time to set his anger aside and consider priorities.

"I see," he said. "It is good that the work got done. The mission objective always comes first. But outside of emergencies, *how* the work gets done is at least as important. I gave Journeyman an order. It was your job to ensure that he carried it out."

"You know how he is, Skip," Gwen said. "What about what you said about honoring each crewman's talents? I thought this applied."

"Part of what makes him an excellent etheric engineer is that he is obsessed with his toys, yes," Grimm said. "But he is also a member of the crew. His duty to his crewmates comes first." He sighed. "Can't have crewmen who won't follow orders. With me."

Grimm strode to the engine room with the XO's boots striking firmly on the fresh deck just behind him. He pushed open the door and let the smell of copper and grease and the waste heat of the ship's beating heart wash over him.

Predator's engine room occupied the mass center of the ship belowdecks. The middle of the room was occupied by the main lift crystal of the ship: a green stone the size of a large bathtub cut into a faceted, rounded oblong. It was nestled into a socket in the main suspension rig in the room's ceiling, and power lines from the engine core carried enough power to it to keep it aloft. This crystal was the structural core of the ship, and the weight of the entire vessel hung from the rig it supported.

Just beyond it were the Haslett cage and the power core of the ship. There, within the collection of copper rods that would be adjusted to collect electricity from the power core, was a crystal about the size of a grown man. It was a lumpy and asymmetrical stone of ancient origin, one of the oldest power crystals grown by the Lancaster vattery, and based upon the configuration of the Haslett cage's rods, it could produce more or less power for use in the ship's systems. Grimm always felt that the Haslett cage looked like some kind of dead spider, its many, many long legs caging the crystal within them.

Mister Journeyman occupied the main core power panel, peering at dials and other indicators, and the engineering crew was scattered around the room at the various panels that moderated power flow to the various systems: the web, the ship's shroud, the lift and trim crystals, and the weapons systems. Journeyman was a medium-sized bear of a man, thick through the shoulders and arms and legs and hands. He wore his dark hair cropped short while he'd allowed his beard to grow enormously, giving him rather the look of a mountain, Grimm thought: craggy slopes up to a nearly bald crown.

"Mister Journeyman," Grimm stated as he entered.

"Skip," muttered the engineer with something approaching courtesy. But absorbed in his work, he didn't look up.

"Give us the room," Grimm said firmly.

The crewmen in the engine room took one look at Grimm's face and departed. Journeyman kept working while they did, seeming to take no notice.

Grimm strode over to the man, seized his shoulder, whirled him around, and delivered an uppercut to his chin that snapped the bearlike Journeyman's head back and left him seated on the deck, his shoulders against the command console. He let out a stunned sound and raised his hand to his jaw, blinking up at Grimm with startled eyes.

Grimm met the man's gaze as he took off his coat and passed it to the XO. "This isn't Fleet, Journeyman," he said in a calm voice. "They have regulations. I have principles. There's a difference."

"Wha?" Journeyman said, scowling.

"I believe I gave you an order, Chief," Grimm said calmly. He unbuckled his sword belt and passed that to the XO as well.

"The damned buoys got built!" Journeyman protested, rising. His huge fists clenched and unclenched.

"But not by you," Grimm replied. "Any alteration to my orders needs to come from me. Not you."

"By God in Heaven, you're right." Journeyman narrowed his eyes. "This isn't Fleet." And he came at Grimm with a quick, hard combination of powerful punches, any one of which could have laid him out.

Grimm ducked one blow, took another properly to the belly,

caught three more on his forearms, and stopped Journeyman's assault with a hard, straight jab to the man's nose. He followed up with three more jabs, driving the chief engineer back across the engine room. Journeyman's shoulder blades bounced off the bulkhead, directly into Grimm's right cross, and the burly engineer went down as if some divine artist had erased his legs.

Grimm stayed on guard for a moment, then lowered his fists, shaking them. Hitting people hurt. Journeyman was still for perhaps the space of a long breath, and then he twitched, groaned, and sat up.

"I keep telling you," Grimm said, "your footwork isn't there."

Journeyman scowled, but there was no longer that same quivering tension in his shoulders. He rubbed at his jaw, wincing. "You know I don't like listening."

"I don't need you to like it," Grimm said. "I need you to do it. Or I'll find a new engineer."

"*Preddy* would never be treated as well as I treat her, Skip."

"Your job is more than simply systems, Chief," Grimm replied. "You have to set an example for the rest of engineering. That means being on time. That means following orders."

Journeyman scowled again, ducking his head. But he nodded. "Okay, Skip."

"Excuse me?" Grimm said, his eyes hard.

Journeyman at least had enough shame to look down after being called out for using the familiar title. "Aye, aye, Captain."

Grimm nodded. "Let's go. We'll test the chase gun. You'll monitor."

"Aye, aye, Captain."

"Mister Journeyman?" Grimm asked, softening his tone considerably.

"Sir?"

"I don't enjoy this," he said. "Let's not do it again."

Journeyman rubbed his jaw again, squinting. "No kidding."

"Five minutes, Chief," Grimm said, and turned to leave.

Gwen paced beside him, frowning.

"Mister Journeyman is a special case," he explained. "The man's a genius with systems. He doesn't know anything about people. And he's so tough and thick-skulled that the only way to get an idea in is to crack it open a little. He'll be sore for a day or so, but he'll get over it. It's the best way to deal with insubordination in his case."

"Fleet would have him flogged and in irons," Gwen noted.

"I'm not Fleet," Grimm said. "And I don't have a contract of obligation with him. Journeyman could quit on me. I'd like him not to do that."

Gwen frowned. "But fighting? I'm fairly sure I'd not care to engage him in hand-to-hand. He'd trounce me."

"Oh, that wasn't a fight. It was more an alternate means of communication Journeyman and I have developed over the years. You never set out to fight someone. What you want to do is confront them and resolve whatever issues are at hand. It doesn't always have to be physical. But if it is, it doesn't matter if you win or you lose," Grimm said. "If you're willing to fight, you make your point and win respect. But." He paused for a moment for emphasis. "Never. Ever. In front of the crew. It would gut his pride and their morale if you won and do worse than that if you lost. Always discipline. Never humiliation. Hear?"

"Yes, Skip," Gwen said, her voice thoughtful.

Installing the chase gun had been complicated. The original forward gun deck was made for a pair of weapons considerably smaller than the one now occupying it, and Journeyman had been forced to add a platform to the airship's superstructure to compensate. His crew and he had needed to install a much heavier gimbal to mount the cannon upon, and the result was a weapon that stood forward from the prow, on the gun deck just below the bridge, giving *Predator* the rakish look of a swordsman at the ready.

Lieutenant Stern was currently under the gimbal, tinkering with a set of tools, but his dark-haired, grease-smudged face was grinning. "Skip! Chief! Come to see the action?"

"That's the idea," Grimm replied.

Journeyman stumped over to the readouts on the control panel for the cannon, then glowered at them. He and Stern spoke briefly, and Journeyman tested the gimbal, then climbed under with Stern for ten minutes of cursing.

After they both emerged, they seized the control handle for the cannon and wrenched it left and right, up and down, and it moved readily enough. A regular cannon would have been able to fire almost straight up and down, but the limited space had similarly limited the chase gun's field of fire.

Grimm wasn't overly worried by that. *Predator* herself was one of the more mobile ships in the sky and could easily adjust. And besides, it was a chase gun; he meant to use it when *Predator* was on offense, which was the posture he always preferred.

The new weapon was also the same size as a cannon on a dreadnought's broadside, so it had the potential to wipe out a smaller ship's shroud in a single blast and annihilate a ship *Predator*'s size with a second shot.

"Ready, Skip," Stern said excitedly.

"Carry on, Lieutenant," Grimm replied.

Stern began shouting orders, and a few moments later the ship's forward speed was cut, and her acceleration dropped to almost nothing. After that, Stern and his crew launched the buoy, essentially a wooden platform supported by a tiny power crystal and a nearly dead trim crystal; a wooden target had been mounted upon it. The wind caught it and began carrying it away from the ship.

"At five hundred yards, Mister Stern," Grimm noted.

"Aye, Skip," Stern said excitedly. The young man paused, and though he tried to disguise the way his face suddenly fell, there was vibrant reluctance in his voice. "Would the captain care to fire the cannon, sir?"

"That's all right, Lieutenant," Grimm replied, firmly suppressing his own grin. He'd been Stern once upon a time. "Take the shot."

"Aye, Captain!" Stern said, beaming, and he settled into the gunner's seat.

By then the crew had begun to gather to watch the test, so many of them coming to the front of the ship that the deck began to tilt a little until Kettle compensated from his pilot's position on the bridge.

Grimm idly took his sword and coat back from the XO as they waited for the wind to carry the target far enough out. "Does that look about right to you, Lieutenant?"

"Just a little more," Stern replied. "There. That's five hundred yards, Skip."

"You may fire when ready," Grimm replied.

"Always wanted to say that to someone," Journeyman muttered.

Stern lined up the cannon carefully and then said, "Firing," and squeezed the handles.

Energy cannon didn't buck or recoil. They shivered and howled, making the decking beneath the crew's feet vibrate disturbingly, the very air screaming in protest as the cannon let out a sizzling bead of white-hot light that moved at ridiculous speed and expanded as it flew forward. The first shot missed the relatively tiny target. Stern adjusted the sights and fired a second round. This one also missed but came considerably closer. Stern adjusted the sights again.

The third shot engulfed the buoy in flame and blew the fragile wooden platform to very small, very hot splinters.

Grimm swallowed. *Predator* herself was, at the end of the day, basically a wooden target. The weapon they had just installed could hammer her just as easily as the buoy. He watched flaming splinters rain from the sky.

"Just remember, sir," Journeyman said. "That's too much gun for *Preddy's* power core. We can't run everything and also use this gun. Either we cut power to the shroud or to the web if we're going to fire this beast."

"Understood, Chief," Grimm replied. "Does the weapon perform to your satisfaction, Mister Stern?"

Stern spun in his seat, grinning. "Oh, it definitely does that, Skip."

"Mine as well," Grimm said, permitting himself a small smile. "Thank you, gentlemen. That was excellent work from both of you. A week's bonus pay at the end of this cruise."

Stern straightened in pride, and Journeyman nodded, smiling.

"All right, Chief," Grimm said ruefully. "Go play with your spanners."

"Will do, Skip." Journeyman gave him an easy grin and a casual salute, and then he ambled away.

Stern checked several more readouts on the weapon, writing down notes furiously. Then he hurried out. Grimm had no doubt the young officer would be every bit as involved with this weapon as Journeyman was with the ship's engines. He'd have to watch Stern for signs of Journeyman Syndrome.

The XO put a fond hand on the forward gun and said, "I like it too."

"Remember that it's just one cannon," Grimm said. "We'll have to use it intelligently and carefully. We must rely on skilled position-ing and use our mobility to maximum advantage."

"That's every cannon," Gwen said, smiling brilliantly. "Your dress uniform has been cleaned and pressed, Skip."

Grimm eyed her sourly. His neck itched already. But making a good showing for Albion upon arrival was critical. "Pass the word among the men. Baths and combs and clean clothes all around."

"Baths and combs and clean clothes, aye," Gwen said. She turned to go and then paused. "You seemed keen to get the new gun up and running."

"Yes."

"Are you expecting trouble?"

Grimm frowned. "War is in the air, XO. I'm not expecting any-thing specific, but . . ."

"But what?"

Grimm shrugged. "Over the course of my command, I've found that it's always better to have something and not need it than the other way around. Let's be ready."

■ ■ ■ Chapter 10 ■ ■ ■

AMS *Predator*, Skyport, Spire Olympia

The sun had burned through the mists in a blaze of light and clear blue sky, so that Spire Olympia's skyport seemed to float upon a sea of roiling cloud. Grimm stood upon the bridge while the XO brought the ship in, working together with Kettle and Journeyman, and tried not to look as if he wanted to take command back and bring his precious ship into port himself. But he resisted the temptation. He was supposed to be training Miss Lancaster. He could hardly teach her how to handle an airship without letting her handle an airship from time to time.

When she ordered a course change a moment too soon, Grimm winced but said nothing. Gwen realized her mistake a moment later and compensated. After pacing to the far side of the bridge to give the XO room to work, he held his hands clenched behind his back until his knuckles ached, and he kept his expression impassive.

Footsteps came slowly up the ladder; then there were a couple of stamping sounds. Grimm turned his head to see who had come up.

A tall, lean man in his late sixties had appeared. He was dressed in a tattered grey bathrobe, deep blue pajamas, and oversized quilted slippers. His silver hair was a rumpled mess, his beard resembled some of the wire brushes Journeyman used to keep his parts clean, and his expression was pleased and dreamy. He carefully turned in a circle to his left twice and stamped his feet. Then he did it in the opposite direction, stamped his feet again, clapped his hands twice, and beamed at Grimm.

"Ah, the grim captain!" he called. "My goodness, what a pleasure it is to see you again."

Grimm turned to face the man, smiled, and bowed. "Master Ferus. We, ah, saw each other at dinner only last night."

"Which was also a pleasure at that time," Master Ferus assured him. The master etherealist walked across the bridge and took up station next to Grimm. "My, my, my," the old man said. "Look at all the banners."

Grimm gave him a quick smile. Olympia's banner, with its golden laurel wreath upon a field of green, blazed from every edge of the Spire and flew from every Olympian ship and flagpole. Atlantea's fabric manufactories had made a great deal of money from Olympia's preparations for the summit meeting.

Granted, *Belligerent* was decked out with so many flags and so much bunting, all in scarlet, white, and azure, that it resembled some sort of bizarre and overdecorated cake in the shape of a warship. Her new name had been blazoned on her prow in letters of polished silver two feet high that could be seen clearly for hundreds of yards, and Bayard had made sure to keep all the decorations clear of the lettering. By comparison, poor *Predator* appeared to be a grocer standing next to a lady in a ball gown, but Grimm took satisfaction in his ship's clean decks and flanks and in the efficiency of her lines and her crew.

The sky blue bars and scarlet stars of Aurora were present on a dreadnought that had already landed. Apparently, His Majesty Tuscarora had decided to make an impression himself. The vast ship—

one whose hull could have swallowed *Predator* whole, masts and all—made even mighty *Belligerent* dwindle into relative insignificance.

But those weren't the only banners. Grimm counted six variations of the flag of Dalos, doubtless from various colonies of that federation; a dozen banners from minor independent colonies and Spires; and a single heavy-cruiser-sized ship draped in funereal black and flying a midnight banner with a grinning white skull centered upon it.

Grimm felt his heart skip a little beat.

Master Ferus glanced aside at Grimm's face and followed his gaze. "Anyone you know?"

"Only a little," Grimm said, "and—"

He was interrupted by an enormous sound—one like an airship's steam horn but far deeper and more melodious. The blast sounded again, deep enough to make the deck quiver beneath the soles of Grimm's boots, and he looked up, scanning the skies for the source of the sound.

"My word," Master Ferus said. "What was that?"

"The Atlanteans like to announce themselves," Grimm replied.

He spotted the source of the sound and nodded toward a heavy cruiser that was descending gracefully toward the skyport about a mile off from *Predator.* The ship had been painted in a bizarre zigzag pattern of white, black, and scarlet; it streamed silken banners of brilliant purple marked with an open silver triangle. The sailors on the deck were all dressed in preposterously expensive pure white uniforms that mostly stood out brilliantly against the dark skin tones of that Spire's people. "That must be their delegation."

"Well, I must say they look quite fine," Master Ferus said. The Atlantean horns blared again as the ship dropped deftly into her docking cradle. "Captain, have you been to Spire Atlantea?"

"Many times."

"Is it true that the ruling class . . . What was it called?"

"The Spectral Congress," Grimm replied, "though most simply call it the Spectrum."

"And they are all etherealists?" Ferus asked skeptically.

"So it would seem," Grimm said.

The etherealist shook his head. "Dear me. I can't help but think I'd be an absolutely terrible ruler. I'm still wearing pajamas. I'm not sure I'd do anything very rulerlike."

"A leader who was conscientious and intelligent about doing nothing would be better than most," Grimm noted. "Of course, you never see anyone from the Spectral Congress without the Crimson Guard around them."

"Elite warriors, yes?" Master Ferus asked. "I read an essay about them once."

"Warriorborn, all of them," Grimm said. "They have almost as much power as the Congress. Some say it's the Crimson Guard who really run the Spire." He nodded toward the banners. "That's why there's a triangle on their banners." Grimm drew a triangle in the air with his finger, starting at the bottom-left corner. "The Congress, the Guard, and the people."

"One notes that the people are on the bottom of that triangle," Ferus said drily.

"I noticed that as well," Grimm confirmed. "From what I've seen, it's easy to be poor in Atlantea."

The horn blared one more time for no reason at all, and Grimm rolled his eyes.

"You don't care for the display," Master Ferus said.

"I'm an Albion," Grimm said simply.

Ferus glanced aside at the utterly bedecked *Belligerent* and eyed Grimm with lifted eyebrows.

Grimm frowned and said, "Bayard is atypical." He glanced around. "Where is Miss Folly?"

"Practicing," Ferus said. "Etherealism requires a great deal of practice." He beamed at Grimm. "Quite maddening, really, but it must be done."

The XO misjudged another angle on her approach, and the deck pitched slightly. It took her a moment to correct, and Grimm muttered to Ferus, "I know precisely what you mean."

"I've been talking to your ship," Ferus said.

Grimm arched an eyebrow. "Oh?"

"She's very fond of you, you know," Ferus said, beaming. "I daresay she'd sacrifice herself for you if it was needful."

Grimm really had little idea if this alleged consciousness in his vessel was a real thing or a metaphoric figment of quirky etherealists' imaginations. He'd certainly never seen anything to make him think the consciousness was real. But at the same time, he had to acknowledge that his little ship had gotten a great deal more done than it had any right to, and he was generally the sort of person who valued positive outcomes. If the etherealists talking to his ship made her perform better, he supposed it didn't matter if *Predator* was truly alive or not. Whatever the case, his behavior would not change, and he still had the same duties to accomplish.

Though, he mused, if it ever turned out that his ship genuinely was alive and aware, he felt he might owe her considerable back pay.

"Master Ferus," Grimm said, "have you read the intelligence packet I dropped off for you?"

"It was mostly guesses," Ferus replied. "Hardly any of them seemed intelligent."

"I think Vincent is making his best estimates," Grimm said.

"Vincent is afraid of everything," Master Ferus replied easily.

"It's what makes him adept at spotting trouble. But it's a very difficult way to live."

"I was curious as to your thoughts on the document," Grimm said.

"Seemed flimsy," said Ferus instantly.

"In what way?"

"The parchment flopped everywhere."

Grimm stifled a guffaw.

Ferus narrowed his eyes for a moment and said, "It seems to me Bayard needs to keep his friends close." He yawned. "These pajamas are making me sleepy. I think I'll change into day clothes."

"That does seem entirely appropriate," Grimm noted, still smiling with his eyes.

Ferus winked at Grimm. Then he did his little dance in reverse order, clapping and stamping and turning, and departed from the bridge.

Then Grimm winced as the XO brought the ship in a little too quickly, setting *Predator* down with a tooth-clacking thump. Everyone staggered a little, and Miss Lancaster shot him an apologetic glance.

"Better than last time," Grimm said with a smile. "As soon as we're secure, I need a runner sent to *Belligerent*. I want to talk to Alex."

Chapter 11

AFS *Belligerent*, Skyport, Spire Olympia

Grimm hurried over to *Belligerent*, but as efficient as he was, before he could step onto the ramp up to the ship, Lady Hinton came sweeping down it. Dressed in a dark red bustled dress and a broad-brimmed black hat often favored by ladies traveling aboard airships, she was trailed by a trio of harried-looking aeronauts carrying her luggage.

"Madison, darling," Hinton said, "Bayard expects you. Excuse me." She kissed the air next to Grimm's cheek. "Permission to board? Is that what they say? I simply must talk to a number of people, you understand." And she whooshed past him and hurried off into the crowded skyport.

Grimm watched her go, smiling, and then went up to the ship. The Marine on duty stopped him, as he should have, and Grimm sent word to Bayard that he was there. Five minutes later, a Marine escorted him respectfully to the captain's cabin, and Grimm knocked and entered.

Grimm pulled up short as he walked into a cabin large enough to hold a table for a dozen people. The ceiling was so high that he couldn't have bumped his head on a beam even if he jumped. He found himself staring around it for a moment, bemused.

Bayard appeared from the next room—a captain's *suite*, apparently—and grinned at Grimm's expression. He swaggered in, wearing his impeccably cut dress uniform in the deep blue of the Aetherium Fleet. His dark gold hair and ready grin were on display. "Roomy, isn't it?"

"How?" Grimm asked.

"The Armada has a captain's cabin and a political officer's cabin in every vessel," Bayard said smugly. "As the good Spirearch makes no such position necessary in Fleet, I claimed the space for both." Alex stretched out to full length, arms overhead.

"Hmph," Grimm said. "Someone your size hardly needs all the space."

"Unfair, isn't it?" Bayard replied in satisfaction. "Good to be working with you again, Mad."

"If you say so," Grimm replied, smiling, and the men traded a warm embrace.

"I've got half an hour or so while I let the XO cut his teeth," Bayard said seriously. "Time for a talk?"

"Done."

Grimm got glasses out while Bayard produced a bottle of his favorite cognac, and the two men each took a finger.

"To good men gone," Grimm said.

"Good men gone," Bayard replied, and the two touched glasses and took their first sips in silence.

Grimm leaned a hip against a sideboard and studied his friend. Only a bit more than five feet tall and built like a cat, Alex was lean, muscular, swift, and far too powerful for his size. Bayard always had a sense of containment to his person that Grimm envied. Regardless of the situation, Bayard would appear calm and graceful in it. There was also always a sense of power to the man's movements as if gravity kept him touching the earth only with Bayard's consent.

His dueling swords, Grimm noted, had been laid out on a table beside the captain's armoire. They were freshly polished; their steel edges had been honed to a razor's sharpness before getting a fine coating of wax to protect them from ironrot.

"What's on your mind, Alex?"

"Abby," he said. "She and I. Actually."

Grimm tilted his head. Bayard was notoriously sensitive about comments on his relationship with Lady Hinton. He had, in fact, been so sensitive about it in the past that several men had bled for making them.

The diminutive captain grimaced and held his glass with both hands, looking down into it. "I should have married her a long time ago."

Grimm sipped his drink and said nothing. Bayard wasn't the sort of person who reacted well to prompts or nudges, and Grimm was accustomed to being patient with him.

"It would have meant the end of House Bayard," Alex said quietly. "But perhaps . . ."

Grimm regarded his friend skeptically.

Bayard rolled his eyes. "Don't look at me like that. Of course I was too stiff-necked to yield it when I was young. But now . . ." He shook his head. "My House is me and my father's sister and brothers. As it stands now, when my time comes, Bayard will die with me in any case. Perhaps it is time to acknowledge that." Bayard stepped to one side to look into a small mirror mounted on the wall, and said with experimental drama, "Please welcome Lord and Lady Hinton."

"If she'd have you," Grimm said.

"If she'd have me," Alex agreed. He looked at Grimm. "Mad. I know of no man more honorable than you." He took a deep breath and then asked seriously, "Would you think less of me?"

Grimm felt his eyebrows go up. "For marrying Abigail?"

"For ending my House," Bayard said seriously. "Its name."

Grimm smiled faintly. "The only way that would happen, Alex, is if I thought you were turning against what you thought was right." Grimm stepped over to his friend and poked him in the heart. "Here. I don't spend much time thinking about what is right for noble Houses. People matter more."

"Populist," Alex accused. "Revolutionary."

Grimm touched a finger to the brim of his—civilian's—peaked captain's cap.

"I'm still thinking it through," Alex said, and stared down into his drink. "But . . . if I decided to move ahead, would you stand with me?"

Alex looked up at him, and Grimm was cut to the quick by the utterly uncharacteristic, searching intensity in Bayard's gaze.

Grimm put out a hand and gripped Alex's shoulder. "Every time."

Bayard clasped a hand briefly over Grimm's, a flicker of relief touching Bayard's face before it resumed its usual confidence. He held up his glass, and the two of them finished the brandy together.

"There's nothing like a friend," Bayard said quietly.

Grimm felt himself smiling warmly. "You always ruin it by talking."

"Hah," Alex said. "I'd like to talk to you about these attacks on colony Spires."

"What attacks on colony Spires?" Grimm asked innocently.

Bayard snorted. "You say that as if you haven't been reading things you shouldn't. I think it offers us a chance to approach Pike. And you know Captain Ravenna."

Grimm's heart stepped out of march for a moment again. "I do."

"The Pikers don't do politics like everyone else," Bayard noted. "They send their fighting people to do all the talking. Lord Lancaster thinks they'd respond better if we did the same."

"He's probably not wrong," Grimm said. "In Pike, political negotiations are frequently settled with fights."

"Duels?" Alex asked.

"Brawls," Grimm clarified. "Their equivalent of Congress will occasionally get frustrated, arrange the brawl, and agree to go with the policy of whoever is the last one standing."

"Rather barbaric," Alex noted.

"I think it's open and honest," Grimm countered. "It might not always result in the wisest policy. It often doesn't. There's a reason Pike is poor. But I'm not sure it doesn't make up for it by being quite healthy for how they relate to one another. There has never been a civil war in Pike. Not in thousands and thousands of years."

Bayard arched his eyebrows. "Are you quite serious?"

Grimm nodded. "In fact—"

He was interrupted by a firm rap at the door. A moment later it opened, and the duty Marine stuck his head into the cabin.

"Captain," he said formally, "a visitor has come aboard and requests a meeting, sir."

Grimm frowned and glanced at Alex, who regarded the Marine thoughtfully. "Interesting. Name?"

The Marine kept a straight face. "Sir Rafael Valesco. Baron Valesco, Captain."

Grimm blinked. "Alex, isn't that . . . ?"

Bayard looked astonished and then slowly smiled. "Why, yes. The man Tuscarora has sent to kill me."

"To be here this soon, he must have been waiting for you," Grimm noted.

"He must have," Alex agreed amiably.

"But what is he doing here?"

"Foreplay," Bayard said. His grin widened and became vulpine, and his eyes sparkled. "Interesting. Send him in at once."

*　　*　　*

Rafael Valesco was one of those rarest of creatures, much like young Benedict Sorellin: warriorborn among the nobility. It was a dubious sort of distinction, to be considered blood cursed toward violence and sexual appetite yet to have the protection of a House's name. It made one the subject of intense legal and social scrutiny, under which one was watched like a cat with a reputation for scratching. Grimm had come to know more than a few warriorborn in his time, and he found the vast majority of them to be little more vicious or lascivious than most people who felt they could get away with such behavior.

But then too, there had been exceptions to that rule. The moment Valesco came through the door, Grimm felt certain that he was one of those exceptions.

The man was dressed in the height of rakish Auroran fashion: black leather trousers, a bloodred tunic spangled with sky blue diamond patterns under a close-fitting black leather waistcoat, and a matching jacket. A black leather hat sporting a two-foot dragon plume was perched precisely at a cocky angle on his head. A cloth blazoned with the Auroran flag was tied close about his neck, and his wrists flashed with broad silver bracers carved in scenes of historic Auroran victories. He wore crossed dueling sword belts at his hips, though both belts were empty of any weaponry.

Valesco was perhaps six feet tall, with long, lean, sinuous limbs and a trunk to match. As a warriorborn, he didn't need large groups of muscles to be terrifyingly powerful; his golden catlike eyes seemed to carry an expression of permanent amusement. His head, including his eyebrows, was shaven clean except for a sandy brown Vandyke beard. His ears had been pierced, and each was set with a jewel the size of Grimm's thumbnail. He wasn't a young man, but he wasn't old either. Grimm had difficulty estimating his age.

As Valesco entered, his eyes swept the room, noting and dismissing Grimm in the same instant—which suited Grimm perfectly—and then they settled on Bayard.

"Oh," he said. His voice was mellifluous bass music. "They said you were shorter than average, but I couldn't quite believe you were that tiny."

Bayard's grin didn't falter. "They never believe it, sir. Not until the end."

Valesco pursed his lips and narrowed his eyes in appreciation. "Oh, well said, Sir Bayard. Your reputation is not without merit, it seems."

"Nor is yours, Baron Valesco," Bayard replied, nodding his head slightly. "You must know I'm aware of who you are and what you've come to do, yet you walk unarmed into my lair regardless."

"Nonsense. I've great regard for you, Sir Bayard." He looked around the cabin. "Lovely ship. Did you know her captain?"

"I know him rather thoroughly," Bayard replied, "though if you mean her former captain, yes. We play chess weekly."

Valesco showed his teeth. "Shall we skip the preliminaries and set a time and place?"

"Oh," Bayard replied, almost as if speaking to a lover, "permit me the anticipation just a little longer."

Valesco's smile faded. "Not that I do not love the dance myself, but there are mutual advantages to my way. We will each have the opportunity to display things for everyone watching to ensure our supporters are in position to take advantage of the results after you're killed in the duel, all sorts of things." Valesco reached into a jacket pocket and produced a small notebook and a coal stylus. "Just looking at my itinerary, I think three days hence might be ideal. Unless you're afraid, of course."

Bayard didn't twitch at the insult. "I confess, I am somewhat anxious as to the possibility of your blood offending my wardrobe. I suppose I shall have to wear red."

Valesco let out a rumbling laugh. "It must have been difficult to learn to fight your way out of all the trouble your mouth bought you," he said, "but I simply can't argue with the results. This is going to be a delight."

Bayard answered him with a lazy grin. "The difference between us, sir, is that I've no need to display anything to anyone, and I don't murder people for sport. If you're serious about your desires, I suggest you behave seriously."

Valesco was entirely still for a moment, and then he narrowed his eyes. Electric tension between the two men filled the air of the cabin. A growl almost too low-pitched to be heard vibrated in the warriorborn's chest, and he began to tap a finger on his belt—exactly where his weapon would have been had he brought it with him, Grimm noted.

Grimm turned to put his glass down. His coat just happened to fall open, exposing the grip of his own sturdy Marine's short blade.

Valesco turned his gaze to Grimm, who felt like he had suddenly heard the growl of a hungry predator. The weight of the Auroran's gaze and the slow heat of his anger were palpable realities.

"Showing off your little sword, Captain Grimm?" Valesco asked. "Are you sure you're in the right company for that?"

Grimm folded his arms, regarded the Auroran duelist calmly, and said nothing as if the other man had not even spoken. But his fingers dangled calmly a few inches from his weapon's grip.

"I believe," Bayard said delicately, "that your business is with me, sir. You know the dance as well as I do." He showed his own teeth in a wolf's grin. "At least buy me dinner first, darling."

Valesco let out a low chuckle and turned back to Bayard, his eyes lingering on Grimm for a slow moment. "I suppose I would have been disappointed if we'd just gone into it cold," he mused. "Very well, Commodore. It's your death, after all. You should have it just as you want it." He swept off his plumed cap, dragon feather glittering through a dozen shades of colors, and gave Bayard a low and dramatic court bow.

Bayard returned a stiff formal bow of his own.

Valesco showed his lengthened canines in a smile at Grimm, then turned and strode from the cabin, not bothering to shut the door behind him. Grimm went to the door, watched Valesco depart from the ship, and turned back to Alex.

"Phew," he said, exhaling slowly and letting the tension out of his shoulders.

Alex shook his head. "He was never going to do anything today," he said. "Too soon."

"Too soon for what?" Grimm asked.

Alex's face was sober. "Valesco isn't a duelist, really. He's a murderer. He simply prefers the form of duels for his killing. They're like a ritual for him. It protects him from the law, provides him with his reputation. He takes pleasure in the process."

"What will he do?" Grimm asked.

Bayard sighed. "Find a way to insult me or Albion in public most likely. Something no reasonable person could let pass. He'll want me to challenge him and set a time and place, and then he'll go to work on me to make sure I'm as off-balance as he can arrange for the duel."

"I thought the idea was to avoid that," Grimm said.

"Mad," Bayard said in a low, passionate voice, "that creature is a predatory monster. He murders at will, and he gets away with it because everyone who has challenged him hasn't been up to the task. I don't particularly care whose flag the man is standing under. Someone should top him."

"And you think that's you?"

Bayard shrugged a shoulder. "I've beaten warriorborn before."

He had, Grimm thought. "You have orders, Alex."

Bayard sighed. "Yes. Obviously." He shook his head. "Thank you, Mad. I genuinely dislike that man. Perhaps it has had an effect on my perspective. I appreciate yours."

Grimm nodded. "Could you beat him?"

"Absolutely possible," Bayard said calmly. "His type nearly always underestimates people like us."

"'Us'?" Grimm said, amused.

"I didn't want to sound immodest," his friend said, grinning. "Opening ceremonies should be interesting."

Chapter 12

Skyport, Spire Albion

Bridget and Rowl went directly to the skyport to take a windlass down the outside of Spire Albion to the surface.

A windlass was a fairly simple affair. Essentially, it was a large, sturdy platform with a modest power crystal and small lift crystals at each corner. An operator worked a simple control: a lever that made the platform rise slowly, descend slowly, or hold still. Windlasses were a vital part of the Spire's economy, moving goods from where they arrived at the skyport down to Habble Landing or else to the fortified enclave at the base of the Spire. Every windlass operator had an interest in making sure his platform was as loaded as possible for as much of the trip as possible.

Bridget and Rowl could have taken one of several spiraling transport ramps within the Spire itself, of course, but the ramps were always thick with commercial transport, wagons loaded with goods hauled by teams of straining men. There were also regular checkpoints for contraband, various tariffs and tolls, criminal activity, and every other problem of a major thoroughfare. It would have taken a day or more to make that trip on foot; a windlass could do it in an hour.

"I do not understand," Rowl said from where he sat perched on

Bridget's shoulder. "Why didn't the Spirearch give me my own ship for this mission?"

"Ships are very expensive," Bridget pointed out to the ginger tabby cat.

"I am a prince," Rowl countered. "It would be appropriate to my station."

"Perhaps it is my fault," Bridget suggested. Experience told her that this reasoning would generally satisfy the cat.

"It would explain much," Rowl said. "You mean well, but you often have no idea what is happening."

"Very true," Bridget said.

She strode through the skyport, ignoring the glances she earned. She was rather . . . exaggerated as a person: taller than most men, and her years in the vattery had left her with as much muscle as many. The fact that she wore the uniform of the Spirearch's Guard and walked with almost forty pounds of cat on her shoulder only made more eyes turn her way, and she found the entire affair unsettling.

When she dodged a platoon of Marines on a training run down one of the avenues of the skyport, Rowl dug his claws into the reinforced padding she'd had built into her uniform jacket. Just then, the sun came out from behind the mists, burning away the grey haze and revealing clear blue skies stretching up and up and up. . . .

Bridget swallowed and fought to keep her stomach under control. Even two years after her first exposure to the dizzyingly open skies, she had the occasional pang of panic when beneath them, so alien after a lifetime of dwelling within Habble Morning, with its comforting spirestone boundaries that (for the most part) kept away the horrors of the surface. If a blue sky was enough to make her breath go short and her heart pound, she could only imagine how she might react to events on the ground.

"You look like a woman desperately trying to think of a way out," came a calm baritone from behind her. "Might I suggest you carry on in the presence of good company?"

Bridget turned so swiftly that Rowl all but pitched off her shoulder. The big ginger tom had to clutch wildly at Bridget's shoulder with his claws to keep from tumbling.

"Benedict!" she gasped. "What are you doing here?"

The tall young warriorborn stood before her wearing one of his favorite personal outfits—a dark jacket and breeches set off by a blindingly clean white shirt and an emerald green cravat. His bandages still poked out past his clothing here and there, and he moved very stiffly. "Word that you were traveling to the surface reached me," he said, smiling. "I've not been down there in some time. I thought I'd see how the place had changed."

"But you're hurt," Bridget said, her tone worried. "I thought you were to be in bed for several days."

Benedict smiled a shade uneasily. "The cuts were shallow and my natural constitution is sufficient to the task."

Bridget frowned up at him. Warriorborn were widely respected for their ferocity and strength in battle, and feared for their aggressive natures and bodily appetites. Any display of "uncivilized" behavior from someone in Benedict's position in society would see him rapidly cast out, and Bridget knew that he labored constantly to maintain in truth and in appearance the demeanor of any gentleman. The fact that he had healed more rapidly from wounds than the physicians had expected would make him intensely uncomfortable.

She peered at him. "Ben, how exactly did word reach you?"

Benedict coughed uncomfortably. "Mirl may have mentioned something when she came by for my lessons in Cat."

Bridget turned and frowned severely at Rowl. "I'm sorry?"

"Do not be upset, Littlemouse," Rowl purred reassuringly. "You

143

know how incompetent you are. And the surface is dangerous. While I am the hardiest creature alive, I might not be able to protect you from everything at once. I require the assistance of someone I don't mind sacrificing, so that I might keep you safe."

"Rowl!" Bridget said, shocked.

Benedict only grinned. "Well, not to put too fine a point on it, but he's correct about the kind of danger you might be facing there. I've been there before. You haven't."

"Have you fought creatures of the surface more than I have?" Bridget asked him.

He smiled at her, a bit of bitterness in his expression. "The difference being that I *am* a creature of the surface," he said seriously. "The people who live in the camps are either warriorborn, criminals, military prisoners, or wildly maladjusted to life in a Spire, and they live a hard, dangerous life. You're in as much danger from your fellow Albions as you are from anything in the wild. You can handle yourself as well as any Guardsman I know and better than most. But it's a different world there, and it won't hurt your mission's chances to have someone who is familiar with it."

Bridget frowned at him steadily and then at Rowl and said, "You two coordinated this."

"If Benedict wishes to mate with you, he must prove he can protect you," Rowl said firmly. "This will be his opportunity."

Bridget felt herself turning beet red, her heart pounding. "I beg your pardon."

"To prove himself worthy to mate," Rowl said more slowly as though she had simply been too thick to understand him before. "I have consulted my father, Maul, upon this. He is confident I am correct."

"Oh, God in Heaven," Bridget breathed, mortified, and eyed the crowd around her desperately for evidence that anyone passing by spoke Cat. Fortunately, hardly anyone did, and none of the passersby seemed to comprehend Rowl.

"I . . ." Benedict said, his face flushed, "was not consulted on that part of their reasoning."

"Yes," Bridget said. "Well." She took a deep breath. "One of us has to be in command of the mission. As I understand it, the medics think you should be in bed. So you can hardly be here in pursuit of your duty."

"Indeed," Benedict said. "Hence the lack of uniform. I am merely Sir Benedict Sorellin-Lancaster today, Sergeant Tagwynn. This is your operation, and I will follow your lead."

Bridget nodded once. She had run a dozen inquisitions— robberies, assaults, even one murder—in the past two years, coordinating as many as half a dozen Guardsmen under her command. "Then my first order is for you to give me an accurate and honest assessment of your injuries."

Benedict grimaced. "The cuts are healing, but there are dozens of them. I am constantly uncomfortable, and that is somewhat of a strain on my temper. If I move too rapidly, some of the cuts will still tear open. I have a mild fever—they are cat scratches, after all—and may require extra food for a day or two yet. I am recovering rapidly and am ready for action meanwhile."

Bridget stared at him hard for a moment. "Are you sure you aren't deluding yourself?"

"Where you are concerned?" he asked her, smiling gently. "No." His arm moved, and when his fever-hot hand touched her forearm, she could feel the heat through her jacket. "I started this when I brought Saza and her people here. I'd like to see it through."

That much, at least, Bridget could understand entirely.

And truth be told, she found the idea of setting foot on the surface somewhat appalling. Even though the hardiest creature alive would be perched on her shoulder. Part of her felt a little ashamed that the idea of Benedict's company was so reassuring, but a more logical part of her mind assured her that the hellish surface was an excellent place for teamwork and additional eyes, hands, and minds.

"Then I suppose we can work together, Sir Benedict," Bridget said, and touched his arm with her hand in reply.

He smiled warmly at her, and for a moment she just bathed in it, like sunshine.

"First," she said, "let's get you something to eat." She took a deep breath. "And then we'll go down."

Chapter 13

Hinton Apartments, Habble Profit,
Spire Olympia

Abigail went directly to her apartments in Habble Profit, the highest habble of Spire Olympia. It was very nearly as well-developed as Habble Morning back in Albion, and her chambers there were as finely appointed as those in her home and in much the same style—rich fabrics of rose and soft sunset colors chased with fine gold. Her Olympian staff had prepared the home for her arrival, and they turned out immediately to meet her as she (and her luggage) swept through the front doors into the light of half a dozen lumin-crystal chandeliers.

"Lady Hinton," greeted her bodyguard, Hamish, a tree trunk of a man a hand over six feet with narrow shoulders and a long, solid body. Dressed in a severe black suit, he wore a short blade at his side, and Abigail knew he kept a number of compact firearms about his person and could draw and employ them with abrupt precision. He turned to the aeronauts bearing luggage, and his hand went to his coin purse. Then he set about tipping and dismissing the men. "Gentlemen, thank you for your assistance."

Mistress Tilde, a small woman with ginger hair and enormous dark eyes, came to Abigail and took her jacket with the absolute, smooth motions of endlessly practiced utility. Lady Hinton noted that she kept an eye on the aeronauts, and she nodded to Abigail when they had departed. Hamish closed the door behind them.

"My lady," Tilde said, her lower-class Albion accent soft, "the house has been under observation for the past two days. I've made a map noting the location of the watchers we have positively identified. It's waiting with your tea next to your bath."

"My *bath*," Abigail sighed. "Oh, Tilde, I really don't see how I could conspire against the enemies of the Crown without you, dear."

The woman smiled with her eyes and said, "Neither do I, milady. Shall I assume Sir Alexander will be joining us?"

"It depends on how difficult he's decided to be," Abigail sighed. "Madison Grimm is sitting on him for the time being. He's a good, sensible man but a man for all of that. I shall be more comfortable when I am on Bayard's arm and our people are watching his back." She reached into her purse and came out with a small stack of letters. "Hamish, be a dear and have these delivered."

The bodyguard stepped forward and took the stack. "Of course, my lady. Opening ceremonies are to begin in a few hours, and you have received an invitation to the Spectral Tea."

Abigail paused, lifting her eyebrows. "And who has the Spectrum sent to represent Atlantea this year?"

"A new representative," Hamish replied, consulting a small notebook he always kept about his person. "One Initiate Hestia."

She frowned and glanced at Tilde. "I'm unfamiliar with the name. What do we know?"

"Newly minted to the Spectrum," Tilde replied immediately. "A young etherealist, ambitious, no known quirks or taboos. She has gained a reputation for cunning within Spire Atlantea, and the Crimson Guard has dispatched a member to serve as her personal bodyguard."

Abigail looked back sharply over her shoulder as she strode toward the bathroom and her people kept pace. "Crimson Guard. Did they assign her a bodyguard or an assassin?"

"My lady," Hamish said with a softly pained voice.

Lady Hinton cast him a quick, winsome smile. "Oh, I don't mean to imply one must necessarily be one at the expense the other. You know that, dear."

"Thank you, milady," Hamish said, mollified.

"A duelist," Tilde supplied, opening the double doors to the bathing room. Next to the claw-footed tub, which was filled with steaming water, was her favorite tea service. "Felicia Montaine. Eleven confirmed kills amongst her fellow Crimson Guard."

Abigail shuddered. "God in Heaven, save Albion from dueling societies." She paused, frowning. "So, Atlantea wants me at their party and, since the Spectral Tea is for women only, away from Bayard at the opening banquet."

"So it would seem, lady," Tilde replied. "Shall I return your regrets?"

"God in Heaven, no," Abigail replied. "That would be like spurning an invitation from the Spirearch. I do not have the standing to deliver such an insult and survive it." Tilde helped Abigail from her jacket and began with the buttons on the back of her blouse. "No, I can't possibly escape that. But we will arrange for an early exit, I think. I can beg fatigue from the journey readily enough."

"Shall I suit your makeup to the rationale?" Tilde suggested.

"Please. But subtly, Tilde."

Tilde gave her a mildly reproachful look.

"I beg your pardon," Abigail said immediately.

"Thank you, lady."

"Hamish," Lady Hinton said, "have you any word on this Valesco creature?"

"He's reserved a table for the Auroran delegation at tonight's banquet, lady."

"Can we poison him?" Abigail asked innocently.

There was sudden silence in the room.

Abigail turned to face them. "The gentleman has been dispatched
to murder Bayard. I shan't be clinging to my scruples to see to it that
no such occasion comes to pass. So. Can we poison him?"

Tilde swallowed and glanced at Hamish.

The big man shrugged his narrow shoulders. "Lady, I should
think poisoning a member of the Auroran delegation might have
some small repercussions."

"Only if we are caught, dear," Abigail said in a hard voice.

Hamish grimaced. "I shall investigate the possibility."

"Thank you. Find out everything about his quarters during the
summit, where he eats, if he sends for women. I want to know when
he passes his food. Everything. We might not choose poison, but I
want to know about absolutely every option available to us."

"Understood, lady."

"The extra security?"

"A dozen good men are standing by," Hamish said.

Lady Hinton frowned. "No more?"

"No more I could trust," the bodyguard replied.

"Everyone is increasing security for the summit," Tilde said
softly. "And everyone wants reliable professionals. Had we brought in
any more, we would have risked hiring informants and doing our
enemies' work for them."

"Ah," Abigail replied. She paused suddenly. Her ears had picked
up a sound so small that she hadn't been sure she'd heard it. "Hamish."

The bodyguard reacted to her tone at once and spun to the
apartments' front door. He was halfway to it when a firm knock

sounded. When he got to the door, Hamish glanced back at Abigail, eyebrows lifted.

"Who is there?" Abigail called. She snapped her fingers softly, and Tilde immediately helped her back into her jacket.

"Not who," came a reply in a rolling baritone speaking voice with a rich Albion accent. "Better to ask what."

Abigail pursed her lips. Tilde had already vanished into a side room and returned with a long gun. She held the weapon the way a mother might her child, comfortably supporting it mostly over one arm, with her hip shot to that side to bear the weight. Her expression curious, she exchanged a nod with Abigail, who said whimsically, "Very well. What is there?"

"Help," came a firm reply. "The Marines. Well, singular. By order of the Spirearch. Miss Folly, this blasted contraption."

"Oh, yes, of course," said a woman's soft, earnest voice. "Of course, it's the same problem today as yesterday." The doorknob turned a bit and then stopped. "It's locked, master."

"Caution, excellent," the man's voice said. "Lady Hinton, please. We cannot assist you if we just stand here in the hallway."

Abigail tilted her head thoughtfully and said, "Hamish, let's see whom we're dealing with, shall we?"

Hamish inclined his head, amusement lurking in his face, and opened the door with a polite yet forbidding mien.

On the other side of the door stood an unlikely pair. The speaker was a person of seemingly vigorous age, perhaps six feet tall, with an unruly shock of iron and silver for hair that poked out from beneath a stovepipe hat in the same bottle green as his ethersilk suit—undyeable ethersilk, Abigail noted. He wore matching glasses, and his right hand rested on a cane whose handle was topped with what appeared to be a power crystal the size of a child's heart. Standing with his feet apart and one fist on a hip, he smiled as confidently as though he were at the head of an army.

The girl beside him made a rather different impression. Her hair had somehow been colored pure white on one half of her skull and pitch-black on the other, making for a very odd braid that fell to her shoulder blades. She was wearing an ethersilk gown in the usual soft silver-grey, along with a forest green youth's waistcoat rather than a proper corset. Her bolero jacket had begun life as a midnight blue Fleet aeronaut's coat and subsequently been tailored to fit the girl, if not precisely to what Abigail would have considered good taste. Her eyes were remarkable: one a gentle blue, the other apple green.

The man grinned up a little at Hamish and said, "Ah, a bodyguard, excellent. Olympian, are you, sir?"

Hamish quirked a mouth at one corner and replied in his flat, twanging Olympian accent, "Consider where we stand, sir."

"And loyal to Albion, are we?" asked the man.

Abigail stepped forward smoothly. "Hamish is a consummate professional, and I am utterly satisfied with his service." She tilted her head. "I don't believe we've met, Master Ferus." She turned to the young woman standing with him. "Which would make you his apprentice Miss Folly, I believe."

Evidently, Abigail's guess had been correct, since the man lowered his glasses and took a long look at her. "Aha! Always such a pleasure to encounter an active mind, Lady Hinton. Your reputation is not without merit, it seems."

Abigail inclined her head. "Only a master etherealist can convince ethersilk to alter its appearance, and Albion lays claim to only three. One is quite ancient and rarely leaves her home in Habble Everhold. I believe she's a consultant on Fleet's designs. Another lives on the surface and heads up the research branch of the Ministry of Surface Creatures. And the third is well-known as a consultant to the Spirearch and was much involved in the raid two years past."

"'Master,'" said the old man with a dismissive flip of his hand, "is but a breath broken into two parts, but a heavy one for all that. There are considerably more people of skill in Albion who choose not to carry the weight of it." He swept off his hat in an elaborate courtly bow a century out of fashion. "Efferus Effrenus Ferus at your service, Lady Hinton. This is, as you have correctly deduced, my apprentice Miss Folly— Oh, I slipped just now, didn't I, Miss Folly?"

"It's all right, master," Miss Folly said immediately. "I was an apprentice for ever so long."

"Still," Ferus said, "we use the different titles for a reason, do we not? And you have certainly earned the right to be recognized as a journeyman."

His dark, gleaming eyes went to Abigail, and she felt immediately uncomfortable, as though he'd caught her in her nightclothes. This was a man who saw a great deal in very little time, she judged.

"Lady Hinton, I find myself surprised that you would be aware of who Miss Folly is."

"Vincent and I have a lovely game where I try to read everything he sends the Spirearch," Abigail replied. "Sometimes he doesn't win." She turned to the young woman and inclined her head. "I am given to understand you triumphed in a duel with a master yourself."

The young woman shifted uneasily, and one of her hands went to a small drawstring pouch she wore on a thong about her neck. "Oh. Oh, dear. I didn't know I was going to have to speak to people. How awkward."

"And so she did," said Master Ferus proudly, "though 'duel' seems a bit prosaic to describe the situation, does it not, Folly?"

"'Desperately needful confrontation,' perhaps, master."

Ferus nodded judiciously. "It was desperate. Certainly needful. Also a confrontation. I concur."

Though the young lady regarded Abigail with a steady gaze nearly as penetrating as Master Ferus's, she continued speaking only to the old man. "And 'triumph' seems too poetical. I survived the situation, which suits me well enough."

"What other triumph is there, really?" asked Master Ferus philosophically. "I think you have a fair claim." Ferus eyed Abigail and said, "So, Lady Hinton, you know who we are. And we know who you are. And we *are* Albions, after all." He paused to bow to Hamish. "Our noble contractors excepted, of course."

"Naturally, sir," Abigail said easily. "Would you care for a cup of tea?"

Once Abigail had them all settled and Tilde had brought tea and a set of lovely local cakes topped with bits of fruit, Hamish and Tilde made themselves invisible except when they were needed, as only the most professional help could.

"You are a most gracious hostess, Lady Hinton," Master Ferus said. He smiled wryly. "Ideal in every particular. Yet skeptical, skeptical. I find that to be wisdom under the circumstances."

Abigail smiled warmly at him and studied his facial features carefully. His face was lined and seamed with the exercise of frequent expression, and it would change much, she judged, under stress—or while prevaricating.

"I confess, I am a bit surprised that Addison would send help by stealth," she said mildly. "Generally, he informs me about such things."

"Gracious," Master Ferus said. "Truth be told, I'm afraid His Majesty is not yet aware that he sent me to aid you. In point of fact, he sent me to accompany the grim captain, follow his orders, et cetera." He ate one of the little cakes in a single bite, and pleasure suffused his face. "Oh," he murmured. "Delightful."

Abigail tilted her head. "Captain Grimm. I see. And he has ordered you to assist me?"

"Goodness no," Master Ferus said, shocked. "That would leave the Crown with no deniability at all, would it not?"

Abigail leaned back slowly. "And why should His Majesty need to deny anything at all?"

Ferus tapped his cane on the floor, frowning thoughtfully. "Difficult to say, but best to plan for as many contingencies as possible," he answered. "In my judgment, your affairs will bring you across the trail of a number of skilled individuals—from the Spectrum, perhaps. And it is quite possible that another former apprentice of mine may involve herself in these affairs as well."

"You speak of Madame Cavendish," said Abigail carefully.

"I do."

Abigail shuddered. What she had read of that madwoman made her skin crawl.

"This Initiate Hestia, for example," Master Ferus said. "Were you aware of what project earned her a place on the Spectral Council?"

"Something to do with textiles, obviously," Abigail replied.

"Mmm," Master Ferus said. "What if I told you that her expertise was in engineering clothing that inspired certain emotions in those near the wearer?"

Abigail felt herself arch an eyebrow. "In what sense, sir?"

"In the sense of compulsion, madame," Master Ferus said calmly. "In the sense of moving energy through ethersilk in such a fashion that it has a physical effect on the brains of those who come within a certain distance."

Abigail frowned. "What sort of emotion?"

"Virtually anything, depending on the intent of the designer," the etherealist replied. He raked a hand back through his hair. "And to what degree such a device can affect a person is also in question. It would, of course, be most efficient if the persons subject to influence did not know such a possibility existed."

"Obviously," Abigail said, leaning forward, fascinated. "You came to let me know to be on guard against it."

"And to help defend you from it, should it come to that," Master Ferus said.

"I am hardly a child who will give sway to my emotions, sir," Abigail noted.

"The strongest of wills and the best of intentions will not prevent enough drink from making one drunk, you know," murmured Miss Folly, her fingers touching the pouch at her neck.

Abigail frowned. "You're saying this is . . . some sort of etheric drug."

"We aren't sure," Master Ferus said smoothly. "But my own calculations indicate that the possibility is a strong one."

"My . . ." Abigail said. She regarded the two etherealists thoughtfully. "I think I believe you."

"That also is wise," Ferus concurred.

Without speaking, she produced the invitation to the Spectral Tea and showed it to him.

"Ha," Ferus said, reading. "Yes, they thought to influence you early. Well, we can't have that, can we?"

"I should think not," Abigail said. "I would prefer to function at full capacity as long as intrigue abounds."

"An excellent idea," said Master Ferus. "One we shall facilitate."

"Very well," said Abigail. "What did you have in mind?"

Miss Folly looked up from her tea, made eye contact with Abigail for the first time, and smiled warmly.

Chapter 14

PAS *Stormmaiden*, Skyport, Spire Olympia

Grimm strode through Olympia's skyport with a rather tediously swelling case of nervous excitement he found entirely inappropriate to his age, his accomplishments, and his station in life. Bayard had been distracted by matters of command, some problem with the wiring to *Belligerant*'s etheric web. He had left Grimm with a promise to be ready to depart for the opening ceremonies an hour before sundown. Grimm, sure the other man would be safe enough aboard his own ship—Bayard had an entire company of Marines there, after all—found himself with time on his hands and the desire to speak to an old friend.

But such things were hardly proper, so he had invited the XO along.

"How different could a Piker ship be?" Gwen asked him as they crossed the skyport. Gwen, a strikingly attractive young woman, ignored the glances she got, and her uniform, sword, and gauntlet evidently forestalled any raucous commentary.

"A very great deal different," Grimm replied. "They pursue a fundamentally different course of tactical operations."

Gwen frowned at that answer. "How so?"

Grimm gestured at the ship as they approached. "Use your eyes, XO. Assume everything about the vessel we're approaching is designed for tactical function. What can you tell me about their intentions?"

Gwen clasped her hands behind her back as they kept walking. "It's that one there, yes?" she asked.

"Very good," Grimm approved. "Always verify your targets."

Gwen pursed her lips. "Well. First off, they intend to be the aggressors."

"True enough," Grimm said. "How do you know?"

"Because their lower hull is painted sky blue, and their topsides are mist grey," she responded promptly. "They want to go unseen until they choose to begin operations." She tilted her head. "That's a heavy-cruiser-sized ship, but she doesn't seem to have armored flanks."

"Exactly."

"That seems odd," she said. "How is she to exchange fire with comparable vessels?"

"She'll avoid it where possible," Grimm replied. "She doesn't have enough lift to support the weight of armor."

The XO's eyebrows went up. "Why not?"

"Pike is a poor Spire—well, not really a Spire at all. More a collection of caves at the top of a very high mountain," Grimm replied. "They have no crystal vatteries to speak of and can afford only smaller or very worn lift and power crystals for their vessels. That's why they're so light as a fleet. You're looking at their largest ship. She's half again as large as *Predator* but her core power crystal probably exceeds ours by only about ten percent, and she'll have a smaller lift crystal. She runs without armor and it makes her as quick and nimble as a light cruiser. If she armored up, she'd wallow like a dreadnought, and remember that she'll do double duty as a cargo ship. She can't afford to carry all that steel."

This information seemed to discomfit Gwen. "Her flanks look lumpy. . . ." The young officer peered. "Are those . . . *gunpowder* cannon?"

"About half her broadside, yes," Grimm replied.

"Don't those explode?"

"From time to time," Grimm confirmed. "But it also means that in battle she can channel more power to her shroud or her web and less to her guns."

"But . . . they're *gunpowder weapons*," Gwen protested. "Why don't they just arm her with catapults?"

Grimm let out a quiet laugh. "They're shorter-ranged than etheric cannon," he agreed. "But shrouds don't stop shells, XO. If they can get close, they can smash directly into the hulls and decks, and some of those shells explode into fragments or incendiary gelatin. Not even a dreadnought could simply ignore a Piker broadside."

"She couldn't survive the reply," Gwen noted.

"Probably not," Grimm agreed. "What else?"

Gwen's steps slowed as they got closer. "Are those cargo doors on her forward hull?"

"Dive doors," Grimm replied, smiling.

"What?"

"Dive doors," Grimm repeated. "Piker ships don't carry Marines. They have divers. That ship will have at least a full company of divers, in addition to the usual crew."

Gwen let out a low whistle. "That's as many Marines as a battlecruiser."

"Smaller ships will have proportionately smaller companies of divers," Grimm replied, "but even a ship the size of *Predator* will have at least a hundred."

"God in Heaven," Gwenn replied. "How skilled are they?"

"Ask Marines who have fought a Piker boarding party," Grimm

replied. "They will tell you that they hate fighting Pikers. They'll carry a dozen gunpowder weapons each, most of them designed for close fighting, and they start shooting before they've even gotten through the shroud. Ethersilk tunics do nothing to stop them. They'll throw grenades—steel shells full of gunpowder—like children tossing fruit at one another."

"That's insane," Gwen said, her voice impressed.

"That's affordable," Grimm countered. "Pikers don't have the kind of economy to support a great deal of etheric technology. They make up for it with cleverness, ruthlessness, and raw courage."

"She isn't made to trade broadsides," the XO said, her tone one of growing respect and discomfort. "They want to swoop down from overhead and drop their boarders. They'll disable their prey's guns or power core, and either fire the ship or have her divers leave her crippled so that they're fighting a maimed opponent."

"Always assume that any Piker that looks like he's squaring up for a fair fight is distracting you, so that an ally can come at you from an unexpected angle," Grimm said. "It isn't a hundred percent true, but it's close enough."

"The ships must be crowded," Gwenn noted.

"Very much so," Grimm said. "Consider the kind of discipline necessary to keep the peace in such a setting. Pikers have a reputation as brawlers and pirates. But if they were simply brigands, they could never hold their crews together the way they do."

Gwen shook her head. "Interesting," she said.

"Here we are," Grimm said. "I suggest you be polite and respectful and follow my lead."

"Aye, Skip," Gwen said, her face eager and interested. "Captain Grimm?"

"Yes?"

"Is that cologne you're wearing?"

Grimm felt his face heat slightly. "It may be."

"It's quite nice." Gwenn looked up at him slyly. "Captain Ravenna commands this ship, does she not?"

Grimm frowned. "And how did you know that, XO?"

"Mister Kettle may have mentioned it," Gwen said. "It is said that she is a great beauty."

"She is a dragon hunter," Grimm replied.

"My goodness," Gwen said, her voice dry. "She sounds very interesting. No wonder you wanted a chaperone."

Grimm gave her a steady glance, sighed, and said, "Kettle speaks his mind entirely too often."

Gwen laughed, a smile brightening her face.

"*Stormmaiden* lives!" called Grimm as he approached the ship.

"*Stormmaiden* lives!" echoed a couple dozen voices on the ship, finishing the traditional call-and-response of Piker aeronauts.

Boots thudded within the hull, and a grizzled man with a braid to his waist, an eye patch, and only four fingers on his left hand appeared at the open dive doors on the lower hull near the ship's prow. He had one hand on the gunpowder pistol at his hip.

Upon seeing Grimm, his face split into a broad grin. "Who goes there?" he called merrily.

"Gunny," Grimm called back, grinning in reply to the ship's gunnery master, a position not required in most Spires' fleets. "Haven't your youngers blown you up yet?"

"They keep trying, but I'm just too damned good," the other man drawled. His hand came off his gun and he extended it to Grimm as he came down the ramp to the skyport's deck. "Good to see you, Grimm."

Grimm shook hands firmly. Gunny was dressed in the Pikers' traditional black leathers. Wound about his head was a costly steel-thistle scarf that would turn steel blades and even some pistol balls, and most of his visible skin was covered in tattoos. Gold flashed in his smile. At his wrists and neck were plain gold links made from melted coins; like most Pikers, Gunny believed that coins were easier to steal than links. His glittering chains were a loop thicker since last Grimm had seen him. As soon as he released Grimm's hand, Gunny unwound one of the chains from around his wrist, and his strong, calloused fingers seized a link and bent it open, slipped it from the chain, and passed it, still looped with three others, to Grimm.

"What I borrowed when ya bailed me out, with interest, and thank ya kindly, Cap'n."

Grimm had forgotten the loan he'd made the man five years before in a Dalosian Federation colony, but he grinned and pocketed the links. "I remember that fight. They had it coming to them."

Gunny's glittering grin widened. "Aye, that they did." He produced a flask, took a quick hit, and offered the flask to Grimm. He took a polite taste and managed it without wincing, which made Gunny laugh as he took the flask back. He turned to Gwen, and his expression smoothed into neutrality.

"And who is this?"

"My XO, Gwendolyn Lancaster," Grimm replied, his voice only slightly roughened by whatever paint-peeling evil Gunny had loaded into his flask. "She's never seen a Piker ship, and I thought it would be good for her education as an officer."

"Nnngh," Gunny said, and winked at Grimm. "Officers. You know how much I like 'em. Present cap'ns excepted, of course." He faced Gwen. "And why should I let you onto my ship, little girl?"

"Your ship?" Gwen asked archly. "Surely you mean your captain's ship?"

Gunny barked a quick laugh. "She don't know a thing, does she?" he asked Grimm.

"That's why she's here," Grimm said.

"Hngh," Gunny said, rubbing his beard. "Then listen here, little girl. Pikers don't work on their ships. We live there. It's home."

"No Albion has ever felt like that, I'm sure," Gwen said, her lips set in a hard, polite smile.

"But you folks got homes elsewhere in your Spire," Gunny said. "We don't. You're in a Piker crew, you're home. That's it." He paused and added, "Little girl."

"God in Heaven," Gwen said. "Captain, you told me to be polite, but . . . permission to shut this person's mouth."

Grimm sighed and eyed Gunny with less-than-perfect tolerance. "Do as you think best, XO."

Gwen squared off against the lean man, her expression neutral, her eyes focused on nothing in particular. "Sir," she said calmly, "call me 'little girl' one more time."

Gunny traded a look with Grimm, then drawled, insultingly, "Little—"

Gwen struck with a foot and a swift combination of blows.

Gunny turned his leg and took the kick on his thigh, rolled out of the way of most of Gwen's attack, and caught her wrist when she failed to draw it back quickly enough. Then he roughly dragged her into him and caught her back against his chest, one tattooed arm slipping around her throat.

"Now, then, little girl," Gunny drawled.

Gwen drew back the hammer on his pistol, which she had taken from his holster as he pulled her in, and pushed it across her body and into his hip. "I'm sorry?" she said. "I'm not sure I heard you, sir."

"Very polite," Grimm noted.

Gunny tilted his head to one side and studied his own gun pressed against his lower abdomen. Then he took a breath.

"So, she's not useless," he said to Grimm.

"Perhaps an apology is in order," Grimm suggested.

Gunny barked out a breath and, raising his arms away slowly, released Gwen. "No one comes aboard a Piker ship without being tested, lass. Nothing personal."

Gwen blinked. "Oh. Rather like Benny at the Temple of the Way, then?"

"Something like that," Grimm said. "Pikers believe that everyone on a ship should be able to take care of themselves. They require proof. It saves time and complications down the line." He glanced down at the gun in her hand. "Ahem."

Gwen pointed the weapon away and carefully lowered the hammer. Then she turned to Gunny, reversed her grip on the weapon, and offered its handle to him. "Do I pass inspection, then?"

"Standing up to me was enough," Gunny noted. "Don't know that we needed to go all the way to weapons."

"You're better than me," the XO pointed out. "No sense in playing fair."

Gunny stared at her for a moment and then slowly smiled. "No, there isn't. Welcome aboard *Stormmaiden*, Miss Lancaster." He nodded to her and then glanced at Grimm. "You're here for Cap'n Ravenna?"

"If she's available," Grimm returned politely. "I take it she's preparing for opening ceremonies."

"Oh, aye," Gunny said, beckoning Grimm casually onto the ship. Grimm winced at the lack of formalities but followed the man into the *'Maiden's* hull.

"You know how cap'ns like getting dressed up for battles and parties," Gunny continued.

"I have taken note," Grimm admitted, smiling. To Gunny, Grimm's everyday standards of dress were needlessly decadent.

Grimm was struck once more by the differences in the interior of the Piker ship. They made more use of tar than paint in Pike, their cultural parsimony reflected in the state of the ship. Though it was scrupulously clean and well-ordered, their function-focused attitude toward the repair of wear and tear and battle damage, with visible seams and splotched seals of tar beside unstained and unpainted wood, made him shudder inwardly.

Gunny led them through the ship; its passageways and holds were crowded for a ship that had released most of its crew on shore leave. The conversations between the aeronauts were loud and raucous, with an even greater deal of cheerful and quite colorful cursing than Grimm expected from the breed.

Grimm checked the XO's face. Two years before, such language would have caused Miss Lancaster to blanch or turn slightly green, but her time on the ship and in several actions had hardened her to such environmental hazards. Instead, she seemed to calmly take note of the more visceral and effective curses as if filing them away for future use, should she ever need them.

"We're not going to the captain's quarters," Grimm noted.

"Nah," Gunny replied. "No room in there to get dressed, ya see. She's in the armory."

He let out a peculiar whistle, and Grimm noted a young crewman who darted off abaft, doubtless carrying word of their coming.

"There are a great many young people," Gwen noted.

"Aye," Gunny agreed, grinning. "We're not letting children run around Olympia without officers and chiefs to supervise them, and we're still working."

"The nature of Piker crews," Grimm said. "Think of each ship's company as a House in Albion, or perhaps a Dalosian clan. It's as close as I can get to an example of something like their arrangement. One joins a crew in much the same way that one might marry into a House, and they begin their basic education in aeronautics quite young."

"Youngers work in the galley, clean, and learn basic maintenance," Gunny said, slipping aside so that a trio of children around the age of twelve could get past him with the loads of laundry they were carrying. "Come battle, they help prepare 'chutes, pass out arms, and help manage the web."

Grimm nodded. "So don't be fooled, XO. A Piker crewman your age has been serving on an airship five times as long as you have."

"I see," Gwen said, frowning as she watched the children go.

A pair of guards lounged outside the door to what was presumably the armory. When Gunny strolled up, he and they nodded to one another, and one of the guards said laconically, "Wait."

Gunny yawned, glanced at Grimm, and then grinned. "Miss Lancaster, perhaps you'd care for a tour of the gunnery deck. You can see some of our gunpowder cannon up close."

The XO looked at Grimm, who gestured his assent. "Try not to enter combat with anyone else if it isn't absolutely necessary."

Gwen suppressed a smile and gave him a sharp salute. "I'm sure it won't be, Captain," she said, and turned to Gunny. "Thank you, Chief. I should enjoy that very much. I've had a brief introduction to gunpowder pistols, but I've no idea how they work on a more . . . dramatic scale."

"Dramatically," Gunny said, and started to engage her in an animated conversation as they walked away.

The guard who had spoken before tilted her head toward the armory door, and then she said to Grimm, "Cap'n's ready to see you now."

"Thank you," Grimm told the leather-clad guard, and entered the armory.

A Piker armory was typically a bifurcated affair: one side was devoted to the Pikers' beloved gunpowder weapons, the other to more conventional etheric arms. On the *Stormmaiden,* the split between gunpowder weapons and etheric arms wasn't equal; it was more like a ratio of three to one, respectively. The gunpowder weapons were stored in neat rows on racks, the better to be taken down and scoured on a regular basis, since even the most efficient barrel plugs could only slow ironrot , not stop it altogether. The place smelled pleasantly of steel and burned gunpowder. In lockers taking up a quarter of the space, Grimm knew, the ship's etheric gauntlets and long guns would be ready at hand, since Pikers were ferocious, not foolish, and acquired modern weaponry whenever possible. Sunlight poured through a row of portholes in warm shafts of brilliance.

At the far end of the chamber, a compact woman stood on a small platform bathed in a beam of light. She was dressed in extremely well-tailored Piker black leather that clung to her closely, leaving her arms bare to the shoulders, showing off both warriorborn musculature and . . . Goodness, Grimm had forgotten the rather extreme degree of observable femininity with which Ravenna had been born, and his heart pounded.

Ravenna's hair was as black as her namesake, and thick enough to fall in waves to her shoulder blades and still bear a number of warrior braids woven with costly dragon plumes that reflected the light in shining iridescence. The breeches she wore were leather as well, laced up the sides, and her skin showed in a long strip up the outer side of each leg, the laces making little impression on the muscle beneath. Grimm could see the watery, rippling pattern of dragon hide whenever the material caught the light.

"Frank!" Ravenna all but bellowed, her face splitting into a wide smile. Her gold-green cat-pupiled eyes wrinkled at the corners, and her elongated canines showed. She bounded lightly down from the platform with the assistance of a couple of women who were apparently helping her dress. She crossed the armory in a handful of enthusiastic strides and promptly threw herself at him in a delighted bounce.

Grimm staggered as her muscular weight hit him and she

wrapped her legs around his hips, but he managed to support her without quite grasping her utterly inappropriately. Ravenna placed an exuberant kiss on each of his cheeks, rested her hands comfortably on his shoulders, and leaned back enough to grin down at him. "By God in Heaven and every pleasant Path, it's good to see you!"

"Ravenna!" Grimm said, laughing despite himself. "Have you no restraint?"

"What for?" she demanded, smiling. She leaned back with a look of humorous suspicion on her face. "You haven't gone and fallen in love again, have you?"

"Alas, no," he replied. "I am still technically married to Calliope."

"The fool who left you," she murmured, and closed on him for a rather serious kiss.

There was, he thought, simply no way to resist her. For one thing, she was at least as strong as he was and in a rather excellent position to bestow the kiss by force. And for another, she knew perfectly well that he had no intention of offering her any resistance. The kiss was searing, her mouth soft and sweet and her lips flavored faintly of cinnamon tea and honey. Her body against his was the most intensely pleasant sensation he had ever experienced, and as he returned her kiss in kind, it was suddenly everything he could do not to let his hands do entirely inappropriate things.

"Ravenna," Grimm murmured into the kiss a moment later, his voice gone throaty. "Your, ah, crewmen are still here."

She let out a merry peal of laughter and unwound herself from him. Her boots hit the deck with hardly a sound as she landed with a bounce that looked extremely fetching. "Nothing happening here they wouldn't enjoy themselves with men they favored," she replied, laughter bubbling under the words. She gripped his upper arms and looked him up and down. "My," she purred, quite literally, "don't you look lovely in black? Have you taken up piracy, then?"

"I have in fact a letter of marque in *Predator*'s safe," Grimm replied.

Still smiling gaily, Ravenna wrinkled her upturned nose. "A pirate for the old spider, then. I suppose it's a start." She glanced over her shoulder at the two women and said, "This is the man I told you about."

One of the women, who looked much like Gunny in only slightly altered tones, snorted and said, "I thought he'd be taller."

Ravenna's catlike eyes met Grimm's as she said, "He's quite large enough to suit me, Marta, I assure you."

Grimm's cheeks heated. "Ravenna!"

She laughed again, warmer this time and more relaxed. "Oh, I love how easy it is to torment an Albion."

The other woman, quite a bit younger, her hair pale as honey, raised a speculative eyebrow and gave Grimm an easy smile. "Oh, so that's why you find him so interesting."

"I saw him first, Hannah!" Ravenna said, still smiling. "Now out, both of you! The captain and I have matters to discuss."

"I'll bet," Hannah drawled easily.

She went past Grimm with a wink. Marta passed Ravenna with a touch on her captain's shoulder, and the women shut the armory door behind them.

"You're a terrible influence on them," Grimm scolded Ravenna, smiling.

She let out her full, throaty laugh again and took his hand in her small, calloused, fever-hot fingers. "I've missed the hell out of you, Frank Grimm. Even the rod up your bum." She squeezed his fingers gently. "Tell me you'll have some time to spend with me."

"I hope so," he said, "subject to the exigencies—"

"Of the service," she finished with a roll of her eyes, "even though you aren't actually in the Aetherium Fleet anymore. Well, you wouldn't be you without an answer like that, I suppose." Her expression sobered. "I'm here on business as well, of course."

He nodded and eyed her outfit. "That's sure to make an impression. They might arrest you on a morality charge."

She positioned her upper body provocatively—though, Grimm thought, he supposed that she would have difficulty doing otherwise.

"Let them try, and see what happens," she said. "And besides, I'm only half dressed." She crossed back to the far end of the armory, where there was a dressing dummy. From it, she took . . .

God in Heaven. She took an entire *cloak* made from dragon plumes and draped it over her shoulders. It covered her from neck to knees in a dazzling ripple of color and light, and when she turned in it in a shaft of sunlight, it sent a dizzying rainbow of colors cascading over the walls of the armory. A rising collar of upright plumes framed her head, casting more radiant colors over her face. Once she had finished, she cocked a hip to one side and rested a fist on it so that the cloak opened to show the silhouette of her curves clad in sinister black leather beneath it.

Grimm stared, tongue-tied for a second, and then said admiringly, "Ravenna, why not sell it and get a bigger ship?"

She let her head fall back for another of her delicious laughs. "The way you've been trying to get rid of *Preddy*?" She rested a fond hand on the wooden bulkhead. "I couldn't leave the *'Maiden* any more than you could your darling. She's my real wife. Just like you."

"There's an image," Grimm replied, lifting an eyebrow.

Ravenna spun once more in the cloak and said, "I'd never sell this. I took every plume the hard way. You know that." She tilted her head and studied him. "Besides. We tested it against muskets and boarding guns, and it held up."

Grimm lifted his eyebrows. "Truly?" He pursed his lips thoughtfully. "How heavy is it?"

"Quite," Ravenna said. "And hot as well. But it's proof against ball and blast alike, and I think I'm quite willing to live with a little discomfort for that." She frowned then and slipped out of the cloak, then carefully replaced it on the arming rack. "Which segues nicely into the next matter. War."

Grimm took a deep breath. "Ah."

"My Senate knows your Parliament's official position," Ravenna said. "But I speak for our fleet. And I need to know what the old spider thinks about things."

"Parliament controls the Aetherium Fleet," Grimm replied, "not the Spirearch."

Ravenna snorted.

Grimm shrugged. "Officially."

Ravenna bobbed an eyebrow at him and prowled back across the deck to slide her arms around his neck. "Since when has our relationship been an official one?"

"I don't know his mind," Grimm said, his own hands coming to rest on Ravenna's hips without him consciously thinking about what he was doing. God in Heaven, it was difficult to concentrate with the woman that close. "But we can all see the shape of things."

"War," Ravenna said.

"Almost certainly. You're aware of what Atlantea's fleet is doing?"

"Naturally," Ravenna said. "Your Admiralty is behaving with ridiculous amounts of caution."

"They're a cautious bunch," Grimm replied.

"They'll still be standing there counting their pennies when Atlantea and Aurora are blowing your Spire to bits," Ravenna said. "You should have attacked them two years ago."

"Your answer to every problem is to attack," Grimm noted.

She showed her canines again. "It's in my nature." The smile vanished. "Our colonies are being hit, of course. Our intelligence service thinks the Aurorans are testing a new weapon on soft targets prior to using it on you."

Grimm inhaled and nodded. "We've had a colony destroyed as well. There's no proof of who is doing it."

Ravenna snorted.

"I concur," Grimm said. "Our Parliament doesn't—not yet."

"Then they're fools," Ravenna said.

Grimm blinked. "They *are* Parliament."

She gave him a quick smile. "We also think that Olympia is going to hold certain indiscretions against us."

Grimm tilted his head.

"The Olympians are bean counters, of course," Ravenna said easily. "And they take a little commercial raiding so personally." Her expression grew serious. "But these attacks have made a great many crews desperate. The Senate has issued orders to curtail raiding, but when captains need to feed their crews . . . well, my people are rather independent minded."

Grimm considered that for a moment. "That drives a rather neat wedge into what would appear to be a natural alliance." He frowned. "Without Olympia's aid, it will be extremely difficult to counteract both Aurora and Atlantea—even if your people decide to throw in."

"Oh, we will," Ravenna assured him. She drew in a breath. "Unless it's smarter not to. We can dance and play merry hell with their shipping, but in the end, we can't go toe-to-toe with either one of them. Our people say you're working directly with the Spirearch now. We want your point of view on things."

Grimm drew in a slow breath. Ravenna, commander of the premier ship in Pike, was as close to a Fleet commander as Pike had. Her words would carry far more weight than those of an admiral in the Aetherium Fleet. "I'm not at all certain I'm qualified to respond to that, Ravenna."

She shook her head. "Not good enough, Captain," she said without rancor. "You're the independent commander of your Spirearch's personal airship. Your word is going to carry weight with those who know the true balance of power in the world."

"Then I say it's too soon to know," he replied.

She narrowed her eyes. "I just knew you'd say something like that." She shook her head. "I'll be open with you. Our people are as close to desperate as I've seen in my lifetime. Eight colonies gone. Eight of them, Frank. The work of two generations. There are Piker families dead, Piker children going hungry, and whoever is responsible for it is going to pay one way or another. We stand ready to fight with you. But if our presence causes Olympia to side with your enemies . . ."

Grimm sighed. "I believe there are many at home who hope war can be avoided."

Ravenna shook her head firmly. "Not for us. Not now." She looked torn for a moment and then said very quietly, "There are those who have argued for flying Albion flags the next time we go a-viking."

"God in Heaven," Grimm said, "the chaos that could cause."

Ravenna shrugged. "Chaos favors the Spire with the smaller, more numerous ships that can be in more places at once," she said calmly. "And it might kick your Parliament into acting instead of sitting on their hands." She held up a hand to forestall a protest. "I'm not one who favors that approach, but that side is getting more and more support as more bellies go empty. The clock is ticking."

Grimm exhaled slowly. "I understand. Thank you, Ravenna."

She nodded once. "Your people should know. I wanted to send word through a channel I trusted."

He gave her part of a smile. "Kind of you."

"Oh," she said, and her catlike eyes seemed to grow larger and darker. "I haven't even started being kind yet."

Then she stepped into his arms and kissed him, hot and sweet, her body pressed against him with full intention, and suddenly he didn't give a solitary damn about what was proper and what wasn't.

He shot the bolt to the armory door blindly with one hand.

Matters between the Spires were becoming dire, but nothing could be done about them in an hour.

They could wait. For a little while.

■ ■ ■ Chapter 15 ■ ■ ■

The Surface, Spire Albion

Bridget leaned out over the railing at the edge of the windlass as it descended. The mists had gotten thicker as they got nearer to the . . .

Bridget took a deep breath.

. . . to the surface, but it had come into sight when they were perhaps sixty feet away, and Bridget found herself suppressing sheer panic.

Life in a Spire's habbles could be, at times, crowded and busy. It could be quite dull and predictable. It could be endlessly trying, continually crossing the paths of those who had been terrible to you in one way or another.

But it was, in general, quite safe.

For her entire life, Bridget had been warned by dramas and novels and songs about the dangers of the surface world—about the hideous beings that dwelt there, about wolves wiser than men, about Greenmen and dragons and a thousand other dangerous predators. She'd listened to tales about poisonous forests whose very air could burn the lungs, about bizarre plant life that rendered solid earth into nearly insubstantial sinkholes, and about the madness that the constant pressure of such an environment frequently forced upon those who called it home.

Benedict's fever-hot hand found hers, and his strong fingers squeezed. She squeezed back gratefully.

"How horrible is it down there?" she asked him, her voice anxious.

"The horrible part is very hard to see," Benedict said quietly. "But as long as we're close to the Spire, there shouldn't be anything that gauntlets and blades can't handle."

His words caused Bridget to reflexively check her own gauntlet, as well as the sturdy short blade at her side. Benedict smiled at her but did not check his own gear while he leaned confidently, if not quite comfortably, on the railing as the windlass slowed and eventually thumped quietly down onto the ground.

God in Heaven, Bridget thought.

Down onto the *surface.*

"Visibility is always low here," Benedict said, his voice subdued. "Five to twenty yards. You'll never see the sun peek through down here. It will be your instinct to search for trouble with your eyes. Don't. It's useless. Use your ears and your nose."

"My nose?" Bridget asked.

Benedict winced. "And lower your voice, please," he said. "Everyone around you is depending on their ears to warn them of danger. Speak softly."

"Oh," Bridget said at once. "I'm quite sorry."

"Don't be sorry," Benedict said, his expression serious. "Be ready to use your gauntlet."

Rowl leaned against her cheek from his seat on her shoulder. "I will hear and smell any danger long before you, Littlemouse, and warn you."

"He's right," Benedict confirmed in a hushed tone. "Trust Rowl's senses. Cats are far better equipped to survive the surface than humans."

Rowl preened smugly. "If you are doing this to flatter me and gain my approval, half-soul . . . you should continue. It is effective."

"Merely being practical," Benedict murmured, suppressing a smile.

"I know you wish to mate with Littlemouse," Rowl told Benedict. "I will of course be evaluating you and will judge your performance while we are here. If you do not measure up favorably, you will obviously be denied."

"Rowl!" Bridget protested, feeling a certain amount of outrage, but mostly feeling her cheeks heat up.

"Obviously," Benedict said soberly.

"He does not need your encouragement, I think," Bridget found herself telling Benedict.

The tall young warriorborn met her eyes and smiled. "I should have thought you were accustomed to feline directness at this point, my darling."

Bridget felt her heart skip a little beat at his smile and at the fondness in his voice, and she held on to his hand harder by the moment.

The windlass's operator casually kicked down the gangway, and it thudded to the ground. "End of the line," he announced quietly. "Everyone off."

"Come on," Benedict said. "They'll be busy with crates and cargo in a moment. Passengers must debark first."

"Of course," Bridget said.

She released his hand reluctantly, squared her shoulders, and followed the stiffly moving young warriorborn down the gangway. She hesitated for only a moment before she drew a breath and stepped off the ramp and onto the surface world.

The ground felt like any other ground. She supposed it was

technically earth and should feel different, but it didn't. There were a number of living green plants growing all around, though she could see that here at the windlass docks the earth had been trampled down flat, which had evidently made it mostly unsuitable for green things to grow.

Stevedores appeared from the mists and gave a few sharp whistles to one another, and then men began rapidly moving up the gangplank to the windlass, where they took directions from a loading master with a sheaf of papers. He directed which cargo was to be carried to a number of looming warehouses constructed from extremely solid-looking masonry.

Bridget and Benedict stepped to one side out of the way of the workingmen, and Bridget looked around, frowning. She took note of a large, low dome of some kind of bony plate covered in spines and protrusions of the same material. It was perhaps twenty feet across and held up by wooden poles to a height of about three feet above the ground at the edges, though there would be room to stand in the middle. Rowl, on her shoulder, leaned toward it, sniffing in fascination.

"What on earth is that?" Bridget asked.

Benedict took note of the building with half-closed eyes and murmured, "Voice down."

"Sorry."

"It's platecreeper's shell," he murmured, "repurposed into an attack shelter."

"A what?"

"They have shelters or covered buildings at least every fifty yards or so," Benedict said, "in case of aerial attack. Mistsharks, dragons, shriekbats, diremoths, and the like."

Bridget's eyebrows went up. "The *like*?"

Benedict smiled faintly. "We never see half of the things that swoop down and take someone. If you hear sharp whistles or cries of alarm or any strange clicking sounds you can't identify, get under a shelter. It makes it less likely that you'll be attacked."

Bridget felt somewhat alarmed. "Strange clicking sounds I can't identify? Are there deadly clocks?"

"Most of the flying predators use pulses of sound to hunt," Benedict said. "It sounds like a series of sharp clicks or taps."

Bridget swallowed. "You're quite serious?"

Benedict nodded. "Deadly serious, my dear Miss Tagwynn." He paused to muse. "Of course, a sword mantis uses clicks as well, and it would happily pop right under the shelter with you—a very disturbing way to meet one's fate, believe me."

Bridget swallowed and gauged the distance between her toes and the shelter. "It would seem there are no guarantees."

Rowl nudged Bridget's head with his. "Did you bring my fighting spurs?"

She reached up a hand to touch his head for reassurance. "Yes, of course."

"I will put them on now," Rowl said, "so that I might slay anything that threatens you, Littlemouse. You need not be afraid."

She leaned her head against Rowl's flank and felt the cat's thrumming purr against her cheek. Then she set him down and took a moment to slide on the cat's fighting spurs—wicked curved blades three inches long that slid over his rear feet and rested in line with his natural claws.

"Most days, nothing much happens," Benedict said, resting a hand on her other shoulder as she worked. "But it is important to be aware that when something does happen, the results can be quite deadly."

"I understand," Bridget said, rising to put Rowl back on her shoulder. "I—"

Something brushed against her ankle and she bounded into the air, letting out a shout that broke off into a squeak. Rowl's claws dug into her tunic, but the motion had been so swift and unexpected, the big cat tumbled from her shoulder and landed with a yowl of annoyance on the ground.

From ten feet away, Bridget spun around, bringing her gauntlet to bear with her left hand while her right fumbled for the grip of her sword.

A small grey-brown tabby cat stood next to the space she had just vacated. "Pardon me," he said in Cat. "Now I see why you are so named, human Littlemouse."

"Fenli," Benedict said, frowning.

"The halfling," Rowl spat, his fur bristling. "Littlemouse, look away!"

Fenli regarded Rowl for a moment and then flicked his ears dismissively. "You could not catch me. You are too fat."

"Oh!" Rowl said, furious.

Bridget rushed to scoop Rowl up and gave Benedict an imploring look.

The wounded warriorborn smiled somewhat whimsically and then stiffly knelt down in front of the tiny Fenli. "Pardon me, Captain," he said. "There are a great many humans who are not terribly aware of where they place their feet in a place like this. If it doesn't offend you, permit me to carry you to save you the trouble of avoiding them."

Fenli considered Benedict gravely and then said, "You are wounded and might fall over. I will ride on your shoulder, as the oversized one does on hers. That way I can jump clear."

Benedict nodded seriously and picked up the little cat very carefully before setting Fenli on his shoulder. Fenli worked his claws into the fabric of Benedict's jacket a few times, drawing only a small wince, and nodded in satisfaction.

"There."

"I . . ." Bridget began. She shifted the growling Rowl around in her arms for a moment, eventually getting the large cat settled. "I am quite surprised to see you here, Fenli. I wasn't aware you had accompanied us."

"Your senses are less keen than mine," Fenli said. "Even Rowl's."

Rowl's keening growl made several of the stevedores look over in their direction.

Fenli closed his eyes and yawned.

"Oh!" Rowl said again, thrashing in Bridget's arms.

"Rowl!" Bridget said in a note of uncharacteristic firmness. "This is not the time or place for such a thing."

"Our leader, Saza, commanded me to accompany you and be sure you did not fail to attain our territory," Fenli said serenely. "She has great respect for the courage and tenacity of the half-soul who saved us, but she does not know human Littlemouse."

"How dare Saza!" Rowl said. "I will box her ears!"

"Now, Rowl," Bridget said. "One can hardly gainsay the fact that Saza has not had time to get to know me. She must provide for her people, after all."

"Halfling sneaks and thieves!" Rowl snarled.

"Clumsy fat cat," Fenli returned calmly. "I am more of a quarterling compared to your belly. And I am not afraid of you."

"Hmph!" Rowl said, tail lashing. Then he seemed to summon some kind of dignity and restraint from the depths of his soul and turned his face away from Fenli with a certain magnificent indifference.

"Gentlemen," Benedict said, looking between the cats, "I trust that we can work together in a spirit of cooperation and courtesy. The surface is not a place for divided loyalties—or attentions."

"Of course," Fenli said smoothly.

"Hmph," Rowl said, managing somehow to insert a conciliatory note into the sound.

Bridget exhaled slowly. "Thank you both," she said. She traded a look with Benedict and mouthed, *Thank you.*

The young warriorborn winked at her and then said to Fenli, "Your tribe's claws are quite sharp, as I have reason to know. I ask that you spare my hide as much as you can, please."

Fenli tilted his head in genial amusement. "When have we not?"

Benedict smiled with genuine whimsy. "I suppose that is entirely accurate."

"Precisely," Fenli said. "Now, I suggest we—" The little cat froze in a crouching position. Then his head suddenly rotated toward the misty sky. "Danger!" he piped.

An instant later, Rowl hissed. "Littlemouse, the shelter!"

A sound that was less like a series of clicks than a tearing of particularly heavy canvas came out of the mists above, and almost before Bridget's ears had registered it, the stevedores and the windlass crew dropped their burdens and began sprinting in frantic silence for the shelter, their faces pale and their eyes wide with terror.

■ ■ ■ Chapter 16 ■ ■ ■

IAS *Mistshark*, Coordinates Unknown

Colonel Espira's new rank and station had gotten him a great deal of respect within the Armada, at least within the Marine forces, but being an officer nearing flag rank or not, he hadn't gotten a bunk. Instead, he swung in a hammock with the rest of his Marines, including a young commander named Menendez and a sergeant named DeLeon.

Ciriaco was in the main hold, running a squad through their knife-fighting drills. Espira would have preferred the warriorborn's solid presence at his side, particularly with the witch's batman, Sark, forever lurking about. Espira had hardly been able to take a step on the *Mistshark* without Sark appearing from around a corner or up a hatchway. The scarred, burr-headed warriorborn with a cast in one eye made him nervous, and he would have preferred to have his own warriorborn on hand to counter Sark. Not that he and his men couldn't handle Sark if it came to that, but a comparable counter-measure would have given him more options to head off trouble before it began.

Espira was understandably nonplussed, then, when Sark appeared at his hammock in the hold of the ship and said in a flat tone, "She wants to see you."

The colonel's stomach churned and twisted, but he had no idea if any impoliteness performed toward Sark might be taken as an insult by proxy to Madame Cavendish. So he opened his eyes, took a steadying breath, and said, "Please inform her that I shall come immediately."

"Hngh," Sark said, and lumbered off, ducking far under a doorway.

"Sir?" piped up Menendez from the next hammock. "Shall I help you dress, sir?"

"I'm almost sure I can manage, Commander," Espira said, failing to keep his voice entirely calm, and the young man looked away quickly. Espira sighed and said, "Sorry, Rory. Keep warm, stay here, and keep an eye on Garcia's cough, eh? And when Sergeant Ciriaco returns, let him know where I've gone."

"Aye, sir," Menendez said, his confidence returning.

Espira grunted and unwound from his heavy blankets, mentally preparing himself for the cold. The ship was riding high above the mesosphere, the perpetual banks of mists beneath it, and at this altitude the winds were constant and blustery, the *Mistshark* all but flying, the air biting to mere human flesh.

Espira dressed neatly in his uniform and then skinned into his chilled, heavily lined leathers, fastening them closed to brace against traversing the ship's deck. Several wooden stoves, always carefully attended, lined the hold, but they merely made the sleeping area a little less than dangerous—for healthy men, anyway. Garcia coughed wetly and seemed to still be fighting his fever.

Once Espira had buttoned up, he went to one of the stoves and turned slowly a few inches from it, doing what he could to warm up the leathers before they leached the heat from his body. Then he sighed, squared his shoulders, and proceeded up to the airship's deck.

Stepping from the sheltered stairwell up onto the deck of the

THE OLYMPIAN AFFAIR

ship was like plunging into cold water, and his ears immediately began to tingle. He turned toward the prow, and the wind chewed at his back, forcing him to clap one hand to his hat to keep it from being taken away. A large round moon rode the sky off the starboard beam, casting the ship in silver light and stark shadows.

Sark was waiting for him on the deck, seemingly inured to the cold. The glowering batman gave Espira a sour look, then turned and plodded forward, his long legs carrying him swiftly enough to force Espira to hurry every few steps to keep up.

Sark led him down the deck to the passenger cabin, and he followed docilely. It rankled Espira that he should have to take such a subordinate role to a bloody Albion civilian, and a servant at that, but the only thing that mattered about Sark's position was its proximity to Madame Cavendish.

They passed perhaps a dozen aeronauts on duty, men bundled against the cold and long used to standing duty in such conditions, though their tasks were limited with the ship running swiftly and surely, both driven forward by the wind in her sails and being pulled strongly by her web.

Espira tried not to think about what was following them, far below and shrouded by the mists. It couldn't do him any good.

Sark took him to Cavendish's cabin, knocked twice, and opened the door.

"Colonel Espira, madame," the batman announced.

"Let him in," came the etherealist's voice.

Tension kept Espira's back straight as he entered absolute warmth and comfort. The passenger cabin, well insulated against the cold and the wind, was almost stuffy with the heat from its stove, and once the door shut behind him, the sound of the wind was cut off almost entirely.

"Ah, Colonel," said Madame Cavendish. She was dressed

185

immaculately in a steel blue dress and matching bolero; her long hair was down, apparently having been recently subjected to a thorough brushing. She lifted a steaming teapot from where it had been suspended over a small brazier. "Tea?"

"Very kind, Madame Cavendish," Espira replied, doffing his hat smoothly and inclining his head to her. "It's a bit brisk tonight."

She gave him a tolerant smile, and once again the odd coloration of her cinnamon eyes made him uneasy. "Of course." She nodded to a compact chair at her small table. "Please, sit down."

"Thank you," he murmured, and took the seat across from the etherealist. He waited until she had poured for them both, took up his cup, and sipped together with her. The tea was at an ideal temperature and, if a bit strong for his taste, excellent as usual.

She tilted an eyebrow at him, and Espira gave her a polite smile. "Lovely, as always."

"So charming," Cavendish said without inflection. "Colonel," she said, taking a slow breath, "I'm afraid I have concerns."

"Concerns, madame?" he asked. "How may I help you alleviate them?"

"By assuring me of your loyalty to Aurora and to His Majesty," she said, her tone suddenly hard, buzzing like the wings of an angry insect.

Espira felt tension like bands of iron creeping into his shoulders. His hands began to shake, so he set down the teacup and its saucer smoothly while directing what he desperately hoped was a calm expression to Cavendish. "Madame?" he asked politely. "I'm not at all sure what you mean."

"Tuscarora has given you an enormous opportunity," Cavendish hissed, her eerie eyes focused on his, cold with anger. "Yet I have the distinct impression that you are uncomfortable with your mission."

Espira thought fast and hard before answering. "Madame Cavendish," he said in his most polite tone, "as you say, this mission does represent an opportunity for me, the likes of which I never dared to hope for in my life. I am a soldier of Spire Aurora, ma'am. Whatever my concerns, they are for the success of the mission itself."

"Mister Sark tells me that you seemed discomfited by our most recent tests," she said, narrowing her eyes, watching him intently.

Espira took up the cup of tea and took a polite sip, rather than swallowing and giving himself away. Cavendish was more than capable of striking him down horribly with a simple thought. He'd seen her incapacitate men before. They'd torn out their own eyes rather than continue to see whatever she'd put in front of them.

"My emotions are of no account in this matter," he said smoothly. "Some portions of a soldier's work are difficult and distasteful, even when practiced upon the enemies of the Spire." He shuddered at the memory of the young man, the civilian boy he'd run through during the last mission in Albion, and he forced himself not to show the shame and regret he still felt for the reflexive act. "That has never prevented me from attending to my duty before. It will not do so now."

Cavendish stared at him for an endless moment. The fingernail of one forefinger tapped repeatedly on the wooden tabletop. Espira forced his shoulders to relax and returned her gaze steadily.

"I very much hope it will not," Cavendish said finally. "This particular operation is critical to the future. I will require your complete and unhesitating cooperation." She took a slow sip of tea, her eyes never wavering. "Commander Menendez would, I think, be an inferior replacement for you."

He tried not to exhale harder than he would have in any other conversation as the threat hit home. "Young officers are often sent along in order to gain experience under a steady hand and learn from wiser heads," he replied.

"Just so long as you remember your duty and your orders, Colonel."

"I would not be here, madame, if I had not cultivated devotion to duty as a foundation stone of my professional demeanor."

"Should that quality change, Colonel," Cavendish said, "you most certainly will not be here."

For a flash of an instant, he felt heat rise in his breast. He was a highly decorated officer of the Auroran Marines. How dared this Albion madwoman level at once both deadly threat and mortal insult and cast them in his very teeth? If she'd been an officer, even a citizen of Aurora, and a man, he would have thrown a gauntlet and demanded satisfaction on a dueling ground at once.

But she was none of those things.

She was a deadly etherealist—and quite insane. Her eyes widened slightly, the corners of her mouth turning up as she anticipated his reaction and waited for his manners to slip. If they did, she would do something to him that would make him tear out his own eyes—if he was fortunate.

So he smothered the fire in his chest with another slow sip of tea and a long blink, and said in a very polite tone of voice, "In my own work, I find it is often best to communicate about matters of discipline clearly, concisely, and in terms that leave no doubt as to what I require of those under my command. I certainly have no objection to you engaging in similar behavior, and thank you for ensuring that I understand your meaning with clarity."

Cavendish's eyes flickered with something like disappointment. She set her teacup and saucer down on the table with a precise movement that resulted in a sharp clink. "Excellent," she said in a cold voice. "Thank you for your visit tonight, Colonel. You have sealed orders from Tuscarora, I believe?"

"If I did," Espira replied with a slight bow of his head, "it would be my obligation to keep them confidential from anyone not in my direct chain of military command."

Cavendish showed her teeth. "Tuscarora made me aware of them, Colonel. Keep them on your person if you please. You will need to refer to them rather quickly when the time comes."

Espira inclined his head to her, giving her no other response, and hoped that she would not construe his professional obligation to maintain operational security as a lack of consideration.

Evidently, she did not. She turned her eyes from him and said in a suddenly weary tone, "That will be all for tonight, Colonel. I find myself unusually fatigued and the company somewhat fragrant. Return to your duties. I will call upon you again when you are needed."

Espira rose in relief, reclaimed his hat, and swept Madame Cavendish a polite bow before retreating to the door of the cabin.

"Colonel," Cavendish added as he put his hand on the door.

He froze, then turned to her with a politely inquisitive expression.

Cavendish stared at him, apparently without seeing another person standing in the room with her. "I will be observing you most closely, sir."

"You will see nothing but a loyal soldier performing his duty, madame," he replied firmly.

She regarded him with empty, odd eyes. Then she flicked her wrist at him once.

Espira flinched, but nothing untoward happened. His cheeks hot, he retreated, glad to be stepping back into the cold if it meant putting distance between himself and the woman seated in the cabin.

He all but propelled himself into Sark. The huge warriorborn let out a low growl and gave him a hostile glare.

Espira met the man's gaze steadily and stepped around him,

turning his face into the wind and hurrying back toward the Marines' sleeping area, eager to have friendly faces around him once more.

A dozen steps later, a slim, straight form almost paced into him in the silver moonlight. Calliope Ransom was inspecting her airship during the third watch.

The captain stepped aside and stared at him as he passed. Her dark eyes narrow and thoughtful, she glanced past him to the passenger cabin, where Mister Sark was just now squeezing in through the door like a spider folding itself into its burrow.

Her hand touched Espira's arm.

He blinked and glanced at her.

She put a finger to her lips and gave him a deliberate wink and murmured, her words barely audible above the wind, "We should talk. Soon."

Espira blinked at her for an instant, then bowed his head and hurried on back toward the warmth of his hammock.

■ ■ ■ Chapter 17 ■ ■ ■

Habble Profit, Spire Olympia

Captain Grimm and Miss Lancaster marched down into Habble Profit alongside Commodore Bayard and Lord Lancaster. The group was flanked by a squad of half a dozen warriorborn Aetherium Fleet Marines in their deep blue–and–snow-white dress uniforms and plumed caps, all lined with yards of silver piping and trim.

"I must say," Miss Lancaster commented to her father as they walked, "I never expected to be walked anywhere with a Marine escort. Except, I suppose, to the gallows."

"God in Heaven," Lord Lancaster said. The tall, lean man's face was suffused with amusement. "I finally convince you to watch your father at his work, and your mind goes directly to executions?"

"Oh, Father," Gwendolyn teased, smiling merrily, "I've seen you try to repair the paneling in the drawing room. How complicated could Parliament possibly be if you can manage it?"

"A fair assessment," Lord Lancaster said gravely, "though I would point out that one could say the same of running an airship, should one compare doing so to, say, an executive officer's ability to solve differential equations."

Gwen burst out into a laugh. "Mercy, Father," she said, lifting her hands in surrender. "I must concede that the mastery in finding the area beneath a curve belongs solely to you."

The old politician smiled warmly at his daughter. "And chess. But I shall give you that you have far more of your mother's spirit of adventure than I have ever managed." He turned, somber in his dark suit, and regarded her in her own dark dress uniform. "Have I mentioned to you, my darling, how proud I am of your accomplishments?"

Some of the merriment faded from Miss Lancaster's face and she studied her father's expression earnestly. "Are you?"

"Oh, yes," he said. "I have grown terribly busy of late, always distracted by the business of the Spire, and for that I perhaps owe you some time and some words of apology. And I've been terrified for you, for no matter that you have commanded the helm of an airship in battle, you are, of course, also still the little girl I once carried on my shoulders."

She found his hand with hers and said, "Of course."

Lord Lancaster smiled warmly. "But yes, no father could be prouder of a child so brave and determined."

Gwendolyn narrowed her eyes at him and said, "Goodness. Tell me this is not some flattery leading up to a plea to settle and marry."

At that, he laughed out loud. "What a fool I would be to bid the wind blow this way or that, eh? Though I suspect your mother would be cross with me for missing the opportunity."

"Tell her to be patient," Gwen advised him. "When I've acquired more experience, I have every intention of securing the future of House Lancaster. And meanwhile I've gained more knowledge of the practical operations of our crystals in the field than any Lancaster in our House's history."

"And so you have," Lord Lancaster said.

After that, they walked along hand in hand, with Lord Lancaster pointing out the features of Habble Profit's architecture and statuary, which seemed quite extensive to his daughter.

Bayard leaned close to Grimm and murmured, "A better conversation than I ever had with my own father, I think."

Grimm nodded, remembering old Lord Bayard's harsh, unyielding, taciturn demeanor. "But he taught you swordplay well enough."

"The one thing he gave freely," Alex acknowledged. "Even to my schoolmates."

"I suppose I cannot complain that he took interest in a fatherless boy. He found me a most mediocre student, I'm afraid," Grimm said as they passed through the Bear Gate, the opening into the habble proper, which was flanked by a pair of fifteen-foot-tall statues of bears rampant, near-mythical beings of the surface world.

"He was a fool about many things," Bayard replied philosophically and without heat. "He never forgave you for not falling in love with the mental strategy of dueling an opponent."

Grimm shrugged a shoulder. "I confess, I never saw the point. I was mad for the Aetherium, for airship battles. I can't remember the last time I fought fewer than twenty or thirty men with at least as many of my own. Smaller fights than that have carried very little weight in my life."

"And I love you for that practicality, my friend," Bayard said, "though it does make it difficult to trade dueling stories with you and makes you dreadfully dull at parties."

"Thank God in Heaven," Grimm murmured drily.

They passed down the Avenue of Heroes, one of the main drags of Habble Profit, where long rows of various fortunate (or unfortunate) figures of Olympian history, relatively brief though it might have been, had been immortalized in stone. Grimm spotted other delegations ahead of them on the avenue, each flanked by its own armed party. The Auroran group sported half a dozen warriorborn

Marines of their own, resplendent in scarlet and black and gold, their gilt helmets shining.

"There. The Aurorans," he noted.

The diminutive Bayard did not attempt to crane his neck. "Do you see my dear opponent Valesco?"

"I can't from here," Grimm reported. "They've got a flag bearer, though."

"Aurorans love to plant those flags of theirs everywhere they go. I wonder what makes it such a national pastime?"

"Perhaps they grew weary of dueling," Grimm suggested.

Bayard threw his head back and laughed.

"I'm surprised Abigail isn't on your arm tonight," Grimm said.

"She writes that she found herself facing another obligation she could not reasonably avoid," he said.

Grimm arched a brow. "Greater than this?"

"The Spectral Tea," Bayard confirmed. "It's where the women get together to work out how they're going to undermine one another throughout the summit, she says."

"I don't understand that kind of fighting," Grimm said.

"All things considered, you should," Bayard noted. "How is dear Calliope?"

"She is an enemy combatant," Grimm said flatly.

Bayard eyed him. "Not even visiting Ravenna can lift that cloud, eh?"

"Alex," Grimm replied calmly, "perhaps you should change the subject."

"That may work with men who are afraid to fight you, old friend," Bayard said. "But I'm not, and I care about you far too much. The woman left you. Stop torturing yourself. Enjoy your time with Ravenna, or, if it suits you, seek a new wife. You owe Calliope nothing and haven't for years."

"Not all of us are so fortunate as to fall in love with an Abigail, old friend," Grimm said. "You shouldn't change the subject because I might take umbrage. You should change it because, in this specific case, you are speaking outside your areas of expertise."

"Not so. I'm talking about my friend," Bayard responded. "And in deference to his pain, my last word is this: occasionally I grow weary of seeing him torment himself."

Grimm eyed Bayard, and the two of them traded ironic nods.

By then they had arrived at Olympia's Great Hall of Commerce, a building seemingly made of pure white marble columns and arches and steps. Like the rest of the delegations, they began to climb the steps to the summit meeting's opening ceremonies. It was rather the most grandiose structure Grimm had ever seen, but then, Olympia, the hub of commerce for half of a continent, could afford to spend money on such things. And honestly, it really was by far the largest and most convenient location for the trade summit within a week's sailing in every direction.

"All this marble," Bayard said with heavy disapproval.

"I rather like it," Grimm said.

"Too flashy."

"It's bright," Grimm countered. "Stone and mortar have a very solid look, I will grant you, but they can be terribly gloomy. There's a reason I spend most of my time on an airship. You're just jealous they have access to better quarries than Albion does."

"Probably," Bayard said, the corners of his eyes wrinkling.

The grand staircase opened onto an enormous domed chamber whose ceiling was spangled with lumin crystals of all colors that cast brilliant light down over the space below, which was filled with hundreds of people. Musicians played somewhere nearby in the bright, up-tempo style of Olympia; their instruments consisted mostly of strings and flutes.

"Bah," muttered Bayard. "A dance floor, and I'm not on it with Abigail."

"I'm sure you wouldn't have trouble finding a partner," Grimm consoled him.

"They're all too tall."

Gwen turned from where she walked arm in arm with her father and said, "I'm not, Commodore."

Bayard frowned at her. "You're too . . . Lancaster."

Lord Lancaster arched an eyebrow.

"Too Lancaster?" Gwen said merrily.

"You'd lead," Bayard deadpanned.

Gwen laughed, and even Grimm found himself smiling.

"Queenkiller!" boomed a large rolling voice, and a man in a green-and-gold admiral's uniform came stomping toward them and engulfed Gwendolyn in a bear hug. He wasn't inordinately tall, but his shoulders, arms, back, and jaw all looked like they'd been sized for a giant of a man. He had a russet brown beard and short-cropped hair. He spun Gwen around in a whirling hug, laughing heartily. "Here I thought I'd never have a chance to thank you for what you did, and you show up at this!"

Gwen laughed as well until she ran out of breath and said, "Pike! Put me down, you great oaf!"

"Right away, lady!" Pike said, and plopped her down promptly.

"Pike," murmured Grimm. "Admiral Pike of the Olympian Merchant Marine? Of the Pike Shipping Company?"

"The same," rumbled the large man looking over their group. "Lord Lancaster, I think, yes?"

"The same," said Lancaster, bemused. "Gwen, when did you meet the admiral?"

"This girl," said Pike, sliding a bearlike arm around Gwen's shoulders, "stood cool and steady when a bloody silkweaver queen that had gone blood mad started tearing up a tavern. Stood her ground and put a gauntlet bolt right down her throat. Killed her dead as a stone when I thought we were all about to meet our Makers."

"Only after you'd charged the thing armed with nothing but a barstool," Gwen said, smiling.

"Pshhh, that," Pike said deprecatingly. "I did what I could. But you killed the bloody thing. Saved us all."

Lord Lancaster stared at Gwen for a long moment, his eyebrows going up. "Gwendolyn," he said in a chiding tone.

"Oh, it's long past, Daddy," Gwen said. "It was back during the attack."

"You never said anything about fighting silkweavers in a tavern, young lady."

"To be fair," Pike rumbled, "it was only one silkweaver. And your daughter saved my life. And the lives of my captains. I'm in her debt." He turned and faced Gwen, his expression suddenly serious. "And Lincoln Pike takes his debts seriously, Miss Lancaster. If ever you have need of me, I'll be there."

Lord Lancaster's eyebrows climbed most of the way to his receding hairline.

"Now," Pike stated firmly, "this tale should be told properly, and that means drinks. Lancaster, you've a reputation as a dry fish, but you need to hear this story with the taste of proper Olympian whiskey in your mouth. If this hero is your daughter, she deserves that much at the very least. Come with me."

Pike took each of the Lancasters by the arm and promptly stomped off, giving them very little choice but to go along. The commander of the Marine detachment looked torn for a moment, and then, at a nod from Bayard, he trailed as discreetly as possible after the Lancasters.

The music swelled and more dancers crowded onto the floor in the center of the large room. Grimm and Bayard drifted over to one side of the hall, and Grimm spotted Ravenna whirling gaily on the dance floor in her dragon-plume cloak with a rather intimidated-looking young Dalosian officer. She spotted Grimm and gave him a gay wave and a brilliant smile.

"Oh, that poor nipper," muttered Bayard. "I hope she leaves him alive."

"Unfair, Alex," Grimm said, grinning. "She's only dancing."

"I'm talking about when he tries to lift her in that bloody cloak. The thing must weigh more than a cannon. Drink?"

"Shouldn't you be on your best game?"

"Oh, a duel won't happen tonight," Bayard said easily, "even if Valesco somehow manages to provoke it in this setting. My second will have to deal with Valesco's second and set a time. Valesco himself will need a while to brag about how he'll kill me where people can overhear it. Believe me, Mad, such a thing takes days."

Grimm shrugged and secured a couple of glasses from a passing server, then offered one to Alex. According to Alex, the wine was light, very dry, and quite excellent.

Grimm disliked it. "If you say so," he said with a faint grimace. He scanned the room slowly, but the assassin in question was nowhere to be seen.

Bayard, he noted, was doing the same thing and frowning.

"Something wrong?" Grimm asked. "If he's not here, he can hardly begin trouble."

"Exactly," Bayard mused, his tone a mix of puzzlement and worry. "Someone like Valesco lives to begin trouble. I wonder. Where is he?"

Chapter 18

The Spectral Tea, Habble Profit, Spire Olympia

Abigail made sure her security team, half a dozen rather formidable-looking men, was in position both walking ahead of her and trailing behind her. She paused outside the vast town house where the Spectral Tea was being hosted so that she might turn and inspect Miss Folly. Abigail had managed to find a dress in cobalt blue to fit Folly in time for the Tea, and enough jewelry to perhaps cover for the lack of a proper corset. Her horrendously dyed hair had been swept up beneath a matching hat, but Abigail had been entirely unable to convince the young etherealist to remove the small pouch from around her neck.

Folly looked intensely uncomfortable. Her eyes were a little too wide, and she was breathing more quickly than even Abigail's brisk walking pace could explain.

"Goodness," Abigail said to the young woman. "Are you quite all right?"

"This dress itches," Folly said, "and it's all . . . fitty. And so normal. It's altogether too normal, and it doesn't fill in any holes at all, but I don't wish Madame Abigail to think that I am not grateful for her efforts."

"Your . . . unique manner of dress is one of your quirks, I take it," Abigail said, frowning.

"I'm not sure what a quirk is," Miss Folly said, looking down at the ground firmly. "Oh, dear. Madame Abigail is going to think me quite ignorant."

"It's how personnel in the Intelligence Service refer to the oddities acquired by etherealists as they age, dear," Abigail replied. "The unique facets of personality that they develop, such as your . . . habitual wardrobe."

"She doesn't understand how important it is that I dress how I feel," Miss Folly breathed. "Oh, this dress is itchy, though I suppose I'm feeling rather itchy now because of it."

"I understand, dear," Abigail said firmly, "but for an occasion such as this, I'm afraid what you had on would not have done at all. You'd not be allowed in."

Folly looked up at Abigail and touched her corset gently with a trembling hand. "I wonder if Madame Abigail is very comfortable in that."

"Most days," she replied. "They're uncomfortable only when not properly fit. I assure you, I am quite used to it."

The young etherealist frowned. "But some days Madame Abigail is not comfortable. Normal people are so odd," Folly said. "They have so many rules and then tell me dressing the way I feel is strange."

"I suppose it can seem that way at times," Abigail replied. "But you said you had to stay near me in order to defend me. That is still a fact, yes?"

Folly looked up and met Abigail's eyes with what seemed like difficulty. Then she nodded.

"Well?" she said. "Miss Folly, can you do what is needed for the sake of Albion? Even in a rather fashionable dress?"

Folly looked down again. "Please tell her I shall try."

"Excellent," Abigail said. "Thank you. And please do not take this the wrong way, dear, but I think it would be best if you said as little as possible. Your quirk of speech is quite endearing, but I'm afraid it would make you rather memorable, and we like to avoid that kind of thing where possible."

Miss Folly smiled demurely. "Oh, Madame Abigail should be assured I'm quite excellent at being seen and not heard. I shall be far too busy for conversation in any case."

"Busy?" Abigail asked. "Doing what?"

"Protecting Madame Abigail," Folly replied. Then she added, "And making her look quite remarkable, I suppose."

Abigail arched an eyebrow. "Oh?"

The young etherealist nodded. "It will be quite important that she keep correct posture and not move her neck very much at all. It might be best if she pretends she's balancing a cup of hot tea on her head."

"My word," Abigail said. "It's been a few years since finishing school, but I daresay I can manage. Precisely what is it that you have in mind, dear?"

"Not my mind," Folly assured the pouch of crystals around her neck. "It was Master Ferus's thought, though he conveyed it to me verbally. Still, I did add a thought of my own to the idea, so that when Madame Abigail sees red, she should be aware that an attempt is being made to influence her."

Abigail blinked at the younger woman. "Sees red? My word."

Hamish loomed out of the shadows ahead, moving in total silence. The bodyguard was a tall and forbidding presence dressed in an excellent suit in shades of color little different from black. "My lady," he murmured, "we need to wait a moment more to allow the Auroran delegation to enter the Tea."

"Hmmmm," Abigail said, pleased, as she came to a halt. "We're going to be later than they are, then. We have an opportunity here. Folly, I don't suppose you could do something for me?"

Folly tilted her head, flicking a quick glance up at Madame Abigail. "Madame?"

"I need to make an entrance," Abigail said. "How creative are you feeling?"

The large and expensive town house where the Spectral Tea was being held had been lit with lumin crystals in dozens of colors, spilling out of their sconces in clusters after the fashion of grapevines. Larger clusters of crystals hung from the center of each room in a similar model, bathing the interior in sparkling colors and opulent brilliance. The light shone upon expensive wooden flooring and walls and fixtures, all whitewashed until the grain of the material could hardly be seen, but the light swathed them in myriad spectra of colors, giving quite the enchanting aura to the event. A chamber ensemble of strings and woodwinds and a very mild drum to keep the beat played unseen in a balcony overhead.

The ladies of the elite strata of their respective Spires (and their ladies-in-waiting, naturally) stood talking in small groups or sat at tables where elegant silver tea service sets awaited their pleasure, at least in the main chamber, though Abigail noted at once that side rooms of art, statuary, and fashion, respectively, were attracting a steady flow of admirers, mostly in pairs. The hosting Atlanteans were distinctive in their vivid silks, each color denoting a stratum of their ruling Spectrum. To Albion eyes, they wore a garish amount of golden and silver jewelry that contrasted sharply with the dark richness of their skin. Their metallic facial makeup had been designed to highlight their luminous, jewellike eyes.

Atlantean servants, also female, hovered near each table and along the walls, so alert that the ladies present hardly needed to lift a finger to attract their assistance. All were dressed in simple white silks, their garments making a statement in their rather common styling, their extremely expensive quality, and their pristine spotlessness. There was not a food or tea stain to be seen.

The Auroran ladies had arrived together. Against all the white, they were like a rather large bloodstain in their various shades of scarlet, and began to spread out through the main room.

Abigail drew up at the entry, indicating calmly to Miss Folly that she should hover at her left side, a step behind her. After recognizing a dozen allies and three times as many potential foes, Abigail felt herself suppressing a wolfish smile of excitement.

"Miss Folly," she murmured, "are you all right?"

"Oh," Folly said, fingering the velvet bag around her neck nervously, "there is enough money in this room to found a new colony."

"Several, I daresay," Abigail said. "Shall we make an impression?"

Folly smiled nervously at her and nodded. Abigail turned to the page by the door, also female, and passed her a simple placard.

The page accepted the card with a smile of her own and turned to announce in a clear and ringing voice, "Please welcome Abigail, Duchess Hinton, of Spire Albion, special delegate of His Majesty Jeremiah Addison Orson Albion, Spirearch of Spire Albion."

Abigail took a step forward, paying special attention to her posture, her back as straight and rigid as any of her finishing school instructors could have wished, her head regally erect.

Behind her, she heard Folly exhale in a slow, controlled fashion.

The lights of the entire gathering dimmed abruptly, plunging the assembled company into deep shadow. There was a whispering sound, and two dozen tiny lumin crystals abruptly flared to life in a cloud of Albion white, red, and blue spread out into a neat coronet that began to slowly, steadily orbit Abigail's head at a distance of approximately six inches. She stood for a moment at the top of a short stairway above the company and let them see her. Indeed, with the lights down, they could hardly see anything else. She found herself rather enjoying the murmurs (some of them doubtless vicious) that spread through the crowd.

She smiled brilliantly at the gathering.

Yes. That would do nicely as an entrance.

She descended the stairs with regal grace, her head held carefully in place, and as she walked forward, flickers of light seemed to flow from her coronet of circling crystals and give light back to the existing fixtures as she passed them. She was acutely aware of Miss Folly proceeding along at a precise distance behind her. The young etherealist's eyes were downcast modestly, but Abigail sensed the intense concentration the young woman was maintaining to manipulate the lumin crystals throughout the chamber.

It was unusual to see floating lumin crystals, so they were making quite an impression on the crowd. Abigail kept her smile fixed in place like armor as she crossed the main floor and said to the first face she could identify, "Victoria, darling, so good to see you. How are Darren and the children?"

While the light was restored to the room over a few moments, Abigail engaged the Olympian lady in pleasantries and began planning her next steps. She was very much on her own at the Tea. Hamish and his security team were waiting outside, along with everyone else's guard dogs. Abigail had no fear of any sort of violent incident happening here; any such thing would draw the instant and immediate wrath of highly protective professionals who would rush in from outside the town house. She had an amusing mental image of a small army of them attempting to wedge themselves through the doors at once, in fact.

No. There were other, far more intangible dangers to be faced here.

Abigail Hinton foremost amongst them, she reminded herself firmly. Hamish might have been a master of his domain, but this arena belonged to Abigail.

A brief conversation with Victoria, Lady Jennings, led Abigail to a longer engagement with Helen of House Harrison, and from there she angled herself neatly into a seat at the right hand of the grande dame of Spire Olympia—Madame Iphigenia, First Lady of House Warren, elder sister of Olympia's Lord President, who was Abigail's own master's opposite number in this Spire.

Madame Iphigenia was a tall and rawboned woman with brilliant red hair now thick with silver and shoulders almost as wide as a man's. Her voice was a rich, throbbing, melodious alto, and she was an accomplished singer of opera who still performed occasionally. She was no beauty, but she was striking and held herself with such poise and grace that one could hardly tell the difference. Madame Iphigenia inclined her head very slightly to Abigail as she seated herself, Folly hovering dutifully nearby.

"Your Grace," she said, her rich voice somehow conveying both welcome and wary amusement, "I see you have not forgotten the importance of a strong entrance."

"First Lady," Abigail replied with a slightly deeper nod of her head. "I was given excellent advice once at an after-party to the finest performance of *The Time of Troubles* I have ever seen."

Lady Iphigenia let out a low, rich laugh at that. "Flatterer. Though that was an excellent production team. Tea?"

"Thank you," Abigail replied, and accepted a cup from the first lady's own hand. "I'm glad to see you again."

"Have you met young Lady Emilia of my House?" Lady Iphigenia inquired, and made polite introductions around the table, which Abigail returned graciously.

"Always a pleasure," Abigail said, finishing with the last of them. "I trust that the fortunes of House Warren remain bright?"

"Unless we find ourselves embroiled in a war we have no desire to entertain," Lady Iphigenia said archly. "My brother tells me that the old spider in Albion is insisting upon it. And now here you are."

"No one wants a war," Abigail assured her. "However, it does become difficult to see how one is to be avoided, given Tuscarora's ongoing actions."

"The Piker colonies, you mean?" Lady Iphigenia asked.

"And one of ours now," Abigail replied, and took a sip of tea.

That comment had the impact she had hoped for. The ladies of House Warren seated at the table exchanged glances and a few quiet murmurs behind lifted hands.

"When did this happen?" asked Lady Iphigenia, her brow furrowing in concern.

"Not two weeks past," Abigail replied calmly. "The laws of war were not followed. There were no survivors, I'm very much afraid."

That drew another round of murmurs. Excellent.

"And how can you be sure it was Spire Aurora who perpetrated such a massacre?" inquired Lady Iphigenia.

"I assure you that investigations that will acquire proof are underway."

"Ah," the Olympian matron murmured. "But perhaps not before the summit."

"These matters are never certain," Abigail responded. "But Aurora was clearly responsible for the attack on Albion two years ago and for the destruction of our docking facilities at Habble Landing."

Iphigenia flicked out the fingers of one hand in an elegant gesture of acceptance, conveying no sense of support as she did. "A devastating stroke," she said in a neutral voice, "though to the benefit of our own trade, as you can imagine."

"In the short term, perhaps," Abigail said. "But Olympia and Albion have been trading partners since your House declared independence two hundred years ago. In the long run, our alliance has benefited us both enormously."

Lady Iphigenia regarded Abigail steadily as she sipped tea. "And that is why you wish me to persuade my brother to enter the war on your side, should it come to that, eh?" She set the cup down and shook her head. "Lady Hinton, most of our fleet is merchant marine. A war does not serve Olympia's purposes, economic or otherwise."

"You know how Aurora and Atlantea both are willing to play cutthroat when it comes to trade," Abigail countered. "Should they gain ascendance, will being constantly skinned by their merchants serve Olympia's purposes?" She softened the sortie with a smile and a blink of her wide eyes, took a sip of tea, and awaited an answer.

Lady Iphigenia gave her a shrewd glance and exhaled a little breath through her nose. "Lord Albion chooses his people well, I suppose." She drummed her fingers on the table exactly once, a precise gesture, as she thought. "Even if I added my weight to your side of the scales, it might not move my brother's mind."

"And yet you are considering it," Abigail noted.

Lady Iphigenia nodded slowly. "Well, let us decide the matter in an appropriate fashion."

"And in what fashion would that be?"

"Dramatically, of course," the First Lady of House Warren said, her dark eyes sparkling with sudden interest. "I believe you should come with me, Lady Hinton."

"And where might we be going?"

"Why, to have a cup with your enemies, of course," Iphigenia said. "Let us see what everyone has to say, and I shall make a judgment for myself."

Abigail's heart began to beat faster. She had hoped to bend Lady Iphigenia's ear and have her well in hand before the Aurorans and Atlanteans could do so, but that plan had clearly been pitched over the side of the Spire. "Face-to-face, is it?"

"I'm sure Aurora and Atlantea chose their people just as well as Albion," Iphigenia said. "I think I should like to hear you all talk and see what emerges from the discussion." She nodded once firmly, set her tea aside, and rose. "Please don't regard me as mistrustful of you personally, darling."

"I should never think of it," Abigail said, mirroring her.

"Excellent," said Lady Iphigenia. "Come with me if you please, Lady Hinton."

"Of course, Lady Warren," Abigail said. "Lead on."

She followed the First Lady of House Warren into the elegant fray of civilized battle to confront her home's most dangerous foes.

Chapter 19

The Spectral Tea, Habble Profit, Spire Olympia

Abigail followed First Lady Iphigenia from her House's tea table toward one of the side rooms. Iphigenia had evidently decided to shield the members of her House from any fallout by bidding them wait for her return, but Abigail could sense the collective gaze of the gathering—at least of those who existed for more than the social swirl—tracking their movement across the main gathering area. Abigail maintained her posture and her slowly spinning coronet of glowing crystals and struggled to keep her pace regal and sedate while simultaneously accompanying long-legged Iphigenia.

Iphigenia led them directly into the sculpture chamber, where a selection of statuary from the various Spires stood ready for admiration—from the painstakingly lifelike depictions of Atlantean art, accurate down to the tiny folds of skin at the corners of the eyes; to the more clean and idealized Olympian stylings; to Albion's traditional stone-and-dye-colorized sculptures; to the primitive depictions of the Pikers, which conveyed raw emotion through exaggerated body language and expression; to the collective mishmash of the loose-knit Dalosian Federation and its many profitable branches. Spire Aurora's sole contribution was what was surely a lionized, nearly seven-foot image of His Majesty Tuscarora naked and spitting a downed and writhing dragon upon a long lance, his foot pinning one of the beast's heavily plumed wings to the earth.

"Subtle," Iphigenia noted as they approached Tuscarora's statue.

"I've never had the pleasure," Abigail said. "Shall I recognize His Majesty from his likeness?"

Iphigenia paused by the statue to consider it. "Mmmm. Seems more or less what he looked like twenty years ago. I suppose if he's kept himself fit, it might do."

"But smaller?" Abigail suggested.

"No. The proportions seem accurate enough," Lady Iphigenia replied. "He honestly is that tall."

"Goodness," Abigail murmured. She regarded the image of the man who had sent a murderer to deal with Bayard and stored the memory of his features. Just in case.

The Atlantean sculptors had taken an entire row of the display room to themselves, with half a dozen Atlantean displays lined up beside the image of Tuscarora. A small group of noblewomen was just gathering about the image of Tuscarora's feet and regarding the statue with interested, dispassionate eyes.

"There," Iphigenia breathed, pausing before a Piker piece of a grieving adult and children. The subjects were so nebulous that one could not be sure of the gender of any of them, though their racking pain and mourning were evident in their posture and body language. "Do you recognize those women at Tuscarora's feet, Lady Abigail?"

"The ravishing young woman with the hair to her knees is Tuscarora's youngest sister, Sarafine," Abigail murmured.

"Twenty years old," Iphigenia said, nodding. "And both of her husbands have died of unknown illnesses of the stomach, one quite recently."

"Perhaps she's a bad cook," Abigail said lightly.

"Perhaps Tuscarora needed a single relative to secure new alliances," Iphigenia replied. "The others?"

"I don't recognize the warriorborn lady in the scarlet uniform by sight," Abigail replied, "but from what I've read, that must be Felicia Montaine, member of the Crimson Guard. She's a killer."

Iphigenia nodded her head slowly once. "Leaving . . . ?"

Abigail regarded the rather average-looking young woman in a gown of the palest, pinkest rose one could reasonably create without bleaching it entirely white. Down her back, the young woman had long, curling hair worn in a long banner tied with a wide cloth that matched her dress. Her dark skin was a rich contrast to the fair silk, and her eyes were a cold and icy blue the color of a clear winter sky. A simple silver circlet around her brow denoted her status on Atlantea's ruling Spectrum; she wore it without a trace of self-consciousness.

"That must be Initiate Hestia of the Spectrum," Abigail murmured. "Newly elevated. Least of the Spectrum but a ruler of Atlantea nonetheless."

"It's so nice to speak with someone of basic competence," Lady Iphigenia noted. "Hestia has quite the presence for one so young."

Abigail arched an eyebrow. "Do you think so?"

Lady Iphigenia gave an eloquent shrug of her shoulders.

Initiate Hestia was studying the statue of Tuscarora quite closely, her plain features revealing little. Abruptly, she seemed to sense Abigail's gaze upon her, and she took half a step to turn toward them, her pale eyes direct and cool. She regarded Abigail for a long, solid breath without reaction, and then she pursed her lips and evaluated Abigail's coronet of floating crystals.

Hestia lifted a hand and put it on her warriorborn bodyguard's arm. Felicia Montaine stopped speaking to Lady Sarafine at once, her own pale green eyes flashing amidst the delicate, fine gold wire of a mask that framed them. Felicia was as beautiful as most of the warriorborn. Her canine teeth showed prominently when she smiled and murmured something to the Auroran lady beside her.

Abigail became suddenly, intently aware of Lady Iphigenia watching her for her reaction.

Abigail fixed on her face a smile like a helmet's visor and swept forward confidently to meet the ladies gathered about the feet of Tuscarora's statue.

"So masculine," Abigail said admiringly, looking up at the statue and then at each of the other ladies. "One hardly knows how to react to such a graven image." She turned to face Lady Sarafine, smiling. "Do you know the artist?"

Lady Sarafine shifted her weight slightly, her long wheat-colored hair swaying behind her. "I adore her, actually. A blind woman with the most exquisitely sensitive touch. She's done the entire royal gallery, you know."

"Amazing," Abigail said. "She must have a truly inspired gift."

Lady Sarafine's smile turned brittle. "Of one kind or another. Lady . . . Winton, is it not?"

"Hinton," Abigail corrected her warmly. "House Winton makes and sells baskets."

"My mistake," Sarafine said drily. She inclined her head slightly to First Lady Iphigenia as that woman approached in Abigail's (and inevitably Folly's) wake. "Still, as much as my dear brother's appetites guide his artistic choices, I must admit that this particular piece is most impressive."

Abigail nodded warmly. "I'm quite certain an executive's ability to murder a surface creature with hand weapons plays regularly into Spire politics. I'm afraid I don't quite see how at the moment, but perhaps that's simply my lack of travel to Aurora showing itself."

Something like dark humor sparkled in Sarafine's eyes. "Much as in Aurora, we do not overly concern ourselves with men who spend more time pursuing books than women. I'm not quite sure I see how an executive with no heirs serves his Spire with endless hours of reading when he should be getting himself a wife, but I'm sure that's simply the result of my own flightiness and indiscipline in never traveling to a place that considers such lack of activity admirable."

The young woman was a bit clumsy and eager to be on the attack, Abigail thought. But then, that was the Auroran character generally. Sarafine was game enough, and that pleased Abigail. "I'm certain that amusements enough to occupy the lady's mind could be found in Albion," she said effusively. "When you do visit, you must be my guest at House Hinton." She met Lady Sarafine's eyes. "I will ensure that you do not find yourself helpless in the jaws of ennui."

The much taller young woman went still and studied Abigail with remote eyes. She covered her wariness well but not entirely. Then she inclined her head slightly and said, "Should I find myself in Albion, I will certainly want to talk to you at the very least, Lady Hinton."

Abigail laughed and touched Sarafine's arm fondly. "Yes, do. Lady Sarafine, such a pleasure to meet you at last."

"Lady Abigail Hinton," purred Felicia Montaine. The warrior-born turned to regard Abigail from her better than six feet of height, smiling down as one might upon a playful kitten. "Rumors are so often unkind, but I find you a perfectly marvelous little person."

Abigail felt a flicker of genuine annoyance at the reference to her height. Not that she was of anything but perfectly functional stature, but she did find the arrogance of tall people occasionally cloying. "Oh, rumor," she said with a wink. "If we listened to rumors, I might think you one of those horrible duelists who has found a socially acceptable means of enjoying the act of murder."

Felicia's dark face split into a wide, genuine smile. "I've heard that you fancy yourself quite the swordswoman."

Abigail let out a tittering laugh. "Oh, darling, I'm sure I'm simply a spoiled wealthy woman whose people flatter her outrageously." She kept smiling but let it fall away from her eyes. "And honestly, as I'm given to understand, there's only one way to know for certain. True?"

Felicia, perhaps unconsciously, moved her fingers, the tips of her nails lengthening slightly. "That is indeed the truth," the warriorborn woman purred. "Perhaps we should have a ladies' day in the salle. All of these parties are sure to grow dull and repetitive after a time."

Abigail let her eyes widen dramatically. "Scandalous! Oh, you Atlanteans and your defiance of convention. What would our poor fathers and forefathers think?"

"They'd think to keep their mouths shut if they know what's good for them," Montaine said with a wink. "I doubt you allowed your own father's choices to guide you very much either, Lady Hinton."

"Guilty as charged," Abigail said. "May I say that you are quite striking in that uniform, Madame Montaine. It really does suit you magnificently."

Felicia took a small step to one side, her trousers drawing tight over a hip, and unconsciously straightened the hem of her jacket. "Between just us girls, I'd prefer skirts, I think, but the Guard has its rules and little tolerance for individual tastes."

"At least it's not that dreadful eggplant and mauve that the Dalosian prefect's house guard is wearing."

Montaine shuddered delicately. "The world abounds with unpleasant things I am glad to have missed." She winked again, dropped the smile from her eyes, and said, "It's definitely gone short of a number of unpleasant things I *haven't* missed."

Oh, thought Abigail, that was a very well-made threat. With yet another reference to my height worked in as well. This one isn't merely good with a blade, and she's at least as arrogant as I am, so she would seem to be worth having as an enemy.

"That sounds so exciting," Abigail replied without showing an ounce of the intimidation she had begun to feel. "When the current difficulties have been resolved, I should love to spend a little more time with you."

"A little," Felicia murmured. "It would have to be." She paused to let the insult sink in and then added deprecatingly, "My duties, you understand. They consume the lion's share of my time."

"Of course," Abigail answered with waxing sympathy in her voice but not in her eyes. "Aspiring to status of one's own in the periphery of the Spectrum must be a particularly exhausting challenge. No matter how tall one is. Or how many people one kills."

Felicia Montaine stared hard at Abigail for a moment, and Abigail could just barely hear the low rumble of a lioness's snarl that had begun to bubble in Felicia's throat as she failed to find an appropriate response to Abigail's sally.

A quiet, rich laugh bubbled forth from the lips of the third woman present.

Initiate Hestia finally seemed to find something interesting beyond the subject matter of the statue of Tuscarora. The youngest member of the Spectrum turned to face Abigail with her expression animated for the first time that evening.

"Oh," Hestia murmured, "Lady Hinton knew where to aim those darts, did she not, Felicia?"

Technically, the tall warriorborn woman smiled, but the muscles along her jaw flexed as she kept her teeth together and gave Hestia a faint nod without ever looking away from Abigail.

Hestia smiled at her bodyguard and said, "Your face vanished when she spoke. You should be careful about such things."

JIM BUTCHER

Felicia Montaine gave Hestia a brief stare, her facial expression fixed. Then she straightened her shoulders and withdrew half a step to stand slightly behind Initiate Hestia and a bit to one side.

Just where Folly was standing in relation to Abigail, in fact.

Hestia turned her attention fully to Abigail. "I cannot see the faces of people who don't matter," the etherealist explained. "Lady Hinton, perhaps I was mistaken about you. At least you have a measure of personal courage to be able to speak such calm insults to one of the warriorborn. What distinctive features you have." She took an uncomfortable step closer into Abigail's personal space, and Hestia leaned forward to peer at her face. The orbiting lumin crystals whirled by less than an inch from Hestia's eyelashes, but the woman did not blink. "Interesting."

"Faces?" asked Abigail, fighting an urge to lean back. "Do you mean to say that you literally cannot see the faces of some individuals?"

"Most of them, really," Hestia replied. "I believe your people call it a quirk when referring to the coping mechanisms developed by etherically capable individuals." She smiled and met Abigail's gaze. Her icy eyes were eerie. "I believe it is some kind of filter my brain has put in place to reduce the amount of incoming information and to help me function more ably."

Abigail resisted the urge to tilt her head in curiosity. "A fascinating theory, Initiate. How do you know which people matter and which don't, do you suppose?"

Hestia smiled warmly. "Why, by whether or not I can see their faces, of course," she replied.

Abigail got a little fluttery feeling behind her ribs, her instincts screaming that she was facing someone who was quite clearly not sane.

"I think," Hestia said, her smile widening, "that it's time you made your excuses and left, Lady Hinton."

Abigail instantly felt chagrined, as she hadn't since she'd committed her many, many faux pas as a schoolgirl. She felt color come into her cheeks in embarrassment, and she drew in a breath to issue a brief and vague apology in preparation for her withdrawal.

Suddenly, the orbiting crown of crystals flared into scarlet light, and her abrupt sense of embarrassment vanished. Abigail took a steadying breath because she felt mentally off-balance, as if she'd been standing on slippery ice and nearly taken a tumble. Her eyes focused on the orbiting crystals and then upon Initiate Hestia.

"But, Initiate," she heard herself replying calmly, "I've only just arrived. And I haven't had a chance to view any of the paintings yet."

Hestia's smile vanished and was replaced by an expression of analytic calm. The etherealist's eyes narrowed, focusing upon Abigail's coronet of orbiting crystals.

And then looking past Abigail entirely.

To Folly.

"I see," Initiate Hestia said, drawing the word out. "Oh, and she's accounted for herself as well as for you, Lady Hinton. Clever child."

Abigail checked over her shoulder and saw that Folly stood in rigid tension, her eyes on the ground, her heels grinding into the floor as if desperate to be put to use.

"Stand fast, Miss Folly," Abigail breathed to her. "I, for one, refuse to be routed like a pair of truants from a chocolate store."

Folly drew in a breath. Then she looked up at Abigail, met her eyes for a fleeting second, and then dropped her jaw in a sharp nod.

"Good lass," Abigail said approvingly, and turned back to face Hestia. "I work only with the best, Initiate Hestia. May I compliment your choice of garments for this evening? That dress is ideally suited to this particular gathering."

Indeed, the ability to induce the genuine-seeming emotion of shame in someone at a ladies' social gathering was a sword of the first order. Well, that would spread. It wouldn't be long before coronets of a more practical, etherically engineered design would be a necessary accessory to her wardrobe, Abigail supposed, and she made a note to get her personal empire's jewelry house into position ahead of the trend.

"In the absence of all the men of the court, I feel the compliment needed to be given," Abigail finished.

Hestia exhaled a breath and flicked her wrist to one side in an imperious gesture. "About that."

From behind the heroic statue of Tuscarora suddenly loomed the tall, sinister shape of Rafael Valesco, the Auroran duelist.

The man took two strides in the time it took Abigail to draw in a breath, and he struck her abruptly, sharply, with a blow of the back of his hand to her face. He did not shirk in the amount of power he placed in the strike, and though Abigail tried to mitigate its force, the differential in their physical capabilities was stark.

The blow was stunning, and she dropped to a knee, dimly aware of the tinkling sound of tiny crystals falling to the floor, Folly's cry of surprise, and an overwhelming sensation of simple shame.

There was no chance whatsoever of preventing the duel between Bayard and Valesco now. Not after this provocation.

With all her faculties focused on the swirl of social battle, Abigail had made insufficient allowance for her enemies to move entirely *outside* those same confines.

She had just been badly used.

Intensely aware of Lady Iphigenia's regard, Abigail knew that her Spire's enemies had just cast down the gauntlet in full view of the world and God in Heaven Himself, and that her reaction in the face of this event might well determine whether or not Albion stood with allies against the combined forces of two full Spires—or stood alone.

But it was more than that.

Abigail had been used.

As a weapon.

Against Bayard.

It simply would not do to strike at Initiate Hestia, Abigail thought. She was a member of the Spectrum of Atlantea. To physically strike her would be tantamount to an emissary striking His Majesty. It would be an unbearable slight to the honor and prestige of the government of a powerful Spire, one that must be answered, possibly even with open war.

No, that response would simply be too shocking.

But Hestia had used Abigail.

Against.

Bayard.

Abigail rose, thought one of her soft leather gloves would do very nicely as a gauntlet with her fist left within it, and fetched Initiate Hestia of the Atlantean Spectrum a blow to the base of her jaw.

Hestia crumpled to the floor in a suddenly boneless heap, leaving both Valesco and Felicia Montaine staring in absolute, startled horror at the furious Lady Hinton.

Abigail stripped off her glove briskly, cast it negligently at Hestia's face, and said, "You have used me wrongly against an honorable man, and I will have satisfaction. You are a vicious, spineless little coward, and I will prove it so upon your blood"—Abigail looked up at Felicia Montaine and met her eyes—"or the blood of your champion. You will have your second contact mine at your earliest convenience." Abigail produced another placard and offered it primly to Felicia Montaine, who accepted it with hard, wary eyes.

Abigail held her gaze and the placard for a moment, her own expression hard. Then she released the card, turned, cleared her throat, and straightened her posture.

Miss Folly took the cue at once, and the coronet of floating crystals flickered back into place around Abigail's head. The instant it had re-formed, she began sweeping out of the building—

—and found herself facing a silent, staring room full of shocked expressions.

"It is not every high-society evening," Folly noted duly into the stunned silence, "that sees one of the leading citizens of Spire Albion insult the Atlantean Spectrum before all of Heaven and then challenge one of its ladies to a duel."

"Well," Abigail noted, "she rather worked for it, did she not?" She nodded good evening to a few familiar faces and strode out, her chin high. "A great many people would even say she'd earned it."

"Please tell Lady Hinton I said yes," Folly said, smiling. "Word of this will spread like wildfire."

"That is rather the point," Abigail said. "Had I done nothing, word of the abuse I'd received meekly would have spread as swiftly. Now it is a much more interesting story, and one we might still write the ending to."

Folly studied her intently as they exited. "Lady Hinton is extremely good at thinking clearly in a moment of crisis."

"Yes, dear," Abigail agreed placidly.

They left the building and Abigail sighed as their security men approached. "Oh, no."

Folly tilted her head. "The lady is upset?"

"Oh. I've gotten myself into a duel and with a warriorborn to boot," she said. "Hamish is going to be terribly disappointed in me."

Chapter 20

IAS *Mistshark*, Coordinates Unknown

Colonel Espira had been asleep for less than an hour before the sentry on duty shook his shoulder and roused him from his rest. Espira struggled to get his thoughts straightened out over the low rumble of the snores of three dozen sleeping Marines—and the coughs of half a dozen more sick men.

Espira held up a hand until he could sort up and down from left and right. Then he blinked his eyes open and said, "Report, Mister Sanchez."

"Sir," the Marine said respectfully, "the captain's compliments, and she requests your presence in her cabin."

Espira grunted without enthusiasm but rolled out of the meager warmth of his hammock and blanket and felt the chill of the high winds instantly leach most of the gathered heat from his limbs. "Well, we mustn't keep the captain waiting, I suppose."

He took down his sword from its peg, slid the cold leather belt across his torso, then gathered up his chilled aeronaut's leather coat and shoved himself into it. He already wore his extra tunic and a second pair of trousers over the first, but the thicker insulation had done little to counter the cold. He was surrounded by miles of freezing air, and there was simply no escaping the discomfort.

The Marine passed the colonel his hat. Espira pulled it on over his ears, dropped a glowing lumin crystal on a chain around his neck—another flutter of cold as the metal touched his skin—and climbed out of the hold to the ship's deck to make his way forward to Captain Ransom's cabin.

Once again, he passed the madwoman's batman, Sark, on the way. The looming warriorborn stared down at him as he went by, and once again Espira missed Ciriaco's balancing presence. Espira slipped past the man without taking any apparent notice of him, though doing so meant walking along next to the airship's safety railing with the wind coming up behind him, propelling his steps forward and sending icy chills slithering beneath his coat.

A shudder in the airship's deck abruptly lifted Espira's heels and made him feel weightless for an instant. He grasped the copper-clad safety railing with both gloved hands in a moment of panic and then closed his eyes and held on until the buffeting of the wind eased and he could move forward again without fear of being tossed over the side.

"What am I doing here?" he breathed to himself. "Renaldo Espira, perhaps you should have been a smith like your mother."

The dead eyes of a young tradesman's apprentice stared at him from the vaults of his memory. Espira had killed the young man in reflexive self-defense when he'd been suddenly attacked in darkness during the mission to Albion. It had been, as such things went, a clean and merciful killing.

But Espira had killed a boy, of perhaps, if he was generous with himself, fifteen years of age.

All but a child.

Espira hadn't been able to see who his attacker was in the darkness. He hadn't been able to stop thinking about those dead, puzzled eyes. Not even while His Majesty himself had draped a medal around his neck. He had gone into the enemy's stronghold and acquitted himself well, accomplishing his primary and secondary mission goals and failing only to destroy the famed Lancaster Vattery, Albion's main production facility for airship crystals.

It had been a clean and orderly place, Espira recalled, and abnormally well defended. And it hadn't made him uncomfortable in the least—unlike what he had seen during his visit with Tuscarora.

He stopped outside the door to the captain's cabin, sighed, and barely breathed, "What am I doing here?"

He knocked on the door.

The door was unbolted. Then it opened into the dim red interior of the cabin, which was lit only by the glow of the wires of an electric heater hooked to the ship's systems. Espira hurried in to keep the heat from escaping and heard Calliope Ransom close the door and bolt it behind him. He took a deep breath and felt he could barely get enough wind, the room's atmosphere was so warm and almost damp. A basin of water big enough to sit in steamed gently in front of the heater.

"I thought you might appreciate a bath, Colonel," Calliope said.

He turned and found Captain Ransom wearing nothing more than a man's white shirt. Her long, pale legs flashed in the red light as she turned toward him and put a finger to her lips with one hand while making a rolling, go-along gesture with the other. She wrinkled her nose slightly and said, "I know I would."

Espira blinked several times. Then he bowed at the waist and said, "That's a very thoughtful gesture, Captain."

"Wait an hour before you make such a judgment, Colonel," Ransom said with a slow smile. "It might give you more perspective."

Espira eyed Ransom warily. "I'm not at all sure what you mean."

In answer, Calliope stepped closer to him, reached out, and started unfastening the belt on his coat, her eyes direct.

"Oh," Espira said, his voice gone suddenly hoarse. He hadn't been with a woman in a goodly while, and he found his body responding quite positively to the notion.

She stepped closer to him so that she could slide the coat from his shoulders and gently remove his baldric and the sword buckled to it. As tall as Espira, she leaned in and nuzzled the side of his neck with gentle lips.

"I tested with my own warriorborn," she murmured quietly. "If we keep things to a whisper, Sark won't be able to hear what we say. We'll be able to talk."

Espira didn't actually remember lifting his hands to rest them lightly on Calliope's hips, but her skin was soft and warm and curved beneath the thin fabric of her shirt. "Talk about what?"

"You know what Cavendish and her machine are doing to those colonies," Calliope said softly.

Espira's belly twisted and he nodded. "And?"

Her fingers calm and steady, she began taking off the rest of his clothing. "And we're going to talk about what we're going to do about it."

Espira stared at her for a moment, his eyes widening.

"I am an airship captain," Calliope said in a calm, certain tone. "A privateer. When needed, a soldier. I am content to kill when my profession requires it, but I am not a mass murderer. And, I think, neither are you."

"What are you talking about?" Espira said, laboring to keep his voice quiet.

"Our target," Calliope said. She bared his upper body to the skin and took a moment to consider him. "Well, this could have turned out worse for both of us."

"Excuse me?" Espira asked.

Calliope smiled again as she calmly knelt and started unfastening his belt. "We'll need a believable excuse to meet and coordinate with each other."

"What target?" Espira demanded as his body started getting firmly behind Calliope's apparent trajectory. "Only Cavendish knows what we're doing next."

Calliope took his hand and Espira stepped gingerly into the tub. The hot water felt scalding against his chilled feet and calves, and his lower legs began to feel warm for the first time in a week. He settled himself into the tub a little at a time.

"Not entirely true," Calliope said. She calmly drew her shirt off over her head and let it fall to the cabin's deck. Then she knelt down by the tub, slipped a cloth into the water, let it swell as it filled, then squeezed it out at the base of his neck, so that hot water sluiced deliciously down his back. She leaned in close to murmur in his ear, "In order to go anywhere, they have to give me a heading."

Espira frowned for a moment and eyed her over his shoulder. "What colony are we heading for next?"

Calliope told him.

Espira's body went numb.

"That's not possible," he said. "Tuscarora wouldn't support that. That's not a few dozens or a hundred people in a mostly empty colony Spire. That's . . . tens of thousands. Women. Children."

"There's no reason to think it won't be hundreds of thousands," Calliope replied in a steady whisper as she continued to bathe him. "It might take a few hours more. That's all."

"God in Heaven," Espira breathed.

She leaned forward, then pressed her naked chest against his back and reached around to sluice more hot water down over his chest.

"You're a soldier and a hero of your Spire," Calliope breathed. "A loyal servant of Tuscarora and an honorable man." Her lips touched his neck just below one ear. "But I know men like you, Colonel Espira. They think you a faithful dog that attacks whomever they will. But that isn't who you are."

"Is it not?" Espira growled quietly. He pictured a young man's empty, staring eyes without willing himself to do so.

Calliope prowled around the tub to stand facing Espira. She casually tied her hair up into a knot, and then, her eyes on his, she stepped into the tub and settled to her knees, straddling his hips. The proximity and hot water made him ache, but even though Cavendish's plan was unthinkable, if it was the will of his King, he would be bound by honor to see it through—or face a court-martial if he didn't.

Calliope shivered as she brushed against him. "You'd have left by now and turned me in if you were their dog," she murmured. "You didn't become a soldier to murder the helpless. You became one to defend them."

Espira's heart was beating faster and not simply because of the woman's damnable appeal.

Protecting the innocent.

Something he hadn't thought about in a very long time.

He pursued his career for the sake of his Spire, but he had long ago realized that meant doing things that did not please him. Still, the thought of those dead young eyes had haunted him and haunted him.

If he went against his orders, it would mean imprisonment at best, and a torturous death at worst.

But if he created tens of thousands more empty, dead gazes, how could he remain himself and sane?

Calliope, meanwhile, kept on bathing him, warm water a blessed relief and caress over his skin. Her naked breasts brushed his chest, and his body was becoming more and more certain how events should play out.

By God in Heaven, it felt good to be clean.

By God in Heaven, it would feel good to *feel* clean.

"I'm listening," he whispered.

Calliope's mouth found his and pressed on him a searing kiss that nearly made Espira howl in pure, primal need.

She tore her mouth from his a moment later, her eyes dazed, and said, "Oh, my." She blinked twice and then focused on his eyes and breathed, "Take me to bed."

Some bit of his rearing in the Church lifted its head, so he growled, "We don't have to actually do the deed for the sake of the ruse, Captain."

In response, she gave him a smile that was as wicked as any villain's from any melodrama. She leaned in close and bit gently at his ear as she whispered, "Sark would be able to smell it if we were with each other. So we really have no choice if we're to sell our torrid affair. Besides, this is my ship and I'm her captain, and I've issued you an order, Colonel."

Espira regarded his body's enthusiasm with some dismay and felt himself precariously balancing wise caution, loyalty to his monarch, and the absolute madness of the alternative she presented.

An alternative that might be free of staring, dead eyes.

With a groan, he rose, taking Calliope with him with casual strength. He pressed her to a bulkhead and returned her earlier kiss with added heat and hunger. Then he spun and all but slammed her onto her bunk with sudden pure, mindless need.

She wrapped herself around him with eager sounds of encouragement, her body complying sinuously with his.

They both gasped, eyes wide.

Espira saw the woman for a moment, then: saw her rage and wounded pride because her ship was being used for something so foul; saw the ego and determination that would drive her to be the mistress of her own vessel under the open sky.

Saw that she was as terrified as he was.

Espira groaned and let his chest fall to hers as their bodies began to move in hunger.

She wrapped her arms around his neck, and her nails bit gently into his shoulders. "That's right, Colonel," she hissed into his ear. "We need each other right now."

Chapter 21

The Surface, Spire Albion

A wounded Benedict was faster than Bridget, but even so, he stopped at the shelter and, his posture perfect, made his usual polite "ladies first" gesture with one hand. Bridget threw herself under the spiked shell of the shelter. Then she glanced around frantically and soon spotted Rowl and Fenli—both of whom sat at the very limit of the shelter's protection, looking outside curiously as men and women threw themselves desperately toward purported safety.

Shortly thereafter, the shelter was crowded with the fragrant bodies of teamsters and woodcutters and millers. The hardworking men and women, who were either felons or those comfortable with them, pressed in tightly, with no regard for social propriety whatsoever.

That strange tearing-canvas sound echoed again through the misty air, and a last set of footsteps frantically approached the shelter, along with the panting, desperate breaths of a grizzled, skinny man whose eyes were dazed with drink or other intoxicants. He ran with a slight limp, and each time his right foot came down, he let out an explosive whimper of pain.

"Run, Roric!" bellowed a beefy-looking man whose chiseled-stone forearms marked him as a smith. "Run!"

Bridget listened to the skinny man's footsteps and pained exhalations. She struggled to see the poor fellow but caught only glimpses of him and then, as the press of the people in the shelter forced her slightly back, the view of his running legs. Step, step-gasp, step, step-gasp.

Then there was the whooshing sound of displaced air, and the footsteps abruptly stopped.

There was a thin, high, desperate moan from somewhere overhead.

Then it was silent except for the panting breaths of the survivors.

Bridget stared out, horrified. No one moved from the shelter.

"Ya see what got him?" one of the men in the shelter asked of the smith.

"Aye," said the smith. "Diremoth. Forty feet if it was an inch."

"Damn stupid, drinking in the morning," a woman noted in a neutral, numb voice, "when he's spending the whole working day roofless."

"Wasn't all he liked in the morning," drawled another woman in a very low-cut blouse.

There was a round of rather puerile chuckles from the gathered surface workers.

"He have kin?" asked another.

"Nah, none he talked about," answered the smith. "Fair hand with an ax, Roric. Was a friendly drunk. Bought the drinks sometimes. Never made trouble."

"Never did," came a general rumble of agreement from the workers.

"He was awfully stupid to get drunk in the morning," insisted the first woman. Bridget noted that after she spoke, she unshipped a copper-clad metal flask from her hip and took a belt from it. "Poor Roric."

Little flasks were appearing everywhere, and as a group the workers drank and then rumbled, "Poor Roric."

"Poor Roric," echoed the first woman. Then she leaned out of the shelter and peered around at the misty air for a moment before she sighed and said, "Our turn soon enough. Back to it."

"Aye, you heard her," the smith said, and started shouldering his way back out of the shelter. "Move it along, you lot. There's plenty of work to be done. Lucky and smart."

There was a generalized back-to-work groan, but then folk started slipping away from the shelter and moving about their day as though nothing of particular note had happened.

Bridget felt slightly sickened. A man had just been killed. Right there in front of all of them. Was his only funeral to be a few murmured memories and a round of quick drinks on a working morning?

She watched the workers departing and concluded that, yes, apparently this was the extent of the memorial the man was to have.

Such deaths, then, had to be common fare here.

Bridget shivered.

"Sir," she said to the smith as he began to leave the shelter, "might I have a moment of your time?"

The burly smith paused and seemed to notice Bridget and Benedict for the first time. "Ah. M'lady. M'lord." He tugged at his forelock uncomfortably. "What are folks like you doing here without guards?"

"We are the Guard," Bridget said calmly.

"Ah," said the smith with cautious neutrality. "Them."

Benedict grinned at the man and said, "We'll do our best not to get you killed."

"Appreciated," said the smith, looking at both Bridget and then Benedict more carefully, and then at the cats. "Surviving down here is work enough without carrying extra weight." He nodded toward the animals. "Nice having the little fur balls to give warning, though. Gave us all a chance to get under cover. Thanks, lads."

Rowl and Fenli looked up at the smith, narrowed their eyes to precisely the same degree, and glanced dismissively away at precisely the same time.

"Humans are mostly helpless," Rowl said calmly. "We do what can be done."

"He says, 'You're welcome,'" Bridget translated smoothly. "Sir, we are looking for a cat in point of fact."

The smith stared at them both for a moment. Then he let out a guffaw and said, "You're serious?"

"Yes," Bridget said.

"The high and mighty sent members of their own Guard down here? To look for a cat?"

"Yes," Bridget said.

His eyes wrinkled at the corners. "Couple of rich children from the high habbles are crawling on the surface with the rest of the bugs? Looking for a cat and hoping not to get eaten?"

"That part is more a plan than a hope," Benedict noted calmly.

The smith grunted. "No one has plans to be eaten, boy. Roric didn't." He shook his head. "Well, you children can't be expected to understand if you haven't lived here."

"I understand that I don't want to be here any longer than I must," Bridget said seriously and without heat. "Sir, are there any cats in residence here?"

"Plenty cycle through," the smith rumbled. "Hell, I got an Arrangement of my own to keep my storehouse clear of vermin. But those cats are all young warriors and hunters from tribes in the lower habbles. They've got more energy than sense, and their tribes send them out to be daring until they grow out of it. But there's only one who stays. A big old lazy tom, huge, a couple stone at least."

"Where might we find this cat?" Bridget asked politely.

"Ah," said the smith. "He lives with the madman. Maybe a mile clockwise of here." He gave them a grim smile. "Just past the prison camp, at the forest's edge."

"Meaning no offense, sir," Benedict said, "I don't suppose you could be a little more specific with the details about the madman?"

The smith grinned a square, strong grin and rubbed his scarred hands over the front of his leather apron. "The etherealist. The one who studies surface creatures."

"Who does what?" Bridget asked in a rather startled voice.

"His rules are on the signs outside his house," the smith said. "He's all right—as long as you follow the rules."

"What rules?" Bridget asked.

"They change time to time," the smith said. "But Master Harbor is good about keeping his signs all proper and readable."

"Master Harbor," Benedict murmured. "What does his house look like?"

"Oh, you won't be able to miss it," the smith said. "Follow the base of the Spire. Stay back, mind you. People toss things out occasionally." The smith picked up a heavy sack, and the muscles of his forearms bulged and distended. He nodded to them. "Lucky and smart, children."

"Lucky and smart," Benedict replied with the instant, reflexive response usually reserved for a service of the Church of God in Heaven.

The smith vanished into the mist, and Benedict and Bridget watched him go before Benedict oriented himself on the clifflike side of Spire Albion, and they began walking with the Spire on their right—always, Bridget noted, moving from covered building to covered building rather than in a simple straight line.

"That man died," Bridget said after several moments.

"Yes, Littlemouse," Rowl said in the tone of a schoolteacher with a slow student. "That is correct. The surface is a dangerous place for humans."

Bridget gave him a frustrated glower and then turned back to Benedict. "Does that happen often here?"

"On average," Benedict said, "someone on the surface is killed every three days or so."

Bridget shook her head as they walked past a mill running a noisy steam saw. The racket was deafening, and she had to wait until they were clear of it to say, "How many people live here?"

"Between forty and sixty thousand at any given time," Benedict replied. "If you lived here for ten years, you'd lose someone you knew every eight or ten weeks on average." He shook his head. "Everyone here is polite. They never know who they might need to help them keep their lives. But no one makes friends quickly or lightly. We're outsiders. Don't expect help if we get in trouble."

"How much danger are we in?" asked Bridget.

"The same as everyone else," Benedict replied, his eyes scanning the mists around and above them ceaselessly. "Well, a little more. They know where all the buildings and shelters are. Be aware that you are in danger. Keep an eye out for it. Do everything in your power to be smart and stay alive, and hope you get a little bit lucky."

"Lucky?"

"Sometimes the smart thing happens to be the exact wrong thing," Benedict replied. "If we'd run into a sword mantis this morning instead of a diremoth, we might have felt quite foolish for crowding into a shelter where it could feed on us quite easily. Best to be lucky *and* smart."

"Lucky and smart." Bridget felt the rhythmic cadence of a blessing come into her voice as she spoke.

"Exactly," Benedict said. "A bit of a prayer for luck and something like an insistence on being smart."

A troop of men carrying a tree trunk on their shoulders and axes in their hands puffed with effort as they walked toward the sawmill. The woodcutters offered the pair of them a series of glares as they went by.

"I take it we are talking too loudly," Bridget noted.

Benedict lowered his voice. "Indeed, we are. Let us pick up the pace a bit."

They did, moving at a brisk walk, and if Benedict's lacerations slowed him down, the deficit in cat-weight borne by each of them resulted in Bridget working very hard to keep the pace. Their journey took them the better part of an hour, with Benedict pausing at occupied buildings—mostly mills, but also a few carpenter workshops, smithies, taverns, and once a dilapidated old church—to ask for directions to the etherealist's home.

Finally, Benedict led them toward the forest's edge.

Trees loomed ahead of them.

Bridget paused to catch her breath.

The forest was . . . imposing, to say the least. Vast tree trunks, bigger around than a dozen people holding hands could reach, stretched up into the mist, swallowed up by the limited visibility before a branch could sprout out. Beneath those enormous trees grew their offspring, which were much smaller than their giant progenitors. Some of their trunks were as slender as one of Bridget's legs, some thicker than her body. Creeping vines covered most of the tree trunks, their broad, dark leaves occluding everything and stretching from trunk to trunk on thick tendrils. Along the ground, low ferns and fronds grew everywhere, battling the creeping vines for ground space.

"Oh," Rowl said, eyeing the thick undergrowth, "I wonder what's in there."

Fenli regarded the forest floor with a slightly different form of interest. "Prey. And whatever hunts it. Things large enough to endanger the humans could be hiding anywhere in that."

"Correct," Benedict said, nodding toward the undergrowth. "Woodcutting crews go out in groups of twelve or more. The heaviest casualties take place inside the forest itself. Lots of times, they never see what takes someone."

Bridget shivered. "Well, at least we're not going there."

Benedict grinned as he pointed ahead of them. "That must be it."

Bridget felt her feet slowing as Master Harbor's house emerged from the mists.

At least, she assumed it was a house.

There was a certain amount of rough wood involved—boards that looked like they had been rejected by the millers for too much warping and too many rough, uneven edges. But some of the more badly twisted boards seemed to fit their purpose appropriately, for they had been used to conglomerate three enormous, strangely shaped skulls, each the size of a cottage, into a single structure. One skull was rather long and full of teeth the size of large portraits. The other two were more rounded and somewhat smaller than the first, perhaps twenty feet across and half as high; they sported the broken stubs of what might have been horns or antlers. The crazed wooden structure used walkways to join the three skulls together. Window settings had been built around the eye- and earholes, complete with colored glass. In addition, a raised porch meandered all the way around the three huge bone structures. To finish the whole thing off, there was an unpainted picket fence made of salvaged and ancient wood that circled the overgrown yard to form a boundary. The fence hardly seemed able to remain standing on its own; indeed, it would have fallen over outright if it hadn't been half swallowed by creeping vines.

"God in Heaven," Bridget murmured. "What kind of creatures grow so very large?"

"I'm sure I have no idea," Benedict replied cheerfully. "But if any approach, we'll hear them knocking down trees for half an hour before they arrive, I daresay."

"So much wood," she breathed, staring at the ramshackle dwelling that in materials alone was probably worth twenty years of her father's labor in the family meat vattery.

Benedict's steps slowed as he approached the fence. There was a sign on a wooden stake in the ground. It had been painted over so many times that the paint stood out a quarter inch from the surface of the wood. On a background of white paint, simple black letters read: **PLEASE MINIMIZE YOUR FUNDAMENTAL HUMAN STUPIDITY BEFORE ENTERING.**

Benedict eyed the sign, then looked over his shoulder at Bridget. "Do we know if any cats have taken up writing yet?"

Rowl yawned. "Why would we? It is boring."

"One must carefully deliver words to humans over and over to even have a chance of them understanding them," Fenli agreed. "Writing the words down and expecting them to get through to your kind seems . . . overly optimistic."

Bridget and Benedict stopped at a broken gate in the little picket fence. A sign five feet beyond the first read, **DO NOT SAY THE WORD** [Over the next word, there was a huge splash of paint that rendered it unreadable.] **I AM SICK AND TIRED OF IT.**

"Well," Bridget murmured, "that's a challenge."

Benedict lifted the gate enough to swing it open gingerly, and the four of them stepped inside. Fenli immediately plunged from Benedict's shoulder and vanished into the fronds and grass in the strange house's yard. Rowl had begun to move but froze in place stiffly when Fenli beat him to the exploration. The larger cat sniffed, turned his head to one side, and ignored the smaller animal.

There was a small path worn into the ground from the gate up to what was evidently the etherealist's front door. Bridget and Benedict started up it, their footsteps soft. The next sign read, **ANYONE WHO DOESN'T STAMP THEIR FEET TWICE AND TURN ONCE AROUND WILL DIE.**

"They aren't very clear directions," Bridget complained. "I mean, given the apparent stakes. Both feet? One at a time? Which direction do we turn?"

"We'll have to hope good intentions count for something," Benedict murmured.

Bridget sighed. She stamped each foot twice, one at a time. Then she turned in a circle, drew in a breath, and kept walking. Benedict echoed her and stayed with her.

"Now I am dizzy," Rowl complained.

They kept walking forward and found the next sign beside the steps leading up to the sloped wooden front porch. It read, **I DON'T SING BECAUSE I'M HAPPY. I'M HAPPY BECAUSE I SING.**

"Hello the house?" Bridget called softly. "Master Harbor?"

Only profound, misty silence answered her.

"There's a note on the door," Benedict murmured.

Bridget was the commanding officer, she supposed. She stepped onto the rickety porch, walked to the door, and found a slate hanging from a peg. On it was sketched a rough little map, along with the words: **TAKING SAMPLES FROM THE POND. BACK BEFORE NOON.**

Bridget read the note aloud. Benedict frowned, glanced up at the sky, and said, "It would appear Master Harbor is late."

Bridget took a slow breath. "Oh, well. It is a good thing he left us a map, then."

Benedict exhaled slowly.

"It seems that he is only about a mile away if this map is anything close to correct."

"Yes," the young warriorborn said. "But it's not really a matter of distance so much as the scenery along the way."

Bridget took down the slate and offered it to Benedict. "I suppose we will have to find out ourselves," she said. "We have to find this cat. To find the cat, we need Master Harbor. Master Harbor is in the forest. Therefore . . ."

Fenli appeared soundlessly from around a corner of the house, his little face lifted, his nose taking in deep breaths as he paced slowly toward them. "I believe the owner of this home went to the forest. I believe the cat went with him."

"We already knew that," Rowl said with vast superiority, "from reading."

Benedict exhaled. "The forest is dangerous. It might be better to wait for Master Harbor."

Bridget shook her head. "Time is fleeting. We need the information Saza and Fenli are holding as soon as it can be had."

The warriorborn winced. But rather than objecting, he checked his gauntlet and blade. "I wish we'd brought long guns."

"How dangerous is it?" Bridget asked.

"We will be your eyes and ears," Rowl said with confidence.

Fenli calmly leapt up and scaled Benedict, winding up on his shoulder. "Yes."

Benedict shrugged his other shoulder and said, "Most crews go in and out without trouble every day."

"Most?" Bridget asked.

Benedict sheathed his sword. "Most."

Bridget took a deep breath. "Well, then," she said, "we shall go into the forest. Most cautiously."

Chapter 22

Habble Profit, Spire Olympia

When a man identifying himself only as Hamish came and murmured in Bayard's ear, Grimm's diminutive friend went nearly apoplectic. Bayard immediately turned and stormed out of the reception even as other messengers arrived, moved through the room with quiet efficiency, murmured to their employers, and caused a low storm of whispers to begin spreading.

Grimm hurried to catch up to his friend, who strode out of the municipal buildings and into the darkened streets at such a furious pace that even long-legged Hamish had to press himself to keep up.

"Alex," Grimm said, "what has happened?"

"That Auroran bastard," Bayard snapped. The man practically vibrated with rage and his voice shook. "I'll kill him."

Grimm turned his head to Hamish and said, "Who are you?"

The man replied in a laconic Olympian accent. "Bodyguard. Lady Hinton. Sir."

"God in Heaven," Grimm said, "is she all right?"

Hamish considered that question for a moment before saying, "Yes and no."

"He struck her," Bayard snarled. "He *touched* her." The duelist's hand fell to his sword again and again as if he were reassuring himself of its presence. "I will carve her name into his *entrails*."

"Alex," Grimm said. "Alex, you're angry. What has happened?"

Bayard's jaw clenched. "I will have his *eyes* for this."

Grimm looked up at Hamish and suppressed exasperation. "Explain, please."

"Due respect," the tall man replied. "Don't know you."

"Grimm, captain, AMS *Predator*," he replied.

"Hello," Hamish said in a neutral tone.

Bayard waved an impatient hand at Hamish.

Hamish squinted at the small man, then back at Grimm. "*Predator*. You know a big-knuckled bastard named Kettle?"

"My pilot," Grimm said shortly.

The Olympian seemed to consider that for a moment before he said, "Tough."

"Very."

"Says you're tougher." Hamish squinted into the distance for a moment, then said, "Valesco came to the Tea. He slapped Lady Hinton in full view."

Grimm let out a groan.

"Gets worse. Lady Hinton fetched the Atlantean high lady a blow to the jaw. Knocked out a tooth."

Grimm all but stumbled over his own boots in shock. "She what?"

"She struck a member of the Atlantean Spectrum," Bayard spat.

"Merciful Builders," Grimm said, "why would she do *that*?"

Hamish shook his head. "Stopped asking things like that a while ago, sir."

"She's never fought a duel!" Bayard said, biting off the words.

"Now she'll be up against the lady's champion. Warriorborn. And Valesco *touched* her. I'll eat his *heart*."

"Alex, not like this," Grimm said.

"Don't, Mad," Bayard snarled.

Grimm took several quick steps and got in front of Bayard, then stopped and put a hand on his friend's chest. "Bayard! Stop! Think!"

Bayard barely stopped. The weight of his body leaned against Grimm's hand; his face was dark with fury.

"This is what Valesco wants," Grimm said in an even tone. "It's clearly his plan. He wants you furious. Off-balance. Not thinking."

Bayard's eyes flashed, and his sword leapt into his hand.

Grimm planted his feet. He met Bayard's eyes, reached up slowly, and opened his coat to bare his heart.

"Is that what it's come to, Alex?" he asked, keeping his voice quiet and even. "Are you so angry you'd bleed a friend? Is that how you fight?"

The smaller man's face was hard, suffused with rage. Grimm wasn't even sure Alex was actually looking at him.

"Think of Albion, my friend," Grimm said. "You can't simply walk up to the man and try to murder him. The entire point of being sent to deal with Valesco is to do so properly, publicly, and in accordance with the law. How would a simple brawl accomplish that?" Grimm let his own voice harden. "Especially if, when you try it, he simply kills you. Or one of his associates shoots you in the back, which would be entirely justified."

"Grimm," Bayard began.

He answered Bayard with icy detachment. "You'll be of no use to Abigail as a dead attempted murderer."

Bayard glared furiously up at Grimm for a moment. Then he let out a sound of disgust, spun a quarter turn on his heel, and stared hard at nothing.

"If you charge up to Valesco right now," Grimm continued in the same steady voice, "what are your chances?"

Standing by passively with his hands behind his back, Hamish watched the two men.

"What have you always said about duels?" Grimm asked. "That one had to have cold blood? That one had to be a bit of a reptile?"

The furious man glowered partway toward Grimm.

Grimm sighed. "Alexander Bayard, can you look at me and honestly say that you are in the proper frame of mind to end this man? Do that and I'll stand clear."

Bayard stood shaking through a long moment of silence. Then he slammed his sword back into its sheath and said, "Damn it, Mad."

Grimm stepped over to his friend and put his hand on Bayard's shoulder. "Breathe. Think. What's the rational move?"

Bayard grimaced. He was silent for a full minute before he said, "We should talk to Abigail."

Grimm nodded firmly. "That sounds like an excellent idea," he said. He glanced up at Hamish. "Will you lead us to Lady Hinton, please?"

The Olympian braced to something like attention, and Grimm recognized the posture of a former Marine showing respect to a captain. "Sirs," he said. "Follow me."

Lady Hinton's apartments were, Grimm thought, rather extravagant. Wooden furniture—much of it either painted white or stained rose, chased and bound in gold, covered in rose cushions with gold embroidery—was everywhere. Expensive art lined the walls, expensive vases held fresh roses and other flowers, and the intricately patterned carpet worked subtle shades of gentle fire into the room's décor with what he felt sure was consummate taste that far exceeded his own knowledge of such matters. Tinted lumin crystals gave the entire place the look of a summer sunset and made it feel warm and inviting.

Grimm did what he always did in such settings. He made sure that his boots were well knocked clean of dirt and dust before entering, calmly folded his hands behind his back, and tried not to touch anything.

A servingwoman in a plain dress showed them into the apartments' parlor, where Miss Folly sat in a rather excellent dress, with her back very straight and her expression somewhat miserable. Master Ferus sat beside her in his trousers and shirtsleeves, his expression vague and his hair rumpled from sleep.

"Oh, it's the captain," Folly said. Her voice was thready and nervous, and she fingered the little pouch of crystals about her throat almost desperately. "I'm sure he knows what a relief it is to see him."

"Hmmm?" Master Ferus said. He gestured at the low table in front of him sleepily. "Ah, Captain. Tea? You'll pardon a lack of decorum, I trust"—he yawned expansively—"but I'm afraid I was already in bed when matters developed."

"Naturally," he said, and turned to Bayard beside him. "Alex?"

Bayard bowed stiffly to Miss Folly, then unbuckled sword and scabbard from their frog and set them carefully to one side. "Fine."

Grimm poured tea and made introductions. "You'll have to excuse the commodore," he said to Folly. "He's rather upset."

"Oh, my, yes," Folly said to her little crystals. "Why, he's practically purple. And his sword is so thirsty."

Grimm frowned at Folly. "Are you all right, dear?"

Folly waved her hands in a small and frantic gesture and looked imploringly at Master Ferus.

"Please, pardon my apprentice, grim Captain," Ferus said easily. "She's had something of a frightful evening."

"It's the dress," Folly told Ferus, her voice strained. "It's so lovely and it does nothing for me."

"Perhaps you should change, dear," Grimm suggested.

Folly reached out for a cup of tea, and he could see the contents of the cup trembling as she lifted it.

"Oh, I couldn't possibly. It would be rude. Lady Hinton went to such trouble."

Grimm set his own cup down calmly and then gently took cup and saucer from Folly's shaking fingers. "Miss Folly," he said gently, "I need your help. The hour calls for steady reason and calm minds. You should go change into something suitable for the hour. You may consider it an order if you like."

The young etherealist's mismatched eyes flashed up toward Grimm's with almost desperate gratitude, and without a word she rose, curtsied stiffly, and hurried out of the room.

Ferus watched her go and then beamed sleepily at Grimm. "That was rather well done, sir. Thank you."

"Hamish," Bayard said, "I don't suppose you've a drop or two about you?"

The mostly silent bodyguard produced a copper-clad flask from his coat and passed it soberly to Bayard, who added a rather generous splash of its contents to his tea. Master Ferus cleared his throat, and Bayard did the same for him. The duelist sipped from his cup, closed his eyes for a moment, and then said, "Bless you," in something like his usual tone and passed the flask back.

A few moments later, Abigail Hinton entered the room, elegant and tiny and resplendent in her evening dress. The men rose at once. Bayard bowed deeply to her and immediately went to her and lifted her chin with one hand. Her left cheek was reddened and slightly swollen, and there was a small cut along her cheekbone—the mark of a ring, Grimm supposed.

"So," Bayard said quietly, "he's right-handed."

Abigail reached up to touch his hand with hers, and she searched his expression silently for a long moment. "When you kill him, Alex," she said calmly, "please be sure his face has been repaid for mine."

Bayard swallowed. "I will, my lady."

"Excellent," she said. "I'm rather shocked you didn't simply storm into the Tea with your sword drawn."

Bayard grimaced. "Mad convinced me otherwise."

"Did he?" Lady Hinton turned her gaze toward Grimm. "Thank you, Captain."

Grimm bowed.

"So," Master Ferus said, returning to his tea, "an agent of Albion physically assaulted a visiting head of state. How covert."

Lady Hinton's cheeks acquired a bit of color. She allowed Bayard to guide her to a seat at the table, and she composed herself while he prepared her tea.

"It was a decision in the moment," she said. "There was no chance Valesco was present without the complicity of the Atlantean delegation. Can you not see the picture they were trying to paint?"

Ferus sighed and nodded.

"I'm afraid I don't," Grimm ventured.

"Their actions are a clear attempt to create a story that would spread rapidly through the other Spires," Lady Hinton said calmly. "Atlantea and Aurora's invincible alliance. The greatest duelist of Albion destroyed by their complicity and his grieving woman—one of Albion's preeminent social and economic figures—humbled and weeping over his corpse. The message to other Spires and their leaders would be entirely clear."

"Bow to them or be humiliated and destroyed," Bayard said darkly.

Lady Hinton waved a hand. "Oh, openly they'd approach other

Spires with smiles and generosity," she said. "But yes, the example they'd have made of us would be the knife held behind their backs, ready for use. I decided in the moment that I could not permit them to position the frame around that picture so advantageously."

"That's why you struck Lady Hestia," Grimm said pensively. "To change the picture."

Lady Hinton lifted her chin, and Bayard mirrored her precisely, though neither looked at the other.

"Quite," she said in a crisp voice. "Albion defies them to do their worst."

"We are not their victims," Bayard said, "nor their prey. To finish the painting, they must finish us both."

"And we shall not let them do that," Lady Hinton said smoothly. "I've doubled the chances of their plan failing. Should only one of us fall, Albion stands defiant of their alliance, and the other Spires will see that they can be fought. Should we both succeed, the bold little couple from Albion has defeated their combined might and knavery with courage and skill, and the newly painted picture humiliates them all."

Grimm shook his head. "But . . . with respect, these are but duels. It doesn't change the balance of power, airship to airship, between the Spires."

"No," Lady Hinton agreed mildly. "It merely changes the balance of power in the minds of the people and the leadership of all the Spires. The Alliance knows this. Fear and despair are powerful tools, Captain."

"As are courage and hope," Master Ferus said quietly. "Lady Hinton has created the possibility of a story that will spread like wildfire amongst the Spires and that could ultimately affect the outcome of the conflict as powerfully as squadrons of dreadnoughts."

Grimm pondered for a moment, then said, "Assuming you are

correct, then, the alliance will realize it as well. They will have no choice. They must see you both dead at any cost."

"Yes," Lady Hinton said plainly.

"No honor will bind them. No law will hold them back. They will do everything in their power to ensure you both fall."

Lady Hinton reached out to cover Bayard's hand with her own. "They will try," she said calmly. "I have some small knowledge of skullduggery myself." She turned to face Bayard. "You will need a second for the duel, Alex."

"He has one," Grimm said at once.

Bayard shot Grimm a fierce smile and the two men bowed their heads deeply to each other.

"And," Lady Hinton sighed, "it appears I shall need one myself."

Grimm found himself smiling. "I know precisely the young woman for the job." He turned to Hamish and said, "Sir, I wonder. Could you arrange to send a messenger to my ship?"

Chapter 23

The Surface, near Spire Albion

God in Heaven, Bridget thought to herself, I have certainly made some interesting choices today.

She and Benedict, Rowl, and Fenli stood at the edge of the mist-shrouded forest. Trees, some of them larger around the base than her father's vattery, towered overhead, vanishing into the mists before their lowest branches could be seen. Their smaller offspring grew in competition with some kind of enormous, pale, wrinkled mushrooms that loomed over them, their broad heads spreading to shade areas the size of small houses. Within twenty or thirty feet of the edge of the forest, afternoon light faded to deep twilight.

In the air, here was a heavy, musty smell made of earth and water and mist and mold.

Eerie calls echoed through the mist. But the thick air made it impossible to say from what directions or from what distances or from what creatures they might have originated. A mournful howl ululated from far away. Echoing clicks drifted back and forth, but whether they were the creaking of trees or the sounds of something living, Bridget could not even guess.

Benedict took half a step ahead of her, his feline eyes everywhere, his head tilting and making minor adjustments at each sound.

Without a word, he drew his sword, and in his left hand his gauntlet kindled to life, emitting a soft white glow that would provide both light and at need deadly defense. He was breathing rather more quickly than usual and through his nose, as though he were determined to scent any danger before it could come close.

After a long moment, he turned slowly back to Bridget, his expression serious.

"Are you sure?" he asked quietly.

She took a slow breath and nodded once before her fluttering stomach and cold spine could make her rethink her decision. "Rowl," she said in a very quiet voice, "you and I will go first."

Benedict frowned. "Are you—"

"I trust you to watch my back," she told him quietly.

He gave her a look that was half exasperation and half warm affection.

"Fenli," Bridget said, "do as you think best."

"Yes," the tiny cat said. "Obviously I was going to do that."

"You are on an official mission of the Spirearch's Guard," Rowl said loftily. "If you knew how these things worked, you would follow orders."

"Why?" Fenli asked.

Rowl's tail lashed. "Because—"

"Also, I am doing what she said to do."

"Gentlemen," Bridget said, a hint of frustration in her tone, "the quieter we are, the more likely we are to avoid trouble."

Both cats turned to regard her with something like disbelief.

"Littlemouse," Rowl said, "did you, a human, just tell cats how to be quiet?"

"That was in very poor taste," Fenli noted.

"You are personally quite incompetent at moving quietly," Rowl said.

Fenli's tail twitched erratically in indignation. "Whereas it is a cat's specialty."

Rowl flicked his ears in agreement. "And you are not a cat."

"Very much not a cat," Fenli agreed.

"Even the half-soul is more of a cat than you," Rowl said.

Fenli pawed idly at the ground. "And the half-soul got himself slashed to ribbons, which none of the actual cats did."

"Gentlemen," Bridget breathed. She hesitated. If Rowl was agreeing with Fenli, and if Fenli was agreeing with Rowl, then the two of them were under a great deal more stress than either of them let on.

The cats were afraid.

"Gentlemen," she continued softly, "I withdraw the comment."

"Thank you," Rowl said magnanimously.

"That is wise," Fenli said.

From somewhere back over the work area of the logging camp, there was another series of rippling clicks like tearing cloth.

Bridget flinched down and lifted her suddenly glowing gauntlet toward the sky, purely in reflex, though she knew on a rational level that the sound had come from much farther away than it had before and was therefore probably not a threat. Nonetheless, she traded a look with Benedict, who had also crouched down and raised his gauntlet toward the sky.

"I suppose we shouldn't stand around out in the open," Bridget suggested.

"I suppose not," Benedict breathed in agreement.

Bridget lowered her gauntlet and let its energy subside as its crystal died away.

Benedict frowned and looked at her.

"The light won't let us see much more," she said. "But it can be easily seen."

He took in a breath and then nodded shortly, lowering his own gauntlet and letting the weapons crystal against his palm go dark.

"Rowl," Bridget said, "shall we?"

She strode forward into the forest as quietly as she could.

The ground was littered with mushrooms, some of which rose to above Bridget's knee, in competition with sickly-looking ferns of deep green striped with yellow. Though very few heavy shadows fell from above, the light dwindled to an umbral gloom after Bridget had taken only a few strides. After a moment, as her eyes adjusted, Bridget could see that the undersides of the mushrooms put out a faintly pulsing, greenish luminescence that did nothing to let her see into the gloom around her, but it at least provided some kind of reference for where she could place her feet.

Some sort of insect, long and low with dozens and dozens of legs, rippled past the toes of one of her boots, and Rowl and Fenli both nosed toward it in fascination for a moment.

"Venom," Rowl noted.

"Venom," Fenli agreed.

"It probably would not taste good in any case."

"I concur," said Fenli.

Both cats studiously ignored the creature and it trundled away beneath the mushrooms.

Benedict sheathed his sword and drew a short, practical knife from a case on his belt. Eyes wary, he carved into the trunk of a tree they passed, peeling away a strip of bark several fingers wide and leaving white wood bared.

"Should we need to find our way back quickly," he noted.

Bridget felt rather foolish for not having considered doing that herself, but she nodded. "Capital thinking, sir."

A low wind passed through the forest, drawing a vast sighing sound from the mists overhead. Pops and creaks echoed everywhere around them. Bridget thought she saw motion from the corner of her eye and supposed that the denizens of the forest had waited for the cover of the sound to move.

She swallowed. It was entirely possible that they were surrounded by many more surface creatures than they could easily observe. The thought made a chill slither down her spine. They need not die a death so dignified as being eaten by a large predator. Many creatures of the surface world bore venom that could readily kill a human being.

Still, as strange as the surface creatures were said to be, certain things were common amongst all predators, such as preferring to attack fearful or uncertain prey. Bridget took a moment to imagine that she was Gwendolyn Lancaster and to remind herself in Gwen's remembered voice that she was not prey. Then she started forward again with steady, quiet steps.

She and the others proceeded through the gloom for perhaps half an hour, moving very slowly and quietly (at least according to human values of quiet), before Rowl, walking just ahead of Bridget, paused and lifted his head, his ears swiveling forward. Fenli, after taking note of this and ghosting up to stand beside Rowl, also focused forward.

"What is it?" Bridget asked.

"A human," Rowl said, "is singing."

They proceeded forward into steadily growing light, which grew brighter rapidly as they passed a last set of enormous tree trunks. Then they moved through a band of smaller trees and mushrooms, the latter seeming to shrink and shrivel as the light grew. Creeping vines and ferns appeared to draw a line against the mushrooms, growing over the dying fungi as if devouring them. At some point, long, thin blades of grass grew over the ground as Bridget and the others passed into a clearing.

At last, a rather deep, pleasant voice came to Bridget through the mist. A man was singing the villain's merry aria from *Las Guerreras*, a very popular Auroran comedic opera. The farther they walked into the clearing, the more the light grew until it was almost painfully bright in contrast with the darkness of the forest through which they had just passed.

Motion stirred nearby, and Bridget flinched as something large and swift bounded by at the edge of her vision. She caught only a fleeting glance of the creature: something four-legged and lean and powerful rushing by in graceful bounds. The animal had dark golden hair or fur over shining, liquid muscle; its long head was crowned with an enormous rack of some kind of spreading horn.

She had rarely seen such beauty in her life.

"God in Heaven," she breathed as the creature vanished into the mist, "was that a . . . a stag? Isn't that what they're called?"

"I haven't read my scriptural stories in a while," Benedict replied, his voice hushed. He stared after the creature much as she had. "But . . . it would seem to be something like one, yes."

She found herself exchanging an enormous smile with Benedict and felt a pleasant thrill run through her at how boyishly joyful it made him look.

Rowl and Fenli trotted a few steps after the departed stag and stood staring themselves, noses lifted into the air and questing.

"Food," Rowl said.

"Delicious food," Fenli agreed. "Let us eat it."

"It's rather large for you, is it not?" Bridget asked.

"Hmmm," Fenli said. The little cat padded over to Benedict and looked up at him. "Half-soul, next time, use your gauntlet to kill it, and we will see if it tastes as good as it smells."

"It seems a shame," Benedict said, smiling down at Fenli. Then he hurriedly added, "That I missed the opportunity, of course."

"You can do better," Fenli said happily. "I believe in you."

"Do not overly encourage them," Rowl said quietly, "or they quickly become unmanageable."

"Rowl," Bridget chided, shaking her head fondly. "I didn't know," she said to Benedict. "I didn't know there would be something so beautiful here."

A rippling set of clicks echoed from somewhere in the mist, and Benedict muted his smile slightly as his eyes searched for threats. "Let us maintain our vigilance nonetheless."

"Indeed," Bridget said, and kept walking forward toward the source of the singing.

They found the singer next to a body of water that stretched out into the mist. It was larger than anything Bridget had ever seen. Gentle wind sent mesmerizing patterns washing across the water's surface, and light sparkled off it in a flickering dance that delighted her eyes. Small trees covered in fruit of brilliant colors, deep dark red swelling to rich purple, grew at the water's edge. In an open space between some of the trees there sat a rough wooden chair that looked as if it had been built from natural logs. In the chair sat a rather large and burly man, his long grey hair, which was thick and mussed, blended in with his similarly luxurious beard. He wore odd leathers, perhaps crudely made but comfortable-looking, and his large feet were bare. He held a long, slender pole of wood in one hand. A line dropped from the tip of the pole to the water, where a large cork floated. A long spear leaned against the chair beside him, its copper-clad steel head gleaming in the light.

On a wooden platform beside him a large black cat slept in a comfortable curl. The enormous beast, its fur frosted in shaggy patches with silver, was even larger than Rowl or Chief Maul. The cat was snoring audibly.

Bridget stepped forward and drew in a breath to speak, and the man cocked his head slightly to one side.

Suddenly, her gauntlet emitted a whining sound, and heat flared against her palm, even through the thick leather of the glove. Benedict let out a hiss of discomfort and thrust his hand out away from him as his own gauntlet began to overheat. The whining of the power building in the weapons crystals of the arms began to grow higher and louder.

Bridget desperately tried to release the etheric weapon's energy buildup, but it did not respond to her at all. She knew that should it not be averted, the gauntlet's crystal would explode with enough force to remove her hand at the wrist.

By the time Bridget looked up from her gauntlet, the big man was standing with the spear gripped in his hands and pointed at them. A crystal mounted in the weapon's head was glowing with brilliant green energy that reminded her with a surge of panic of one of the light cannon upon *Predator*. The man's expression was set in stone, hard and unforgiving, and the cat, which had risen from its place and crouched with narrowed eyes between the man's feet, let out a low, yowling growl.

"Five," snarled Master Harbor in a burly, resonant basso. "Four. Three. Two . . ."

Chapter 24

IAS *Mistshark*, Coordinates Unknown

Espira stood on the deck of the *Mistshark* in the evening, his goggles on, watching a sight only aeronauts and Marines saw with any regularity: a flaming orange sunset, colors spreading as the sun sank toward the horizon, expanding enormously as its lower edge settled from the clear skies of the aerosphere and seemed to set the mists of the mesosphere on fire.

Boots paced toward him and Espira turned to find a goggled Ciriaco approaching, his expression bleak. He leaned his forearms down on the guardrail beside Espira's and grimaced toward the sunset. "Colonel."

"Sergeant." Espira glanced up and down the deck, seeing who was nearby. The nearest aeronauts were forty feet away, coiling ether-silk web cables neatly onto one of the ship's replacement reels. They were singing a droning work song. Between that and the wind, Ciriaco and he were as safe from eavesdropping as they were likely to get. "Do you regret your choices in life?"

"Sir?"

Espira's sword hand seemed to itch beneath its glove as if he could still feel the weapon quivering in his grip back in that shop in Spire Albion. "When you look back," Espira said, "and you see the whole of your life, do you ever wish you had taken a different path when you were young?"

The big warriorborn rolled a shoulder and frowned out at the sunset, briefly perplexed. He seemed to consider Espira's question for several moments. Then he said, "My mother was a hostess in a wine hall. I only had three choices, sir. The Navy, the Guilds, or the surface. Most Guild enforcers don't make it past thirty before they're killed or replaced. Longtimers on the surface build up injuries and sicknesses, just from the work and conditions, until something eats them. Don't even get a grave." He shrugged. "Few enough of the other warriorborn boys I grew up with are even alive. And I'm a Hero."

Espira had never heard the larger man speak so many words together. He considered him for a time. "So, no regrets," Espira said.

Ciriaco's canine teeth showed briefly. "There was a woman."

Espira smiled faintly.

"This is about that boy in Albion," Ciriaco said.

Espira felt his jaw clench. He jerked his chin in a nod.

The warriorborn exhaled. "Hard one. We join, we join to protect people. Fight anyone who wants to hurt them."

Espira's chest felt a strange, slow pang as he remembered a much younger version of himself. "Yes."

"Raid on Albion didn't feel like that."

"It did not."

Ciriaco grunted. "I was there. That boy had a weapon. He was old enough and strong enough to kill you with it. He tried. It was dark. You reacted fast, or it would have been you on the floor. That's what war is."

"It's not so much the moment," Espira replied. "It's why we were there."

"You did what the brass said," Ciriaco said. "You hadn't done it, someone else would have. You're a soldier. Means following orders."

"Insufficient," Espira replied.

Ciriaco grunted. "I'm just a soldier, Colonel. My world is smaller than yours."

Espira's heart pounded as he turned to the Hero of Aurora. "What if I wanted to do something different?"

Ciriaco lifted his goggles and squinted at Espira. The silence hung between them. Espira had never said anything so overt as "Betray the King," but Ciriaco was an experienced soldier of Aurora. He had been to enough posts, seen enough disobedience and mutiny with their ugly consequences, to know what Espira was talking about.

The warriorborn slipped his goggles back down and watched the last of the sunset vanish into the mesosphere, turning the eternal mists brilliant orange and leaving the skies above them plunging into deep blue and purple as the evening stars were born of night.

"Like I said, sir," Ciriaco said, "my world is a lot smaller. I follow you, Ren."

Espira kept the surge of relief from his expression. He inhaled and exhaled very deeply. "The men?"

Ciriaco shook his head. "Need time. Tell you more."

"Understood," Espira said. "Beware of Sark. The witch is suspicious."

Ciriaco grunted. Then his tone of voice changed, became more businesslike. "Colonel, it's Garcia. He's taken a turn for the worse."

Espira tilted his head. "How so?"

Ciriaco shook his head. "Best see for yourself, sir."

Espira tilted his head and then straightened and gestured for Ciriaco to lead on. He followed the warriorborn sergeant down belowdecks to the Marine quarters and found their medico and the sick man alone on one side of the compartment. The other Marines were casually cleaning weapons, sealing blades with wax, or otherwise occupying themselves with the details of Marine life, but they were as close as they could be to the far bulkhead without actually crowding together. Espira swallowed and marched across the compartment after Ciriaco.

"Morales," the colonel greeted the medico.

The man was a veteran and one of the men Espira had taken into Spire Albion and out again. He had saved several of his fellow Marines who might otherwise have lost their lives to wounds on their way home.

"Sir," Morales said. The man's face was a little pale and sweat beaded his upper lip.

Garcia burst out in a fit of heavy coughing. The private's eyes were closed, his skin flushed, and his breathing labored.

"Report."

"Fever is up," Morales reported. "His cough is worse. He lost consciousness about an hour ago and I haven't been able to wake him." He swallowed. "And, Colonel, his hands."

"Sergeant," Espira said.

Ciriaco fetched a lumin-crystal lantern from the wall and brought it closer. Espira took a steadying breath and then reached down to lift the sick man's hands into the light.

His fingernails were outlined with a thin trickle of blood.

Small, orangish . . . growths were erupting up through the nails.

Crystals, Espira realized.

Small orange crystals.

"God in Heaven and Merciful Builders," Espira breathed. He let Garcia's hands down gently. "What do you know?"

"Sir," Morales said, "I've treated blast wounds. Burns. Splinters from ship-to-ship fire. Wounds from knives and swords and axes. Broken bones. Infections. Once I had to draw a piece of a man's skull from his own brain, and he even lived to sort of talk about it. I've dealt with fevers, parasites, dysentery, pneumonia, consumption, and poisoning." He shook his head. "I've never seen anything like this."

"You saw?" Espira asked Ciriaco.

"Aye, sir," growled the towering sergeant. "If the colonel wishes an observation?"

"He does."

"This looks like some kind of etheric business to me, Colonel."

Espira nodded. "That's not a foolish theory, Sergeant." He rolled his shoulders uncomfortably. "Some kind of toxic by-product perhaps?"

"From *what*?" Morales asked quietly.

"Garcia was on rotation guarding the cargo hold, sir," Ciriaco said, "with Menendez's detail."

"He was guarding the witch's tank," Espira said. He nodded. "Get me Menendez. Then go strike up a conversation with Mister Sark. Make sure he won't overhear us."

Ciriaco grinned. "That's going to be a one-sided talk, sir."

Espira tilted his head for the man to go, and Ciriaco flicked a casual salute and departed.

Commander Menendez came over a moment later; the young man was visibly nervous. "Colonel."

Espira held up a hand until he heard Ciriaco's booming rumble of a greeting ring out from above decks. Then he drew Menendez in close and spoke quietly.

"Commander, did anything untoward happen during any of your men's guard rotations?"

Menendez swallowed and replied in kind. "I didn't think it was worth talking to you about, sir. I thought I handled it."

Espira shot the young officer a hard glance. "Why don't you start at the beginning, Commander?"

"Sir," he said, "Privates Garcia and Delgado were bored, so they started heckling each other. A fight developed. Garcia was pushed against the tank, and some of the . . . water, fluid, whatever is in there, splashed out onto him. I rushed in and broke it up. Disciplined both men."

"When was this?"

"Just before dawn day before last. Sir, I don't think—"

Commander Menendez burst out into an abrupt, heavy cough. Exactly like Garcia's.

He recovered a moment later and looked quizzically at Espira's expression. Then his eyes widened, and the blood drained from his face. "Sir?"

"Steady, man," Espira said quietly. He glanced past Menendez to the other men, who had surreptitiously taken notice of Menendez's cough. "Remember that you are an officer."

Menendez began to breathe fast, but he clenched his jaw and nodded.

"Morales," Espira murmured, "see to him. And I want Delgado here too. Keep an eye on all of them. Keep Ciriaco informed. I'll want to know about any changes immediately."

"Yes, sir," Morales said.

The young commander licked his lips. Espira remembered being that young, that unsure. He remembered looking up to the officers above him as if they'd had the ear of God in Heaven Himself.

"Sir? What are you going to do?"

An excellent question, Espira thought. But he found himself speaking aloud almost before he'd had the chance to make a decision. "I shall speak to Captain Ransom when I take dinner with her this evening," he said, "and see if she will loan me her physician."

When the galley bell rang for dinner, Espira went directly to the captain's cabin. Her steward, a stocky older man with calloused hands and suspicious lumps under his coat, served dinner as always. When he began putting out plates with overt and obvious clattering, Espira leaned toward the captain and quickly explained his concerns.

Calliope Ransom narrowed her eyes while Espira murmured his explanation into her ear. Then she tapped her fingernails in rapid rhythm on the tabletop while she mulled over what he had told her. It didn't take her long.

"Mister Mason," she said.

"Cap'n," said the steward, setting out silverware with more clattering.

"Sark still takes Madame Cavendish her meals, yes?"

"Aye."

"Once he does, bring Doctor Calloway here, as well as Chief McCormick. Ask the bosun to conduct a security sweep of the hold below my cabin and make sure no one is listening in."

"Aye, Cap'n," the steward said. He finished setting out the meal and then rapidly vanished.

The two of them were silent while Captain Ransom made and poured tea, and they waited for it to cool. Moments later, there was a double thump on the deck beneath them—the bosun signaling the all clear.

"Calloway studied etheric theory in school. McCormick is a trained etheric engineer," Captain Ransom said. "We'll have them take a look at your men. Perhaps it is something one of them is familiar with."

Espira toyed a bit with his food, his stomach unsettled. "Do you think that's likely?"

"No," Ransom said frankly.

"I suppose you don't find it coincidental either."

"That the same color crystals are growing from your man's nails as in Cavendish's eyes?" Ransom asked. She snorted delicately.

"What do you think?"

"I think," Ransom said thoughtfully, "I should never have allowed Tuscarora to remove the scuttling charges from beneath Cavendish's quarters." She exhaled and then began eating her evening meal decisively.

"You understand," Espira said quietly, "if it comes to it, her first targets will be the two of us."

"Obviously."

"And we've no etherealist of our own to counter her."

Ransom's face turned expressionless, and she nodded. "I imagine that whatever she has in mind would be a bad way to go."

"I've seen it," Espira said, remembering the poor fellow tearing out his own eyes in desperation. "Quite."

Ransom studied his face for a moment, her dark, intelligent eyes intense. Then she reached out and laid her hand on his, fingers gripping tight.

Espira turned his palm to hers and returned the grasp. He would say that Madame Cavendish terrified him beyond reason—except that, going over his logic, he could find nothing unreasonable about his fear. How could he strike at her without either having his mind torn apart by her power or facing a court-martial and subsequent hanging when he returned to Spire Aurora?

Ransom nodded firmly at him, her jaw set. Then she released his hand and turned her attention back to her meal.

"I suggest you eat up, Colonel," she said. "The time is coming soon, and you'll want to have all your strength."

Chapter 25

Auroran Embassy, Habble Profit, Spire Olympia

Grimm strode along at Bayard's right hand. He wore his black civilian version of a dress uniform to complement his friend's splendid appearance in his Aetherium Fleet full mess dress of vibrant blue and gold. Half a dozen warriorborn Albion Marines in their dark blue–and-gold dress uniforms accompanied them as they marched through the streets of Habble Profit and toward Valesco's quarters at the Auroran embassy in the Grand Square.

Morning foot traffic was brisk and busy in the Grand Square, perhaps the most public space in all of Habble Profit. The embassy itself was an expensive building all of wood stained a deep, dark red and polished to a low glow. The flag of Spire Aurora hung above the doorway to the embassy, four red stars between sky blue bars upon a white background. A pair of Auroran Marines at attention on either side of the entrance glanced at each other warily as the Albion party approached.

Bayard came to a stop with a stomp of one foot, echoed by Grimm and the Marines, who came to parade rest.

"Are you quite sure about this, Alex?" Grimm murmured under his breath. "There's still time to reconsider."

"He dared strike my Abigail, old boy," Bayard said calmly. "Are we sure he's here?"

"Abigail's people say he is."

"Then he is," Bayard said with certainty.

"You know what this is going to do."

"The arrogant bastard, to lay a finger on her. I'll have him look-ing down at his own spilled entrails or my name isn't Bayard."

"I meant more the way you intend to drop the gauntlet."

Bayard's teeth showed wolfishly. "Oh. That."

And without hesitation, he raised his gauntlet, weapons crystal glowing brightly, and sent three blasts into the Auroran flag, promptly setting it aflame.

After a startled second, the Marines at the door of the embassy began to lift their own gauntlets.

Grimm had already held up his hand, and the half dozen Albion Marines with him snapped long guns to their shoulders.

"Don't be fools," Grimm said in his hardest captain's voice. "Let us not make any hasty mistakes."

The Auroran Marines froze.

So did the crowd in the Grand Square, perhaps three thousand people, who would excitedly spread word of what had happened. Foot traffic in the square came to an abrupt halt as the Auroran flag blazed and smoldered, briefly threatening to set the embassy aflame before sputtering out.

"Gentlemen," Bayard's voice rang out with scorn, echoing through-out the square for all to hear, "you have amongst you a puling coward and sell-sword known as Baron Rafe Valesco." He paused for effect and repeated the name. "Rafe. Valesco. I am His Excellency Count Commodore Alexander Blaine Balthazar Bayard, Count Bayard, Master and Commander AFS *Belligerent,* and personal champion of His Majesty Spirearch Albion. This is my second, Captain Francis Madison Grimm, AMS *Predator.* I forthwith deliver challenge to this lawless scoundrel Valesco for striking a lady of Albion, and bid him come forth to give me satisfaction, or I will declare him an impotent coward to all the world."

Silence weighed heavily on the square, and Bayard glanced back without turning his head, a small smile on his mouth.

"Impotent?" Grimm murmured under his breath.

"Abigail's idea," Bayard murmured back.

Grimm lowered his hand, and the Marines relaxed their long guns and grounded them in perfect unison.

"Go on, then," Bayard said, waving his hand at the Auroran Marines on guard. "Run and tell him."

"Sir!" said one of the young Marines in a heavy Auroran accent. "What you have just done is beyond the pale."

"You know who I am," Bayard responded, his face hard. "I've killed Aurorans enough. Send for your champion if he has the stones to show his cowardly face."

The two men goggled at the Albion delegation and the scorched flag for a moment. Then one of them turned and pounded up the stairs to the embassy and ran inside.

"Subtle," Grimm noted.

"Aurorans are often impressed by dramatic displays," Bayard noted calmly. "I want to make sure I have the man's attention."

"*Aurorans* are," Grimm clarified.

Bayard's mouth twitched up at the corner, and the two of them waited.

It took perhaps five minutes for Valesco to appear, and before he did, tension gathered in the air as the crowd waited, breaking into excited murmurs as more people poured into the square.

Then the embassy doors opened and quiet fell. The tall warriorborn Auroran prowled out of the embassy wearing tights and a billowing white shirt stained with wine, his hair mussed, his eyes apparently bleary, but Grimm took note that his expression was steely.

"Oh," Valesco drawled, his own voice pitched to carry, "it's you. The little man."

"You struck a lady of Albion, sir," Bayard said. "And you will answer for it."

"That tart?" Valesco said carelessly.

Bayard's gauntlet hand twitched, and Grimm moved only his arm, seizing the duelist by the wrist. "Alex," he said gently, "don't let him."

Grimm's friend took a slow breath through his nose and then nodded. "Of course." And Grimm released his wrist carefully.

Valesco let a slow smile spread over his face and strolled lazily down the stairs toward the Albion party. If he were at all concerned with their weaponry and formal finery, he did not show it. He stopped to loom over Bayard and studied him with an arrogantly cocked eyebrow, his lips lifted just enough to show his slightly lengthened canines.

"So, little man," Valesco said, "it would seem I have found your weak spot."

"I'm sure you'll continue thinking that until the very end," Bayard replied. He deliberately reached into his coat, produced one of Abigail's white leather gloves, and flicked it calmly into Valesco's face.

The warriorborn caught the glove before it could strike him, his hands so quick Grimm could scarcely see them move. A slow smile spread over Valesco's lips as he lifted the glove to his nose. His nostrils flared as he inhaled.

"The woman likes fighters," he said quietly. "Perhaps after you're dead, I'll introduce myself. If she's still alive, of course."

"You're fortunate to be facing me instead of her," Bayard shot back. "My second will contact yours and arrange the details."

Valesco glanced aside at Grimm, his eyes dismissive. "I'll send word to my second, and he'll be out in a little while," he told Bayard.

"Captain Grimm, I do hope you'll take breakfast with me while we wait. I'm told aeronauts have iron stomachs."

"Sir," Grimm said with a very small, very stiff bow.

"Excellent," Valesco replied. "I'd invite you as well, Bayard. But you do seem so excitable. I'd hate for anything untoward to happen— at least before we can do this properly."

"In that, sir, we agree," Bayard said with a sneer. "I want everyone to see how you are repaid for your behavior."

Bayard turned to Grimm, who faced him. The two bowed briefly to each other and shook hands. Then Bayard nodded to his complement of Marines and strode off, his men following him with formal precision, leaving Grimm standing with Valesco.

"So bright and shining," Valesco murmured. He glanced at Grimm. "Whereas you are already dressed for his funeral. I think I shall put my sword just beneath his medal with the red ribbon. The one he got for capturing *Itasca*."

"Bayard isn't afraid of you, sir," Grimm replied calmly. "Neither am I."

"Then both of you are rather foolish," Valesco said calmly. His handsome face spread into what almost seemed a genuine smile. "What a piquant and theatrical morning this has been, Captain." He turned and gestured grandly for Grimm to join him. "Please, this way. The cook at the embassy is really quite excellent."

The Auroran embassy's dining room was large, spacious, luxurious, and filled with growing plants and flowers beneath appropriate lumin crystals. Tables at slightly different levels were scattered throughout the room on various platforms, and the sounds from a stone fountain burbled and chuckled throughout.

His movements leonine and lazy, Valesco went to a table in the center of the room, settled into a chair, then gestured for Grimm to join him. Grimm did so with stiff formality, and a servant in plain garb appeared with tea and coffee almost at once.

"As a well-traveled man, I assume you've had coffee, Captain," Valesco said.

"Indeed," Grimm replied. "I prefer tea."

"Albions," Valesco murmured, pouring himself a large cup of coffee from a carafe. "I've read all about your involvement in the raid two years ago, Captain. You're something of a hero."

"Merely a man who knows his duty," Grimm replied, pouring tea into his cup and sampling the embassy's blend. It was quite good, though not excellent, but it tasted just as tea ought to taste.

Valesco let out a laugh. "I'm hardly going to have you poisoned, Captain."

Grimm smiled faintly. "Perhaps. Perhaps not."

"Tell me, Captain Grimm," Valesco said. "Have you fought many duels?"

"None," Grimm replied.

Valesco seemed fascinated by the answer. "Really? That's terribly interesting. Do you not have the stomach for it?"

"I don't have the time," Grimm replied calmly. "When I kill men, there's rarely been an appointment made for it."

The servant returned with cakes and scones and morning pies filled with eggs and bacon. Valesco and Grimm made their choices. The food was excellent.

"For how long were you Bayard's friend? I wonder, Captain."

"Since Fleet Academy," Grimm responded. "We were roommates and later served together. I expect we shall be friends until old age."

The Auroran duelist smiled. "Such optimism."

"Hardly. Alex has dueled many times—including dueling warriorborn, sir. Yet there he stands."

"Half-wits and drunken oafs," Valesco said with a dismissive wave of one hand. "Not an expert. Not me."

"For someone who wishes to appear confident," Grimm said mildly, "you seem to spend a great deal of effort reminding those around you of your prowess, sir."

That remark earned Grimm the flash of an ugly expression and a venomous glare. "A rather large complement of dead men would beg you to reconsider that thought if they could."

"I beg your pardon, sir," Grimm said without rancor. "I am not, as you have noted, an expert duelist. I am sure my opinion must be uninformed as to the proper protocols around duels. No offense was intended."

Valesco stared at him with feline eyes for a long moment before he nodded slowly.

"You're a fighter," he mused.

"When necessity demands it."

Valesco's teeth showed. "Well, I take it you understand that as Bayard's second, should he fail to arrive at the duel or should he be forced to withdraw for whatever reason, you, and not he, will be facing me. Have you a dueling blade, Captain?"

"Only my service weapon," Grimm replied. He drew back his coat to show the hilt of the short, heavy blade of an aeronaut. "And my friend is looking forward to your meeting. I'm sure he wouldn't miss it for all the world."

Valesco grinned, a surprisingly boyish expression but for the cold steel in his eyes. "Excellent. He seems a man well worth killing."

At that moment, the door to the dining room opened, and an older gentleman in an Auroran Armada officer's uniform approached their table and bowed politely to Valesco and then to Grimm. There was a sturdy look about him, and he wore a beard shot with streaks of silver through dark hair. His eyes were an unusual pale grey, odd for an Auroran.

"Ah, Captain Chavez," Valesco said with pleasure. "Captain, do you know Raoul Chavez?"

"Indirectly," Grimm replied, nodding to the man as he rose. "You command the *Conquistodor*, do you not, Captain?"

Chavez bowed from the waist, not looking away from Grimm's eyes. "Correct, sir. A rather merry chase you led us upon not so long ago."

"Luck was with me," Grimm said calmly, returning the bow. "It could as easily have gone your way."

"Much more easily," Chavez said, smiling faintly. "Perhaps next time."

"One never knows," Grimm replied.

"When this unpleasantness is over, Captain," Chavez said, "I should enjoy buying you a drink and discussing the capture of *Itasca*. I commanded her, you see, earlier in my career and trained her captain. I should, I think, enjoy hearing your perspective on the battle."

"Perhaps," Grimm said noncommittally.

"You Armada types," Valesco said with an ugly laugh, "you talk like old women."

Chavez's eyes flickered with irritation, but he smiled at Valesco and nodded. "Captain Grimm, shall we sit and arrange matters for our principals?"

"Of course."

"Excellent," Valesco said, rising. "I shall leave you both to it. There are a number of girls in my bed who will wake disappointed if I am not there."

And without so much as a courteous farewell, the warriorborn padded out of the dining room.

But not without one last hard, speculative look at Grimm.

Chapter 26

The Surface, near Spire Albion

Bridget stomped each foot twice and turned in a circle.

Upon seeing this, Master Harbor fell silent, and the whine of the overloading gauntlet stopped scaling higher. He shot a suspicious glance at Benedict from beneath shaggy brows.

Bridget turned to him and jerked her chin toward his feet.

His eyes widened in sudden understanding, and he did the same little pantomime.

"Ah," said the burly etherealist. "Well, at least one of you is literate, I suppose. That's a start." He lowered the spear with a negligent flick of one hand, and Bridget felt the vibration from the weapons crystal in her gauntlet ease and settle back into stillness.

"Ah," Bridget said. She took a steadying breath and tried not to let her severe trembling show. "Master Harbor, I presume?"

The burly man snapped to attention, clacked his heels together after the fashion of some of the lower habbles of Albion, and bowed at the waist. "The same. I receive very few visitors out here, miss." His eyes raked over her uniform. "Probably for the best, honestly. My compliments to you both for having such spine."

More weird clicks echoed through the sunlit mist. Bridget found herself tensing, but Master Harbor gave them no more than a twitch of a glance from beneath his shaggy brows and grounded the spear.

"Thank you, sir," Bridget said. She cleared her throat carefully. "Need my feline companions . . . comply with the text of the signs outside your house?"

Harbor snorted. "No one tells cats to do anything."

Rowl tilted his head thoughtfully at the etherealist. "He seems reasonably intelligent."

"Rowl," Bridget sighed. Then she straightened and said, "I am Sergeant Bridget Tagwynn, Spirearch's Guard, as you can see."

Master Harbor grunted. "Tagwynn. Do you know Franklin? Big man. Muscles like a bear."

Bridget blinked. "A what?" She shook her head quickly, a little disoriented. "He's my father, sir."

"It's a surface animal. Huge and furry and a damned sight smarter than it appears to be. Just like Franklin. I knew him when he was a Marine. Taught him his first words of Cat."

His eyes raked over Bridget again, and she felt uncomfortably . . . observed.

"And you," Harbor said to Benedict. "Warriorborn. Surprised you didn't try that sword while I was counting. Or the knife."

"Benedict Sorellin-Lancaster, sir," he replied with a small, polite bow. "It seemed like it would be rude. And that you were being polite by counting."

"Hah. So, you're not a fool. And you're cut to ribbons under that suit, eh? That had something to do with it." Harbor studied them both for a long moment and then exhaled. "I'll warn you both right now. New people make me cautious. And stupidity gives me a headache."

"I strive to avoid idiocy wherever possible," Benedict assured him. "With mixed results, but I think I can manage for a little while."

Bridget felt herself begin to smile at the remark, but Master Harbor seemed to take it very seriously and nodded several times. "I'd appreciate that, little brother. Pretty as it is, this isn't the sort of place where I'd like to be blinded with pain. There's a reason I live the way I do." He glanced back at his bobbing cork and sighed. "What does the Spirearch want with me this time? He's already got my most recent reports."

"Well, sir," Bridget said carefully, "not to be too pointed, but we didn't actually come to speak to you, as such."

Harbor's craggy brows rose. "Oh." He looked briefly baffled. "I'm not sure what to do with that. Did you wish to try your hand at fishing?"

Fishing? What on earth was that? Ignorance and stupidity weren't exactly the same thing, she supposed, but it was probably best not to show the etherealist either if what he said about himself was true. Bridget did her best not to look lost at the strange word. "No, sir. We were sent to speak to Chief Farr of the Shadow Stripes."

The big, dark cat had been still for some time, and Bridget had begun to think that the old beast was perhaps deaf, but at the mention of his name—of course—the tip of his tail began to twitch.

Harbor barked out a laugh and said to Farr in Cat, "Did you hear that, little brother?"

Farr stirred slowly and rose to stretch and yawn. He was a magnificent specimen of his breed, still sleek and firm with muscle, if aged and somewhat stiff. A stray shaft of nearly clear sunlight played over his fur, revealing a subtle pattern of lighter and darker grey stripes.

"Of course I heard," Farr replied in a surly voice. "Ask the human why it has interrupted my nap."

Bridget turned to Farr, bowed politely, and said in Cat, "I apologize for not sending word ahead, but our mission is urgent. Longthinker sent me to ask a favor of you, great Chief."

Harbor beamed at that, then pursed his lips, and his gaze shifted shrewdly between Farr and Bridget as he took a small step back.

Farr prowled forward, in no hurry whatsoever, and regarded Bridget, Benedict, and the two cats with a steady, disinterested gaze. "I suppose I need not ignore you, human. Have you a proper Name, then?"

Rowl stood up in front of Bridget defensively and arched his back, displaying his own size, which was not quite as impressive as Chief Farr's. "She is called Littlemouse by the Silent Paws."

Farr flicked his ears in dismissal of Rowl's stance, his words, and his very existence.

"Oh!" Rowl said in indignation.

"I have no time for disrespectful kittens," Chief Farr said, and began to turn away.

"Rowl," Bridget said urgently, "our mission."

Rowl looked up at Bridget in protest. "My father did not win a war against this old bag of bones and his tribe to have me humiliate myself for the sake of his wounded pride."

Chief Farr, without ever hurrying, turned back to eye Rowl. "This one," he said, looking up at Bridget. "He is the kit of Maul?"

"Yes," Bridget said. "Chief Maul and my father have an Arrangement."

"Ah," Chief Farr said. "I do not care for Maul. But he is worthy of respect." He eyed Fenli. "And the halfling?"

Fenli regarded some insect that flitted from one particularly high blade of grass to the next, and otherwise ignored Chief Farr.

That seemed to amuse the old cat. He padded slowly over to sit beside Fenli and regard the insect. They both sat there beside each other for a while, ignoring each other. Bridget felt a flash of frustration, but she waited. Cats were cats, and there was no use trying to rush them. A glance at the other two humans with her told her that they both understood the process and were willing to wait for it to play out.

Rowl fumed.

After only a quarter of an hour or so, Fenli turned to Chief Farr and said, "I am called Fenli, of the Swift Slayers. I am not afraid of you. I do not seek combat."

Farr lashed his tail in acknowledgment. "Fenli of the Swift Slayers, I am Chief Farr of the Shadow Stripes. I have no reason to wish you harm."

"Chief," Rowl said derisively. "He is chief of only himself."

"Rowl!" Bridget said.

Chief Farr regarded Rowl steadily. "I at least command myself, kit of Maul. That is, it would seem, more than you can say."

"Rowl, a word," Bridget said, and took several steps over to one side.

The ginger cat padded after her through the grass, his tail lashing. "What is it?"

"Rowl," Bridget said, struggling to keep her tone patient, "my home Spire may soon be at war with a deadly foe."

"I know that," Rowl said. "I live there."

Bridget steadied herself with a breath. "Fenli and his people have information that may be vital to that war effort."

"Yes. And?"

"Chief Farr," Bridget continued steadily, "is the key to securing their cooperation."

Rowl's whiskers twitched in disgust. "Yes, it is unfortunate that he is being so maddening."

She clenched her fists. "I merely suggest," she said, "that perhaps the fates of a quarter of a million human beings—and more than one hundred fifty tribes of cats—may be more important than your pride."

Rowl stared at her for a moment, and then said, "I am not sure I follow you."

Bridget shot an exasperated glance back at Benedict, but the warriorborn was firmly facing away, struggling to keep a straight face and slowly turning red, though whether from frustration, suppressed laughter, or both was not immediately apparent.

She turned to the cat and said, "I wish you to do me a favor. I will be most grateful if you should do so."

The cat's head tilted to one side. "Littlemouse, for you, I would . . ." He paused. "Not trim my whiskers. Not shave my tail. But I would eat food that was not good at the very least. Or get all wet."

Bridget knelt down and nodded seriously, looking into Rowl's eyes. "I need you to let me deal with this problem for you. I know you could handle Chief Farr yourself, but this is the first mission under my command, and it is very important to my personal honor that I handle matters myself."

"I treasure your honor as if it were my own," Rowl said seriously. Then he looked toward Chief Farr and narrowed his eyes. "But the honor of my tribe is at stake as well."

"That is the favor I ask," Bridget said. "That you trust me with this matter. I need you to . . . be more important than these petty squabbles."

"Ah," Rowl said pensively. "I am, of course, very important."

"Of course," Bridget said.

"And this is a matter of your personal honor, you say?"

"I must return to His Majesty with success in my own right. I cannot have you constantly fighting my battles for me."

Rowl sighed and then rubbed his shoulder against Bridget's stomach as she knelt in the grass. "My Littlemouse. It has taken years and years, but finally you are growing up into a hunter. Naturally, you must succeed on your own."

"Thank you, Rowl," Bridget sighed.

"Due to my excellent supervision and mentorship, obviously."

"Oh, very obviously." She rose and said, "Wish me luck."

"Why?" Rowl asked. "You do not need it. You have had *me*."

With that and a long stretch to show off his magnificent fur, Rowl turned his back on the entire matter, seating himself in the long grass and curling his tail calmly about his paws.

Bridget strode back over to the little gathering, acutely conscious of Master Harbor's bright gaze upon her.

He gave her a small bow as she approached and murmured quietly, "That was well done."

Chief Farr's tail tip flicked back and forth in amusement. "Very well, then, Littlemouse. What favor does Longthinker ask of me?"

Bridget quickly explained their predicament. "And so we need to ask if you will cede your territory to the Swift Slayers."

Utterly still, Chief Farr stared at her for a long moment. Then he said, "But if I do that, then I will have no territory."

Bridget blinked. "I . . . I rather thought that since you weren't using it in any case—"

"Using it?" Farr asked. "I do not understand. The territory is mine. It is my territory."

"Yes, but you have not actually been there in several years, and—"

Farr rose to his feet, indignant. "And? And what? The territory is mine, and that's the end of it. The Shadow Stripes bought it with blood. What matter that the tribe is scattered? It is still the tribe's territory. While I yet live, it is still mine."

Bridget blinked. "But . . . you live here with Master Harbor, do you not?"

"Hates Strangers," Farr said, then paused to bump against the etherealist's knees, "is a friend, and I am visiting his home. That bears no relation whatsoever to the territory under my rule. And in honesty, it pleases me to frustrate the kit of Maul."

"But . . . surely there is some way to come to some kind of Arrangement," Bridget protested.

Farr sighed in frustration and looked at Fenli. "Do you have any idea how to explain it to her?"

"I see no reason why such a thing should need to *be* explained," Fenli replied. "Your position is entirely obvious. And Rowl is most undeniably frustrating."

"Fenli!" Bridget protested. "Whose side are you on?"

"Littlemouse," Fenli said primly, "my people may be small and homeless, but we are neither poachers nor thieves. We respect tradition and the rule of law. If Chief Farr does not wish to cede his territory, he is well within his rights to refuse."

"Yes," Bridget said, "but we need to know what you saw."

"Then return to Longthinker," Fenli said patiently, "and see what alternative he may offer my people. Once you have the information you wish, you may not see a need to grant us a home of our own. We will not be either foolish or used for human advantage."

"This is only proper," Farr interjected.

"It is," Fenli said.

"We may well not have time to begin again," Bridget protested.

"That," Fenli said reasonably, "is not a thing that is within my control."

Bridget looked helplessly between the two cats and then at Benedict. His expression had sobered, and he shook his head helplessly at her. Bridget turned to Master Harbor.

"I'm sorry, little sister," the etherealist said, shaking his head regretfully. "But no one tells a cat to do anything. You know that as well as I."

Bridget clenched her fists in frustration and felt close to tears. "I am well aware how useless it is to issue orders," she said. "But there must be some accommodation to be had here somewhere."

"None," Fenli said.

"None," agreed Chief Farr.

"Augh," Bridget said. She thought frantically. "What if—"

A rapid burst of clicks echoed through the golden mist; they were so intense and loud that Bridget felt them thump against her back like a series of little pats from unseen hands.

Master Harbor's face suddenly went pale and grim, and he seized his spear.

"What was that?" Bridget breathed, whirling.

A second series of heavy clicks issued from the mist—this time against her rib cage on her left side.

Benedict's sword appeared in his hand and his gauntlet flared with light.

"Sword mantis," Master Harbor barked. "A mated pair. You children had best get behind me. Now!"

■ ■ ■ Chapter 27 ■ ■ ■

The Surface, near Spire Albion

Bridget hurried to comply with Master Harbor's command, with Rowl surging through the grass at her heels while little Fenli had to travel in great plunging leaps in their wake. Benedict was at her side at once, sword in hand, gauntlet primed.

"Damn the things," Harbor growled. "They came from your back trail. They're probably following the scent of your blood, Sir Benedict."

"What are we up against?" the warriorborn asked the etherealist.

Master Harbor stood with his spear held level, wavering back and forth between the approximate directions of the clicks. "They're about eight feet tall and twice as long and deucedly fast. Imagine a berserk warriorborn coming at you with two swords and nothing to lose."

"I'd blast him," Bridget said at once.

"The eyes, mouth, and antennae are about the only unarmored spots," Harbor said. "Those little things won't get through anywhere else. Steel is better, especially on the neck. I'm sure I can handle one. Two might be an issue."

"Ah," Benedict said, released the charge on his gauntlet, reached into a belt pouch at his back, and produced a compact gunpowder pistol. He cocked the hammer, bounced the sword in his hand a couple of times, and waited.

"You carry a gunpowder weapon around all the time?" Bridget asked him quietly.

"Since all that business with Madame Cavendish, yes," Benedict said.

"Those things explode!"

"Rarely," Benedict allowed. "Mine is in excellent condition. It probably won't."

"'Probably'!?"

"Just between us, children," Master Harbor rumbled, "a weapon of last resort is exactly what this situation calls for. Now be quiet."

More clicks thumped against them through the mist, and then dark, lean, tall forms appeared, gliding forward with smooth, somehow spectral motion. They were monstrous, insectlike things with six legs moving smoothly to propel them forward with slow, eerie grace. They kept the long trunks of their bodies moving on perfectly level planes.

Their forequarters rose to the vertical and supported massive shoulders and long arms that terminated in inwardly curving serrated blades that gleamed in the glowing mist. Their heads were massive triangles speckled with four bulbous, gleaming eyes; they supported macerating jaws that bore the same gleam as the claws and looked like they could snap through a man's thigh without effort. The sword mantises indeed stood high over even Benedict, and each probably weighed three or four of him.

The sword mantises glided silently toward them and then crouched. Their jaws snapped together too rapidly to be seen, producing another burst of thudding clicks that sent Bridget's heart into a near panic, and from their backs spread almost translucent leathery wings that fluttered and buzzed excitedly. Moving in perfect synchronization, they shot forward ten feet, froze, and then darted another ten feet, wings buzzing with more and more frantic energy.

"Good God in Heaven," Benedict breathed.

From the ground beneath Master Harbor's legs, Chief Farr let out a slowly rising cat's warning snarl.

Rowl and Fenli joined him.

"They'll pounce," Harbor growled. "The one on the left is the male. The big one is the female. I'll take her. The male is yours. I'll help you if I can."

"Understood," Benedict said. "Bridget, I'll go in first and distract it. Try to get a shot into its eyes."

Bridget had practiced diligently with her gauntlet, but such a shot in combat conditions was for an expert with far more actual experience than she had. Her mouth was suddenly dry, and she felt a horrible weakness in the fingers that gripped her sword.

Bouncing his extra-heavy blade in one hand, Benedict took a couple of steps toward the male sword mantis. The warriorborn used a weapon three times heavier than Bridget's own sword, and his prodigious strength allowed him to wield it without difficulty. Gwen had told her about how he had systematically chopped apart a silkweaver queen with the very sword now in his hands, and Bridget had to hope that he could visit similar consequences upon the predator now approaching them.

Bridget stepped out behind and just beside Benedict, lifting her shaking gauntlet hand, willing the weapons crystal against her palm to life.

Both sword mantises froze in perfect unison again. Then the male tilted its head, chittered weirdly, and *looked* at Bridget, its four eyes somehow focusing on her with frantic intensity.

It's identified me as the weakest link, Bridget thought to herself. And it's going to come after me.

Her stomach twisted horribly, and she fought feebly against every nerve and instinct in her body screaming that she should turn and run at once.

But she had felt this way before, in the midst of a burning monastery, when her life had been in danger and when there had been no one to help her—and she had survived, victorious.

By God in Heaven, she would survive this too.

Her hand closed hard around the grip of her sword; she clenched her jaw and raised the weapon to a ready position.

And then, with another ripping-canvas burst of clicks, the sword mantises bounded thirty feet through the air, buzzing wings carrying them in a partial glide that brought them down atop their would-be prey.

Bridget's heart lurched as everything seemed to slow.

The female sword mantis came crashing down upon Master Harbor, but as it did, the crystal set into his spear flashed with light so brilliant that the sun itself seemed to dim, and a force almost the equal of one of *Predator*'s main guns smashed into the descending sword mantis.

The blast of energy tore through the sword mantis's leathery wings as if they had been made of paper, forced its head to one side, and caused its leap to veer in midair, bringing it crashing to the ground—and onto the spear that Master Harbor had grounded against his foot and now leaned into.

The spear spitted the sword mantis through the center of its thorax, and its crossbar caught the weight of the hideous beast. Then Master Harbor guided the bowing spear through an arc that flung the mantis off the blade and sent it tumbling to the earth behind him.

Even as that happened, the male mantis soared over Benedict entirely and directly at Bridget. She raised her gauntlet to shoot, but the buzzing and the clicking and the sheer massive presence of the surface creature shook something in her. So, instead of shooting, she flung herself to one side as the scythe-bladed arms of the mantis came whipping toward her. She avoided one of the scythes with her movement, but the mantis's flaring wings altered its course in midleap, so she raised her sword to block the other scythe.

There was a ringing sound that began at a low pitch and rapidly screeched higher, and Bridget's sword went tumbling away in two separate pieces while a sudden hot pain shot across her back and shoulder. Then something flung her viciously through the air and to the grass.

"Littlemouse!" Rowl screamed, and let loose with his yowling war cry.

Fenli bounded away through the tall grass.

Bridget gasped with pain as the sword mantis turned with horrible speed and grace and plunged down its scythes. She rolled to avoid one, but a white-hot lance of agony shot up her leg as the other speared through her calf and boot and into the soil beneath her with almost contemptuous ease.

The Prince of the Silent Paws snarled and bounded through the air, bounced off the limb of the mantis that pinned Bridget to the earth, and flung himself at the mantis's head. He sank his jaws into one of the thing's antennae and began slashing at a bulbous eye with his front claws and raking at a second with his wickedly sharp battle spurs. Greenish ichor sprayed out.

The sword mantis recoiled, its jaws jittering and clattering like some kind of steam-powered machinery. Its wings made a low thunder of furious energy while a whistling shriek emerged from its thorax. It thrashed wildly left and right, tearing its scythe free of the earth but not from Bridget's leg. As she was dragged across the ground in unbelievable agony, she could not stop herself from screaming. Her blood sprayed scarlet over the long green grass, and some of it got into one eye, half blinding her.

The mantis flung its head about, and Rowl's jaws lost purchase. The cat flew clear of the creature and tumbled in midair. Then the sword mantis's other scythe lashed out and, even at an awkward angle, struck hard enough to send the cat to the earth with a piteous cry of pain.

"Rowl!" Bridget screamed.

And then Benedict caught up to the sword mantis. With a coughing, leonine roar, he whirled his sword in a powerful arc and simply swept it through one of the mantis's rear legs at the knee joint. The creature chittered and staggered, then whirled about its long axis with vicious speed, dragging Bridget in a dizzying half circle.

The warriorborn fended off a strike of the mantis's scythe with his heavy blade. Then he lashed out with a blow at its torso that left a long green streak of a wound but did not slow the mantis down. Bridget's leg shook violently, tendons and joints crackling with the sheer strength of the thing, and she realized that the sword mantis was trying to draw its limb free of her, the better to maul Benedict.

With a cry of fury and terror, Bridget lurched forward and seized the length of the scythe. Though the ridge of steely chitin immediately began slicing into her palms, she hung on with both hands in order to trap the mantis's second vicious weapon.

Somewhere behind her, there was a flash of green light, a howl of etheric energy, and a thunderous explosion like the impact of a shipboard cannon.

The sword mantis swiped again at Benedict, forcing him back, and in the half second of time afterward it lifted the scythe pinning Bridget and dropped its jaws at her head.

She barely saw the grey-and-brown blur of tiny Fenli, who

emerged from the tall grass and sprinted up the wounded mantis's abdomen, bounded onto its head, and seized in his own little jaws the same antennae that Rowl had already bitten.

Hissing and writhing, the mantis threw Bridget clear before, without one of its legs for support, it overbalanced and toppled to one side. She fell to the grass and, desperate to see what had happened, pushed herself up with her freely bleeding hands. As the mantis fell, Fenli calmly leapt away, then vanished into the tall grass like a wisp of mist.

With another roar of pure fury, Benedict fell on the mantis. He struck twice, his weapon whirling, its sharpened edge ripping through the mantis's scythe limbs where they joined the trunk and sent them spinning away into the meadow's grass. The mantis struggled up, green ichor spraying, staggering on its unbalanced limbs, and Benedict swept off another leg at the knee.

The mantis tried to retreat, its long limbs now moving desperately as it hobbled backward through the grass, but the warriorborn offered the creature no quarter. He pursued it, leaving more wounds and taking another limb, until the mantis leapt into the air, wings frantically beating, and came down with its terrible jaws.

Benedict met the attack with his suddenly pointed pistol. A crack of miniature thunder roiled through the clearing as he sent the shot directly into the creature's mouth. Green ichor exploded out the back of the monster's head in a spray of fine mist, and Benedict leapt back as the thing crashed down to the earth.

Even then, horribly, the thing wasn't dead. It struggled to rise again, jaws now thumping together slowly and awkwardly.

Benedict's next strike took its head from its neck.

The body staggered around for another moment even as the jaws kept clashing together.

Bridget turned her head wearily to see Master Harbor approaching at a run that slowed as he took in the results of the battle. Behind him, there was a smoking, burning mess that had once been the female mantis, its body exploded into a blackened, charred circle twenty feet across.

Chief Farr came padding along after Master Harbor and considered the conclusion of their fight.

"Under my leadership," the cat declared, "we are victorious."

"Thank God in Heaven you were here," Master Harbor said absently. He eyed Benedict. "And thank the Merciful Builders for warriorborn. Well done, little brother."

Benedict grimaced, sword and smoking pistol still in hand. "Bridget!" he said, and ran toward her.

"I'm alive," Bridget said. She fumbled at her equipment belt, but since her hands were covered with blood, she couldn't get the clasp on her medical pouch to open. "Oh, bother," she said blearily. "I can't get to my bandages."

"Easy, easy," Master Harbor said. The burly etherealist stood over her with his spear gripped in strong hands. "See to her, little brother. I'll stand watch. There's too much blood in the air. We need to get her bound up and move her immediately."

"On it," Benedict said, kneeling beside Bridget and setting his weapons aside.

"Rowl," Bridget breathed. "Where is Rowl?"

Fenli's little striped tail bobbed through the tall grass, and then the tiny cat's ears and eyes appeared just above it. "Here," Fenli said. "I am sitting on him." His eyes bobbed up and down a bit. "He is breathing but unconscious. He is not bleeding. He must have been struck with the blunt side of the scythe."

"Hah," said Chief Farr. "Bold but stupid, Prince of the Silent Paws." The great dark cat tilted his head at Bridget. "Littlemouse, it seems that Prince Rowl thinks you worthy of him losing his own life."

"He is my friend," Bridget said. She was having trouble breathing. Her ribs on one side hurt abominably. "Fenli, are you sure he is all right?"

Before Fenli could answer, Rowl said in a bleary voice, "Insolent halfling, get off of me."

Fenli obligingly hopped down. His little tail proceeded through the grass until he emerged at Benedict's side. He rubbed his shoulder against the warriorborn's leg as the tall man knelt and began rapidly bandaging Bridget's wounds.

"You see?" Fenli said calmly. "I told you he was all right. And Tribesaver was there to protect you."

Benedict smiled at that and gave Fenli a fond look.

"Not half-soul?" Bridget ventured.

"He has earned a Name," Fenli declared.

"So he has," Chief Farr concurred.

"My head hurts," said Rowl sullenly, emerging wearily from the tall grass. He came and rubbed against Bridget, purring in concern.

"Do not worry," Fenli said. "I saved her when you failed."

"I did not fail!" Rowl declared indignantly. "I made a frontal assault so that you could get into striking position."

"And you failed," Fenli said. "You need not reward me for saving your human. Any cat of honor would have done so."

Rowl's tail stiffened in indignation. He sputtered for a moment, then turned exhaustedly back to Bridget, ignoring Fenli.

"Hah," Chief Farr said. "You have put my old enemy's prince in his place." The big, dark cat flicked his ears contemplatively. "I like that. I like that very much." His eyes narrowed in thought. "I will not cede my territory to you."

"Naturally not," Fenli said.

"But," said Chief Farr, "as you have shown both honor and skill at battle, I will accept you as guests of the Shadow Stripes. You will have full run of the territory with rights to hunt and raise kits, as much as you can manage for yourselves. I hereby designate your chief as my heir, and she will have full responsibility for managing the territory while I am away, which I presume will be always. And when I have no further need of territory, she will have care of it and manage it in whatever way she chooses."

"That," Fenli said, "is generous, fair, and wise."

"Of course it is," Chief Farr growled. "I have done it."

Benedict removed Bridget's gauntlet, the leather of which was slashed to bits, and bandaged her hand.

"Wait," she said wearily. "Does this mean what I think it means?"

Fenli turned to her. "It means," he said, "that the Swift Slayers have a home. It means that Longthinker has fulfilled his end of the bargain. And so, we will fulfill ours."

Bridget blinked at the little cat, tears of exhaustion and pain and relief in her eyes. "Oh?"

"Yes," Fenli said calmly. "You wished to know how Spire Dependence was destroyed."

Bridget nodded wordlessly.

"The skyport, the upper habble, its defenses, and all its people were devoured," Fenli said, calmly licking one paw, "by a mistmaw."

Chapter 28

IAS *Mistshark*, Coordinates Unknown

Colonel Espira stared at his sealed orders. They were not to be opened until the *Mistshark* had carried Madame Cavendish to their final target after the tests were complete.

"I can't believe it," he murmured to Captain Ransom. "That can't be the course."

"This is my airship," Calliope pointed out archly. "I have been steering her around the sky for a number of years now. Over time, I have gained a vague understanding of how navigation works, Colonel. As a result, I can make a fair guess at where she is and where she will end up on a given heading."

He grimaced at her. "How many of your people are down?"

"Forty-three as of this morning," she said, "according to Doctor Calloway. Yours?"

"Twenty-two," Espira said.

"Merciful Builders," Ransom spat. "Better than half your complement. They must have started with your men. Our galley staff went down first, so Calloway thinks they must have poisoned the water."

"If so," Espira said, "it's only a matter of time before it spreads to all of us."

Ransom's tone turned acidic. "That had occurred to me, Colonel." She raked her fingers through her hair, her eyes a little too wide, and paced back and forth across her cabin while he sat at her small table. "Ren," she said more gently, "you saw those weird ships. The creatures on them. And what Cavendish did to them and that poor merchantman. I don't know what Tuscarora's game is, but I'm not going to stand by while the witch destroys another Spire with that monster."

As if the creature had been listening, the misty sky beneath the *Mistshark* reverberated with a low, shuddering moan that scaled slowly up to a lonely wail that lasted several moments and then faded away into echoes and silence.

Espira shuddered. "How did she do it?" he asked. "As if the world isn't dangerous enough, how did Cavendish take control of a bloody mistmaw?"

Ransom shook her head. "Some people think that if they're simply insane and ruthless enough, they can accomplish anything."

"Terrifying," Espira said.

"Oh, that's not the terrifying part," Calliope said.

"No?"

"The terrifying part," she murmured, "is that sometimes they're right."

"God in Heaven," Espira sighed.

Ransom ceased pacing and settled down in the other chair at the table, facing Espira with a serious expression. "Your orders are going to tell you what Tuscarora has in mind," she said, "or at least what he wants you to think he has in mind. This is no time to waver, Colonel. You see what's happening. Whatever Cavendish is doing, it's going to kill your men and mine. I won't stand for it. Neither will you. You're simply being precious, worrying about the instructions of a sealed order in the face of tens of thousands of lives."

Espira shook his head slowly. He stared at the envelope. Thus far, his actions had not amounted to anything irretrievable within the legal structure of the Armada. He had been that cautious, at least. Part of him remembered what he had felt when he was young—the pride and the excitement and the joy of first donning his uniform. The camaraderie of the academy; the other young men who were, like him, striving to achieve, to fulfill their potential, to place their lives, their fortunes, and their honor into the service of Spire Aurora. He remembered the triumph of being accepted into the academy, of the long walk up the spiraling transport ramps to the halls of Flamecrest.

In those days he felt heroic. Invincible. Unstoppable. Fiercely proud of who he was and what he was doing.

When had he lost his faith?

His right hand twitched. As if he could still feel that Albion apprentice's heartbeat fading through the steel of his sword.

Was there any going back?

Opening that envelope, breaking the personal seal of His Majesty Tuscarora himself, would constitute a direct violation of military law. It would shatter the oaths he had sworn as an officer. It would mean that he had stepped beyond a line.

Oh, he could conceal it, he had little doubt. He could, most likely, avoid the consequences of his actions.

But he would know.

He would always know.

Colonel Renaldo Espira had ascended through the ranks of the Armada through hard work, competence, integrity, and loyalty. He had believed, believed with such passion, in the honor and righteousness of his path. God in Heaven, he had given blood, sweat, and tears in droplets beyond counting to attain his position.

Those colonies. He hadn't been able to see clearly what the mistmaw had done to them. But he had been with the teams that observed the results after. The skyports wiped clean. The stone and wooden buildings of the first several habbles of the tower smashed into ruin, empty of life. All that had been left behind were the tools of the workers and the furniture they'd sat upon.

And the children's toys.

His hand twitched harder.

There was no honor here. No honor in what he had been sent to do.

No honor. No faith. No righteousness.

Then Colonel Renaldo Espira squared his shoulders, forced his right hand to move, and tore the envelope open. He withdrew the folded vellum within and read the secret orders thereupon. His jaw tightened and he swallowed as his world dropped away from beneath him.

"Upon reaching our final destination," he said, "I am to execute you and the other officers of the *Mistshark* and give command of the ship to Madame Cavendish and Mister Sark."

"Oh, that *bastard*," Ransom snarled. "I will cut the price of this out of Tuscarora's flesh. And from somewhere dear to the arrogant son of a bitch."

Espira let the hand holding the letter fall into his lap. The only reason Tuscarora could have for such an order was to return the *Mistshark* and its secret weapon to Spire Aurora so they could be used again in the future. His mind tracked down the various trails of logic and came to a single conclusion. He had little doubt that in order to preserve the secret, Tuscarora would have anyone not named Cavendish or Sark promptly executed upon their return to Spire Aurora.

Espira could live with being sacrificed—even knowingly sacrificed— for the good of his home Spire if it meant that others had a chance at life. That was part of a soldier's duty.

But . . . to be thrown away like a pail of refuse—merely to keep a secret.

For his *men* to be so thrown away.

A low and terrible rage began to burn in his chest.

He looked back at the young man he used to be. He stared at the hope, the optimism, the loyalty, the utter naivete.

How *dared* they turn that young man into their attack dog?

It ended here.

No more.

It might well mean his death to stand this ground.

But perhaps that young man—and the other young men like him—was worth it.

No more.

The tremble in his right hand vanished as he folded the page, returned it to the envelope, and left the envelope sitting in the open on Calliope Ransom's table.

He looked up to find her staring at him, her mobile face focused as it searched his expression. She leaned forward intently. "What are you going to do?"

"How long before we arrive at Spire Olympia?" he asked quietly.

"Forty-six hours," she answered.

He considered that information, and a plan began forming in his mind. "Captain," he said, "I shall require your assistance."

Calliope tilted her head, and her eyes widened slowly. Then they sparkled with sudden ferocity, and her mouth lifted into a wolfish smile.

"I intend," Renaldo Espira said, "to become a pirate."

Chapter 29

Dueling Platform, Habble Profit, Spire Olympia

I t's not that I mind wearing a dress precisely," Gwendolyn Lancaster said. "It's just that I haven't done so in quite some time." She smoothed down the plain, dark, badly fitting dress and settled the skirts a little more to her liking, fumbling only slightly because of her sprained and bandaged wrist. "Though honestly, I'm not sure how much of a disguise this is for either of us."

Abigail sighed and fussed with her own dress. Both had come from Tilde's closet, and they were modest, plain, and practical, much as Tilde herself. Abigail was, however, even smaller and slimmer than Miss Lancaster, and the dress hung upon her as though she had draped herself in a brown-and-grey flag. At least the black cape and hood would hide her identity, or so she hoped.

Being in disguise, after all, was the point.

"Nonsense. They're perfectly common pieces of clothing."

"Duchess Hinton," Gwen said calmly, "you would be unmistakably a duchess were you wearing a burlap sack." She sniffed. "And I am a Lancaster."

Abigail had found, in their brief acquaintance, that Miss Lancaster made that fact rather impossible to forget, but she had to admit that the younger woman had a point. Any operative would spot them without difficulty, though Abigail supposed there was no point in her laboring to appear nondescript while Miss Gwendolyn was in her company, and naturally, once she had agreed to be Abigail's second, there was simply no being parted from her.

The pair of them were walking toward the eastern gallery of Habble Profit, a large open space that included a public park featuring fountains and large planters of actual bushes, flowers, and trees. At one end of the gallery, a medium-sized crowd had begun to gather near the dueling platform set up for exactly such activities, and the habble's marshal, sober in his black suit, was already standing upon it.

"Duels are so problematic," Gwen sighed. "Lady H— Abigail, are you quite certain this is wise?"

Abigail fingered her handbag idly, making sure that she still had the vial of poison within it ready. Honestly, there was very little chance she would get to use it, but she did like to be prepared for all contingencies.

"That beast Valesco is doing us the service of fighting another duel today," she said. "Hamish found out about it two hours ago. I want to get a look at him."

"I understand the tactics of it," Gwen said calmly. "But I should think Count Bayard would want to see it for himself."

"Alex has duties aboard *Belligerent* he cannot simply ignore," Abigail sighed. "And your own Captain Grimm is meeting with Valesco's second and arranging details."

Gwen arched an eyebrow. "Valesco has a second second?"

"As many duels as he fights," Lady Hinton replied, "I suppose he might even have a third second standing by."

"Perhaps whoever he's dueling today will save Bayard the trouble and dispatch Valesco for him."

"I should think that hopelessly optimistic," Abigail said, again touching the poison. "But perhaps fate will favor us. At the very least,

I will have a chance to analyze Valesco's stances and his style and to convey them to Alex."

"Do we know the details of Commodore Bayard's meeting?"

"Within another day, I daresay," Abigail said. "Tomorrow morning or tomorrow evening at the latest."

"Where will Bayard want to fight?"

"He's an aeronaut, dear," Abigail said, "and Valesco is not. He'll choose the dueling platform in the skyport."

Gwen raised her eyebrows. "Ah," she said. "How . . . very gladiatorial of him."

Abigail suppressed a smile. Dueling platforms were regulated within the Scriptures by the Merciful Builders and God in Heaven Himself, with standard sizes and surface compositions. The dueling platforms in a Spire's skyport hung out over open air, with yawning two-mile drops beneath them and nothing like safety railings.

Of course, the point of duels was to wound or kill at least fifty percent of the participants, so she supposed safety railings might have been counterproductive to that end. Aeronauts like Alex routinely operated in hazardous conditions in which a fall would give one more time to appreciate impending death but have the same grisly ending. Fighting on the skyport's platform, Bayard would, if nothing else, possess a psychological advantage of confidence and familiarity.

Though, Abigail supposed grimly, it seemed certain that in more than three hundred duels, Valesco had fought on them before. Still, in everything, there was a difference between professionals and amateurs.

"Which protocol shall be engaged, do you think?" Gwen asked.

"Oh, the Protocol Mortis, of course," Abigail replied. "Bayard fights only when he feels it is a matter worth killing a man for."

Or worth dying for, she added mentally, and suppressed a shiver.

For all of her intrigues, her financial empire, and the lives and charities and workers it supported—for all of the balls and dramas and operas and arts—it was her relationship with Bayard that made her life truly worth living. He was a naval officer, so they had always spent long periods of time apart, but she could often afford to travel to meet him, and it only made their reunions the sweeter.

Fear for his safety had always been a part of her world. When he had set off with three light ships in pursuit of the battlecruiser *Itasca*, her heart had been in her throat for the space of a day, but, as always, he had returned victorious against a larger and more powerful foe. That was his habit, in fact.

But the cold logic of reason told her that every time he did so, he was gambling with his life—and good fortune always ran out sooner or later.

She touched the poison in her bag again and had to will herself not to bite her lip.

"You still intend the Protocol Sanguis, I take it?" Gwen asked.

"Yes. My quarrel is with Initiate Hestia, not her champion, and there need not be a loss of life over it. Mistress Montaine should have a chance to yield."

Gwen lifted her eyebrows. "Mistress Montaine should?" she asked with gentle emphasis on the name.

Abigail glanced up at Gwen and for a second let the steel show in her face. "She's quite young."

Gwen looked baffled at that. But then, Abigail supposed, at least she was wise enough to know she should be baffled. Most youths didn't get that far.

"I see," Gwen said.

"I very much doubt that, dear," Abigail said. "But you will."

They had reached the crowd near the dueling platform, and Valesco mounted the platform in an aeronaut's leather breeches, shirtless. He was, to be frank, a magnificent specimen of a man, combining lean grace with obvious muscular power, a warriorborn at the peak of his abilities.

"Oh, my," Gwen murmured. "He's even more muscular than Benny."

Valesco spread his arms to the crowd, and there was a mixture of cheers and derisive jeers. He turned and an Auroran Marine captain tossed him a dueling sword by its handle. Valesco swept it through a couple of arcs, making the air whistle with its passage, its long and flexible blade describing whipping circles and flicking the wax sealing from its razor steel edge.

"Why, um," Gwen said. "Why is he shirtless?"

"I suspect because he likes to show off," Abigail replied. "If he was like most men, it would be to prevent pieces of his own shirt from being driven into a puncture wound and causing infection." She shook her head. "It's sensible. But look at him."

"Hmmm?" Gwen said, not looking away. "Oh, yes. Look at what, exactly, Your Grace?"

"All his scars," Abigail said.

"He has none."

"Precisely," she replied. "He is not in the least afraid of being wounded. So I assume he's taken his shirt off in order to make an impression on young ladies."

"He is . . . rather statuesque," Gwen noted. She sighed and looked back at Abigail. "Would you like me to shoot him? I brought a gun."

Abigail blinked several times and lowered her purse out of easy line of sight before saying, "Miss Lancaster, what a shocking suggestion."

"I could shoot him in the leg, I suppose. Just a little."

"You're carrying a gunpowder weapon and you want to shoot him a little," Abigail said. "Am I understanding you correctly?"

"It was a gift from my dear coz, and I've never yet used it," Gwen said, reaching a hand into her purse. "Honestly, it wouldn't be any trouble."

Abigail choked briefly and then said, "We can't do anything so overt. We're merely here to watch."

"I dislike watching when I can act," Gwen said, removing her hand from her purse. "But I suppose reconnaissance is nearly always wise."

The second duelist, a young man in the green coat of the Olympian merchant marine fleet, arrived along with his second, a slightly older gentleman in a sober suit. He too removed his coat, waistcoat, and shirt and accepted a dueling sword from his second. He drew the blade through a tightly held handkerchief to remove the sealing wax, and waited at his edge of the platform while the two seconds went forward to confer with the marshal.

The marshal went through the public ritual of asking the two seconds whether they had attempted to resolve the dispute peacefully and if there was any recourse but blood. Both dutifully nodded and then shook their heads in turn.

"Does anyone ever back down at this point?" Gwen wondered aloud.

"Oh, of course, often," Abigail replied. "Young people who suddenly see their enemies' swords or pistols or gauntlets realize that they have pressing business that requires them to be alive and unmaimed. They'll usually request another meeting of the seconds to resolve the dispute, perhaps the next day. Then they'll make some appropriate apology or conciliatory gesture, and the matter is done. Sometimes, with pistols or gauntlets, they'll face each other to avoid any accusation of cowardice but discharge their weapons into the air. With blades, at the last moment, they'll change to the Protocol Sanguis, only fight to the first blood, and thus avoid any risk to their reputations that way."

Gwen pressed her lips together. "In my professional experience, 'first blood' and 'to the death' are generally the same thing."

"In boarding actions on airships, I daresay," Abigail agreed. "Duels are an entirely different species of combat—they rely as much upon the mind as upon skill at arms. On the dueling platform, with long, light weapons, sometimes there's hardly a scar. Pistols or gauntlets make that different, of course. But Valesco loves his blades."

Indeed, the Auroran held his blade cheerfully, balancing his weight on his toes as he flexed the steel back and forth in his hands as though impatient to begin.

The grizzled marshal looked between Valesco and the young Olympian. "Gentlemen, in the interests of peace and harmony, would either of you care to remonstrate before bloodshed begins?"

Both men shook their heads.

The marshal nodded. "Very well. Would either of you care to change the protocol of the duel from mortis to sanguis?"

Valesco shook his head, but his opponent hesitated.

Abigail leaned forward. If either participant wished to fight to the first blood or surrender of their opponent, the law required both duelists to adhere to the Protocol Sanguis—though, as Gwen had pointed out, there were ways around that.

Valesco said something that she could not hear to the young man, whose face darkened with fury. The Olympian then firmly shook his head.

"Very well, gentlemen," the marshal sighed, and withdrew a handkerchief from his waistcoat pocket. "Remain in your corners. When this cloth touches the surface of the platform, you may begin. Salute each other."

The Olympian made a textbook salute. Valesco waved his sword in a vague, lazy motion.

The marshal gave Valesco a brief, level look. "Salute me," the marshal said.

Both men did so.

"God in Heaven be with you both, whatever the outcome," the marshal said, and flicked the handkerchief into the air.

Abigail leaned forward, watching intently. She half expected Valesco to bound across the platform and spit his opponent at the moment the handkerchief touched down, but instead he spread his arms, with his sword wide and to one side, and gave his opponent a mocking smile of invitation.

The young Olympian took the bait, taking a bounding crossover step into a long lunge. Had Abigail been attacked so, she could have stepped off the line of attack, crouched low, and punished the overly aggressive assault by skewering her opponent's heart. But instead of ending the duel, Valesco swept the thrust aside with contemptuous ease and struck the young man in the face with the back of his free hand before stepping away from a slow counter slash and opening the distance once more. Again the Auroran said something quietly, and the young Olympian reacted with fury, pressing forward with a more balanced but still aggressive series of attacks that Valesco countered with relaxed precision.

Abigail paid less attention to Valesco's weapon than to his feet and his balance as she hunted for a weak spot in his technique. The man was excellent, perhaps the finest swordsman she'd ever seen. At one point, as the young Olympian pressed forward again, he simply lowered his arms to his sides and laughed mockingly as he stepped in smooth arcs away from the young man's sword, its wickedly sharp tip missing the Auroran by the width of a fingernail.

"This isn't a fight," Gwen said angrily. "Look at that. There's no honor in behaving that way."

"I think we can safely assume that anyone who feels a need to kill three hundred people in duels has, at best, an incomplete understanding of the concept of honor," Abigail said in a hard voice. "He's enjoying it."

The duel went on for several moments more, and both men became covered in a light sheen of sweat. But Valesco was simply smiling and occasionally making comments, and the young Olympian was breathing hard and grunting with fatigue. The young man, his sword arm slowing, made a final burst of effort, a series of deft thrusts and parries that amounted to a credible and formidable attack.

Valesco defeated them methodically, and then, for the first time, his sword lashed out in a blurring, full-speed counterattack. Its sheer speed and power smashed through the Olympian's skilled but imperfect parry.

The young man reeled back, the skin of his forehead opened to the bone. Blood sheeted down over one eye as he staggered, then raised his sword in desperate defense. The crowd gasped and tensed.

Valesco's smile widened and he held his hand up to the marshal. "Respite!" he called, allowing his voice to carry. "I call for respite!"

The young Olympian stared at his opponent with a dull, sickened gaze. Then he nodded his bloodied head once.

The marshal stepped forward between the two men. "Respite has been sought and granted. Return to your starting corners." He drew a pocket watch from his waistcoat and clicked it. "Three minutes' rest."

Abigail's eyes immediately darted to Valesco's corner. He would of course take water, which she could potentially flavor from her vial, but the Marine captain held the canteen warily, eyes alert to any such mischief, and he passed the closed canteen directly into Valesco's hands.

Valesco stared at his opponent as he drank. His stance and expression had changed from blithely amused to something harder, more dangerous, more predatory. His feline eyes focused on the wounded man, and he took slow, catlike strides back and forth in his corner.

"Oh, the bastard," Gwen breathed. "The utter hubris."

Abigail kept her lips pressed firmly together as the Olympian's second tried desperately to stanch the blood flowing into his friend's eye.

A cold feeling flowed into her stomach.

Bayard was not as skilled as Valesco.

As a fighter, Alex was a technician, an engineer, intimately familiar with exact forces and counterforces. He won his fights, despite his size and his lesser reach, by discipline and focus upon the cold mathematics of a duel. She knew his mind in these matters as intimately as she did her own.

Valesco held every advantage, and the man's skill was, even if only slightly, superior to Bayard's. Even had their skill levels been equal, Valesco's greater height, reach, and speed—leaving aside entirely his warriorborn strength and endurance—would overcome Bayard. Perhaps not quickly but inevitably.

She remembered with a shudder the advice of her father's master-at-arms when she had learned her basic self-defense: *A good big person beats a good small person.* Bayard, if he fought this man to perfection, would eventually weary and slow down. The warriorborn wouldn't. It might make for an epic duel of song and tale, but she knew with a sickened certainty the most likely ending.

Oh, certainly, there was always the chance that outrageous good luck would favor Bayard or that foul fortune would fell Valesco. But chance played no favorites and could as easily reverse that balance and seal her love's fate. Some deceptive stratagem might suffice, she supposed, but Bayard had always eschewed such things in favor of focusing on pure skill. He had spent a lifetime victorious by doing so, and it seemed unlikely that he would—or could—change course now.

But worst of all, Valesco had found the chink in Bayard's psychological armor—namely, herself. By openly and publicly treating her with such outrageous cruelty and disrespect, he had stoked Bayard's ire to dangerous levels. Hamish had told her of Alex's fury when he had been given the news, how only Grimm's intervention had saved Alex from rushing into what would have amounted to a blindly furious brawl.

Alex was more contained now, but her people had been watching his challenge at the embassy, and once again Grimm had been forced to restrain him after a comment from Valesco. The Auroran had probably done something similar to the young Olympian: created an emotional and psychological vulnerability and then goaded the young man with it until he had been too furious to consider his circumstances.

Valesco wasn't a fool. He knew Bayard's skill, and the Auroran would treat him with the respect such a dangerous man deserved. He would seek every advantage, lancing Bayard with one comment after another. Alex's strength in a duel was his cool, calm intellect. His weakness was his sense of honor. Valesco would know what to say to enrage a man like Bayard, and even a flicker in Alex's discipline would be opening enough for Valesco to exploit. Enough to kill Alex.

Lady Hinton knew enough of swordplay and of Bayard to realize a single crystalline truth: if Alex fought this man, she would in all probability lose him. It was as simple as that.

And she herself had become the weapon that Valesco would use to kill him.

Her heart began to beat very quickly.

Steps would have to be taken.

A tall woman in a dark cloak stepped up to their side and said, "God in Heaven, he's phenomenal, is he not?"

Gwen's hand plunged into her purse as Felicia Montaine, the Atlantean champion Abigail herself would be fighting, lowered her hood and regarded them with cool feline eyes. "Fast. Strong. Perfect technique. I wouldn't care to fight that man, even being warriorborn."

Abigail put a restraining hand on Gwen's arm and said calmly, "Even warriorborn bleed, Mistress Montaine." She exchanged a small bow with the much taller woman.

"Bayard should have waited for Valesco to issue a challenge," Montaine noted clinically, her eyes going to the wounded man in the ring. "He could have chosen pistols or gauntlets. He might have had something like even odds in that kind of duel." She looked down at Abigail. "So might you."

Abigail smiled faintly. "Does Initiate Hestia's mouth hurt very much?"

Montaine smiled widely. "Oh, well said. Still, you understand that the Spectrum cannot allow you to simply walk away after such an act. Protocol Sanguis or not."

Lady Hinton arched an eyebrow. "I assure you that I am aware of the realities in our bout."

Montaine looked down at Gwen. "Mistress Lancaster, is it not? I am told you are Lady Hinton's second, as I am Initiate Hestia's."

Gwen faced the warriorborn woman stiffly. "I am, Mistress Montaine."

Montaine's nostrils flared. "Goodness. Carrying a gunpowder weapon in your purse? You're a serious woman."

"I've not gotten to shoot anyone with it yet," Gwen replied. "I'm interested to see the difference in effect between pistol and gauntlet."

The Atlantean woman's smile became a trifle uneasy. "Well, it is our duty to arrange the details. To that end, I thought I would offer you lunch."

"I'd sooner dine with silkweavers," Gwen said calmly. "But I'm willing to set terms."

"Oh, excellent," Montaine purred. "Ah, excuse me, ladies. The respite period is nearly up."

All three women turned back to face the blood-speckled dueling platform as the marshal once more stepped forward with his handkerchief and received the salutes of the duelists, this time in earnest by both parties.

The young Olympian, his head wrapped in an improvised bandage made from his own ripped shirt, faced Valesco with his face pale. He was shaking.

Valesco gave the young man an approving nod.

And when the handkerchief touched the ground, the warrior-born duelist blurred across the platform in a lunge that could scarcely be seen, defeated the younger man's parry with a liquid dip of his blade, and slid his sword quite easily into the Olympian's heart.

The young man gasped and stared, his eyes losing focus.

Valesco twisted the blade and withdrew it with smooth, professional ease.

Abigail looked away as the young man fell to the platform's surface. There was a physician standing by, and he rushed to mount the platform, along with the Olympian's second, to go to the young man's aid, but there was no need. Not with that strike. Valesco had killed the young Olympian. It would simply take a moment for his body to realize it.

In her mind's eye, Abigail could see Bayard in precisely the same state, eyes unfocused and confused, face rapidly turning corpse grey as the life bled out of him.

Oh, God. Oh, God in Heaven.

Bayard.

Valesco was already leaving. A group of men appeared around the Marine captain and the duelist and hurried them from the platform. That escort was customary to avoid sudden and passionate reprisals from the loved ones of the fallen.

"Does the sight of blood disturb you, Your Grace?" asked Felicia Montaine a moment later, a small smile on her lips.

"Always," Abigail replied. She pushed thoughts of her lover from her mind for the moment. She had a duty, after all, and her own part to play. She took a steadying breath, then looked up and met her opponent's eyes. "Even when it is necessary. Mistress Montaine, I am requesting the Protocol Sanguis for reasons I'm sure you would not understand. I shall give you every opportunity to preserve your life. Don't force me to take it."

Montaine blinked at that warning, and her expression gained an edge of wariness.

Abigail lifted a hand in a signal, and Hamish and his trusted men appeared from the crowd to bracket her.

"Mistress Lancaster," she said, "I trust you and Mistress Montaine will arrange things to the mutual satisfaction of myself and Initiate Hestia."

"Of course," Gwen said, inclining her head to Abigail. She turned to smile sweetly up at Felicia Montaine. "Shall we walk and talk? I find my stomach doesn't turn so much if I can move a little."

Montaine looked uneasily from Abigail to Gwen, and her expression turned into a frown. Then she nodded, and the two of them walked off together as the crowd, muttering darkly, began to disperse.

Abigail watched them go.

On the platform, the physician asked the fallen duelist's second for his coat and laid it gently over the dead young Olympian's head and shoulders. The second laid his hand on the corpse's chest and bowed his head, shoulders shaking.

Abigail stared at the dead man and his sobbing friend.

That could easily be two other men she knew.

Indeed.

Steps would have to be taken.

"Hamish," she said in a cold, hard voice.

"Ma'am," the big bodyguard said easily.

"We're going to the skyport, to AFS *Belligerent*. I want to speak to Alex at once."

■ ■ ■ Chapter 30 ■ ■ ■

AFS *Belligerent*, Skyport, Habble Olympia

G rimm strode through the skyport toward *Belligerent*. The meeting with Captain Chavez of the *Conquistodor* had gone smoothly enough and as expected. Valesco had asked for blades, the duel would be held upon the skyport's dueling platform, and Protocol Mortis would be in effect.

Chavez had genuinely tried to seek remonstration, inquiring if an apology from Valesco would suffice to end the matter, but Grimm's instructions from Bayard had been clear: the only acceptable redress of his grievance would be taken from Valesco's body. Chavez, after inquiring after the possibility of Valesco apologizing to the lady and making other restitution in the form of remuneration, seemed to accept Bayard's position as inevitable.

Footsteps, purposeful and quick, approached from behind Grimm, and he made sure he had a hand on his sword before he turned to look over his shoulder.

Captain Ravenna of *Stormmaiden* wore her black dragon hide and a long leather coat, and her hair bounced left and right in a braid festooned with small dragon plumes as she walked. She gave him a wide, sunny smile and fell into step beside him. "Captain Grimm."

"Good morning, Captain," he said. "I trust you enjoyed yourself at the reception?"

She heaved a theatrical sigh. "I barely got warmed up with a little dancing." She gave him a direct look. "I was hoping you and I could find some quiet time to try a few steps, but I suppose politics ruin everything."

"Generally and specifically," Grimm confirmed. "I hate them."

"How is Bayard?"

"Furious," Grimm said. "Heatedly so. I've never seen him so angry."

Ravenna's smile became a sober, serious look. "You Albions, you're so reserved. You act as if by simply having enough will, you can control every reaction, every facet of human nature." She shook her head. "People don't work that way, Frank."

"I suppose your recommendation is unbounded licentiousness and revelry?" he murmured.

She flashed him a quick, bright smile. "God in Heaven, a joke? From you? Perhaps there's hope after all." She shook her head and said, "You can't hold yourself stiff as a board all the time. Human beings are animals too. We're built that way. We respond to animal things, no matter how badly we wish it were otherwise."

"'Animal things'?" Grimm inquired.

"Mating," Ravenna said frankly. "Territory. Protecting those under our care." She shook her head. "This duel with Valesco targets all three. Valesco made it personal, not some matter of airy honor. Once Bayard is under threat of his life, he'll react like an animal defending his mate, no matter what reason might say.

"I've seen Bayard fight," Ravenna continued. "He's like some kind of warrior from the old dramas. He comes straight at you and beats you fair and square because he's better and more disciplined. But this time he isn't. I've seen the Auroran kill two Pikers in duels in Spire Aurora. He's the single deadliest swordsman I've ever seen. I wouldn't send any of my warriorborn up against him in a fair fight—and that includes myself."

Grimm frowned at Ravenna but . . . he couldn't exactly gainsay her. "I wish they were using pistols or gauntlets."

"They're not," she said bluntly. "And if I were betting my ship, I'd put my money on Valesco."

The calm statement hit Grimm like a punch in the belly. He glowered at her and said, "Tell me what you truly think, Ravenna."

She shrugged easily. "It accomplishes nothing to kill the messenger, Frank, however bad the news." She grimaced. "And it gets worse."

"Worse?"

She dropped her voice to a lower volume and stepped closer, so that their bodies pressed together. She slid beneath his arm. Grimm's face heated up as if the entire skyport were staring at the both of them, but he couldn't deny how pleasant she felt there.

"Word from our chief of naval intelligence is that the Auroran Armada sailed three days ago with damned near every destroyer and light cruiser they have running screen. They chased off everything in sight, dipped into the mesosphere, and no one knows where they are now."

"Merciful Builders," Grimm muttered, glancing around. "Are your people sharing information with the Aetherium Fleet?"

"And with the old spider," Ravenna confirmed. "But the Aetherium dreadnoughts are still positioned around Albion."

"Whatever has been wiping out these colonies," Grimm said, "I suspect Fleet wants its heaviest guns ready to defend against it."

"Or they want them ready to sail against Spire Aurora the moment they know that a sizable portion of the Armada is out of position," Ravenna noted.

"Possibly," Grimm admitted. "Tuscarora's aggression leaves him prone to overextending himself."

"Yes," Ravenna said wryly, "his aggression has been such a handicap thus far." She shook her head. "War is coming. Tuscarora knows it. If your people won't see that, he's going to send you all down in flames."

"Albion has stood for a very long time," Grimm said stiffly. "It will not fall to a pack of Auroran wolves."

"Albion was stupid enough to cast you from their precious Fleet," Ravenna countered. "If they do fall, I can find a berth for *Predator* in Pike. You and your crew would be welcome."

Grimm exhaled through his nose. His arm around her tightened slightly and he said, "Thank you, Ravenna. But I hardly think it will be necessary."

She rolled her eyes. "I'm trying to tell you, Frank—that's the problem." She shook her head. "When is the duel?"

"Noon tomorrow."

"On the skyport platform, I take it?"

"Obviously."

"I'll be there," she said. She squeezed his waist with a surprisingly strong arm and said, "I hope I'm wrong. I hope we have something to celebrate after."

"Thank you," he said.

She swung into him and drew him down firmly for a kiss that was utterly inappropriate for the venue, squeezed his arm, and turned to stride away, her braid swinging, the plumes in it sparkling in many colors in the light.

Grimm watched her go.

Damn the woman. He appreciated the intelligence she'd shared, but he wished that she would bring good news into his life on occasion.

Worse, she wasn't wrong about Bayard. If she was also right about Valesco . . .

He blew out a breath and turned to find a trio of Atlantean aeronauts in their dull grey leathers looking after Ravenna and then staring at him with broad grins.

He gave them a stiff, polite bow and then continued on to *Belligerent*.

After a sentry challenged him and then waved him by almost before he'd identified himself, Grimm went up the long ramp onto the battlecruiser. He was met by Bayard's XO, a brawny commander named Waggoner, who looked uncomfortable.

"Sir," he greeted Grimm calmly. "Ah, the captain is in a private meeting."

Grimm pursed his lips, put his hands behind his back, and kept walking toward Bayard's cabin. "With Lady Hinton, I take it?"

"Yes, sir," Waggoner said, his expression distressed as he kept pace. "Captain, I don't think you want to interrupt."

"I'll manage," Grimm said calmly. "Thank you, Commander."

Waggoner grimaced and shook his head but waved for Grimm to continue, then peeled off as though he himself wanted nothing to do with whatever was going on. That seemed ominous.

Grimm realized why as he approached the cabin.

Raised voices shouted within.

He paused outside before knocking. The ship's armored walls were too thick to make out any of the conversation from inside, but Alex was speaking in his command voice, which Grimm could only assume was a last resort and likely to be a futile maneuver when dealing with someone like Abigail.

Indeed, she answered Bayard in a sharp, passionate tone that

Grimm had never heard from her before. He had never known them to have more than the gentlest and most reasoned of conflicts with each other. Certainly, Grimm had never known them to do verbal battle to the degree he could now hear.

Grimm supposed that he had very little to say to anyone when it came to matters of relationships. The last time he'd seen his wife had been after airship-to-airship combat, and he'd been preparing to accept her surrender after she'd commanded transport in the devastating raid upon the skyport of Habble Landing that completely destroyed it, along with a dozen airships—*Predator* very nearly one of them. But she'd managed to escape, which was no great testament to his strength as a captain—or as a husband either, he supposed.

The voices rose to an even higher pitch, and he debated whether to simply depart. He felt awkward and out of place. But he had genuine business here as Alex's second. He couldn't simply walk away.

He tried to ignore the very reasonable voice in his mind that sounded a great deal like Ravenna's and that pointed out that this conflict between Bayard and his long-term lover was more evidence that Alex was not in the proper mental state to handle a creature like Valesco.

He couldn't walk away.

Grimm clenched his jaw and knocked sharply on the cabin's door.

The voices came to an abrupt halt, of course. A moment later, the door was unbolted and opened, and Bayard, in his shirtsleeves, glowered up at Grimm. He all but vibrated with energy, and Grimm had the distinct impression that had he proven to be Waggoner, Bayard might have chewed him up one side and down the other.

"Mad," Bayard said, his expression slipping into something less hard and more haggard. "Ah, yes. I suppose you've dealt with Valesco's second."

"Indeed," Grimm said in a gentle voice. "I'm sorry. I wouldn't have interrupted except that . . ."

"Of course, of course," Bayard said. He drew in a breath and checked over his shoulder, then stood aside. "Please, come in."

Grimm entered, his eyes adjusting to the cabin's comfortable dimness. "Ah," he said, "Abigail. I'm very sorry to interrupt."

Lady Hinton, dressed in oddly plain and ill-fitting clothing, was clutching her purse and staring hard at Bayard, who stood stiffly, not facing her. "Not at all, Madison. I believe we have more or less exhausted useful conversation at this point in any case."

Bayard exhaled through his nose and shot her a hard look. Then something in his expression softened and he said, "Abby, I shouldn't have raised my voice. You do not deserve such treatment. I apologize."

Lady Hinton's expression twisted into something Grimm couldn't properly identify. Then she sighed and said, "I'm hardly some recruit to be frightened by a barking officer, Alex. I gave you reason to be frustrated. I will not apologize for what I had to say." She glanced at Grimm and then down, and her voice softened. "But I am sorry I did not say it with more kindness."

The two faced each other for a moment, and clearly neither was willing to budge an inch. But neither were they incognizant of each other's feelings. Bayard offered her a proper bow, which she returned with an equally careful curtsy.

"Dinner tonight?" he asked. "We can both . . . attempt to improve upon today."

"I will look forward to it," she said in a subdued voice, and lowered her eyes in what Grimm could only believe was weariness. "Madison, would you excuse me? I am quite certain Initiate Hestia will attempt some kind of etheric mischief, and I must consult Master Ferus and Miss Folly regarding countermeasures."

Grimm bowed to her deeply and said, "Of course, Abby. This is a difficult time for all of us."

She gave him a wan smile without ever quite meeting his eyes and swept rapidly out of the cabin.

Grimm watched her go, frowning.

Bayard closed the door behind Abigail and shot the bolt. Then he leaned his head against the copper-clad steel with a long, slow sigh.

"Alex," Grimm said, "are you quite all right?"

"We haven't fought like that in a very long time," Bayard replied. "God in Heaven, I need a drink. Will you join me?"

"Not this early," Grimm replied. Then he added diffidently, "Nor should you be drinking the day before a duel."

"Merciful Builders," Bayard cursed, going to his liquor cabinet. He roughly seized a bottle of his favorite cognac, tore the stopper from it, and sloshed some liquid into a tumbler. His voice was hardened with frustration when he spoke. "As if I had not fought more duels by the age of twenty than either of you have fought in your lives. I know precisely what I am doing, Captain Grimm."

"I'm aware of that," Grimm said gently. "Alex, you are already engaged for dinner. Do we really need to retread the ground you and Abigail have already covered?"

"That depends," Bayard snapped. "Are you here to tell me that I can't beat Valesco as well?"

Grimm lifted his chin. "He's younger than you, Alex. He's fought more duels. He has the advantage of height and reach. And he's warriorborn."

Bayard downed the cognac with a defiant glare. "I know that."

Grimm frowned. Then he squared his shoulders to Bayard and said, "You wouldn't be this angry if you weren't afraid."

Bayard's face went red, and his eyes flicked to where his sword hung over the back of a chair. Then he closed his eyes and took a deep breath through his nose. When he opened them again, he poured a modest amount of cognac into his glass and slumped back against the liquor cabinet in a more relaxed slouch.

"Of course I'm afraid," he said quietly. "I know what Valesco is."

Grimm nodded and waited. It seemed the time to listen.

"He's . . . God in Heaven, man, the man is a murderer. A monster. Abigail watched him duel some poor Olympian boy today. He tortured him to death." Alex shook his head. "And I'm not as fast as I used to be. Oh, good technique makes up for that. And it wouldn't be the first time I fought a warriorborn. But it's been years since then, and those fights were very close things." He opened his shirt to show an ugly puckered scar over the left side of his chest. "Through the lung. If I'd been wearing boots with thicker soles, he'd have gotten my heart."

"Then how are you going to beat Valesco?" Grimm asked.

"His arrogance is his only weakness," Bayard replied. "But . . . I'm afraid my reputation works against me there. I'm one of perhaps half a dozen men who has beaten warriorborn in duels with blades. If he doesn't take me seriously or if he slips up, I'll take him—and he knows it." He shook his head and sipped from the glass. "And damn it, the man knew where to strike to provoke me."

"Abigail."

Bayard nodded. "Even now I can't . . . I want him dead, Mad. More than dead. Beaten. Humiliated. I know that my anger is a weapon that will turn in my own hand and yet I cannot set it aside."

"Even knowing it was done entirely to manipulate you," Grimm said quietly.

"You've been in love," Bayard said quietly. "I notice that it may have had some small effect on your judgment two years ago. You let her go."

Grimm exhaled slowly. "I suppose you aren't wrong."

Bayard smiled wanly. "Naturally." He finished the rest of the small drink and set the glass down with a decisive click. "All of this discussion is academic at this point in any case."

"Is it?" Grimm asked.

"My friend, I feel obliged to point out to you that the duel is already arranged. Should I fail to fight, it will fall to you to do so." He looked up at Grimm frankly. "Do you even own a dueling blade?"

"No," Grimm answered quietly.

Bayard lifted his hand, palm up. "There it is," he said. "To lose the duel would be a devastating public blow to Albion. To refuse to fight it at all would be to announce to all the world that we are afraid of Aurora. We would stand alone."

"You knew," Grimm said quietly. "From the beginning."

"Yes," Bayard said. "I knew the odds were long. I discussed the matter with His Majesty. He considered sending Benedict Sorellin-Lancaster in my place, but the young man is a novice. Valesco would eat him without salt."

Grimm settled down on a chair at the small table, his elbows on his knees, and took a moment to think. Then he nodded and said, "Then how will you beat him?"

Bayard smiled faintly. "Abigail's play has already reduced the impact, should I lose."

"I note," Grimm said, "that she too is fighting a warriorborn."

"She's fighting a bravo," Bayard said absently. "Felicia Montaine has dueled only young hotheads and fools. There are hundreds like her, and I judge Abigail will acquit herself ably."

Grimm blinked. "You're that confident in her?"

Bayard's mouth curled up at one corner. "Oh, yes."

Grimm nodded, taking that in. "Then how," he repeated with gentle emphasis, "will you beat him?"

"How are dragons slain, old friend?" Bayard asked. "With will, skill, and steel. I am no stranger to the dueling platform. Valesco shall have the fight of his life. In the end, win or lose, that is what will matter most to Albion."

Grimm thought about the opinion of the only dragonslayer he knew and suppressed a shudder. "But not to you, Alex."

Bayard looked down and nodded. "I didn't swear my life to the defense of myself, old boy. And there is always the chance that fortune will turn on Valesco. If he slips up in the least, I'll put my steel in his heart."

Grimm nodded and clasped his fingers, frowning down at his own square hands. "Alex, I must insist that you have no more drink. Have you broken your fast for today?"

"Not yet."

"Then as your second, I will send for food. You will eat it with copious amounts of water. Then you will stretch and rest. I shall return at sundown and give you a light workout. Then you shall have a healthy supper with Abigail and go to an early bed."

Bayard's eyes wrinkled at the corners, and he waved a hand. "As you wish . . . Admiral Grimm."

"Hmph," Grimm said, and set about sending for a meal.

They ate together in companionable silence, with Grimm pointedly refilling Bayard's cup with fresh water every time he so much as sipped from it. Alex tolerated this treatment with good nature.

"Mad," he said quietly at the end of the meal.

"Yes?"

"It is a great honor to be your friend," Bayard said. "Should . . . tomorrow not go well, there are letters in my bureau."

"Should you reduce me to a mailman, Alex, I do not think I shall forgive you."

Bayard chuckled. He lifted his cup to Grimm and said, "To fortune. May she be with and against the proper individuals."

"To will, skill, and steel," Grimm answered. They touched cups and drank.

Bayard began to choke.

Grimm looked up at his friend.

Bayard's cup fell from his hand and clattered to the deck. Bayard began to cough, his face reddening. He stared up at Grimm for a moment, his eyes very wide, shocked. Alex stared at his hand, which was trembling violently.

Then his eyes rolled up and back, and Bayard collapsed to the deck beside his spilled cup.

Chapter 31

Skyport, Spire Olympia

Abigail met Hamish in the skyport, and his security detail fell in around them as she headed back for her apartments.

"Well?" he asked her. "Shall I put Tilde and her long gun in position, Your Grace?"

She grimaced. "Bayard wouldn't hear me," she said. She dropped her voice to its deepest register and mimicked his inflections. "'God in Heaven, woman. The entire point of the duel is to show the world we do not fear them. If Valesco turns up dead after I've dropped the gauntlet, there will be no end to the suspicion and questions. I have not lived a lifetime in service to Albion to blacken her honor now.'"

Hamish took that in without changing expression and then repeated in exactly the same tone, "Shall I put Tilde and her long gun in position, Your Grace?"

"Bother, no," Abigail sighed. "And let us hope Valesco doesn't choke on his dinner. Alex would never let me forget it. I will find some other course. I hope."

"Ah," Hamish said with no particular emphasis. He tensed for a moment as someone approached the security detail through the crowded skyport, but it proved to be one of his men, who nodded to him and, while breathing hard, spoke in a low, quick voice.

"Lady Gwen has returned to the apartments, Your Grace," he said. "She has completed negotiations with Mistress Montaine."

"Excellent," Abigail said. "At least one thing is going smoothly."

"Your Grace," Hamish said in a tone of mild rebuke.

Abigail smiled briefly at him. "I know. You hate it when I tempt fate."

"Pride goes before destruction, Your Grace," he said firmly. "And I'll be the one standing between it and you, ma'am."

Abigail waved a hand as they paused while a team of men went by hauling a loaded wagon toward an old Albion merchant ship. "Fate is simply the accumulation of choices, Hamish, and choice is a matter of will. I will not permit these . . . predators to have their way."

"When you say it, Your Grace," Hamish said in a very neutral tone, "it sounds so simple."

She pressed her lips together and gave him a look that he did not seem to notice. "Yes. Well. It is all rather simple."

He gave her another expressionless look as they passed a slow line of monks of the Way in their saffron robes who went by murmuring a quiet chant in relaxed unison.

Abigail sighed. "I will allow that simple is not the same thing as easy."

At that, Hamish's eyes wrinkled at the corners, and he almost smiled. They were just passing a Dalosian merchant ship that had recently docked and was unloading.

"Most employers would not tolerate such insouciance, you know," she told him fondly.

"I'll work on that, Your Grace," he said. "We should talk about my pay when this business is done."

"Hamish!" she said, feigning shock. "I am but a poor maiden aunt!"

"Man has expenses," he responded calmly. He cleared his throat. "When he's getting married."

Abigail stopped and stared up at him in shock. "Hamish, is some poor girl now distressed?"

"No, Your Grace," Hamish said easily. "It's Tilde."

Abigail found her face lifting into a smile and her heart lightening for a moment. "What? You know my rule about fraternization between my people, Hamish."

"Well, ma'am, my mother was a Piker. You know how they are with rules."

She burst out in a merry laugh and put a hand warmly on his shoulder. "I knew I should have fired you years ago."

"Yes, Your Grace," Hamish said. "Now, about that raise—"

Someone shouted, and Abigail saw motion out of the corner of her eye. She began to move, but Hamish was faster. The tall, narrow-shouldered man seized her unceremoniously by the belt and the hand that was on his shoulder, and hauled her off her feet as if she were a toddler. They both wound up on the spirestone floor of the skyport while a great crashing thud turned into the rippling cracks of shattering iron, and she was suddenly inundated by a spray of something warm and wet and reeking of alcohol.

"Go, go, go!" Hamish roared to his team.

Two men pulled Abigail and Hamish to their feet and immediately enveloped her on either side as the point man of the security team raised his gauntlet and fired a howling blast into the air, causing enough confusion to clear some of the crowd from in front of them. The wedge of large men immediately seized momentum and charged forward into the opening, blades out, gauntlets glowing. Others in the crowd scattered from their path, and those who were too slow got none-too-gentle encouragement from the team.

Abigail looked back over her shoulder to see a shattered cask nearly as tall as herself upon the spirestone ground. Its contents of spirits had spewed everywhere. Above, she saw the cargo crane on the deck of the Dalosian merchantman they'd been passing. Its ether-silk loading net had torn right through, the ripped ends swinging wildly.

God in Heaven. If it hadn't been for Hamish, she would have died in a hideous accident.

Then her stomach went cold.

No.

If not for Hamish, she would have been *murdered*.

The thought stunned her as it went through her head. Fighting to look back at the crowd through the looming forms of her body-guards, she tried to take note of everything.

A slight figure in the grey leathers of an Atlantean aeronaut, probably a female, vanished into the busy skyport in the direction opposite the one in which her men were taking her.

"Wait!" she shouted. "Hamish!"

But her voice was lost in the barking commands of the security team and the cries of the panicked crowd. Her men would be focused on getting her out alive, and they wouldn't stop until they were sure she was safe. There was no way whatsoever she could keep them from carrying out their duty.

Abigail wanted to howl with frustration.

Sturdy Tilde in her plain gown handed Abigail tea in a fine cup, and then immediately passed over a copper-clad metal flask. Abigail took both gratefully and dosed her tea with a bit of the spirits. Hamish's favorite, she noted with a small smile.

"Thank you, Tilde," she said.

"Of course, Your Grace," Tilde said. "I'll get my long gun and put an end to this Atlantean problem, shall I?"

Abigail sighed. She felt safe back in her apartments for the most part, but Hamish lurked near enough to seize her again as though expecting another attack. Miss Folly stood at the door with her eyes half closed and one hand on the pouch of little burned-out lumin crystals at her throat.

"It is extremely unwise to attack an etherealist with etheric weapons, dear," Abigail said. "If they're at all aware of it—and from what I've read, they nearly always are—they can turn them back against you without particular effort."

Tilde considered that and then nodded firmly. "My gunpowder rifle, then."

Abigail blinked. "Goodness."

"Swapped it for an old gauntlet with a Piker last year," Tilde noted. "For just such an occasion as this."

"Now, now," Hamish said. "We don't know it was an assassination attempt."

"Don't you tell me what's what, you great, dark lummox," Tilde said fiercely. "It's obvious the Atlanteans tried to kill Her Grace."

"She's safe now," Hamish said soothingly.

"Oh, aye. Until she walks out the door of her own apartments," Tilde said.

"Can't assassinate a visiting head of state, Tilde," Hamish said.

"And why not? I've not had much opportunity to practice with the rifle, but I daresay I can get close enough that it won't make a difference."

"That's enough of that kind of talk," Abigail said decisively. She looked at Tilde and Hamish fondly, warmed by their protective instincts. "Though should I change my mind, I shall consult with both of you without delay."

From the doorway, Miss Folly said in a dreamy voice, "Oh, I should tell Her Grace that they've returned."

Hamish drew a gunpowder pistol and held it by his leg. He went to the door and opened it carefully. He exchanged words in low tones with one of the men on guard and then opened the door to admit Gwendolyn Lancaster and Master Ferus.

The old etherealist bustled in and went immediately to the heater and warmed his gnarled, strong hands by it. "Well," he said. "Well, well, well, well, well. That was interesting."

Lady Lancaster, now dressed in her shipboard leathers, grimaced and said, "Is there any tea?"

"Of course, Lady," Tilde said, and provided some immediately.

Gwen accepted it with a smile and sat down across from Abigail. "According to Master Ferus, the netting holding that hogshead of spirits was . . . etherically snipped somehow."

"Simple application of forces," Master Ferus said, and rubbed his temples with an unsteady hand. "Folly, I'll need a dragon plume, please. Oh, and tea. Oh, and my dueling suit. Lay it out for me if you would, please."

"Of course, master," Folly said, and went to the tea service and poured Ferus a cup. He accepted it with a faint smile, and she left the room.

Master Ferus sipped the tea and said, "I'm very much afraid that an etherealist tried to murder you, Your Grace," he said.

"Initiate Hestia," Abigail said darkly.

"In all probability," Ferus replied. He paced back and forth, cupping his tea in both hands. "Some things become clear."

Abigail frowned. "Do they?"

"Her Grace refers to the unique psychological traits and compulsions of etherealists as quirks, I believe."

"Her Grace does," Abigail replied.

Master Ferus nodded. "I'm not sure that you're aware of how severe they can become with the ongoing practice of etherealism. One of the more skilled etherealists I know will quite literally attempt to murder anyone he meets who does not immediately accede to an irrational demand, for example. Which, at least in my opinion, goes a few steps further than quirky."

"Oh, my," Abigail replied. "Yes, that does seem . . . like it would make life rather awkward."

"Indeed. He must live on the surface because of it." Master Ferus shook his head. "The practice of the ethereal arts is inherently damaging to the human brain. We understand it only incompletely, but when etheric energy passes through it, some areas of the brain simply stop working." Thoughtfully, he took another sip of tea. "Marvelous engine, the brain. It seeks out ways to continue to pass thought and energy through, although often by more circuitous routes. Depending upon one's life experiences and personality and so forth, those routes can pass through any number of portions of the mind, such as Miss Folly's centers of social interaction."

"Which is why she has such difficulty making eye contact or speaking directly to another person," Abigail suggested.

"Precisely," Master Ferus said. "And why I need the reassurance of my collection. Excuse me." He rose and paced back to the guest chambers in her apartments, returning a moment later with a satisfied look on his face. "All there, except for a dragon plume. Apparently, my alternate routes run through the part of my brain that keeps inventory."

He shook his head bemusedly. "I should judge that, for Initiate Hestia, continuing to function mentally means a greater use of whatever portion of her brain controls her reaction to danger."

Lady Lancaster frowned. "In what way, Master Ferus?"

"Rumor has it that at least three members of the Spectrum immediately superior to Initiate Hestia have died in the last three years," he said. "All of them women. All of them in terrible accidents. The first of them her own mother."

Abigail shuddered. That seemed ominous. "You think she was compelled to kill them," she said quietly.

"I suspect so," Master Ferus said. "That's an instinct, of course. It could be that she's simply a horribly murderous individual. I haven't lived as long as I have by ignoring my instincts, but whether she's driven to it or simply enjoys the exercise of power, Your Grace, I judge that you are in danger of etheric methods being used against you during your duel."

"If Her Grace is not killed somehow even before then," Tilde said, outraged.

Ferus bobbed an eyebrow, took a sip of tea, and said, "Quite."

Abigail set her tea down and folded her hands in her lap. The idea of a mad etherealist out to claim her life was more than a little disquieting. "Master Ferus," she said, "what would you suggest?"

"That depends," the old man said. "When is the duel?"

"Tomorrow at sunset," Gwen said, "on Habble Profit's dueling platform." She gave Abigail an apologetic grimace. "The skyport's platform is already being used."

"Just as well," Abigail assured her. "I've no particular head for heights."

"Gauntlets or blades?" Ferus asked.

"Blades," Lady Lancaster replied, and Abigail serenely nodded approval.

Ferus blew out a breath. "Well, then, I shall, if Folly can find that damned dragon plume, accompany you to the appointment."

"Do you think you can prevent any kind of etheric mischief?" Abigail asked.

"Oh, I should very much doubt that," Master Ferus said. "But I shall endeavor to provide enough counter mischief of my own to keep Madame Hestia occupied. Then all you need worry about is outfighting a warriorborn with a number of kills of her own on the dueling platform."

Abigail found herself smiling at that. "That should indeed be my problem."

"If you like," Lady Lancaster offered, her face sincere, "I can try my hand. I'm better with gauntlets than blades, but—"

"Nonsense," Abigail said. "If I let you do any such thing, your parents should never speak to me again, and it would make socializing at home most awkward. We'd have to sit at different tables at every event, it would be an absolute nightmare."

Gwen smiled faintly. "Then I suppose I shall settle for my duties as your second."

"Thank you," Abigail said seriously, "for offering to be my champion. But I am not ignorant of the blade, and I very much knew what I was doing when I struck Initiate Hestia."

Gwen looked around the room and awkwardly said with care, "Your Grace . . . are you quite sure you know what you're getting involved with here? I've had ample opportunity to train with my warriorborn cousin, and I assure you that you are overmatched in terms of speed and power."

"We shall see," Abigail said calmly. "Well, I don't suppose we might find something to eat? I can't do battle on an empty stomach, after all."

Gwen chuckled and started to say something, but there was a rapid knocking at the door.

Hamish calmly took up his weapon again and went to see what was the matter. He returned a moment later, leading a man in an Aetherium Fleet commander's uniform: Bayard's second-in-command, a tall and powerful man named Waggoner.

Abigail took one look at his haggard expression and rose from her seat, a cold feeling trickling along her spine.

"Lady Hinton," Waggoner said, bowing, his body rigid with tension, "I'm afraid I am the bearer of bad news. The commodore has . . . been stricken. Captain Grimm asks that you come to him at once."

■ ■ ■ Chapter 32 ■ ■ ■

Spirearch's Chambers, Habble Morning, Spire Albion

Bridget rather forgot how to be conscious for some indistinct length of time. She felt this only reasonable, since the sword mantis had impaled her calf and dislocated everything between there and her hip. The pain in her leg was bothersome in the extreme.

She awoke sometime later in a bed. The dark room was cold enough to tell her that she was back inside Spire Albion, with its constant temperature. She first became aware of a bad taste in her mouth, and then of the dull throbbing in her slashed hands, which she found to be wrapped in thick white bandages. Rowl was nestled in the curl of one of her arms, all two stone of him; he purred a slow and lazy purr even in his sleep. He sported around his head a bandage that had been wound so that his ears had been left clear of it.

There was a small lumin-crystal lamp sitting on the bedside table, and in its wan light, she could see a dresser, a rather large and old-looking wardrobe, and shelves and shelves and shelves of books. More books, most of them bookmarked or lying open to certain pages, were scattered over two bedside tables—and in a chair beside the bed sat an exhausted Benedict, his long, lean form stretched out in a doze.

Bridget stared at him for a moment and found herself smiling. This was usually quite the reverse, she thought, and it seemed odd to be seeing him from the vantage point of the wounded rather than from that of the nursemaid.

The man had fought a veritable terror of the surface for her sake and slain it before it could kill her or either of the cats. Even though he'd been wounded and in pain, he'd stood to battle like a hero of old.

Her response to that valor would bear thinking upon.

Fenli was curled up in Benedict's lap, sleeping contentedly, holding his little striped tail over his nose with all four paws. As Bridget looked at him, the little cat's eyes flicked open as if he'd felt her gaze, and he promptly rose and stretched, then prowled up Benedict's chest and pawed gently at his face.

The young warriorborn nobleman frowned in his sleep and murmured something vaguely reproving in what might have been Cat. Then he blinked his eyes open. "Yes, yes, Fenli. You can't possibly be hungry again."

"Littlemouse wakes," Fenli chirped.

Benedict blinked his eyes open even wider and focused them somewhat blearily upon Bridget. Then his face lifted into the boyish grin that always made her feel as if there were a part of her chest that hadn't quite been filled in yet.

"Oh. Oh! There you are. I was starting to get worried."

"He was asleep," Fenli told Bridget calmly. "I was worrying for him."

"*You* were asleep," Bridget murmured, amused.

"I gave the matter its due attention," Fenli said with a yawn. "Tribesaver is excitable where your well-being is concerned. Rowl and I knew you would be fine with some rest." Then he closed his eyes and went back to sleep.

"I suppose he's not entirely wrong about that," Benedict murmured. "How are you feeling?"

"Everything hurts," Bridget reported. "What kind of shape am I in?"

"You look like a bruise with eyes," Benedict said frankly. "The Spirearch's physician thinks the bones of your leg have been fractured in several places. He's concerned that you may not regain the full use of your fingers for a while, and it seems you have cracked a number of ribs."

"My," Bridget said, closing her eyes briefly. "You paint a . . . rather colorful picture."

"You're a rather colorful person at the moment," Benedict said, smiling gently. "Do you need anything?"

"Water," Bridget replied. "I'm parched."

"You can have some if you're cautious," Benedict said. "I'm afraid the physician said that the painkillers she gave you will have ill effects if you try to gulp anything down." He produced a mug of water and passed it over to her, careful not to disturb Fenli. "Sip slowly, please."

Bridget found her bandaged hands clumsy but functional, and she needed only a little steadying from Benedict. She wanted to gulp the water down, but the throbbing, pleasant euphoria that seemed to surge through her limbs warned her that it was likely best she took his advice.

After a long, delicious moment of sipping slowly, she blinked around the room and asked, "Benedict?"

"Hmm?"

"Where are we?"

"I should think that would be obvious," said a voice from the doorway, and the Spirearch appeared in it. He paused there, his forehead seeming to gain a few more lines as he studied her and sighed.

"Oh, my dear Miss Tagwynn," he said, "you have paid a stiff price for your service to me."

"It could have been much worse," Bridget assured him, and dropped the mug of water from her clumsy hands.

Benedict was there and caught it before much could spill. "She did her duty, sire."

Albion came into the room and inhaled deeply. "So she did."

"Did they tell you?" Bridget asked abruptly. "Sire, we know what wiped out Spire Dependence."

"They told me," Albion assured her. "A mistmaw. God in Heaven help us."

"I confess," Bridget said, slurring her words slightly, "I'm not quite sure what one of those is. A great beast, I know."

"A beast that is etherically enabled to fly," Albion said gently, "or at least to float upon the etheric currents, which is why they can be such a menace to shipping that enters the mesosphere. They're vast, a mile across or more, and have hundreds of terrible tentacles thicker than a dreadnought's spinal masts. Sometimes they'll come up to the edge of the mists and drag ships down like a spider catching so many flies."

Bridget shuddered. "That's awful."

"They're not very clever beasts," Albion noted. "But the notion of one under control is . . . a matter of concern."

"'Under control'?" Benedict asked.

"It stands to reason," Albion said firmly. "Much as Madame Cavendish bade the silkweavers to do her bidding two years ago, it would seem she has found a way to extend that manipulation to larger targets."

"Maker of Ways," Benedict breathed. "Then those things I found inside Spire Dependence . . ."

"Its larvae, I suspect," Albion said, nodding.

"What on earth can be done about such a creature?" Bridget asked.

"Albion's defensive batteries are strong enough to bring one down, now that we know what to be on guard for," the Spirearch said. "And it is possible our dreadnoughts could deal with one." He shook his head. "That's why Tuscarora has it attacking colony Spires—the defenses there are lighter and less likely to be able to harm his pet monster."

"The mistmaw or Cavendish?" Benedict asked wryly.

Albion flashed him a fleeting, close-lipped smile.

"Is that what's happening?" Bridget asked. "Is the mistmaw coming for Albion?"

The Spirearch frowned. "I don't think so," he said quietly. "Our defenses are heavier, and such a beast would not be swift. We'd blast meat off it as fast as it came in." He inhaled slowly. "I suspect Tuscarora has a less heavily defended target in mind."

"The trade summit?" Bridget asked.

"Spire Olympia's defenses are lighter than any other Spire her size," Albion said quietly. "And the shipping around the summit is likely to interfere with the speed of any reaction." He looked pained. "Which is why, my dear, I'm afraid I must ask you for even more than you have already given."

Bridget blinked and felt slow. "Sire?"

"We must warn them," Albion said.

"They won't believe us," Benedict said. "I can scarcely believe it myself."

"Which is why we must send eyewitnesses," Albion replied. "You've seen the results of an attack, Sir Benedict. You're in. And we have a witness who has seen the attack itself."

In Benedict's lap, little Fenli made a tiny snoring sound.

"I need someone to translate accurately for Fenli. And frankly, my dear, your physical state will make an impression independent of other factors. You have paid for this knowledge, and anyone who looks at you will be forced to see that."

When Albion lifted a hand and beckoned, Vincent appeared in his dark suit. He was pushing a wheeled chair.

"Oh," Bridget said a bit dazedly. "I'm . . . going on an airship, then."

"It will take us days to get there," Benedict objected.

"You'll be taking my personal transport," the Spirearch said. "She's an unarmed yacht, but . . . she's rather swift."

"We'll be there in less than thirty-six hours," Vincent said quietly. "Sir Benedict, if you would assist me."

"I would *not*," Benedict said firmly. "Sire, Bridget needs rest."

Lord Albion gave Benedict a pained smile. "You're right, lad. She does." His eyes became intense, almost burning. "But *Albion* needs her in Olympia. It is imperative that we give the Olympians warning enough to position their dreadnoughts to protect their Spire."

"And what of protecting Bridget, sire?" Benedict asked calmly.

"I know," Albion said. "What I am asking is not kind. Nor reasonable. Nor easy. I can assure you both only that, to the very best of my judgment, it is something more important than any of that." He looked each of them in the eye and enunciated his words carefully. "It is necessary. Tens of thousands of lives could depend upon this message being communicated successfully."

"Of course I'll go," Bridget said as firmly as she could manage. "Ben, you know he's right."

Benedict glowered at her for a moment and then fixed Lord Albion with a steady gaze. "You will do everything in your power to assure she has adequate medical care immediately upon completing her duty."

"I agree to your stipulation, sir," Lord Albion said.

Benedict looked like he'd swallowed a silkweaver but he reluctantly nodded. "Very well, then. We shall leave as soon as the ship is prepared, sire."

"It's ready now, young sir," Vincent said quietly. "Letters of introduction and passport have already been written, and the doctor for Miss Tagwynn in Olympia has already been chosen. Please, help me move Miss Tagwynn to the chair, sir. It will be easier on her with two of us."

"Rowl," Bridget said urgently, nudging the orange tabby cat with her elbow. "Rowl, wake up."

"Waking up is stupid," Rowl complained, and yawned. "What is it, Littlemouse?"

"Our work isn't done," she explained to him. "We're going on an airship to save another Spire."

"Two?" Rowl demanded. "In one day? Why cannot humans solve their own problems without my help?"

"God in Heaven knows," Bridget said. "But I need you and Fenli to go with me."

"Pfeh," Rowl said. "Must we continue associating with the halfling?"

"For now," Bridget said.

"Oh, very well, Littlemouse. You should know by now that I go where you go."

Bridget gave Rowl a very undignified cuddle and sank her face into his fur. Then she set the cat aside and rose with a pained grunt, even with help from Benedict and Vincent, and settled in the wheeled chair to be whisked away to her next mission.

Chapter 33

AFS *Belligerent*, Skyport, Spire Olympia

Grimm took his dinner beside Alex's bunk. He found that years of being cast out of Fleet had not altered his dislike for its cooking, and he found himself forced to attack the meal—honestly, what incompetent vatterist had provided this rubbery chum that passed for meat?—with the same sense of duty he would have used for inspecting a ship's bilges or scraping mold from its hull.

The tipple of rum, at least, was acceptable, and mixing some with the unidentifiable brown sauce Bayard's cook had created improved the meat dramatically.

"I was thinking," Bayard said suddenly, weakly, "watching you eat, of that horrible food we had to sustain ourselves with on board the old *Perilous*."

Grimm looked up from his meal at his friend and exhaled slowly. "Alex. How are you feeling?"

Bayard hadn't risen. He lay on his back, his expression distant, his eyes unfocused. His face was pale but for scarlet blotches on his cheeks and forehead. "Do you remember, Mad? That hideous soup?"

"Mistsharks aren't very good eating," Grimm replied quietly. "But we were so far off the currents we had to take what we could get."

"Either we ate them or they'd have eaten us," Bayard said with a small chuckle. "I'm still not sure we got the better end of that bargain." He looked around the cabin blearily. "I collapsed, didn't I?"

"Yes," Grimm said calmly. He set down his eating utensils, untucked the kerchief from his shirt, and stepped away from the alleged sustenance to settle on the edge of Bayard's bunk. "Your physician has been in an agony of terror and confusion."

"It's his first tour," Bayard responded. "The first time he's had to deal with more than books and dead rats—" He broke off in a wretched-sounding cough for a few moments and then closed his eyes. "Bother. Water, please?"

Grimm had already fetched the cup left for precisely that and offered it to Bayard to drink. Alex tried to sit up twice and then let out his breath in a miserable sigh. Grimm, without comment, set the cup aside and hauled his friend up, then propped pillows beneath him.

"Your doctor says you're not to sit up."

"Blast his flat belly and pimply skin," Bayard said easily though a trifle breathlessly. Grimm passed over the water, and Bayard drank, albeit shakily. "What else did he say about me?"

"He suspects poison," Grimm replied.

Bayard passed the cup back as though he might be too weak to keep holding it. "Tower of intellect that he is." He shook his head. "Well. That bastard Valesco was right here in this cabin only days ago. He probably slipped the poison into something then."

Grimm studied Alex for a moment before he said, "I'm sure that is the case." He turned to retrieve a basket from beside the table. "I've had some beef bone broth from *Predator*'s galley brought for you. Don't know how the cook does it, but it's delicious and brings life to the dead on a regular basis. I just wish I'd known to ask for enough for two."

Alex smiled weakly. "Still don't like the nourishment provided by the Aetherium Fleet handbook, eh? You've gone soft." Bayard eyed the basket. "Hangover cure, is it?"

"First thing the men get when they seem out of sorts. Doctor Bagen says he wants to bottle it."

"Well, who am I to contradict an experienced doctor?" Bayard murmured. But his eyes closed, and a second later a low snore came out of his mouth.

Grimm stared helplessly at his friend for a moment. Then he sighed and turned dutifully back to his meal.

The ship's doctor, a young and anxious-looking man named Shipley, came and examined Bayard briefly. Grimm informed him that Alex had woken and taken some water.

"Well," Shipley said, "consciousness and drinking are both good. But the commodore needs his rest even more." The young doctor fretted for a moment and then said, "I don't like his color at all."

"Shall I fetch some paint?" Grimm asked mildly.

Shipley grimaced and shook his head. "If he needs to eliminate, let me know. It might tell me something."

"The color," Grimm said with no expression at all.

"Yes, precisely."

"I'll be sure to send for you," Grimm assured him.

As Shipley made his way out of the cabin, there was a movement at the door, and Lady Hinton finally arrived.

Grimm rose at once and said quietly, "Abigail."

"Madison," she said, and moved at once to Bayard's bedside. "Oh, God in Heaven. How is he?"

"He seems to have come out of his unconsciousness," Grimm said. "He's sleeping and had a little water. The doctor wants to examine the color of his, ah, effluvia as his next step."

"What happened?"

"He was, apparently, poisoned."

Abigail closed her eyes for a moment and then said calmly, "He said that Valesco came to the cabin when he first arrived."

"Indeed, he did," Grimm said. "I was here."

She sat down on the side of the bed and took Bayard's hand in hers. "How was it done?"

"I'm not sure," Grimm said. "It did not seem that Valesco had much opportunity, but I was not watching his every move for such a thing."

"I'm told that Auroran agents store such things in assassins' rings," she said.

"Perhaps that was it," Grimm said.

Bayard stirred again and opened his eyes enough to smile faintly at Abigail. "Ah. My lady. There you are. Forgive me if I do not rise."

"Alex, you poor fool," Abigail said. "How could you let such a thing happen to you?"

"I'm very much afraid he got to my cognac."

Abigail gave him a wan smile. "The fiend."

"I was just talking to Mad about *Perilous*. . . ." Bayard shook his head weakly. "We were talking about how bad it was. How afraid we were. How afraid I was . . ."

"Alex, hush," Lady Hinton said quietly. She shook her head. "You need your strength. You need to rest."

"Mmmm. Duel tomorrow. Should sleep. But in the morning, we'll . . ." His voice trailed off into a mumble, and then he was asleep again.

Lady Hinton bowed her head and then turned to Grimm.

"Madison," she said quietly, "he's never spoken to me about what happened on *Perilous*. He's never spoken to anyone about it as far as I know. But he wakes up from nightmares sometimes."

Grimm chewed down a mouthful of the substance accused as food and shook his head. "I thought all of Albion knew what happened."

"I know that you were cashiered for cowardice unbecoming an officer," Abigail said, "and that Alex always said it was nonsense."

"It was necessary," Grimm said quietly.

Abigail rubbed Alex's hand silently. Then she asked, "What happened?"

Grimm stared at the lovely noblewoman for a long moment. Then he sighed. "Alex was a midshipman on his first tour. I was a fresh lieutenant on my third. *Perilous* was one of the last of the old frigate-class airships, even smaller than a destroyer, and it was the two of us, Lieutenant Stanton, and Captain Haggerty as ship's officers. Ship's complement of only forty men, plus the four of us."

"Quite a responsibility for such young men," Abigail suggested.

Grimm shrugged. "Haggerty wasn't a bad man. But he was a drunk. Stanton was . . ." He shook his head. "There was something wrong with him. He liked his authority too much. And he would give lashes to any aeronaut who seemed to contradict him, even on small matters. Like coiling webline or tying knots."

Abigail studied him, listening.

"We were on a deep patrol, antipiracy operations. We'd hit a couple of rogue ships and given them hell: sent one down into the mist and burned another's web so badly that they had to sit there floating until a cruiser could come and fetch them. We were all the way out by Pike when we came upon three Pike merchantmen under attack from half a dozen light ships. Captain Haggerty called us to general quarters, and then he just grabbed his chest and"—Grimm spread his hands—"died."

"Heart attack?" Abigail asked.

"Looking back, maybe Stanton doctored his drink. I honestly couldn't say. I was seventeen years old, with everything that goes with it." Grimm smiled faintly. "Stanton immediately ordered us to prepare to attack. Outnumbered six to one. The first mate protested, and Stanton blew the front half of his skull off with his gauntlet."

Lady Hinton shivered.

"In we went," Grimm said. He felt his eyes slide out of focus. "That was my first bad action. The pirates weren't much for gunnery, but they had us six to one. They burned through old *Perilous*'s shroud in less than a minute and set us afire. The ship's pilot tried to dive into the mist to get us out of sight of all the pirates. Stanton split his skull with a boarding ax and—"

He broke off, staring at the sleeping man.

"Alex was almost two years younger than me. His family connections got him a post faster than I got one. He wasn't yet sixteen years old." Grimm swallowed and felt his eyes unfocus. "Stanton was furious. His veins standing out. His face all but purple. He screamed at Alex. Ordered him into the pilot's station to wheel about and attack again. Alex was mostly a child. A very gentle young man. He had no scars on his knuckles. He . . ." Grimm swallowed. "He'd never been in a fight."

Abigail blinked. "Alex? Truly?"

Grimm nodded. His jaw worked several times, clenching and unclenching. "Stanton drew his sword and beat him with the flat of it, screaming. Beat him badly. He broke Alex's arm. He was a big man. Eyes like ice in a purple face. And Alex was all but a child. He was terrified. And . . . he did what Stanton said."

Abigail's eyes filled with tears. She said nothing.

"This man," Grimm said, "this . . . monster. I watched him beat and break my friend. Take my captain's crew and order them into a hopeless battle for no reason. He was willing to throw their lives away in his pursuit of command." Grimm's face twisted. "For glory. Or power. I never understood him."

Abigail's expression had turned compassionate as she stared at Grimm. The cabin had grown darker as the sun set, the light turning orange and red as fire filled the mists outside Spire Olympia. "What happened?"

Grimm took a deep breath and said, "I drew my knife and cut Lieutenant Stanton's throat."

Abigail stared at him in slowly dawning horror.

Grimm continued in a slow, steady voice. "I was strong by then. Stronger than Alex. I cut both arteries and the windpipe at once. And I threw Lieutenant Stanton over the side of the ship. He was trying to scream on the way down." Grimm nodded. "Alex told me later that I was screaming the whole time. But I don't remember it."

Grimm's mouth filled with bitterness. He seized a cup of water and drank it.

Abigail looked down. "Oh, Merciful Builders. Madison . . ."

Grimm continued in the same quiet voice. "I had seniority on Alex. And he was in shambles. So I assumed command. The merchantmen had gotten away, and the pirates were determined to take it out of our hides. We dove into the mists and got away with our lives, but our etheric systems were damaged, our web burned away. So I ordered the men to raise sail, and we ran." Grimm stared at the sleeping Alex for a moment before he said, "A storm came up. Blew us so far off the shipping lanes that even if we'd had our web, there might not have been current enough to drive us. And we were lost.

"It took us better than three months to blunder back into an etheric current. By then we were out of food, out of water. We had to land on the surface to look for both. We lost eleven of the crew— mostly to mistsharks. But we managed to trade with some scavengers and rigged a makeshift web, and we were able to get back to Albion after we'd finally gotten our bearings."

"What happened?" Abigail whispered.

"I told the truth," Grimm said. "Alex and the men backed me up. Kettle especially. The Admiralty had selected an incompetent drunk and a madman as the ship's commanding officers. Political picks, I'm fairly certain at this point, but if word got out about everything that happened, their sponsors would have been publicly humiliated. So instead they blamed it all on me. Said I lost my nerve in the heat of combat and mutinied against Stanton when they knew damned well why I had to kill him."

"They threw you to the silkweavers," Abigail breathed.

"That is precisely what they did," Grimm acknowledged. "It was going to a court-martial. One of the aides to Admiral Williams wanted me hanged, so Alex challenged him to a duel. His first. After what Stanton had done to him, Alex was determined never to back down again. And he was determined to defend me as I had defended him. The aide—Regent, his name was—deferred to the Protocol Sanguis, but Alex killed him where he stood with a single stroke."

"I heard about a little of that," Abigail said.

Grimm nodded. "It was quite a scandal within the Fleet back then. More than anything, they wanted it to go away. So I made a deal with Williams. I claimed responsibility for everything. Admitted to the charges and accepted being cashiered out. It was the least I could do to protect Alex, after all we'd been through together. So I got run out of Fleet, and he got promoted."

"Which is why he financed the purchase of *Predator* for you, I take it," Lady Hinton said quietly.

"Yes, Your Grace," Grimm said. "He said I'd taught him courage and protected his honor and his House's honor. So he ruined his financial prospects to make sure I had a ship to command."

"You're not telling me everything, are you?" Abigail said.

"No," Grimm said. "I glossed over the bad parts."

She closed her eyes. "Oh. Oh, Mad."

He smiled faintly. "That was when I met Calliope."

Abigail blinked several times and then let out a breathless exhalation of a laugh. They exchanged world-weary smiles.

Grimm sighed and nodded toward the recumbent Bayard. "Is he going to recover?"

Abigail looked up at Grimm for a long, silent moment. "What does his physician say?"

"I thought I would ask his poisoner," Grimm said.

Lady Hinton didn't move. She might have been a statue.

"Is he?" Grimm pressed gently.

Her chin moved up and down once.

"Good." He looked up at her and met her eyes. "Alex is my friend, Your Grace. Like few human beings ever get to have. That's why I trust him. Why I stood as his second. And why I will face Valesco twenty-four hours from now."

She looked down. "Did . . . Does he know?"

"I didn't say anything," Grimm said. "I won't speak of it. You have my word."

Her eyes filled with tears. She closed them, her face never moving. "Thank you."

"I understand. You wanted to protect him. And he wasn't the right man for this task."

Abigail took a slow breath and nodded. "And . . . you are the right man?"

"Alex knows dueling: the tactics, the stratagems, the techniques." Grimm shook his head. "I just know killing. And what killers are like."

"Valesco is a killer," Abigail said.

"Miss Lancaster told me about the duel with that boy earlier today," Grimm said. "Valesco uses the rules that are meant to create order as a sword and a shield. He's never been where I've been. He hasn't seen what I've seen."

"Do you really think you can best Valesco?" Abigail asked.

"No," Grimm replied calmly, "I think I can kill him."

Chapter 34

IAS *Mistshark*, Coordinates Unknown

Colonel Espira and Captain Ransom were in the throes of passion. To a degree. The ropes of her bunk creaked in steady time.

"Sixty-four down," Calliope whispered into his ear, breathing hard. "That leaves me with a hundred twenty still healthy."

"I'm down to fifteen Marines," Espira panted back. "We can't wait any longer."

"Hah," Ransom said, and shuddered. "You're right, of course. How?"

"I will send my men at her cabin," he breathed. "Ciriaco will go first. His job will be Sark. I'll follow with the men armed with knives and gunpowder weapons. We will take the witch."

"You say she can take a man down with a thought," Calliope said.

Espira found it increasingly difficult to concentrate. "Yes. Horrible."

"Then she'll take Ciriaco out first," she said. "And the rest of you will be dealing with a warriorborn in close quarters."

"It can hardly be helped," Espira said, hardly able to help himself.

Calliope's teeth flashed in the dark. "Tuscar—oh—ora made me

350

remove the scuttling charges beneath her cabin," she panted. "But he didn't say I had to throw away my grenades."

Espira's eyes widened. "What?"

"I've a dozen Piker explosives," she breathed. "We throw them into her cabin through the portholes first. Then you can go in after . . . they've . . . exploded."

Calliope gasped—and then they exploded.

Espira collapsed slowly atop Calliope a moment later, breathing hard. She wound her arms around his neck sinuously and kept her lips close to his ear. "God. Auroran men. It must be the egos."

Espira let out a low chuckle against her throat. "Perhaps," he replied. Then he dropped his voice to a whisper again. "The explosives. They will not damage the ship?"

"Woodwork can be repaired," she whispered back. "That's not true for whatever the witch has in mind."

"She'll know once my men start moving. Sark will be able to hear us coming."

"So?" Calliope countered. "It isn't like she's coming forth to do battle. She'll fort up in her cabin with her pet monster and dare you to come at her. Exactly what we want."

Espira thought through the plan for a few moments while his frantic heartbeat slowed down to a normal pace. Then he nodded. He couldn't really add much to Calliope's reasoning. It was everything an assault plan should be: simple, unfair to the point of being entirely one-sided, and very likely to succeed.

"When?" he whispered.

"The men are dropping left and right—the sooner the better," she breathed back. "Tonight. As soon as you go back to the crew quarters."

Tonight.

Colonel Espira's heart pounded.

She looked up at him, her dark eyes calm, but he could see the fright dancing far back in them. She was terrified too.

But it felt good. It felt good to be fighting a foe worth risking his life to defeat.

Fear and excitement and something suspiciously like hope surged through Espira. He lowered his mouth to Calliope's, body singing with energy again, and she gasped in surprise, her hips rising to meet his with ardor.

"Damned Aurorans," she moaned, her eyes closing. "Perhaps we can take . . . a few moments more. . . ."

And they did.

Espira readied his men in silence. Captain Ransom had her men singing raucously after dinner that night, having issued an extra ration of rum, and the sergeant had the still-healthy Marines remaining divided into two squads, one under Ciriaco's command and one under Espira's.

Every man had been ordered to leave gauntlets behind, and two in each squad had grenades ready, their fuses trimmed short. Two more had gunpowder pistols. The rest were armed with long knives and boarding axes. Espira and Ciriaco each carried match lines, their ends smoldering cherry red in the night.

Espira led his Marines out of their quarters in the hold and onto the deck. Boots had been removed despite the bitter cold of the winds at this altitude; the men knew that their stealth might well determine who lived and who died this night. Espira split off to the left side of the ship as Ciriaco's party went right, and they moved forward in low, tense crouches, blades already out. The men made almost no noise at all.

They converged on Madame Cavendish's cabin from either side. Ciriaco clenched his match line in his teeth and held a boarding ax lightly in his broad, scarred hands. From ten feet away, he exchanged a nod with Espira. The colonel carefully eased up to the window, trusting the darkness outside the cabin to turn the glass reflective within, and chanced a brief glance inside.

Cavendish sat in a chair, in a blue dressing gown, reading from a small volume held in one hand, with a porcelain teacup in the other. Sark, wearing all black, was tending to the cabin's brazier, taking a teapot from it and pouring into two more cups, the big warriorborn's large hands moving with spiderlike grace.

Espira eased back down, gave Ciriaco the hand signal to proceed, and turned with his match to his two grenadiers. They both lit their fuses from either side of the match line, the grenades' fire sparkling to life.

"Go, go, go!" Espira hissed.

Four men hurled heavy metal spheres through the cabin's portholes. The sound of shattering glass tinkled sharply through the night, and heavy thuds sounded against the cabin's far wall as the grenades hit.

Pistol in one hand, knife in the other, Espira crouched, bracing for the thudding explosions of the grenades to come.

One second went by. Two. Three, and he readied himself.

But there was only silence.

And then Madame Cavendish laughed. It was a low, quiet sound at first, but it scaled up in pitch and volume and viciousness as it went on.

Espira's belly fell out and he traded a look with Ciriaco, but not before the whine of two dozen gauntlets kindled to life in the darkness of the rigging above them and flooded with etheric light his Marines where they crouched along the deck like perfect targets. Even as he realized that, half a dozen of *Mistshark*'s aeronauts appeared along the deck behind them, gauntlets glowing.

And they were led by Calliope Ransom, slim and dangerous in her shipboard leathers, her auburn hair bound beneath a scarlet cloth.

Ciriaco let out a low growl that vibrated the surface of the deck around them, and Espira saw him tensing and preparing to move. Espira rose abruptly, dropping his knife so he could hold an open hand out to Ciriaco. "Sergeant, no," he said firmly. "Stand down."

"Sir," Ciriaco began, his voice feral.

"No," Espira repeated, his voice hard.

There were too many gauntlets on his men. Even Ciriaco would have done well to take more than three or four before he was brought down. The trap had been well laid, and Espira had led his men straight into it. He imagined that there was little chance a crew of pirates would leave his Marines alive, but at least there was a chance. He might be able to talk Calliope into some kind of . . . well, ransom.

If they tried to fight, there would be no chance whatsoever.

He slowly set his pistol down on the deck and said to his Marines, "Lay down arms. This isn't a fight we can win."

Calliope snorted quietly. She and her men stayed ready while the Auroran Marines put down their weapons.

"Gentlemen," she said, stepping forward, "one at a time, you will walk over to the first mate there. He will put you in irons and you will offer no resistance. If any of you so much as coughs too loudly, you'll catch a gauntlet blast at point-blank range. Do you understand?"

"They understand," Espira said.

"Excellent. I'm glad this could be civilized, Renaldo."

"My name," he replied stiffly, "is Colonel Espira. Captain Ransom."

Something flickered in Calliope's eyes and her mouth twitched at one corner. But she inclined her head to him politely.

"Colonel," she said, "I am willing to accept your surrender without irons if you give me your parole as an officer."

Espira fought down a flash of utter fury at her betrayal and wished for nothing so much as to rush her and carry her over the side of the airship and into the glorious, deadly ecstasy of the fall that would come afterward.

But that would not help his men. If he could speak on their behalf, it might.

He clenched his teeth over his rage and said, "You have my word as an officer and a gentleman, Captain Ransom."

Calliope stared at him warily for a long moment. But then she nodded her head and lowered her gauntlet to half ready.

The door to the cabin opened and Mister Sark suddenly loomed there, lean and hard-looking, the short fuzz of hair over his head, lower face, and visible body all the same length. He stared at them with his crooked gaze, a low growl to match Ciriaco's bubbling in his chest.

"Sark," Madame Cavendish said, her voice calm and soothing, "no. I need you to be a gentleman for exactly as long as the good colonel is."

Espira's stomach twisted. Cavendish was mad, yes. But she was mad in a very specific way. His manners were excellent. As long as they remained so, it seemed to have some kind of restraining effect upon what she would allow to happen.

"Most kind, Madame Cavendish," he said loud enough to carry.

"You are very polite," she called back, "for a man who just tried to murder me."

"Even when we have our differences, there is no reason we cannot be civil," Espira replied calmly.

"I suppose there isn't," Cavendish all but purred. "Do come in, Colonel. And you, Captain. I've asked Mister Sark to be so kind as to make enough tea for all of us. Yours should be almost ready to drink."

✢   ✢   ✢

Espira traded a last glance with Ciriaco on the way into Cavendish's cabin. Having mastered himself, the warriorborn Hero wore a calm, resigned expression as he offered his hands to be put into irons. Like most irons meant for warriorborn, the bracelets were thick enough to cover most of his forearms, and their interiors were lined with dull blades that would nonetheless cut him to the bone if he tried to shatter the chains.

Espira entered the cabin with Captain Ransom following him at a distance too far for a casual lunge; her primed gauntlet was not quite pointed at his back.

Cavendish sat in a comfortable chair, one leg crossed over the other. She held her saucer in one hand, her teacup in the other, and she watched them enter with unsettling eyes somewhere between the colors of a sunset and honey. Espira had the uncomfortable sensation that they might have been emitting a little of their own hellish light.

Light the same color as the vatteries he had seen at Flamecrest, in fact.

"Colonel, Colonel, Colonel," Madame Cavendish murmured. "You poor naughty boy. Please be seated."

"Madame," he replied, and took the indicated seat, his posture precisely correct.

The airship cabin was a trifle closer than the average sitting room, but he supposed simply being within sight of Madame Cavendish was every bit as dangerous as being close enough for her to reach out and touch him.

"You too, Captain," Cavendish said, and her tone brooked no dissent. "Sit."

Without even looking at her, Espira could feel Calliope bristling after she'd been so addressed on her own vessel, but she was wise enough, at least, to keep silent as she followed Cavendish's direction.

Sark served them tea, with the barest hint of a low growl in every single exhalation he made. Calliope took hers impatiently. Espira gave the witch's batman a small nod of polite acknowledgment.

"Drink," Cavendish said with a small smile, meeting Espira's eyes.

He regarded the tea warily. Captain Ransom was watching him, and he glanced at her. She looked uncertainly from her tea to him, to Cavendish and back.

Espira felt a sudden little surge of anger at Calliope's betrayal. Yes, it seemed likely that Cavendish might have put into the tea whatever was making his men sick. Certainly, the witch was enjoying his discomfort. It was also certain that he had little choice if he wanted to play this matter through to something other than disaster for his men.

So, without breaking eye contact with Ransom, he sipped calmly from his cup. "Quite excellent, madame. Thank you. Wouldn't you agree, Captain?"

Madame Cavendish's perhaps glowing eyes shifted quite noticeably, swiveling like cannon turrets toward Ransom.

Calliope looked down at her tea, her expression a bit sickened. But she took a quick sip, swallowed, and said, "Delicious."

Cavendish let out a low, throaty chuckle and gestured to Mister Sark. The big warriorborn went to a dresser, took up a silver hairbrush, and then stood behind Madame Cavendish. He started brushing her hair slowly and carefully.

"It soothes him," Cavendish said calmly. "Colonel Espira. What a treacherous thing you are. And you as well, Captain Ransom. Turning on your lover like that. For shame."

"You have my men," Calliope said stiffly. "You said they'd be restored to me if I cooperated."

"And so they shall be," Cavendish said calmly. "Once I am sure you are . . . committed to this choice, Captain. You are, after all, rather treacherous." She tilted her head and studied Espira closely. "Colonel, I once believed you to be a loyal soldier. A man of principle."

"I am still one of those things, madame," Espira said stiffly.

Something dangerous, waspish, came into Cavendish's voice. "Men of principle," she said. "Righteous men. Pfaugh. Irrational fools. One cannot count upon such flighty creatures. What ever happened to loyalty and obedience as values, Colonel? They seem so rare these days."

She reached up a hand to touch Sark's wrist fondly.

"Obedience, like loyalty, should never be blind," Espira replied.

"And you are the one who should decide which of the King's orders should or should not be obeyed?" Cavendish asked almost playfully.

"Everyone should," Espira replied. "I should have confronted you long before now, madame—the first time you unleashed that thing on a Spire. It is to my great shame that I did not do so, orders or not, I am afraid."

Cavendish pushed out her lower lip in a mock pout. "Oh, Colonel, how drearily conventional of you. What difference does it make where I send my pet to do your King's will?"

"Military targets are one matter," Espira replied. "Destroying civilians and children is something entirely different."

"Sophistry," Cavendish spat, her eyes glittering. "Military conflict is merely the first step in a process. The entire point in destroying a Spire's military is to leave it helpless, so that its resources can be extracted, its economy cannibalized, its civilians pillaged a bit at a time. When a Spire is left vulnerable to raiders and pirates, to starvation and disease, to more powerful Spires, its traditions will end, its culture will be crushed, and it will be generally wiped from the pages of history." She shrugged elegantly. "My method achieves exactly the same results quickly, cleanly, and without prolonging the suffering."

"Your argument is not without merit," Espira replied. "But yet there is a difference."

Cavendish narrowed her eyes. "Do elaborate, Colonel."

"You have already murdered hundreds. If you have your way, it will be tens of thousands. There is an inherent value in preserving human life. There is an inherent loss to all of humanity in choosing to end life when doing so might otherwise be avoided. Those who stand forth to use violence in defense of their Spire understand that value and choose to hazard their lives so that others might be saved."

Cavendish tilted her head, studying Espira with an opaque expression.

It took him a moment to realize that she simply did not understand him. That his words had baffled her.

His stomach twisted in fear.

"I am here," he said carefully, "because I wish to preserve the lives of my men."

"Your men are problematic, Colonel," Cavendish replied. "Much like yourself."

"And yet you have allowed the conversation," Espira replied. "I assume because you have some sort of resolution in mind."

Cavendish's face turned into a slow, slow smile. "Oh, very good, Colonel. I do admire it when the purity of intellect can trump such things as moral outrage or the vexation of pride." She turned her face to Calliope. "Captain Ransom, I wish you to combine the crew quarters of your unwell men with those of Colonel Espira's. Let's have them all together where they can be cared for more effectively, hmmm?"

"Madame?" Calliope said warily.

"I cannot force you to do it, of course, Captain," Cavendish said mildly. "But I invite you to consider the consequences to your men if you do not." She leaned her head back and closed her eyes briefly as Sark completed long, slow strokes down the length of her hair with the silver brush. "Mmmm. Honestly, you people of pride and principle, how readily you turn. You, Colonel, grew squeamish and decided to betray Tuscarora. You, dear Calliope, are even worse—for you there was never any question whether or not you would betray someone's trust. And you blinded the colonel with carnal pleasures while you decided which of us would take your dagger in the back. I have to admit, I wondered about those grenades until the last second."

She let the room be silent for a moment.

"Consider," she continued, "that at least *I* have not betrayed anyone. I have not wavered from my course. I have been precisely who and what I am this entire while. Unswerving. Certain. In control." She opened her eyes and gave them both a venomous look. "I want you both to consider that during these last hours before we arrive at Spire Olympia."

She pointed at Espira. "Mister Sark, place the Colonel in chains and confine him and his remaining men in the forward hold." Her eyes swiveled to Calliope. "Captain Ransom, I imagine that no more of your men will fall sick as long as all proceeds smoothly. When we are finished, I should expect a number of remarkable recoveries. Am I quite clear?"

"Quite clear, madame," Calliope said in a hushed voice.

"Excellent," Cavendish said, and let out a low laugh.

Outside, the mistmaw moaned somewhere in the mesosphere beneath them, its basso rumble rising slowly to an eerie, whistling wail.

Chapter 35

PAS *Stormmaiden*, Skyport, Spire Olympia

"*Stormmaiden* lives!" Grimm called up to the watch aboard the Piker vessal.

"*Stormmaiden* lives!" called the officer of the watch, a brawny bald man in black Piker aeronaut's leathers and sporting a bristling beard. "Come aboard, Captain Grimm! The skipper said to expect you."

"Appreciated," Grimm replied, and came up the gangplank onto the deck of *Stormmaiden*.

The crew was abustle, coiling lines, scrubbing and retouching the sealing on the deck, and doing a hundred other tasks required of an airship before she got underway. Grimm nodded to the officer (more a loosely held concept of seniority amongst Pikers than a hierarchical reality) and asked, "Getting ready to ship out, eh?"

"By evening," he said. "Skipper wants us ready to put sky around us."

"Did she say why?"

The officer shrugged. "She didn't, and no one asked. Instinct, I reckon. We all of us trust her by now. This way, Captain."

Grimm followed the officer to Ravenna's cabin. The warriorborn dragon hunter's taste in décor for her personal quarters . . . would have made a Landing harlot blush. Rich fabrics hung everywhere, including colored silks in strips over the cabin's portholes, which let in light in a vibrant, gentle rainbow. Rather than the traditional brazier, Ravenna used an electrically powered heater, a sturdy box of copper-clad steel mounted on stylized dragon feet. The implements of a small but complete kitchen were stored in cabinets on either side of and above the heater.

Ravenna herself was seated at her writing desk, dashing off a missive with terse, brisk motions, but she looked up with a grin when Grimm entered. Not yet in her shipboard leathers, she wore only a rather short sleeping gown and a perilously thin silk robe that clung to her intriguingly.

"Frank," she said, rising. "Mmm, and here I was just thinking about breakfast. Sanders!" she called. "Have Cookie send up enough for me to cook for two."

"Aye, Skip," drawled the officer from outside the cabin, and he padded away.

"So, Frank," Ravenna said with a lingering look up and down his black uniform, "did you come to make me a happy woman?"

"You knew I was coming," Grimm replied amiably. He walked over to her and slid his arms around her. She came up against him readily, and they exchanged a slow kiss. "Word is out about Bayard, I take it."

"The whole of Spire Olympia was abuzz about the great duelists meeting," she said with a sigh. "Did you really think a development like that wouldn't get out?" She drew back her head and stared at him searchingly. "I rather assumed that Bayard had realized what everyone else with a brain had already figured out. Tell me you aren't going through with dueling Valesco."

"Hmmm," Grimm said.

Her eyes widened. "Maker of Ways, save me from men and their pride," Ravenna said. "Frank, you can't be serious."

"On the contrary," Grimm replied. "I need a second."

She gaped at him for an instant and then closed her eyes and exhaled. "Tell me you'll opt for the Protocol Sanguis."

"I cannot do that," Grimm said.

"Of course you can't," Ravenna sighed. "And what? You expect me to come stand by dutifully while he spits you?"

"Yes."

"Are you out of your mind?"

"Possibly," Grimm said, and explained his plan.

Ravenna listened, her expression shifting from dismayed to skeptical to thoughtful over the course of a minute.

"Only an Albion," she declared, "could possibly conceive of something like this."

"But do you think it can work?" Grimm pressed.

Ravenna looked around the cabin as if searching for some reasonable way to deny the possibility. Then she looked up, sighed helplessly, and said, with heavy doubt, "It might. It will all come down to one moment."

Grimm nodded once. "What I need is for you to watch my back during the duel. The Atlanteans have already shown that they're conspiring with the Aurorans. I'd prefer that someone be ready to interfere with them, should they decide to interfere with me."

"As if they would if this insanity works out," Ravenna said. "And if Valesco kills you?"

Grimm raised his eyebrows and exhaled. "Then I suppose I shall desire pleasant company for my last moments, and I can think of no one more pleasant."

She gave him a look that was half smile, half exasperation.

"Frank, if you didn't have a fight coming up, I'd react to that compliment in a very specific way." She shook her head. "I'd say we will celebrate after the duel, but even if you live, you'll be in no condition. This bargain looks worse and worse for me."

"You like fighting almost as much as . . . ah . . . ardor," Grimm pointed out. "And I need to practice for it."

She grinned. "Foreplay without follow-through isn't precisely what I had in mind." Ravenna's expression turned serious. "Frank, you understand that even if everything goes the way you would wish it, I'd not bet the airship on you. It's a coin toss at best, and it might kill you even if you win."

"I've already consulted with Doctor Bagen about what is necessary," Grimm assured her.

"Excellent, a physician has sanctioned this madness, and that makes it all right." She shook her head. "Albion madmen."

"Quite possibly," Grimm acknowledged. "But will you help me?"

The officer of the watch arrived with a covered tray. Ravenna took it from him and shut the door to the cabin. She walked over to the heater, set the tray on the small counter beside it, and began to get down her cooking implements.

"Sit down," she said firmly. She uncovered the tray to reveal fresh eggs, thick slices of bacon, and a warm loaf of bread, along with a number of fruits from several different Spires. "We will start with a decent breakfast. Then we'll go to the armory and get out a foil and practice until you can do it at speed."

Then she gazed at him over her shoulder with her feline eyes heavy-lidded, her dark hair spilling down in soft waves.

"Frank," she purred.

Grimm felt his heart literally skip a beat at the look. "Ah. Ahem. Yes?"

Ravenna moved her arm, so that her silk robe and her sleeping gown slowly slipped down enough to show off the smooth muscle of one shoulder. "When you survive this, I'm going to demand . . . consideration from you. For several days."

Grimm suddenly felt like ripping off his leathers and possibly screaming at the top of his lungs. Instead, he took a deep breath, rose with something resembling composure, crossed the cabin to stand over Ravenna, and lowered his mouth to hers very slowly.

"Done," he murmured somewhat breathlessly.

She kissed him with languid heat, and she went on for several moments. Then she laughed and nudged him away with her hip.

"Make yourself useful and get me the salt," she said, nodding toward one of the cabinets. "Then you can make us tea, which is something I'm told Albions feel confident about. We'll eat, and after that"—she nodded at him seriously—"we'll get to work."

▪ ▪ ▪ Chapter 36 ▪ ▪ ▪

Hinton Apartments, Habble Profit, Spire Olympia

Abigail woke up the next morning feeling wretched. She had been awake, silently weeping, for hours the night before, terrified.

Not of the duel, not especially. She had placed herself at hazard for the sake of Albion on more than one occasion, if never quite so visibly as this. Yes, she was fighting a warriorborn bravo, and Felicia Montaine would possibly be the most dangerous opponent she had ever encountered. But she had fought with both sword and knives in dark alleys and once upon a pirate-boarded airship, and had—thanks to Bayard's preparation and training—acquitted herself not just ably but disdainfully well. She had killed men before in circumstances far more desperate than this, and she regarded Felicia Montaine much as she would any other difficult day's work.

What terrified her was losing Bayard.

She had never been able to give him a child—or, perhaps, he had never been able to give her one; there seemed to be a frustrating amount of uncertainty on that account—and she had always been afraid that he would break things off to seek someone who might provide him an heir for his House. This, however, was something different. She had, with her actions, perhaps sentenced his best friend to torture and death, for Valesco would certainly torment and humiliate poor Grimm before the end.

But Alex would be alive. God in Heaven, Merciful Builders, and Maker of Ways, at least Alex would be alive. She had taken the most logical course when it came to preserving their relationship, she told herself. Anything might be recovered from as long as Alex was alive.

But she had a sick feeling that should Captain Grimm die at Valesco's hands, it would cause Alex to shut a door that would never be opened again.

Oh. Her Bayard.

Damn it all, she wept again despite her efforts to control herself.

She scarcely noticed when plain, competent Tilde entered, carrying her long gun and morning tea. The housekeeper set down her weapon and then the tea, and calmly settled on the edge of Abigail's bed. She took one of Abigail's hands and pressed a kerchief into it. Then she took Abigail's other hand in both of hers and held it steadily.

"Oh, Tilde," Abigail said.

"Milady," Tilde replied compassionately, "Hamish has a report for you when you're ready. And after that, the etherealists are waiting for you."

Abigail took note of Tilde's unusual assertion of the order in which things should be done.

"Blow your nose, milady," Tilde said, quietly businesslike. She rose and fetched a cool, damp cloth and returned with it. "Here. You're a mess. Wipe your face. Then come and take some tea while I see to your hair."

Abigail found herself smiling at Tilde and followed her directions dutifully. "Honestly, Tilde, I don't know what I would do without you and Hamish."

"You'd be helpless, milady," Tilde replied with quiet cheer.

"Obviously. It's always folks like Hamish and me who get the foundation work done while you see to your highborn matters. There's a rather large breakfast coming, milady, as you've exercise today." Tilde gave her a firm look. "You'll be needing to eat it all."

"Thank you, dear," Abigail said, and set about forcing herself to move. Matters with Bayard would certainly go poorly were she to lose focus and be killed in a duel, after all. It would be best to deal with one thing at a time.

So she took the terrified, sobbing person she wanted to be and shut her quite firmly into a closet in her mind. She could be that person again after work.

Once she was seated and sipping tea, with Tilde working on her hair, Hamish knocked and entered when summoned.

"A group of bravos challenged our men while you slept in the early hours of morning, Your Grace," he reported without preamble. "There was swordplay and a bit of weapon fire."

"Hmph," Tilde said.

"We ran them off. They left two dead behind them, with Atlantean silver coins in their pockets."

Abigail felt her eyes widen. "Hamish, you should have told me."

"Her Grace needed her rest," he said firmly. "And I picked our men well. One man needed some stitches, but he's been seen to by your physician here and will recover in a few days." He sniffed. "I believe I told you a few days ago, there was a limited number of competent men available. I also told you I hired them."

"What did it cost me?" Abigail asked him, smiling over her teacup.

"Less than your life, milady," Hamish said.

"Quite correct, I suppose," Abigail said. "Well done, Hamish."

He bowed slightly at the waist. "I also took the liberty of sending a runner to inquire after the commodore."

Abigail felt her shoulders tense. "How is he?"

"Out of sorts," Hamish said carefully. "He threw a cup at my runner and told him to get out."

Abigail closed her eyes. "Oh, thank goodness."

She had used no more than a tenth of the dose intended to kill Valesco, because Alex wasn't warriorborn and was perhaps two-thirds the other man's mass, but even so, the poison could have done more work than she had meant it to—such things were never certain. The fact that Alex had energy enough to be angry was an excellent sign.

It was an excellent sign of his recovery.

It might mean something else sometime after today.

She felt utterly sick.

Abigail turned the key on the lock in the closet door in her mind and focused on the positive: Bayard would live. He would live, thank God in Heaven.

"I don't suppose we can prove that Initiate Hestia hired the men who attacked us?" Abigail asked.

"I'm sorry, Your Grace," Hamish replied. He glanced at Tilde. "One man lived briefly but he'd been shot with a long gun, which sent the others running. He bled out before I could get anything out of him. I spent the rest of the night speaking with the constabulary, and they're content that we acted appropriately."

Tilde nodded firmly.

"Hamish, Tilde," Abigail asked archly, "when do you sleep?"

He smiled slightly. "When the work is done, Your Grace."

"Don't worry, milady," Tilde said practically. "I'll see to it he gets his rest whether he wants it or not. But this is a time for all hands on deck, if you take my meaning." She went to her long gun, slung its strap over her shoulder, and said, "Now, Master Ferus and Miss Folly are waiting for you with breakfast."

Abigail felt as if she might have preferred to spend some time retching instead.

But there was a heavy day's work ahead of her.

She squared her shoulders and nodded firmly. "Tilde, my dressing gown, please. Let us see what Master Ferus has to say."

"I went down and examined the dueling platform last night, didn't I, Folly?" Master Ferus said over breakfast.

"We both did, master."

"I put some thought into how I might interfere with Your Grace's duel, were I nefariously inclined," the old etherealist said, "and I reached a few conclusions." He took a generous bite of a scone and gulped down some tea enthusiastically. "I think that there are limited avenues of attack and that we can defend against them to a reasonable degree."

Abigail watched the old etherealist hammer away at breakfast with the manners of a soldier, which was to say none at all, faintly alarmed. "Do tell, sir."

"First," Ferus said through a mouthful of bacon, "that damned clothing Initiate Hestia developed. Folly got quite a good look at it during the Spectral Tea."

Miss Folly ducked her head, her cheeks bright pink, and nibbled at the edges of her own scone. Her black-and-white hair made her mismatched eyes seem oddly imbalanced.

Master Ferus beamed at her. He was wearing his bottle green ethersilk suit, and his crystal-headed cane rested on the table beside him. "As long as Your Grace avoids the enemy corner of the platform, you will be out of range of any sort of influence. And if you are pressured into that corner, you can be assured that any emotion you feel is of external origin and may be safely discounted."

Abigail nodded her head firmly. "At the Tea, once I was aware that the feelings were not my own, it became possible to disabuse myself of their influence, thanks to Miss Folly."

"Oh, oh, really, she's very kind to say so," Folly murmured to the little jar of crystals next to her teacup. "But the mental discipline the duchess displayed was certainly impressive."

Abigail smiled at her and took up her own breakfast. Her stomach rebelled, but she began with a plain scone and tea, and she was a daughter of Albion. She mastered herself in short order.

"The only etheric pathways near the platform are those running to the lumin crystals that light the area," Master Ferus continued. "However, Initiate Hestia may attempt to manipulate those streams to influence the lighting."

"To what end?" Abigail inquired politely.

She set the half-finished scone aside. Tilde cleared her throat and firmly put the scone back down in front of Abigail and gave her a stern look. Lady Hinton took the scone back meekly and continued working on it.

"The human eye doesn't work the way everyone seems to think it does," Master Ferus said. "It actually sends quite a messy picture to us, and our brains, marvels that they are, fill in the empty spots and connect things smoothly. If she causes the lights to flicker at precisely the correct rate, it could have a disruptive effect on your mind and severely inhibit Your Grace's ability to track the movements of her opponent. Warriorborn eyes don't work quite the same way, so Mistress Montaine would likely not be nearly so affected."

"That could be . . . problematic," Abigail noted.

"Quite so," Master Ferus said seriously. "So we whipped up something to assist you. Folly?"

Folly reached into a pouch at her belt and produced a small copper case. She opened it. Inside, upon a green velvet cushion, rested a pair of golden wire-rimmed spectacles with blue-tinted glass. She offered the case to Lady Hinton without ever looking up.

"I . . . ground up one of my crystals to a fine powder for the glass," Folly said in a rush. "And I told the dust how to line itself up properly to protect your mind from outside etheric influence." She swallowed and her lower lip trembled. "I explained everything to the crystal, and they don't precisely feel pain, but I beg Her Grace not to drop or lose the spectacles and to take great care not to scratch them."

Abigail blinked at the girl, who seemed to hover on the edge of tears. Then she looked at the little jar of expended lumin crystals that the young etherealist constantly talked to. She had a horrible feeling inside, as if she were talking to a mother who had just sent one of her children off to war.

"I will take great care with them, Miss Folly," Abigail said. "I assure you."

Folly flashed her a very quick glance and a relieved smile. "Oh. Oh, that is good to hear. I'm so glad Her Grace understands."

Master Ferus beamed at them both. "Finally, Your Grace, Initiate Hestia might attack your mind directly if she has the skill. It isn't common amongst etherealists, and those who can manage it are frequently . . . Well, shall we say, they don't fit in with pleasant company with any great facility?"

"My mind?" Abigail asked, mildly alarmed.

Master Ferus waved an impatient hand. "She might affect your balance, slow your reflexes, or otherwise impair your ability to act appropriately."

"Or she might make her claw her own eyes out of her head," Folly murmured to Master Ferus.

"Yes, well," Ferus said, and cleared his throat uncomfortably. "Should she present such a threat, Your Grace, and should the glasses prove insufficient, I will be near enough to sense it and to take action to distract her."

"I . . . see," Abigail said carefully. "Master Ferus, if I may ask . . . what will you do to attain such ends, precisely?"

"Oh, I'm sure I don't know the specifics at this time," Master Ferus replied breezily. "It will depend on the circumstances. But I daresay I might set her on fire."

Abigail blinked several times.

Master Ferus's lean, weathered face became stern. "Etherealists have a great deal of power, Your Grace, and thus a responsibility to use it with restraint and good judgment. It is a principle by which I have lived my life, and etherealists such as Initiate Hestia make a mockery of that principle." He shrugged one shoulder. "I won't have it. If she turns her power against you in that fashion during a lawful duel, I feel I shall react with considerable animosity."

"Just so long as I don't go up in flames myself," Abigail said.

"Your Grace," Master Ferus said firmly, "I should never do such a thing. You and Initiate Hestia have quite disparate appearances."

Abigail found herself laughing, and her stomach began to settle in earnest. She nodded to Tilde, who smiled and provided a plate of wholesome food. "It would seem, Master Ferus, that I am in good hands."

"God in Heaven, Your Grace," Ferus said, shocked. "You are about to duel a warriorborn. And on that score, I can do nothing to help you."

"Leave Mistress Montaine to me," Abigail said. "If you can manage her superior, I will deal with her."

"You have my word that I will do my utmost," Master Ferus said, bowing his head.

"Oh, Her Grace should know that she has my word as well," Folly added.

"Of course she does," Master Ferus said, and turned to Tilde. "I don't suppose you have any more of those scones, my dear? And perhaps some kind of berry preserve?" He beamed at Abigail. "After all, Her Grace is eating—"

Folly quite swiftly kicked Master Ferus in the shin.

"—eating for an athletic contest," the old etherealist finished smoothly. "And shall need ample energy."

Abigail eyed the two etherealists, but Folly had begun murmuring in an earnest whisper to her jar, and Master Ferus had turned to a bowl of oatmeal and begun using a spoon like a coal shovel to deliver it to his mouth.

"Thank you both," she said finally. She looked around the room and said, "Thank you all, actually. I . . . I feel myself quite fortunate, to be surrounded by so many decent people."

Hamish, silently looming in the corner where he'd been standing still for the entire meal, simply said, "I've never regretted my service to you, Your Grace. You've always been kind, reasonable, and professional with me." He cleared his throat. "If I may offer a word of advice on the duel?"

"Of course," she said.

Hamish grinned and growled, "Hand that Atlantean wench her head, Your Grace."

"Hear, hear!" Master Ferus said, and raised his cup of tea. "Ladies and gentlemen? Let us drink to Albion, His Majesty, and Lady Hinton." The old etherealist's eyes glittered. "Good fortune go with you, Your Grace."

They laughed and drank together, and Abigail tried to ignore the quiver of anxiety in her belly as she set about filling it with breakfast.

■ ■ ■ Chapter 37 ■ ■ ■

ACS *Sunhawk*, Bound for Spire Olympia

Bridget had only limited experience on airships. Honestly, when they had loaded her aboard Vincent's yacht, proclaimed the ACS *Sunhawk* in modest white letters across her dark prow, she had scarcely been cognizant. The boarding had all been done in a rush in the dark, and her body had simply been hurting too much for her to take much notice of anything but the relative comfort of the bunk she was lowered onto.

What she noticed most, when she awoke sometime the next day, were the cold, the breathless thinness of the air, and the constant powerful rush of wind around them. Her breath congealed into mist in front of her face when she exhaled. She was all but smothered under layers of thick quilted blankets, which were held down by netting that was evidently intended to keep her in the bed in the event of abrupt maneuvering. Rowl was curled up under her left arm; over her belly, Fenli was stretched out as if boneless, rising and falling with each breath Bridget took.

She was in a cabin, all of dark wood, that reminded her greatly of the Spirearch's study. There was a single large bed, where she lay, and a triple rack of bunks stood on the opposite side of the cabin, only a few steps away. At the foot of the bed was a table that folded out from the wall, along with bench seating for the same, and a step beyond that were an expensive-looking electric cooking stove and a miniature galley. Brilliant sunlight streamed in through the small portholes along both sides of the cabin, and beyond them were blue sky and the tips of the little ship's port and starboard masts. The *Sunhawk* rocked and rattled and strained with the speed of its passage.

"Rowl," she muttered.

The ginger cat lifted his head at once. "Ah, Littlemouse, good. You are done sleeping. Tell someone to make me some food."

Bridget exhaled slowly and extricated an arm so that she could rub the cat's broad head. He nuzzled into her hand, purring. "I feel somewhat terrible," she said. "I wonder if you could find Benedict. Perhaps he can be helpful."

Rowl considered her request for a moment before he said, "You are indeed wounded from the battle." He raised his voice to a yowl and said, "Fenli! Get up and go and find Tribesaver!"

Fenli opened one eye, then stood up and stretched and yawned, making rather a show of it all. Then he said, "I do not enjoy the wind. You do it."

"I asked first," Rowl pointed out.

"She is your human. You care for her," Fenli responded. And he promptly lay back down on Bridget's stomach and went to sleep.

"Useless halfling," Rowl grumbled, and rose to his feet, stretching and yawning. Then he went to the cabin's door, into which a smaller door had been built. He pushed down on a lever and nudged the door open so he could go out on deck. Bridget saw the wind flatten his fur almost instantly. He dug his claws into the wooden deck and began pacing steadily down it while the little door was held open by the wind for a moment, then sprang shut.

A moment later, Rowl returned through the lower door, and Vincent opened the cabin's door and followed the cat. Vincent was bundled in aeronaut's leathers, a safety harness, a scarf, and the om-nipresent goggles necessary to an aeronaut. There was a howl of wind. The cold followed him in and the temperature in the room dropped noticeably. Vincent stripped off his goggles and tight-fitting leather aeronaut's cap and beamed at Bridget. "Good morning, Miss Tagwynn, or rather, good noon."

"Mister Vincent," she replied, unsure of the man's title.

His smile widened, and he doffed the cap, revealing a tangled mess of grey hair. "Sir Vincent Grant of Habble Hagland, if we must use titles. Though my knighting days are far behind me. 'Vincent' will do nicely."

Bridget found herself returning his smile. "Vincent. I wonder if . . ." She felt herself blush awkwardly.

Vincent took in her expression with perfect grace and opened a door she hadn't noticed. "The privy. Here, allow me."

He came to the bedside and unfastened the safety netting, and with him helping her to get around on one leg, Bridget availed herself of the privy, somehow less uncomfortable than she should have been in the presence of a man while she was wearing only her nightdress.

The little chamber was not quite freezing, and she emerged, shivering, to find that Vincent had turned on the heater and flooded the compartment with quickly rising heat. He assisted her back to the bunk, and Bridget found herself hurting too much to be worried about her modesty.

"I do apologize for the inconvenience," Vincent said, "but Sir Benedict is at the helm with the pilot learning the controls and seemed to be enjoying himself very much. My understanding of Cat is limited, but Prince Rowl said something about breakfast, I believe?"

"You see?" Rowl said to Fenli. "At least Longthinker's whisker is making himself useful."

Fenli rolled over onto his back and yawned again. "*I am very useful,*" Fenli said, settling down on Bridget again. "I am a witness to important events. You are simply Littlemouse's hanger-on in this matter."

Rowl growled and fluffed his tail indignantly.

Vincent looked back and forth between the two cats and then smiled again at Bridget. "Do I want to know?"

"They would both appreciate food," Bridget said tactfully. "As would I, Vincent."

"Of course," Vincent said, and set about making a perfectly delightful little breakfast including meats from her own father's vattery.

"Oh," she said. "You buy Tagwynn."

"Only the best for the Spirearch," Vincent confirmed. "Your father does excellent work. His beef, fowl, and pork are second to none."

Bridget beamed at him. "Why, thank you. Many people don't seem to think twice about it."

"Mastery of any important skill is worthy of respect," Vincent said firmly. "Without people like your father, others would go hungry. Or at least be forced to eat that rubbery chum from Camden's chain. The poor boys in the regular Fleet." He gave a delicate shudder.

Bridget burst out in a laugh, though she wound up wheezing slightly in the thin air.

Vincent beamed. "There, excellent. I have done at least one worthy thing today."

"If you don't mind me asking, Vincent?" Bridget began hesitatntly.

"Certainly not, Miss Tagwynn."

"I'm unfamiliar with the requirements of a ship like this one," she said. "How many are aboard?"

"Ten, including yourself and Sir Benedict," he replied calmly. "The pilot, engineer, navigator, myself, and four mast hands."

"Oh!" Rowl said.

"Twelve," Vincent amended smoothly. "Twelve all told, including yourself and Sir Benedict and our fine furry friends."

Fenli flicked his tail in amusement at Rowl's outrage.

"And how fast is she?" Bridget continued.

"The *Sunhawk* is a fast courier," Vincent said. "Essentially, she's a ship with the bare minimum of systems necessary for a voyage of any length, with the lightest and most streamlined design possible. Without any need to devote weight to armor or weapons, she can be made considerably lighter and faster than any warship, and she travels at somewhat more than twice the maximum velocity in a strong etheric current."

"And if she must travel outside one of the currents?" Bridget asked.

Vincent smiled as though pleased to be answering questions about his vessel. "*Sunhawk* bears a single turbine system that can drive her quicker than all but the fastest warships in the same circumstances. It's also useful for maneuvering and docking."

"No weapons? Isn't that . . . rather daring?"

"At the speed she flies, Miss Tagwynn, weapons would only be a temptation to foolishness. There is an arms locker aboard in the event of the rare mistshark attack."

Then a warning bell began ringing sharply on the deck of the little ship.

Vincent snapped to attention and strode quickly to a speaking tube on the wall. He held it to his mouth and bawled, "Vincent!" Then he held it to his ear. His expression hardened. "Miss Tagwynn, I suggest you secure your safety netting and perhaps take the cats beneath the blankets so they will be protected should we need to dive suddenly."

Bridget felt her weary shoulders stiffen. "What's happening?"

"That's what I'm going to find out." Vincent snapped his goggles down over his eyes, wrapped his scarf around his neck, and strode out of the cabin into another blast of freezing wind.

As Bridget waited nervously, she held open the blankets for Rowl and Fenli. Fenli slipped under them willingly, but Rowl looked at her in disgust.

"I am the prince of my tribe," said Rowl. "I do not hide under blankets."

Bridget sighed. "Do you want another broken leg?"

"Feh," Rowl spat. "Humans are so undignified."

But he leapt up on the bunk and got under the blankets.

Bridget sat impatiently and wished she were in the condition to go find out for herself what was happening. Running bootsteps sounded on the deck, and an indistinct crew member went by the portholes, heading to the bow of the ship from the stern. The alarm bell stopped ringing.

"Bother," said Bridget, "next time I shall not get wounded."

Footsteps approached the cabin. Then Benedict opened the door and came in, dressed in ill-fitting aeronaut's leathers, goggles, and a leather cap. He slipped the goggles up to his forehead, nodded at Bridget, and said, "I think you should see this."

Bridget plucked somewhat helplessly at her nightgown with her bandaged hands. "I am not sure I am dressed to do so."

Benedict nodded and produced a pair of goggles and a cap. "Put these on," he said.

Bridget found the leather cap to fit close to her head; its long flaps hung down to cover her ears. The cap's interior was lined with soft quilted material. After Bridget pulled the cap down over her hair—which was a perfect mess, she was sure—she donned the goggles, and the cabin darkened immediately.

Benedict unfastened the safety netting and, with seemingly no effort in particular, scooped Bridget up, wrapping the layers of blankets around her as he did.

"Tribesaver!" snapped Fenli. "Please!"

"Oh, I beg your pardon," Benedict said, and allowed Fenli and Rowl to escape from the blankets.

"He's small enough that I worry about the wind," Bridget said. "Fenli, if you would be so kind as to reassure me, I will hold you."

"What about *me*?" demanded Rowl indignantly.

"I will trust you to guard me from attack while we are on deck," Bridget said. She made a sound of not-at-all-feigned discomfort. "Please, Rowl, I need your help until I heal."

"Yes," Fenli said as he leapt with seemingly weightless grace up into Bridget's waiting arms and snuggled beneath the blankets. "Do not be insensitive to your human's needs, Rowl."

Rowl grumbled and rubbed against Benedict's legs. "Do not drop her, Tribesaver."

"I will not," Benedict told him, "provided you do not trip me."

"I am not responsible for your clumsiness," Rowl said airily and then walked to the door, always just a few inches in front of Benedict's shins.

Benedict looked up at the cabin's roof and muttered, "Maker of Ways, give me patience."

Bridget found her chest heaving with laughter, but she kept it silent and leaned against Benedict fondly. "What are you going to show me?"

He paused to slide his goggles back down, then carried her out onto the deck of the *Sunhawk*.

The wind whipped against them with sudden, startling strength and cold. Bridget found herself hiding her face against Benedict's neck. It was a fine, clear day, as days often were this high up above the mists of the mesosphere. The sun was a searing golden sphere almost directly above them.

The deck of the fast courier was . . . shockingly small, really. She realized that the ship must consist of little more than the crew cabin, the engineering compartment, and a tiny hold for supplies. The ship's masts were angled sharply forward, and its prow was unusually pointed, giving the vessel a rakish, angular look. The ethersilk web stretching out before the ship from the tip of each mast glistened in the overhead sun. It rippled now and then with blue flickers of electric static and spread out nearly as far as *Predator*'s webs might have. Powered by electricity from the ship's core, the web was caught by etheric currents that hauled *Sunhawk* forward with literally breathtaking velocity.

In a dozen steps, Bridget and Benedict reached the prow of the ship, where the ship's complement was gathered around the pulpit of the pilot's station, up against the safety railing, staring down.

Benedict joined them, and Bridget found herself looking at a number of sharply edged black shapes far below them.

"What are they?" she asked Benedict. "Airships, yes?"

"Not just airships," he replied, his voice hard. "That is Spire Aurora's Armada."

Fenli craned his head to look, and Bridget had to wrap her hands around the little cat securely. "Oh," she said. "I . . . take it we are in danger?"

"Surprisingly, no," called Vincent, who stood on her other side. "We are fortunate. We are directly above them and in the sun from their viewpoint. By the time the sun has moved far enough to reveal us, we will be well ahead of them. They have nothing that can catch us." He pointed, evidently indicating ships. "This is the bulk of the Armada. See? Their dreadnoughts."

Some of the tiny shapes far below were bigger than the others, so it stood to reason that they would be the ships he indicated. She counted six or seven of them. "I see them."

"The Armada can move no faster than their slowest ship," Vincent called. "*Sunhawk* can move at three times the flank speed of any dreadnought in the world. And even if they send their destroyers after us, we'll leave them eating our wake." Vincent nodded firmly and put his hand on the pilot's shoulder. "Full speed ahead, and don't change course," he called to the man. "I estimate we'll arrive at least four hours ahead of them."

"Ahead of them?" Bridget called.

"Indeed, Miss Tagwynn," Vincent said. "The Armada is headed for Spire Olympia, just as we are."

"God in Heaven," Bridget breathed.

The war between Albion and her allies and the mighty Spire Aurora, it seemed, would begin today.

Vincent gave her a serious look and nodded again. "Sir Benedict," he said over the wind, "perhaps Miss Tagwynn should return to the cabin. We won't have much time to talk them into preparing, miss. You should get your rest."

Chapter 38

Dueling Platform, Skyport, Spire Olympia

Grimm strode through Spire Olympia's skyport with Ravenna at his side and a dozen sailors from *Predator* and *Storm-maiden* at his back. The members of Habble Profit's constabulary were at their wit's end, trying to control the crowds who had turned out to witness the duel, but a fortunate side effect of their presence was that they had cleared a path to the dueling platform for both parties.

Ravenna had chosen to make an impression. Rather than her shipboard leathers, which were already scandalous by Olympian standards, she wore . . . rather more recreational ones that more ably showed off her impressive physique, leaving her shoulders and upper back mostly bare and drawing stares from every man with eyes. Her thick dark hair was worn down, with narrow braids worked in and festooned with dragon plumes; on either hip, she wore a sword, each beside a large gunpowder pistol. The men she'd chosen to accompany Grimm and her were universally large, scarred, muscular, and heavily armed. The contingent in black leather looked entirely piratical.

Grimm, for his part, wore his black leather shipboard uniform and peaked captain's cap, so he supposed he could cast few stones about looking like a pirate, especially given the letter of marque still stored in *Predator's* safe. At his side, he bore his short, heavy combat blade and no other weapon whatsoever. Kettle had chosen the most seasoned fighters from *Predator's* crew, all men who had survived the raid on Spire Albion two years prior and the subsequent actions after and who had proven their ability to fight like demons and to keep cool heads under pressure. They walked through the crowd carrying boarding axes and long guns. Grimm felt a brief pang of sympathy for potbellied, balding Doctor Bagen, who kept pace in a properly modest suit and carried his leather doctor's bag.

Grimm could see the wooden dueling platform as they approached. It was lifted to the regulation height of five feet above the floor of the skyport—but a narrow walkway led out to the simple wooden platform that protruded off the edge of Spire Olympia itself, a two-mile drop yawning beneath it. The end of the day was fast approaching, and faint droplets of rain had begun to fall through the misty skies, giving the entire place a gloomy, funereal air.

Planks and crates and boxes had been set up in an improvised arena in a half circle about eighty feet back from the platform and they were crowded with observers, while the open ground in front of them was packed with more onlookers, who were barely being held back by members of the constabulary. Vendors were enthusiastically hawking food and drink, as well as rain ponchos and caps, all for exorbitant prices. Bookmakers were taking bets as fast as they could hand out receipts. Thousands would witness the duel. Grimm found the entire affair to be in rather poor taste.

His contingent reached the dueling platform and stopped opposite a similarly sized group of Auroran Marines, brilliant in their scarlet uniforms and led by burly Captain Chavez . . .

And Rafe Valesco.

Grimm's eyes locked on the Auroran duelist as the two contingents faced each other from a distance of perhaps twenty yards. Compared to Grimm, Valesco was taller and leaner, with longer arms and legs. His cat-pupiled warriorborn eyes seemed unnaturally golden in the dimming light of evening, and his handsome face was relaxed into a polite smile as he took in the crowd.

Lightning flashed somewhere out in the mist, sending a coruscation of light through it. A long moment later, a low grumble of thunder followed.

"Hmph," Ravenna said, her voice pitched to carry to Grimm alone. "You would think your ambassador would be here at least."

"The Parliament of Spire Albion's official stance on dueling is to frown and righteously condemn it as a barbaric inheritance we should be rid of," Grimm replied. "Lord Lancaster could have shown up for Bayard—ancient House, hero of Albion, et cetera—without causing problems for himself back home. I'm simply a merchant captain, and a problematic one at that." He grimaced. "Besides, he'll be at the duel where his daughter is the second, as he should be. Duchess Hinton is far more important than me back home."

"When this is over," Ravenna said, "come to Pike. I'll put you in command of a quarter of our fleet."

"That would be rather like being given command of a thousand cats," Grimm said. "I'm not sure I desire that kind of futility as a professional career."

Ravenna gave him a sharp look and opened her mouth to answer, then frowned and shrugged a shoulder in acceptance.

The faint speckling of rain became a slow, light drizzle.

Ravenna looked around. "That's going to make the deck slippery," she noted.

Grimm continued to stare at Valesco, who was conversing pleasantly with Captain Chavez, taking in the crowd, and apparently ignoring him. Grimm's shipboard boots were well suited to such conditions. He noted that Valesco was wearing similar, though newer, footwear.

"I've worked in the rain before. I'll not melt."

Ravenna looked up at Grimm and gave him a fierce smile. "I'll do that for you later," she said.

"Don't distract me, I'm fighting for my life," Grimm said calmly.

A dark-suited marshal appeared from the crowd. An older man and warriorborn, he bore a worn service gauntlet on one arm and a blade not too different from Grimm's own at his hip.

The crowd hushed.

Grimm fought down a quivering tension in his stomach and forced his shoulders to relax. It was important that he appear to Valesco as confident as possible.

The marshal strode to a point midway between the contending parties and extended his hands to either side.

"I'm merely making sure you'll be well motivated," Ravenna said airily, and swaggered forward toward the marshal. Captain Chavez mirrored her, frowning as he approached.

The marshal nodded to them, his eyes lingering briefly on Ravenna, but his sober expression never changed. He looked around at the crowd with firm disapproval and then raised his voice and mouthed the ritual formulas. "Today, we are gathered to bear witness to the armed dispute between Baron Rafael Valesco of Spire Aurora and Count Commodore Alexander Bayard of Spire Albion, in the person of his second, Captain Francis Madison Grimm."

A hearty cheer went up from the crowd. At least some of the vendors had been selling pennons, and various folk waved the scarlet and sky blue of Aurora or the red, blue, and white of Albion in approximately equal distribution. Horns blew, few of them well managed, in approximations of Auroran or Albion tunes, assuming the musicians tried for any melody at all.

The old warriorborn marshal rolled his eyes and raised his hands for silence. It was given grudgingly by the crowd.

"Kettle?" Grimm asked over one shoulder.

"Skip," Mister Kettle said.

"How are my odds running with the bookmakers?"

"Aw, Skip . . ." Kettle began.

"Kettle," Grimm said reprovingly.

"Well, Skip," Kettle drawled, "let's just say I stand to make enough money to afford me as many teeth as I want and damned pretty women for a long damned time when you put this Auroran bastard in his place."

Grimm glanced over his shoulder and took note that Kettle's extensive jewelry had vanished entirely. Kettle grinned at him. There was even a gap in his smile where the gold tooth had been.

"Gambling is a sin, Mister Kettle," Grimm said with sober severity.

"Said the man gambling with his life, Skip?"

Grimm took that in and turned back to the front. "Your point is taken."

"As may yours be, Skip, if you get the drift of my sails. Or I'll be begging for work."

Grimm found himself suddenly showing his teeth as the marshal continued the ritual, asking each of the seconds if there was any other course available.

"Thank you, Everett," Grimm said. "For your faith."

"Captain Grimm," Kettle said firmly in reply. "Sir."

The marshal listened to each of the seconds and nodded, raising his voice to the crowd. "There being no other recourse, by the power vested in me by Spire Olympia and Habble Profit, I declare this conflict lawful and allow it to proceed under the Dueling Code as enumerated in Holy Scripture and Spire law. Let no one interfere under penalty of swift and summary response. Let the principals come forward."

The crowd went wild, shouting and blowing horns and clapping and stomping their feet. Chants for the two Spires rose in the background.

Grimm walked forward to join Ravenna, with Doctor Bagen accompanying him. Valesco mirrored him, bringing his own physician, a rather watery-eyed young man in an expensive suit with pale, long-fingered hands. The parties joined the marshal, who glanced down at Grimm's blade, looked at his face for a moment, and then nodded to both men.

"Gentlemen," he said, "please prepare yourselves for the platform."

"It's a bit late for that, isn't it, Captain?" Valesco drawled easily. He slipped out of his coat, passed it to Chavez, and then took his time about unfastening the lace-covered cuffs of his shirt and the long row of buttons down its front. He admired Ravenna openly as he did. "Hello, darling. Now, why haven't I ever made love to you before?"

Ravenna looked him up and down, gave him a sultry smile that showed her pointed canines, and said, "Because I have a certain amount of self-respect."

Valesco laughed easily. "Perhaps when we are finished here, you will let me explore that thought with you." He glanced at Grimm. "Unless you've brought in your second as a ringer, Captain. Hmmm? Another warriorborn to balance out the scales?"

Grimm met Valesco's eyes and said nothing. He took off his coat, folded it meticulously, and gave it to Ravenna.

"Ah, a stoic soldier," Valesco said calmly. He turned to the people in the crowd and shrugged sinuously out of his shirt, held out his arms, and spun in a slow display for them to their rising cheers. "I've fought many of them, Captain. They die so blandly. I trust you'll at least put on a bit of a show? All these people did come out into the rain, after all."

Grimm unfastened his shirt without comment or exhibition, folded it calmly, and passed it to Ravenna as well. The cold air and colder rain sent chills racing across his skin and down his spine.

Valesco tugged a fine leather glove onto his right hand, making a show of stretching his fingers into it and examining it in minute detail. "I've learned a little about your past, Captain. The confessed coward. Is this your redemption, Lieutenant Grimm? Hmmm? Your absolution for murdering your superior officer aboard *Perilous*? And then leading half her complement to their deaths?"

In the years since *Perilous*, Grimm had often heard worse from those whose opinions he valued more. He simply stared at Valesco as Ravenna passed him one of his well-worn shipboard gloves. He pulled it on in a smooth motion, rolled his wrist once, and then dismissed Valesco from his gaze. Grimm turned to the marshal and said, "I'm ready."

"Sir," the marshal said calmly to Grimm, "by law, I am authorized to loan you a dueling blade if you do not have one of your own."

"Yes, Captain," Valesco said pleasantly. "Let's at least make this sporting. It is, after all, for the honor of our Spires."

Grimm ignored Valesco entirely. "Thank you, Marshal. But I know what I can do with this one."

The grizzled warriorborn narrowed his eyes and then inclined his head to Grimm. He glanced at Valesco and asked, "Are you ready, sir?" Then, without waiting for an answer from the Auroran, the marshal turned and strode up the steps to the dueling platform.

Grimm and Valesco faced each other at the bottom of the stairs.

Something ugly lurked in the Auroran's eyes, something that he kept hidden most of the time. It was there for only a second: a flash of cold, inhuman hunger.

This man, Grimm knew, wanted to kill him. Wanted it as badly as other men wanted wealth or women or wine. There was something inside Valesco that needed to end Grimm's life as much as the Auroran needed to eat and drink. And there was nothing—nothing whatsoever—to stop him from doing it.

Except for the heavy combat blade at Grimm's side and the hand inside his glove.

Well.

Grimm had made do with less.

"This is going to hurt, Captain," Valesco said quietly with no showmanship to his voice at all. "Bayard I would have killed cleanly. But for Albion to send *you* against the pride of Aurora? Without even a proper blade?" He shook his head minutely. "I'm going to make an example of you. I'm going to bleed you. I'm going to hurt you. I'm going to show them what defiance of Aurora costs. And in the end, Captain, be most assured—I will kill you. In agony."

Grimm felt the thrill of terror go through him. Felt his body aching to respond. Felt the leashed lightning of adrenaline course into his limbs. But he showed none of that. Grimm faced Valesco and gave him nothing. Not words, not defiance, not arrogance, not anger, not fear, not confidence, not respect.

Nothing.

The rain drizzled down. A small trickle slithered along the inside of Grimm's wrist and into his glove.

He ignored that as well.

Because Valesco was right—this was going to hurt.

"So," Valesco purred, and bowed to his opponent, making a grand gesture for the sake of the crowd. "After you, Captain Grimm. It's the least I can do for a dead man."

Chapter 39

Dueling Platform, Habble Profit,
Spire Olympia

I really do hate that such a show is made of these things," Abigail said to Miss Lancaster as she prepared to mount the dueling platform. "Honestly, people should have better things to do."

"Better things to do than watch highborn ladies stab each other with swords, or better things to do than physically assaulting visiting heads of state?" Gwen wondered politely.

"Yes, well," Abigail said, giving her an arch look. "Politics being what they are."

Gwen glanced around them. The eastern gallery of Habble Profit had filled with onlookers, a great many of them in the finery of the noble classes, visitors from every major Spire on the continent. A few raised box seats had been erected, and were occupied by the red-headed former opera singer Madame Iphigenia, her husband, and their immediate circle, though her brother, the Lord President, was not in evidence.

On the far side of the platform, Initiate Hestia was standing calmly, staring directly at Abigail. Behind her, Felicia Montaine bounced lightly on her toes and stretched her arms, her eyes focused in the middle distance and her expression impassive. The crowd was getting thicker by the moment as more people pressed in to see the proceedings.

"It's not as bad as at the skyport platform, I suppose," Abigail sighed. "Duels there are mostly viewed by aeronauts and teamsters and they can become quite raucous. Here it's mostly local citizens."

"And visiting dignitaries," Gwen noted. "Oh, look, there's Father."

Abigail glanced up to see the lean, greying form of Duke Lancaster settling near Madame Iphigenia in the box seats. He peered at the platform, his expression tense; then he murmured something to a page and passed him an envelope. Abigail watched as the page waded through the crowd until he approached them at the base of the platform and offered her the envelope.

Gwen took it, looked at its exterior, and handed it to Abigail with a sigh.

It read simply, "Lady Hinton." Abigail opened the envelope and read the brief note.

"What does he say?"

"'Abigail,'" she read aloud. "'Don't be a hero. Fight to the first blood and yield. That is victory enough. PS Please, give my love to Gwen.'"

"Oh," Miss Lancaster said, pleased. "That's nice."

Abigail continued. "'And inform her that this dueling penchant she seems to have taken up the past few years is highly unbecoming of a Lancaster.'"

"Ah, yes, that's more like it," Gwen said with a dry smirk. She lifted her chin until she apparently caught Lancaster's gaze, and then she deliberately stuck out her tongue at him.

Abigail glanced over to see Lord Lancaster sigh, shake his head, and give Gwen a reproving glower that was somewhat undermined by the smile lines at the corners of his eyes.

Gwen looked pleased. "He wanted to marry me off years ago, you know."

"As if your mother would have permitted it," Abigail said. "Here comes the marshal."

"What about Master Ferus?" Gwen asked, scanning the crowd around them uncertainly. "I thought he was supposed to be here."

"He said he would be, and the Spirearch trusts him," Abigail said. "I'm sure he's about."

"Well, then," Gwen said, "I'll go through the formalities as soon as the marshal calls us out."

"Just like we talked about," Abigail said firmly.

"Are you?" Gwen asked.

"Am I what, dear?"

"Are you going to take my father's advice?" Gwen asked. "He's often rigid and stuffy, but he's never, ever stupid. I mean, he left it to Mother to try to convince me to go to finishing school."

Abigail arched an eyebrow. "You mean, let that Atlantean bravo cut me? I think not."

Gwen pursed her lips. "You've seen warriorborn fight in earnest? I have. They're like a force of nature."

"This is a dueling platform, darling. I'd never cross that woman in a dark alley. But on the platform, there is structure. There are rules."

"Like the Protocol Sanguis?" Gwen asked. "If her first successful thrust spits your heart, your death will fall quite neatly within the rules."

"That is precisely what's going to shackle her."

"I don't follow."

"If she's careless and pinks me, I'll have given a mortal insult to Atlantea's ruling body and walked away. Her every attack must be an attempted killing stroke, and there are a limited number of available targets for a dueling sword: the eyes, the mouth, the throat, the heart, major arteries—those kinds of things."

"But mustn't you do the same?" Gwen asked. "The Protocol Sanguis means that she can withdraw after any wound that draws blood, but she need not do so."

"True," Abigail said. "But there are a great many more targets available to me than to her." She gave Gwen a direct look. "And even warriorborn bleed."

Gwen looked uncertain for a moment, as though she had never actually seen Abigail clearly before.

"The marshal," Abigail noted calmly.

The dark-suited marshal, the same one from Valesco's duel with the Olympian boy the day before, raised his hands and beckoned the two seconds forward. Gwen drew in a steadying breath, squared her shoulders, and approached him while Felicia Montaine matched her, and the standard ritual before the duel began.

You are going to die today, said a voice quite clearly in Abigail's ear.

She twitched and looked over her shoulder, but no one was there.

Amusement entered the voice. *How frightened you look right now. You should be.*

Abigail turned to look at the other side of the platform, where Initiate Hestia was staring steadily at her, a small smirk quirking the corner of her mouth.

You begin to understand, came her voice, though her mouth did not move. *I can do things you cannot imagine. This isn't a duel. It is an execution.*

Abigail yawned and covered her mouth politely. She unfastened the buttons of her shirt. The close-fitting, fine black leather chemise she wore beneath would cover her torso with some small amount of modesty, and it had no threads to be pushed into a wound. Montaine would probably be wearing something similar.

Abigail shrugged out of the shirt, feeling the constant, cool air of any Spire pressing against the bare skin of her shoulders and upper back. She unfastened her skirt and let it fall aside as well. She wore trousers of the same fine leather, shamelessly formfitting, and the comfortable aeronaut's shipboard boots she'd had made for herself after her very first trip on an airship and its unsteady deck.

She unbuckled her sword belt and let it fall away while she held the hilt of her weapon. The long, light dueling blade was the same length as her opponent's, though the Atlantean's arms were admittedly much longer than Abigail's. The weapons were in fact identical in every specification, though Abigail's lacked gold chase and elaborate carvings on the regulation wire handguard. Much like Bayard, she believed in coldhearted business when it came to blades: weight, length, balance, sharpness. Any other considerations were useless distractions.

Foolish noblewoman, came Hestia's voice. *Do you really think you stand a chance against the warriorborn of Atlantea? I can see your face now, Your Grace. But not for much longer.*

Abigail took a small handkerchief from her pocket and met Initiate Hestia's eyes as she pressed thumb and forefinger together, and with a sweep of her arm removed the sealing wax from the weapon's scalpel-sharp edge.

I wonder, came a quite different, cheerful voice, *what you will look like with your pretty dress on fire, Initiate.*

From the crowd appeared Master Ferus in his bottle green ethersilk suit and bottle green spectacles, complete with a matching top hat, the whole ensemble perhaps three decades out of style. He stepped up to stand beside Abigail and rapped his cane sharply on the ground. The heavy power crystal at its end flared with a subtle green glow that slowly died away.

Hestia's expression twisted with open hatred. *Would you challenge a member of the Spectrum with your wandering thoughts, old man?*

You and I are not involved in a duel, madame, came Ferus's answer. *Whatever made you think I intend a fair fight?*

Good evening, came a third voice, and Abigail felt her mouth tilt up into its own smirk as Miss Folly appeared from the crowd just behind Initiate Hestia. *I do hope that we can be civil. Because if not, it's going to be very difficult for Initiate Hestia to defend herself from multiple attackers.*

Initiate Hestia stiffened and looked over her shoulder at Folly for a second, staring hard. Then she said, *Have you any idea what the Spectrum will do to you amateurs for this?*

Master Ferus bared his teeth and bowed toward her, doffing his hat and taking it beneath his arm in a smooth little flourish from an earlier time. *But, madame, the Spectrum is not here. At the moment, you are alone. We are not. Now, let us be reasonable and allow the duel to proceed. Otherwise, if you take action, so will we.*

Hestia bared her teeth in an open snarl of frustration.

"Some people are so unpleasant," Master Ferus said firmly. "And they really needn't be, but there's only one language they understand. I think the education system could use an overhaul."

"You arranged for me to hear all that, didn't you?" Abigail murmured.

"It was important that you know, Your Grace."

"Know what?"

The old man looked at her, his eyes wrinkling at their edges. "Why, the most important thing any of us can know. The only thing any of us truly have." He leaned forward and winked at her. "You are not alone."

And Abigail's heart pounded with something deep and strong that welled up from far down inside her—something that drove away her fear and left her filled with energy and determination.

No. She was not alone.

Not yet.

She held out her hand to Gwen, who passed her the spectacles Folly had made for her. She donned them calmly, making sure their wire hooks were settled firmly over her ears.

The marshal beckoned, and Abigail mounted the stairs to the dueling platform while the crowd began to shout excited encouragement. She waited, bouncing lightly on her toes and stretching her body as Felicia Montaine returned to Hestia's side and slipped out of her crimson coat. Hestia, her expression furious, pulled Montaine's head down to her level and spoke rapidly into the warriorborn's ear.

Montaine stared at the etherealist for a moment, then at Abigail.

Hestia hissed something harsh.

Montaine didn't quite flinch, but Abigail got the distinct impression that she wanted to. The warriorborn inclined her head to Initiate Hestia and then sprang lightly up to the platform without bothering to use the stairs.

The marshal went to the center of the platform and beckoned them both.

"Ladies," he said, nodding to each, "I must once more ask if remonstration for the given insult may be possible with any means short of shedding blood. There is no dishonor in working out your differences peacefully."

"There is no other way," Montaine said firmly. With a sharp snap of one wrist, she flicked her sword hard enough to make the steel flex and send the sealing wax bouncing away in dozens of pieces.

"I agree with my opponent," Abigail said. "Thank you, Marshal."

The marshal nodded at their answers. "Then the Protocol Sanguis is hereby engaged. At the drawing of any blood, you will cease hostilities and retreat to neutral corners. I will ask the wounded if she is satisfied or if the match should continue. The match will end when one of you yields—or falls to the blade. Do you understand these guidelines as I have described them?"

"Yes," Montaine said impatiently.

"Yes, thank you," Abigail said.

"This is a contest of blades," the marshal said, his glance perhaps lingering on Montaine slightly longer than on Abigail. "Not one of blows. I will not tolerate kicks or punches. When blood is drawn, withdraw to your corners at once. I have been bidden by no less than the Lord President himself to enforce my authority by gauntlet fire. Do you both understand?"

"I do," the warriorborn said, staring down at Abigail from quite a height above her.

"Yes, of course," Abigail confirmed.

"Then, ladies, take two steps back and present arms."

Abigail took a pair of steps back and came into an easy guard position, weapon held ready. Montaine mirrored her, though with longer strides.

The marshal stepped out from between them. "Salute each other," he commanded.

Abigail Hinton and Felicia Montaine pointed their swords at each other, then swept them to the side and up to the vertical in acknowledgment.

"Salute me," the marshal continued.

They both pivoted to face him and did so.

The marshal withdrew a white handkerchief from his pocket and held it aloft. A hush fell over the gallery as the crowd looked on, seemingly holding its breath.

"When this cloth touches the platform," the marshal said loudly enough to be heard, "you may begin."

And he released the cloth.

Chapter 40

Dueling Platform, Habble Profit,
Spire Olympia

Abigail came forward the instant the cloth touched the dueling platform's rough-sanded surface, her blade flashing in a blindingly quick but conservative sequence. Even though she was quick, as quick as she'd ever been in her life, Montaine's speed was greater. She met Abigail five feet past the center of the platform, defeating her attack with excellent discipline and riposting for the heart.

Abigail barely slid the attack aside, and it missed scoring on her by less than a finger's breadth. Her return slash made Montaine lean far back to avoid taking a cut of her own, and Abigail took advantage of the warriorborn's off-balance posture, following up with a blinding series of cuts and thrusts and driving the taller woman back toward the edge of the platform.

"God in Heaven," Montaine muttered as her heels fetched up at the platform's edge. "You're feisty for such a tiny thing." She beat Abigail's blade aside and sprang laterally in the same motion, escaping her precarious position in a single graceful bound and dropping into a more cautious guard. "You've had real training."

"Why do people like you insist on talking and talking during duels?" Abigail sighed, and stalked carefully forward, keenly aware of the difference in her reach as compared to Montaine's.

The warriorborn lunged from a good foot farther than a common human would have been able to manage, and Abigail only just deflected a thrust that would have plunged into her throat.

Montaine defeated Abigail's counter and backed off, circling. "Because we have the extra wind and the time. You people. You normals. If you had any idea what you looked like to us. How slow and predictable you seem."

She came in hard and fast, her slender blade darting toward Abigail's throat. Abigail parried and came back with a riposte to the shoulder that Montaine countered—just as Abigail's scalpel-sharp blade dipped down beneath the counter and left a thin, brilliant scarlet line on Montaine's forearm.

The warriorborn backpedaled and Abigail did not follow. Montaine paused to examine the small wound on her sword arm. Her expression had gone from confident to entirely neutral.

"I'm sorry, dear," Abigail said. "You were saying?"

The marshal stepped between them. "Hold!" he called, holding his open hand out between them.

Abigail straightened calmly and stepped back to her corner.

The marshal turned to Montaine. "The statutes of the Protocol Sanguis have been met," he said. "Has honor been satisfied?"

Montaine stared at Abigail for a long moment. Then she glanced over her shoulder to where Initiate Hestia stood beside the platform. Montaine licked her lips and studied Initiate Hestia's expression. "No, it has not," she said firmly.

The marshal nodded and turned to Abigail. "Your Grace, are you prepared to continue?"

"Yes," Abigail replied.

The marshal grimaced, nodded, and lifted his hand decisively. "The bout will continue."

And the two engaged again. Again Montaine came forward with bold, strong attacks—always striking to kill. Of course, any decent training would have been quite certain to teach its students to defend most strongly against the deadliest strikes, and Bayard had trained Abigail quite thoroughly. She defeated one attack after another with textbook-perfect form. It was rather frustrating. Even though her defenses were quite strong, the simple fact of the matter was that Montaine had a good seven inches of reach on her, so when the tip of her enemy's blade menaced Abigail's body, Abigail's sword would wave short of Montaine.

Montaine knew it too—and those inches, seemingly a small measure to the unschooled observer, were a yawning chasm on the dueling platform. The warriorborn was quicker than she should have been for her size too, and she could match Abigail's advances and retreats with perfect compensatory grace.

But Montaine was young. And the young were rarely patient.

After a dozen deadly strikes had been defeated with the same calm competence from Abigail, Montaine grew more aggressive, putting more power behind her attack. Abigail set a rhythm of small retreats, circling around the platform as Montaine attacked, forcing Montaine to keep advancing to close the distance even as her attacks grew stronger. It didn't take long for Abigail to sense that her opponent had gathered too much momentum, and when Abigail abruptly advanced instead of retreating, Montaine was thrown wildly off her balance. She was so quick that Abigail's cut at her belly missed, but that had never been Abigail's real goal—merely the move that would force Montaine to draw her hips back and leave her weapon arm extended and vulnerable.

Abigail's sword flashed and left another streak of scarlet on Montaine's sword arm—and this one left a sprinkling of blood on the platform's surface.

"Hold!" called the marshal, again breaking up the flow of the bout.

Abigail retreated to her corner, but this time she paced back and forth in a short line, her weight on her toes, her eyes focused on her enemy.

Again the marshal asked Montaine if honor had been satisfied. The warriorborn shook her head. She was covered in a light sweat. Her aggressive posture had demanded more physicality while Abigail's calm, energy efficient defense had cost her relatively less metabolic strain. Steady, Abigail thought. She simply needed to continue steady on, holding her defenses firm and waiting for the openings and miscalculations that the warriorborn's aggression would inevitably produce.

The marshal signaled for the bout to continue, and Abigail sensed that her foe was very slightly slower than she had been. The wounds to Montaine's forearm, though hardly life-threatening, were sapping some of the spring steel from her attacks and parries—unless, of course, she was feigning weakness. Abigail decided against testing Montaine's defenses with a serious offensive of her own. Instead, she limited her responses to simple, snapping ripostes that did not threaten her balance or overextend her defenses.

Montaine was not talking now, and Abigail's patient restraint was drawing her opponent into more and more ferocious assaults, but her wounds had taught her caution, and she was far more on balance now. Even so, with the light weapons of the dueling platform, power and speed alone were not a match for Abigail's patient technique and skill, and after several minutes Montaine reeled back again with a cry. She clasped her left hand over a shallow puncture wound to the biceps of her weapon arm, and a trickle of blood slithered out from beneath her fingers.

"Hold!" called the marshal.

Montaine kept her expression from showing any pain, but the set of her shoulders told Abigail that the warriorborn was hurting from her wounds. She was bleeding more freely now, the wounds on her weapon arm seeping more blood with the effort of fighting. It was really rather ghastly, Abigail supposed, though she had shut the part of her that could feel such things away until the fight was done.

The marshal offered Montaine the chance to back down. The warriorborn, her eyes closed, shook her head several times. Then she set her jaw in determination and came on guard again, almost visibly walling away her own pain and moving forward to engage Abigail once more.

"Did you know," Montaine panted as their blades crossed again, "that you are pregnant?"

And her sword blurred toward Abigail's belly.

The words hit Abigail like a blow. She caught and countered the attack, forcing Montaine back by sheer, drilled reflex, but she stared at the other woman, stunned.

Montaine pressed in again, sword menacing Abigail, who reeled back, trying to gather her concentration as strike after strike drove toward her.

"You're lying," Abigail spat.

Montaine gave her a tight smile. "I can smell it. Hestia can see it. Didn't your pet etherealists tell you?"

After all, Her Grace is eating . . . For two, Abigail realized. Ferus had nearly told her she was eating for two. Her sickness that morning . . .

And overhead, a lumin crystal exploded into a shower of blue sparks.

Both fighters flinched, but the warriorborn recovered quicker and came at Abigail mercilessly, putting the smaller woman back on her heels and driving her toward the platform's edge. Another lumin crystal burst, and another, and another, and bright purple blurs speckled Abigail's vision even as the gallery began to grow dimmer and dimmer.

Night vision, Abigail realized. If enough lights went out, she would not be able to see, but Montaine would be. Her warriorborn eyes would pierce the gloom, growing sharper while Abigail's vision dimmed.

She caught a glimpse of Initiate Hestia giving her a hard smile, staring at her without blinking, without moving. Behind the Atlantean ruler, Folly stared up uncertainly at the dying lights.

"Folly!" shouted Master Ferus's voice from behind Abigail somewhere. "Your bag!"

Abigail fought furiously to preserve her life as Montaine's breaths began to burst forth in a lioness's snarl, her wounded arm moving with almost inhuman speed and power. It took every bit of skill she had ever earned for Abigail to merely stay alive under that assault, and she knew that if she stumbled or faltered, Montaine would run her through.

A child? Surely it was a lie but . . .

Every parry, every block, seemed to ring through her whole body, the sound and impact magnified by sudden fear. Fear that sent chills of weakness down her arms and legs, fear that made something inside her scream and gibber, fear that began to erode her defenses.

Hestia's expression grew gleeful.

Folly fumbled at the bag hanging around her neck, opened it, and flung dozens of tiny expended lumin crystals into the air.

Behind Abigail, there was a flash of green light, and in her peripheral vision, she saw Master Ferus raise his cane, the crystal at its head glowing brightly. That light enveloped the flying lumin crystals and they seemed to catch its green fire like tiny stars, whirling and dancing in an unseen wind, rising in a glowing green halo that surrounded the dueling platform, bathing it in pure green light.

Your Grace, hammered Master Ferus's voice as though directly into her mind, *YOU ARE NOT ALONE.*

Abigail's terror went through some kind of alchemical transmutation. She felt it happen, felt it as she saw her enemy moving, as time slowed, as thoughts crystallized.

A child. Bayard's child.

A tiny life beneath her heart.

A life her enemy now threatened.

Had tried to use against her.

How *dared* they do such a thing?

How dared they!

Abigail's fury suddenly filled her limbs with living lightning, but she remembered her years of training, what cold experience had taught her. Her rage was tempered by that experience, and she allowed it only to lend her strength within her center of balance. But that strength was enough to halt Montaine's momentum as Abigail defeated attack after attack, returning them with counterblow after counterblow, always aimed at the same point in Montaine's defense, so she would have to lift her wounded arm and flex her damaged muscles to defend herself.

Abigail felt the momentum shift. She felt Montaine's blade give way as wounded muscles failed her, as her leaking blood began to take a toll. Abigail pressed forward again, flicking one strike after another aside with smooth circling deflections while the tip of her blade menaced Montaine's body. She pressed her offensive inside Montaine's advantage of reach, her thrusts menacing the warriorborn's heart, her eyes, until at last, with a final flourish, Abigail took a long lunging step on the diagonal, flicked out her blade, and sliced through the tendon behind Felicia Montaine's forward knee.

The warriorborn fell with a cry, and Abigail, her eyes furious, her expression cold, was atop her, pinning Montaine's blade back against her body with superior leverage while Abigail's razor-sharp sword lay against the warriorborn's throat.

"Hold!" the marshal choked out, but held his rush forward, hardly daring to move.

Abigail breathed heavily, rage suffusing her. A shift of her balance, a flick of her wrist, and she would lay open the artery in Montaine's neck and spill her life out like a fountain.

The young warriorborn stared up at her, eyes wide, her face set in a grimace of pain, fear, and rage. She looked aside at Initiate Hestia, at her mistress's pitiless face, and then back up at Abigail, her expression set in despair.

Montaine would not yield. She could no longer fight Abigail, not on one leg. She would die on the platform, but Abigail could see that the warriorborn would face that death rather than yielding, than accepting what Hestia would do to her.

Abigail let out a slow breath.

Felicia Montaine was not her enemy. She was merely a weapon. And while Abigail might fight for her Spire and her people, she was not a murderer.

Lady Hinton exhaled a slow breath and raised her gaze to stare at Initiate Hestia beneath the whirling carousel of glowing green crystals that lit the dueling platform.

Then, very calmly, she reached out her free hand and touched the tip of her forefinger against Felicia Montaine's sword. She lifted her finger away from the sword and showed the single drop of scarlet blood there to the marshal.

"The Protocol Sanguis has been met," she said loudly enough to carry to the entire gallery, never looking away from Initiate Hestia. "Honor has been satisfied."

A moan of released tension went through the crowd as the marshal straightened and declared, "The bout is over! Let no more blood be spilled!"

Abigail saw Montaine's expression shift into puzzlement and then sudden understanding. The young warriorborn sagged and closed her eyes, the resistance going slowly out of her blade. Abigail eased up on her own sword as her opponent yielded; then she stood away from the wounded warriorborn.

Initiate Hestia's face went dark with fury, and suddenly Master Ferus was facing her, his walking cane's crystal glowing, his expression hard.

Initiate Hestia's glare went from Abigail to Master Ferus. Then, furiously, she spun and stalked away into the crowd with her guards, leaving her champion bleeding on the platform behind her.

Felicia Montaine stared after her mistress for a moment, her expression strained. Then she sagged in something between relief and defeat. She bowed her head briefly. Then she looked up at Lady Hinton and nodded her head deeply.

"Thank you," she said simply, "for my life."

Abigail's fury hadn't simply vanished. It had been put aside for further use later. But she could admit to herself that the woman she had bested hadn't lost for lack of courage. She nodded her head regally back to Montaine and said, "Stay still, dear." Then she turned back to her corner and called, "Physician!"

Her doctor had been standing by, of course, and he was hurried up the stairs by Miss Lancaster, who followed him closely, coming up to offer Abigail a mug of water.

"Not me," Abigail said. "Her."

Gwen looked at Abigail intently for a moment and then approval glittered in her eyes. She nodded to Lady Hinton, and then went to Felicia Montaine's side and held the cup to the wounded woman's lips. The doctor opened his bag and bent over the warriorborn's leg.

Abigail turned away from the tableau and let her dueling sword fall from her fingers to clatter on the platform. She pressed her sword hand over her belly.

The growing murmurs of the crowd made her look up. The people were all staring up at the platform, at her.

Ah, she thought. Yes. The show. The entire point of this whole stupid mess.

She stood over her bloodied foe and held up her wounded fingertip, smeared with a single scarlet droplet of blood, and called simply, "Albion!"

And the crowd broke into cheers.

She saw Lord Lancaster turn to Lady Iphigenia, one eyebrow quirked in a silent question. Iphigenia stared at Abigail for a moment, then inclined her head to Lady Hinton and turned to Lord Lancaster. The two put their heads together and began speaking. She had demonstrated that Albion's enemies were not invincible. She had given Lord Lancaster the opening he would need to secure a real alliance with Olympia.

Abigail wanted nothing so much as to go somewhere dark and quiet and have a good hard cry. But instead, she forced herself to smile and stand calmly, her hand lifted into the air, while the citizens of Spire Olympia cheered for their new ally.

■ ■ ■ Chapter 41 ■ ■ ■

IAS *Mistshark*, Bound for Spire Olympia

Colonel Renaldo Espira and the men from his raiding party had been locked in the freezing forward hold for hours. Night had given way to morning and become afternoon, and still no food or water had been brought to them, furthering Espira's certainty that the lives of his men and him alike were forfeit.

Only if that were so, why had they not been killed yet?

Orange and scarlet twilight filled the sky, the light slipping between the planks of the *Mistshark* agreeing with the watch in his waistcoat, which told him sundown should be fast approaching.

The men had piled together for warmth, a lump of humanity that generated a comforting heat and a less-than-pleasant smell, but it kept them alive. A number of men had been carrying their flasks and had managed to keep them secret, along with a small knife that one of the Marines had managed to keep concealed in a boot. Every man who had been bound had been cut free of his cordage, then had it loosely reapplied so that they could slip free of it without trouble. They had already tested the door to the hold, but it was sealed fast as well as guarded, and even had Ciriaco and the men managed to burst through it, they'd have been cut down as easily as children.

At least no more of the men had gotten sick.

Espira had ordered the flasks rationed about evenly and had tried his hand at opening Ciriaco's manacles with the point of the knife, but to no avail. He could have carved at the door or one of the bulkheads, but the tough wood would have resisted the little knife, and it would have been easily heard. Beyond that and demanding food and water from his unresponsive captors, there had been little to do but wait.

Orange and red lines began to slide across the hold's walls and the snoozing men in their overlapping pile. Ciriaco lifted his head sharply, nostrils flaring.

"Sergeant?" Espira asked.

"We're descending," Ciriaco said quietly. And indeed, after a quarter of an hour, they saw tendrils of sunset-colored mist curling into the hold as the shadows lengthened and the light dimmed. *Mistshark* had descended into the misty mesosphere. The chirruping call of a cruising mistshark echoed through the oncoming twilight and was answered by sporadic calls in the distance.

"Colonel," the warriorborn warned, shifting his arms uncomfortably in his manacles, "boots coming."

"On your feet, lads," Espira said quietly.

The seasoned Marines, in their stocking feet since the night before, rose in silence and divided themselves to either side of the door at Espira's hand signals. If the door opened, it would probably be to admit that damned treasonous Ransom and her men, shooting. Or perhaps they'd throw in some live grenades this time and leave it at that. The men would rather go down rushing forward for their lives than be killed like rats in a trap.

"Colonel," Ciriaco said quietly, "been a pleasure."

Espira gave the big man a brief smile. "The same."

Ciriaco grinned, showing his short fangs, and stretched his jaws in a lazy yawn. The warriorborn's hands might have been bound, but

Espira supposed that Ciriaco would see to it that at least one man was going to pay with his life for what was coming for his men.

But instead of the hold door opening, someone rapped quietly three times, and Captain Ransom's voice came evenly through it. "Colonel, rather than anything wasteful happening, I should like to speak with you."

Espira and Ciriaco exchanged a look. The warriorborn shrugged.

"Certainly, Captain," Espira called back. "Come in. We'll have a polite chat."

"I prefer to remain unstrangled," Ransom shot back in a wry tone. "But if you'd care to come speak to me and are willing to give me your word that you'll limit it to that, I may have options for you."

Ciriaco gave Espira a highly skeptical scowl.

Espira rolled his eyes and nodded. "Captain, I'm not sure we're in a position to be giving each other our word about anything."

"Nonsense," Ransom returned. "Renaldo, you haven't betrayed me, after all. Your word is obviously still good."

"And why should I assume you will do anything but shoot me and toss me overboard?"

"That's a simpler matter. Perhaps you're expecting a better offer from Cavendish?" Ransom asked.

Espira glanced at Ciriaco, who snorted softly through his nostrils.

"I don't like it either," he muttered to the warriorborn, but clapped him gently on the shoulder. "You're in command until I get back." Then he raised his voice and said, "Very well, Captain, you have my word that I come to parley in peace."

"Have your men stand away from the door if you please," Ransom murmured.

Espira signaled the men back.

The door opened, and Espira squared his shoulders and his coat and walked through it.

413

Ransom and a dozen of her aeronauts were gathered around beneath the light of a single lantern in the hold. Espira at once picked up on a silent tension running through the men, something in their shoulders and faces. They were quietly terrified.

Espira clasped his hands behind his back and eyed Ransom. "Did your treachery not turn out as much to your liking as you had hoped? Pity."

Ransom grimaced. "I'm sure you've made nothing but excellent choices in your life, Colonel. Those of us who are merely human sometimes make mistakes." And without another word, she passed the butt of a gunpowder pistol over to him.

Espira calmly took it, cocked it, and leveled it at her head.

A round of tight breaths went through the aeronauts. Hands went to weapons, but Ransom held a hand up to her men and said, "Hold. No one move."

Espira mused, "Likely this weapon has no priming charge. Is that it, Captain?"

Ransom swallowed and said in a level tone, "If you pull that trigger, you end my life. And as you have only the one shot, your life as well."

Espira tilted his head slightly. "That seems poor judgment on your part."

"Colonel Espira," Ransom said evenly, "you gave me your word."

Espira almost did it out of a sheer flash of rage.

But she was right. Her men would finish him. And likely would turn on his Marines afterward.

"Colonel?" Ransom asked softly.

Espira held a finger from his free hand to his lips and murmured, "I'm thinking."

Her eyes went a little wider.

414

Espira finally, slowly, tilted the gun very slightly to one side. The bullet would perhaps graze her cheek if he pulled the trigger. "I suppose, if nothing else, my word still means something to me. Very well, Captain Ransom, I'm listening."

"You . . . aren't going to lower the gun?"

"I'm thinking while I listen," Espira shot back with a tight smile. "Perhaps it is a good time to be careful with your language."

At that, Calliope's teeth flashed in the dim light. "I bet on the wrong throw," she said simply. "More of my men are sick, including my warriorborn. There are barely enough of us left to man the ship. Cavendish has locked herself in the aft hold with her tank and ordered me to hold course. And that thing is coming along right in our wake. You hear the sharks? They follow it in schools. I've got a ring of men with pikes around the pilot. I can't have anyone in the masts or we'd lose them."

"You've made your bed, Captain," Espira said stiffly. "I'm not sure how any of this is my problem."

Ransom gnashed her teeth. "The witch has betrayed me."

"I hardly think you should torture yourself over it, Calliope. After all, who could have seen that coming?" Espira wondered lightly.

"This isn't the time to be petty," Ransom snapped, her dark eyes flashing. "I assume you would prefer it if you and your men survived."

"Yes," he admitted.

"As would I," she said. "We have common cause, Colonel."

"Ah," he said. "You want my help."

"It may already be too late," she said.

And coughed.

She swallowed it down, her expression going pale in the lantern light, and said, "But I'd rather go down fighting. Wouldn't you?"

She reached a hand back behind her. One of the aeronauts passed her a blade—Espira's sword, in fact. She offered the hilt to him.

"Renaldo," she said quietly, "please. The aft hold is adjacent to the engine room and we don't dare use the grenades. I need your warriorborn to handle Sark. That means I need you. If we get out of this alive, I'll take you and your men wherever you want to go."

Espira tilted the pistol back to level and said in a deadly quiet voice, "I would not make any further promises, Captain, if I were in your position."

Ransom's eyes focused on the end of the pistol, and she stifled another cough, trembling.

Espira closed his eyes for a moment. He should never have gotten on this damned ship again. He should never have accepted the mission in the first place, the King's third cousin be damned. He certainly shouldn't have trusted Calliope Ransom.

But damn the woman, she was right about Cavendish. He wasn't going to get a better offer from the madwoman. And by God in Heaven, he was not going to simply stand by and let the etherealist murder the inhabitants of entire habbles with her pet monster. If Tuscarora didn't like that, he could damned well take a running leap from his own Spire.

"I'm in command of the attack, period," he growled. "Get weapons for my men. And I'll have the key to those manacles this instant."

Calliope reached into a pocket and produced the copper-clad key without a word as if she'd been waiting for the request.

Espira took it and then his sword. "Best you let me go explain things to Ciriaco. You know how . . . impulsive warriorborn can be when they've been starved for a night and a day."

Ransom exhaled slowly and nodded. She jerked her head at her men, and they withdrew farther down the passageway. The frightened aeronauts started passing weapons—blades and gunpowder pistols, exclusively—down from the darkness and stacking them against the bulkhead.

"The weapons your men will need, Colonel," she said. "Are you going to help me?"

"Captain," Espira said, finally lowering the pistol and giving her a small bow, "it would seem I have very little choice."

■ ■ ■ Chapter 42 ■ ■ ■

Dueling Platform, Skyport, Spire Olympia

Grimm stood bare chested in the cold drizzle. The wind whipped back and forth uncertainly over the creaking wooden dueling platform. Grimm glanced over the edge to the yawning abyss below. It would be a two-mile drop to the surface if one of the contestants fell. It took a man a relatively long time to fall two miles—long enough to regret a great many decisions.

Below, in the flame-colored mist, a flight of dark birds went by, making raucous sounds that got caught up in the yells of the crowd in the stands observing the platform.

Grimm turned to face Valesco, who stood at the other side of the platform holding his blade by the handle with one hand and between the fingers of his other hand. He bent the supple steel back and forth with lazy indifference.

"Gentlemen," the warriorborn marshal said, his voice rough, "you have chosen to engage under the Protocol Mortis. By law, I am obliged to ask you both if you would be willing to change your minds and engage in the Protocol Sanguis instead."

"I will not," Valesco said almost before the marshal had finished speaking.

Grimm's strategy required the Protocol Mortis. He tried to say that he would not either but found his throat too dry to speak, so he met the marshal's eyes and shook his head deliberately.

The marshal's thick, grizzled hair was being plastered to his head slowly by the persistent drizzle. "Then we will proceed. The duel will cease only at my command or the death of one or both combatants. Requests for respite may be made if agreed upon by all parties and myself. Are these rules understood?"

"Yes," Valesco said impatiently.

Grimm nodded in silence.

The marshal nodded and withdrew a clean white cloth from his jacket. "Draw steel."

Valesco already had, so he dropped into a casual fighting stance. Grimm drew his combat blade with its large steel guard. More suitable for slamming into an enemy's face than dueling, it was dented and scarred from exactly such use. He used a handkerchief to strip away the wax sealant over the finely sharpened, nicked, battle-scarred edge of his blade.

"Salute me," the marshal said.

Both men did so.

"Salute your opponent," the marshal continued.

Grimm did so, extending his weapon's point toward Valesco, then raising it to the vertical.

The marshal gave Valesco a sidelong glance, then raised the cloth overhead. "You may begin when this cloth touches the surface of the platform." He took a step back from between the two men, looked at each of them, and then dropped the cloth.

Valesco turned his back on Grimm and deliberately stretched and yawned.

Grimm's combat reflexes cut in and, blade held ready, he advanced smoothly over the wooden platform. He was tempted to simply deliver a heavy slash across Valesco's spine, but he was certain the move was a feint, and he went for a far more conservative and balanced thrust instead.

It was a ruse. Valesco spun as Grimm covered the critical distance of the warriorborn's superior reach, due both to the length of Valesco's arms and the length of his blade. Grimm barely managed to sweep his heavy sword up in time to prevent taking a lightning slash to his face.

Valesco followed up with a sweeping series of thrusts and slashes with the whipping steel of his dueling sword. Grimm shifted his momentum, dropped his weight slightly, and circled away, defending. His blade, though shorter, was several times heavier than Valesco's, and required no additional momentum other than its own mass and inertia to effectively parry the lighter sword effectively. Grimm kept his motions quick and short, moving the heavier blade as little as possible, pivoting his body around his blade's axis as he tracked the edge of the platform behind him.

Valesco engaged Grimm's blade with his own and tried a short rush to simply push Grimm off the platform's edge as he approached it, but that was a fighting trick of which anyone who had done battle on an airship was well aware. Grimm bent and rolled before the attack, and had Valesco been less agile, he would have gone over the edge. Instead, the Auroran recovered his balance, deflected Grimm's counterthrust with a roll of his blade, and whipped his sword straight out and back.

Grimm felt a sensation like a mild electrical shock in his left shoulder as Valesco's slender sword plunged an inch into his flesh and withdrew again. He reeled back several steps as the larger duelist stood his ground, simply watching Grimm's reaction.

"This is going to be messy," Valesco noted calmly. "The rain is going to make it take less time for you to go into shock, Captain. Pity you didn't opt for the Protocol Sanguis. It would have been seen as cowardly, but I'd have had to make it quick." He swept his sword once to each side, came on guard, and advanced again.

This time, Valesco came in earnest. The man was damnably fast—faster than anyone Grimm had ever crossed blades with before. Grimm defended against the first three thrusts, then tried a counter that was half an instant slower than it should have been. Sudden lightning leapt across his right cheek.

He fell back, and again Valesco gave him time to feel his injury as slow fire spread across his face. The drizzling rain fell a little harder, and his wounds stung. Grimm swiped his left hand over his face, and it came away covered in blood.

Well. He had known this was coming, hadn't he.

He stifled the sick spiral of fear that was spreading through his belly and, after lifting his sword again, extended his arm a little more. Placing the weapon a shade farther from his body would mean that he would need to move it a slightly shorter absolute distance to intercept incoming attacks.

Of course, doing so also made the sword feel that much heavier, which would tire him faster. His wounded shoulder throbbed in time with his face, and the drizzle began to feel slightly colder.

"Honestly, I'd have loaned you a spare blade, Captain," Valesco said politely. "That cleaver you're holding must be getting heavier by the moment."

And again he came. This time, Grimm kept a bit more distance open between them. That meant that he had no opportunity at all to reply to Valesco's attacks, but he was better able to defend against them. The noises of the crowd, shouts and trumpets and drums, rose with every successful parry, but Grimm knew that there was an absolute truth about his tactics. He was being hunted like prey.

The exchange went on for perhaps a minute, a subjective eternity, and Grimm felt his arm begin to burn and tire. Again Valesco scored on him, this time leaving a long cut over the lowest rib on his left side, and instantly a sheet of blood and more burning pain washed over him.

"Still silent," Valesco said. "I suppose there's courage in that, Captain." The Auroran tilted his head, and Grimm realized that the warriorborn was enjoying the fact that the light rain was keeping his body temperature down. "But let's see if we can't make an impression."

This time, Valesco was even faster. Grimm danced around the edge of the platform and managed to stop the first couple of attacks. Then the Auroran pounced, closing the distance with abrupt speed, and scored on the slope of muscle that joined neck and shoulder beneath Grimm's left ear. As Valesco withdrew the blade, he flicked it into a light cut across Grimm's temple—and then, as Valesco ghosted away from Grimm's counter-slash, he plunged his sword's razor-sharp tip into the calf muscle of Grimm's forward leg. Valesco sneered as he twisted the blade and withdrew the sword, dancing back out of range of Grimm entirely.

Grimm couldn't stop a short cry of pain from escaping his lips. The injuries were not large ones, but his blood was turning his body scarlet in the rain, and the pain of his wounds throbbed through him, steadily draining away his concentration and speed. He was slowing down a little at a time while Valesco moved lightly, his long, slender blade dipping and swooping with ease.

The wound to Grimm's calf was the worst. He had no choice but to put his weight on that leg, and while the injury was minor, pressure sent the muscles around it into spasms. He had been lamed— not much, but enough to cost him his life the next time Valesco came at him in earnest.

He couldn't just take the hits. No man in his right mind would. And though he knew it was foolish and knew it would cost him, he could not afford for Valesco to realize that things were more or less proceeding the way he had expected. So Grimm huffed out a wordless, brief cry and lunged forward on his increasingly faltering leg, whirling his heavy blade in a quick combination of attacks that could have left gaping wounds in Valesco's flesh.

The Auroran was a superb swordsman. His light blade could not directly counter the power of Grimm's battle sword, but he rolled the little weapon in circular blocks that deflected the momentum and power of Grimm's weapon.

"Excellent, Captain! Make a good show of it!" Valesco cried, smiling broadly as he defeated one attack after another, his technique perfect, damn the man. As Grimm's attack slowed under the serious energy requirements needed to move the heavy blade at speed, Valesco found an opening and planted yet another shallow thrust to the aeronaut's right pectoral muscle.

Grimm staggered back, his throat burning with shortened breath, pain spreading across his entire upper body. He nearly fell, the sword suddenly awkward to balance in his hand.

The crowd's cheers abruptly fell silent as though a great invisible wind had sucked the breath from thousands of lungs.

A hush fell.

Valesco bared his teeth and raised his hand toward the marshal.

"Respite!" he called. "Marshal, I call for respite!"

The marshal, his face grim and seamed in the rain, turned to Grimm. "Captain," he said quietly, "do you agree?"

Grimm was laboring too hard to breathe to form words. But he gave the marshal a short nod.

"Retire to opposite corners," the marshal said.

Grimm limped heavily to the indicated corner and dropped to a knee, his sword point down. He leaned on his weapon to keep from falling. Blood droplets fell from his body to the platform's surface.

Boots sounded on the platform as Valesco's second, Captain Chavez, went to him. Then more rapid steps sounded, and Ravenna knelt beside Grimm.

"God in Heaven, Frank," she said.

He managed to turn his head enough to look up at her. His neck ached and his shoulder burned where his trapezius had been punctured. His whole body felt quite fiery, really, and at the same time, he was getting colder by the moment. He had to will himself not to begin shivering.

Ravenna had brought bandages. "Where?"

"The leg is worst," he managed to grate out. "Bind it as tight as you think it can take."

"You're a bloody mess," she said.

"Mostly the rain," Grimm said. "Making it worse than it looks."

"Pull the other one," Ravenna said. She cut his pants leg open with a small knife and set to binding his calf. Her quick, strong hands made short and efficient work of it, but it hurt like ten kinds of torture. Grimm was shaking by the time she was finished.

"Can you lift your arms?" she asked. "That cut on your ribs is bleeding too much."

It hurt like blazes, but Grimm lifted his arms. The left burned with pain from the injury, the right with muscular exertion. They shook badly as he held them up. Again she was quick, winding around his torso bandages from a long roll. They turned dark red almost immediately, but they seemed to stanch the worst of the flow from the wound.

"Good," Grimm groaned as Ravenna tied them off. "That's fine."

"Maker of Ways, Frank," she said. She cast a glare over her shoulder toward Valesco's corner, naked fury on her face. "Can you still do it?"

Grimm huffed out a short breath and gave her a faint smile. "We'll . . . know soon . . . won't we?"

She lifted a cloth and wiped at the blood on either side of his face. "Damn you, Frank. Don't waste energy on trying to make jokes. This man will kill you."

"Is that . . . what he's doing?" Grimm panted.

She handed him a flask and he took a blessed drink of water, which eased some of the burning in his throat. He finished the whole thing and passed it back, nodding his thanks.

"Frank," Ravenna breathed.

He met her eyes for a moment. And for just a moment, he allowed the fear pounding through his chest and belly to show. He didn't remember joining hands with her, but he did, squeezing her left hand tightly in his.

Then he turned his gaze across the platform.

Valesco was pacing back and forth in his corner like a restless animal, his eyes focused solely on Grimm. He had been drinking lightly from a flask as well, and he passed it back to Chavez without ever looking at the man. He took a cloth from his pocket and wiped his blade clean with it. Then he inspected the nicks Grimm's heavy sword had left in the blade. Evidently, he found the weapon still serviceable. Then he whipped his sword through a pair of arcs and came out of his corner, flicking a glance at the marshal.

The grizzled warriorborn nodded, but instead of calling out he took the time to walk over to Grimm's corner, giving him a few more seconds to rest. Then he nodded to Ravenna and said, "Captain Grimm, the three minutes are up. It is time to continue."

Grimm nodded. He put his bound leg beneath him and tried to rise, but he had to lean hard on his sword to manage it. Ravenna helped steady him or he might have fallen.

The crowd gathered energy again, crying out, cheering and jeering and shouting and clapping. Horns blew wildly. Drums pounded.

Ravenna gripped Grimm's arm hard and said low, "It's coming. Remember what I told you."

"Ouch, dear," Grimm complained in a very mild tone. "There's a hole in that one."

She gave him a frustrated look but relented at once, her grip instantly turning gentle. "Are you ready?"

He met her feline eyes for a long breath and gave her a firm nod.

"Darling," Valesco caroled toward Ravenna, "do you enjoy wine? I think after this, I'll have a nice, rare steak and an excellent red I brought with me from Aurora for the occasion. I'd love your company."

Ravenna shot him an absolutely murderous glare and opened her mouth.

"Don't," Grimm said firmly. "Don't give it to him."

The muscles in her jaw bunched as she clenched her mouth shut. Without a word, she strode back toward the platform's stairs. She met Chavez there. The Auroran captain gave her an apologetic grimace and gestured for her to go first down the stairs.

And then there were only Grimm, the marshal, and Valesco on the bloodied platform in the gathering darkness.

The birds flying circles beneath them sent up another chorus of raucous cries.

Grimm limped out to meet his opponent one slow step at a time. Valesco watched him come. Grimm didn't look away from the man's eyes.

The Auroran's smile widened. "I'll give you this, Captain. You're no coward." He lifted his sword and pointed it at Grimm's heart. "Shall we finish our dance?"

Grimm tried to lift his heavy blade, but the muscles of his arm seemed to refuse to cooperate. He had to take it in both hands.

The marshal looked at Grimm and nodded firmly. Then he lifted his dampened cloth and said, "When it touches the platform, gentlemen."

Grimm took a deep breath and relaxed every muscle in his body but those needed to hold up the sword.

The marshal flicked the handkerchief into the air and it plummeted damply down to the platform's surface.

The crowd howled.

Valesco came forward like a striking serpent, his sword blurring, driving hard toward Grimm's heart.

Grimm felt sick with terror.

But this was the exact moment he'd been preparing for.

The secret to speed was relaxation, focus, and commitment, Ravenna had told him. They had practiced this precise parry over and over again.

Grimm engaged every muscle needed to drop his blade down in the single fastest move he'd made in the entire duel. The heavy sword was aided by gravity and by the slight bending of his knees. It caught Valesco's thrust in a parry no sane man would make.

Grimm didn't try to slide the blade aside. He didn't try to avoid its point.

He simply moved it.

With desperate speed and absolute focus, Grimm parried Valesco's thrust down into his own thigh. The needlelike point of the blade pierced the heavy muscle and sank in deeply. The tip erupted out the other side of Grimm's leg. Agony like none he had ever known raced up through his body, lanced up his spine.

And with a scream of pain, Grimm twisted his leg, his hips, trapping the slender, flexible dueling blade in his own flesh.

Caught off-balance by the sheer alienness of Grimm's tactic, Valesco followed the blade forward, holding on to the handle, trying to wrench the dueling sword free—but the meat of Grimm's thigh held it trapped.

Grimm's left hand snapped out to seize Valesco's wrist, and with a simple, brutal twist of his shoulders and his good right arm, Francis Madison Grimm swept the short, heavy battle blade up the length of Valesco's trapped limb.

Even in this circumstance, though, Valesco's reflexes were unmatched. He was a creature perfectly adapted to the dueling platform. His left hand lashed across, attempting to deflect the blade.

And had Grimm been wielding a dueling sword, the reaction would have been perfect. Valesco would have traded a moderately severe cut to his off hand for protecting his throat.

But Valesco's reflexes had been built for the dueling platform. And Grimm wasn't wielding a dueling sword.

The sharp, sturdy battle blade went through Valesco's fingers like so many sausages and hacked brutally through the meat of the Auroran's neck to sink with an audible crack into the bones of his spine.

Grimm met Valesco's shocked, unbelieving eyes and snarled, "Sir. You talk too much."

And then, shaking in agony and screaming in fury, with four or five brutal hacks, in a fountain of gore, he chopped off the Auroran champion's head. It fell through a sudden, stunned silence, and landed with a thud on the platform.

Grimm dropped his sword. He bent over and wearily took Valesco's shaved head by one ear and, with a negligent gesture, tossed it over the edge of Spire Olympia. The screaming birds gathered in a cloud that dove after the falling head, vanishing into the mists below.

Then, his balance wavering, Grimm turned to the marshal and slurred, "I believe that concludes the matter, sir."

He felt himself begin to collapse. He never felt the platform rise up to meet him.

The warriorborn marshal caught him.

He saw Ravenna rushing up the stairs, felt footsteps on the platform as she ran forward with Doctor Bagen in tow. The crowd erupted in frenzied howls.

Grimm closed his eyes and stopped worrying about the entire affair.

▪ ▪ ▪ Chapter 43 ▪ ▪ ▪

IAS *Mistshark*, Bound for Spire Olympia

The main hold of the *Mistshark* was full of moaning, coughing, dying men.

Espira led the way, with Captain Ransom coming along behind him and Ciriaco behind her. They glided through the hold without a word, and all around them, strung up in hammocks and stretched out on the deck, were dozens and dozens of men too sick to do anything but cough and shake and moan quietly.

Espira had to do something for them, if anything could be done. But to do that, he had to get rid of Cavendish and Sark—and deal appropriately with Calliope Ransom.

He glanced over his shoulder at the woman, who moved as quietly as any of his Marines. In return, she gave him a level look that told him nothing. He would have to hope that his own expression was just as opaque.

They reached the hatchway to the rear hold and heard the sound of voices. Espira held up a hand, motioning for stillness. The moans and gasps of the sick men filled the air with a constant rasping susurrus that would mask the sounds of their movements if they were cautious enough.

"If you would please just let me see to them," came a man's pleading voice.

Espira didn't recognize it. He glanced aside at Ransom.

She leaned close and whispered, "Doctor Calloway."

Espira nodded and listened.

"Please, ma'am. Those men are in pain," Calloway continued.

"There is nothing you can do for them, Doctor," Cavendish replied. "I do apologize for what is happening to them, but the construct is not as easily recalled as I would have preferred it to be. Just be glad you've proven to be naturally immune. Not even direct exposure to the fluid seems to have had an effect on you. Are your parents of Auroran extraction by any chance? No matter. You might simply have a natural immunity. Mister Sark, please, put the doctor's blood sample into cold storage as soon as we have a moment to spare."

There was a low growl and the sound of glass clinking gently.

"Your pardon, ma'am, but I . . . I don't understand what you're talking about," Calloway said.

"You shouldn't feel bad about that. How could you? It wouldn't be fair to expect you to understand what no one does—myself and the Tyranima excepted, of course."

"The . . . the what, ma'am?"

"Doctor, Doctor, Doctor," Cavendish tsked, "beware of asking questions whose answers would haunt your sleep. Suffice it to say that the Tyranima is the future and this"—she gave a patient sigh—"*all* of this . . . this *nonsense* is nothing but the burned-out remnants of a desperately chaotic past. One that will soon be mercifully laid in its grave."

"Ma'am?" the doctor said, a tremor of fear in his voice.

"Doctor," Cavendish said in a compassionate tone, "you cannot be expected to understand how pathetic humanity has become, huddling in its great stone towers. The heights from which we fell since the Merciful Builders"—she spat the sacred words—"sentenced us to our imprisonment. The Archangels were the last thing standing in the way, and they are all dead. . . ."

Well, a finer time than this to begin the fight could scarcely have been imagined. Espira had no idea what the madwoman was babbling about, but as long as she was working herself into a good rant, he had no objections to using it to his advantage. He nodded toward Ciriaco and made a quick gesture at the door to the rear hold.

The rather grouchy-looking warriorborn ghosted across the floor, set his shoulder as though preparing for an explosive movement, then frowned to himself and tested the handle.

It turned readily. He glanced back at Espira and lifted an eyebrow.

Espira held up three fingers, then two, then pointed the last one at the warriorborn, and the big man exploded into the rear hold with a coughing roar.

Espira went in on Ciriaco's heels, figuratively speaking—the warriorborn was three steps into the hold before Espira had taken his first stride. The other Marines were right behind him, and he led them to the left. Ransom would be taking her people to the right. As he ran, he tried to take in the situation as best as he could, pistol up and questing for a target.

Centered at the rear of the hold was the great copper-and-glass tank, sloshing full with water. Its power leads ran down through a control panel nearby, then down through the floor to the engine room below. Cavendish stood in front of the tank, next to a young man with his arms bound behind his back. Over to one side, near a large cold-storage cabinet, was Mister Sark. The crooked-eyed warriorborn surged into motion in an instant with a coughing roar of his own; he headed directly toward Ciriaco.

Strewn against the rear bulkhead of the hold were the rest of his men. Poor Captain Menendez looked like death, with one of his arms thrown across his eyes and blood dribbling from his nostrils and the corners of his mouth as he labored to breathe. Sergeant De-Leon lay facedown beside him, and Espira could not tell from here if the man was alive or dead.

He turned his pistol on Cavendish.

The two warriorborn met in a blur of steel and flashing hands and feet. Ciriaco and Sark both carried heavy warriorborn blades, and the weapons met with such power and fury that they spat sparks and sent chips of steel flying forth from each impact.

Espira lined his pistol up on Cavendish's heart and squeezed the trigger.

The gun roared and bucked in his hand.

Cavendish was already moving, so the bullet went wide of her, smacking into the wooden bulkhead behind her. She darted behind Doctor Calloway and made a wide hurling gesture with one hand.

There was a sound of rushing wind, and then the air filled with hideous, biting flies the size of Espira's palm. Those creatures inhabited the swampy surface near the abandoned Spire Mobia, where as a young commander he had led a company of Marines in a recovery mission for the crystals of a downed destroyer. The flies hurtled for his face, hitting with stinging impacts, their puncturing mouths plunging into his face and forehead and eyes, their buzzing wings clogging his nostrils.

Espira bucked and staggered, his body thrilling to a sudden tide of panic, and could hear men screaming behind him and around him. He managed not to simply fall, but staggered to a halt, dropped the expended pistol, and clawed at his face with his free hand, trying to clear it of the vicious and hungry insects.

He struggled for several seconds, his throat clogging with the things, which somehow got in through his clenched jaws. Then they were gone, gone as if they had never existed. The pain from their bites vanished, and Espira thrust his hands down. He lifted his head and goggled about the room in confusion to find his men, Captain Ransom, and her aeronauts in almost exactly the same condition—staggered, stunned, and dazed but whole.

Sark stood with a roar, lifted a similarly startled-looking Ciriaco overhead, and flung him into the nearest bulkhead with bone-shattering force.

Espira shouted as he drew his second pistol from his belt. This time he aimed true, fetching Sark a lead ball to the belly. The enemy warriorborn screamed and doubled over, then dropped to a knee.

There was a splash from the tank, and Espira whirled to see that Cavendish had plunged into the murky fluid. Her long hair spread about her in a dark cloud as dirty yellow gel began to stir from the bottom of the tank and swirl around her legs. Her head immediately snapped to one side.

Toward his downed Marines.

The men began to scream.

Espira shouted and began to rush forward, his limbs feeling leaden and far too slow. He could only watch as Commander Menendez thrashed in pain. Menendez's arms flew down to slam against the floor and pushed him up to a sitting position, even as a nest of crystals the color of glowing embers and as thick as Espira's little finger began to burst forth from his eyes, sprinkling blood everywhere. Beside him, Sergeant DeLeon gagged and retched as the same thing happened to him, and the other Marines came to their feet, howling in pain until their throats rasped.

And then they lurched forward toward Espira.

"Colonel!" shouted one of the Marines, a man named DelRio. He fired a shot from his pistol past Espira and into Menendez's chest.

The young commander didn't so much as wobble. He took the round like a light push of the hand and continued forward, gathering momentum as he went. With his sword in hand, DelRio shoved past the stunned Espira to meet Menendez, then swept his weapon in a brutal horizontal slash.

Menendez caught the blow on his forearm, and the heavy battle sword sank into the bone—and stuck there. The young captain didn't so much as flinch. He just ripped the sword from DelRio's hand by leaving it trapped in the bone of his own arm, and struck out with his other hand. The blow landed on DelRio's chest with a sudden wet crackling of breaking ribs, and DelRio dropped in place, clutching his chest and gasping.

Then Menendez ripped the sword out of his own arm, gripped it in his uninjured hand, and turned toward Espira.

But that wasn't the worst of it.

Rasping screams came howling in from the hold behind them. The hold where nearly the entire ship's complement had lain groaning and coughing and sickened.

The crystal-eyed revenants slammed into the small group of Marines and aeronauts, delivering crushing strikes and ignoring bullets and blows with almost equal contempt.

Floating in the tank, Cavendish stared at the results of her work, her smile growing almost inhumanly wide, her eyes casting out a glow the same color as the crystals that had made puppets of his men.

Poor, bound Doctor Calloway had no chance at all. He was overwhelmed by three of the revenants and rapidly, mercilessly torn into several pieces.

"Ciriaco!" Espira screamed. "Sergeant!"

The Hero of Aurora shoved himself up off the deck with one arm; the other was a pulped and bloody mess, oddly misshapen, after Sark hurled him into the bulkhead. His expression was horrified and stern at the same time as he recovered his heavy sword. A revenant got in his way, and when he tried to block the warriorborn's sword, Ciriaco simply deprived the revenant of its arm and, rapidly thereafter, its head.

That seemed to do the trick. The thing dropped to the deck, where it suffered a series of rapid spasms.

"Sergeant," Espira said, drawing his sword, "take the lead. Get us to the ship's launch. We'll try to keep them off your flanks."

Ciriaco, pale and clearly in pain, simply nodded. "Got it," he said, and laid into the nearest revenants with a will, taking legs and arms with great sweeps of his heavy sword.

"Captain Ransom!" Espira screamed. "Follow me!"

Calliope looked up at him desperately. Then she discharged her pistol into the head of an approaching revenant, flipped the weapon to grip it by the doubtlessly hot barrel, and used it to club a second crystal-eyed thing off of one of her aeronauts. Screaming orders, she shoved the man into Ciriaco's wake.

Espira rallied his remaining Marines. There was nothing to be done for the men who had been injured, damn it all. If they didn't clear the main hold before the men there finished becoming revenants, they would all die there in the darkness.

It was a short, desperate, wildly vicious fight. Some of the men's eyes burst into crystals faster than those of others, perhaps based upon how sick the men had been. Espira and the others made it thirty feet before the revenants pressed against them, and even then the warriorborn made the difference. Even though Ciriaco was wounded, his blade was an unstoppable force, cutting down revenants with every sweep.

But the enemy numbers around the stairs were simply too many, and the revenants began to gather more thickly as the group's progress slowed.

"The forward hold!" Espira called. "Bear left, Sergeant!"

Ciriaco altered his direction, and there was less resistance. Calliope's people brought the last few loaded pistols forward; they employed them barely at arm's length and shot for the eyes. While an accurate shot wouldn't end a revenant, it would send them writhing to the floor.

Espira lost four more men before they got back to the forward hold. Calliope did even worse, as only she and two of her aeronauts survived. The last of her men was killed just as he came through the door but then was ripped back out into the darkness of the main hold. He screamed. Loudly. But not for long.

After Espira slammed shut the door to the room that had been their prison, he shot the nearside bolt, then staggered back from it as the last light of the sundown faded and the room sank into gloom.

"Quick!" Calliope said. "The boards from the benches!"

Ciriaco and a couple of the stouter Marines made swift work of dismantling the benches along the bulkhead. One of the surviving aeronauts had nails in a pouch on his belt. They hammered the nails in as best they could with the hilts of knives and the handles of empty pistols, fortifying the door for whatever it was worth.

But Espira had seen the strength of the crystal-eyed revenants. He knew the door would not hold for long.

"My God in Heaven," Calliope breathed. "My God, what have they done to my men?"

"I don't know," Espira said. "I've never seen anything like that."

Calliope shook her head. "They . . . they were still screaming."

"Steady," Espira said, keeping his voice hard. "We need boarding axes to fight those things. Something with more cutting power."

"The armory is on the deck next to my cabin," Calliope said.

Something slammed into the door to the forward hold. Then again. And again.

Outside the ship, the mistmaw let out its moaning cry, this time so loud that it rattled Espira's teeth in his head and sent his heart skipping into a rapid beat as fear shot through him.

Calliope turned to him, but he could barely see her pale face and wide eyes in the dimness.

"Renaldo, what do we do?"

He glanced at Ciriaco. The Hero of Aurora was leaning against the door, more in weariness than with any intention of reinforcing it. His broken arm hung loosely at his side. He met Espira's eyes and shook his head in exhaustion.

Espira nodded slowly.

"What do we *do*?" Calliope pressed.

"We hold out," Espira said quietly. "For as long as we can."

Chapter 44

ACS *Sunhawk*, near Spire Olympia

Bridget woke up in near darkness, as the *Sunhawk*'s bell began to ring and the deck pitched beneath her bed. She was somewhat startled to realize that a couple of men she had not met came tumbling lightly out of two of the bunks on the far side of the room, donned their caps, and shambled out onto the ship's deck.

Benedict appeared in the doorway a moment later, and this time he didn't bother to hurry in and out. The ship had apparently descended from the upper aerosphere, because swirling mist went by outside.

"Bridg— Ah, there you are, already awake. We've arrived at Spire Olympia."

Bridget tried to sit up, found herself held down by the restraining straps on the bed, and sighed. "Oh, bother."

Benedict came over and freed her. "Vincent says he thinks he can get you in front of the Lord President within the hour," he said urgently. "We need to get you as presentable as we can manage."

"The Lord President! Benedict, that's like being brought before the Spirearch!" She looked at him aghast as he helped her sit up. "I look like stale death."

"Part of why Lord Albion sent you, remember?" Benedict fetched a brush from a drawer built into the bulkhead near the bed. "I'm very sorry, but we don't really have time to be as careful as I'd like to be."

"No, go ahead. I don't always have time either," Bridget said, and bent her head forward slightly while Benedict took the brush to her hair.

Despite his words, he managed to balance efficiency with gentleness and at least brushed her hair out straight rather than leaving it in a tangled gold-brown thundercloud.

Outside the cabin's portholes, light streamed around the ship as they came down into the enormously busy skyport of Spire Olympia, its spotlights tracking the incoming vessel. There was light rain falling, and thunder rumbled somewhere in the distance. The maneuvering of the courier vessel was nimbler and swifter than Bridget was accustomed to on an airship, and her stomach lurched several times.

"Rowl!" she said. "Where are Rowl and Fenli?"

"With Vincent and the pilot at the prow," Benedict replied calmly. "They wanted to see Spire Olympia and observe our landing." Benedict mocked a scowl. "And Fenli was entirely too interested in the controls. If he were actually big enough to operate them, I might be concerned."

Bridget's wearied brain was treated to a sudden vision of Fenli, complete with an eye patch and a buccaneer's hat, standing on top of several other cats and piloting the ship off into the sunset. She found herself bursting out in a series of very undignified giggles.

Benedict helped her into a robe and a long coat that went over it, and while Bridget did not feel at all properly dressed, she allowed that at least she would be modest. As Benedict helped her, the *Sunhawk* glided down while the various lumin-crystal lights of the skyport rose up outside the cabin's portholes. The ship thumped very gently down into a landing cradle, then settled in place with a creaking of stressed timber. Benedict brought in the wheeled chair and gentled Bridget painfully into it, taking great care to settle her wounded leg in the brace that propped it out straight.

"Now we wait," Benedict said. "Vincent will send us to the appropriate people."

"I would say that you should kiss me," Bridget said, panting lightly. "But I suspect it would hurt."

Benedict's face colored slightly. "Miss Tagwynn, I believe the pain has made you forward."

"I find myself quite inspired by the sight of you battling a sword mantis."

"I did have a bit of help," Benedict said. "If it had had both of its limbs available to it, I'm not at all sure our fight would have turned out the way it did."

"I'll take the assist," Bridget said firmly. "And you'll take the victory. Among other things."

"Bridget!"

"Don't chide me, Ben," Bridget said, thrusting out her lower lip mockingly. "In my fragile condition, it might make me cry."

"You're turning wicked on me," Benedict murmured, and knelt down beside the chair to put a gentle arm around her shoulders and press a long, slow kiss against her hair.

Bridget sighed happily, despite her general discomfort, and leaned against him for a time. It was, she dimly realized, perhaps half an hour later before she lifted her head and said, "Benedict?"

"Hmmm?"

"It isn't that I don't adore the . . . intimate time with you. But shouldn't someone have come by now? Time does seem to be a bit of a concern."

He straightened, blinking his eyes several times, and Bridget realized that he had not had a chance to properly sleep since the battle; the poor man had to be exhausted.

"I'll go see," Benedict said, and padded quietly out of the cabin.

He returned with Vincent a few moments later. Rowl and Fenli followed them into the cabin.

"We have a problem," Vincent said. "My contact is Lord Lancaster, but apparently he's not at the embassy and they're being quite cagey about where he is. My backup is Duchess Hinton, but she's not in her quarters, and apparently neither are any of her people. I've got my people looking for her now, but the skyport and the nearest streets of Habble Profit are a bit of a madhouse. Apparently, the Auroran duelist Valesco was defeated at sundown, and there's a rather raucous celebration happening. There's some mad rumor that the duchess fought a duel as well—"

"My goodness!" Bridget said.

Vincent shook his head wearily. "But I'm not sure precisely what's happening. I think it might be best if we proceed directly to the Lord President's manor and hope that a personal letter from the Spirearch will get us inside."

"You don't look confident in that plan, my lord," Benedict noted.

Vincent ran a hand through his silver hair, his expression harried. "Getting through the skyport will be an issue. It's a carnival out there."

"Send word to our people here," Bridget suggested. "Surely Captain Grimm will send some men to assist us. Or the commodore."

"I don't have that many people," Vincent said, a frustrated edge to his voice. "My crew is already out trying to find out what's going on, and I'm not sure where either *Predator* or *Belligerent* are berthed."

"Send the prince," Benedict said diffidently. "He knows *Predator*, and Captain Grimm knows him. He can carry a message."

"Prince?" Vincent said vaguely.

Benedict cleared his throat and nodded toward Rowl.

The big ginger cat sighed. "Now I must save the day. Again."

"Oh, Rowl, we truly do need your help," Bridget said.

"Again," Rowl pressed.

"Yes," Bridget said. "Again."

"Very well, Littlemouse. I am, after all, a hero."

"True heroes," Fenli noted, "do not need to talk about their status in order for people to realize it." He hopped up onto Bridget's lap in the wheeled chair and sat down primly. "Now, run along and do errands so that I can save the day."

Bridget rubbed at the space between her eyebrows, where a cat-inspired headache was forming. "I find myself quite sick of this cabin," she said abruptly. "Benedict, would you very much mind pushing me out on deck? There's no room in here, and I suspect I will only be in the way of Vincent using the writing desk where I am."

Vincent nodded and, as he carefully took out his pocket watch, said, "In fact, you are in my way, Miss Tagwynn. It's raining. Take a cap."

Benedict snagged one off a rack by the door and passed it to her. "Thank you," she said. "How much time have we left before the Armada arrives?"

Vincent looked up with a careful, calm expression. "Just over three hours, I should say. Given that it takes an airship time to prepare to lift off, even less . . . If you will excuse me, Miss Tagwynn, I will write the note for . . . Prince Rowl."

"The hero," Rowl said sullenly. "In the rain."

Benedict pushed Bridget out of the courier ship's little cabin and onto the deck. The evening air was chilly, and the rain was coming down in sparse, large droplets that were having trouble deciding whether or not to become ice. Bridget almost instantly regretted her request. But then Benedict draped an oilcloth over her lower body, and the rain spattered off it in fine droplets without soaking in. Fenli trilled a protest and wriggled until he was out from under the cloth and could observe the skyport beside Bridget.

She stared out at the top of Spire Olympia, which, despite the weather, was full of people, mostly aeronauts in their shipboard leathers, but also traders, craft folk, entertainers, vendors, merchants, musicians, jugglers, and dancers, all moving about in a dull roar of laughter and merry talk and good-natured business. Goodness, it was a veritable stampede of humanity, the like of which was seldom seen outside Winterfest, Midsummer, or the solstice festivals. The teamsters and longshoremen who had brought the ship into its berth were hurriedly departing into the crowd to rejoin the impromptu celebration.

"Ben," she said, "are we in time?"

"Honestly, I have no idea," Benedict said easily.

"What happens," she asked, "if the Armada arrives and no one is ready to meet it?"

He stared out at the night for a moment, his eyes scanning the rows and rows and rows of grounded airships. "I can't imagine that it would be anything good. Ships in port are a legal target of war."

"Oh," Bridget said quietly. She looked up at the sky, but in the rain and the mist, she couldn't see farther than the lights of the skyport.

"The real problem is," Benedict said, "that I can't really imagine someone as aggressive as Tuscarora going to the trouble of enslaving a mistmaw to attack his enemies, as well as dispatching his Armada to battle, and *not* sending both to the same place."

Bridget felt a little flutter go through her throat. "You mean . . ."

"Here. Yes."

"Oh," Bridget said. "Oh, my. If we're in the skyport . . ."

"I'll get you to shelter," he said quietly. "Vincent and his people know what they're doing. We'll get it all sorted out."

She fumbled for his hand with her clumsy bandaged fingers. "I think . . . I think I'm too tired to be very afraid."

"That's quite all right," the warriorborn said softly, his feline eyes scanning the skyport. Then his fever-hot fingers closed on her hand harder than she expected. "I've sufficient energy to be frightened enough for both of us."

Chapter 45

AMS *Predator*, Skyport, Spire Olympia

Grimm would much rather have been entirely insensible during the process of having the sword removed from his leg. When Doctor Bagan swabbed out the wound with alcohol, Grimm would rather have been enduring some lesser form of torment, perhaps being soaked in oil and set aflame. By the time Bagen got to cleaning Grimm's other wounds, with all of the concurrent necessary stitching, the captain was quite certain that any true friend would have struck him unconscious, and he told Ravenna so.

"Nonsense," she told him, holding his hands firmly. "I might have broken a nail."

"Quite right," he said weakly. "What was I thinking?"

Bagen, his sad-eyed face set in concentration, worked with steady, professional speed, cleaning the wound sites and stitching them closed with quick, efficient motions. When he got to the long cut over Grimm's ribs, Ravenna placed a roll of leather between Grimm's teeth. He bit down on it and tried not to jump off of the bunk as Bagen's needle flashed.

"Not even Mister Kettle has ever given me this much work, Captain," Bagen sighed when it was over.

Grimm spat out the leather and sank back onto what turned out to be a bunk. He looked around blearily. He'd been taken to the infirmary aboard *Predator*; when he realized where he was, he felt himself relax somewhat at once.

He was home.

"I do apologize, Doctor," Grimm said. "I had hoped to make you use fewer of your medical supplies, but the Auroran was damned disagreeable."

"*He* was," Bagen said with subtle emphasis. He turned to his basin and washed his bloodied hands. "I'm afraid I don't understand how you took him at the end like that."

"He made assumptions, Doctor," Grimm said wearily. "Mostly about me but partly about himself. Very dangerous not to know oneself in a fight for one's life."

Ravenna put a placating hand over Grimm's and said, "His mistake was thinking of it as a game. A game he was quite good at playing and winning." She smiled slightly. "Frank understood that there's only one person who wins at this kind of game."

"The one who survives," Grimm said firmly. "I may have been holding back a bit until the very end. And even then, it would never have occurred to someone like Valesco that I would make such a sacrifice to win." He swallowed. "Ah, how much did I wind up sacrificing, Doctor?"

"Most of the wounds aren't too terribly bad," Bagen reported in a neutral voice. "If none of them go septic, you should recover. You lost quite a bit of blood, but the wounds are not the worst I've seen by any means. The leg . . . well, Captain, you might consider what sort of cane you'd like to use."

Grimm felt himself quail a bit at the thought but pushed it away. He'd made the choice, now, hadn't he? And he would live with it. The operative word being "live." "I see."

"You're healthy. It's possible you'll regain some portion of use if you exercise your leg carefully. I'll write a fellow I know in Dalos who has had good results with such rehabilitative measures, and we'll work out a daily regimen for you."

"That would be very fine, Doctor," Grimm said. "I wonder if I might have some water now. I'm parched."

"Sip it slowly," Bagen admonished. "Captain Ravenna, if you would help him with that? I'll go get him some broth."

"Broth," Ravenna scoffed. "He's lost blood enough. He needs a nice, rare steak."

Grimm quailed again but in an entirely different way, and he suggested, "Perhaps water first."

Bagen left calmly, and Ravenna, despite her brusque tone, was very gentle about helping Grimm sit up and take a few sips of water. She let him have only enough to coat his tongue at any one go, and Grimm felt entirely too weary to argue with her. Eventually, he found the cup removed from his lips, and her own replacing it. He returned the kiss with as much ardor as he could muster—approximately none or very little more.

Ravenna sat back from the kiss, grinning, and said, "That's all right. You'll heal."

He felt a corner of his mouth tilt up, and he murmured, "So it would seem. What have I done?"

"You have earned nights that the skalds would sing about if any of them dared," Ravenna replied smugly. "God in Heaven, Frank, that was boldly done."

"It was necessary," Grimm replied quietly. "I took no pleasure in it."

"Well, you're not going to be able to say that about what I do to you," she replied in a practical tone.

There were frantic bootsteps along the deck, and a young woman's voice called stridently, "Make way! Make way!" Then the door to the infirmary flew open and Gwendolyn Lancaster burst in. "Skip!"

Grimm nodded to her. "XO."

Gwen stared at him for a moment and then said, "You're . . . going to live, Skip?"

"And then some," Ravenna said with an arch smile.

The young woman looked back and forth between them, then let out an explosive breath of relief. "Well, thank the Merciful Builders for that at least."

"Lady Hinton's duel?" Grimm asked wearily.

"She lost in the most spectacularly domineering way imaginable," Gwen replied promptly. "Humiliated Atlantea. No one died."

"Ah," Grimm said, "good."

"Skip?" Gwen asked. "Valesco?"

"Your captain threw his head off the side of the Spire," Ravenna said calmly.

Gwen blinked several times and then said, "Well done, Skipper."

"Thank you, XO," Grimm said. "Are the men back aboard yet?"

"According to Mister Stern, all but a handful," Gwen said. "We're making ready to sail now just in case, and I made sure word was taken to *Belligerent* before the duel."

"Excellent. Thank you, XO."

Ravenna nodded and rose. "Then I'd best make for *Stormmaiden*."

"The men want to be out carousing. I'm placing quite a bit of trust in your instinct, Ravenna," Grimm said quietly.

"Name one time that's gone wrong for you before," she said.

Grimm extended his hand, and Ravenna gripped it hard and shook it.

"Thank you for your help, Captain," he said.

"My pleasure, Captain," Ravenna replied. She flashed him a

happy smile and said, "I love seeing a smug bastard put in his place. Miss Lancaster."

"Captain," Gwen said.

Ravenna padded out with quick, silent movements, vaulted the handrail outside Grimm's cabin, and vanished down toward the spire-stone of the skyport.

Gwen watched her go thoughtfully, then turned back to Grimm. "Captain, if you don't mind me asking?"

"The entire point of the past two years has been for me to answer your questions, Miss Lancaster," Grimm said, his mouth quirking in amusement.

"How in the world did you defeat Valesco?"

"He underestimated me and overestimated himself," Grimm replied. He attempted to shift his hips and a spike of pain went through his wounded leg, causing his whole body to clench for a moment. "Nnnngh. Miss Lancaster, should we need to take to the sky, I'm going to trust you to command *Predator*."

Gwen stared at him for a moment, her expression serious. Then she nodded her head and squared her shoulders. "I'll take good care of her, Skip."

"You'll command her," Grimm corrected her.

"What are you expecting?"

"There's politics on the wind," Grimm said, grimacing. "God in Heaven only knows. But Ravenna is making ready to lift off at a moment's notice. She says it's an instinct, but I suspect she knows something she isn't supposed to tell me."

"An attack from Pike?" Gwen suggested.

"On a major port like Olympia?" Grimm asked. "It would start a general war if someone did that. It would take every ship Pike had, and it would be against their operational style and bloody as hell."

"Then what?"

Grimm shook his head slowly. "Perhaps her government has given her intelligence she's not allowed to share with Albion directly." Grimm nodded sharply. "There are half a dozen Albion-flagged merchants here. Have Lieutenant Stern send runners to them and advise them to make ready to sail on short notice, identifying me as the captain of the Spirearch's personal vessel. And I want you personally to send word to Admiral Pike, advising him to do the same."

Gwen nodded firmly. "What about the Olympian Fleet?"

"We can only hope that the admiral takes us seriously," Grimm said. "If he does, perhaps he can talk the other Olympians into going along with him."

"Skip," Gwen said, "with your permission, I'll send word to my lord father as well."

"Capital thinking, XO," Grimm said. "If Lord Lancaster lends his weight to a general state of readiness, the Olympians might well listen to him."

"I'll get right on it, Skip," Gwen said. She tossed him a salute and turned to go, but paused at the door to smile back at him. "I placed quite a bit of money on you to defeat Valesco, you know."

Grimm blinked at her. Miss Lancaster's idea of a lot of money did not line up with most people's notion of the same. "You've been spending too much time around Mister Kettle, XO."

"I daresay the local Guilds are going to take a serious hit to their bottom line this year," Gwen said smugly. "And . . . I'm glad to see you victorious, Skip."

"Hmph," Grimm said, smiling at her. "Get to work."

"Aye, aye, Skip," Gwen said, grinning, and turned to leave, nearly bumping into the returning Doctor Bagen. The two danced around each other, Bagen juggling a steaming mug and a bowl of broth. Then Gwen hurried off down the deck, yelling for Lieutenant Stern.

"Captain," Doctor Bagen said calmly, bringing in strong tea and the promised broth, "you'll need to drink these. And, sir, there's a cat standing on the deck at the top of the gangplank, yowling. I believe he may be Prince Rowl."

Grimm sat up straight in surprise, and grimaced at the pain that shot through his leg. "Rowl? What in the name of God in Heaven would he be doing in Olympia?"

"I'm sure I don't know," Bagen said seriously. "But he's got some kind of message tube around his neck."

"Hah," Grimm said. "Well, don't just stand there, man. Send him in."

Chapter 46

Warren Manor, Habble Profit, Spire Olympia

Abigail stood by the window of Lady Iphigenia's parlor, staring out at the streets of Habble Profit. They were high enough up that she could see several blocks of the habble, which was abuzz with activity. As a major trading hub, every bit the equal of Habble Morning in Albion, Habble Profit was always busy, but this time of the evening was generally much quieter. Hamish had brought her word of the rather spectacular ending of Captain Grimm's duel with the late Valesco, and she had breathed a huge sigh of relief.

At least she hadn't been responsible for the death of Alex's best friend.

"And I'm sure, Lord Lancaster," Lady Iphigenia was saying, "that my brother will be glad to meet with you in the morning."

"Lady Warren," Lord Lancaster said with stiff formality, "I'm very much afraid that half a day's delay may matter a great deal."

"Perhaps," Iphigenia replied frankly, "to Albion. But this is Olympia, sir. And Olympia does not currently stand on the brink of war with Spire Aurora."

Lord Lancaster made a visible effort to compose himself and took up his cup of tea. Because of course they were all having tea,

Abigail thought. The fates of entire Spires were in the balance and here they were sipping tea and being polite.

She took up her own cup and drank. Ten minutes of dueling and here she was, desiring to solve problems in the Bayard tradition. Draw a sword, set sail, run out the cannon. She sipped her tepid tea and kept her silence. Lord Lancaster was an able politician and would most likely get through to the Olympians in time.

"Nor is it ready to fight Aurora, should Tuscarora decide to attack," Lord Lancaster pointed out. "Your fleet is mostly merchant marine. You have but four dreadnoughts to match against the Armada's heavy squadrons and a similar disparity of light and medium warships."

"Our merchant fleet has a martial tradition at least as significant as your own, Lord Lancaster," Iphigenia replied stiffly.

He lifted his hands. "Of course it does. But in Albion, perhaps only one captain in ten can match his crew's skill against a professional warship, and the differences in the capabilities of purpose-built military vessels and ships meant for trade are not insignificant, particularly over the course of a military campaign."

Lady Iphigenia's mouth quirked. "Are you trying to frighten me into compliance, Lord Lancaster? Do you think I'm going to shiver in my corset and feel dread at the proposition of fighting Aurora?"

Lord Lancaster shook his head. "Of course not. Olympia's resources are outstanding. Your merchant fleet is the largest in the world—almost double the size of any other Spire's, even Dalos's. And you could have them worked up to a near-military level of preparedness in less than a year."

Lady Iphigenia frowned and leaned back in her seat, motioning with one hand for him to continue.

"But there is one resource you do not have in any greater abundance than anyone else, madame: time. Consider that Aurora has been testing upon Albion colonies a new weapon—a weapon that has completely destroyed entire skyports and wiped out the inhabitants of the upper levels of a Spire within the space of a few hours. Suppose that weapon was turned upon Olympia—and upon Habble Profit, which very well might be its purpose."

Her frown darkened. "And why would Tuscarora use it here instead of in Albion?"

"Our skyport defenses have always been heavier, to the detriment of the number of berths we can offer trading ships," Lancaster pointed out. "Habble Landing made up for that difference, but after Aurora's surprise attack two years ago, that advantage was lost, and our trade has been considerably throttled since then. Even so, I managed to convince the Council that we needed to maintain those defenses. Those batteries are sufficient to make an attack upon Albion too costly to consider, particularly with the Aetherium Fleet ready to defend the Spire. Can you say the same about Olympia's defenses?"

"Olympia's defenses are her value as a trading partner and her skill at diplomacy," Iphigenia said frankly.

"Yes, Olympia is incredibly valuable. And only moderately well defended in order to discourage independent raiders," Lord Lancaster said gently. "You've read as much history as I have, Lady Iphigenia. You know which kinds of targets attract aggressive leaders."

She opened her mouth to speak and then seemed to think better of doing so. She took a sip of tea instead.

Abigail's figurative ears perked up. That had been the plan, of course. Lord Lancaster was to engage her, and Abigail was to observe and glean whatever she could from Iphigenia's reactions. Or rather, that would have been the plan had she actually spoken to Lancaster about it, but naturally neither of them had.

"Diplomacy is your defense," Abigail murmured. "You seem

remarkably undisturbed at the possibility of Auroran aggression. And the Lord President isn't available until morning. Where, I wonder, is the newly single Princess Sarafine?"

Iphigenia and Lancaster both turned to stare at her. Lancaster looked back and forth between the two ladies and took note of Iphigenia's rather caught-out expression. He would understand the ramifications at once, of course.

"Ah," he said quietly, "I think I see. Tuscarora has tendered an offer of alliance—perhaps marriage between his sister and your brother?"

"My brother," Lady Iphigenia said firmly, "is unavailable for the night."

"Of course," Abigail said. "I see it now."

"The duels were a distraction," Lord Lancaster said, nodding. "Or rather, they were the sword we were supposed to focus upon. This is the dagger aimed at our guts." He shook his head.

"Please, Lord Lancaster," Lady Iphigenia said, her tone mildly caustic. "Was it such a coincidence that the very attractive and single daughter of the prime minister of Albion also happened to be present at the summit?"

Lord Lancaster blinked at Iphigenia a couple of times and then said, "My God, I hadn't even considered that."

Lady Iphigenia gave him an openly skeptical look.

Lord Lancaster waved a hand. "You'd have to know Gwen better. Believe me, I'd rather surrender to Tuscarora than try to arrange a marriage for that young woman."

"Forgive me for saying so, but that seems a very convenient explanation," Iphigenia said.

"It does if you haven't met her. My God in Heaven, she's decided to become an aeronaut," Lancaster said acerbically. He blew out a breath. "I take it negotiations with Tuscarora have begun."

Iphigenia seemed to consider her answer for a moment and then said, "My brother is quite taken with Lady Sarafine."

"Especially if her tailor is providing her with the latest Atlantean fashions, I'd wager," Abigail said, her voice hard.

Iphigenia frowned, her expression suddenly pensive. "Meaning what, precisely?"

"You recall your comments about the strength of Initiate Hestia's presence?" Abigail asked.

"Of course."

"That presence was being enhanced by a new ethersilk design that incorporates etheric principles in order to generate an emotional response in those nearest the wearer. The personal etherealist to His Majesty is downstairs in your dining room with my retainers. He could explain it to you."

Iphigenia shook her head. "That seems a rather large pill to swallow, Lady Hinton, if you will pardon me."

Abigail frowned. "Didn't you wonder why my serving girl was so inept? Mine? When have my people ever been incompetent?"

The Olympian frowned.

"She is also an etherealist. Our intelligence picked up word of Hestia's new design, and I reasoned that she might well test it at the Spectral Tea. I wasn't making a fashion statement with those crystals. Miss Folly was using them to protect me from being influenced."

Iphigenia shook her head slowly and looked sharply at Lord Lancaster. "Is this true?"

"To the best of my knowledge," Lancaster said frankly.

Iphigenia exhaled slowly, her expression suddenly worried. "Princess Sarafine is currently in a private dinner with my brother. They are . . . becoming acquainted with each other."

"And?" Abigail asked.

"And she was wearing an Atlantean-styled silk gown," Iphigenia said, "as she has been for days."

"Except at the Tea," Abigail said.

"Except at the Tea," Iphigenia confirmed. "She wore them . . . only when she was near my brother."

A commotion arose outside, and Abigail glanced out the window. "That's the fourth runner I've seen in the last hour," she said. Then she stiffened. "Did you ask your staff to make sure we weren't interrupted?"

"Of course," Iphigenia said. "I know you may not like the fact that we may become a neutral party in this war, but you both still have my personal respect. I wanted to make sure you had my attention."

"God in Heaven," Abigail said, and strode for the parlor door, "someone is desperate to get through to us. I think we need to speak to these runners at once."

"Abigail?" Lady Iphigenia asked.

"If I'm wrong, I'll owe you apologies, dear. But if I'm right, I think we have all underestimated Tuscarora and what he is willing to do."

Lord Lancaster rose and extended a hand to Lady Iphigenia. "Your Grace? Regardless of Olympia's intentions, I think it would be best for your brother and for your Spire if we gathered as much information as we can as quickly as we can. Shall we?"

Iphigenia's rawboned face hardened in a sudden decision, and she extended her hand. "Absolutely."

Abigail was in the hallway and striding for the stairwell when she heard voices ahead of her.

"Her Grace Lady Iphigenia has given orders that she not be interrupted," said a man in a hard voice.

"And I'm telling you, Guardsman," Hamish said in a very patient and reasonable tone, "that top-priority dispatches for Lady Hinton and Lord Lancaster have arrived and must be delivered immediately."

"Hamish," Abigail called, "I'm coming. Under no circumstances are you to render that man unconscious."

She turned a corner and found Hamish standing before a trio of House Warren's guards. "Your Grace," he said, and held up a hand with a number of envelopes, "Sir Vincent just arrived on a fast courier ship. He's got top-priority envelopes marked for you."

Abigail drew in a breath as Iphigenia and Lancaster arrived behind her. "Sir Vincent," she said to Iphigenia, "is Lord Albion's personal minister of intelligence."

Iphigenia blinked at that. "I thought he was his valet."

"Iphi, please," Abigail sighed. "I have worked with Vincent and Addison for many years. The Spirearch would not have sent him if it weren't a matter of life and death."

Iphigenia searched her eyes for a moment and then said, "All this time, you've been a spy?"

"No, dear," Abigail said, "I have *also* been a spy."

Iphigenia frowned down at her. "You come in here with wild tales about new etheric devices that can influence minds when simple lies can do that job quite effectively. Why should I believe you?"

Abigail exhaled. "Why on earth would I lie about being a spy, knowing that doing so would end our friendship and my ability to keep doing it?" She spread her hands. "I told you that because I'm telling you the truth, Your Grace. If you believe me and there is no threat to Olympia, you've wasted nothing but a little time. But if there *is* a threat, if Tuscarora is daring enough to strike at you now, you could save thousands of lives and the freedom of your home Spire."

Iphigenia hedged visibly.

"Guardsman," Abigail snapped toward the security man in front of Hamish, "by any chance, did the Lord President leave instructions that he not be disturbed under any circumstances?"

"Answer her," Iphigenia instructed calmly.

"He did, Your Grace," the security man said hesitantly. His cheeks reddened slightly. "Ah, 'Randolph, don't you dare let anyone knock on that door until breakfast' were his exact words."

Abigail turned back to Iphigenia and folded her arms.

Iphigenia frowned and then beckoned Hamish. "Come forward, sir."

Hamish hurried over. Abigail tore open the missives and read them in frantic haste, needing only a pair of seconds per page before she passed each on to Lancaster. "God in Heaven," she breathed. She whirled on Iphigenia and said, "Your Grace, the Armada will be here in a matter of hours. Your brother needs to order your Fleet ships into the air immediately." She thrust the relevant missive at Lady Iphigenia.

"Maker of Ways," Iphigenia breathed, reading. "Randolph, I need to meet with my brother at once."

"Your Grace," the guard said carefully, "he gave very clear orders."

"I changed his diapers when he was an infant," Iphigenia said firmly. "I *think* I know when it is necessary to invade his privacy as an adult. Take me to him this instant."

The guard winced. "Yes, Your Grace," he said, and started purposefully down the hall with the others in tow.

Lord Lancaster finished scanning the papers and looked up at Abigail, somewhat stunned. "We know how he was wiping out the colony Spires, Your Grace," he said somewhat breathlessly. "There are witnesses to the fact who have been sent along to give testimony."

"We'll give it all to the Lord President," Iphigenia said firmly. "He's the commander in chief of our military." She blinked. "Who would have been unavailable to issue any orders at all if you hadn't intervened, Abby."

Abigail had opened her mouth to answer when the very walls around her and the floor beneath her vibrated with a low, moaning sound that buzzed higher and higher and ended in a long, eerie shriek so loud that it echoed through the habble and even into the halls of the presidential manor.

Lady Iphigenia stopped in her tracks, her eyes wide. "Maker of Ways," she breathed, "what was that?"

Abigail felt her heart begin to beat in sudden, frantic terror. "Tuscarora's secret weapon," she said in a voice that came out with far more matter-of-fact serenity than she felt. "A mistmaw."

Lady Hinton turned to Lord Lancaster and said simply, "It's already here. We're too late."

Chapter 47

AMS *Predator*, Skyport, Spire Olympia

Pain had kept Grimm from falling into more than a light drowse. When the mistmaw's wail came, from nearer than he'd ever heard one, it shook *Predator* so hard that his empty broth bowl tumbled off the nightstand and shattered on the floor. The sound was as deafening as the howl of cannon in battle.

Fear went through his body like lightning.

Pain vanished.

Predator was in danger.

"General quarters!" he bellowed, flinging himself out of the bed and hopping on one leg to fling open the cabin's door to a night of that same cold, drizzling mist and rain. "General quarters!"

From the bridge of the airship, he heard Gwen's voice ringing out like the high notes of a trumpet, and an instant later the ship's bell began clanging frantically.

"Kettle!" Grimm shouted as the pilot came pounding down the deck, his neck and shoulders burdened with perhaps fifty pounds of layered gold chain. "Get me to the bridge!"

Kettle stopped and blinked at him. "Skipper, get back in bed!"

Grimm shoved his arms into his coat, seized his safety harness from its peg by the door, fastened it on with the ease of a lifetime of practice, and slammed his peaked captain's cap over his brow. "Damn it, man, that's an order!"

Kettle looked briefly torn, then spat, "Maker's balls," and seized Grimm under his left shoulder, put the captain's arm around his neck, and dragged him toward the bridge while the captain wore nothing but his coat and hat, half a pair of pants, and bandages.

"My God, Kettle," Grimm grated as the chains pressed into his arm, "you look like a pirate king."

"I won't say what you look like, Skip. But my winnings wouldn't all fit in my trunk," Kettle said cheerfully. "Like as not those scoundrels in engineering will help themselves before they get to stations."

"Good God in Heaven, man," Grimm said.

"The odds were pretty long against you." Kettle grinned ferociously. "Haven't gotten anything but richer following your orders, Skip."

They reached the bridge, and Grimm seized the handrails on either side of the precipitously steep staircase up to the bridge and hauled himself up with his arms and his good leg. Kettle went up the other staircase and beat Grimm there by only a second.

Gwen was standing next to the piloting station, shouting into the speaking tube, and she noticed Kettle first. "Damn your blocky ass, Mister Kettle!" she snapped. "Get to your post!" Then she saw Grimm and an unmistakable expression of relief came over her features before being rapidly replaced by outrage. "Captain Grimm! What do you think you're doing?"

Kettle helped Grimm over to the command station. They'd upgraded the station with its own shock frame, like on the pilot's station, and Grimm clipped himself into position with the attachment points on his safety harness.

"I'm not sitting in my cabin," he said.

Behind him, he heard the gunnery officers getting men into place and unshipping *Predator's* cannon. More men were leaping into the dorsal rigging, while other aeronauts were hurrying to be ready to rush to their stations on the lateral and ventral rigging as soon as *Predator* gained air and could sweep out her other three masts.

Gwen gave Grimm a hard look for a second and then said, "Mister Kettle, if the captain starts bleeding through his bandages, I'm relieving him of duty."

"Aye, aye, XO. Or if he can't stand," Kettle said with a firm look at Grimm, and strapped himself in. "Pilot stands ready, Skip."

"I can bloody well stand for this," Grimm said firmly. "Crew to the forward chase gun as well, double time."

Gwen bawled the orders down the deck, and men called back as they raced to respond. "The chase gun, Skip?"

"It's the only thing we've got that will do more than tickle a mistmaw," Grimm said evenly. "What's the status on the crystal array?"

Gwen strapped into the frame beside Grimm's and calmly checked her pocket watch. "Ready in forty-five seconds from . . . mark."

"Journeyman always pads his time estimates," Grimm said. "We'll go in thirty seconds, Mister Kettle."

"Aye, aye, thirty seconds, Skip."

The gunnery officers port and starboard called out their readiness. Crews stood by the web reels at each mast, ready to play out the ethersilk webbing that would, when charged with electricity from the power core, give the ship its drive.

Grimm seized the speaking tube for engineering and shouted, "Bridge to engine room!"

"Engine room, aye!" came Journeyman's response.

"The sky is shortly going to be crowded, Chief. Maximum power to the running lights."

"Running lights, aye!" came Journeyman's sour reply. "I've got nothing better to do, Skip."

Grimm snorted and hung up the speaking tube, counting silently when a very clear, calm voice said, *Captain*, Predator. *Miss Folly is approaching. She needs another thirty seconds.*

Grimm twitched in pure, startled bewilderment and glanced around him. Gwen was watching the second hand of her pocket watch intently. Journeyman was poised to lift off. Neither had reacted to the voice.

Grimm looked around wildly and spotted Miss Folly's stark black-and-white hair. The young woman had fought her way through the suddenly panicked crowds on the skyport somehow, and she was pelting down the starboard side of the ship in another one of those mismatched outfits that made her look like a badly dressed doll.

"Belay takeoff, Kettle!" Grimm snapped. "Lieutenant Stern!"

"Aye, Captain!" came the young officer's call from the starboard-side gunnery officer's position.

"Lower a line for Miss Folly and get her aboard!"

"Aye, sir!"

With the crew of the chase gun, the slender young officer rushed down the deck, seized a coil of rope, whipped a loop in its end, hurled it down, and called out to the young woman.

As he did, there was a flare of lights as the lumin crystals mounted along the hull of *Stormmaiden* burned to life, and Ravenna's lean, wolfish ship leapt swiftly into the air and began to rise, her running lights shattering to rainbows through the rain and mist. Alarm bells were ringing on most of the airships in port now, and the carnival atmosphere had turned to sudden horror.

The docking berth beneath *Predator* abruptly shook as if kicked by a giant, and only the safety harness and shock frame kept Grimm from being toppled from his one good leg. Incredibly, everyone in *sight* staggered. People fell into one another across the entire surface of the skyport as though the Spire itself had been suddenly shaken. The rain itself rippled for a moment, so vast was the energy involved.

A sound so deep that it threatened to turn Grimm's guts to water reverberated through the night air.

The mistmaw had struck the Spire itself.

Grimm turned in near panic to see his men haul Miss Folly aboard, and the moment she was over the railing, he snapped, "Take her up, Mister Kettle, best speed."

Kettle didn't respond with a confirmation. Instead, he simply hauled back on the elevation controls. *Predator* sailed up as swiftly as a bird would for the open sky, her own running lights flaring as power flowed through the ship's systems.

"I don't understand," Gwen said, her voice shaking. "Mistmaws don't attack Spires."

"But if one did," Grimm said, "I can imagine that it would be capable of wiping out an entire skyport. Like the one we saw at Spire Dependence."

Gwen's eyes widened as she understood. "This isn't a coincidental attack."

"You yourself witnessed Aurora's agents using silkweavers against us two years ago, I believe. Perhaps they've found a way to expand their control to other creatures."

Gwen's eyes flashed with anger and her jaw set in a hard line. "God in Heaven preserve us."

Other ships began to rise. *Belligerent*, still dressed like a debutante at a ball in her red, blue, and white bunting, hauled herself into the sky. Half a dozen Olympian ships, including a pair of heavy cruisers, were already rising.

And so was the Atlantean heavy cruiser with its red, white, and black zigzag-painted hull whose nameplate read *Achilles*.

And so was the Auroran dreadnought *Conquistodor*.

Gwen followed Grimm's line of sight and asked calmly, "Do you think she's about to open fire?"

It was an excellent question. *Conquistodor* had the firepower to destroy every ship lifting out of Spire Olympia's skyport in rapid order. She could blow every Albion and Olympian vessel present out of the sky without breaking a metaphorical sweat.

"She hasn't run out her guns yet," Grimm replied. "My guess is that Captain Chavez retired to his ship after the duel and simply reacted. He seemed a decent enough sort of fellow."

Below them, the skyport was pure chaos. A crowd had gathered around the entrance to the spiraling transport ramps that ran the length of the Spire. People pushed and shoved in an instinctive attempt to seek the safety of the spirestone shelters that had provided haven for humanity against the surface creatures for millennia. Aeronauts fought and pushed to move in more or less the opposite direction, struggling to get through the crowds to their airships from all across the skyport.

A few of the smaller merchant airships, corvette-sized vessels crewed by a few dozen, were lifting off, though even they were shorthanded. One of them suffered a failure in its port-side lift crystal array and listed badly to the side, then slowly careened into an Olympian destroyer whose crew was making frantic preparations to lift off. Wood splintered with earsplitting cracks, splinters flying. Men screamed. Some portion of the electrical system on the destroyer failed in a cascade of crackling bolts of blue-white lightning and sparks that showered the wreckage of both ships.

"Skip!" Kettle said, his voice gone suddenly hoarse with fear. "Starboard, four o'clock!"

Grimm whipped his head around as Kettle obligingly pitched the ship slightly to starboard, and saw the greatest beast of his mist-covered world emerge from the darkness into the frantically sweeping lumin-crystal spotlights of Olympia's port defenses.

It was like watching an enormous, leathery mountain rise out of the mist, and there was no way the spotlights could illuminate even a portion of the creature. Fog and rain roiled and sluiced off the vast beast's flanks as a gargantuan bubble of cracked hide appeared, then drifted upward through the night sky on its own etheric power.

Grimm stared in awe and horror as the defense guns of the skyport oriented on the target illuminated by the spotlights and opened fire. Cannon howled as lances of boiling-hot energy lashed out almost too quickly to be seen and exploded into spheres of green-white flame as bright and hot as miniature suns against the thing's hide, spilling fire across the mistmaw's back and flanks and drawing an air-shuddering moan of reaction out of it.

The mast of one luckless merchantman intercepted a cannon bolt. Her crystal array silent, without any of an airship's shroud of protection to defend her, the mast vanished into a boil of light, and every wooden surface within twenty yards burst into flame.

It took the mistmaw nearly half a minute to rise fully into sight, and when it did, it towered hundreds of feet over the skyport. The mountain of flesh began to glow with fire-colored light spilling out from beneath its cracked hide. The skyport's guns poured fire onto the creature with furious abandon, and Grimm saw that the thing somehow generated an etheric shroud of its own, shrugging off fire and energy as it spilled across its skin without sinking in, like raindrops on an oilcloth.

And then the mistmaw's underside appeared, and great ropy tendrils of flesh, thicker than a dozen of *Predator*'s masts, coiled and roiled and lashed out in mindless fury. Grimm saw one of them strike the armored turret of a defense battery and smash it like a fine teacup. Others swept into a warehouse and sent it flying off the edge of the Spire and into the abyss while the poor, unfortunate men and women hiding inside screamed their way to their deaths. Still more hanging tentacles smashed down as the mistmaw began to move, gliding over the skyport, bringing more and more and *more* dangling tentacles to bear on the ships and buildings—and people—beneath it.

Smaller, lither tentacles in fantastic abundance swept down as more of the mistmaw's bulk warped slowly over the skyport. With indiscriminate hunger they began hauling up barrels, boxes, and terrified, howling people, all of which were drawn into the ember-colored glow of the creature's underbelly.

Great smashing sounds and screams and the useless howl of Olympia's light defenses vanished beneath another moaning wail from the enormous beast.

"Masts out!" Grimm bellowed down the ship as the sound faded, and the deck officers took up the call, relaying orders. *Predator's* port and starboard masts swept out like great wings, and her ventral masts would be dropping into place even more quickly. "Run out the maneuvering web!"

"Skip!" Gwen called over the tumult as *Predator* continued to ascend. "*Conquistodor!*"

Grimm snapped his head around to see the Auroran dreadnought. Her huge masts stretched out all around the clock, her wide maneuvering webs spread like glittering motes of silver—and her flanks suddenly bristled as she ran out her multiple decks of guns. Her horns caroled the high-pitched, brassy blasts the Aurorans loved so much. The sound was almost a rival to the mistmaw itself.

"My God," Grimm said, instinctively understanding at once what he saw. "Chavez is challenging the thing."

Conquistodor's spotlights suddenly focused on her own stern lines, and Grimm saw the signal flags being run up. Though each Spire's Navy would use its own coded flags, there were universal signals shared amongst all airships to make ship-to-ship communications practical.

Gwen stared, her mouth open, and said, "Captain, *Conquistodor* signals a general order to . . . form up on her for an attack."

"By God she does, XO," Grimm said.

Belligerent, still fitted with Auroran-style horns, aggressively trumpeted her reply. Then her blowers roared to life, turning the Albion battlecruiser with elegant grace and sending her on a lateral course that would take her directly beneath *Conquistodor* on the vast dreadnought's flank. Her own spotlights shone on her stern lines, where simple flags of compliance were being run up.

"Is this a trick to get us to lower our guard, Skip?" Gwen demanded. "Why would the Aurorans send that thing to attack and have their own ship square off on it?"

Grimm stared at the dreadnought for a long moment and thought about the plain, stocky man who commanded her. "Wars are fought by men, XO," he replied slowly. "Captain Chavez probably doesn't know what's going on. Or maybe he does, and he isn't going to stand around and let that monster kill thousands of unprotected souls in the skyport when he has a ship under him that might stop it." He clenched his jaw and nodded. "And, by God, neither are we!"

Gwen stared at the captain for a second, then flashed a ferocious smile and said, "Of course we aren't, Skip!"

Grimm answered her smile in kind, turned to Kettle, and said, "Pilot, take us into formation on the extreme flanks astern of *Conquistodor.* Keep our nose to the thing." He raised his voice. "Lieutenant Stern! Ready the chase gun!"

"Powering up the chase gun, aye!" screamed Stern's tenor from behind Grimm.

The Olympian ships were responding as well, if not as crisply as Bayard's vessel.

"What if it's a trick to get us in close to all those guns, sir?" Gwen said quietly.

"Well, then, XO, we will be in position to send broadsides lengthwise up *Conquistodor*'s arse while she can reply only with her stern guns. And Bayard will drop *Belligerent* onto her side and send a broadside directly up into her guts."

"Will we even be able to get through her shroud, Skip?"

"I've never given much thought to how *Predator* might fare against a dreadnought at point-blank range, to be perfectly honest with you," Grimm replied whimsically. "I think it best if we do not learn the answer to your question."

It took the Olympian ships another two minutes to get into position. During that time, the mistmaw eclipsed more of the lights of the skyport beneath them. From the quadrant that contained the Olympian fleet and that was nearest the approach vector of the mistmaw, a few more vessels struggled to rise. They were seized and crushed in the dangling jungle of tentacles of all imaginable shapes and sizes, their crews hauled up to vanish beneath the monster's mass. Dozens of human beings. Then scores. Then hundreds.

Meanwhile, the mass of the creature cruised steadily and slowly toward the panicked crowds trying to force their way down the transport ramps.

Some of the defensive fire was at least able to do damage to the dangling tentacles, singeing and burning them away like curls of fatty bacon over an open flame, but it was like opening fire on individual trees in a forest, and the thicker tendrils shrugged off cannon fire like an armored warship.

"Signal from *Conquistodor*, Skip!" Gwen sang out. "Ahead and north! She wants us to circle around to its flank!"

Grimm stared at the monster and the destruction it was wreaking for several seconds and then said, "Chavez wants to draw it away from the transport ramps before it reaches the people there!"

"Will that work?" Kettle asked.

"We find ourselves in strange skies, Mister Kettle," Grimm replied, then bellowed back down the deck, "Signal flags! Compliance!"

"Signal compliance, aye!" the deck officer screamed, and began relaying the command.

Grimm nodded. "Follow *Conquistodor*, Mister Kettle, if you please."

"Flying the bloody ship sideways, aye, Skip," Kettle growled. "The masts ain't made to be pulled straight out from the ship, Captain."

"I'm sure you will handle it with your usual finesse," Grimm said. "Lieutenant Stern!"

"Aye, Skip?"

"Mark wherever *Conquistodor* targets and concentrate your fire there! The damned thing is shrouded and we'll have to punch through!"

"Concentrate fire with the Auroran, aye!" Stern shouted.

Conquistodor's blowers roared to life, and the ship surged ahead through the mist and rain. Kettle worked the controls, reversing the current flow to the port maneuvering web and causing that mast to press against the hull of the ship, and sending more power to the starboard web, pulling that mast away from the hull, and *Predator*'s decking groaned as the lateral masts took the tension in an unusual direction.

Only the fact that *Predator* was a light ship little larger than a destroyer enabled her to keep pace with the dreadnought. Turbine-powered blowers, with their adjustable nozzles, enabled dedicated warships unparalleled ability to spin and adjust their arcs of fire, a necessary trait should battle become a close-quarters affair. It also allowed for ease of adjustment within a close formation. *Belligerent* kept its place in the formation beautifully, her own blowers thundering, while the Olympian ships, most of them the size of large merchantmen or heavy cruisers, had more trouble keeping their spacing around the dreadnought. But if the Olympians weren't quite up to

Aetherium or Armada standards, they were at least competent, and they managed to keep the pace set by the ponderous *Conquistodor*.

The improvised task force sluiced around a ninety-degree arc, until the Auroran signaled for a stop and then raised the universal yellow signal flag.

"Signal from *Conquistodor*!" Gwen called. "Prepare to engage!"

"Stand ready, Lieutenant Stern!" Grimm thundered. "Fire with the dreadnought!"

"Can't hardly miss the thing, Skip!" Stern called back excitedly.

And then *Conquistodor* opened fire, and night turned to brilliant, blinding noon.

Predator was three hundred yards off the stern of the dreadnought. Even so, the heat from the blast of *Conquistodor*'s mighty broadside sent a hot wind washing across her command bridge and down her deck. Forty-five of the heaviest cannon humanity was capable of creating poured their fury out at the mistmaw, and they were all focused on a surface area of the monster perhaps twenty feet square.

After a few seconds, *Belligerent* and the Olympians added their fire to *Conquistodor*'s. The battlecruiser's guns, though fewer in number, were nearly peers of the dreadnought's. The Olympian ships' light and medium cannon added their thunder and fury—though, compared to *Conquistodor*, they poured out perhaps a fifth of the energy on a gun-for-gun basis.

And for the first time, *Predator*'s heavy chase gun spoke in anger.

Green-white fire exploded from her prow like a newborn sun, blinding bright. Grimm had to throw up his hand to shield his eyes against the sudden spike of painful light, even as the heavy gun's howl pressed against his eardrums like knives. The various lumin crystals around the ship dimmed as *Predator*'s power core focused most of its output on the single weapon. Grimm could feel the very deck under his boots—well, boot—shivering as the heavy cannon bucked in its mount.

Gwen shouted something, and Grimm squinted through the haze of hellish light to see *Conquistodor* run up the flag for continuous fire. Then, with everything the ships had, the little makeshift fleet hammered the monstrous thing destroying the skyport. Again and again the heavy chase gun spoke, and even Kettle had to let go of the controls with one hand to shield his eyes.

Ruinous energy poured into the mistmaw, punched through its shroud in a matter of seconds, and burned and gouged into the creature's flesh, tearing out an area the size of the Aetherium Fleet Academy campus from the mistmaw's hide and sending showers of green-brown ichor spraying into the air, where it was vaporized into hideous steam by the following salvo.

The mistmaw bellowed in earnest now, the sound so loud that Grimm found himself swaying in his shock frame; only the well-fastened safety harness kept him standing. A forest of tentacles rose to shield the beast's wounded flesh, and hundreds or thousands more flailed out toward the source of its agony.

With another furious moan, the mistmaw changed course, and the great mass of the creature began to swell and grow higher and larger. Seconds before the first tentacles would have started ripping at the panicked crowds, the enormous mistmaw lurched toward the little fleet. The beast began rotating on its axis, turning the breach in its shroud away from the fury of the human weapons, whose blasts began to skip and dance across the monster's glow-cracked hide once more.

"Skip!" Gwen cried. "We've done it!"

"We have indeed, XO," Grimm replied. "And now the bloody thing is coming straight for us."

Chapter 48

AMS *Predator*, near Spire Olympia

Signal from *Conquistodor*, Skip!" Miss Lancaster called. "Ahead flank, prepare to turn south-southwest!"

"He wants to draw it away from the Spire," Grimm confirmed.

The mistmaw wailed and approached them rapidly. The great creature was using the etheric current flowing past the Spire to accelerate very nearly as rapidly as a dreadnought, if not slightly quicker.

"Skipper, I can't keep pace with them flying sideways at flank speed," Kettle noted. "We'll tear the mast right off."

"Understood, Mister Kettle," Grimm said calmly. "Spin us ninety starboard and we'll catch up to them."

"Ninety degrees starboard and fly the ship proper, aye," Kettle confirmed, adjusting the power flow to the maneuvering webs and tilting the ship nearly thirty degrees to help with the differential in applied rotational force between the four masts. "Without thrusters, she's not exactly going to be turning on her axis like a dancer here, Skipper."

Grimm judged the distance between themselves and the oncoming mistmaw, estimating its speed. "Steady, Kettle. We should have time."

A high-pitched woman's voice, tight with strain, came drifting up to the bridge from the deck. "Oh, oh, tell them to let me through! I must see the captain so that I can make sure he knows something very important!"

Captain, Predator, came the calm, measured voice that Grimm had heard earlier. *Miss Folly comes bearing intelligence.*

"Damnation, that's eerie," Grimm muttered, and raised his voice to bellow at the starboard-side deck officer. "Mister Johnson?"

"Aye, Skip!"

"Is that Miss Folly you've got there?"

"Yessir!"

"Send her up at once!" Grimm said. She had the bloody ship talking to him on her behalf, after all. It wasn't as if adding one more voice to the conversation on the bridge was going to make the situation any worse.

Miss Folly came puffing up onto the bridge by way of the steep staircase on the starboard side. She was dressed in civilian clothes that were rather thoroughly soaked in the rain. Should the ship rise into the high, cold aerosphere, she would go into hypothermia in short order. At least she had strapped on a safety harness, though it hitched her skirts up between her legs rather comically.

"Miss Folly," Grimm said politely, "over here in front of me, and strap on to the lateral attachment points at least."

"Oh, oh, he means me," Folly said breathlessly, and did as he had directed. She clutched her little jar of crystals rather desperately and said, "Please apologize to the captain on my behalf. Master Ferus sent me running to be on board so that I could tell *Predator* what we might need, and I needed her help to make it aboard before you lifted off."

Captain, Predator, came the calm female voice again, *Miss Fol-*

*ly's compliments, and she apologizes for having me speak out of turn,
but she says it was necessary.*

"I can hear her," Grimm said to the air next to him somewhat
desperately. "Honestly, there's no need to repeat her."

Kettle and Miss Lancaster both shot Grimm very sharp glances
and then traded an uneasy look.

"Ah, Skip?" Kettle said. "Are you feeling all right, sir?"

"Rot and ruin, Mister Kettle," Grimm swore. "Haven't you a ship
to pilot?"

Kettle blew out a breath between nonplussed lips and turned
back to his controls. *Predator* warped rather slowly on her axis, her
nose gradually turning away from the onrushing mountainous mass
of the mistmaw. Tentacles by the hundreds lashed out desperately
toward the ships that had been the source of the beast's pain.

"Miss Folly," Grimm said, forcing calm back into his voice, "please,
report whatever you've learned to your jar of crystals in a loud, clear
voice."

"Oh, thank goodness, the captain is so understanding," Folly
said with a sort of desperate relief. She held up the jar in her hands,
her back against Grimm's chest, and projected her voice at it. "Master Ferus says to tell the captain that he can sense someone sending
a signal to the mistmaw via etheric current. He wants the captain to
know that just as he was attacked two years ago by silkweavers under
outside control, that the mistmaw is being similarly directed by an
outside source." She took a deep breath. "And he should know that I
can feel it too. There is someone nearby who is commanding the
beast."

Grimm frowned, thinking hard. "Nearby? In Spire Olympia?"

"Tell the captain that is not an unreasonable assumption, but no,
the signal is coming from outside of the Spire."

"It's certainly no one in the skyport. An airship, then," Grimm concluded.

"He really thinks terribly well for someone who hasn't had formal training," Folly said admiringly to the jar.

Miss Lancaster scanned the sky around them. "One of these ships, Skipper? I don't see *Achilles* anywhere in the formation."

Grimm shot his eyes around the skies and cursed silently. No, the Atlantean vessel had not joined in defending the civilians. In fact, he spotted her far to the southeast, a blur of running lights in the mist. Streaks of colored light began to flicker up from her into the mist, emerging into the lower aerosphere.

She was launching signal rockets.

Grimm clenched his teeth and shook his head. He could well imagine whom *Achilles* was signaling: the Atlantean fleet ships that had been holding in the general area. The rockets could be seen for miles and miles. *Achilles* would not be launching them if she didn't expect someone to see them and respond.

Well, focusing upon only one insurmountable problem at a time was likely a wise policy.

Predator's prow finally oriented upon *Conquistodor*'s stern, and Kettle gave full power to the maneuvering web, causing it to catch the flow of etheric current around the Spire and sending the ship leaping forward.

Off the ship's port side, one of the enormous tentacles of the mistmaw flailed angrily through the air close enough to send a stiff breeze across the deck of the ship. Grimm's heart began to pound harder. A single blow from one of those thicker tentacles would smash his ship to kindling.

Though, he supposed, at least the mistmaw was keeping his mind off his leg.

Gwen turned a pale, wide-eyed face to Grimm and said in a

shaky voice, "Signal from *Conquistodor*, Skip. Forty-five degrees to starboard, resume fire."

"Forty-five degrees starboard, Mister Kettle, and in formation," Grimm said, keeping his voice calm.

It was a trick he had learned long ago. He had to breathe all the way into his belly and then hold the air like iron. It was perfectly all right for the crew to be frightened; airship battles were the most destructive known to man, after all. But their commander could afford no such luxury if he was to lead as many of his men as possible out the other side.

"Port batteries!" he barked. "Open fire! Keep the beast's attention on us, lads!"

The port-side gunnery officer echoed the command, and *Predator*'s seven light cannon angled toward the stern of the ship as Kettle banked her into a turn. The weapons began to howl, spitting their lances of energy out at the mistmaw and spilling green-white fire over the thing's skin and flailing tentacles. For the most part, their fire only splashed off the shroud around the beast, but now and then a shot blasted a section of the thing's hide or found one of the smaller tentacles and wounded it, causing that particular tendril to writhe in agony.

"Oh," Miss Folly said, her voice thick with compassion, "poor beast."

"Poor beast?!" Kettle demanded.

"It seems to me," Miss Folly said to her jar, "that the creature doesn't want to be going through this any more than we do. It would much rather be gobbling up a tasty nest of silkweavers or a school of mistsharks."

"It's welcome to!" Kettle snapped, his head whipping quickly from point to point as he kept the ship's distance from *Conquistodor*, marked the distance to the mistmaw, and scanned the sky ahead of them.

Keeping most of his focus on the mistmaw, Grimm felt some of the tension ease out of him as *Predator*, even running on the shorter maneuver webs, began to pull slowly away from the beast.

"Engineering to bridge!" came the tinny call from the speaking tube.

Grimm seized the tube and shouted, "This is the captain!"

"Sir!" came Journeyman's half-angry roar. "The core is running hot! We're sending too much juice to the maneuver webs in combination with firing the chase gun and keeping up fire from the port cannon!"

"Acknowledged!" Grimm shouted. "Reduce power to the shroud, Journeyman!" He hung up the speaking tube. "Kettle, ease off on the throttle just a touch. We're out of its range. We just need to stay there."

"Captain," came Miss Lancaster's hard voice, "if we reduce power to the shroud and the Aurorans turn on us, we'll be defenseless."

"Understood, XO," Grimm said. "I'm gambling that Chavez doesn't have that in mind. A good portion of the captain's duty is coaxing the most performance possible out of the ship. Vessels our size don't carry heavy cannon for good reason. We've put too much strain on the core crystal, and now we must ease *Predator*'s burden as much as we can."

Gwen stared at him hard for a moment and then set her jaw and nodded. "All right, Skip."

"Now, then," Grimm said. "Miss Folly, is there any way you can tell where this enemy vessel is? Perhaps if we can down her, the mistmaw will wander off on its own."

"Oh, goodness no, the captain trusts me far too much," Folly told her jar of crystals. "But it's possible that *Predator* can."

"Excellent," Grimm said. Miss Folly had used her talents to elicit a number of surprises from *Predator*'s systems on several occasions in the past. "If you would be so good as to have a word with her, please."

"Oh, yes, of course," Folly said, and began to murmur under her breath.

Gwen glanced at Folly and said in an aside to Kettle, "I don't know about you, Mister Kettle, but it's difficult for me to think that *Predator* might somehow be alive."

Kettle glanced over his shoulder at Folly and then at the executive officer. "Begging the XO's pardon, but it's difficult for me to think she's *not*. All ships are." Kettle put a broad hand on the main throttle's housing fondly. "Don't you worry, darlin'," he murmured. "The skipper will get us through."

The mistmaw moaned again, shaking the air, and then began abruptly to recede. It began falling away rapidly off the stern port. Good Lord, the thing had reversed its direction seemingly almost instantly. Backlit by the lights of the skyport that it had obscured with its sheer mass, the mistmaw had stopped flailing its tentacles toward the retreating airships and now thrashed them at a lower elevation, pushing itself back and adding to its momentum with great sweeps through the air.

In the sky beyond the enormity of the creature, lights shone through the mist as airships, gifted with precious minutes by the improvised defense fleet's actions, managed to take to the sky. Behind the beast, more light flickered from where the skyport would be. Fires, Grimm thought. There had likely been more crashes and accidents as panicked crews tried to lift off with insufficient hands and unready systems.

"Captain?" Gwen asked, staring at the retreating mistmaw.

Thinking, Grimm stared after the thing too. "Cease fire!" he called. "Cease fire!"

Predator's cannon fell silent as the order was echoed up and down the deck. The sudden silence left a ringing in Grimm's ears as he thought furiously.

"It would seem," he said slowly, "that the level of control of whoever is directing the beast is less than perfect. I think our first volley angered it and triggered an instinctive defensive response. Now whoever is commanding it has resumed control and is sending it back to its true target: Olympia's skyport."

"More flags from *Conquistodor*, Skip," Kettle growled.

Gwen peered at the dreadnought and said, "*Conquistodor* orders ninety degrees to port now, Skip. She wants us to close distance again."

"Contact!" called a voice from the stern. "Port side, ten o'clock!"

Grimm craned his neck, stared up, and spotted a brilliant emerald green glow approaching at a breathtaking rate of speed through the mists above the ship.

"What on earth is that?" Gwen murmured.

"Oh," Miss Folly said. "Oh, thank goodness."

The green glow grew brighter and more focused as it approached, then resolved itself into a single brilliant, shining crystal that dove toward *Predator*'s bridge. An instant later, a dark shape formed around it, and then Master Ferus, lanky in his bottle green ethersilk suit, the green crystal on the end of his cane casting emerald light, descended lightly to the bridge. His shock of grey hair had been plastered to his head by the rain and mist. He immediately donned the bottle green top hat he'd been carrying under one arm and nodded to them politely.

"Permission to board, grim Captain?" he asked.

"Permission granted," Grimm said faintly. "Ferus, did you just fly through the air to my ship?"

"That's what a dueling suit is for, sir," Ferus said with a faint bow. "Folly, have you worked things out with *Predator*?"

"Almost, master," Folly replied firmly. "The range is long, but she thinks she can show it to the captain."

"Show me what?" Grimm demanded.

"The enemy control ship, of course," Master Ferus said, his voice darkening. "There have already been a great many lives lost. Madame Sycorax Cavendish has a great deal to answer for."

"Cavendish?" Grimm said sharply.

"Remember two years ago," Master Ferus asked, "when I had to change my mind to avoid her sensing my approach?"

"Of course."

"I'm afraid her mind has remained very much the same," Ferus said, his voice certain. "She's here."

"Then we're likely looking for *Mistshark*," Grimm said. "Damn it all, Calliope."

Captain, Predator, came the calm voice in Grimm's thoughts.

Grimm blinked and then held up a hand to forestall anyone else there from talking and said, "*Predator*, report," as he would to any crewman.

There is a vessel a thousand yards below us, in the thick mist about a mile off our starboard stern, the ship reported. *I cannot be certain from this distance, but I remember* Mistshark, *and it could be her.*

"Understood," Grimm said. "Well done, *Preddy*. Keep me apprised of any change in her position, please, and prepare to change course."

The ship's silent voice somehow sounded pleased and politely ferocious at the same time. *Aye, aye, Captain. I'll find her for you. We've taken her once. We can do it again.*

"Hah!" Grimm said, and found his lips stretching out into a fierce smile. "Mister Kettle, bring us onto a due southerly heading, best speed."

There were no odd looks this time. Kettle immediately banked the ship. Master Ferus's staff began glowing and he planted his feet on the deck, standing there as steadily as if he were strapped in with a harness.

"XO, raise signal flags for *Conquistodor* and *Belligerent*," Grimm said firmly. "Signal enemy contact low. We are engaging."

Gwen immediately began barking orders to send down the deck, and when she was done, Grimm said, "Down planes thirty degrees if you please, Mister Kettle. Take us into the mist."

Chapter 49

IAS *Mistshark*, near Spire Olympia

Espira and Ciriaco had led the remaining men to barricade the hatch to the forward hold of *Mistshark*. They simply pressed their bodies against it to hold it firmly in place. Ciriaco employed his greater-than-human strength to bear the sheer force of twenty-one men leaning against him and lending their weight to his strength to keep the hatch shut.

The battering had stopped abruptly.

And there had been for a time nothing but silence, the occasional mournful wail of the mistmaw, and the thin, racking sounds of Calliope's coughs.

Espira ordered the only exit from the chamber tested, but the copper-clad steel hatch had been bent in its frame and was stuck shut.

"I don't understand," Espira said after a while.

Ciriaco grunted. "They could have gotten boarding axes and come through the bulkhead by now. We've been penned."

"We have a few axes," Espira mused. "We could cut our way out."

"And go where?" Ciriaco countered. "Out there with those crystal-eyed things? They're maybe three times as strong as most men, Colonel. Couple of them are pretty near as strong as me."

"We can't stay here either," Espira said quietly. "Not for long. We've no water."

"Colonel," Ciriaco said quietly.

The big warriorborn glanced over at Captain Ransom, who was among her men and lying back weakly against the curved bulkhead of the outer hull of the ship. She was using a folded coat for a pillow.

"Hmm?"

"Don't know how long. But we're going to have one of those things in here with us soon. Maybe they're just waiting for that. Come in when people start screaming."

The mistmaw let out a moan and then the ship rocked, bobbing sharply up and down as though her lift crystals had received an uneven surge of energy. The beast cried out again, farther away, and then there was a low thud so deep and heavy that Espira did not so much hear it as feel it thump against his chest. The men in the hold fell silent and became tense, and then moments later there was the sound of distant thunder.

"Is that what I think it is?" Espira asked.

"Cannon," Ciriaco confirmed quietly.

"We've reached Olympia."

"Ungh," Ciriaco grunted in the affirmative. "Maybe the port batteries. Or maybe they had patrol ships in the air."

"Port batteries would be heavier than that," Espira objected.

"Olympians took out their heavy emplacements to make more room for traders."

"Oh, yes," Espira said. "That was foolish."

"Apparently."

The mistmaw moaned again. There were crackling sounds far away.

Captain Ransom went into a spasm, thrashing wildly, and her people let out exclamations of startled surprise.

"Watch it!"

"Hold her head!"

"—something between her teeth before she bites off her tongue—"

Ciriaco put a hand on the borrowed sword in his belt and looked at Espira. The colonel glanced from the sword to Calliope and back. He drew in a breath to speak, but suddenly Madame Cavendish's voice rang out quite clearly in the room—coming from Calliope Ransom's throat.

"Colonel Espira. I assume you survived, Colonel. You seem to be both fortunate and resourceful."

The room fell into shocked silence. The men around Ransom fell back as if seeming to realize the danger all at once.

Calliope lay as if poleaxed, her entire body limp. Her face was distorted in a grimace of pain and the muscles on her neck stood out starkly, with deep shadows between them.

"Oh, come now, Colonel," came Cavendish's voice, and Ransom's eyes went wide in panic, though she did not—perhaps could not—move. "Don't make me take her eyes as well. Do be so kind as to answer me."

"I am here," Espira said warily.

Ransom's head rotated toward Espira jerkily, as though someone had seized her by the hair to move it like a puppet. "Ah, there you are, Renaldo. As you see, I have control over most of the men aboard *Mistshark*."

"I did notice something to that effect," he said.

"Allow me to assure you," Cavendish's voice said, "that if I wanted you dead, you would already have been torn to pieces."

Ciriaco looked at him and then motioned with his sword hand questioningly. Espira gave him the silent signal for "Stand by" and continued talking.

"If I assume that is the case, madame," he said, "then I must also assume you want to have this conversation for a reason. What do you want of me?"

"To the point. I can appreciate that at a moment like this." There was a sensual edge to Cavendish's voice. "Oh, I can feel them going into my mouth—" She broke off into a girlish giggle, then said, "Your men are still themselves—at least on the inside—until they're too damaged to keep functioning. But they have very little personal initiative, and I have to send them on their little tasks every time I need something done. I need to focus on other things. It would be useful to have officers to command them."

Espira felt his mouth fill with water as his stomach began to revolt. He swallowed the liquid down, mastered himself, and said, "You want me to join you?"

"I want you to take command of the ship, yes," Cavendish purred. "See your mission through."

Ciriaco rolled his eyes. Espira grimaced and motioned him to remain silent. "Intriguing, madame. I should inquire as to how I profit in such an arrangement."

"You get to live," Cavendish said bluntly, "as do any who remain unconverted. I can finish the mission on my own, but I have more options if I don't have to split my attention quite so many ways. To say nothing of the fact that . . ."

Captain Ransom's body quivered in a slow shiver that shook her in a ripple from her toes to the crown of her head.

"Faugh," said Cavendish a second later. "My old master is somewhere near somehow. The enemy may be able to find us. The ship would fight better with officers to command my crew."

"You've killed twenty of my men," Espira said in a hard voice.

"I haven't killed them, Colonel," Cavendish's voice countered soothingly. "I've made them better soldiers. Stronger. Fearless. Perfectly disciplined. And a great deal more polite than they were before."

"What of Ransom's crew?" Espira demanded.

"The evening bridge team and the engineering crew are still . . . unimproved," Cavendish said. "They threatened to stop cooperating if their captain was harmed, and their tasks are reasonably complex, so here you all are. I can be reasonable, Colonel. You want to live. You want those who remain to stay as they are. I have control of the ship, and I am now in a position to grant a certain amount of license to a defeated foe, provided you are wise enough to grant me your cooperation."

"I notice you didn't make such an offer to Captain Ransom," Espira said quietly.

"She lives, as per my agreement with her pilot and engineer. She is even largely unchanged. But she's a treacherous, fickle creature, and as I've no desire to feel her knife in my back, it was important to me that she not be allowed to hold one." Ransom's back suddenly arched fantastically, almost inhumanly, and the woman let out a very real scream of agony in her own voice before subsiding into absolute limp stillness again. Cavendish's voice purred out of Ransom's throat. "Now she understands that actions have consequences."

Espira tilted his head and pursed his lips suddenly.

Cavendish had a weakness after all. A chink in her armor over which she had no control.

And he had no intention, no intention whatsoever, of working with that witch ever again.

"There is one good thing about our position, Sergeant," he said quietly to Ciriaco.

The warriorborn looked at him and then spread his mouth into a wide grin, showing his pointed canines. He kept his voice to a low growl. "It can't get any worse, sir."

"It can't get any worse," Espira agreed.

"I'm sorry," Cavendish said, twitching Ransom's head back and forth. "What was that, Colonel?"

Outside the ship, there were the distant sounds of the mistmaw letting out its haunting call and the sudden thunder of what could only have been a coordinated broadside.

"Madame Cavendish," Espira suddenly said in a cold, clear voice, "I find your person repulsive, your actions reprehensible, and your offer selfish, insulting, and in the main unremittingly stupid. Only an idiot would so much as consider extending anything like trust to you, and only a fool would believe your simplistic blandishments. Moreover, madame, while I am sure your opinion of yourself is very high, I cannot help but think that such an opinion can only be the result of an intense denial of reality so severe that you actually believe that you rise to the level of the most debased humanity. I can assure you that a creature of your nature can never aspire to such giddy heights as that of the most pathetic wretch exiled to the surface of the world. You would do me and the rest of the world a great kindness, madame, if you should exit your disgusting, stinking, venomous tank, proceed to the main deck, and hurl yourself over the side of the ship."

There was an instant of startled silence.

And then Ransom opened her mouth and screamed in Cavendish's voice.

Screamed in fury.

Cavendish screamed.

Outside the ship, the mistmaw screamed.

And every crystal revenant on the ship opened its mouth and screamed in Cavendish's voice, screamed in primal, wordless fury, screamed in absolutely berserk rage.

"The hatch!" Ciriaco shouted, and men rushed to brace it as something slammed into the metal a dozen times.

Blows sounded on the bulkhead. Wooden planking began to crack.

"Well," Espira said, "if her mission requires concentration, I'd say that rather puts a damper on it."

"Well done, sir," Ciriaco snarled, grunting as he leaned into the hatch. He flashed his teeth at Espira. "Couldn't you have said something about her mother too?"

"She talks too much. Now we know where allies are," Espira said. He seized a boarding ax and handed it to one of his Marines. Then he pointed at the ceiling and gestured for the aeronaut holding the other ax to join him. "The main deck. Cut us a hole up and we'll make for the bridge! Do it, men! Hurry!"

Ciriaco stood clear of the hatch while others braced it. His cat eyes alert, he drew his sword and stalked up and down by the bulkhead. When one of the revenants smashed open a hole in the planking, he rammed his sword out through the small opening, scored, twisted the blade, and withdrew it to the sound of a furious scream from outside.

"There a plan, Colonel?"

Espira drew his own blade and took up position beside the sergeant. "We get control of the bridge and take the ship straight down. Smash Cavendish and her creatures and her machine to pieces on the surface."

Ciriaco stared at him for a second, then flashed his teeth in a grin and said, "I can't go no higher than I have anyway, Colonel. Gotta die of something. Might as well be doing something worthwhile."

■ ■ ■ Chapter 50 ■ ■ ■

ACS *Sunhawk*, Skyport, Spire Olympia

When the mistmaw arrived, Bridget thought that she had never seen a more terrible, overwhelming sight in her life.

She was still waiting on the deck of the *Sunhawk* with Benedict, Rowl (who had only just returned, seemingly Vincent's sole messenger of the evening to complete his mission), and Fenli, along with a near-frantic Vincent, who had sent runner after runner to Lord Lancaster and Duchess Hinton with no detectable success. There had been an enormous sound running from a basso so deep that it rattled her teeth against one another to a high-pitched, whistling wail that made her feel that some titanic dentist somewhere had begun pedaling up the rotations on his drill.

"That," Fenli informed them calmly, "is the mistmaw."

"We worked that out," Benedict snapped. "Both cats into Bridget's lap at once! We're moving!"

"Fenli shouldn't be in Bridget's lap in any case," Rowl complained from the ground. "I think that— Oh!"

Benedict scooped Rowl up without preamble and deposited him on Bridget's lap. She gathered the two cats in close before they could start quarreling. Benedict seized the handles on her wheeled chair, tilted it back, and, before he all but sprinted down the gangplank, paused to seize the sleeve of a wildly staring Vincent to haul him into motion to follow them.

Bridget held on to the cats and stared in numb, fascinated horror as the mistmaw rolled up the side of Spire Olympia and loomed over its skyport.

It was huge, simply enormous, more like some kind of weather phenomenon than a living creature. In the rain and mist, she could see only a portion of the beast, and that view was further obscured by the way the Spire's spotlights could pick out only bits and pieces of the creature at a time—though the general lighting of the skyport gave her a dim view of the mistmaw's overwhelming outline.

The mistmaw's body was a flattened sphere almost a mile across, and from it hung a ridiculously thick network of tendrils and tentacles, all stirring and curling as if in anticipation of the meal the monster was about to devour. Most of the tendrils and tentacles hung down out of sight, past the edge of the skyport, like a woman's long hair falling below the edge of a dining table.

Bridget had never felt so much like an appetizer.

Dim ember-colored light emanated from the mistmaw's underbelly; the hellish glow made the tentacles look like writhing black serpents. Droplets of something fell from the monster like rain, but they spattered and sputtered and hissed when they struck the obdurate invincibility of the spirestone. A foul odor wafted by on the breeze, and Bridget dimly noted an urge to gag.

The port's defensive emplacements opened up on the mistmaw. The howl of cannon split the air and bursting spheres of white-hot fire splashed up against the vast creature with little or no effect. She was dimly aware of a handful of airships lifting off, brilliant lights against the night sky. Several of the ready military vessels in Olympia's Fleet quadrant of the skyport tried to lift off but were smashed to pieces by the mistmaw's limbs.

"My God in Heaven," Vincent breathed. "It's eating people."

Bridget blinked and then took note that the limbs of the leading edge of the mistmaw were now dragging over the nearest edge of the skyport. One tentacle smashed a wooden warehouse over the edge of the Spire. Other, lither limbs were extending like elastic bands, wrapping around objects and people with blind indistinction, and lifting them up toward the sullen glow of the mistmaw's underbelly, where they vanished into the beast.

It was eating them.

"It's going to eat us," Bridget breathed.

Her thoughts went still. Her tired body ached. She sat limply in the chair, staring at her end, while a vague shadow settled over her thoughts. Her terror and her protest and her babbling anger became nothing more than idle clockwork machines somewhere in her head, where they clicked away at their business with no connection to anything else.

"We've got to get under shelter," Vincent said urgently.

"There's no shelter up here from *that*," Benedict countered. "Our only chance is to get to the transport spiral and down several levels."

"Several?" Vincent asked.

"At Spire Dependence," Benedict said calmly, "there wasn't a soul left on the uppermost habble but for Fenli and his people, and they were small enough to hide in the smallest ventilation tunnels, where the tentacles couldn't fit."

"Some of them are miles long," Vincent said, his tone numb, neutral. "And there's a crowd at the transport spirals. Everyone in the skyport will be trying to get there."

Benedict's steps slowed as he watched the progress of the mistmaw across the skyport. For all that the vast creature seemed ponderous and slow, it was still approaching at the speed of a running man, more and more tendrils blindly smashing buildings, airships, and people.

"Parachutes," Benedict said. "We get back to your ship, strap into parachutes, and jump."

"For the *surface?*" Vincent blurted.

"Some of it was quite pretty," Bridget said in a detached voice, even as some part of her noted that she was saying that after being beaten half to death on the surface and now sitting in a wheeled chair as a result of her visit there.

Vincent stared at her and let out a half-hysterical laugh.

"Our chances there will be better than up here," Benedict said firmly.

"One minute back to the ship," Vincent said like a man adding up a list of figures. "One minute to unship the parachutes. Another minute to put them on, accounting for needing to strap an invalid into one. Another minute to reach the Spire's edge . . ." He shook his head. "It's coming too fast. There isn't time."

"The ventilation tunnels," Bridget said.

Benedict leaned down. "What, love?"

Bridget stared at people who were incapacitated and writhing in pain on the ground after being spattered by the fluid falling from the mistmaw's underside. They were rapidly swept up by pale tendrils, plucked up like tomatoes taken from their vines by water farmers.

"That's how the Aurorans got into Albion two years ago," she said. "They came in through the ventilation tunnels on the outer rim of the Spire."

"We won't be out of the thing's reach there," Vincent noted.

"No," Benedict said. "But we could potentially climb down the vertical shafts until we were, like the Aurorans did."

"They worked in coordinated teams and had climbing equipment," Vincent said.

"It's either the tunnels," Benedict said, "or the drop."

"Untrue," Fenli said from Bridget's lap. "You can also be eaten."

For a moment, both men blinked at the little cat, who stared at them with feline unconcern.

"Either way," Vincent said, "it will take time to get rope from the airship. Time to reach the edge of the Spire and locate a vent. Time that we do not have."

Staring at the oncoming mistmaw, Benedict opened his mouth. Then he sagged and closed it again. His posture slumped, and his eyes shut.

Bridget's heart went out to him. But with her mind under a shadow, that too was simply an object in motion, purposeless and undirected.

"Bridget," Benedict said, his voice rough, "I love you. I had intended my courtship to last a little longer to be proper, but under the circumstances . . ." He let go of the chair's handles, came around to the front of it, and knelt down as close to her as the awkward positioning of her wounded leg would allow.

Her eyes widened, and her heart began to beat very quickly. Although terror had been unable to reach through her numbness, Benedict's gently yearning expression struck a chord somewhere deep inside her. He took her hand gently.

"I am Benedict Michael, warriorborn of House Sorellin-Lancaster, knight of the Order of Albion," he said formally. "And, Bridget Muriel Tagwynn, I should be very much honored if you would agree to be my wife."

Bridget sat thunderstruck for a moment while cannon blazed and the monster roared and buildings splintered and men and women screamed and ran for their lives. Amidst all that horror, the simple sincerity in Benedict's face, the calm and quiet pride with which he'd made his proposal, and the love shining in his green-gold feline eyes ignited a sudden, furious fire in her, an abrupt beacon of joy and love and hope in the darkness that obliterated the shadow over her thoughts, drove her body's pain far away, and sent up and down her spine a bolt of lightning that made her feel as if the very Spire beneath their feet could crumble to sand before her will would flag.

At once, the world came back into focus.

Rowl reacted immediately. He rose to his feet in her lap, his head high, his fur bristling with pride.

"I am Bridget Muriel of House Tagwynn, last of my name," she said firmly. "I will be your wife upon a single condition, Sir Benedict."

Benedict's face shone, his mouth turning into a rare smile wide enough to show his elongated canine teeth. "You have only to name it, my lady."

There were the valiant, furious sounds of trumpets—the steam horns of an Auroran airship. They blared a brassy challenge, and Bridget looked up to see that several of the airships had managed to lift off and rapidly maneuver into formation, a vertical wall in the air around the copper-clad armored shape of an enormous Auroran dreadnought.

One of the airships had the familiar lean, graceful shape of *Predator*.

Suddenly, the night turned to noon under the blaze of dozens of cannon.

The mistmaw bellowed, its tentacles writhing as the airships gathered around the dreadnought slammed their fury into its vast body. The ships continued in volley fire, round after round, and the night was filled with green-white flame and thunder like nothing Bridget had ever seen. The beast roared, its pain causing its tentacles to wreak even more destruction upon the skyport as they thrashed.

Wailing in fury, the monster rotated and began rushing with gathering speed and momentum at the airships.

Surely, surely, they could not stop the monster.

But they'd given the people of Spire Olympia—and Bridget—something they hadn't had a moment ago: precious time.

Bridget leaned forward and took Benedict's face in her bandaged hands, then turned his head from the battle to meet her eyes. She stared at him, pouring every bit of that sudden fire of her love, of her newly kindled hope, into him with nothing but her will and the vibrating passion in her voice. "Get us all parachutes," she commanded him. "And get us out of this alive."

The warriorborn's face went incandescent with ferocious joy, and he snarled, "Vincent, get in the chair with her."

"I beg your pardon?" Vincent said.

"Sir, for your own good, I'll be giving the orders for the duration of the emergency." Benedict gave Bridget a swift, hard kiss on the mouth that made stars swim into her vision. Then he straightened and said, with an unmistakable warning growl in his voice, "We'll be doing this at my speed. Sit. Down."

Chapter 51

AMS *Predator*, near Spire Olympia

Kill the running lights," Grimm said quietly. "Let's not announce to them that we're coming."

"Lights out, aye," Kettle replied, and turned a dial on the
control panel, plunging the ship into near-total darkness. Grimm
waited patiently for his eyes to adjust. The mists around them were
suffused with a ghostly luminance from the lights of both Olympia's
skyport and her surface installations below. It provided just enough
contrast to allow movement about the ship, at least above decks.

Captain, Predator, the ship reported in a hushed tone. Grimm
had no idea why the ship should communicate in a hushed tone that
only he could hear. Perhaps she was getting into the spirit of the
thing. *We are level with the enemy contact. A thousand yards more
and she'll be off the port beam. It's definitely* Mistshark.

"Port-side gunners ready," Grimm called quietly, and heard the
orders echoed in hushed tones down the length of the ship.

"Master," Folly said in a strained voice. "Master, do you feel that?"

"I do indeed, Miss Folly," Ferus said grimly.

Grimm glanced over at the etherealists and asked, "Is there something I need to know?"

Ferus grimaced and said, "Captain . . . the Enemy exudes certain etheric energies when its agents are active. Folly experiences them as a sensation. I hear them as a kind of buzzing sound. Cavendish has used these energy fields before—to control the silkweavers two years ago, I believe, as well as to guide in the enemy troop transport that dropped off the Auroran Marines who attacked Habble Landing. Think of it as a by-product of the etheric energies they are working with. It spreads out around them in a large area—something like a ship's shroud."

"This . . . energy field, is it dangerous to us?"

Ferus squinted and tilted his head slightly as though enduring an unpleasant noise. "It's . . . a great deal more intense than we've ever experienced before."

There was a sharp snapping sound and a sudden spark leapt up off the crystal at the head of Ferus's cane.

"Skip, engineering," came Journeyman's voice through the speaking tube.

Grimm lifted it and said, "This is the bridge. What is it, Chief?"

"Damnation if I know, Skip," Journeyman said. "The power core is sparking up something terrible. Lift and trim crystals too. We're getting a lot of fluctuation in the power output. Getting worse as we keep going."

More sparks began to leap from Master Ferus's crystal. The master etherealist lifted the cane and held it by the very end at arm's length, at the maximum possible distance from his body. He swept it far off to the right, and the snapping sparks slowed slightly. Then he swung his cane in a slow arc until it was pointing ahead, off *Predator*'s port beam, and more intense and frequent sparks began to fall from the end of the crystal.

"It would appear," Master Ferus said, "that the Enemy is this way, Captain."

"Chief?" Grimm asked. "Are you having any trouble with the lift crystal array?"

"Not moving this slow, Skip," Journeyman replied warily. "At least not yet. But I increased the output by about five percent to try to stabilize and we started a fire. It's out, but I recommend we throttle way down."

"*Predator*," Grimm said, "report."

The ship's voice came back to him and sounded under strain. *Captain,* Predator. *I feel very strange. I do not recommend employing my weapons at this time. I believe the release of that much energy in such a limited amount of time would result in unpredictable results.*

"The ship," Grimm said, "is concerned that if we use her weapons, we might not like what follows."

Miss Lancaster was staring at Master Ferus's crystal intently. "That makes sense, Skip."

"How so, XO?"

The Lancaster vattery was one of the premier crystal production facilities in the entire world. By the time she was fourteen, Gwen had been as thoroughly schooled in their creation and function as any etheric engineer, and she'd shown her expertise repeatedly over the past two years. "Because power crystals and weapons crystals are essentially the same pattern, Skip, but weapons crystals are simpler and easier to grow because they need to release only the energy they generate in a single burst rather than a variable stream. If *Preddy's* core crystal experienced dangerous interference at a five percent increase, imagine if we opened her up all the way. That's what a weapons crystal does. It's either on or off. There's no throttle."

"Excuse me, pilot," Master Ferus said.

"Kettle," Grimm supplied.

"Mister Kettle," Master Ferus said, "may I borrow your gauntlet?"

Kettle gave Ferus a suspicious look over the gold chains mounded around his neck. "I like this gauntlet."

"Oh, for goodness' sake, Kettle," Miss Lancaster said, and stripped her own gauntlet from her wrist, then offered it to Ferus.

"I feel I must inquire as to what you are doing," Grimm said.

"Oh, I mean to toss the gauntlet over the side and trigger it and see what happens," Ferus said, beaming. "They use the same weapons crystals as the ship's guns, only smaller. Rather important to know what will happen, after all, what?"

"The enemy is half a mile off," Grimm pointed out.

The ongoing thunderous crackling of cannon fire still drifted down from the embattled Spire, along with the continued bellows of the mistmaw, and Ferus extended his hand toward the noises as if that were all the explanation he needed to offer.

"Point," Grimm said. "Very well, proceed."

Ferus held the gauntlet up to his face, peering at it intently and muttering beneath his breath. Then he gave it a quick toss over the side, gesturing with his cane as he did.

Brilliant light flared from the gauntlet as it fell. It had barely gone out of sight in the mist below before the telltale whine of a critically overheated crystal filled the air, along with a flicker of green-white light and a crackling detonation.

No one said anything for a moment.

Then Kettle said, "Well, then," and calmly unstrapped his gauntlet and shoved it into his pants pocket.

"That's *better*?" Gwen asked incredulously.

"XO, let's ship the guns," Grimm said mildly.

"Aye, Skip," she said quietly. "Well, we have a problem, Skipper."

"Albion has a problem," Grimm said firmly.

Ferus gave Grimm a sharp look and nodded rapidly. "Quite so, Captain, quite so."

"Skipper?" Miss Lancaster asked.

"The enemy can project a field that renders our ship's power systems, shroud, and cannon useless," Grimm said. "Yet we had no issues using gauntlets against the silkweavers Cavendish was controlling at Albion."

"She's found a way to massively expand the field," Ferus said. "It is several orders of magnitude more powerful than it was in Albion."

"An etheric device?" Grimm asked.

"Almost certainly, Captain, with a power core of its own. It seems reasonable to assume that it is the device she's using to control that creature by amplifying the field."

Grimm exhaled slowly, thinking. Then he said, "XO, after you ship the guns, stow gauntlets and long guns, arm all hands with whatever gunpowder weapons we have, and prepare for boarding."

Everyone on the bridge turned to stare at Grimm.

"Sir?" Gwen asked.

Grimm tilted his head. "We can't use our cannon. It stands to reason that the enemy can't use theirs either."

"That's a large assumption, Skip," Miss Lancaster warned.

"Supported by the fact that *Mistshark* is holding position, likely so it doesn't overload its own systems while the field amplifier is in operation. It is imperative that we capture whatever technology they are using, so that Albion's etheric technicians can find a way to counter it. Even if our guns worked, we couldn't afford to send *Mistshark* down now."

"Your reasoning seems sound, Captain," Ferus said supportively.

"You hear that?" Kettle asked Miss Lancaster. "The etherealist who can't function without his huge collection of random things being safe just told the captain—who is taking reports from his ship—that his reasoning is good."

"Don't be insubordinate, Kettle," Gwen sighed. "I would hate to brig you."

"Heh-heh," he said. "Just putting things in perspective, ma'am."

"People are dying while we delay. You have your orders, XO," Grimm said gently. "Off you go."

Gwen blew out a breath and turned to head down to the deck. "Aye, Skip. Shipping etheric weapons, arming the crew with grubby antiques, preparing for a boarding action."

Grimm checked in with *Predator* and then told Kettle, "Another thousand yards, Kettle. Bring us right up alongside her. With any luck, we'll be on her before they have a chance to arm and repel us."

"Damnation, Skip," Kettle said cheerfully. "With your luck, they'll be carrying the Armada payroll too."

Luck always runs out, was Grimm's immediate thought. He far preferred professionalism and efficiency to luck. But they had the opportunity here and now to both stop the enemy's control of the mistmaw and to recover the technology that allowed them to do so and that could be used for further devastation if it was not countered. If he delayed, *Mistshark* might slip away to wreak havoc another day. The chance had to be seized at once.

His men were not Marines, although a great many of them were veterans of the action in Albion two years past, and most of the rest had been blooded in the two years of privateering since. He would match them against Calliope's crew of miscreants. But Grimm had no illusions. If Aurora had sent professionals to escort her, matters could swiftly become dire.

Miss Lancaster had participated in a number of boarding actions, but she didn't have the experience or the personal inclination to realize when a fight had turned irrevocably against her. In addition, *Mistshark* carried more crew than *Predator,* so the only chance Grimm had was to commit every single hand to the attack.

There would be no room for inexperience or errors of judgment in the leadership of this action. For his crew's sake, he had little choice.

"Slow ahead, Mister Kettle," Grimm said. "Give me the wheel. Then arm yourself with as many pistols as you can carry. I'll need you."

"Skip," Kettle said warily, "tell me you aren't planning on going over with the boarding party."

"Tut, Kettle," Grimm said. "Ask yourself: Would I do such a thing?"

Like a ghost through a wall, *Predator* came out of the mist upon *Mistshark*. One second there was nothing but grey before *Predator*, and then the black lines of the smuggling-painted ship swam into view.

There was the sound of fighting aboard her.

Grimm traded a look with Kettle as he heard steel chiming on steel, the thud of a boarding ax against a deck or bulkhead, and the shouts and screams of men locked in mortal combat.

"Skip?" Kettle asked. "What in the name of the Merciful Builders is happening?"

"An opportunity," Grimm said, and raised his voice. "Port-side mast in!"

Orders were snapped down the ship and the crew standing by the port mast reeled it back into place snug against *Predator*'s flank.

"Bring us alongside, Kettle. Commander Lancaster," Grimm called, "on your mark!"

"Aye, Skip!" Gwen called back. "Stand by boarding ramps!"

Grimm wished for a moment that *Predator* had turbines like proper military ships, but Kettle made up for the difference with sheer deft skill and glided her to within a handspan or two of *Mistshark*'s starboard side. Grimm scanned the enemy vessel's deck, taking note of the crowd around the stairs to the bridge. An embattled and hopelessly outnumbered knot of what could only have been mutineers was trapped against the bulkhead of the forward cabins beneath the bridge.

"Cut throttle," Grimm said.

Kettle, now wearing crossed bandoliers and a belt, all bristling with gunpowder pistols, killed the slight forward drive that *Predator* carried at her reduced speed. He finished only a breath before Gwen shouted, "Boarding ramps down!"

The boarding ramps had been mounted into the copper-clad steel frames of three of the port-side gunports, locking them into the skeletal structure of the ship. They were heavy devices equipped with a row of six-foot serrated steel spikes upon their ends. The ramps fell, smashing straight through *Mistshark*'s starboard railings, and the spikes struck cleanly down through her deck like so many nails and stuck fast in the enemy vessel's deck planking and crossbeams.

As *Predator*'s forward momentum was arrested by the boarding ramps, she lurched, jerking *Mistshark* as she did, and for a second there was silence except for the ships' frames creaking and groaning with stress.

Then Miss Lancaster bellowed, "With me!" and leapt up onto the center ramp. With a roar, the leather-clad aeronauts of *Predator*'s crew bounded up to the ramps and surged onto the enemy's ship. The pace of the leaders was frantic and headlong, because they knew that their best chances of both survival and victory lay in naked aggression. If they didn't move ahead, the aeronauts coming behind them would pile into their backs and trample them, and if they didn't get as many people onto the enemy ship as they could as rapidly as they could, *Mistshark*'s crew would overwhelm them with sheer numbers.

Or at least, Grimm thought, that was what should have happened.

After the boarding ramps came down, no cry went up from the enemy crew. No bells rang, no officers bellowed orders, and no one tried to hack loose the boarding ramps with axes. The fight at *Mistshark*'s prow carried on, and Grimm heard the unmistakable coughing roar of a warriorborn in battle as a dim shape flew into the air and over the railing of the ship to fall toward the earth.

Miss Folly had retired to the guest cabin, as was her custom during battle, but Master Ferus stood on the deck beside Grimm and his mouth opened in a sudden, shocked expression. His eyes went wide behind his bottle green spectacles.

"My God. My God, the monster, she's actually done it. Captain, *look at their eyes.*"

And with a gesture of his cane, a shower of brilliant sparks erupted forth, and an intense mote of green light leapt from the cane's crystal and shot overhead, where it hovered, illuminating the *Mistshark*'s deck like a flare.

Grimm unstrapped his harness with reflex-level practice and lurched to the port rail.

The crew of the *Mistshark* wore what at first glance he took to be goggles, an odd and unnecessary precaution at night, but the brighter light of Ferus's flare showed Grimm the horrible truth.

Their eyes were gone.

Crystalline growths had replaced them, refracting the green light in oddly muted shades of yellow where they were not smeared with dark stains, and the men's cheeks and cheekbones beneath were thickly coated with masks of dried—and not-so-dried—blood. A full two dozen of the crew simply stood calmly on the deck, hands at their sides, while forty or fifty more pressed toward the ship's forecastle, where the fighting was hot. The enemy bridge was littered with the forms of scattered—literally, limbs torn asunder and scattered— dead.

A door in *Mistshark's* stern slammed open, and Grimm's head whipped around to see the backlit figure of Madame Cavendish's warriorborn bodyguard, Mister Sark, with one hand clutching at his heavily wrapped stomach. He staggered out and bellowed, "All hands, repel boarders!"

Furious screams erupted from the deck and mad chaos ensued as the *Mistshark's* crystal-eyed crew whirled, screaming like berserkers, and flung themselves forward into the fight.

Chapter 52

Warren Manor, Habble Profit, Spire Olympia

Abigail followed Lady Iphigenia toward the Lord President's apartments as the explosive power of the skyport's defense cannon came rumbling down through the spirestone like thunder. It was close enough to be felt through the soles of her boots.

Randolph, the tall security captain, strode ahead of them, seized a speaking tube on the wall, and called into it, "Guard room, lock down the residence at once."

There was no answer.

"Guard room!" the captain called, his voice tense. "Respond!"

Only silence answered him.

Abigail thought she heard a sound echoing up the stairs and shot a glance at Hamish.

The dark-suited man had heard it too, and he confirmed, "Gauntlet fire, Your Grace." He looked at Randolph. "They're inside."

"Who?" Lady Iphigenia said intently.

"That hardly matters, Your Grace," Abigail said. "There are a number of high-value targets within the residence. The Lord President, Lady Sarafine, Lord Lancaster, yourself, and I daresay I might seem like a valuable hostage to the casual observer. We can safely assume that one or more of us are the objective."

"Those stairs we just climbed are the only way up," Iphigenia said. "Randolph, gather whatever men you can and secure the stairs. I will warn my brother."

"Aye, my lady," Randolph said. He beckoned the two men with him.

"Ma'am," Hamish said, his voice tense, "our etherealists rushed out just before I came up to find you. But Tilde's down there."

"Go," she said. "Find her and do whatever you can to defend the house."

The tall man put his hand on her shoulder, clasped it firmly, and then strode away with Randolph and his men.

Iphigenia nodded to Abigail rather deeply and then began moving briskly down the hallway. "Your people are capable."

"I wouldn't be here to speak to you at the moment if they weren't," Abigail said.

The lumin crystals lighting the hallway suddenly dimmed. A second later there was a sharp report from lower in the house, and the floor shook hard enough to make Iphigenia put a hand against the wall for balance.

"What was that?" the tall woman demanded.

Abigail felt her stomach quail as she looked at the lumin crystals. "An etherealist at work, unless I miss my guess."

"God in Heaven," Iphigenia breathed. "Then this is a proper attack."

"So it would appear," Abigail said. "Your men have gunpowder weapons as well?"

Iphigenia looked stunned. "I . . . I assume so. I don't handle security personally."

Abigail nodded shortly and produced the small, fine pistol she carried in her bolero pocket and offered its handle to Iphigenia. "Here. Should you need it."

The noblewoman's eyes widened. "I . . . I'm very much afraid I don't know how to work it."

Abigail nodded and put the weapon into Iphigenia's hand. "Hold here. Your thumb here on the hammer. When it is time, pull the hammer back until it locks. Put the end of the pistol within a foot or so of your target, or better yet right against it, and pull the trigger."

"That close?"

"It makes things simpler, dear," Abigail said firmly. "Otherwise, you might miss, and then what would be the point of having a pistol?"

Iphigenia swallowed and then nodded. "I see. Are you armed as well?"

Abigail put her hand on the hilt of her dueling blade and said, "I am."

"Oh. Of course." Iphigenia nodded and said, "This way, then."

She led Abigail down another pair of hallways to where a last security guard, a rather tense-looking young man, sat outside a pair of grandiose double doors chased in polished silver. He bounced to his feet from the chair as they rounded the corner and said, "My lady? What's happening?"

"We are under attack, Edmund," Iphigenia said shortly. "Both the Spire and the Lord President's residence. Open the doors."

"But, my lady—"

She gestured with the pistol. "I'm well aware of my brother's orders. There's no time for this. Open the door and then join Captain Randolph in defending the stairwell."

The young man goggled for a moment and then said, "Y-yes, my lady." He produced a key from his pocket.

Iphigenia stepped forward and took it from him, then said, "Thank you. Go, go, go."

Edmund hurried off, and Iphigenia unlocked the doors to the apartments, calling, "Ambrose! I'm very sorry to disturb you, but I'm afraid there are matters requiring your attention."

She stepped forward after she opened the doors and said, "I'm very sorry but . . ."

She froze, and Abigail watched her look warily around the room. Light flickered over her face from some combination of lumin crystals within. Abigail held utterly still and was entirely silent.

"Hello, Iphigenia," said a young woman, her Auroran accent marked. "This is somewhat awkward."

"Your Highness," Iphigenia said quietly. "Yes . . . it is."

"You're staring, Iphigenia," came Sarafine's voice. "Do you like my dress?"

Iphigenia seemed caught up in thought. She frowned faintly, and her right hand twitched the gun in a little movement.

"I know, I know," Sarafine said, her voice dulcet. "It's very difficult to think just now, isn't it? Do you like my necklace? Ambrose loves it. He's been staring for hours."

"Wh . . ." Iphigenia licked her lips, frowning, and said, "Why?"

"To keep him from ordering your fleet into the air, of course," Sarafine said. "My brother's new weapon is going to devastate your skyport. Our allies will signal the Armada to proceed. They will sail in, finish any remaining defenses, land, and oversee a peaceful transition of Spire Olympia to a joint protectorate of Aurora and Atlantea. You'll need us, of course. I don't think you're going to have much of a Fleet left."

"N-no . . ." Iphigenia said, blinking slowly. "That's . . . It isn't . . ."

"Hestia is quite fashion-forward," Lady Sarafine said with a little laugh. "She provided both the dress and the necklace for me. Fascinating, isn't it?"

Iphigenia simply stared, saying nothing.

"I imagine that's her downstairs," Sarafine said. "She and her people have been preparing for this for several months."

Abigail thought quickly. Sarafine had clearly taken the Lord President hostage by some rather unique means. Abigail had no reason to think that if she tried to enter the room, she wouldn't be affected herself—

Except that Miss Folly and Master Ferus had provided her with a possible defense.

She took the spectacles from her jacket's pocket and put them on, tinting her vision slightly blue. Still, there was no sense in not seeking every advantage, and Sarafine seemed content to continue prattling on.

There was no such thing as a ruler's home without a servants' entrance. Abigail considered the portion of the room she could see from where she stood beside the wall, and then ghosted down the hallway. She found a side entrance down the hall and around the corner. It was locked, so she took out the small tools from the concealed pocket in her coat's hem and opened the lock as quickly and quietly as she knew how. Then she opened the door soundlessly, drew her sword, and padded into the royal apartments.

The door had opened onto a butler's pantry, and she stalked through it, silent on the thick carpeting, her weight on her toes. A service hall led to an opening into a lavishly decorated great room with a definite masculine flare—all deep green curtains, rich dark wooden furniture chased in brass and gold, and a large masonry fireplace that was burning wooden logs that popped merrily.

A man in his late thirties lay on a plush green divan, his eyes glassy, and astride him in a sensual embrace was a young woman in a white silk gown that draped and rose to show beautiful limbs and skin. She was quite possibly the most desirably feminine thing Abigail had ever seen.

No, she thought. That was the dress itself having an effect on her perception, she reminded herself. The person wearing it was simply Lady Sarafine. She was facing away from Abigail, speaking to Lady Iphigenia, who seemed overly large and rough-hewn in comparison to the exquisite Auroran. Iphigenia stood with the gun now lowered at her side, her expression quite blank as light of several subtle colors played over her face.

"For some reason, the words are important," Lady Sarafine said in a slow, dulcet voice. "Something about keeping the mind engaged. As long as I keep talking, you're quite helpless. And all I have to do is hold you here for a few moments more, until Hestia and her people arrive or until our Marines do. At which point steps will be taken to ensure your cooperation. Hestia also has clothes that do things to the person wearing them, you know. Clothes made to fit you and your brother both."

Something about the cadence of Sarafine's voice and the light playing over Iphigenia's face made Abigail want to stretch out, relax, and perhaps take a nap. Perhaps while curled up next to the delightful Sarafine.

Then she frowned and pushed the spectacles more firmly up onto her nose, banishing the impulse and ignoring the imposed desire. Goodness, these were terrible people she was dealing with. Simply terrible.

Abigail's first thought was that, given what she knew of Hestia, the plan that Sarafine suggested was in place seemed utterly horrifying. Her second was that she might well rid herself of any ethersilk clothing in her wardrobe for a goodly while.

And her third thought was that it was important to be completely silent as she crossed the floor, aimed the tip of her sword most carefully, and slipped it along Lady Sarafine's flawless skin and into the hollow of her collarbone.

Abigail flicked her wrist and the razor-sharp steel blade of her dueling sword neatly clipped through the fine silver chain holding up the crystal necklace. It fell to the floor, and crystals scattered everywhere, their light abruptly dying out.

Sarafine gasped and whirled toward Abigail. Both Lady Iphigenia and the Lord President blinked and shook their heads. Sarafine began to lunge for the low table in front of the divan, where a sheathed dagger, some decorative piece, sat in a little display rack.

Abigail calmly laid the blade of the dueling sword across the Auroran beauty's throat and said, "That was an absolutely riveting necklace, Your Highness. Duchess Abigail Hinton, Spire Albion. What a pleasure it is to take you hostage."

Chapter 53

AMS *Predator*, near Spire Olympia

Kettle, with me!" Grimm shouted. He flung himself down the staircase from the bridge, slowing his fall with the pressure of his hands on the railings and taking the landing on his good leg. Even so, when he landed, the pain in his wounded leg was enough to take his breath away. Kettle came down after him and caught Grimm as his balance wavered. Together they rushed as best Grimm could move over the nearest boarding ramp, where his men were still piling onto the enemy vessel.

Kettle pulled Grimm up sharply before he could attempt to lower himself down onto *Mistshark*. "Far enough, Skipper. You can command from here."

"At them!" screamed the XO, and Miss Lancaster raised her pistol and calmly sent a ball into the heart of the nearest approaching crewman.

She might have blown him a kiss for all the reaction he showed. He seized her by the coat and dragged her forward.

Kneeling on one of the other loading ramps, Lieutenant Stern lifted his rifle from forty feet away and sent a three-quarter-inch ball into the head of the thing that had grabbed her. Grimm saw that the shot did the trick. The ball struck the crewman in the crystalline eye and took most of the back of his skull with it as it passed through. Gwen managed to break the dead man's hold on her coat and stagger back.

She fared better than most. The crystal-eyed things shrugged off gunfire and thrusts from swords and daggers alike. They seized several of Grimm's aeronauts with terrible strength, dragged them down, and . . .

God in Heaven.

And tore them apart.

"Kettle! Pistols!" Grimm screamed.

Grimm accepted a weapon from Kettle, took aim on the nearest enemy crewman, and sent a shot through his head. "XO!" he screamed. "Axes! Aim for the head!"

Gwen let out a scream as she brought her battle sword down hard into the skull of an enemy crewman. The man staggered back, crystal eyes glinting as he thrashed his head back and forth and, with frantic fingers, pawed at the sword stuck in his skull. He did not scream.

"Aye, sir!" she shouted back. "The heads, boys! Take their heads!"

Kettle aimed a shot, missed, cursed, and then simply passed the pistols to Grimm, explaining, "Never had the money to practice with these things."

"Quite all right, Mister Kettle," Grimm replied. He felled another foe, tossed the pistol back onto *Predator*'s deck, and accepted the next one from the pilot. "I've always found the practice rather relaxing."

Boarding axes rose and fell. They were the most effective weapons against the . . . things that had once been human. They had the weight and the momentum to shear off limbs, and while the loss of an arm or leg did not drop the inhuman things, it left the foe maimed and less capable of doing harm. Men screamed and cried out.

Wounded, felled by the hammering blows of fists like sledgeham-mers, were dragged back to *Predator* and simply thrown to her deck, where Doctor Bagen and his sick-berth attendant raced back and forth, doing triage.

Grimm, meanwhile, lifted his wounded left arm parallel to the plank he sat upon, bent his elbow, braced on his forearm the barrels of the pistols Kettle handed him, and chose his shots with careful precision. Farther down the deck on the next boarding plank, Lieu-tenant Stern was working with a crewman who was reloading one rifle while Stern aimed and fired a second. Grimm found himself firing shots into the bizarrely silent crystal-eyed crewmen whenever one of his own men went down and provided him with an opening.

He saved some. He avenged a few. But at a range of about twenty feet at the most, he rarely missed.

Then one of the crystal-eyed things, a huge man whom Grimm recognized as Calliope's warriorborn first mate, broke through the lines of *Predator*'s crew and flung itself at Grimm.

Kettle let out a shout and met the first swing of the crystal reve-nant's arm with the blade of his boarding ax. Kettle knew what he was about, and the weapon took the arm off at the biceps.

The revenant staggered, and Kettle whirled the heavy weapon straight up and took off the revenant's other arm at the shoulder.

The revenant silently crashed into Kettle, overbearing him by sheer mass. The two went down as Kettle's boarding ax tumbled along the deck. Warriorborn fangs raked at Kettle's throat as the burly pilot tried desperately to defend himself against the revenant's tremendous power and ferocity.

Grimm had three pistols left. He took a brace of them in hand, raised them both from a distance of less than a yard away from the struggling pilot, and barked, "Up, Kettle!"

The pilot let out a scream and pushed, levering the revenant away from his throat with both hands. Links of gold chain went flying everywhere, and Grimm pulled both triggers, sending heavy shot through an eye and a cheekbone. The warriorborn revenant jerked twice in violent spasms—and then toppled limply to the side.

As he heaved in great breaths, his eyes wide and wild, Kettle scrambled out from under the inert revenant and returned to Grimm's side. Several of the gold chains around his neck had been bitten through by the revenant's teeth, and they dangled down like the tail of a scarf, but he seemed unhurt.

"Obliged. Skip, this isn't going well," Kettle panted, the veteran aeronaut's eyes sweeping up and down the *Mistshark*'s deck. "If they hadn't been so slow off the mark and we hadn't gotten so many on board in the first few seconds, they'd have repelled us already."

With his last loaded pistol, Grimm dropped a revenant wearing the scarlet tunic of an Auroran Marine. The shot smashed through his teeth and out the back of his head, stopping him in his tracks. Then Grimm took a look around for himself.

Kettle was right. Grimm's men were no longer pushing forward. *Predator*'s crew had been halted in its tracks and was being pressured back toward the railing. Now wielding a boarding ax in her grip, Gwen led surge after surge against the enemy, but each time, she was driven back with losses, and she was bleeding from a ragged rake mark across one cheek.

There was the rushing sound of many feet, and suddenly more of the mutilated crewmen were pouring up out of the ship's hold.

Grimm's crew could not hold out against numbers like that. The things were apparently as tireless as they were indifferent to pain. Worse yet, the ships were now locked together. The boarding ramps were meant to detach easily from *Predator*'s side, but the damned things rarely worked as well as intended. Only a little bad luck would mean those crystal-eyed nightmares were all over his own ship.

"Captain," called a voice from behind him, and he turned to see Master Ferus standing calmly on the boarding plank near him as though there weren't a fall of several thousand feet waiting for him should his balance waver. He had a brace of apparently reloaded pistols, and he offered the handle of one to Grimm.

The captain took it. "Ferus, what the hell are those things?" Grimm demanded as he aimed and fired again.

"Shells," Ferus said. "Husks. The remains of dead men."

"Can you do anything about them?"

"I dare not," the etherealist said seriously, "for fear that my power crystal might react the same way as the weapons crystal in that gauntlet."

Grimm squinted back at him and said, "It might overload and explode?"

"Yes, with a great deal more released energy."

"Kettle," Grimm said, "your gauntlet, now."

"Aw, Skip," Kettle said, but he produced the weapon from his pocket.

Grimm seized it and passed it to Ferus. "Toss it over them to the far side of *Mistshark*'s deck and set it off."

"Oh!" Ferus said with a blink as he passed Grimm the other pistol. "Oh, I see. Rather an improvised grenade."

"That's the idea," Grimm said. "Right there where all the rein- forcements are coming up."

Ferus nodded seriously, hefted the weight of the gauntlet in his hand with his eyes narrowed, and then flung it in a high arc with a textbook straight-armed throw. The gauntlet tumbled through the air, its crystal glimmering and letting out a high-pitched whine, and fell onto the steps leading down to the hold.

The explosion that came next sent out a blinding flash of light and a deafening crack of thunder. It tore the deck to shreds for five feet in every direction, sending out a cloud of splinters largely absorbed by the bodies of the crystal-eyed husks. Fire followed, a sphere that charred twenty bodies to so much blackened meat and sent dozens more staggering across the deck as though walloped on the heads with truncheons.

There was a stunned moment of silence on the deck. Then came the coughing roar of a warriorborn, and suddenly a knot of perhaps a dozen men, most of them wearing the scarlet tunics of Auroran Marines, burst through the wavering line of crystal husks that had formerly pinned them against the forecastle. With exhausted, professional intensity, they linked up with Grimm's people on that end of their line. They were led by a wounded warriorborn Marine and a medium-sized man in the uniform of an Auroran colonel.

Two of the men, who were wearing aeronaut's leathers and had frightened pale faces and terrified human eyes, dragged the limp form of Grimm's wife. Calliope hung boneless, though her expression was one of agony. Grimm couldn't tell how she'd been wounded.

"Bagen!" he shouted. "Get to that woman and help her!"

Bagen's sad eyes snapped up and focused on Calliope at once. "God in Heaven, Captain!" He thumped his sick-berth attendant on the shoulder and shouted, "Come on!" The two men sprinted down *Predator*'s deck toward the Aurorans.

"Stern!" Grimm bellowed. "Get more gauntlets to Master Ferus now!"

"Aye, Skip!" Lieutenant Stern shouted, and rushed back aboard *Predator* as fires leapt up from *Mistshark*'s crystal-blasted guts.

But Grimm saw that it was already too late. Though Ferus's attack had bought his men a little time, it wasn't enough. Still more of the crystal husks were emerging from *Mistshark*'s aft stairwell. As he watched incredulously, scorched hands seized at the burning wooden planks of the deck, and husks began hauling themselves up through the hole.

The pressure was simply too great, the foe too relentless. In a matter of seconds, Grimm knew, some point in his men's line would buckle. Then the husks would be among them, tearing them limb from limb.

Grimm lifted his last pistol and felled a husk that was reaching for Gwen's throat. Then he growled, "Kettle, for the record, this boarding action was a terrible idea."

"Yeah," the pilot growled. "Just as I got rich."

"Master Ferus," Grimm said, "our position appears untenable. And we cannot allow the enemy to continue with their plans."

"No, Captain," Ferus said. "No, we certainly cannot."

"I assume that if you can trigger a small weapons crystal, you could do so to a larger one as well. Say, our chase gun? It's the largest weapons crystal aboard."

Ferus stared hard at Grimm for a second and then exhaled. "Aye."

"I assume the subsequent explosion would destroy both ships."

"Oh, my, yes," Ferus sighed. "Honestly, overloading any of the cannon crystals would produce enough energy to destroy both ships several times over, Captain."

"Can you do it from a distance?"

Ferus shook his head. "Not from far enough away to make any difference, I'm afraid."

Grimm inhaled deeply. "Then please make ready to do so, sir."

Ferus turned to stare up in the direction of the mistmaw and the embattled Spire for a moment. Then he nodded his head decisively. "Very well, Captain."

Grimm turned to Kettle and said, "Get Miss Folly and as many wounded aboard the survival buoys as you can and get up above this mist. Take signal rockets for *Belligerent*. We'll buy you as much time as possible."

Kettle's expression grew sickened. "Aw . . . aw, Skip."

"That's an order, Kettle," Grimm said. "There's no time to argue."

"Aye, sir," Kettle said quietly.

Grimm's leg hurt. For a moment, he bowed his head against the pain, and then he steeled himself. He had to do whatever he could to delay the inevitable. Perhaps he could at least give the wounded time enough to get clear.

Then there was a sound.

A beautiful, beautiful sound.

A trilling, yipping war cry that came from somewhere off in the mist and was joined by dozens more like it. And then dozens more.

Grimm looked up and his eyes widened. "It can't be."

"Pikers!" Ferus shouted.

A gliding parachute appeared from the mist over *Mistshark's* prow, and a compact, muscular figure in black leathers and a dragon-plume cloak hit the release on her harness and dropped six feet onto the planking of the bridge. As her chute flew off into the night, Ravenna bounced to her feet, hefted a short, bell-mouthed arquebus to her shoulder, and, with a roar of exploding powder, sent a cloud of scrap metal slashing into the mass of crystal husks below her, felling four.

More Pikers came gliding down, then landed on the bridge beside their captain, upon the aft tower, or atop the central cabin. Others alighted in the masts and rigging. They bristled with swords, knives, axes, and gunpowder weapons. It was a glorious mess as parachutes tangled in the rigging or fell across the crystal husks. With the roar of a tigress and an ax-handled billhook in her hands, Ravenna flung herself from the bridge and into the opening she'd blown in the fray with her arquebus. She began scything the foe down like wheat, the wicked inner curve of the hook slicing off limbs with contemptuous ease.

The crew of *Stormmaiden*, grim and eager in their black leathers— more of them arriving by the breath—came piling down after her, bellowing their terror and fury, their weapons crackling thunder.

And with a clarion battle cry from Gwendolyn Lancaster, the crew of *Predator* surged forward against the foe, renewed hope lending them strength and ferocity.

"By the Maker of Ways and the Merciful Builders and the golden streets of Heaven itself," Kettle breathed, "I will never tell jokes about Pikers again for as long as I draw breath."

"Kettle," Grimm said intently, "belay my last order. Master Ferus, you as well. I want to know where that Cavendish woman is."

"Belowdecks," Ferus supplied instantly, "in the stern. Whatever device she's created, it is near the engine room."

Grimm fought off a wave of nausea from the pain in his leg and nodded. "Then that," he growled, "is where we're going next."

Chapter 54

Skyport, Spire Olympia

Bridget didn't hold on to the chair so much as get pushed down on it by acceleration. Because Vincent had settled his weight across the arms of the chair, very little of it was actually upon her. They had managed to get Rowl and Fenli with their front legs perched on Bridget's shoulders and their hind limbs braced upon Vincent. Then, guiding the chair, Benedict sprinted across the skyport to *Sunhawk* to secure parachutes.

The place was in chaos. Bridget saw perhaps a dozen more airships lift off. Another ship crashed as it made the attempt. A second made it perhaps five hundred feet up, then listed sharply as the trim crystals along her port side failed. That ship broke in half around its main lift crystal. The pieces came spinning down just to one side of the Spire, where they vanished beyond the lip of the skyport into the mists below.

People ran in every direction. Most were rushing for the shelter of the transport ramps down into the Spire. Others were running in different directions, presumably for their airships. More were simply fleeing the oncoming mass of the mistmaw.

The monster had covered the airspace back to the Spire every bit as quickly as it had moved away, and its vector of approach brought it over the Olympian Fleet's home berths. Most of the ships that had made it into the air were light military vessels. The larger ships simply didn't have sufficient numbers of crew members to lift off, and as the tentacles of the creature smashed across the surface of the Spire, the grounded ships were reduced to splinters and kindling.

Benedict got the group to *Sunhawk* in under a minute. Then he calmly seized Vincent by his coat, grimaced briefly in apology, and flung him up over the railing and onto the deck.

Vincent staggered to his feet and gave Benedict a sharp look. Then he vanished into the ship's cabin and began slamming things around in his haste.

"Oh, look at that," Fenli said, peering over Bridget's shoulder. "It is almost to the humans."

Rowl flicked his tail back and forth with interest. "They're just screaming and pushing one another. That hardly seems useful. They should be looking for parachutes or flying away in their airships."

"Like a nest of mice when one knocks it over," Fenli noted.

"Oh, just like that," Rowl said. "You'd think humans would do better."

Fenli blinked and looked at Rowl. "Why?"

Rowl flicked his ears in acknowledgment. "True. Present company excepted, naturally."

"Yes," Fenli agreed. "Littlemouse and Tribesaver seem to be doing better than most."

"Did you hear?" Rowl said proudly. "Littlemouse is taking Tribesaver as mate."

"Yes, I was there," Fenli said. "Perhaps they will breed children of adequate competence."

Benedict made a choking sound, but when Bridget looked up at him, his eyes were shining. He was also shaking. He was trying hard not to show it, but the run had taxed him tremendously. Bridget desperately wished that she could sit him down under a blanket for a cup of tea and some scones.

There would probably need to be less cannon fire lancing overhead, she supposed. The constant flashes of green-white fire continually lit him up from varying angles, casting shadows on the nightmare form of the mistmaw still approaching behind him.

"It seems as if you will not be warning anyone about the mistmaw now," Rowl said with a smug flick of his tail. "So you do not get to be heroic."

Fenli's whiskers twitched in irritation. "It is hardly my fault that it took the humans so long to meet our reasonable and plainly stated conditions."

Rowl's fur fluffed up in satisfaction. "I suppose that is true," the ginger cat said magnanimously. "But then, humans do not seem to function well under pressure."

"Present company excepted, of course," Fenli said hurriedly.

"Oh, of course," Rowl said, patting Bridget's (injured, she noted) leg absently with one paw. "But where would they be without management?"

"Where, indeed?"

Bridget sighed. "Gentlemen," she pointed out, "I observe that you are in just as much danger of being devoured as we are."

Both cats leaned back to stare at her with expressions somewhere between astonishment and pity.

"We are cats," Rowl said with towering confidence. "We will think of something."

"There is, after all, a reason my tribe survived when the humans of Spire Dependence did not," Fenli said. Then his eyes focused intently behind Bridget, and in a suddenly quiet voice, he said, "Oh. The poor mice."

Bridget did not want to look.

The howl of the port's defensive batteries redoubled to the point at which several defensive cannon overheated and went up in furious fireballs. Bridget had neither the energy nor the desire to see what both cats were now staring at so intently. Instead, she looked up at Benedict, who took one slow glance back and quietly reported, "The mistmaw has gotten to the ramps. It's descending so more tentacles can reach them. It looks like it's slowing down a little while it . . . feeds. But it's still coming."

Feet pounded on the courier ship's deck, and Vincent reappeared, grunting and dragging several large packs and standard shipboard safety harnesses with him. He stuffed them into a large aeronaut's canvas shoulder bag and tossed it down. Benedict caught it and slipped the strap across his chest while Vincent sprinted down the gangplank and resumed his awkward position on the chair, panting, his expression grim.

With his additional burden, Benedict started off again, pushing for the nearest edge of the Spire. He wasn't moving as fast as he had earlier. Bridget could feel him trembling wearily through the frame of the wheeled chair.

Vincent noticed too. "Sir Benedict," he said quietly, "perhaps I should push the chair while you carry the chutes."

It was a mark of Benedict's exhaustion that he made no argument. He simply came to a stop. Vincent got up, took the chair's handles, and started forward at a trot. Benedict bowed his head, adjusted the strap of the aeronaut's duffel, and shuffled forward without speaking.

"Endure, sir," Vincent said firmly. "There's a package of hardtack and jerky at the bottom of the bag. Once we're down, we'll get some food into you."

Benedict looked up, gave him a fleeting smile, and ducked his head in a vague nod.

"Good man," Vincent said.

Bridget said nothing but reached across her body with one bandaged hand and patted Vincent's hand gratefully.

They didn't move as fast as earlier, but neither did the mistmaw. Bridget could hear distant screams between the bursts of cannon fire, which was slowing as the weapons grew too hot to fire frequently. Great clouds of steam were arising around the perimeter of the Spire where gunners desperately employed their water tanks to try to coax as much fire as possible from the weapons. The flash of energy fire and the sullen glow of burning buildings lit the steam in a spectrum of colors, giving the world a surreal look, as if it were some kind of horrible, haunted painting.

Bridget and the others approached the edge of the Spire and found it occupied. It was, in fact, crowded. With their backs against the low spirestone wall around the Spire's edge, desperate-looking men and women stood staring at the mistmaw with funereal expressions on their faces. A great many, dull eyed and hopeless, were drinking from crocks and bottles. Some were shuffling slowly along the outer curve of the skyport to get to the maximum distance away from the mistmaw, but there was little urgency in evidence. The people looked dully terrified. Stunned. Crushed under the weight of terror and spectacle and imminent death.

Bridget knew exactly how that felt.

Of course there would be a crowd, Bridget thought. Plenty of desperate people must have realized that there was no escape down the transport ramps. Where else would they go but as far away from the monster as possible?

Vincent drew to a halt slowly, staring around. Benedict came to a stop beside him. Their expressions were grim.

"If we show that we have parachutes," Vincent said quietly, "we will be attacked."

"Surely they wouldn't," Bridget said anxiously.

"Everyone wants to live, love," Benedict contradicted her gently. He drew in a deep breath. "To that end, some of them will do anything they must."

Vincent turned the chair and wheeled it into the space between a warehouse building and a darkened, deserted airship. Judging from the mess and debris on the ship's deck, it had already been ransacked.

"So?" Vincent asked, turning to Benedict.

"I can get . . . us to the edge," the tall young warriorborn said quietly. "It won't be pretty. But if we move fast enough, I can do it."

Vincent stared at Benedict for a long moment, then asked, "Are you sure?"

"Yes. Can you get Bridget over the wall?"

"I believe so, yes."

Bridget looked sharply between them and then said, "Gentlemen, did you both just decide to sacrifice yourselves to ensure the young woman got the chance to fall two miles on a parachute and land on the surface at night, crippled and alone?"

The two men exchanged a guilty glance, and Vincent said, "Actually, miss, Benedict agreed to get you and me over the edge. I agreed to look after you on the surface."

"My God," Bridget said. "You communicated all that with a glance and yet you can't simply speak your minds. And, Sir Vincent, I believe in this situation you should address me as Sergeant Tagwynn."

Benedict smiled faintly and leaned down to kiss her hair. "I can't fight in a parachute, love."

"Fight?" Bridget demanded. "Innocent people?"

"The operative word there," Vincent said quietly, "is 'people.' Sir Benedict is correct, Sergeant. They will fight to live."

Benedict nodded. "I thought I'd throw my parachute out into the open and let the hungriest rush for it and fight one another. That should thin out the worst of them. Then I can get you both to the edge and you can go over. The cats can go down with you in the duffel."

"I do not like this plan," Rowl and Fenli both said at the same time. Then they looked at each other suspiciously.

Vincent ignored them and nodded several times. "Precisely. Sir Benedict is strong enough to get us through without doing severe harm. I'd have to kill people to do the same."

Bridget stared at them both and then said, "You sound like you're talking about a game of chess."

"There is a reason to practice such thinking," Vincent confirmed. "For moments like this."

"With all due respect, Sir Vincent," Bridget said, "chess presumes that you know every factor within a very limited theater."

"Love," Benedict said, "is that not what we are faced with at this very moment?"

Bridget stared up at the airship above them and said, "How long are the reels of etherweb on a ship this size?"

Benedict blinked at her, then up at the ship. "She's about *Predator*'s size. Several hundred yards, I believe."

"And the web is extremely strong, is it not? And the ends are secured to a rather solid, heavy object?" Bridget said.

"By God, they are," Vincent said.

"And the ventilation tunnels are spaced around the outer surface of the Spire about fifty feet below us, yes?"

"Yes," Benedict said with sudden certainty. "But they're closed with steel grates."

Bridget met his eyes and showed her teeth. "If only we had a warriorborn to tear it open." She turned to Vincent and said, "Sir Vincent, provide Sir Benedict with food immediately. We aren't going to sacrifice anyone, and we aren't going to fight these people, gentlemen," Bridget said. "We're going to save ourselves. And we're going to take them with us."

■ ■ ■ Chapter 55 ■ ■ ■

IAS *Mistshark*, near Spire Olympia

Colonel Espira stared around the deck of the *Mistshark*, his home for the past weeks, and could hardly believe his astonished eyes.

They were alive.

Against all odds, against all expectations, against all fortune, he and some portion of his command were still alive. The arrival of the Pikers—who had brought three warriorborn of their own, including their exquisitely distracting commander—had turned the tide of the battle. The revenants had not reacted to the new circumstance quickly enough, and by the time they had adjusted their attacks, their numbers had dropped too low to hold the ship.

Espira and his men were alive.

His decision had cost all but eight of his men their lives. He'd had to follow his conscience. But by God in Heaven, he felt horrible about the men who had fallen while trusting his orders.

But these last few had come through. They had followed him into the fire and come out alive.

Well, for the moment at any rate.

The deck of the airship was covered in blood and the remains of corpses. The survivors were dumping the dead over the side as quickly as they could. The trilling chirps of actual mistsharks, the ship's namesakes, had begun closing in almost as soon as the combat had ended, and every Marine and aeronaut there knew they couldn't leave bodies and blood on a deck without drawing attacks. With a will, Espira and his men pitched in with the Albions and Pikers, clearing the crystal revenants' remains as rapidly as possible and dumping them over the side to plunge toward the surface.

"Sergeant," Espira said quietly, "how are you?"

Ciriaco looked up from where one of the surviving Marines was splinting his arm, and he said, a growl in his voice, "Back hurts a bit, Colonel. Did some heavy lifting there. Cracked some ribs, I think. Belly's worse."

"It's been too many hours since you've eaten," Espira said, and turned to the next-highest-ranking Marine on his team—a corporal named Martinez. "See to it that the sergeant gets food."

"Sir," the Marine said respectfully, "we already ate what we had in our pockets. The food from the galley might be tainted. Our packs are still down in quarters, but I can go down for mine."

"Month-old rations," Ciriaco said whimsically. "Just throw me over the side."

Espira put a hand on the warriorborn's shoulder and said, "No, Corporal Martinez. I'm not sending anyone belowdecks until we know there aren't more of those things lurking in ambush." He glanced up at the Albions, who were a little way down the deck and seeing to their own wounded. "I'll . . . speak to our, ah, allies."

He approached the man who was obviously in command of the Albion ship. Of unimpressive height but sturdy build, he was wearing the remains of a civilian shipboard uniform. One of his legs was heavily wrapped in bandages that were easily visible since that leg of his trousers had been cut away. There were recent stitches in a swollen wound on his face, and he was peppered in lighter dressings over most of his visible body. His face was gaunt, with pain showing beneath a well-kept beard, and there were dark circles beneath his eyes. But sitting on the deck with his back straight and his eyes alert, he was giving directions to his crew. A petite and lovely young woman in an officer's uniform and a burly aeronaut festooned in a rather ludicrous number of golden chains stood over him like personal bodyguards.

Espira approached the other commander, who was speaking to one of his officers, a slip of a young man with dark hair and a cocky grin. Then Espira braced himself to attention. Odd, Espira thought, that the reflexes of a Marine before a ship's captain were not in the least different simply because that captain happened to be a civilian from another Spire. This fellow wore confidence and command so comfortably that his ragged clothing hardly mattered.

The Albion captain sent the young officer off on a mission to fetch kegs of powder to reload the gunpowder weapons. Then he turned his attention to Espira, his dark eyes intent. "Ah, Colonel, allow me to compliment you and your men for seizing the initiative and joining us during the fight. I saw what those things could do. I'm impressed that you and your men survived."

"Thank you, Captain," he said. "I am Colonel Renaldo Espira of the Royal Auroran Marines. My men and I owe you our lives. You came out of nowhere."

The man snorted. "The Pikers came out of nowhere," he said. "I just happened to come by to borrow a cup of sugar."

Even as he spoke, a lean, dangerous-looking Piker ship the size of a heavy cruiser came swanning slowly down out of the rain overhead. Painted mist grey on the top and sky blue on the bottom, she loomed over the *Mistshark* and the Albion vessel like a diremoth frozen in the moment of a swooping attack. At least a platoon of assault troops stood by at her drop doors, and her gunnery crews were in position at their weapons.

The other man squinted at Espira thoughtfully for a moment. "A pleasure to work with you and your people, Colonel. Captain Francis Madison Grimm of the Albion merchant ship *Predator*."

Espira felt his eyes widen slightly. Ah, he was *that* civilian captain. The one who had led a counterattack against a critical portion of Espira's raid upon Spire Albion two years past. The man who had very nearly blown *Mistshark*—and with it, Espira and his command—from the sky when they were trying to escape. Only the intervention of the AAS *Itasca* had saved them from capture or death.

"I recognized your name as well, Colonel," Grimm said quietly. "You led the raid that nearly destroyed my ship—and did destroy better than forty airships, along with the docks at Landing."

Espira bowed slightly from the waist. "The same, sir."

"It was an effective mission," the man said with the kind of professional detachment Espira would honestly only have expected from a career military man.

"It was my duty," Espira replied calmly.

Captain Grimm stared at him for a moment, his eyes narrowed. Then he nodded his head sharply once. "Just so. Just as I was doing mine today."

"I thank you nonetheless," Espira said. "Captain, my warriorborn was starved before the battle. The food aboard this ship is probably tainted. Might I impose upon you for something for him?"

"Of course," Grimm said at once. "XO, see to it immediately."

The young woman beside Grimm tore her eyes away from staring at Ciriaco and said, "Aye, Skip." She hurried away briskly.

"Colonel," Grimm said, "I think we both know that you and your men are engaged in hostile action against Spire Albion and Olympia. By all reason, I should take you and your men as prisoners of war and interrogate you."

"War has not yet been declared, Captain," Espira observed in a neutral tone.

Grimm tilted his head and gave Espira a frank look. "Colonel, please."

Espira felt a certain amount of shame, for of course the man was correct. But at the same time, he found it difficult to so much as consider speaking to an officer of the enemy about his Spire's actions. "Captain," he said after a moment, "you are a man who understands duty, are you not?"

Grimm gave him a faint smile and said, "For the moment, Colonel, keep your sword. You will please consider yourself and your men to be my guests. I will have your parole, sir, while you are."

"You have it," Espira said immediately. "We will comport ourselves with courtesy and respect—as much as young Marines are capable of, at any rate."

"Hah," Grimm said. "I don't suppose you'd care to share any details of your mission with me?"

"Captain," Espira chided gently.

Grimm shrugged a shoulder. "And how is Madame Cavendish these days?"

Espira stared at him for a moment. Grimm knew. If he knew about Cavendish, then he would know about her pet as well. Either that or he had deduced what was happening and then acted with superb initiative. God in Heaven, how foolish was the leadership of the Aetherium Fleet to cashier such a capable commander?

Strictly speaking, Espira should have respectfully declined to answer any questions from an enemy officer.

But.

Espira was a soldier, not a mass murderer. And the thunder of

Spire Olympia's port guns, coming slower now, told him that Cavendish's monster was still murdering civilians.

"Regrettably," he said carefully, "when last I saw the witch, she still drew breath."

"Mmmm," Grimm said thoughtfully. "I mean to correct that the very moment the firearms are reloaded. I don't suppose you have any idea if there were more of those crystal-eyed things aboard?"

"I would be startled if she hadn't kept some in reserve for her personal protection," Espira said. "She is quite capable."

"Not for long," Grimm said calmly. "Captain, it is clear to me that you and your men somehow earned Madame Cavendish's malice, and I find myself inclined toward amity for that reason alone." His eyes thoughtful, he looked away into the distance, then nodded. "Your men have fought enough for one day. They will remain on deck while I finish this. You, however, are welcome to accompany me, provided you keep to your parole and are willing to follow my directives while it happens."

Espira felt a tension he hadn't recognized as a strain easing out of his shoulders and spine. He glanced over at his physically and mentally exhausted troops and closed his eyes. "Captain Grimm," he said formally, "I cannot speak to the future. But today, until this matter with the witch is settled, my sword—and the hand that wields it—is yours to command."

"Excellent," Captain Grimm said. "Ah, Kettle, here comes Lieutenant Stern. Get the firearms loaded, bring Captain Ravenna over, and then help me up." His dark, sunken eyes glittered with a predator's hunger. "It's time we settled with Madame Cavendish."

Chapter 56

IAS *Mistshark*, near Spire Olympia

Grimm fought down a desire to snarl in pain as Kettle hefted him up from the deck. If he survived this, he promised himself, he would take a day to rest.

He saw Espira studying him as he rose. The Auroran officer, a few inches taller than Grimm and built with that lean power the Aurorans were famous for, frowned as Kettle helped his commander up.

"You didn't get those wounds in this fight, Captain," Espira said.

"No, they came courtesy of Rafael Valesco," Grimm answered.

"The duelist?" Espira asked.

"The late duelist," Kettle corrected him. "Captain threw his head off the side of the Spire."

Espira blinked mildly at that, then frowned at Grimm more deeply. "A dangerous man," he said.

"A proud man," Grimm corrected him. "Dangerously so."

"Mmmm," Espira said.

Ravenna approached, light glittering gorgeously in a hundred colors from her dragon-plume cloak. She frowned at Grimm and said, "Frank, don't be an idiot. Get back in bed at once."

Grimm gave her a look.

The warriorborn woman rolled her eyes and said, "Oh, for pity's sake. You and your people have done enough. I'm taking point."

"By all means," Grimm said, "ladies first."

"Frank," she said, "a word."

Grimm tilted his head and studied Ravenna for a second, then nodded to Kettle. The pilot propped him up against the *Mistshark's* railing and withdrew, making a point to crowd the Auroran officer some distance away as he did.

Ravenna waited until the Auroran was standing off, then said to Grimm, "Did you see the Atlantean ship sending up rockets?"

"Yes," Grimm said. "Just before we came down."

"They were answered," she said. "Maybe ten miles out. The Auroran Armada is here."

Grimm's head rocked back as if she'd slapped him. "What? Are you sure?"

Ravenna's jaw tensed. "Yes."

"How do you know?"

She shook her head and looked away from him. "I can't . . . Frank, I need you to trust me. I know it the same way I knew to be ready to lift off at a moment's notice."

Grimm narrowed his eyes. "This isn't an instinct, is it?"

Ravenna let out a little laugh that was brittle around the edges. "You wouldn't believe me if I told you. But it isn't. Once the Armada shifts formation, they'll be coming for whatever is left of Spire Olympia. And not only did the mistmaw beat the hell out of their Fleet while it was in port, their guns are overheated. You can hear that their fire rate has slowed."

She glanced up and Grimm listened. Ravenna was right. Though the guns of Spire Olympia still thundered, their tempo had slowed, and there were fewer of them than there had been before. Broadsides from the improvised defensive fleet had slowed as well.

"I don't suppose," Grimm said, "that your instincts also told you to have every Piker ship in the sky available to fight them."

"Even if they had," Ravenna said quietly, "we can't stand up to the Armada alone. You know that. What about Albion?"

"The current Admiralty is not known for its stunningly aggressive philosophy," Grimm replied. "The Aetherium Fleet is being held close to home."

Ravenna nodded. "Then it's over. We need to finish business here and run. Whatever they're using to interfere with our power cores, we turn it off, back away, blow up their ship, and live to fight another day."

Thinking, Grimm stared into the distance as the mistmaw wailed again.

"Perhaps not," he said. He raised his voice. "Master Ferus, may I consult with you, please?"

Ravenna and her two warriorborn aeronauts descended first into the *Mistshark's* lower decks, followed by several Pikers bristling with gunpowder weapons. In the middle were Grimm and Kettle, with Ferus, Espira, and Miss Lancaster. Behind them were more Pikers and several of Grimm's own veterans.

Here and there were inert crystal revenants scattered in pools of blood. Apparently, while the poor men who had been taken over could keep fighting through any kind of pain or maiming, the machinery of their bodies would still break down eventually, given enough blood loss.

"These are the ones we fought when they first . . . happened," Espira said quietly. "Ciriaco did for most of them. We didn't see this many fall. It must have happened later."

"Good to know they aren't invincible," Gwen said quietly.

"Aye," Kettle said a bit sourly, tucking the loose end of a gold chain into the mound of them still around his neck. "You cut off an arm, you can be sure the damned things will die a few minutes after they've chewed your throat out."

"How many could she fit into the rear hold?" Grimm asked.

"There were maybe fifteen of them there when we went in," Espira said. "The hold is about as big across as the ship. Call it thirty feet. It's about twenty feet from the door to the tank. The tank is on the right. The machine is on the left. Cavendish will be in the tank, I think. Don't get any of the fluid on you, or you'll get sick and become one of those things."

"Oh, it's a great deal worse than that, I believe," Master Ferus said. "I expect that once enough of the Enemy's structures have propagated inside a body, they can be used to accomplish any number of effects. I suspect that's how Sycorax was able to control the mistmaw—by infesting it in some way."

"Two years ago," Grimm said, "you told me that structures had infested my blood as well."

"Exactly correct, grim Captain," Ferus said.

"But you were able to destroy them."

"Yes."

"Can Folly do the same?" Grimm asked.

"I believe so. For Captain Ransom's sake, let us hope Folly believes it too," Ferus said. "She's attempting it as we speak."

Grimm stared for a second. "Calliope . . . has those things inside her?"

"Did I not mention that I saw them? I apologize, Captain. The past half hour has been rather distracting."

"Quiet," growled Ravenna from the front. "If it's all right with the discussion group, I'd like to be able to hear."

Grimm clamped his mouth shut after resisting the urge to curse at himself. Ravenna might have been more correct than he thought, if he had so little discipline in this moment. His damned leg hurt on a level he had previously associated only with being very, very drunk. Perhaps it stood to reason that the pain was affecting his judgment as well.

He had to focus. Concentrate.

Ravenna ghosted up to the door in the kind of total silence that came only with the grace of the warriorborn. She had her arquebus in hand, her boarding billhook hung on a strap over her shoulder. She put her head close to the door while each of the two warriorborn behind her drew a broad combat knife in one hand and hefted a heavy double-barreled pistol in the other. Ravenna made eye contact with each man, nodded, and leaned back in preparation to kick the door open.

"There's no point in destroying a perfectly good door," called a woman's voice from the other side. Grimm recognized Madame Cavendish's rich alto at once. "Come in, Efferus. Come in, Captain Grimm."

Ravenna glanced back at Grimm and lifted her eyebrows in question. Grimm felt quite certain that if he gave her the signal, she'd simply shoot the woman through the door now that she'd spoken and given away her position to the excellent hearing of the warriorborn.

Grimm glanced at Master Ferus. The old etherealist's face was grim. He held up a hand and called back, "Sycorax, you know why we are here."

"To kill me," she said firmly. "I assure you, I have arranged matters so that doing so will result in the deaths of everyone aboard both ships. Though, to be perfectly honest with you, Efferus, I'm not at all certain that killing me will put an end to me. I am far too useful to my master."

Grimm turned at once to Gwen. "Get word to Journeyman's

people," he said quietly. "I want two of the boarding ramps detached right now."

Gwen nodded and turned to Lieutenant Stern. After she whispered to him for a moment, the slim young man departed on quick, quiet feet.

"Then why don't you simply destroy us all, Sycorax?" Ferus asked, genuinely curious. "Especially if you think you will somehow survive it."

She let out a girlish laugh. "Because I've had very little conversation these last weeks. And I want to see the look on your face. Do come in. I won't strike first."

"Said the snake to the scorpion," Kettle muttered. "Snakes bite, Skip. Scorpions sting. It's what they do."

"If Ferus has the capability to destroy both ships, so does she," Grimm said quietly.

"Yes," Ferus said, "but if I am in the room with her, I may be able to counter her, Captain. I believe we have little choice."

Grimm turned to Ravenna. "Get a rifle. If she looks distracted for an instant, put a bullet through her head."

Ravenna passed her arquebus off to one of the men with her, held out a hand, and caught a gunpowder rifle carried by one of the other Pikers.

"Sycorax," Ferus called, "we're coming in."

"Just you and the captain, Efferus. Don't make me end this conversation in a way we'll all regret."

"Skip," Kettle said warningly.

"The captain is injured," Ferus said. "He needs someone to help him walk."

"So much the better," Cavendish replied. "It will keep your mind that much more occupied."

Grimm calmly began transferring pistols from Kettle's belt to his coat pockets and the waistband of his ruined pants.

"You must think me a thoroughly dangerous woman, Captain," Cavendish said, her voice amused. "By all means, bring your weapons."

Gwen stared at Grimm with her face going pale. "How . . . how did she know?"

"She's learned quicker than I expected," Ferus said quietly, his eyes somber. "Much quicker." The old etherealist gave Kettle a wan smile. "I'll take good care of him, Mister Kettle. And perhaps we will need you at *Predator*'s helm."

Kettle let out a frustrated sound. Then he changed places with Ferus. The old man was surprisingly sturdy as he slipped under Grimm's left arm, supporting his weight on that side.

"Very well, Ravenna," Grimm said. "Open the door."

"Don't cheat me out of my vacation, Frank," Ravenna said sternly. Then she opened the door to the rear hold.

Grimm and Ferus went forward slowly. Ferus was not as strong as Kettle, who, Grimm realized, had mostly dragged him everywhere. It was a great deal harder to move without that strength assisting him, and he found himself breathing harder just moving forward a few feet.

To their right was a great tank, a cylinder of thick glass and copper-clad steel, full of some kind of clear liquid mixed with a yellowish substance that looked like mucus. To their left, a heavy control panel sat with wires running to the tank and off to the power systems of the ship.

Clad only in a wet white shift that clung to her skin transparently, Cavendish sat on the floor next to the tank. Sark lay on the floor beside her, his head in her lap. He was quite dead, his crooked eyes staring blankly, his form unnaturally still. Cavendish's long, fine, damp fingers stroked the dead man's cropped hair. Her expression was relaxed and quietly amused.

The bare ends of copper wires had been thrust directly into her chest, over her heart; small trickles of blood marked where they pierced her skin. Grimm tracked the wires back to the control panel she rested against.

"My poor Sark," Cavendish said. "Endlessly reliable. Endlessly useful. Colonel Espira shot too well. But even so, he died trying to protect me." Something ugly flickered in her face and she said, "If he survived, please tell Renaldo that there shall be an accounting for that."

"I don't think either one of us is going to be in a position to do much talking for very long," Ferus said gently. "Sycorax, what have you done?"

She looked up and laughed, and the lumin crystals in the room seemed to pulse along with her voice.

No, Grimm realized. They were pulsing along with her *heartbeat*.

The etherealists' gazes met, and they stared steadily at each other.

"You can see it, can't you, Efferus?" Cavendish asked. "If you remove the wires or should my heart stop beating, the ship's power core activates. And if that happens, its core crystal overloads. Not a simple explosion, Efferus. An energetic release."

"What's the difference?" Grimm asked.

"Several orders of magnitude," Efferus said without blinking. "It would badly damage or destroy Spire Olympia."

"God in Heaven," Grimm said. "If she's telling the truth—"

"I assure you, Captain," Cavendish said waspishly, "I am."

Ferus narrowed his eyes. "You've learned very quickly, Sycorax. This new master must be an able teacher—and you an able lackey."

Cavendish let out a low, quiet cackle. "You cannot dream of the things I have learned, old man."

"Small favors," Ferus murmured. "I assume you didn't ask me in here just to trade insults."

"Naturally not," Cavendish said. "I'm actually going to offer you a different kind of trade."

"Oh?" Ferus said. He winced. "Captain, my back. Would you very much mind sitting on the floor?"

"Not in the least," Grimm said.

Truth be told, he felt slightly dizzy. In his arms, there was a queer, warbling sensation that made him think they might be about to start shaking. Ferus lowered him gently to the floor, and Grimm sat with his leg out in front of him. He held the bandages briefly so his hands would be close to his waistband.

"Very well, Sycorax," Ferus said, rising. "What is your offer?"

"Live and let live, of course," Sycorax said. "Your own life's philosophy. Let us see if you cleave to it under pressure."

"We're here to stop the mistmaw," Ferus said quietly.

"You can't," Cavendish said with a small smirk. "The mindless thing has been guided to a rich feeding ground. That's why I need not be in the tank any longer. Its instincts are keeping it in place now. It will endure a few stings for the honey it's taking."

Ferus's expression darkened. "And after killing so many people, you want us to . . . what? Simply let you walk away?"

"The Armada is here, Efferus," Cavendish purred. "And your ships are flying the wrong flags. I have already directed a strike force to our location. If you leave me in peace and depart at once, you may escape them. Otherwise, I cannot be held responsible for what a very anxious and aggressive group of Marines will do to you and your people, assuming they do not simply send you burning to the surface with their cannon."

"I didn't realize Tuscarora was such a mentor of the ethereal arts," Ferus said.

"Tuscarora," Cavendish said dismissively, "is merely a means to an end. He has no idea of what is truly at stake. And he is easily distracted by shining baubles such as destroyed fleets and conquered Spires." She turned to Grimm. "Captain, let me sweeten the deal with more than simply your lives and the lives of your friends and crew." She smiled brilliantly. "I'll give you a gift."

"What gift, madame?" Grimm asked quietly.

"There is a power crystal in this control panel," she said. "Sufficient to run a small vessel. And grown in mere weeks."

Grimm frowned. Power cores sufficient to run ships, even small ones, took decades to form. Not weeks.

"I make it a point not to tell lies," Cavendish said as if she'd followed his very thoughts. "The older I get, the more they seem a waste of time, creating more problems than they ever solve. Upon my love of power and upon the Tyranima itself, I swear to you, Captain, I am telling you the truth."

Upon the what? "What would I want with one small crystal?" Grimm responded calmly.

"To grind it to dust and use the fragments as seed crystals, obviously," Cavendish replied. "Imagine, doubling the size of your dreadnought fleet in just under a year."

Grimm felt his mouth fall open. He closed it again.

"After all," Cavendish said, "I gave Tuscarora his seeds almost a year ago. What's coming for Spire Albion is going to be entirely overwhelming—unless you counter them, of course."

The woman was lying. She had to be. And yet, for Aurora to take the risk of sending out its home fleet to attack Olympia . . .

They had to have something left behind. Not even Tuscarora was that aggressive.

If they'd found a way to massively increase their fleet in a fraction of the time . . .

Then Grimm's world had just changed.

Rapidly.

Completely.

And damn it all, the woman spoke with the ring of truth.

"I know men like you, Captain," Cavendish said quietly. "You're willing to die in defense of that rabble who cower behind you and never lift their eyes from their own little lives. And what I'm offering you will be your Spire's salvation. As well as the salvation of your ship. Your crew. And your own life."

Grimm stared at her for a long, silent moment.

"So must the Serpent have spoken to the First Mother and Father," Ferus said quietly.

Grimm found himself smiling slightly. He might be about to make a mistake. But at least it would be a mistake made by a man he could respect.

"Madame Cavendish," he said gently, "I cannot think of anything you have ever offered that was not full of pain, death, and suffering. No, I think we will take other action. Master Ferus."

Ferus took off his hat, his spectacles, and his jacket, then folded them and left them in a neat pile on the floor. He laid his crystal-headed cane down gently over them. Then he started walking calmly toward the tank.

"What exactly," Cavendish asked, naked contempt in her voice, "do you think you're doing?"

"I observed the energies you were using rather closely as we approached, dear Sycorax," Ferus said. He mounted the steps built into the side of the tank. "Rather foolish of you, really, to bring the Auroran Armada directly into the reach of a creature so readily capable of smashing them."

Cavendish's eyes widened. "You wouldn't."

The old man, his wild hair drifting in the updraft from the tank, smiled faintly at her. "You aren't nearly as talented or clever as you seem to think you are, Sycorax. The only question at the moment is whether I can't or whether I can. And I believe I can."

And with that, he swung his legs neatly over the lip of the tank and sank into the fluid within. The yellowish gel immediately began to stir and swirl around Ferus's legs and lower body.

"No!" Cavendish said, and reached out a desperate hand for the control panel.

Grimm drew his pistol, moving with sure, perfect instinct, and the weapon barked and bucked in his grip.

Cavendish let out a high-pitched wail of pain and clutched her hand back to her belly, blood pattering down onto Sark's dead face.

"Madame Cavendish," Grimm said calmly, "I'm afraid I must ask you not to move."

She looked up at him, her face twisted into a mask of hatred. "Or *what*, precisely?"

Grimm discarded the spent pistol, took up another one, and drew back the hammer.

There was a quiet chorus of clicks from the doorway from a dozen weapons—held by Kettle, by Ravenna, by Gwen, by Colonel Espira, and by the Pikers—trained on Cavendish.

"Or there are a great many more places to shoot you that won't kill you, witch," Espira said in his soft Auroran accent. "At least not right away."

Cavendish narrowed her eyes, and they *shifted*, changed color and shape slightly, like embers glowing through the wavering heat of a particularly intense fire.

"Captain," she hissed, "you are going to regret this."

"Madame Cavendish," Grimm replied, "you have two choices. Either withdraw the wires from your chest or keep your teeth to-gether."

She stared at him, her lips twitching up from her gnashed teeth in a weird, erratic rhythm. The lights in the room pulsed swiftly.

And she did not move.

"I thought not," Grimm said. "Well, then." He looked back at the doorway. "Can anyone fix some tea?"

Chapter 57

Skyport, Spire Olympia

Bridget watched as Benedict and Vincent (to be honest, mostly Benedict) got the crowd moving to help them.

It had been simpler than she had thought it would be. Benedict had simply approached a group of four hopeless-eyed men in aeronaut's leathers and told them to come with him and help him unreel the etherweb sail from the deserted airship. The men had stared at him for a moment, and one of them had said something caustic. Benedict replied. The men had stared at one another for a second with widening eyes, and then Benedict stalked off toward the airship, and they followed with a will.

In that crowd, the purposeful movement stood out like a candle in an unlit chamber, and it had drawn eyes at once. While some folk jeered and made rude noises at the men, others suddenly came on alert. More men in aeronaut's leathers appeared to understand what was happening, and they came rushing over to help. Others followed them. Within two minutes, there were a hundred people working together, mostly under Vincent's instruction and organization, and they had formed a pair of lines about sixty feet apart that led from the airship to the nearest edge of the Spire. Together, they began hauling out the ethersilk webbing.

While they did that, Benedict appeared with a coil of line and three burly men. While the three men held the rope, he secured the end around his waist and calmly went over the edge, bracing his legs against the spirestone. It took Bridget only a moment to realize that he was scouting out the nearest opening to Habble Profit's ventilation tunnels, and when he came back up, he shouted for Vincent and marked where the webbing, a woven net of squares about two feet on a side and sixty feet across, would need to go down. Then he went a bit farther down the Spire's wall and came back a second time. Bridget saw blood on his hands. It took her a moment to realize that he must have wrenched out the grating over the ventilation tunnel openings each time he had gone down.

And all the while, the mistmaw came closer. Bridget kept track with a kind of fascinated indifference. The thing was simply too big to consider it to be some kind of animal. It was more like watching the progress of a storm, or worrying about a funnel cloud or an earthquake. Frightening, yes, but impersonal. Either they would be out of its way when it arrived, or it would destroy them. They were simply waiting to find out which it would be.

It was even beautiful in its own way, she supposed. The orange-red glow emanating from its underbelly lit the entire skyport like a low-burning fire that was assisted by the actual fires raging across wide avenues of ruined airships in port. The tendrils and tentacles moved with a sort of slow, mindless, random grace, simply reacting to whatever they touched, coiling and uncoiling, lifting and then reaching out again. She could still see people being swept away— mostly over toward the transport ramps. But as more and more of the beast floated toward her, the writhing tendrils blocked out much of that view, and she could hear only the screams.

The fluid pattering down from the beast was what worried her. It smoked and smoldered on the spirestone and chewed holes in the hulls of airships and in any people unlucky enough to be touched by it. When it got to within about two hundred feet of her current position in the wheeled chair, her heart began to beat faster.

She saw other things too. There were . . . large lumps of some fleshy substance that fell from the lowered mistmaw and curled up into spheres. One of them dropped exactly in the center of the street down the nearest row of airship docking slips. Fascinated, she watched as it uncurled into a wormlike creature perhaps ten feet long and glistening with slime. A mouth opened at one end of the thing; it featured a couple of serrated ridges of some kind of hornlike substance.

As she watched, a young man darted out of concealment nearby, screaming as he was burned by the falling fluid. The worm thing reacted with unexpected speed, its neck snapping out with rubbery fluidity; then it bit down across one of the man's hips, while its slime-covered body snapped forward with elastic power and curled around him. The young man screamed horribly for a few seconds, pounding down on the rubbery flesh beneath him, but his arms quickly lost their strength. He fell limp while the wormlike creature wrapped him in a ball of flesh that pulsed and quivered and slowly grew tighter around him.

"Those things burn and paralyze by touch," Fenli reported to her, watching with interest. "Tribesaver said they are the mistmaw's spawn. It left many of them behind in Spire Dependence."

"A tribe with fighting spurs could kill one," Rowl said with certainty.

"The slime would eat away their paws," Fenli said quietly. "They are not good for anything. Not hunting. Not eating. Not fighting. They have no purpose. Best avoided and ignored."

Bridget shook her head and looked away from the bountiful variety of horrible ways to die that now approached them. She moved her gaze toward Benedict, the sight of whom she found far preferable.

"If you're strong enough, climb down the center and help the people on the edges!" Benedict was shouting. "Mind your footing! Hold on with two hands and keep one foot supported before you try to move down! Make sure both feet are settled before you change your grip!"

Vincent was doing the same thing, only on the far side of the netting. People were moving now, crowding in, all striving to hang on to their lives. Benedict and Vincent had created two lanes leading to two ventilation tunnels that were side by side, she realized. By doing so, they had doubled the number of folk they would be able to save.

Of course, Bridget noted, she would not be able to make the climb down herself, not with her leg and her wounded hands.

The nearest tentacles were following the falling slug-worm things by about fifty yards. The slugs seemed to occupy themselves thoroughly with the first food they could find. She wondered if it would be one of those things or a tentacle that would reach her first. Or the falling acidic fluid that led the way.

She'd rather be eaten by the mistmaw proper, she decided. Burned to death by acid seemed a messy way to go, and being dissolved and absorbed by a ten-foot slug when she might have been devoured by a creature a mile across seemed disappointing. At least she would have a lovely view for a few moments as she was drawn up into the mistmaw, she supposed. Or she could jump. She wondered if it would feel like she was flying. Momentarily.

To prove how bored he was, Rowl looked away from the mistmaw with a yawn and suddenly peered out into the night.

"Littlemouse," he said, "what is that?"

Bridget turned, frowning, and saw . . .

What *was* that?

Airships, she realized. A wall of airships with their running lights blazing was out in the distance and coming closer through the fine rain. Dozens of them, their etherweb sails glittering in the rain ahead of them, sending out coruscating spectra of lumin-crystal light.

No, not dozens, she realized. Hundreds.

It was a *fleet*.

And now Spire Aurora's plan seemed clear.

It was simple enough. First, send the mistmaw in to cripple Olympia's skyport, defense fleet, and defense guns. It had, after all, come in from exactly the right vector to wreck the Fleet Quarter first. Then, once Olympia was reeling from the monster's attack, send in the Armada to wipe out any remaining defenses. The port batteries were running hot, if they hadn't already exploded due to overload, and there was not a chance that the already light defenses could provide serious resistance to that many ships.

Olympia was the largest port of trade in the world, even larger than Spire Albion, at least until the subordinate skyport at Landing had been rebuilt. Control and taxation of that trade would fill the Auroran war chest to overflowing, and the Olympian merchant marine, while it would be impressive when gathered together and organized, was currently neither. If Aurora could take Olympia's skyport and upper habbles in a lightning attack, many Olympian ships would learn what happened only when returning to their home port, so their crews would have little choice but to accede to Aurora's control of their home Spire.

Bridget felt suddenly exhausted. Everything she had gone through in the past few days had been for nothing, she realized. They had brought their warning too late.

The Aurorans would claim Olympia and her riches. And then

they would turn their eye upon her home. Her people would be unable to resist the combined forces of Aurora and Atlantea for long.

"That's the Armada," she said quietly. "Aurora has come for Olympia."

"That is not fair," Fenli said with mild indignance. "They are already fighting a predator. No cat would do such a thing."

"Indeed," Rowl said. "We have proper priorities. If your tribe was under attack, the Silent Paws would assist in destroying the predator."

"Of course," Fenli said. "It would someday be a threat to your own kits if it was not stopped, and it is best dealt with in numbers." He glanced back over Bridget's shoulder. "Oh, tentacles."

Bridget looked back to see one of the vast tentacles smash down onto an airship construction slip, destroying wood costing a lifetime of a shopkeeper's earnings in a single blow. Splinters flew out from the ruined airship, some of them clattering across the spirestone floor near Bridget. Flames from some banked fire caught on the new-made kindling and fire began to leap up despite the cold drizzle.

Benedict suddenly appeared at the wheeled chair, grimly looking up at the oncoming mistmaw, and said, "I believe we've cut this quite close enough."

"I can't make the climb," Bridget said.

Benedict snorted. "If only you'd brought a warriorborn strong enough to carry you down himself. You put on the harness?"

"Yes, of course," she said.

Benedict got behind the chair and started pushing them away from the oncoming mistmaw. "Vincent is standing by to clip your harness to mine, back-to-back. Then I'll climb down."

In only a little more time than it took to explain the procedure, Vincent had her lean forward, and Benedict snapped the back of the wheeled chair off with a single sharp motion. Then the warriorborn crouched behind her while Vincent took several carabiner clips and attached the two harnesses together, doubling them at every connection point.

There were very few people besides themselves left on the surface of the Spire now, and all of them were hurrying over the edge on the ethersilk netting.

Benedict said, "Brace yourself, love," and stood up.

Both cats leapt down from her vanishing lap to the spirestone. Bridget went breathless with pain and managed not to make any noise as the harness took her weight and distributed it mostly across her hips, which had been through quite enough in the past days, thank you.

"Gentlemen," Vincent said, and held open the aeronaut's shoulder bag for the cats, "I apologize for the crudity of your conveyance, but time presses."

"I take issue with being called a 'gentleman,'" Rowl said, his tail fluffing up indignantly.

"Oh, for the love of God in Heaven, Rowl!" Bridget said very crossly. "Get in the sack!"

Rowl blinked at Bridget, startled.

"Now, Rowl!" Bridget said. "Or I will tell Benedict to put me down and let that thing eat me!"

Rowl looked aghast and, of all things, at a loss for words. Then he straightened his whiskers and marched into the proffered bag with massive dignity. Fenli followed him, amused.

"Right, then," Vincent said. He took up the sack and slung it over his back, then turned to the waiting webbing without glancing back at the vast predator above them all, swung his legs out over the edge of the Spire, turned carefully, found his footing, then began descending.

"All right, love," Benedict said, "perhaps you should close your eyes for this part."

"I'm not sure I would think well of myself later if I did," Bridget said. "Go."

As Benedict bent over, her view shifted, and her gaze lifted to the sky. The oncoming curtain of dribbling acid was less than thirty feet away. One of the weird slug-worm things was not thirty feet beyond that, its eyeless head and mouth straining slowly toward them as its jellylike body slid forward, gathering and elongating in mesmerizing rhythm.

Then Benedict bent forward, and Bridget's gaze perforce settled on the oncoming mistmaw itself. She could see, from here, the fate of those taken up by the vast creature. The tentacles pressed them against the surface of its mucus-covered underbelly, where the slime covering it started . . . simply dissolving them as hundreds of thousands of tiny frondlike cilia drew them in. They sank into the mistmaw as if slowly drowning in reverse, screaming and thrashing until their heads vanished into the beast.

And then the mistmaw . . . stopped.

It simply froze. No tentacle moved. For a bizarre second, everything about it was completely still.

Then the great beast shuddered and hundreds of tentacles descended again, still bearing their human captives. Bridget stared in wonder as an acid-burned woman was brought down not fifty feet away and deposited roughly onto the surface of the Spire.

Other tendrils were moving. One of them near her curled around the base of a water tower and tore the supports out from it, so that the tower overbalanced and sent water flooding across the surface, quenching a number of small fires. Other tendrils smashed down upon burning buildings, collapsing them into dust and rubble ill-suited for combustion. Smoke and dust billowed up across a mile-wide section of skyport.

And then the mistmaw moaned. It turned.

It oriented itself on the Armada currently taking formation in the distance, and then the creature let out a long and bugling cry as it surged forward.

"Benedict!" Bridget cried in horror as the current of falling acid swept forward.

The warriorborn did not ask questions. He swung out over the edge of the Spire, and Bridget suddenly saw the vast expanse of empty air spreading in front of her as Benedict flung himself down the hanging netting. Panting with effort, the warriorborn moved with sure and certain speed as he scrambled down the side of the Spire.

Bridget's stomach dropped entirely out of her and she felt her body clenching in desperate response to being held over such a drop. She fought not to move and threaten Benedict's balance as he plunged down the netting, panting and snarling as the fantastic strength of his body fought to hold them both up against leaden gravity.

"Here!" Vincent shouted somewhere behind Bridget, and a sudden force pulled them horizontally, even as the acid fluid began pattering down around them.

Then they were suddenly inside the mouth of a spirestone ventilation tunnel, the cool, comforting darkness of the unyielding black material rising up around her on four sides as Benedict collapsed to his knees with racked, heaving gasps of exhaustion.

Bridget could only watch as the mistmaw glided out like some vast and horrible airship and swooped down into the mists and out of sight with another wailing bugle of challenge.

"Out!" called Rowl from the bag. "Enough of this indignity!"

Bridget, still bleary with pain, turned to Vincent and said, "Let them out of the bag."

Vincent wearily doffed the shoulder bag and opened it up. Rowl wriggled out at once, looked around with vast annoyance, and then went to Bridget's side. "You look ridiculous," Rowl said. "And I do not think you should have spoken to a prince the way you did."

Bridget, rising and falling with Benedict's heaving breaths, looked wearily at Rowl and said, "Possibly you're right."

"What happened?" Vincent demanded, staring intently out past Bridget at the retreating mistmaw. "Why did it leave?"

Bridget shook her head. "I'm certain I don't know. I'm equally certain that I do not care."

Vincent looked faintly annoyed at that answer and said, "The Aurorans. Perhaps they're whistling their beast away so that they can attack."

Bridget thought of the tentacles releasing their prey and of the quenched fires. "I . . . I am not at all sure that is the case."

Benedict hauled himself upright with a groan and managed to turn his body enough to let them sit back-to-back on the floor. Bridget managed to get her leg into a position that wasn't excruciating; then she leaned back against Benedict wearily as they both stared at what passed outside the Spire.

It took the mistmaw only moments to reach the Armada.

Then vast tentacles began rising out of the mist, smashing against airships, wrapping around the smaller vessels and crushing them with contemptuous ease, while even the heavy ships were badly battered.

"Why aren't they firing?" Benedict wondered aloud.

"Presumably," Bridget mused, "they weren't expecting to be fighting a mistmaw."

"There are too many ships," Vincent said. "Stacked up in a battle wall, in the dark, they can't propagate flag signals from one to the next quickly enough. Mass fleet tactics rely upon a similarity of training and thought for individual commanders to know their places in the battle formation and coordinate their actions sensibly. I believe there are simply too many of them to coordinate a response to a . . . novel situation."

The Armada began firing salvos, but it was operating in groups of six and eight and twelve, rather than en masse. The wind began to rise, driving cold rain into the ventilation tunnel, which Bridget could now see was lined with weary survivors stretching as far back as the light reached. There must have been hundreds here.

Thunder rumbled across the night as a proper storm began spinning up. Clouds and mist rose sharply as the mistmaw bugled, and the last thing Bridget saw of the Armada, before the mists swallowed Spire Olympia, were ships reeling out of formation and rising sharply, desperate to get out of tentacle range and occasionally colliding with one another in midair.

"Hmmm," Vincent mused. "I'm not at all certain they'll be able to bring enough firepower to bear to bring the beast down."

"Meaning what?" Bridget asked.

"Meaning," Vincent said, "that the Auroran Armada is in for a very difficult evening." He took a slow breath, watching until the rising storm drove down more cold rain and greater winds and hid the Armada from sight. "My God, if the Olympians turn out their lights, I daresay the Aurorans might not even be able to find them in good order, much less press an effective attack." Then he shook his head slightly and looked around them. "Not that we are in any position to do anything about that, should it happen. But we can help the survivors, beginning with you, my dear Sergeant Tagwynn. Sir Benedict, if you would turn slightly."

Benedict did not respond.

"Ben?" Bridget asked. "Ben?"

There was a sound from him. His breath dragged through his nose and mouth in a soft, exhausted snore.

Her fiancé, it seemed, was finally and entirely knackered from his efforts.

Her. Fiancé.

She tried out the thought again.

Her fiancé. Benedict Sorellin-Lancaster. Her husband-to-be.

Despite her exhaustion and discomfort and pain, Bridget found herself smiling.

She leaned her head back against Benedict's while Rowl's familiar weight settled against her lap, and then she closed her eyes as well.

Chapter 58

IAS *Mistshark*, near Spire Olympia

Grimm sipped tea with one hand and kept his pistol leveled at the motionless Madame Cavendish with the other. Within the great tank, Master Ferus floated with his limbs loose and flaccid, only occasionally rising to surface and take in a slow and measured breath. Ravenna was still present, along with her two warriorborn fighters and Colonel Espira. The Pikers were staring in fascination at Master Ferus where he floated in the tank, but Grimm ignored the man.

Certainly, the Auroran Armada was a threat.

But Madame Cavendish was just as much so, and she was a great deal closer and either brilliant enough or insane enough to be far less predictable. He did not for a moment believe she was finished fighting, despite her seemingly helpless position on the floor. It was merely a question of when she would act, and what she would do.

Espira watched her with a similarly sharp eye, Grimm noted with approval. The Marine commander also had his priorities in good order.

If Cavendish truly believed herself more than mortal, as she had said, Grimm could not be certain that their current situation was survivable. She might find some way to act, and his options for stopping her were limited. If he killed her when she made her move, she would certainly destroy both ships—and the nearby *Stormmaiden*—and though it seemed unthinkable, perhaps she would harm Spire Olympia as well. Yet he couldn't be certain that any action that was less than lethal would be sufficient to obviate her intent.

There was nothing for it but to look sharp and trust himself to make the right decision when it came to it.

There were footsteps behind him.

"Skip," Gwen said nervously, "report from Journeyman."

"Go ahead," Grimm said.

"Two of the boarding ramps are jammed," she said quietly. "He'll have to use explosives to free them."

Grimm winced. That would mean expensive repairs to the ship, though he supposed he could always bill the Spirearch for the damage. "Very well," he said. "Tell him to make ready the charges. And I want everyone off *Mistshark* and moved onto *Predator*'s deck."

"Already done," Gwen said confidently. "And *Stormmaiden* is moving into position below us on the far side so that her people can skin down lines and get back to her."

"Well done, XO," Grimm said. "You'll be ready for your own command in no time."

Gwen paused and then said thoughtfully, "A year ago, I'd have agreed with you, Skip," she said. "Now that I know more, I'm not as sure."

"That is an excellent frame of mind to maintain, Miss Lancaster," Grimm replied, his eyes steady on the motionless Cavendish still cradling Mister Sark's dead body. "Always assume there is something you do not know and proceed accordingly."

"Captain," Espira said quietly, "I'd like to request that my people be transferred to the Piker ship. They've been through enough, and if *Mistshark* is destroyed . . ."

"Understood, Colonel," Grimm said at once. "XO, see to the colonel's request."

"Skip," Gwen said cautiously, "I should point out that our Spires are certainly now in a state of war. The testimony of the captured soldiers will mean quite a bit when the Admiralty is sorting out exactly what happened afterward."

Grimm considered that for a moment. The Admiralty would indeed have many, many questions, and he had been consistently misfortunate in his choice of allies in the upper echelons of that body. Some of the men who disfavored him would certainly try to use the situation to worsen his lot.

He glanced aside at Espira, who stayed steadily focused on Madame Cavendish, with the attention to purpose for which Marines were notable.

"We are a civilian vessel, XO, and have no knowledge of any declaration of war," Grimm noted. "Additionally, we have only a scant idea of what is happening. What we do know with certainty is that Colonel Espira and his men have behaved with exemplary discipline and courtesy and fought beside us against a terrifying foe. Colonel, may I have your word that you will remain at my side and present yourself as an honorable officer in the wake of whatever transpires today?"

Espira nodded. "You have it, Captain. To the best of my judgment and ability."

Grimm nodded. "That suits me well enough," he said. "XO, provided Captain Ravenna has no objection, see to the transfer of his men."

"Aye, aye, Skip," Gwen said quietly, and glanced at Ravenna. "Captain?"

"*Stormmaiden* always welcomes brave fighters, Colonel," Ravenna said. "If Mad Frank Grimm thinks it's all right, we'll look after them for you for a while."

Espira closed his eyes tightly and bowed his head for a moment. Then he nodded and said very quietly, "Thank you."

Ravenna nodded toward Gwen. "Tell my XO I've ordered it, Miss Lancaster. He won't give you any trouble."

"This would be easier with physical visualization," Master Ferus said abruptly from the tank, his voice strained. "By any chance does anyone have a model airship? Or a rubber duck?"

Grimm glanced at the old man. Ferus made a vague roaring sound and smashed in slow motion at the surface of the tank with his hands, then looked up as if that had been a sufficient demonstration of his intent.

"My God," Gwen sighed, "there are days when this job is nothing but madness, aren't there?"

"We serve the Spirearch, Miss Lancaster," Grimm replied. "It would seem to go with the territory. Off you go."

"Aye, Skip," Gwen said, and hurried out.

Grimm turned to Ferus and said, "I'm very sorry, but no."

"Pity," Ferus said. "I must remember to add them to my collection." His eyes went out of focus for a moment. "Excuse me, Captain. I am engaging the vessels of the Armada."

Ferus's eyes rolled back as he took a deep breath and sank down into the fluid in the tank. The yellow gel gathered thickly around him. There, he began to thrash in seemingly random spasms, his hands opening and closing constantly, his face contorted into a rictus of pain.

Grimm felt the deck beneath him shiver almost imperceptibly as the distant thunder of shipboard guns roared far away in the darkness and the moaning wail of the mistmaw drifted through the night.

Cavendish opened her eyes and regarded Grimm calmly. "Tell me, Captain," she said. "Does that pistol make you feel as if you are in control of this situation?"

"It would seem to be a reasonably good indicator, madame," Grimm replied.

"Don't, Frank," Ravenna warned. "Don't engage with people who are mad. No good can come of it."

Cavendish gave both of them a pained smile. "Precious. Do you think I simply left the machine in operating order for no reason?"

Grimm tilted his head and looked from Cavendish to the control panel beside the tank, to Ferus, and back. He got a sudden sinking feeling in his stomach.

Cavendish let out a girlish giggle, shaking her head. "Honestly, it's quite complex. The balance of electrical current running through it has to be adjusted just so or it will kill anyone who goes in. It would have been child's play to simply take the resistors out of the circuit and let whoever went into it boil."

"Meaning what, precisely, madame?" Grimm asked.

Cavendish's eyelids became heavy and a slow smile spread over her mouth. "Meaning that everything is proceeding according to the Tyranima's design, dear Captain."

"Shoot her," Ravenna said. "Just shoot her."

"If we do, none of our ships will survive," Grimm responded.

"So shoot her a little," Ravenna suggested. "In the knees."

Cavendish laughed again. "Warriorborn trash," she said easily, "I could rend your mind right now if I wished it. Captain Grimm would shoot to stop me." She gestured toward the wires plunged into her chest. "And my death would detonate *Mistshark*'s power core."

Grimm narrowed his eyes. "You have been working for Aurora for years, Madame Cavendish," he said. "It seems rather foolish of you to attempt to convince me that suddenly you wish their Armada wrecked."

"Tuscarora was useful for a time," she replied. "Now he will be useful in an entirely different capacity."

Feeling the tension rising in Colonel Espira beside him, Grimm said in warning, "Colonel."

"I should be pleased to beat her unconscious, Captain Grimm," Espira said. "Simply give the word."

Cavendish pursed her lips. "Daring, Colonel. Rendering a person unconscious without killing them is not a simple task. Tell me, have you been trained in it? Because it seems to me that you are quite simply a killer." Her voice hardened. "I recommend you stick to your realm of expertise. Should you wander from it, I will be pleased to see you tearing out your own eyes. I do not think Captain Grimm would sacrifice his crew for you, however much a kindred spirit he is."

"Frank—" Ravenna began.

"Quiet, both of you, please," Grimm said. "The Tyranima, madame. Tell me more about it."

Cavendish's eyebrows went up. "You do possess a formidable amount of cunning, Captain," she murmured. "Enough to ask the proper questions. But why should I tell you anything?"

Grimm met her eyes. "Because it has to be tearing you apart inside. You must be bursting to talk about it with someone, or you'd have said nothing at all. When will you have another opportunity— particularly when you are, allegedly, so much in control of the situation?"

She narrowed her eyes.

Grimm smiled. "Tell me more about it. Please. Given the day I've had, it seems only polite."

Cavendish stared at him for a long moment, and several times her lips moved as though she was about to say something. Then she gave him a slow smile and said, "Oh, Captain, you *are* a clever boy." She shook her head. "Suffice it to say that this . . . this sham of a world we share is not now as it ever was." Her eyes went distant. "It was beautiful once. And we, our kind, were its undisputed masters. We roamed the surface at will and took our bounty from the open earth beneath blue skies. We took our meat from living creatures, not from great stone vats. We grew our fruits in the earth itself. We built great cities and traveled at speeds that made even airships look slow." Her eyes grew distant. "The Tyranima has shown me our past, Captain: vast rolling hills; plains covered in farms; cities that glowed in the night like jewels, illuminated by power of our own devising. Crystals were naught but a curiosity for the mystically inclined. Our numbers, Captain. Our numbers were all but beyond counting."

Grimm tilted his head and tried not to let his skepticism show on his face. "I do not recall mention of much of this from my history classes. Perhaps I was inattentive that day."

Cavendish smirked. "The leaders of that day made many mistakes. They were as vain and foolish and arrogant as those we enjoy now. They engaged in needless wars and the capricious use of power, and destroyed all, in their hubris. They blackened our skies and burned our forests, poisoned the waters and filled the air with the ash of cremated humanity. You call them the Merciful Builders, but they were nothing but fools who struggled at the end merely to provide shelter in which a few could survive. And memory of our world vanished as we huddled in our black towers." She leaned forward, eyes bright. "But the Tyranima has come to give us a chance to redeem ourselves, Captain. A chance for the blasted cinders of our kind to rekindle. To rise again. To once more be the masters of our world, instead of scrambling to survive this . . . this hell it has become."

"That sounds quite altruistic," Grimm noted.

"There will be a cost," Cavendish said, nodding. "A terrible cost. But the price must be paid, Captain. The cleverness of the Merciful Builders is fading. You have no idea how much our society utterly depends upon their unseen devices for our very survival. Time has worn them down. Ten thousand years of our struggle have finally battered them to the breaking point, and we are about to be utterly alone. Humanity must rise together—or fall to inevitable chaos and darkness."

There was a splash and a gasp from the tank as Ferus surfaced, gulped in more air, and sank into the fluid again.

Cavendish looked at him sadly, almost fondly. "The poor old man. He tries so hard to hold himself together. It has left him unable to face the concept of such great change. I wanted him to stand with me. But he wasn't strong enough to face what needed to be done."

"I see," Grimm said quietly. "And that has been your goal this entire while, the salvation of humanity itself?"

Cavendish's eyes looked haunted for a moment. She bowed her head and used her good hand to stroke Sark's dead face. She smeared streaks of her drying blood along it. "My God in Heaven, Captain. What sane person would do what I have done for anything less?"

When she looked up again, there were tears in her eyes. She stared at one of the walls, eyes unfocused as if looking far beyond it, and said, "The Armada has been broken. Excellent. Farewell, Captain Grimm. You have been a troublesome adversary."

And with no more warning than that, the deck of *Mistshark* pitched wildly to port, her wooden frame groaning and creaking and cracking.

Grimm found himself sliding along the deck, pain from his leg rising up like a red mist to cloud his vision. He lost his pistol as his arms flailed. Seeking balance with an aeronaut's reflexes, he managed to turn himself so that he was able to catch most of his weight with his good leg as they slammed against the bulkhead on the bottom end of the suddenly akilter compartment.

The great tank overbalanced and overturned, spilling clear fluid out in an enormous rush and sending the sopping-wet form of Master

Ferus to smash against the bulkhead twenty feet from Grimm like a rag doll beneath a hammer. Grimm struggled with horror as the sloshing fluid rushed toward him, and he felt a small, strong hand hook against his collar and haul him up the steep slope of the deck, so that only the heels of his boots splashed against the fluid.

Grimm whipped his head around to see Ravenna holding him above the vat's fluid, the nails of one of her hands sunk into the wooden deck. Her other hand and forearm were stark with muscle and shadow as she strained to hold them both in place.

"Grab me!" Ravenna shouted. "I'm slipping!"

Even as she spoke, Grimm saw one of her fingers come free of the decking, the sharpened nail tearing. Ravenna snarled at the pain.

There was the sound of a body sliding on the decking, and then Colonel Espira was there, driving a short combat knife into the deck and halting himself by hanging on to it. He twisted his body around and unceremoniously slipped his boots beneath Ravenna's arms, curled his toes up, and grimaced with effort, straining to take some of the weight off Ravenna's tenuous grip.

Ravenna let out a whoop of excitement and flashed the Auroran officer a sharp-toothed smile. "Viva bloody Aurora!"

Espira shot her a quick smile back as he held on to the knife with both hands.

"Colonel!" shouted one of Ravenna's warriorborn. He had been close enough to the doorway to hang on to it when *Mistshark* listed; he had snapped one of his safety harness lines to an attachment point with the reflexes of a seasoned aeronaut. He promptly disengaged one of his lines, clipped it to the end of the third, and tossed it down toward Espira.

Grimm watched all this and felt quite like a piece of fruit dangling from a vine, though somewhat less useful than a vegetable in this current circumstance.

Espira released a hand from the knife and caught the line. He wrapped it around his wrist with a few practiced flicks of his hand and said, "Go!"

The forearms of the warriorborn Piker flexed as he hooked a leg in the doorway and began to haul the three of them with slow, steady power up the sharply pitched deck. Grimm tried as best he could to push along with his good boot, sparing Ravenna the use of whatever strength he could.

"*Mistshark*'s port trim crystal array is gone!" Grimm called to her through a haze of pain. "Cavendish has cut it off from power somehow."

Espira reached the warriorborn, clipped himself to an attachment point, and hauled with his legs, dragging Ravenna and Grimm up the slope.

"Aye!" Ravenna replied. "She's going to break apart!" She reached the doorway, clipped her own harness to an attachment point, and then hauled Grimm up so that he could do so as well. It took him three tries to get the clip to attach, so much had pain and weariness drained him.

"Master Ferus!" Grimm gasped.

"I'll get him," Ravenna said.

The second warriorborn had appeared at the doorway with a coil of line. Ravenna ran it unceremoniously through a ring on her harness, braced her legs far apart, and started hopping down the steep slope of the deck toward the motionless old man.

"Captain!" screamed Miss Lancaster somewhere above him.

"Here!" Grimm said. "Send down lines!"

"On the way!" Gwen called back. "Captain, *Predator* is still locked to *Mistshark*! She's dragging us down! We can't run more power to the lift crystal without setting her afire!"

Grimm shot a glance around the compartment. Mister Sark's

corpse had slid down into the fluid now gathered at the bottom of the slope, and it floated there. Madame Cavendish was half wrapped around the machine's control panel, holding herself there, gasping as she kept one hand on the wires running into her chest. She faced Grimm with an otherwise calm expression, eyes alight, and looked down to the wires and then back up at him.

Colonel Espira cocked his pistol and leveled it at the etherealist, his arm stretching out past Grimm's head. "Give the word and she dies, Captain," he said calmly.

Nothing had changed. Grimm had once heard Master Ferus describe the practice of etherealism as simply etheric engineering without all the trouble of wires and devices. Madame Cavendish could still destroy them all with a thought—or if all thought ceased—and Grimm had no intention of letting his crew be incinerated in the blast of an overloaded core crystal.

"It seems she has chosen her own fate, Colonel. Stand down." He raised his voice and called back to Miss Lancaster, "Tell Journeyman to prepare to blow the separation charges!"

"Aye, Skip! Lines are down! Get out of there!"

Grimm turned back around to see Ravenna reach out and pluck the limp old man out of the water. Ferus coughed weakly and let out a quiet moan of pain as Ravenna slung him over one of her shoulders, took the line in both hands, and began scaling her way back up the sharply pitched decking.

Once *Predator* was clear of *Mistshark*, Grimm decided, he would take her out to the edge of vision and blow the crippled ship, and Madame Cavendish, out of his sky.

"We're leaving," he said. "Captain Ravenna, shall we?"

Ravenna passed the badly wounded old man over to Espira, who passed him along to one of the warriorborn. Together, Ravenna and Espira dragged Grimm through the doorway and down the slope of the deck to where they could each get a shoulder beneath him. Then they dragged him down toward the hatch to the main deck, where dangling lines were waiting for them.

The pain of his wounds became something living that all but destroyed his vision of anything beyond a few feet away and thoughts of doing anything more than a few seconds into the future. Grimm suddenly had all he could do to keep his gasps from becoming screams. Later, he would only dimly remember being hauled out of *Mistshark*'s hold by his safety harness, and the next thing he knew, Ravenna's people were dragging him across the boarding planks and back onto *Predator*'s deck.

"Doctor Bagen!" screamed the XO. "The skipper's wound is open and bleeding! Get the doctor out here now!"

"Wait," Grimm said, or tried to say. He found himself lying on *Predator*'s sloping deck, though he didn't remember getting there. He turned his head and saw Kettle at the pilot's station, where he was visibly straining to keep *Predator* upright. Mist flowed up past them, around the ship's deck and over the ventral mast. Without the power of *Mistshark*'s trim crystal array, the enemy vessel was sinking.

And she was taking *Predator* with her.

"Is that everyone?" Ravenna demanded.

"I was the last out," Espira confirmed. "Only the witch was left behind."

"Where's Journeyman?" Ravenna said. "There, man. Blow those bloody charges and get us unhooked from *Mistshark*!"

"That's what I've been trying to tell the damned XO for the past minute!" exclaimed Journeyman, his voice pitched high with annoyance and terror. "All the sideways maneuvers opened a seam in the powder room roof! The rain and mist got to the charges! They won't blow, and there's no time to get new ones made up!"

"God in bloody Heaven," Ravenna swore.

Grimm had thoughts, but they were curiously distant and difficult to untangle from the haze of pain and sheer exhaustion. One
floated by clearly—he should probably have stayed in bed after all.
There was quite a bit of his blood running in a slow stream down
Predator's slanted deck.

Then Bagen was there, and fire blossomed in his leg and wiped
out thought for a time.

When the world reassembled itself, Grimm saw the survival buoys
being broken out and loaded with the surviving aeronauts. Two of
the buoys were already drifting up, dangling beneath their small lift
crystals. They were barely able to rise with the weight of all the men
they carried, but they floated slowly and steadily up from *Predator*.

"Captain," Miss Lancaster said. "Captain, can you hear me?"

Grimm shook his head and stared at the XO. Bagen and his attendant were crouched over his leg, wrapping it up again. He felt
almost ferociously cold and was shaking so hard that it was a wonder
he could lift his head. He nodded as vigorously as he could at Gwen,
though his effort to speak utterly failed.

"Captain, I've given the order to abandon ship," Gwen said
calmly. "She's going down, and there's nothing to be done about it
except set ourselves on fire trying to hold position."

"Understood," Grimm said, or mostly said. He nodded at her
again.

"If possible," Gwen said, "I'm going to try to bring her down
somewhere clear and mostly in one piece."

"What?" Grimm demanded. "N-no, Gwen."

"There's a war on, Skip, and Albion needs every ship and every
crystal it can get," Gwen replied firmly. "If I can, I'm going to light
beacon fires so a recovery ship can locate *Predator* right away.

"Someone has to stay at the helm or she'll overturn," Gwen continued. "If that happens, *Predator* will shatter in the lithosphere and

be scattered everywhere. Her only chance is for someone to guide her down to something like a controlled landing."

Grimm shook his head, but Gwen gave him a firm look. "Skip, you're out of action. This is my responsibility now." She looked up and said, "Kettle, take the captain aboard the last buoy."

"Aye, aye, XO," came Kettle's roughened voice.

"And, Mister Kettle," Gwen said, "please take word to my father. Once he knows who is with the ship, I believe you'll see the most rapid recovery mission in history unfold."

"Aye, Miss Lancaster, I reckon we will." The pilot offered her his hand. "Good luck, ma'am."

Her expression set, Gwen shook his hand and said, "Thank you. When he's coherent again, please thank the captain for me. I value every day I've spent aboard *Predator* learning from him."

"Will do."

Grimm shouted at them to stop, because he should be the one at *Predator*'s helm, but his lungs barely wheezed in enough air to keep his vision from becoming a grey tunnel, and his mouth refused to take orders. He lifted a hand toward Gwen and only just managed to touch her arm.

She clasped his hand, and Grimm was shocked at how warm she felt to his chilled flesh. She said something he didn't quite catch, and she squeezed hard. Then he was being rolled onto a stretcher and carried somewhere, the rain still on him.

His ship.

His home.

He hoped the rain hid his tears from the men around him as he was settled onto the light planking of the survival buoy.

Grimm faded out, and he didn't come back until there was a distant crash, crunch, the sounds of tortured wood splitting and shattering from somewhere far below.

The men were staring down over the side of the survival buoy, which was little more than a large square deck with a modest safety railing. Their expressions were sober, serious. Lieutenant Stern was there, tears in his eyes. Caps came off all around as the aeronauts stood silent.

Pain that made his wounded leg seem as nothing ripped through Grimm's chest.

And then he let the darkness take him.

▪ ▪ ▪ Chapter 59 ▪ ▪ ▪

AFS *Belligerent*, Skyport, Spire Olympia

Grimm awoke in an unfamiliar place. It was a ship's infirmary, he could tell by the curve of the hull-side bulkhead and the scents of wood stain and scorched rubber from hard-worked wiring, but it was not one that he knew. Outside, there was a storm—a proper thunderstorm—and the sound of heavy rain falling on the ship was a constant, steady drumbeat intermixed with rumbles of thunder.

"Not like that," Doctor Bagen said firmly to an exhausted-looking young Shipley. The novice doctor wore a Fleet uniform with caduceus pins on his collar, and a bloodied apron. "Reverse that stitch or it will come loose before you've finished closing. Good. Like that. Well done. Get the rest of it done up and we'll finally get to sit down."

Grimm's throat burned with thirst. He looked around blearily and saw a mug of water on the stand next to his bed. It took a shocking amount of effort, but he reached out to pick up the mug and managed to sip some of the liquid. He reminded himself to go slowly, taking a slow five count between sips while he studied the room.

There was space for a dozen beds, so he was on a larger ship. *Predator*'s sick bay had only four. The two physicians, along with a pair of sick-berth attendants, were working on an unconscious man on the surgery table. Nine of the twelve beds were filled, and the men in them were either unconscious or asleep.

In the bunk next to Grimm, Master Ferus was recumbent, his lips grey, his breathing ragged. A breathing tube ran from a heavy copper-clad steel tank; the leather mask at the other end of the tube covered his mouth and nose. Folly sat in the chair beside the bed, her back ramrod straight, her eyes closed. She held one trembling hand out over Ferus's chest, and her face was creased with strain.

Bagen glanced up, his naturally sad-looking eyes making his exhausted face look haggard. He summoned a faint but genuine smile for Grimm. "Ah, Captain. Good"—he checked his pocket watch—"morning."

While an attendant hurried out, Grimm swallowed a bit more water, then croaked, "Where?"

"Sick bay, AFS *Belligerent* in port at Spire Olympia," Bagen supplied.

"The men?"

"We lost fourteen," Bagen said soberly. "Eight more are maimed. The rest will recover."

Grimm closed his eyes, feeling a greater balance of relief than remorse. He wouldn't enjoy writing fourteen letters to fourteen grieving families, but all things considered, it could have been so much worse. "Captain Ransom?"

"In recovery," Bagen said. "I had nothing to do with that. Apart from my helping with severe dehydration, that was all Miss Folly. It seems Calliope will live to betray people another day."

Grimm's mouth twitched at one corner. He also exhaled slowly. He gestured to his left and said, "Master Ferus?"

Bagen's face sobered. He came close to Grimm's bunk and leaned down to speak quietly into his ear. "The fall probably killed him. He broke several ribs and they punctured one of his lungs. We did everything we could, but he's got a horrible fever. I think it's only a matter of time now."

Grimm closed his eyes and sighed.

"Miss Folly claims that there are Enemy structures in his blood and that if they can be purged, he might have a chance. She's been at it for the last"—Bagen checked his watch again—"eighteen hours."

"Get her some food and drink."

Bagen shook his head. "Tried hours ago. She won't take them."

Grimm nodded and clenched his jaw. "Is there any word on *Predator*?"

Bagen exhaled slowly, his weary face compassionate. "She was last seen going down with *Mistshark*, Captain. Mister Kettle took word to His Grace, Gwen's father, and a courier left for Albion within the hour despite the storm. I suspect every recovery ship and fast Fleet vessel will be on the way here by tomorrow."

Grimm nodded slowly. *Predator*. His home. And Gwen. He was responsible for them both. And he had, in all probability, lost them both. Tears burned at his eyes, but he recognized the other wounded men in the bay as members of his crew, and he didn't let his tears fall. "Very good, Doctor. But we must attempt to find someone to scout for *Predator*'s location at once. The XO is alone on the surface, and that cannot be allowed to—"

"Captain," Bagen said in a pained voice, "I believe His Grace her father is both better positioned and far more capable at securing such aid than we will be. And you are to stay. In. Bed."

"Ah," Grimm said. He fought down a sharp spike of outrage at the feeling of helplessness he now enjoyed. "Yes. Of course." He slowly took another sip of water, and a thought occurred to him. "Oh. How am I?"

"Extremely foolish and apparently resilient enough to get away with it," Bagen responded promptly. "This time. But you sprained your right wrist and the ankle on your good leg somewhere along the line, and Mister Kettle has orders not to help you do anything else idiotic. You're staying in bed for several days at least, Captain. And you'll not be running any races on that leg if I'm any judge."

"How bad is it?"

"The wound itself wasn't so bad," Bagen said. "Running around and fighting a boarding action on it made it worse. The muscle is badly torn. I stitched it up as best I could, but I can't promise you anything. Get yourself a cane. You'll need it for six months to a year."

"That long?"

"At *least* that long," Bagen said quietly. "You might need it, period."

Grimm closed his eyes. "Ah."

Rapid footsteps sounded outside the sick bay, and Commodore Bayard strode into the room. The small man had rings beneath his eyes even deeper than Bagen's, but he moved with energy and strength as he came to the bunk and studied Grimm.

"Steals my thunder right out from under me in front of half the world, and then has the gall to take up a bunk in my sick bay," he said, shaking his head. "If I'd known you were such a drama queen, Mad, I'd never have asked you to be my second."

Grimm smiled faintly. "Someone has to take care of you," he said. "You're feeling better?"

"I feel terrible," Bayard said cheerfully. "But I can walk again."

"What happened?" Grimm asked. "After *Predator* dropped out of the formation, I mean."

Bayard shook his head, his expression going neutral. "Bad business. The mistmaw flew back over the skyport and killed somewhere between two and five thousand people. By all reports, it's . . . difficult to sort out the remains. They're still running up a tally of the missing. But every hospital and hospice in the top ten habbles of the

Spire was full, so you and your people are recovering here on *Belligerent*."

"Thank you, Alex," Grimm said.

Bayard put his hand on Grimm's shoulder. "After that," he said, "we saw the signal rockets from the Atlanteans, and the Auroran fleet came in. Apparently, Atlantea was supposed to show up with their ships too, but they didn't arrive for several hours. Seems they had their own ideas about who was going to run Spire Olympia after this affair was over."

Grimm grunted. "When will they attack?"

"They won't," Bayard replied promptly. "The mistmaw did for the Auroran dreadnoughts—all but *Conquistodor*, apparently."

Grimm's eyes flew open wide. "What?"

"Mmmm," Bayard replied. "And Aurora lost at least one battlecruiser, two dozen light cruisers, and ten heavy cruisers, and God in Heaven knows how many destroyers and frigates. All those crystals are just littering the ground in the near vicinity. Lord Lancaster is negotiating a joint recovery operation with Olympia now."

"The Aurorans won't like that."

"My heart bleeds for poor Tuscarora," Bayard said breezily. "Olympia's surviving ships launched, and the task force they had keeping tabs on the Atlanteans returned. They're overhead now. They aren't as strong as the Atlantean fleet—four dreadnoughts to eight—but they've got almost enough tonnage of armed merchantmen to make up for it, and the skyport's batteries are on their side too. Seems the Atlanteans didn't have the stomach for a stand-up fight. They had counted on an obliterated Olympian fleet and a damaged and demoralized Armada."

"And they got an angry beehive instead," Grimm mused.

"An angry beehive expecting reinforcements from Albion, yes. They withdrew in good order. Meanwhile, the Olympians have

Tuscarora's sister in custody. Apparently, she made a move to assassinate Lord President Warren and his sister using some kind of new etheric devices." A muscle in Bayard's jaw twitched. "Abigail put a stop to it."

"Ah," Grimm said. He paused delicately and then asked, "And how is Abigail?"

Bayard's back stiffened and his eyes hardened. "We haven't spoken."

Grimm's heart flickered with a little pang. Alex had worked out who had poisoned him. "Alex," he said gently, "I bear no grudges."

"Because you're a damned fool, brother," Bayard said quietly. "She could have killed us both."

"But she didn't," Grimm said. "Here we are."

Bayard's eyes went distant, and he said, "Some things are over the line. She put my best friend in front of the sword I'd chosen to face."

"Talk to her," Grimm said. "You owe her that much."

Bayard inhaled and exhaled slowly. "You're probably right. But what she did, Mad . . ." He shook his head.

Beside Grimm, Master Ferus coughed weakly and opened his eyes. He looked around blearily, then reached up and fumbled feebly at the mask over his mouth. Folly blinked her eyes open as though coming out of a deep sleep. Then she let out a little gasp and helped Ferus move the mask, her fingers as gentle and exquisitely tender as if handling individual snowflakes.

"Blasted . . . contraption . . ." Ferus wheezed. "Grim Captain. Was waiting for you."

"Well, here I am," Grimm said. "You can get some rest now. We'll talk again in the morning."

Ferus's eyes twinkled, though his expression was sad and his lips had darkened to a bluish grey. "When we meet again, it will be morning indeed, Captain," Ferus said. "Or rather, a great and terrible new dawn." He shuddered and took a moment to catch his breath. "I have a request to beg of you."

Grimm met the man's eyes and nodded. "Of course."

"Folly," he said. "She needs a home."

"I'll see to it."

"Not just a house," Ferus said intently. "Someone she can talk to."

Grimm swallowed. "I don't know how much I have left to me, Efferus. But what I have shall be at her disposal."

Ferus smiled at Grimm and whispered, "Good man. Oh, and give her my cane for me, would you? She will need that as well."

Grimm knew that Ferus's cane had gone down with *Predator* and *Mistshark*. But he supposed it might be recovered if he could arrange for it. "Of course."

"Now, then, Folly," Ferus said, smiling gently.

"Master, I'm so sorry. I keep trying to destroy them, but there are too many of them, and they keep building more, and they're building them out of *you*, and the more I destroy, the more they take away from you—"

"Oh, Folly, my sweet Folly," Ferus said. He moved his hands weakly to take hers in his. "My dear little gnatcatcher, it has been my singular pleasure to teach you what I know of life as an etherealist."

Folly looked down at him and smiled, but tears flowed silently from her eyes. "I know, master."

"I love you very much, child."

Folly wept and laid her forehead down against Ferus's. "I love you right back."

The old man reached up and touched her black-and-white hair gently. Then he said, "I won't really be gone. I'll just be one room over. You can still talk to me, you know, even if I don't talk back."

"Master," Folly said, and shook with weeping.

"Oh, child, I am so sorry to leave you now, of all times." His hand fell back weakly. "Remember, the Enemy is out there. Remember what I taught you. My task falls to you now."

Folly nodded and said, "Yes. Yes, it's all right. You've taught me so much."

"Keep friends," Ferus said, his voice fading. "Keep them close. Treasure them. Friends are all the difference between a life of joy and a life of madness. Between you and your mother."

"I will, master."

"I'm really very sorry, Folly," Ferus said, barely any breath left in his voice. His lips had gone deep blue. Tears ran from the corners of his eyes. "But I'm so terribly tired."

"I'm here," Folly said, and took both of his hands between hers. "I'm here with you. It's all right. You've worked so hard. It's all right to rest now."

The entire sick bay had fallen utterly silent.

"My dear child," Ferus whispered, eyes closing.

And he died.

Everyone who was awake bowed their heads.

And the only sound was that of Mistress Folly, heartbroken, weeping.

"Get me over to her," Grimm said.

"Captain," Doctor Bagen said in warning.

"Out of the way, man," Bayard said, and with surprising strength he picked up Grimm from his bunk and carried him to the chair beside the sobbing etherealist.

She never looked up from weeping over the old man's body. But Grimm did everything he could. He put his hand on her back, patted her gently, and said, "I'm here, Folly. I'm here. You aren't alone. You are not alone."

*   *   *

Colonel Espira and Sergeant Ciriaco strode through the Olympian skyport, taking note of the destruction. They had traded their scarlet uniforms for civilian clothing, though since they had come courtesy of the Pikers, with their unbleached homespun and black leather, they still got trepidatious glances on a regular basis.

Ciriaco was walking very carefully, his ribs bound up in layers of bandages, his arm in a cast from elbow to wrist. He was reading even more carefully from a notebook that looked tiny in his broad hands. He had learned to read only recently, so sometimes he sounded like a schoolboy with his halting progress. "Two broken legs, six broken arms, one concussion. Guess everyone else who got hit in the head died. Those crystal-corpse things were strong, Colonel."

"Hngh," Espira replied. "Nine of my men left out of thirty. Hardly legendary leadership."

"That was weird etheric crap, sir," Ciriaco said philosophically. "We both knew Cavendish was bad news. And Ransom stabbed us in the back. You made some good calls too, or everyone would be dead."

"If not for those pirates, we would be," Espira said. "I've been thinking. I think you should sign on with the Pikers. I've already spoken to Captain Ravenna. She said she thought you'd do well there. They have warriorborn officers, you know."

"Lifetime of rolling my eyes at officers. Now you want me to be one." Ciriaco grinned. "That your plan, Colonel? Turn pirate, see how it goes?"

Espira gave him a tight-lipped smile. "Well, the other men seem to want to go back to Aurora. They have families."

"They gonna be killed to keep them quiet?" Ciriaco said.

Espira shrugged. "Quiet about what? There's no secret about the mistmaw to keep. The Albions and Pikers both saw what was going on. The secret's already out. And otherwise, the men all did their duty."

"But you defied orders," Ciriaco said.

"I defied orders," Espira confirmed. "Orders from His Majesty himself, no less."

"If you go back," Ciriaco said, "they'll hang you."

"I am an Auroran Marine," Espira said calmly. "Aurora is my home. Tuscarora is my King. I have done my duty as best I saw fit, and I will face the consequences for the manner in which I carried it out. I owe it to the men to make sure they get home. And I could never be content with the Pikers. Perhaps Tuscarora will merely sentence me to the surface."

The big warriorborn shook his head. "They do something to people's heads at the academy. Glad I never went there." He scrunched up his nose and said, "You're thinking something else."

Espira shrugged. "I think that Cavendish's mission was known only to Tuscarora himself and that he wanted deniability for Aurora. That's why he hired Ransom's ship. Used an expatriate Albion etherealist. I'm betting that he won't want attention brought to what happened—especially since it backfired and caused the destruction of much of the Armada. The Lords and Commons would use it to peck away at his authority."

"So maybe he just breaks your neck with his own hands and tosses you down a privy."

"Another possibility," Espira said. "But since the raid on Albion, I have a certain standing among the Commons, and the Lords took note of me as well. Should I simply vanish, awkward questions will be asked."

Ciriaco looked at him for a moment and then said, "And you

might have an even higher profile if a Hero was hanging around with you all the time."

"You're better off with the Pikers," Espira said firmly.

"Oh, Colonel," Ciriaco said easily, "don't make me break your jaw and interpret all your noises for everyone as orders."

Espira let out a short, sharp laugh and looked up at the larger man. His expression sobered. "Are you sure? It will be dangerous. Very dangerous. I'm not at all sure it will play out the way I would like it to."

"Are you more likely to come out on top if I'm there?"

"Generally, and specifically, yes."

"Then why are we still talking about it?" Ciriaco said. "I'm with you, Colonel."

Espira stopped in his tracks. He turned to Ciriaco and simply offered the man his hand.

Ciriaco shook it.

"I owe you for this," Espira said.

Ciriaco grinned. "You sure as hell do. I'll think of something good."

Espira nodded and started walking again. "Captain Ravenna tells me the *Conquistodor* has been allowed to have their wounded seen to and to water and reprovision here since they fought to defend the skyport. We will go speak to Captain Chavez."

"Lead on, Colonel," Ciriaco said. "I'm right behind you."

Bridget continued brushing Rowl as gently as she could. They were in her room in one of the pricier inns in Habble Profit where Vincent had secured them quarters. Her bandaged hands made her movements clumsy, but she did her best to carry on.

"This entire affair has been very dissatisfying for me personally," Rowl said. "Humans can do nothing properly."

"Is that so?" Bridget asked.

"We went to such trouble for the halflings," Rowl said with a sneer. "Little cats. They're unnatural. Their heads are too small."

"I suppose we did."

"And I battled an epic monstrous beast for you and dispatched it."

Bridget was not at all sure she remembered that fight the same way Rowl did, but she felt no urge to argue.

"And then we flew in human Vincent's horribly uncomfortable ship, and it was cold and terrible."

Bridget remembered Rowl snuggling comfortably into the bed beside her, but she supposed he had spent some time on the high-flying ship's deck as well.

"And after all that trouble and enduring the horrible Fenli for hours and hours and hours, it was not even necessary because Vincent flew his ship too slowly."

"We had to try to stop it from happening, Rowl," Bridget said. "And because we were there, we were able to save others."

"Yes," Rowl said irritably. "I did save a great many other humans. And you, of course."

"Of course," Bridget said contentedly.

Rowl looked up at her rather sharply and said acerbically, "Goodness, Littlemouse. You have not tried to argue with me even once. It is almost as though you no longer misunderstand how constantly right I am. But that cannot be true. You are wonderful and I love you, but you are also quite blind to some basic facts."

"Bridget Tagwynn Sorellin-Lancaster," she replied happily.

Rowl sighed heavily and shifted his hips, so she could work along his spine more easily. "It is far more honorable to earn a Cat name," he sniffed. "New names simply because you decide to become mates.

Hmph. But Tribesaver seems as adequate as a human can be when matters become dangerous."

"He's kind and courteous and gentle and thoughtful and wonderful," Bridget said.

"I suppose that has value for humans." Rowl settled all the way down and began to purr, the sound contented. "I am pleased that he makes you happy, Littlemouse."

"Thank you, Rowl."

"And I think it is sad that we did not arrive in time and that so many of your people were harmed and that you had to suffer so much to so little gain. But none of it was your fault. You even had the guidance of several cats. If that did not make it possible, then it was impossible from the beginning."

Bridget set the brush aside. It fell from her clumsy fingers and clattered onto the side table. "At times, that does not feel true. But I suppose you may well be right."

Rowl snuggled down a little closer. "Of course I am right."

Bridget closed her eyes. She had been working hard to ignore the pain, which was terrible even though a harried physician had examined her and dropped off a tincture that made the discomfort matter far less than it had before she'd taken it. Sleep had come in fits and starts over the past day, but she was gradually feeling better. The storm outside was large and violent enough to be heard even within the Spire, and between Rowl's purring and the intermittent rumbling of distant thunder, sleep stole up on her again.

Voices in the hall outside roused her sometime later, and though Rowl's ears twitched toward the door, he neither raised his head nor opened his eyes, and his purr continued steadily.

Bearing a covered tray, Benedict appeared in the doorway with Fenli sitting calmly on his shoulder. He peered in, then was careful to move quietly until he made eye contact with Bridget.

"Oh, you're awake," he said. "I brought you some food."

"I'm not really hungry," Bridget said.

"You haven't eaten for fifteen hours," Benedict replied firmly, "and you're hurt and need food to help your body heal, so I want to see you try to nibble at something. Start with the soup, and we'll try to convince your body to take some proper nutrition in. Then you'll be due for more painkillers." He came over to the bed and leaned down to kiss her hair. "Technically, we are still on a Guard mission and I outrank you. Don't force me to make it an order."

"I could always resign," Bridget suggested, smiling.

Benedict set the tray down on a side table and said, "Well, in that case, you would drive me to my last resort: I'm bigger than you."

"Brute," Bridget sighed happily. Then she frowned. "Tell me, what did you learn? What is happening? How are Gwen and Captain Grimm?"

"You'll eat?" Benedict challenged her.

"Yes, very well."

"Tribesaver is wise," Fenli said happily. He leapt lightly from Benedict's shoulder to the bed, where he promptly settled himself next to Rowl on Bridget's legs. "I will help hold you down so that you do not go running off."

"Mmmm," Rowl said without opening his eyes. "She can be troublesome."

The next few moments were spent in getting broth into a mug for Bridget, and after the first few sips, her stomach began to remember what it had been missing.

"My lord uncle is deep in negotiations with Lord President Warren," Benedict reported. "I don't know the details, but Vincent tells me to expect a formal alliance between Olympia and Albion. Dalos and the Pikers were invited to join it as well. The Pikers have to convene a Council of Captains to decide on the matter, and that could take a while, but that's because most of them have already set out to start preying on Auroran and Atlantean shipping."

"What about the Dalosians?" Bridget asked.

"They're so much farther south of us, and Atlantea is their major trading partner, so they're staying neutral."

"There's neutral and there's neutral," Bridget fretted. "Which are they?"

"Vincent thinks that remains to be seen," Benedict replied. He took a deep breath. "It turns out that the mistmaw was indeed controlled by Madame Cavendish from aboard *Mistshark*. *Predator* fought a boarding action against her but got badly tangled up with her in the process. *Mistshark* went down and took *Predator* with her."

Bridget's eyes widened. "What?"

He nodded. "Apparently, we lost Master Ferus."

"Oh," Bridget said. "Oh, poor Folly. I've got to see her." She felt herself begin to panic a little. "What about the rest of the crew? Captain Grimm?"

Benedict lifted a hand. "The crew had time to abandon ship," he said. His jaw worked. "Except for Gwen. She went down with the ship to try to bring her in to a safe landing."

Bridget felt her hands start shaking, but she ignored them to focus on the sudden strain in Benedict's eyes. "Oh, Ben, do we know anything?"

"Nothing whatsoever," Benedict said in a numb voice. "Not even the precise location of where *Predator* was last seen. They were in the mist." He swallowed. "Vincent says every recovery ship in Albion will be here in three days, along with a significant portion of the Aetherium Fleet."

Bridget thought about the danger the two of them had faced in perhaps three *hours* on the surface. "Three days?"

Benedict nodded slowly.

Little Fenli got up, padded over to Benedict, and began purring, arching his little back to rub his fur against Benedict's limply dangling fingers.

Benedict petted him absently. "I've sent a message to my lord uncle. If he'll loan me the money, I'm going to try to hire a private ship to take me down at dawn to find my coz."

"Of course you are," Bridget said, and bit her lip. "Ben, Gwen is very determined and tough-minded. I'm sure that if anyone could survive that long on the surface, she could."

He looked up and offered her a faint smile. "Yes. Yes, of course."

She reached out and gingerly took the hand Fenli wasn't paying attention to. Benedict's fingers were cold. "I'm sorry," she said quietly. "If there is anything I can do to help, name it."

Benedict took a deep breath and said, "Yes, you can eat."

She sighed and shook her head, smiling. "You're relentless."

A faint growl came into his voice. "Just you wait."

Bridget thoroughly enjoyed the shiver that ran down her spine at his tone. "Oh. Oh, yes. Yes, please."

He handed her a dinner plate with some meat and bread and cheese upon it. Then he frowned. "Bridget?" he asked her. "What's that?"

"What's what?"

"On your hand."

Bridget blinked and said, "Is there something on my—"

She broke off as Benedict took her left hand, lifted it up to peer at it closely, and shook it a little. "Yes. Can't you see it?"

She felt his deft fingers slide something cool around her ring finger, and her heart suddenly beat very quickly.

She reclaimed her hand and stared at a slim silver band studded with three green stones side by side. The stones were not large, though their quality seemed quite excellent, and the shining silver that supported them sparkled in the room's low light.

"Oh. Oh, Ben," she whispered. She felt her eyes welter with tears. She started shaking. "It's beautiful."

"You're crying," Benedict said warily. "Bridget, you're crying. Did I hurt you? Is it too tight?"

"It's perfect," she said, and cried harder. "I've just had . . . had a very extreme week."

He moved to her then, settling his arms around her, and Bridget realized with a start that he was going to be traveling to the surface in the morning. She managed to get an arm around him and squeeze herself as close to him as she could. "I love you very much, you know."

His arms tightened. "I love you too."

"This . . . all this means war, doesn't it?"

"Yes," Benedict said. "And soon."

"Oh, my," Bridget said quietly. "I find this . . . It's all rather large. And I am suddenly aware that I am not."

"But it's not just you, is it?" Benedict asked. "Nor just me. Nor even you and I together." He squeezed her tighter for a moment. "But you and I are together. And I do not think those great events can change that as long as we wish it so."

She leaned against him. Fenli returned to her lap.

"Together," she said. "You promise?"

"My lady," he said firmly, "I am yours."

Bridget had no idea how long the two of them might have together. Or if she might lose him when he went to the surface to hunt for Gwen.

"We have tonight," she said.

Benedict drew in a breath of surprise. "What?"

"And this is what is going to happen," Bridget said. "I am going to eat my food. And then you're going to give me more of that pain-soothing tincture. And then we're going to ask the cats to leave us alone for a time."

"Finally," Rowl said, and promptly heaved himself up from Bridget's lap. "Fenli, we must go. They're going to mate, and I do not wish to embarrass Littlemouse by laughing."

"Rowl!" Bridget exclaimed.

Fenli rose, stretched, and said, "Oh, of course. It's . . . unfortunate when humans mate. So awkward. But I also find it endearing. They have no idea how foolish they look, so they feel very confident afterward."

"Fenli!" Bridget burst out.

Benedict's arms tightened around her, and though she could still feel the tension of his worry and his anticipation of his next task, he began to laugh.

Abigail dutifully wrote down the required edits to the last of the disputed clauses and read them back in a clear, firm voice.

"Yes," said Lord Lancaster. "Excellent. Thank you, Lady Hinton. Have a fresh copy penned with all the changes and review it for accuracy before you bring it back this evening?"

"Yes," Abigail said. "Of course."

"Thank goodness," said Lady Warren, who sat across from Abigail at the council room table and kept notes for her brother. "The details grow so tedious. Abigail, you'll have a copy sent to me for review before the ceremony?"

"Naturally," Abigail said. She made an additional meticulous note.

She didn't trust herself to be able to focus on a single thing if she wasn't meticulous about her notes.

Alex hadn't come to speak to her.

Lord President Warren settled back into his seat with a weary expression. Like all of them, he hadn't slept the night before while the attack on his Spire commenced. The day had been occupied with coordinating recovery and defenses, as well as dispatching couriers to Olympia's several colonies. His evening had been occupied with negotiating the terms of an alliance with Spire Albion. His blunt, rugged features were excellently suited to scowls, Abigail thought, but he'd been remarkable even under extraordinarily trying circumstances.

"I wonder if we aren't causing that much more competition for ourselves by helping you rebuild the skyport at Landing," the Olympian leader mused.

"With that docking system of yours, you already had the upper hand, even when we had both," Lord Lancaster said, rubbing at his forehead with the fingers of one hand. "I'm sure you'll be back to besting us the moment hostilities cease."

"I have word that your daughter is missing," Warren said.

Lancaster smiled briefly. "A Piker crew offered to find her for an extortionate sum of money. I doubled it and told them to find her faster. They're attempting to spot any signal fires now. A recovery expedition will leave at first light, with her cousin overseeing the operation."

Warren and his sister exchanged a look, and Abigail could read their expressions easily enough: Lancaster's daughter would have to endure more than twenty-four hours alone, exposed on the surface. It would require a heavily armed and exceptionally experienced expedition to manage that feat reliably. Her chances were not good.

"What of the princess?" Iphigenia said to her brother. "Have you decided her fate yet?"

Abigail remembered Princess Sarafine's furious expression as the

Warren house guard had marched her away to lock her into quarters far less comfortable than those to which she was accustomed. Thanks to the guard's efforts and those of Abigail's people, the attack on House Warren had been stymied, though if Initiate Hestia had been behind it, she had managed to escape in the confusion.

Abigail was going to double Hamish's pay. Tilde's too.

"She will be our guest," Warren said thoughtfully.

"In our heaviest security cell, I take it?"

The Lord President shook his head. "I can't put her in a cell without arresting her and trying her under Olympian law, for which she would earn banishment to the surface at the very least. That would close too many possible options."

Iphegenia frowned. "Which options would those be?"

"A marriage might be instrumental in a peace agreement at some point," Warren said.

"*Marry* her?" Iphegenia demanded. "After what she tried to do to us both?!"

"I never had any illusions that I would be able to marry for love," he replied easily. "Nor would I have any illusions about trusting the lovely little snake. Nor did I say that she would be married to *me*, dear sister. She's a valuable asset to Tuscarora. I reduce his options simply by keeping her away from him for now. Later, well . . . we will see what the future brings."

"By keeping her," Iphigenia said, "you make war an absolute certainty."

Warren's eyes glittered. "War was certain the moment Tuscarora's pet monster began killing my people. Men like him understand only one language."

"Perhaps you should consider, at the least, replacing her wardrobe," Lord Lancaster said acerbically.

Warren laughed. "That goes without saying."

"Your Grace," Abigail said, rising and tapping her papers into an even stack, "with your permission, I will have these documents amended."

Lancaster yawned, running a long-fingered hand back over his receding hairline. "Make sure you get some sleep yourself, Abigail. You look exhausted."

She smiled tightly. "Thank you, Your—"

The door opened abruptly, and Alexander Bayard strode into the room, resplendent in the blue and silver of his uniform coat. He was carrying his shipboard hat beneath one arm. He walked directly to the conference table, his boots thudding in firm rhythm on the floor, stopped in front of the table, and gave them a stiff bow.

Abigail could not bring herself to look at him. She suddenly felt very tight in the throat and fought to swallow.

"This must be Commodore Bayard," Warren murmured.

"Indeed. Count Alexander Bayard, may I present His Grace Lord President Warren of Olympia and his sister, Her Grace Iphigenia Warren?"

"Lord President," Bayard murmured, bowing to Warren. Then he faced Lady Iphigenia. "Lady, I beg that you will excuse this intrusion." He turned, and Abigail felt the pressure of his gaze like the tip of a knife against the nape of her neck. His jaw flexed twice, and then he said in a firm, polite voice, "I require the room, gentlemen."

Iphigenia's sharp gaze shot between Bayard and Abigail shrewdly.

The Lord President of Olympia and the prime minister of Albion blinked at Bayard and then at each other.

"Excuse me," Warren said. "Your Excellency, did you just . . . dismiss us?"

"It is late," Iphigenia said, rising, "and we are all exhausted. Brother, would you mind terribly walking with me back to my chambers? I find myself leery of doing so alone."

Warren frowned at that, looking back and forth between Bayard and Iphigenia. The Albion commander's gaze had settled unwaveringly upon Abigail.

"It is very late, Lord President," Lord Lancaster suggested. He was studying Bayard carefully and had quite obviously decided that he was not going to stand between Alex and his objective on this particular night.

Warren blew out a breath, clearly dismissing the entire situation as something unlikely to prove a fruitful investment of time and attention after the day he'd been through. "Yes, of course. Come, Iphi."

The two Olympians left the room as Lancaster rose. He nodded to Abigail and began to leave, pausing only to murmur to Bayard, "We are guests of a sovereign nation, and she hasn't slept in two days. Whatever this is, bear those two facts in mind, please."

"Of course, Your Grace," Bayard said.

Lancaster nodded wearily and walked out of the room with the deliberate movements of a man who was about to fall asleep on his feet.

The door closed behind them, and Abigail was alone with Bayard.

"When did you realize?" she asked quietly.

"The moment I started thinking properly again," he replied. "Do you understand what you have done, Your Grace?"

Abigail flinched at his use of her title instead of her name. "Oh," she said quietly. "Yes. Of course."

He took a deep breath. She could only just hear the furious growl that underlay his next question. "Why?"

"Isn't it obvious?" She still couldn't look up at him. "I couldn't bear to lose you."

"You couldn't bear to lose someone dear to you," Bayard said slowly. "But you had no qualms about putting me through pain every bit as intense had I lost Mad. Hypocrisy does not flatter you, Your Grace."

"Valesco would have killed you," Abigail whispered.

"It's a bloody miracle he didn't kill my best friend," Bayard said in cool, calm reply. "Grimm has been maimed. He may never walk without a cane again. Did you know that?"

She closed her eyes. "No. But he will live, Alex."

"Small thanks to you," he said without heat. "If Grimm had died, I would never have spoken to you again."

Abigail's heart fluttered in a panicky rhythm. This must be what being torn in half felt like, she mused. "But he didn't die."

"No," Bayard said gently. He exhaled a slow breath. "It would seem that I have some thinking to do."

"About what?" she half whispered.

"Whether I am capable of forgiving what you have done to me and to my friend," he said. "I am sure the Fleet will have work aplenty for me. We were going to be apart for a while in any case." He paused, then sighed. "Even if it did turn out to be the right choice with regard to Valesco, you had no way of knowing that."

"No," she said, "I didn't."

His voice shifted, the faintest note of pleading coming into it. "Have you *nothing* else to say in your defense? Anything?"

She closed her eyes and folded her hands over her stomach.

I carry your child, she wanted to say. I carry the answer to all your hopes for a family and an heir, my lord.

But while Her Grace Abigail, Duchess Hinton, was more than capable of manipulating others when need be . . . she could not do it to him.

Not to Alex.

When he received this news, it should be joyous, not a slap in the face, not an anchor to keep him at her side. This conflict was not about their child. It was about the choices she had made and the actions she had taken.

"I won't lie to you, Alex," she said, closing her eyes. "The only thing I have to say is that in the same circumstance, I suspect I would do exactly the same thing again."

There was an endlessly yawning moment in which he did not respond.

Then, finally, he said, "Do you see the problem yet?" He shook his head. "I need time to consider my next steps. I will find you when I've had enough. We will continue this discussion from there."

"But, Alex—" Abigail began.

He bowed stiffly to her at the waist and said, "Your Grace. Duty awaits."

She began weeping silent tears now, despite all she could do. She felt so very tired.

He turned to go.

Then he hesitated, his expression torn.

And then he left.

Abigail continued weeping, holding her belly gently in both arms.

It would seem that for the time being at least, she was on her own.

■ ■ ■ Epilogue ■ ■ ■

Spirearch's Chambers, Habble Morning,
Spire Albion

The last of the expeditionary force departed from Albion, leaving her with the lightest screen of defensive airships possible. Six of her dreadnoughts had departed with the expedition. All seven recovery ships, floating fortresses nearly the size of dreadnoughts, had departed with them.

As Lord Albion watched them go from his suite overlooking Albion's skyport, the ships' running lights vanished into the misty night, though the lightning of distant storms showed the vessels as a cluster of vague black smudges against ghostly skies now and then.

"So," he said quietly, "the war begins. And the next phases of it will be shaped by how successfully the Fleet recovers downed ships."

From the back of his suite, a form stirred, and Chief Maul let out an indifferent growl. "The war was to come. We knew this. Don't whine about it. Fight it."

Albion snorted and took up his cup of tea, though he thought he'd almost prefer something stronger. "Human wars are not like cat wars," he said to the chief cat. "We leave ourselves plenty of time built in. That way we have ample opportunity to doubt ourselves before matters are resolved."

"Foolish," said Maul without rancor.

"Most war seems to be," Albion replied. "But somehow only in retrospect." He glanced at the third person in the room and said, "You're sure that Tuscarora won't send his new fleet to attack Albion?"

The figure shook its head and spoke in a vernacular of Albion so old that it was barely understandable. "Nay, O King. Verily, Tuscarora's own blood was threatened by the actions of the Tyranima—his sister subjected to an attack that might e'en have cleansed every last soul of Habble Profit, leaving it bereft of life. Tuscarora seeks influence and wealth, not extermination. Now he needs must question his newfound bounty and find himself bebothered by the possibility of treachery in each shadow. It is his wont to move boldly, like a lion. But now he must be as cautious as a heron 'mongst the reeds, and 'twill burden his mind like iron chains."

"And you are sure," Maul asked skeptically, "that the Ancient Enemy of the Builders rises anew?"

"Verily," said the tall, broad-shouldered figure in the grey cloak. "The very ending of days, or their new dawning, is upon thee, bold Maul."

"The Tyranima," murmured Albion. He shook his head. "An outside force that drives men to seek to subjugate others. My study of history suggests no such alien awareness is needed."

"Sooth," agreed the grey-cloaked figure. "But envision, if you will, a spirit, an awareness, well acquainted with the weakness of mankind. Well able to tempt them with what they most desire, and devoted utterly to bringing about their doom. It has awoken. And it will lay this world to ruin as it did in elder days if it is not fought."

"We are but men," Albion said.

"Precisely," Maul agreed sadly.

Albion gave the muscular cat an arch look but turned to the

cloaked figure. "If the reports I have read about even a single mist-maw turned against us are true, how can we hope to prevail?"

The figure in the cloak turned and put a wide, strong hand upon Albion's shoulder. "The Tyranima is not the only ancient power 'pon this wide world," he said quietly. "Thy people are stronger and wiser and more dangerous than thou knowest. Countless worlds fell to this evil, but here, by thy people, it was fought. It was baffled. It was banished into the earth. And for ten thousand years, it has licked the wounds your forefathers wrought 'pon it and savaged your world to inflict."

A hand of metallic golden flesh squeezed Albion's shoulder gently.

"Lord Albion," said the figure in a gentle, resonant voice, "know thou this: thou, thou personally, and thy people. You do not stand alone. I will return anon with more word when it is given."

And with that, the Archangel turned to the window, shed its cloak, and leapt out into the night. There was the single sound of great wings sweeping down once, and a flicker of gold in the ambient light from the emptied, subdued skyport.

And then silence.

Albion stared out into the night after the Archangel. But, as always, there was nothing to mark the being's passing. If not for the way Maul had interacted with it, he might have considered it entirely a figment of his own stressed and worried mind.

"Hmph," Maul said, unimpressed, as he came to sit down on the windowsill. "It would seem that wherever such a creature comes from, it is *not* the custom to close the windows behind them."

Albion shook his head, unable to stop a smile from touching his lips. He rested a hand on the cat's shoulders and decided to wait for the sunrise before he went about his day.

He wanted to feel the light on his face.

＊　　＊　　＊

Lady Gwendolyn Margaret Elizabeth Lancaster, executive officer of AMS *Predator*, slowly came to consciousness in a swimming haze of nausea and pain.

Her head hurt horribly, as did her leg. She supposed she could do very little to examine her own head, lacking a mirror. A quick probe with her fingers confirmed that blood had matted her hair and she had a thickly clotted cut along her scalp, but her skull, apart from a knot half the size of her fist, otherwise seemed intact.

She opened her eyes. She lay beneath the bulk of the ship, it would seem. She had a vague memory of *Predator* sinking amongst massive trees and towering mushrooms half a mile high, sliding off one of them, and crashing down to the ground. The ship had wound up almost completely overturned, so she lay under its shelter as a steady rain came down, dripping all around her and drumming on the shattered planks of the hull.

She was quite cold, and it was a wonder she had not frozen. She supposed the insulated aeronaut's leathers she wore explained most of that. There was the dim light of predawn filtering through the mist, but from the aches of her stiff body, she judged that she'd been unconscious for a goodly while. She might have lost a day.

She managed to lift her head and turn her body enough to see that her left leg was horribly twisted at the ankle. Her foot had swollen inside its boot and hurt terribly, the flesh bulging out like a muffin where the boot ended. The sight made her stomach surge with nausea, which she fought off grimly.

Well, she was in a spot of trouble, it would seem. She still had her sword on her and a knife to go with it, and her pistol of course, but none of them seemed remotely helpful for mending a broken ankle. Her basic instruction in medical care in the Guard had been somewhat augmented by assisting Doctor Bagen after several actions, at the captain's insistence, but though she might have dared to set someone else's broken bone, she did not quite see *how* she might set her own under the circumstances. And her wrist still troubled her from being sprained at the beginning of all this mess when they were picking up Benny. Bother.

She felt faint with hunger and thirst and vaguely dizzy, and she realized that she was running a fever.

The wounds were quite likely infected. And here she was, trapped on the surface, lamed, concussed, quite likely unable to walk.

Bother.

Footsteps sounded.

Gwen drew her pistol and knife all but instantly, dropping the hammer back as someone approached. The steps were unsteady and shuffling. They approached slowly. There was a wet, slithering sound that proved a moment later to be damp skirts dragging across the ground as a human figure, a woman, knelt down and leaned forward. One of her hands was on the ruins of the ship above to keep her balance, the other wrapped in bloodied rags.

Because the pale, barely lit mists outside the ship behind the other woman cast her into little more than a dark silhouette, Gwen could not see the woman's face, but she did not have to.

Madame Cavendish's profile was unmistakable.

The mad etherealist went still as she heard the gun's hammer cock back; then she tilted her head to one side.

Gwen thought that with all the rain, it seemed quite likely her pistol wouldn't fire, but there was no need to trouble Madame Cavendish with that. "Try anything," Gwen said, keeping her voice as steady as she could, "anything at all, and I will leave a hole the size of my fist in the back of your skull, madame."

Cavendish inhaled slowly. "Miss . . . Lancaster, was it not?"

she asked in a rasping voice. "I think we are a bit beyond hostilities here."

"You strike me as a person who is unused to being proven wrong," Gwen said. "Please be assured that your assumption is entirely inaccurate."

"Ah," Cavendish said, her voice wry, "I see."

There was sudden motion in the mist behind the etherealist. Over the trunk of a new-fallen tree slithered a creature, something long and sinuous with several sets of legs and rippling scales and a narrow, wicked-looking head. It rose up behind Cavendish, head rearing back, scales rippling as tension gathered in its body. Though Gwen had never seen such a thing before, she knew a predator when it was about to strike.

"Behind you!" Gwen snapped.

Cavendish whirled with eerie speed, raising a hand. Ember-colored light flared from her and spread over the hunting creature, which snapped forward in a blinding lunge that covered the space between it and Cavendish almost faster than Gwen could see it happen. The creature seemed to smash into something that flung it back from Cavendish with the force of a battering ram, slamming it into the trunk of the fallen tree with a series of brittle snapping noises.

The creature fell to the ground, its sinuous body writhing in a dreamy, slow-motion spiral—quite dead, Gwen judged, even as its reflexes continued to fire despite its head being crushed almost flat.

Cavendish remained absolutely still for a long moment, statuelike. Then, as if exhausted, she seemed to shiver and slumped down to sit upon the earth. As the light grew, Gwen got a better look at the woman.

Her face was a ruin.

Madame Cavendish's eyes were gone, her nose a broken, swollen mess. Both had been claimed by some kind of slashing wound that had probably been caused by splinters from the shattering ship. She had bound torn, blood-soaked cloth clumsily across the injuries, but she had made a botch of it, though Gwen supposed she could see why.

"You warned me," Cavendish said in a low, intent tone. "Why?"

"We're on the surface," Gwen replied. "You're human. I suppose."

Cavendish frowned at that. She seemed to struggle with herself for a moment and then blurted out, "Th-thank you. That was kind." She tilted her head and felt at the fallen ship. "You're still under there. You can't walk, can you?"

Gwen saw little point in lying. "No."

"But you can see. Something that, obviously, I cannot do."

"Yes," Gwen said warily.

"There are more creatures coming," Cavendish said quietly. "The *Mistshark*'s ruin is perhaps fifty yards to *Predator*'s stern. They came for the bodies last night." Her expression twitched. "I couldn't keep them from Sark. I had to hide in a storage locker. And listen." She swallowed. "There was plenty for them to eat there. I suspect that's the only reason they didn't get around to eating you, Miss Lancaster. They will remedy that shortly."

"They'll try," Gwen said defiantly.

Cavendish shook her head. "It took me an hour to get here from the *Mistshark*. And I was nearly taken a moment ago."

"I thought you weren't afraid of death," Gwen quipped.

Cavendish's mouth quivered. "Let us say that I desire to explore that option only as a last resort, Lady Lancaster."

"I am startled to say that we have something in common, then," Gwen sighed.

"As you say. We are trapped on the surface," Cavendish said. "I need your eyes. You need my legs. I believe we can reach an accommodation."

"A truce?" Gwen asked.

"That is my proposal," Cavendish rasped. "It may not do us any good. But otherwise, our lives are numbered in moments. Hours, at most."

Gwen pulled the trigger.

The pistol sparked, but the powder in the pan had been dampened by the rain, and it did not flare to life. The gun remained silent.

"Bother," Gwen muttered, and dropped the useless weapon.

Cavendish stared to one side of Gwen with her empty eyes and grinned. It showed her teeth and the cords in her neck unnaturally. "Whatever you may think of me, I am good to my word, Lady Lancaster. I will give you whatever aid I can and protect your life as I would my own until we are returned to civilization, if you will give your word as an officer and a Lancaster to do the same."

"My word as an officer and a Lancaster?" Gwen said carefully. "Why on earth would you trust that?"

"You were trained by Captain Grimm. Your House has a fine reputation. And I have little choice."

"Vexation," Gwen swore.

"Then I have your word?"

"You do," Gwen said. "I have yours?"

"You do," Cavendish said serenely.

"Bother and vexation," Gwen spat. "Rust and rot. Very well. Give us your hand."

ACKNOWLEDGMENTS

Poor Anne Sowards. I made her and the good people at Penguin wait so long for this one, between the last lengthy Dresden project and my own personal life becoming so problematic. Here's to a brighter and smoother future, and to more books getting done faster. I think we would all be happier with that.

My dear readers, thank you for being so patient and enthusiastic about this story. I was on the verge of dropping this tale and trying a new one, but fans at DragonCon and online were so eager to know when the next Spires story would be done that I would have felt like a perfect monster to leave you all Rowl-less, and in writing this I have rekindled my love of this story and its world and characters. I hope you will join me for several more installments to come.

Thank you, Priscilla Spencer, for the map and the endpaper art! It's difficult for me to picture my creative process without your enthusiasm and participation.

And as always, I owe a great deal of thanks to my friends at the Beta Foo Asylum, readers and nerds extraordinaire. They had to read this one in the most spaced-out and irregular fashion as a novel was ever written, and they did so with their usual welcome enthusiasm and highly useful insight. Thank you all.

Of course, the reward for work well done . . .

Captain Grimm's
Battle Sword